THE TRIAL TRILOGY

DAVID B LYONS

❀ Created with Vellum

The Trial Trilogy comprises three novels all set inside the courtrooms of Dublin's Criminal Courts.

She Said, Three Said
by David B. Lyons

The Curious Case of Faith & Grace
by David B. Lyons

The Coincidence
by David B. Lyons

PRAISE FOR DAVID B. LYONS

BOOK I

SHE SAID, THREE SAID

The jury don't know who to believe....

will you?

For Kerry

... as always.

♦

THEY LINE up to enter the room like school children. Brian stops in the doorway to wave everyone through as if he's the conductor of this orchestra. In general, this would be viewed as a polite gesture. But at this stage – five weeks in and with patience stretched – his eleven peers just think he's acting like a twat.

None of them offer him a thank you. The politest reaction he receives is a twitching of the lips from Number Three as she wheels past him.

Number Ten sits down, then stands immediately back up and walks to the far side of the oval table, settling on a seat next to Number Four.

'Jee, undecided already?' Brian says as he enters the room. He chuckles. Nobody else laughs. They're not in this room to laugh. But spitting out a joke only to be met by silence is nothing new to Brian Hoare.

A lack of humour isn't the only blemish he has. Hell no! Brian's unfortunate in a multitude of ways. He's awful looking for starters. He was bald by the time he was twenty-one. Some guys can carry off a shaved head, not this guy. The top of his crown is too bulbous and the bottom of his head... well, it just doesn't seem to exist. He has no chin. His lower jaw just sinks into his neck. The overbite doesn't help either. Nor does his lisp. He produces a squelching sound as if he's bursting saliva bubbles with his back molars when pronouncing a lot of 's' sounds. It doesn't happen all the time, but it is quite a harsh squelch when his lisp does take over. He also has really bad breath. He doesn't know he has; only people who happen to be within a two-foot radius of his mouth knows he has. And right now,

Number One and Number Eleven are the unfortunate ones within that vicinity.

'Ah – six-all again,' Brian says, leaning over to tick his box on the lunch order. He regrets it as soon as he's said it; is aware he has already overstated his fascination with voting numbers over the course of the past five weeks. This wasn't the first time he'd counted up the lunch orders and barked the 'result' across the table as if it held any sort of significance.

'Jusht my idea of a bit of humour,' he whispers to Number Eleven when he sits down. Number Eleven smiles at him sympathetically; not hiding the fact that it's a sympathy smile either. She kinda just throws the smile at him, hoping it will shut him the fuck up. This lack of respect would sting Brian had he not grown thick skin years ago. You'd have to grow thick skin to be a politician. And you'd certainly have to grow thick skin if you looked like Brian Hoare.

He could've compensated for his unfortunate appearance had he developed some sort of personality over his thirty-two years. Aside from his mistimed jokes, Brian takes himself way too seriously. When Number Four gave birth to the idea that the jurors should be known by their juror number rather than their real names over the course of the trial, Brian just had to be the awkward twat he always seems to be by going against the grain.

Most of the jurors were well aware that this trial would be splashed over the front pages of every national newspaper for weeks on end. Some of them were paranoid about the effect it could have on their lives. When this was all over they just wanted to return to normality; out of reach of the press, out of reach of the public, out of reach of each other.

They took a vote at the time. Nine voted *for* the use of juror numbers – three against. So they went with it. All except Brian. He opted to scribble his real name on his sticker badge. It sparked a succession of tuts around the table when he first stuck it to his chest, but his flaunting of the first rule the jurors made inside this room was never mentioned again. Nobody wanted to give Brian the satisfaction of having to explain himself.

He would have liked to have shared his reasoning though. His take on it was he didn't have anonymity anyway. He assumed everyone in the room already knew who he was.

They didn't.

Far from it.

Before this trial started, only Number Eight recognised Brian Hoare. Brian is a long way away from being as important as he thinks he is. By the time he was twenty-four, Brian made waves within the Labour Party; running for the party's leadership having shown drive and ambition when helping his hometown of Ongar pull through the financial crisis unscathed.

Seventeen separate businesses opened in his small constituency through the crash over a three-year period. Most in Ongar knew he was just a jammy bastard, though. He happened to be in the right place at the right time. The plans for the majority of those businesses were in place well before Brian was elected as local TD.

But Brian wasn't backward in claiming credit for the successes, gloating about his achievements in the national press at any given opportunity.

The positive PR didn't go unnoticed by the big wigs in the Dail and suddenly Brian was climbing the ranks of the Labour Party. Though that didn't mean he wasn't deluded when he ran the leadership race in 2011. He never stood a chance. After six weeks of bluffing to the press, he eventually fell out of contention. He's been back in Ongar ever since; half hated, half adored by his constituency and becoming more and more frustrated in his attempts to be re-elected as the local representative. He easily could have been excused from jury duty as of right – being a former politician – but he relishes the prospect of judging too much to pass on such an opportunity.

Brian's self-delusion was highlighted to his fellow jurors within the first twenty minutes of meeting them. He challenged Number One for the position of Head Juror as soon as they entered this room. In a secret ballot for the position, Number One thrashed Brian eleven-to-one. Everyone shifted awkwardly in their fake leather chairs when it became apparent that Brian was the only person around the table to vote for himself.

As soon as all jurors have taken their seats around the table, Brian is the first to pipe up.

'I propose we conduct an early verdict vote just to shee—'

'Scuse me,' says Number Five, cutting Brian's sentence in half. 'You're not the Head Juror. Let Number One do the talking.'

Brian rubs at where his chin should be, then motions towards Number One to get the ball rolling.

The trial ended just over ten minutes ago, the judge's closing statement ringing fresh in their ears, yet they still hadn't begun deliberations. Ticking a box on the lunch order and finding a seat in the jury room took a hell of a lot longer than was necessary.

'Okay everybody – this has been a long, drawn out five weeks,' says Number One after clearing his throat. 'And it all boils down to our discussion in this room. The fate of those three men lie in our hands.'

'And hers,' snaps Number Five.

'Yes. And Sabrina's too,' says Number One, swinging his jaw. 'I was just about to say that, thank you. I've been thinking of the best way for us to approach these deliberations from the get-go and it is my opinion that we should go through the whole night in chronological order. We should start our discussions about what we think happened just gone seven o'clock, when they all first met each other. Then we can continue through to the end of the night... until the incident is believed to have taken place, somewhere between midnight and half-past midnight.'

'We need to do an early vote,' Brian calls out, disrupting Number One's flow.

'What do we need a vote for?' Number One asks, his brow furrowing.

The rest of the jury begin to mumble; Number Ten doing nothing to disguise her annoyance by holding her two palms over her face and sighing heavily into them. Number Four holds one finger to the middle of his forehead and stares down into his lap. This kind of body language is standard practice in a jury room. But very rarely before deliberations have even begun.

The jury rooms in Dublin's Criminal Courts are specifically designed to spark discussion and debate – and they work. Debates arise in here all the time; like ping pong back and forth across the table. But it just so happens that a large percentage of those debates have fuck all to do with the trial they've been tasked with examining.

When twelve random strangers are forced together, the chances of no ego making itself known in the room is extremely rare. It turns out that way more people than you would actually imagine love the sound of their own thought process. In fairness to most of them, they *are* in these rooms to share their thoughts. It's just that the majority of people placed in this situation don't know how to filter between a significant thought and an insignificant thought.

'We need a vote because it'sh important we take note of how we are feeling at every point of the deliberations,' Brian says, trying to justify himself. 'It would be beneficial if we all gave our gut instinct after five weeks of listening to the evidensh. The evidensh is fresh in our minds now. Fresher than it will ever be. I propose that it'd be advantageous to us as a jury if we all knew where everybody stood before we even begin deliberating. It's the besht place to start.'

A mumble of discussion fills the room; a nodding of heads almost running around the table like a Mexican wave. Most of the jurors agree with Brian's sentiment, but they also loathe to give him the satisfaction of gaining a minor victory. Number One sighs before raising his voice again.

'Listen... hands up if you think we should start with a verdict vote?' he asks.

'Hold on... we're having a vote about whether or not we're having a vote?' says Number Twelve, shaking his head. The delivery of his line produces a snort of laughter from a few around the table. Others just sigh.

Four jurors raise their hands in the hope that it will quicken the process. And then four more swiftly follow.

'Okay... so that's eight of twelve. Majority rules. We *will* have a verdict vote to start proceedings,' Number One says.

Brian smiles into his chest. His obsession with voting has bordered on fanatical at times. But this isn't an ordinary vote; it isn't a lunch order, it isn't a vote about the juror's name tags, it isn't about electing a Head Juror. This is the real deal – a verdict vote. Brian can't wait to see what way his fellow jurors have been swayed over the course of this trial. He is dying to know how many agree with him: *not guilty*. He'd made his mind up half-way through the trial and isn't for changing. Brian is adamant the prosecution didn't do enough to prove the case.

'No need for formalities,' continues Number One. 'This will be an open vote. So we'll just raise our hands. There will be three options for now: guilty, not guilty or undecided.'

Number One takes a deep breath, then bounces the butt of the paperwork he's holding off the table.

'Okay... so raise your hand if – at this stage, immediately following the trial – you feel strongly that these three men are guilty.'

Each juror's head pivots around the room. Three hands fly up; Number Five's, Number Three's and Number Six's. Silence fills the air for a moment, in anticipation of any other hands being raised. None are.

'Okay, and those who at this early stage feel that the three men are innocent, please raise your hands.' Brian's hand shoots up, followed almost-reluctantly by Number Twelve's.

'And those undecided at present?' asks Number One, pointlessly. He even proceeds to count the hands in the air aloud, including his own. 'Okay,' he says, scribbling down the result on the sheet of paper in front of him. 'That's three guilty... two not guilty... seven undecided.'

He coughs, scribbles nonsensical notes on the paper just to bide time and then falls silent again. He doesn't know where to take things from here.

'Let's do what you were gonna do,' Number Twelve speaks up. 'Let's go through the night in chronological order. Starting with when Sabrina first bumped into the three lads... or when the three lads first bumped into her – depending on who you believe.'

'Yeah – there's disagreement from the outset,' says Number Ten. 'Sabrina says the three guys approached her first. They claim she approached them. Who do we all believe made the first move?'

I tug at the V in my jumpsuit again, adjusting it for what must be the fiftieth time since I left my apartment half-an-hour ago. I don't know why. My breasts aren't going to fall out. But because it's cut so low, almost down to my belly button, my eyes are constantly catching the end of the V and I instinctively keep running my thumb under the fabric to pull the two sides tighter together.

It's a beautiful jumpsuit, but I really don't feel comfortable in it. It's making me feel too self-conscious. I'm normally self-conscious, but particularly so this evening. Perhaps I overdid it, especially for this place. I've never been to the Hairy Lemon before; assumed it was a bit classier than it actually is. It's just a basic old-school after-work inner-city pub; after work for everyone else in here, the beginning of work for me.

'You do a non-alcoholic wine?' I shout over the other voices to the barman.

He bends down, pops his head back up in a matter of seconds, holding a small bottle of Ebony either side of his face.

'The red, please.'

'You alone?' a boy-cum-man asks, squeezing behind a girl at the bar so he can talk to me.

'I am,' I reply, 'but not for long. Sorry.'

He trundles away, his head bowed. It's tough for men. What are they supposed to say when they see girl in a bar they find attractive? Where would you even begin? I've heard it all over the years; from cheesy one-liners to outright advances. None of it works. Certainly not with me. There's just an unnatural chemistry that ignites as soon as somebody attempts a chat up line. It makes the process unattractive. Chat up lines are cheesy. Cheesy is uncool. Uncool is unattractive. Or maybe I'm just a fussy bitch. Probably why I've only ever had one-and-a-half boyfriends my whole life.

I hand over the five-euro the barman asks for, pick up my glass of red and make my way towards the stairs, slaloming through a host of bodies as I take my first sip. This place is pretty much packed. It's not going to be easy to locate my target tonight.

When I reach the top of the stairs I check my phone. Still no text message. But it'll come through soon enough. It always does.

I soak in the atmosphere. Most people in here likely arrived just gone five o'clock, as soon as their working week ended. They're all out for fun.

But I don't envy them. Not at all. The idea of being cooped up in an office all week doesn't sit right with me. Never has. I can't understand why that's the route most people in this city take to earn money. It seems like slave work to me; working forty hours a week to make somebody else rich. How does that even make sense? I guess it's just routine, tradition, conditioning. Everybody feels they have to have a career and rather than thinking outside the box, they all just do as their parents did: work for somebody else.

It's a real shame. Though I do sometimes feel that if I wasn't genetically blessed I'd probably have to join everybody else in that rat race too. I don't earn an awful lot of money – a modest amount, enough to keep fresh food in the kitchen and a roof over my head. But I guess I'm as happy as I've ever been. I'm managing to stave away my depression most days – and that's probably as good as I can ever do. There are times when I feel down, but I don't feel as lost in life as I have done in the past. There's a tiny glimmer of light at the end of my tunnel. I just have to fixate on it, keep walking towards it.

I pull at the V again as I reach the top of the stairs; noticing a man stare me up and down, licking his lips in appreciation. I've never fully known for certain whether men lack subtlety in these situations or whether or not they genuinely just don't give a shit about getting caught staring. I don't even laugh when I clock the wedding ring on his finger and watch him stroll over to a table on the far side of the room, kissing a girl I hope is his wife. She's pretty – certainly better looking than him. He should count himself lucky. He doesn't need to be perving at me.

I check my phone again and let out a sigh. Still no text. I probably should have waited outside, until the message came through. It's not a great idea for me to be in here before him. Especially in a packed bar. I'm courting way too much attention. I polish off my glass of wine, plonk it on a shelf next to the toilet and make my way through the swinging door; not because I need to use the loo, but because I'm getting a little too self-conscious standing out there on my own. I'll hide out in here for a while, until my phone buzzes.

'Nice jumpsuit,' a young girl says staring at me through the reflection in the mirror.

'Oh thank you.'

'Yeah, ye look deadly. Jaysus, I hope I look as good as you do when I'm … eh… sorry, what are ye twenty-nine, thirty?'

I look into the mirror, just to see if her estimation is justified. She over-shot my age by five years. Bitch. That stung. Maybe she meant it as a put down. I'm used to girls being jealous of me; but to portray jealousy within five seconds of seeing me is probably a new record.

'Just gone twenty-five,' I say. She holds a hand up to her mouth in apology.

'Well... if I look as good as you in seven years I'll be over the moon,' she says, twisting the nub of her lipstick back down. She wings the door open, leaves me in peace – just me and my reflection. Maybe I do look older than I am. My depression has added those years, I'm sure.

The lack of sleep when you suffer with bouts can be torturous. But I still look good. I know I do. I just don't feel good. And I'd take feeling good over looking good any day of the week. Looks are overrated. I know that for a fact. I'm living proof of it.

I touch up the winged tip at the sides of my eyes and purse my lips at my reflection. Eyeliner is the only make-up I ever wear. I'm lucky; I don't have any blemishes on my face to hide. In fact, I don't have any blemishes on my body at all. I'm not quite sure where myself and my sister got our sallow skin from – neither of our parents have it. I guess we just won some sort of gene lottery. We got looky, but not lucky.

I hover inside the middle cubical, trying to kill time. But time doesn't want to be killed – certainly not quickly enough. I check my phone: 7:16. Lorna said I should receive the text anytime between seven and seven-thirty. Another sigh. I can't stay locked up in this little cubicle for much longer. I'll just head back outside, try to blend in. I sigh as I push through the swinging door, my eyes focusing on a group huddled into the far corner of the pub. None of them were there before I went to the toilet. I place my phone back into my purse and pace over to see what the fuss is all about. A group of lads seem to be lining up to take photos of a tall red-haired guy. I feel a wave of excitement wash through me. I bet he's famous. I squint to focus on his face, but can't place him. I always wanted to be famous... in fact I always felt destined I would be. But it never happened. Not yet anyway. Though sometimes I wonder why I hold on to that dream; parts of the celebrity lifestyle must be horrendous. I can't imagine I'd have the patience to pose for a hundred photos and sign a hundred pieces of paper every time I walked into a pub. Though this fella seems to be enjoying it. Either that or he has mastered the art of maintaining a fake smile. He's been handed two pints of beer in the one-minute I've been standing here. That's kinda ironic. If this guy is super famous then surely he has money. Why do the people feel the need to help fund his night out?

'Sorry love, who is that guy?' a girl asks over my shoulder, her eyes squinting as much as mine.

'No idea.'

'He's cute.'

I take in his face again. Yeah... he is kinda cute. I mean... I don't think

I've ever fancied a red-head before, but he wears it well; the beard offsets the ginger somewhat – it actually suits him.

'Yeah he is kinda good looking... kinda has a–' I stop, realising I'm talking to myself. The girl who approached me has gone. I take a step forward and focus on his face again. How do I not know who he is? I stay on top of celebrity news. I could even name all of the past contestants on *Big Brother* if they were lined up in front of me.

'I'll get you a selfie,' a guy says startling me, his Dublin accent not fitting his Asian appearance.

'Sorry?'

'C'mon... I'll introduce you to Jason,' he says.

We laugh out loud walking up South William Street. It's been so long since the three of us have been out together and it always paints a grin on my face when I realise just how seamlessly we fall back into the old routine of slagging each other's mothers.

We've been stinging each other with 'yer ma' jokes since we were fourteen. After I just said I never get sick of the Hairy Lemon, Zach replied 'yer ma never gets sick of my Hairy Lemon' and the three of us literally burst out laughing; the laughter rasping from our mouths like fart sounds.

We know that line isn't funny to anybody else in the world but it happened to be the humour our friendship evolved on. I couldn't care less if anyone labelled us immature. That kind of humour isn't immature to me. It's golden. It's rare. Not every group of best friends from primary school are still best friends thirty years on. I'm proud of our banter. I actually find it quite magical that when the three of us are together we can turn easily back into those innocent little kids we were when we first met.

For some reason the three of us decided to be mates on our first day at Mourne Road primary school. There must have been about three hundred kids in the school at the time, but on day one the three of us somehow happened to cower in to the same corner of the large playground. I often think we found solace in each other because we were the three strangest looking kids in the playground that day. Jason's hair was orange. Not ginger. *Orange*. Bright orange. I don't know why Mrs Kenny didn't have it cut short. She just let him walk around with a giant orange bush on the top of his head. He kept it that way until he was fourteen.

Zach looked like a midget. Still kinda does. He's small, though he always seemed to be the one who got the girls. Before Jason became famous, that is.

There was no doubt I was different. 'Chink' they called me all the way through primary school. 'Chink', I'd later find out, derived from the word 'Chinese'. I don't think the lads understood there was a difference between Korea and China. I'm just certain anyone with Asian eyes in Dublin those days was called 'Chink'. It used to bother me, but all in all I think I survived being of a different race pretty well. I wasn't really bullied at school... just made fun of. Things could have been a lot worse.

'Ah, Jason Kenny,' the bouncer calls out, throwing his hand out for a shake. Zach and I get offered a grabbed handshake too. That's not one of the perks of having a famous friend. I'm a bit of a germaphobe. I wipe my hand against the inside of my blazer as we step inside. It's busier in here than I thought it'd be.

'Whatcha want?' Zach shouts over the chatter, muscling his way towards the bar.

'Here, I'll buy,' Jason pipes up.

'T'fuck you will, big shot.'

'Go on then, get us a pint of Heineken.'

'Same,' I say, even though I hate beer. I only drink it because I feel that's what I'm supposed to drink. I'd love a cocktail. Some bright red, iced concoction that tastes like a Slush Puppie. I could drink that kinda stuff all night. But there's no way I'd order one. I'd look like a right mug.

I sip on the beer Zach hands back to me wondering how the hell my gut is going to feel in the morning after I've poured about seven pints of this piss into it.

'Will we go upstairs?' Jason asks, pinching his shoulders in so he doesn't bump into anyone.

'C'mon,' Zach says, leading the way.

Heads cock as Jason walks through the crowd. He's often said his height helped make him a success, but that it's a bastard to be tall and famous. He gets noticed everywhere he goes.

A bout of 'Boom, boom, boom, lemme hear ya say Jayo' sounds out. This is nothing new. The Irish fans started chanting that when Jason was in his prime, about eight years ago. It follows him everywhere he goes. Only me and Zach know that Jason genuinely hates that chant. It makes him cringe. He hates being called 'Jay' or 'Jayo'. He only answers to Jason.

We shuffle up the stairs without anyone asking him for an autograph or a selfie and manage to squeeze ourselves into a corner of the pub opposite the toilets. The chatter's not so loud up here. Gives us the chance to do what we came out to do: catch up. Jason hasn't been home in almost a year.

'How's Jinny?' he asks me.

'Great. Doing her Leaving next year, can ye believe that?'

'You're fuckin joking me!' he says, holding his fist to his face in surprise.

'Yeah... she's seventeen in a couple of months.'

'Jaysus Christ. I still imagine her being four.'

Jason's always had a soft spot for my little sister. Well, he kinda has a soft spot for my whole family. We're an odd little bunch, us Xiangs. My mam and dad met pretty much the night I was conceived. They're still together... sort of. He mainly lives in Korea, and has still barely bothered to ever learn how to speak English. I've tried to learn Korean; can just about get by to share a polite chat with him whenever he decides to come to Dublin. But I'm not great at it. It's a tough language to nail. Jinny hasn't bothered. She doesn't seem as interested as I am to get to know Dad better. She just can't forgive him for being away from us for most of the year. Mam gets by. She's used to it. Everybody loves my mam. She's just one of those loveable oul dears. The type that would do anything for anybody. She runs the community centre on Mourne Road; helps out at the charity shop on Galtymore. All for nothing. Just for the reward of being part of a community.

'And your ma?' Jason asks.

'Still the same. Hasn't changed.'

'Good to hear it. Tell them I was asking for them.'

'Sure, pop in to them before you go back.'

'Yeah, I'll—' he stops, distracted by somebody holding a pint of Heineken in front of his face.

'Here ya go, Jason. For that goal against Holland, ye legend ye!'

'Thank you, mate,' Jason says smiling back at the stranger.

'I knew as soon as you shaped up to hit that, that the ball was gonna fly—'

'Sorry, my friend,' Zach interrupts. 'It's just Jason here is trying to have a quiet night out with his buddies. We haven't seen him in ages and—'

'Course, sure thing, sure thing,' the fella says, reaching out for Jason to shake his hand. 'I'll leave ye to it, Jason. Have a good night, me oul mucker. Ye fuckin legend ye!'

We're used to it. But the unfortunate thing about the first person approaching Jason when we're out is that it opens the floodgates for everybody else. I'm pretty sure that within the next five minutes, Jason will have at least three more pints of Heineken handed to him and will have signed a dozen autographs and appeared in a dozen selfies. He handles himself so well. I know he hates all this shit, but it's par for the course.

I raise my eyebrows at Zach as a crowd begins to form around us.

'We'll just have the one here,' I whisper into his ear as Jason does his thing. 'I didn't think this place would be so busy this early. Forgot about all the work crowd on a Friday evening.'

'No problem,' he replies. 'We'll just play it by ear.'

'Here mate, will ye take a pic of me with Jason Kenny?' a young fella who must be just about bordering on the legal age limit to drink asks Zach.

Zach doesn't hide his impatience with these fans. He sighs while taking the phone off the young fella. I take in the crowd gathering. It's small – only about eight or nine people. It'll all be over in five minutes. Then we can get back to catching up.

I sip on my pint as I'm forced out of the pack. This always happens. Me just standing aside.

I turn around, take in the artwork on the walls. It's not much to look at, just framed posters of old movies. Most of them are of John Wayne. I'm not quite sure why the pub's decorated this way. I don't see the connection.

I squint, then blink at the reflection in one of the glass frames, barely believing what I can see.

Now that *is* a work of art.

I spin to look at her. She's gorgeous. The white suit she's wearing is really hot. Cut all the way down to her belly button. She has a sheen right down her cleavage. It's like she's bloody photoshopped. But that's not what's most attractive about her. It's those big brown eyes. I'm not one for approaching girls, have never had the courage, but I find myself walking towards her and I can't stop.

'I'll get you a selfie,' I say to her.

'Sorry?'

'C'mon... I'll introduce you to Jason.'

'Who... who is he?' she asks me.

A lot of girls do this. Play dumb; pretend they don't know who he is – thinking that's how he would like it to be. It's all very transparent, though. I don't expect everyone to know who Jason is, but if you've been queuing up looking for an autograph or a selfie, then it's not particularly logical to play the I-don't-know-who-you-are card. But she's super cute. So she can kinda get away with it.

'Hey Jason, this is... this is...?' I ask turning to her.

'Sabrina,' she says, smiling. 'Sabrina Doyle.'

'LISTEN,' Number Twelve says. 'We won't know for certain, but if you sorta boil it down to logic, it's more logical that she approached them. People were approaching Jason. We know that. There's evidence to support that.'

'They cudda approached her,' Number Five says rather dismissively, turning to look Number Twelve square in the eyes.

'Yeah but...' Number Twelve pauses. 'Where's your logic?'

'Where's *your* logic,' Number Five snaps back.

'But that's what I said... I said it's more logical that she approached Jason because Jason is famous – people must approach him all the time.'

'Well you need to look up what logic stands for in the dictionary,' Number Five says.

It's rather ironic she said that. She may have said it as a reflex of what she was thinking, because she isn't entirely sure what the word logic means herself. She always thought she did, but Number Twelve's use of it just now kinda threw her. Number Five isn't normally this stupid but she's been overwhelmed by jury duty. Her anxiety has played up over the course of this trial. She's not entirely sure what her role is supposed to be. She feels a bit out of her depth amongst the eleven others serving alongside her. Feels she has to compensate for her lowly-paid shopping centre shelf-stacking job by ensuring she has one of the loudest voices in the room.

Number Seven speaks up, more so to ease Number Five's discomfort than anything, though she did have a valid point to make.

'I don't want this to sound wrong, sexist... I suppose,' she says. 'I guess it's best I say this rather than a man. But... I kinda think there could be some logic in the boys approaching her. I mean... we've seen photos of the night in question right; how stunning was Sabrina? She doesn't look that striking in the courtroom – still a lovely looking young woman... but on the night—'

'What the hell has this got to do with how hot the girl is?' Number Five snaps back, her voice all high-pitched. She hadn't realised Number Seven was actually supporting the point she was initially trying to make. Number Seven sucks air in through her teeth; an attempt to stop her blood from beginning to boil.

'That's not what I'm saying,' she says as calmly as she can, a polite smile on her face.

'It's exactly what you just said. You were comparing how hot she was on the night to how she dressed in court. We're not here to judge that kind—'

'Number Five, please!' Number Seven finally snaps, placing both of her palms face down on the table, almost standing up. 'It *does* have a lot to do with what she looked like on the night, okay? It does.'

All of the jurors except Number Five stare at Number Seven. She hadn't been exactly shy over the past five weeks, but nobody would have predicted she'd be the first one to lose patience. And the jury are only twenty minutes into their deliberations.

Number Seven is a secondary school teacher from inner-city Dublin. Her real name is Roisin Gorman; a twenty-two-year-old who shares a small two-bedroom apartment in the centre of town with a work colleague. Number Seven is nearest in age to Number Five in this room; they're the only two still in their twenties. Their maturity levels are decades apart, though. Number Seven raised her hand as undecided in the initial verdict vote about twenty minutes ago, but is veering towards the not guilty camp; though she loathes the idea of Jason, Zach and Li getting away scot free, if they did in fact rape Sabrina.

'Ish it even conceivable that both parties just happened to bump into each other and therefore nobody necessarily approached anyone first... they jusht struck up conversation in passing?' Brian asks slowly, trying to cool the temperature of the discussion.

'None of the witnesses allude to this,' replies Number Twelve.

That was accurate. Six witnesses from the Hairy Lemon were called to the stand over the course of the trial. The defence found three witnesses who were willing to testify that Sabrina deliberately made a bee-line towards Jason as soon as he arrived at the bar. But the prosecution were also able to call on three witnesses who testified in complete contrast to that. Two of them said Sabrina was led towards Jason by his friend Li. One other said that he was pretty sure Jason signalled to Li that he should bring Sabrina towards him.

It's justifiable that the jurors are genuinely torn on which side to believe in this instance. There was no CCTV footage, just three witnesses on each side cancelling out each other's perception of what really happened.

'The problem here is,' Number Twelve continues, 'one party or the other is lying all through this case. Straight from the bat somebody is lying and that could, conceivably, lead us to believe that they are lying about everything else.'

The jurors begin to talk over each other, most debating against Number Twelve's argument. But he raises the palm of his hand to silence them. He hadn't finished what he was saying. 'Sorry, if you don't mind me just finishing my point with this... the truth is, if we look at all the evidence, little that there is in this case, we don't and never will know who approached who first. All we have is our gut feeling. Our opinion. And that's not enough in this room.'

The jurors soak in Number Twelve's last sentence. They know this, were told this by the judge. Yet it's so easy to lose track of such instruction; so easy to be swayed by instinct, by opinion.

The judge had eyeballed each and every juror before setting them off on their deliberations after the trial ended this morning. He tried to get through to them that they could only convict Jason, Zach and Li if they felt the prosecution proved beyond all reasonable doubt that non-consensual sex occurred on the night in question. But some of the jurors still aren't entirely sure what 'reasonable doubt' means exactly. Number Twelve and Brian made attempts at defining the phrase for them, but at least five people sitting around this table are still genuinely confused by the phrase. This is not a new phenomenon in these jury rooms. This lack of understanding of the legal processes occurs on a daily basis in here; jurors unclear on the exact protocol they should follow when examining a trial. The judge had told jurors that they shouldn't use their gut instinct, shouldn't use opinion, should only go by the evidence they heard at the trial. Number Five has been totally thrown by this. She can't comprehend that her opinion holds no value.

'It can't be proven,' Brian raises his voice again, his Dublin accent thickening, 'beyond reashonable doubt that Sabrina approached the boys or that the boys approached Sabrina first. So we'll have to chalk this down as an even reshult.'

'What the hell do you mean even result?' Number Three asks. 'It's not a bloody football match here. We're each entitled to our own individual feelings on this and I genuinely believe that the lads were on a mission – as they probably are every time they go out – to find the hottest girl in the pub to bring to Jason. There is a witness who confirms this.'

'There are witnesses who say the opposite,' Number Twelve bites back. But his point is barely heard over the murmurings of everybody else around the table. They all have their own views. And they all want to be heard.

'Can we calm down please?' Brian says, standing to attention. 'Number One, please...' he says to his nemeses, almost embarrassing the Head Juror into curtailing the behaviour around the table.

'Okay... okay,' Number One says, shuffling the butt of his paperwork off the table again. 'We have heard from six witnesses and this matter of who approached who first practically evens itself out, just like Number Twelve said. We will not know who approached who first. Perhaps we should move—'

'If we believe – as Sabrina testified on the stand as well as in her original police statement – that she didn't know who Jason Kenny was, then surely we can believe that she didn't approach him,' Number Three says, opening up another branch of the same argument just as Number One seemed to be bringing it to conclusion. Number Seven sighs as the debate ripples around her. Then she rises from her seat.

'I'm pouring myself a tea, anyone want one?' she calls out, hoping a quick break will offer everyone a chance to digest the argument and calm down.

'Go on,' Number Four says. He's the only one who paid any attention to her question.

The rest of them are still mumbling their views on who approached who first in the Hairy Lemon.

Number Four rises from his seat and follows Number Seven towards the tiny table that stands just inside the door. The only facilities the jurors have inside the jury room rest on this table; a silver dispenser that produces both cold and boiled water, different flavoured tea bags, a jar of instant coffee, a jug of milk and a choice of either plain or chocolate digestive biscuits. The only other object taking up floor space is the mahogany conference table. It's oval, a bit like a rugby ball; six chairs either side of it. A black carton, about shoe-box in size, rests atop it. The carpet's bright red, just as it was in the courtroom – the exact shade of red you'd normally find a movie star gliding across at a premier. Everything else is white; the walls, the ceiling, even the modern rectangular lampshade hovering over the table is a bright white. The bulb is always switched on, shining an unflattering light down on to the top of the jurors' heads. They will be given a break in the corridors soon, just to stretch their legs. At lunch time they'll be brought to a different room, left alone to further discuss the trial over their beef or chicken dish if they so wish. But that won't be for another three hours.

'Whaddya think of this handjob?' Number Four whispers to Number Seven as he pushes down on the tap, releasing cold water into his glass.

'Not a chance. Four minutes?' she replies, raising an eyebrow.

'Ah... I don't know,' Number Four says, shaking his hand side to side. Number Seven snort-laughs, then holds up an apologetic hand over Number Four's shoulder towards the rest of the jurors. Their faces had swivelled towards her at the sound of her snort. She waits until they all resume talking, then whispers back into Number Four's ear.

'That how long it takes you, yeah?'

'It does actually.'

They both stifle their laughs. Number Four and Number Seven had already decided to be friends via body language within the first week of the trial. Their friendship had now developed to a level where they would make eye contact with each other whenever one of the other jurors produced a tic; like when Brian would talk over somebody, or when Number One would bounce his paperwork off the table, or when Number Five would say something close to outlandish, or when Number Twelve would use the word 'logic'. When any of these tics occurred, Number Four and Number Seven would stare at each other, then twitch a muscle in their cheek to signal a stifled smile.

'So what do you two think then?' Number One directs at the pair of them from the far side of the conference table.

The whole table stares at them.

'Sorry?' Number Four says, turning to look back over his shoulder.

'Will we leave that discussion there? I mean we could get back to it at some point... but shall we move on?'

'Sure,' says Number Four. Number Seven nods her head, mouths a silent 'yeah', then sits back down. She offers a purse of her lips to Number Six who is sitting directly across from her; has felt sorry for the woman since the first day of the trial. Number Seven has an inkling that Number Six really doesn't want to be here. But she couldn't be more wrong. Number Six is revelling in this. Nobody has been able to put an accurate age on her. Physically, she looks older than her sixty-eight years; her face is worn, wrinkles wedge deep into her forehead and cheeks – most likely because she has smoked at least twenty cigarettes every day for the past half a century – but although she is mostly quiet, she's not bored, just observant.

'Unless... Number Six, do you have anything to add?' Number Seven suggests, directing her hands across the table.

Number Six peels her back, vertebrae by vertebrae, from the fake leather chair in almost slow motion, pokes her chin out so that it's parallel to the table, looks at the faces of all six jurors sitting on the opposite side to her, then forgets to speak. Everybody sits wide-eyed, staring at her... waiting. She picks up the cold glass of water in front of her, sips from it, swirls the water around her mouth – making much more noise than most would deem appropriate – then places the glass back down with a thud. She lets out a gasp of satisfaction.

'I'd like to move on to the handjob,' she says.

I'll never understand why grown men and women don't have enough cop on to leave Jason alone when he's out with his mates. I've already brushed one of them aside, but there are too many gathering now. Too many to hush away without making Jason look like a prick.

'Here mate, will ye take a pic of me with Jason Kenny?' some youngfella asks me. I sigh, let him know this isn't why I fucking came out tonight, but take the phone he's offering anyway, guide him towards Jason and call Jason's name so they're both facing the lens while I take the pic.

'Here ye go,' I say, handing the phone back. The youngfella pinches at his screen.

'Ah, will ye take another one, mate, my eyes are half closed in—'

'No,' I snap back at him, turning towards Li.

Li normally laughs at how short I can be with Jason's fans. But he's not there. He's scooted away from the small crowd, pretending to stare at shitty movie posters on the wall instead.

I don't know how Jason has the patience to keep that fake smile on his face while he does this shit. I wouldn't be able for it. It's a good job he's the one who made it as a professional, and not me. I'd probably be locked up by now for punching fucking idiots who felt it was appropriate to ask me for an autograph while I'm out having fun with me mates.

Getting an autograph just seems so tedious to me. It used to be bad enough when people wanted just that – Jason's name scribbled on a piece of paper – but camera phones have changed the game. All people want now is a photo – proof that they've actually bumped into Jason as if it's some kind of achievement for them. Sad fuckers.

The frustrating thing about the camera phone is that the cunts never have the bleedin' setting ready. They're always fumbling around with their buttons, trying to find the camera app while Jason stands there waiting with a fake smile plastered across his face.

Maybe I got lucky missing out on all this shit. I was always a better player than Jason. He'd even admits that himself. But he got the breaks. I didn't. I think it's to do with the fact that he grew into himself. I'm still the same height I was when I was fourteen. His natural physique is more in tune with being a professional footballer. Plus – and I only realised this later – Jason had more support from his family. His da practically coached us from when we were about nine years old. His family would be on the sidelines of every home match in Benmadigan Park, cheerin' us on. He had a stable upbringing. Mine was shite in comparison. My ma and da couldn't even tell you what position I played in. My brothers used to play a bit themselves, but by the time I was fourteen, fifteen – that kinda age – they'd already fucked off to live in different corners of the world.

They couldn't stand living in our fractured home, couldn't stand living under the same roof as our folks. Callum moved to Sydney when he was just eighteen. He was supposed to go travelling for a year – is still there twenty years later. Brad was twenty-one when he fucked off to Toronto. I've often felt like following one of them overseas. To get away from Drimnagh, get away from Dublin. But I don't think running away from problems is what will make me happy. I genuinely think my older brothers are cowards. I face up to my problems. I've even told me ma and da that they are the reason I didn't make it as a professional footballer. But they couldn't give a shit. They've no interest in what I'm doing, let alone what I'm not doing.

I sip on my beer, wait for the small crowd to go away and try to dream up an epic night out for the three of us. It's been ages since we've been out together. Jason barely drinks anymore. Just on the odd occasion that me and Li persuade him to. We always have a session in Dublin when the footie season ends. It's the only time each year that we get to spend some quality time doing what we used to do. A few times over the season myself and Li fly over to games, sit in the VIP area of some of the best stadiums in England to take in the games. But the novelty of that died off years ago. It's actually a bit of a slog to go over now. Almost boring. Jason has to be super professional. So when we do call over to see him, it's normally beans on toast suppers while watching Netflix in his gaff. Pretty much the same as I do at home with me bird.

I sigh as another youngfella offers me his phone.

'Sorry mate, it's not my job,' I say before he leans in towards Jason, holds his phone out, fumbles with the button and tries to take a selfie.

'Ah, here – gimme the fuckin thing,' I say before taking a picture of him with a footballer he probably doesn't even rate that much.

After handing the phone back, I decide to walk away from the crowd, do as Li normally does; step aside and pretend it's not happening.

I look towards Li, notice him walking the most amazing lookin bird towards us. Fuckin hell. She's deadly. I love brunettes. There's something more naturally sexy about a brunette than any other hair colour.

I shuffle towards Li, try to eyeball him, try to say well done, mate. But his eyes haven't left the girl's face. That's unusual for him.

I watch her shake hands with Jason and as I approach I hear him offer to buy her a drink. Bastard. He got in there before me.

I'm sure there are worse things to be experiencing than having a queue of people lining up to take a picture with you. I try to remind myself of that on a consistent basis. But the awkwardness of this never fades. Especially when someone mumbles the word 'legend' in my direction. I hate being called that, as stupid as that sounds. I'm far from a legend. Nobody in the football world would class me as a legend. But people just want to say that word to me when they meet me, as if they feel a need to sensationalise my ability. It's just verbal diarrhoea. Utter bullshit. And it makes me feel instantly awkward.

It happens a lot more here than it does in the UK. Probably because the Irish are a lot friendlier by nature. But it's probably more to do with the goal I scored for the national team against Holland. A saucy half-volley that guaranteed we qualified for the 2012 European Championships. It was a freak. I'm not a goal scorer, never was. It's rare Irish supporters have much to celebrate, much to remember. But that goal is up there. If I tried that half-volley another hundred times, it wouldn't end up in the net once. But that's football. It's much more a game of luck than anyone cares to admit. And I'm one of the luckiest fuckers around.

I watch Zach take another phone from another fan and almost laugh out loud as he takes the pic. I'm well aware he'll be boiling inside. I've often joked with him that it's a good job I became famous and he didn't. He doesn't have the patience to be a modern-day professional footballer. Truth be known, he didn't have the ability for it either. Not that I've ever said that to him.

'Hey Jason, this is... this is...?' Li says to me, pointing out one of the most stunning-looking girls I've ever seen.

'Sabrina,' she says, flashing a smile. 'Sabrina Doyle.'

Wow. She's hot.

'Lemme get you a drink, Sabrina Doyle,' I say. It's probably as unoriginal as opening lines go – offering to buy a drink – but it was the first thing that popped into my head.

'Eh... sure. A... red wine,' she says.

'C'mon,' I say, ushering her towards the bar with me. She seems as nice as she looks; shy almost. Actually reminds me of the first girl I ever fancied. Valarie Byrne. She went to Mourne Road primary school with us. All the boys fancied her. But I didn't stand a chance. A pretty little brunette with a dimple on each cheek was never gonna look at the pasty-skinned, freckly ginger kid.

I actually never had a girlfriend until I found fame. I'll never know what it's like for somebody to actually like the real me, not the celebrity. My therapist tries to drill into me that I *am* a celebrity, it's part of who I am and that if fame is attractive to some people, then that's great; because I have fame. He says I shouldn't be too paranoid about it. I don't know... celebrity is just so complex that I'm of the thinking it's pointless even trying to understand it. And fuck knows I've tried for long enough.

I'm ninety-nine per cent certain I wouldn't have wound up depressed if it wasn't for my celebrity, though. All I remember from before I made my first-team debut for Everton is happiness. Even when my brother Eric was born – and diagnosed with his heart condition – our family were still happy. It was a big blow, but us Kenny's just bandied together. We didn't let the fact that one of us had a ticking bomb for a heart get in the way of us all enjoying our lives – however many years they were going to last.

Mam and Dad's outlook was always positive. I'd give up all of the money I have now, all of my fame, in return for an ounce of their positivity. I don't know where mine went. It's almost like I had to sacrifice my happiness to become a successful footballer.

FifPro released a survey they carried out a couple of years ago about depression in footballers. Their research found that thirty-eight per cent of professionals end up clinically depressed within a decade of retiring from the game. That shocked the world. Didn't shock me. I pal around with pro footballers. Most of them are unhappy. Not that they'd admit it though.

'So, what do you do?' I ask Sabrina as I hand her the glass of red.

'Me? What do you do more like? Why is everyone keen to get a picture taken with you?'

'I'm a green grocer,' I tell her. It's my usual line. Especially to girls who play dumb.

'Well your apples and pears must be the best in the business if people feel they need to get a photo with you,' she says laughing. Fuck. That's a helluva laugh. I could fall in love with this one.

'I'm a footballer,' I tell her, giving in.

'Ah... who do you play for?'

'Well... actually, y'know what,' I say, puffing a small laugh out of my nostrils. 'I don't play for any team anymore. But don't tell anybody that. Nobody knows. That can be our little secret.'

I wink at her. Not sure why I feel the need to be so honest with a girl I met literally two minutes ago. Perhaps a pretty face is more powerful than I ever thought it could be.

'It's eh... difficult to talk in here,' I say, leaning towards her. 'Fancy going outside for a minute?'

'Eh... sure. A eh... red wine,' I answer before checking the time on my phone. 7:25. My text should be coming through any minute now, but fuck it – it's not every day a celebrity ever offers to buy me a drink.

I'm supposed to stay sober when I'm working, supposed to only drink non-alcoholic wine. But it's impossible sometimes. The target almost always wants to buy me a drink.

I stare at the back of his head after following him to the bar. One or two people call out his name, wanting to be heard to acknowledge him. It must be great being a role model. I've probably dreamt of fame more than I've dreamt of anything in my entire life, though I know that doesn't make me unique. I'm sure most people have fantasised about being a celebrity. I play the name over and over in my head. *Jason Kenny*. It doesn't ring any bells.

'So, what do you do?' he shouts at me as he hands me my drink. It's difficult to hear in here. The bar area is a lot louder than where we'd been standing.

'Me? What do you do more like? Why is everyone keen to get a picture taken with you?' I shout back, cupping my hand towards his ear.

'I'm a green grocer,' he lies, a big grin stretching across his face. He's getting better looking the more I stare at him. I like his freckles, they look like they belong on his face; as if his face wouldn't work without them.

'Well your apples and pears must be the best in the business if people feel they need to get a photo taken with you,' I shout back, aware it's getting quite obvious that I'm flirting. I'm so uncool. I've never had the nerve to be flirtatious. Unless I'm on the job, of course.

'I'm a footballer,' he relents.

'Ah... who do you play for?'

'Well... actually, y'know what. I don't play for any team anymore. But don't tell anyone that. Nobody knows. That can be our little secret.'

I don't really know what he means by that. Assume it's some football transfer thingy. He's probably waiting on another club to buy him or something. But I feel quite chuffed that we have our own little secret. It's such a shame I'm working tonight – it'd be really cool to hang out with Jason; see how the other half live.

'It's eh... difficult to talk in here,' he shouts at me. 'Fancy going outside for a minute?'

I agree by nodding my head and standing aside, letting him lead the way. I notice the crucifix on his chain as he brushes past me. Jaysus, my dad would be delighted if I brought this fella home; not only a footballer, but a bible believer too. They're the only two boxes a man would need to tick to make Dad happy. Dad still goes to church every Sunday. Myself and Amanda would join him on the rare occasion, especially around Christmas and almost certainly around the time of Mam's anniversary. But that's it. They both tried their best to raise two Catholic daughters, but they raised two atheists instead; probably by trying to force us to be Catholics. In truth, it wasn't anything they did or didn't do – it's just a generational thing. The difference between our generation and their generation is that a world of common sense opened up to us. Media, TV, the Internet – our generation don't have to believe fairy tales to explain some of life's mysteries. We have all the answers at our fingertips. Dad is hugely disappointed that we don't believe the fairy tale he happens to believe in. And he *really* believes it – is deluded enough to think he's going to spend eternity with Mam, even though we burnt her body to a crisp eight years ago. But neither Amanda nor I would ever debate the subject with him. We're happy that he's happy to believe. Perhaps believing is the key to happiness. Because there's definitely a key to happiness somewhere that I've not been able to find.

I can't hold his faith against him though. Not when he has an ass like that. I stare at both of his cheeks snuggled into his jeans as he leads me towards the door. The crucifix is a bit cringe... would most likely put me off most other fellas, but when am I ever going to be flirted with by a professional footballer again?

Jason motions for us to walk around the corner when we get outside, to the side of the pub, and I already know I'm going to kiss him. Jesus, if I still kept a diary this would be one hell of a Dear Diary moment. Before either of us offers up another word, his lips are locked onto mine; his tongue circling my mouth. This all happened so fast. I shouldn't be enjoying it so much; shouldn't be giving myself over so easily, but I am enjoying it. Lots. So much so, I can hear the little devil on my shoulder giggling. It's unusual he gets his way.

My stomach flips a wave of excitement through me. This guy is so cute; he's a footballer; he's famous; he's rich; he's mine – for this moment anyway. He'll probably be snogging someone else in ten minutes time. But right now, all of his attention is on me.

'You're so hot,' he whispers into my ear after gnawing his mouth away from mine. But then he's back in, his tongue now circling in the opposite direction. It's a cute technique; new for me. His left arm squeezes me closer, his right hand working its way up my back, then around to my chest. I allow him to cup me, because the thrill is working. I haven't felt this wanted in a long, long time. Certainly not by anyone I want to want me.

'Touch me,' he whispers. I just continue kissing him, unsure of what he's asking exactly. Until I feel him unzipping his jeans.

I don't move my hands. Not at first. I just continue to kiss him, until I notice my right hand slipping inside his zip; rubbing at his dick through his boxer shorts. Average size. I think. This is only the third dick I've ever touched. It's certainly the average one by my experience.

'I can't,' I say, pulling my hand away. I'm not sure how long I had it in there. Seconds, I'm sure.

I sigh, place my hands either side of his face and bring him in for more of that tongue circling. He wrestles his zip back up, then stops kissing me so he can fasten his top button. I hear the phone vibrate in my bag; a quick buzz that lasts less than a second. But I know it's going to take me away from this moment forever.

'Sorry,' I say, leaning off Jason. I unzip my bag, take out the phone and open Lorna's text message.

'I eh... need to go back inside,' I say, tilting my head and pursing my lips. 'This has been... well... it's been lovely.'

Zach strolls back to me, a beer in each of his hands.

'Here y'are, fella,' he says holding one towards me. Now I've got one and a half pints. Zach's already downed his first. That's nothing new. It's almost as if he sees drinking alcohol as a sport. A competition. I try to swig back the rest of my first pint, but I almost regurgitate it back into the glass.

'I didn't see Jason at the bar, where'd he go?' Zach asks.

'Signing autographs,' I say. 'We came to the wrong bar. I didn't think it'd be this busy this early. Fancy heading somewhere else?'

'Relax Li, we've only just got here.'

He seems worlds away, his head cocking around the room. He hasn't even looked at me since he got back from the bar. Zach and I have always had a strange relationship. We're definitely best mates. But I think we'd both admit – even though we never have out loud – that we're best mates by default. If Jason wasn't living in England, he'd be both mine and Zach's best mate. But as it is, me and Zach are the ones who regularly get to see each other these days. Yet, bizarrely, we've never been really close. Like *really* close.

I know everything about Jason, and he knows everything about me. Not only about our families, but about everything: our feelings, opinions, insecurities. I don't really know Zach that intimately. But only because Zach isn't interested in talking about himself. Well, aside from how good a footballer he used to be. He would never share anything about his feelings. Would never ask after my family, ask how I'm genuinely getting on. I think it's because he had a bit of a shitty upbringing. He's just used to keeping everything bottled up. I've had a shitty upbringing too though, in fairness. Hasn't stopped me from opening up.

My mam raised Jinny and me on one hundred and ninety pound a week. That's how much she got off the social welfare when we were younger. I'll always remember that figure. It just sticks in my mind. Mainly because I remember transitioning from thinking that's a lot of money to realising 'that is nothing!' as I slowly began to fathom how much things cost.

I watch as Zach pivots his head around the room again.

'Where's yer one gone... that Sabrina bird?' he asks.

'Oh... haven't seen her in a while.'

'She's not with Jason, is she? I'm into that. Don't want him getting his hands on her first.'

'Don't think so,' I say, finishing off my first pint, staring at my second as if it's going to be responsible for me feeling like shit tomorrow. 'I think he's signing autographs somewhere.'

That's just an assumption. Jason often goes missing when we're in pubs together, only for us to find him in the middle of a tiny scrum, scribbling his name down on peeled beer mats.

'Where do you wanna go anyway?' Zach asks.

'Somewhere a little quieter. Didn't think this place would be so jammed. I wanted to have a word with the two of you.'

'About what?'

'Ah... I'll tell you later.'

'It's not... it's not about...' Zach says, his eyes narrowing. 'It's not about the secret is it?'

'Jesus no!' I say, noting further evidence that the secret never really leaves Zach's mind. It has affected all three of us, massively. But Zach, I'm sure, is the one who has suffered the most.

Jason and I can keep the secret to the back of our minds. But I just know Zach carries it around with him on a daily basis. He's still as paranoid about it now as he was back then. He still thinks we're all going to get found out. Put behind bars.

'Fuck sake, mate. You've gotta let it go. That was years ago. It's over. No... I just have something to say to my two best mates. We haven't been out in – ah here he is now,' I say, nodding as Jason strolls towards us.

'Where've you been?' Zach asks him. 'Y'haven't seen that Sabrina bird have ye? I'm dying to chat her up. She's amazing lookin'.'

'Eh...' Jason hesitates. I know he's about to lie. I know Jason inside out. 'Nah, haven't seen her since I bought her that drink, mate,' he says.

I usher her around the corner of the pub, along the pathway. And as soon as she stops walking, I kiss her. Couldn't help myself. I actually brought her outside to have a chat, to get to know her a little better, but she just looked too pretty to not kiss.

I squeeze her tighter, feeling her breasts against my chest, then bring my hand back around, just to feel one. It would be a lie to say I haven't moved this fast before – I have – but certainly not with anybody I genuinely like. This just feels right.

'Touch me,' I say, almost regretting it as soon as the two words come out of my mouth. My dick has shot up since I started kissing her. It's almost calling out for her to touch it. But what a stupid fucking way to ask a girl to give you some intimacy. *Touch me.* Jee... I'm such a twat. I cringe inside. Yet for some reason I've popped the button of my jeans open, and pulled my zip down. I leave my jeans hanging on to my hips, wondering how stupid I've made myself look. I contemplate zipping back up and apologising when Sabrina's hand slips inside my jeans, her fingers twiddling at my balls, working her hand up to my shaft. Jesus, this is a hell of a turn on. How the fuck can one woman be this good looking and this dirty?

'I can't,' she says, taking her hand back out, killing my bone instantly. She goes rooting in her bag, picks out her phone.

'Sorry,' she says, offering me a little smile. 'I eh... need to go inside. This has been... well... lovely.'

Bollocks! I'm a fuckin idiot. I've treated this girl like one of the little sluts who hang around nightclubs in the north east of England; the ones who don't hide their ambition to spend the night with a footballer. Shagging a footballer is almost like a badge of honour to these girls. I would consider that really sad if I wasn't the beneficiary of a thousand orgasms because of that reality. Though I'm pretty sure that kinda thing has led to my depression. I sometimes hate myself for how easy it is for me to have sex. Literally any time I want it.

'I need to check through this,' she says pointing the screen of her phone towards me just after we arrive back inside the pub. I cringe again. Maybe she has a boyfriend. Maybe she feels guilty and is pretending she got a text message to cool things with me before they got out of hand.

'Okay, I'm eh... gonna go back up to the lads upstairs,' I say. 'Come see me before you leave.'

I curl my fingers back into my palms and stab with my nails into them as

I watch her walk towards the toilets on the far side of the pub, my gaze only disturbed when somebody behind shouts out my name.

'Ye fuckin legend ye!' a stranger says, pointing his two thumbs up at me after I turn around. 'Me cousin used to play for the Bosco as well y'know? Was coached by your old man.'

I'm famous throughout the breadth of this country. But me dad's more famous in Drimnagh than I am. Anyone who has any relationship to Drimnagh always talks to me about my old man. He must have coached three hundred kids, I reckon, at St John Bosco. He gave up his Saturday mornings playing golf with my uncle to coach my team when I signed up for the under tens. He coached me and Zach for years. I'd say I think of my dad about five times a day, every day. I miss him like crazy. Feel like I have nothing to prove if I don't have him to prove it to.

'Ah here he is now,' I hear Li say in the middle of his conversation with Zach when I stroll up the stairs.

'Where've you been?' Zach asks. 'Y'haven't seen that Sabrina bird have ye? I'm dying to chat her up. She's amazin'.'

Shit. I fucking knew this would happen. It's not the first time hot birds have come on to me, that Zach assumes he could just have for himself. I can't have this argument with him now. Not again.

'Eh... nah, haven't seen her since I bought her that drink, mate,' I tell him. 'Well, he wants to head off somewhere else,' Zach says, nodding towards Li. 'But I ain't going till we see that bird. I'm not leaving without her number. She's was a fuckin' ten!'

'Where d'ya wanna go anyway?' I ask Li, trying to change the subject.

'Somewhere quieter. We were supposed to come out for an early drink so we could catch up... have a chat. It's too noisy here.'

'Yeah – let's head off then,' I say.

But Zach's having none of it, his head swivelling in search of Sabrina. He's not gonna find her up here. She's down in the loo. Probably with tears pouring down her face because she cheated on her fella.

BRIAN RAISES his voice the loudest.

'Can we all jusht calm down one moment, please?' he shouts.

It's slightly ironic. It was he who started the jurors off on the tangent they were currently on. He then raises his eyebrows towards Number One, gesturing outwards with his hands.

'Yes... yes,' Number One says, taking the hint and rising from his seat. 'Let's keep perspective.'

He undoes one more button on his shirt, showing a bit more chest hair than most would deem appropriate. He is one of a few jurors who is finding the temperature in the jury room too hot. But while Number One is loosening buttons on his shirt, Number Six is pulling her cardigan tighter around her shoulders. She's freezing. Isn't the only one.

'Number Six, you mentioned you were keen to get to this stage of deliberations, do you mind giving us your take on it?' Number One says, sitting back down.

Number Six grabs her glass of water again, sips from it, lets out another gasp and then sucks her lips, making a bizarrely loud pop sound.

'It's just... it's just,' she stutters. 'As Number Twelve said earlier. Somebody is lying through the whole night. And I feel that the handjob is the key aspect of the trial because whoever is lying about this, is lying about what happened at midnight... lying about the rape.'

'Yes,' Brian pipes up, resuming control from Number One. 'But what is your take on the handjob specifically – what do you believe happened just outside the pub?'

'Well, I'd rather hear from others on this,' Number Six says, her voice almost shaking.

'Number Six, at some point you have to realise that you are part of this jury too. Your thoughts count as much as anybody else's in this room.'

Number Seven says this sympathetically across the table. It isn't so much that she values Number Six's opinion, it's just that Number Seven wants everybody to be involved as much as they possibly can. She's a typical teacher and is tired of listening to the same two voices all the time. Both Brian and Number One had gone beyond irritating her weeks ago.

'Well, I think that maybe he wanted her to give him a handjob but she refused,' says Number Six, giving her first genuine opinion of the trial.

'Why didn't she say that in her teshtimony, or to the police when she first made the allegations?' Brian retorts. 'If it was a case that Jason tried to get a handjob from Sabrina, why didn't she mention this? Trying to get a handjob ishn't what we have to deliberate here. Nobody argued about trying to get a handjob. Jason is saying she *definitely* gave him a handjob, while Sabrina is saying she kissed him and that was it; that she didn't go near his... eh... his penis.'

'Well in that case, I don't believe it happened,' Number Six says, reaching for her glass again, her fingers shaking.

'So you've changed your mind in the space of—'

'Calm down, Brian,' snaps Number Five. 'You asked for her thoughts, let the woman speak.'

The room falls silent as Number Six finishes her sip, then lets out another gasp that almost turns into a burp. Number Four has to stifle his laugh at the sound.

'I just think four minutes is just not... I don't think much happened in that time,' she says.

The jurors have just finished watching three re-runs of the CCTV footage from the entrance of the Hairy Lemon pub that showed Jason leading Sabrina outside the main door at 19:32 p.m. and then back inside at 19:36 p.m. Unlike the earlier argument of who approached who first, there was at least some hard evidence of this encounter. But it didn't really help either side of the argument.

Sabrina admitted, even as early as her first interview with police almost eighteen months ago, that she did share an early kiss with Jason Kenny on the pathway to the side of the pub. She insists he was trying to kiss her more passionately than she felt appropriate, given that they had only just met. She confirmed that at one point she gave in and kissed him, testifying on the stand that it was 'a very small kiss, didn't last long.' Jason's testimony was quite different. He said he was surprised they were only outside for four minutes, because he remembers them kissing for quite some time, said Sabrina even went so far as unzipping his jeans, fondling his penis outside of his boxer shorts before reaching inside and performing manual stimulation on him.

'If I may raise my concerns here,' says Number Eight, looking at the plasma screen hung on the wall, still showing a paused image of Sabrina and Jason arriving back inside the pub. 'Sabrina doesn't look embarrassed or at any kind of unease coming back in. Don't you just think that if she had given a stranger a handjob, then she might be a bit self-conscious? A bit embarrassed, perhaps?'

'But sure it's black and white footage. She could be red-faced for all we know,' says Number One.

'True. But she's not even trying to hide her face. She shows no sign of unease at all. I genuinely think from this evidence,' Number Eight continues, pointing at the screen, 'this handjob never happened. I think he's making it up. It suits his defence. I wouldn't be surprised if his whole expensive defence team just made this part up.'

Number Twelve lets out an audible sigh before getting to his feet.

'I know we're all frustrated at this particular juncture. But what do we have – apart from the CCTV footage which only proves they went outside for a few minutes... which neither side actually deny? We have her word against his. It's not much to go on.'

'Well I think I may have a good point to raise,' Number Ten says, before clearing her throat. 'Don't forget that the defence are brilliant, right? They are an expensive, operation – we all know this. Think about this for a second... if Sabrina opened Jason's zip, why didn't they try to prove this? Why didn't they have the jeans examined to gather confirmed evidence of her finger prints on his zipper?'

The jury room falls silent, only the noise of a couple of jurors shifting their seating positions creating any sound at all.

'That's a very good point, Number Ten,' claims Brian. 'You're right. If these guys are the besht of the besht in terms of defence lawyers, surely they would have looked into that. And I'm sure they did look into it. But why wasn't it brought to court?' he says, shrugging one of his shoulders.

'Because they didn't find her finger prints on his zip,' says Number Ten. Number Eight stares at Number Ten, meets her eye and then raises his eyebrow in appreciation of her nous. Number Ten is proving that first impressions shouldn't count; certainly not in jury rooms.

Number Ten's real name is Janice Dean, she's a thirty-two-year-old self-labelled geek from Mulhuddart in west Dublin. She's a massive superhero fan. Like her dad, Number Ten read both Marvel and DC comic books as a kid. She has worn an overly big T-shirt for every day of this trial, normally emblazoned with the name of a rock group she's into. Today's T-shirt is blank, but throughout the course of the trial she had worn T-Shirts with the logos of Black Sabbath, Led Zeppelin, AC/DC and Deep Purple – bands her dad had forced her to listen to as a child, bands she still listens to today. She has her face pierced in seven different places; two piercings on each ear, two on her nose; one on the side of her right nostril, the other a ring that forms a bridge between both nostrils like a cute dairy cow. And she also has a rounded stud just below the centre of her bottom lip. It would be difficult to tell from looks alone that Number Ten is one of the highest earners in the room. She works as an engineer on construction sites – again, influenced by her dad. She remains undecided on a verdict in this trial, but is tipping towards not guilty because she thinks the expensive defence team would have done a better job of proving the rape had it in fact really happened. That's how her brain operates. No other juror has looked at it from that point of view.

She sits back on her chair and wallows in the praise that is coming her way from fellow jurors.

'Yeah... why didn't they do that?' Number One asks. 'Really good point, Number Ten. Very smart.'

'Well why didn't the prosecution prove that the jeans didn't have Sabrina's fingerprints? You could argue both sides,' rasps Number Twelve.

'I applaud the point being made', Brian says. 'But given that that is circumstantial, does anybody feel particularly strongly about this handjob claim? Is there anyone here who feels this definitely happened or definitely didn't happen? Let's do it this way... quick and easy. Hands up if you feel strongly that Sabrina did *not* give Jason a handjob just past seven-thirty on the night in question.'

Number Three, Number Five and Number Six raise their hands. This is no surprise. The three of them had already let it be known that they were in the guilty camp from the outset.

'And hands up if you think Sabrina *did* give Jason a handjob at this juncture?' says Brian as he reaches his own hand into the air. Number Twelve also holds his hand aloft. So too does Number Eight. At least there's been some movement on their earlier verdict vote. But not necessarily a move in the right direction. If anything, the jury room is more split down the middle now than it had been at the start.

'Three for, three against,' says Number One. 'Six undecided.'

'It's not undecided,' says Number Ten. 'It's just that we have no way of knowing for certain. I'm not undecided. I genuinely don't know – and neither does anyone – whether or not Sabrina gave Jason a handjob outside the pub. So I find it quite interesting that anyone would raise their hand for any of those verdicts with any degree of certainty at all.'

'Hold on... I am entitled to my—' Number Five begins to argue. An argument she doesn't even need to have.

'Calm down, Number Five,' Number One shouts, interrupting her. It was the first time the Head Juror properly raised his voice.

Number Five sits back in her chair, folds her arms across her chest. She was just about saved by Number One from uttering the word 'opinion' once again. She lets out a sigh that only she can hear. When talk resumes around the table she lifts her head, takes everybody in and begins to wonder why she feels as if she is the dumbest in the room when she certainly doesn't look the dumbest. She stares at six female faces, five male. Then pictures her own face, and tries to imagine what the other jurors are thinking when they look at her. Her sentiment is skewed though. They weren't making judgements on her looks, they were judging her based on what she was saying. She's beginning to wish she hadn't been picked for this trial at all.

The prosecution had tried hard to lean the jury selection gender-wise. They were determined to have as many females on the jury as possible; assuming that women would be more sympathetic to Sabrina's story. The defence did a fine job in limiting the number of female jurors to just seven; almost celebrating the seven:five gender ratio the judge settled on when jury selection was completed. Both the defence and prosecution were actually flawed in their ambitions though. Contrary to the long-held assumption that female jurors find in favour of a female victim of rape, research of over one-hundred rape cases in Dublin's criminal courts show that female-dominated juries are less likely to convict in this type of circumstance. It's almost difficult to believe. But the understanding is that women are more fascinated by this subject. They watch this type of trial through their television screens on a regular basis. Between *Law and Order*, *The Good Wife*, *LA Law*, *Crime and Punishment* and plenty of other Americanised TV courtroom dramas, women – who are the main target audience of such shows – are exposed to trials more readily than men. But the trials they watch on TV are dramatised versions of the real deal. And when set up in a real jury dock, suffering the endless silences of a trial and putting up with legal arguments that can go over most people's heads, they find themselves presented with a scenario that does not match their perception. They are not granted the same indicators and clues that pop up on TV dramas, and – as a result – they are less likely to convict. Though in truth, the toying between both sides pre-trial when it comes to selecting a jury can be a largely pointless exercise. Jurors are mostly swayed, not by their gender or even their past experiences, but by the most dominant voices in the jury room.

In this instance, the Number One versus Brian Hoare arguments – that continue to enrage most jurors, most of the time – hold a lot more significance to the outcome of this case than anything else.

Zach can get a bit like this. Manic. Obsessive.

He won't shut up about that Sabrina girl all night now. I'm sure Jason lied to him, told him he didn't know where she was. Zach would have had a little strop if he knew Jason had got in there before him. That's how nuts he can be.

'Where d'ya wanna go anyway?' Jason asks, trying to pull the three of us together; to stop Zach's head spinning around the room.

'Somewhere quieter,' I say. 'We were supposed to come out for an early drink so we could catch up... have a chat. It's too busy here.'

'Yeah – let's do it then,' Jason says.

He clinks my glass, then holds his towards Zach, waiting a brief moment until Zach tunes back in to clink glasses.

'C'mon man, we're gonna head somewhere else,' Jason tells him.

'Ah wait... lemme see if I can find that hot brunette. Not leaving here till I try it on with her.'

I want to tell him he's wasting his time, that she's way out of his league. But Zach's sensitive about things like that. I mean, he's a nice guy, the funniest guy I've ever met – doesn't take himself too seriously most of the time. But there are two things in life he can't seem to get over. One, Jason becoming a pro footballer while he didn't even get picked up by a League of Ireland club and two, the fact that Jason is now the one who gets all the girls.

'Go and have a quick look for her then,' Jason says, sighing. He looks at me; knows that I know. Is aware the night could turn into a bit of a fuck up if Zach figures out Jason has already put a marker down on Sabrina.

Zach swigs the rest of his second pint down, gasps out loud then claps Jason on the back and sets on his way.

'Have you already been with yer one?' I ask Jason after Zach has disappeared into the crowd. He clenches his teeth and nods his head.

'Ye shudda just told him, for fuck sake.'

'Ah... thought it best if he didn't know. He didn't even tell me he fancied her. The usual shit. Thinks he has first dibs on everything.'

'Poor Tina,' I say.

'And Scott. And Callum.'

Zach's been married around ten years now. Him and Tina have two sons; one they had before they wed, the other straight after. He's often told me and Jason that he wouldn't have married Tina if she hadn't fell preg-

43

nant. As if it was all her fault. But I actually think they're a good couple. Zach needs Tina. He'd go off the rails without her. He'd be fucked.

Still, it doesn't stop him cheating on her almost every time he goes out. He can't help it. Feels a night out isn't a night out unless he's pulled. He's always felt that way. He's the only one of us who cheats. Jason's only had one serious girlfriend, which lasted about two years, but all through that period he stayed faithful to Jessica. I still can't quite figure out why they broke up. 'We just grew apart,' has never really been fully explained to me. That's because Jason can't fully explain it to himself, I bet. My genuine feeling is Jessica got sick of him moping around the house. Jason used to be always in good spirits, certainly was when they first met, but his happiness seemed to erode a few years ago. He's become a lot more introverted. I think it's because his career is coming to an end. Think he might even be suffering from a touch of depression these days.

His current state of mind reminds me of the Jason immediately following The Secret. He shut down back then, kept all of his thoughts to himself. His depression didn't last too long though. Hopefully it doesn't now.

Getting away from Ireland helped after The Secret. So did the excitement of a promising Premier League career. He was sixteen when Everton snapped him up. Three years later he was making his first team debut against Manchester United; with me and Zach chanting his name from the stands of Goodison Park.

'Can't find her. She must be gone,' Zach says arriving back to us. That's a relief. I had visions of him coming back here after her telling him she'd already snogged his mate. It would mean Zach would be breathing heavily through his nose for the rest of the night, barely talking to either of us. It's happened before. Lots of times.

'She must be gone. Sorry mate,' I say. 'Plenty more fish in the sea.'

He spins his head around one more time, then shrugs his shoulders.

'You done with that pint, Li?' he asks.

I stare at the drink in my hand. It's still full. The two lads' glasses are empty.

'Ah... fuck it, I'll leave it,' I say, stretching to place it onto the shelf next to us.

'Fuck that,' says Zach, swiping the pint from me. He takes a deep breath before swigging from the glass, swallowing it all in one go. Then he looks at both of us, his eyes watering.

'Let's get the fuck outta here, boys,' he says.

I click the latch of the door, slap down the lid of the toilet and sit on it. Then I open the text message, squinting my eyes at the photograph. The face doesn't ring a bell. I definitely haven't copped this bloke since I've been here. Maybe he's just arrived. The text message isn't clear on that.

Target in place. Downstairs bar in Hairy Lemon. Be careful. Best of luck. Lorna. x

The guy looks pretty handsome in the pic. Not normally my type, but it helps my job if they're good looking because it makes everything more believable and less awkward. I click into my emails and recall the notes, even though I've read through them at least eight times already today.

Niall Stevens. Age 27. Car mechanic. Lives with his fiancée. Hobbies include watching Formula One, TV shows like Top Gear & Robot Wars. Loves Will Ferrell movies.

I stare at his picture again. Then place my phone back into my bag and stand up, open the lock and pace towards the mirrors. This toilet is pretty packed now. I have to stare over some girl's shoulder to get a good look at my face. I still wish I had worn something a little more comfortable, though this little number certainly worked on Jason Kenny. That was quite intense; never had somebody grab me up against a wall before, throwing their tongue in my mouth after literally meeting them two minutes prior. I enjoyed it. Probably shouldn't have put my hands down his pants though. It's most likely put him off me. He's probably moved on to his next girl already, thinking I was too easy – not enough of a challenge for a professional footballer. It's a pity work called for me when it did. If he's still around when I'm finished with Niall, I might go and speak to him. He did invite me to, after all.

I take one last look in the mirror, pull the V in my jumpsuit closer and decide to just get on with it. I almost see Amanda staring back at me. I think the older I get, the more I look like her. Amanda was a known model in Dublin. Signed up by Assets Agency when she was just seventeen. She used to appear on morning television all the time; me and my folks crunching on our Corn Flakes as she posed on our screens wearing the latest trends for some five-minute fashion item.

I used to think she had the most glamorous existence anyone could ever have. I was crazy jealous when I was a young teenager, though everyone kept assuring me my time would come. Apparently I was even better looking than my older sister. That's what they used to tell me. My time never really did come, though. I did a couple of those morning TV shows after I was signed up to a much smaller agency than Assets about eight years ago. It wasn't the glamorous gig I had assumed it would be when I was younger. Far from it. While Amanda spent ten years modelling, I only lasted two. Not even two. About twenty months. Casting agents used to tell me on a regular basis that I was 'too pretty' and 'too commercial' to land the jobs they were specifically looking to fill. I took myself way too seriously. Barely cracked a smile all through my teens. I'm sure this had an impact on casting agents. It's not just about looks – personality comes into it too, no matter how hard that is for anyone who's not a model to believe. It's a shitty business, modelling. And that's exactly what it is – a business. It's not glamorous from the inside at all. Modelling isn't about being pretty, it's about being a saleswoman. It's too corporate. Takes itself way too seriously. And I became a mirror of it. I'm pretty certain my aspirations of becoming a model, which I held from the age of twelve – when Amanda first started out – is the reason I'm introverted; the reason I haven't quite figured myself out; the reason I don't have much of a personality; the reason the prude angel on my shoulder always wins out over the devil. It's also the reason I don't have many friends.

School was torturous for me, though the torture happened long before I became a mirror image of the modelling industry. One day – my memory tells me it was in the first year of secondary school, but that may be fuzzy – I accused Thomas D'Arcy of punching me on the arm, just so the teacher would move him away from me. I hated sitting beside him; he smelt. I punched myself in the arm repeatedly, until it bruised, then walked into the classroom, sat beside Thomas and raised my hand. 'Miss, Thomas just punched me,' I said, forcing some tears out of my eyes. My plan worked. I was moved. But because Thomas was more likable than me, the students took his side. I was left alone in the playground for pretty much the next six years until I got secondary school out of the way.

I pull open the door of the ladies, the noise of the music causing me to tut. I'm sure somebody's turned the volume up since I've been to the loo. I suck my lips, take in every face before me, searching for the guy who's into Formula One, who's into Will Ferrell movies.

'Wow,' says some guy, standing back a bit so he can take all of me in. I just purse my lips at him in an almost sorrowful way, then walk on by. Turning lads' heads isn't a thrill for me; it never has been. I thought being good looking was a blessing when I was younger, only because it would help in my ambitions to become a model. But it genuinely isn't any advantage whatsoever. Anyone who thinks being good looking is advantageous is one of two things; either they are an idiot or they've never been good looking themselves.

Amanda and I are perfect examples of looks not counting towards happiness. We're both genetically blessed; both miserable at finding love. Sure take the hottest women on the planet: Halle Berry, Jennifer Aniston, Angelina Jolie, Charlize Theron... All hot as fuck. All miserable in love.

I'm pretty sure being good looking is a disadvantage because if you are good looking then that almost seems enough for most guys. They don't need to look past that initially, they don't need to go deeper. Once the novelty of the good looks wears off, which it inevitably does in every relationship, then the guy who hasn't bothered to get to truly know you doesn't know why he's dating you anymore. If it can happen to Halle Berry – constantly – then it can happen to anyone. I'd love to trade my looks for a better personality. I'd love to lighten up, be more outgoing. My new job is helping me come out of my shell, though. I'm getting better at it. I feel more confident now than I've ever felt in my life.

I rub at my palms. They always get a bit sweaty moments before I have to approach a target. They'll stop sweating once I'm talking to him. That's always the way; like an actress waiting backstage before she goes on. She shits herself behind the curtain, is cool as a cucumber as soon as that curtain rises. It's just adrenaline clamming my hands up. I'll be fine. I always am.

'Lookin' for someone, love, it's not me is it?' some fat guy asks me. I just smile at him. Walk on to the end of the bar. And that's when I see him. Niall Stevens. Taking a sip from his pint, before continuing a conversation with his mate.

I take a deep breath and think through my plan. I've got this.

I mutter the words 'excuse me' as I brush between a couple talking and make my way to the bar leaning into it beside Niall.

'Non-alcoholic red wine,' I say to the barman. I notice Niall has already clocked me. He took a peak over his shoulder after his mate pointed me out. I pretend not to notice. Then, after another deep breath, I knock into him – jarrin my elbow into the small of his back just as he's taking a sip of his pint.

'Shit... I'm so sorry. So sorry,' I say, holding my hand up to my mouth. Then I reach out and brush my fingers through his shirt as if I'm trying to wipe away the beer he's just spilt.

'Please, lemme buy you another drink,' I say.

Li leads us down the stairs. He seems overly keen to get out of here; thinks it's too busy. He says he wants to have a talk with us, somewhere quieter. That's nothing new. Li likes to open up, values the opinion of his two best mates. Especially me. We're almost like brothers, Li and I. We share every-thing. Zach's a bit more insular. A bit reluctant to open up.

When we're half-way down the steps I notice her. On the far side of the bar. I turn to Zach, just to try to block him from seeing her. I pull him in for a headlock, keeping his eyes down.

'C'mon Zach, cheer up, mate, this is gonna be a great night.'

'I'm alright, I'm alright,' he says into my armpit. 'Lemme go, for fuck sake.'

I only let him go after we've both reached the bottom of the stairs, Sabrina out of sight. Another bout of 'Boom, boom, boom... lemme hear ya say Jayo,' sounds out. I acknowledge it by holding my hand in the air, but head straight towards the exit without stopping to shake anyone's hand or signing another autograph. I turn to my two best mates as soon as we get outside.

'Hang there one more sec, will ye lads?' I say. 'I told a bloke in there I'd sign a quick autograph for his son before I left. He's just at the far side of the bar. Won't be long.'

I jump back inside. The chant starts up again, but I keep my head down and pace towards Sabrina. I can't let a girl like her go. But it dawns on me quickly that I have to. She's talking to some other guy. Probably her boyfriend. I watch as she laughs at one of his jokes. Damn it. I shudda known.

I turn on my heels, head for the exit again.

'Jason, can I have a quick pic—'

'Sorry man,' I say, rushing by.

It's unusual I'd snub a fan. But he just caught me at a wrong time – in a moment of self-pity. Those moments seem to come to me more often these days.

'Right!' I say, rubbing my palms together as soon as I get back outside, trying to jee myself up for a rare night out with my two besties. 'Where we off to?'

'Your call, Li,' Zach says as he lights up a cigarette.

'I just fancy a nice quiet Irish pub, somewhere we can sit down, have a chat. I thought it'd be quiet in there,' he says nodding back at the Hairy Lemon.

'Jaysus... a quiet chat? Are you sure this is not about... y'know, The Secr—'

'It's not about The fuckin' Secret,' Li snaps back at Zach.

My stomach turns itself over. It's been ages since any of us have talked about that. At least a couple of years since the subject's even been broached by any of us. Not that it's out of our minds. Jesus no. All three of us still live with it most days, I'm sure. I pray about it every night; offer my apology to God and thank him for his forgiveness.

The three of us agreed years ago that we'd stop letting it consume us; that we'd stop talking about it with each other. It was over half our lifetime ago now. Twenty years ago this summer in fact. It happened just a couple of months after I'd signed for Cherry Orchard. I'd been putting in great performances for the Bosco for five seasons. Either me or Zach would end up with the Player of the Season award every year. In fact, I won it three times, him twice in the five years we played together. A few scouts from bigger teams around Dublin started to turn up at our matches. It was obvious they were looking at us two. Cherry Orchard offered both of us a trial, the chance to play in the highest divisions of schoolboy football. A chance to be spotted by proper scouts – scouts from England's biggest clubs.

They ended up asking me to sign for them. But not Zach. I had to lie to Zach. Tell him that the only reason the Cherry Orchard coaches didn't want him was because they already had too many strikers and didn't need another one. He couldn't understand it. Couldn't quite get his head around the fact that I'd leapfrogged him; that I was playing at a standard much higher than he was.

We were fifteen at the time. There's only two weeks between me and Li. Zach's four months younger. Me and him had to stay disciplined at weekends if we wanted to make it in football. But Zach started to slide. He felt we needed more fun; that we needed to let our hair down at the weekends. He started drinking and smoking. Li gave in to the pressure, started drinking himself. But I didn't. I had no intention of throwing away the opportunity I'd been given at Cherry Orchard.

Zach used to wait till his dad went down to the Marble Arch for his usual Saturday night drinks before stealing his car keys and taking the three of us out for a joy ride. We'd head to the coast, out towards Howth, just for something to do. The two lads would be swigging back warm cans of cider. Zach would drive out, I'd normally drive back. But it didn't happen that way this night. Li took the wheel. He just said he fancied it. And I let him. Even though he'd downed about four cans.

Though in fairness to Li, she appeared from out of nowhere. We genuinely didn't see her. Not until the car skidded to a stop.

♦

BRIAN HOLDS his palms flat to the wall and pushes his left calf back to stretch it as if it's half-time in a football match. The judge did tell the jurors they would receive five-minute breaks 'to stretch their legs', but it's not supposed to be taken so literally. It certainly can't be literal in Number Three's case because she doesn't have the use of her legs. She's wheeling her wheelchair up and down the corridor, humming to herself while most of the other jurors have huddled themselves into different corners of the corridor, talking. Not about the trial – they're all staying loyal to the rule that they can only discuss the trial when all together – but about their lives. Weirdly, although they don't know each other's names – for the most part – they know an awful lot about each other.

'Okay jurors,' says a young man dressed in all black, opening the door to the jury room with an overly-big bunch of keys. They file back in one-by-one, Brian deliberately standing at the door and motioning with his hand that everybody should enter ahead of him again. He read about this approach in a self-help book about how to treat the general public and felt it would help him become a more popular politician.

'So...' Number One pauses, gazing down at his notes. 'We... eh... move on to ... yes, Copper Face Jacks. Did Sabrina or did she not—'

'Hold on for one second... if you don't mind me interrupting you, Number One, sorry everybody,' says Number Twelve. 'I just found a small flaw in the way we are deliberating. If we are going through the night in chronological order, then we are missing some of the picture. We're missing out some of the background of these four people. Some of the eh... the...'

'The character witnesses,' says Number Ten.

'Exactly,' Number Twelve says, sitting more upright. 'Like the photographer and the journalist. The fella who testified against Sabrina, and the other fella who testified against Jason and Zach. This kind of evidence – if you can call it evidence – gets ignored if we are just talking about the night in question.'

'Good point,' Brian says. 'We should discuss the character witnesshes at some point. What do we even think of the first, photographer, teshtimony – about Sabrina?'

'Yes... a Mr Patrick Clavin. Does anyone even find his testimony that pertinent?' Number One asks nobody in particular. It's been one of his biggest flaws as Head Juror – he doesn't direct his questions at anyone specifically. He just thrusts them out there, to the middle of the conference table.

Patrick Clavin has had a photography studio on Thomas Street in Dublin since the late eighties. He started off photographing weddings, communions, confirmations that kinda thing; made quite a few quid for his troubles. But as he evolved his business, he evolved his clientele and has been working with top talent agencies for the past decade. He is a genuinely nice guy, never once even considered cheating on his wife or their four kids, though he still gets a kick out of photographing pretty actresses and models for a living. He testified on behalf of the defence that Sabrina Doyle had been a client of his back in 2012, seeking nude shots. He proved to be a very honest witness, certainly amongst the jurors. But some wondered if his testimony was even worthy of being heard during the trial. The defence, doing their due diligence in search of some dirt on Sabrina, contacted a number of people she had worked with over the years, many not able to help their cause. Nobody had anything bad to say about Sabrina Doyle, aside from the fact that she could be a bit moody every now and then. But Clavin let slip that she had done some nude modelling for him six years prior and suddenly they pounced on him, believing his testimony would paint an image in the minds of the jurors that Sabrina was in some way fascinated with both sex and celebrity.

Clavin believed he was just following protocol by agreeing to confirm this information at the trial, but as he sat in the stand giving his evidence, he began to feel really guilty. He looked at Sabrina, knew he had been spun by the defence into painting a negative picture of the claimant. And he actually liked Sabrina. He just answered the questions coming at him as honestly as he could and then kept his head down as he exited the courtroom. Sabrina insisted his testimony was 'mostly made up' when she was called to the stand. 'I did indeed attend Patrick Clavin's studio in August

2012, but I never posed nude,' she said. The jurors were perplexed by this, couldn't understand why Clavin would lie. Unless, perhaps, he was coerced by the defence. It was an argument worth raising.

'I don't know,' says Number Eleven. 'He was definitely nervous on the stand, but I just got the impression he was telling the truth. Let me hold my hands up now and say I am genuinely leaning towards guilty – I think those lads took advantage of Sabrina that night, raped her. But I actually feel she might be lying in this particular instance. I don't know what it is... I believe her every time she speaks, but not here... not about the nude photos.'

'Clavin's testimony was believable,' agrees Number One. This also went against what Number One believed overall – that Jason, Zach and Li were all guilty of raping Sabrina Doyle. But he too found it difficult to dispute the photographer's testimony; didn't believe the defence were evil enough to ask somebody to just make a story up in order to discredit a claimant. Number One's real name is Albert Dwyer, a fifty-five-year-old car mechanic from Rathcoole in Co Dublin. He looks wise – sports glasses, wears his thick head of silver hair neatly split from left to right. It was on appearances alone that led to his fellow jurors electing him over Brian as Head Juror. But Number One hasn't been great in this role at all. He's too indecisive, and lacks the balls to keep everybody in line. Another example of appearances being deceiving.

Number One found himself feeling the defendants were guilty pretty early on in the trial. He couldn't bring himself to believe a beautiful young woman like Sabrina Doyle would consensually have sex with three men in one night. Number One is married with two daughters. It had been advised by the judge that personal experiences shouldn't enter the consciousness of the jurors when considering a verdict, but that's impossible advice to curtail. Number One's daughters aren't far off Sabrina's age. He sees them in her. Her in them. For that reason, more than any other, it would be extremely difficult to persuade him into the not guilty camp. He's adamant that Jason, Zach and Li deserve to do time behind bars.

One of the big questions jurors find themselves stewing over their mind when it comes to rape cases is the difficult-to-comprehend notion that a woman would cry rape when in fact she hadn't been raped at all. Jurors find this more difficult to morally accept than they do actual rape. For some reason, crying rape when you haven't been raped constitutes as a harsher crime than actual rape in the mind-sets of the general public. It's bizarre. Sabrina's case is a fascinating one to consider under these terms: what does she have to gain from claiming these three men raped her? Is she after Jason's money? Or – as is the question most jurors morally ask themselves when examining trials like this – did Sabrina have consensual sex with all three men and then only afterwards feel she was raped? Number Nine raises this point to the room.

'It's possible,' Number Eight answers first, staring straight ahead.

'Yeah, I think that kind of thing is a big possibility,' Number Twelve follows up with. 'A girl feeling guilty the next morning for the... y'know... whatever happened the night before.'

'You can't rule it out,' says Brian. 'Ugh... I don't know. I just... I genuinely think we have to find them not guilty. There jusht isn't enough evidensh—'

'Hold off, Brian,' scoffs Number One. 'We aren't having a bloody verdict vote at the minute... we're not saying what we think overall.'

He sits more upright, elbows on the table, staring down at Brian. He's almost sporting a grin as if he has something in his armoury that will bring Brian down a peg or two.

'So you think not guilty overall, yeah?' he says, swinging one of his hands as if he has adopted a teenage attitude. 'So do you believe Sabrina Doyle is lying about not approaching the three men initially in the Hairy Lemon?'

Brian nods his head slowly, sits back in his chair, almost welcoming the test.

'And you believe she is lying about the nude photos... about the hand-job... about going to that nightclub Copper Face Jacks?'

Brian nods again, shrugs his shoulders too.

'You believe she's lying about the rape too, yeah? Lying about everything?'

'Yesh, yesh I do,' says Brian, leaning forward again, placing both of his elbows on the table to mirror his nemesis in body language.

'Why?' asks Number One, his face glowing pink.

'Why what?' asks Brian.

'Why would she lie about everything? What does she gain from making all of this stuff up?'

'Well that ish one question I can't answer,' Brian says.

Number One scoffs, but Brian continues.

'And I know I can't answer it because I have had that question running through my mind all through this trial. For weeksh I've had that spinning around in my head. And for weeksh I've failed to justify an answer.'

It is believed, though it can't be proven, that in ninety-two per cent of rape cases the claimants are not lying. A massive majority of women who claim they were raped, claim it because they were indeed raped; or certainly believe they were raped. Only a tiny fraction of rape claimants have ulterior motives. Sadly, even though it's believed that ninety-two per cent of rape claims are genuine, only a pitiful eighteen per cent of rape trials end with a guilty verdict, though those numbers are growing – both the number of rape claims and the percentage of guilty verdicts. Unfortunately the former is growing rapidly, the latter very slowly. This particular trial is the two-hundredth and sixty-sixth rape trial that has taken place in Ireland this year, and yet it is occurring in the first week of July: the half-way point of the calendar year. Last year Ireland saw a significant spike in rape reports. In 2016, five hundred and twelve claims of rape were reported, there were six hundred and fifty-five in 2017. This year there is projected to be over seven hundred and twenty. The graph line is practically pointing north on rape claims throughout the country. But sadly that is not the most alarming statistic when it comes to rape. The most jaw-dropping fact is that these growing numbers only take into consideration rapes that are reported. A vast majority go unreported. It is believed, although impossible to prove, that up to eighty per cent of rapes are never reported to police.

'She may have just wanted his attention, his money, his fame,' says Number Eight.

'Well, she's not getting any of that is she?' Number Ten says. 'She's been hiding – and rightfully so – behind the name Ms X in the newspapers, she's not getting any attention, not getting any money, any fame.'

'I don't know... I'm just trying to answer the question,' Number Eight shrugs. 'Maybe she's planning on selling her story down the line. I mean, she must try to court attention in some ways, right? She's a model after all. And if she did do these nude shots, then what sort of attention are you trying to court?'

'Yeah, but that's only if you believe she did the nude shots,' says Number Ten.

Every time I mention the two words *The* and *Secret* I get hushed. It's been twenty years since we first labelled it 'The Secret' and vowed never to talk about it again; decided to leave what happened in the past exactly there – in the past. But sometimes I wish we could all sit down and talk about it... get it all off our chests.

The three of us stroll towards Aungier Street almost in silence; the fact that I mentioned those two words playing on all three of our minds. I wonder how often Jason and Li think about it; wonder if they think about it more than I do.

I recommended The Swan Bar, felt it would be one of the quietest pubs around. Li can tell us whatever the hell he wants to tell us in there, then we can get on with our night. Have some fun. We'll probably end up in Copper Face Jacks now that we're heading in this direction. I know it has a piss-poor reputation, but I love Coppers. It's rare I'd leave there without scoring some bird. Everyone who goes there is practically out for their hole. I certainly am tonight. I'm sick of the same pussy every night. Ye can't beat a bit of strange. I genuinely don't believe in monogamy; think asking a male mammal to stick with one female is asking a bit too much. We're just not cut out for it.

I didn't cheat on Tina for the first four months after meeting her. I was kinda proud of that, but four months was my limit. I love sex, certainly sex with strange birds, but it's more the chattin' them up that is the drug for me. I just love the back-and-forth of the chase; the flirting, the bullshit. I'm a great bullshitter. I'm pretty sure I could bullshit any bird into bed. If I saw Margot Robbie out in a club, I'd have no hesitation in chatting her up. And I'd probably score her too. When it comes to scoring birds, it's not about looks – that's not what they look for in a man. They just want to be charmed, made to laugh. No better man to make a woman laugh than me. I wish that Sabrina bird hadn't left the Hairy Lemon so quickly. She was definitely a few levels above me when it comes to looks, but I'm pretty sure I could have scored her.

'Where is this place?' asks Jason. He doesn't really know Dublin as well as me and Li. Never really took advantage of the nightlife this city has to offer. Even when he lived here, he stayed in at the weekends. Football always came first for him. Fun comes first for me. Always has. I'm sure some think that's why he made it over me, but I don't buy that bollocks for one second. Some of my favourite ever players could handle a few drinks as well as a football career. If Ireland's greatest ever player – Paul McGrath – could balance a social life and a professional football career, then so could I. I just didn't get the breaks. No point in wallowing in it now anyway. At least that's what I tell myself regularly.

'Just on the next corner,' I reply, pointing up Aungier Street.

'Don't think I've been in this place before, is it rough?' Li asks.

'Yer ma's rough!' I fold my fingers into my palm, hold it out, and take a fist bump from both Li and Jason for the gag.

'Ah, it's just a quiet bar. We'll have one in there, then head up to Harcourt Street, will we?' I say.

'Coppers?' Li asks.

'Fuck it, why not!'

'Yeah – fuck it,' says Jason, laughing.

I swing the door of The Swan open and spot a free table at the front window.

'Right, big shot,' I say to Jason, 'your round, mate. Three Heinekens.'

Li and I take a seat at the table. I stare at him, wonderin' what the hell he has to tell us. I love this fella to bits, I'd do anything for him. But he can kinda do my head in sometimes. He takes everything too seriously. I don't know why he feels the need to be formal all the time; don't know why we all have to be sitting around a quiet table when he has somethin' to tell us as if we're havin' a bloody office meeting. If I had something to say to my two best mates, I'd just bloody say it to them.

It's too far back for me to remember fully, but when we were kids I'm pretty sure Li was as outgoing as I was. But ever since The Secret, he lost his edge. But maybe he carries more guilt than me and Jason. He was the one driving after all. I can still hear the thump of her hitting the car. I opened the passenger door, stared at her lying on the ground in front of us. It all seemed to happen in slow motion after that. I don't even recall hearing sounds as Jason got out of the car and ran towards her. Li followed him. I just stayed in my seat, a wave of sobriety splashing me in the face.

'Get the fuck back in the car,' I screamed at them when I clicked back to reality. They did. Both of them.

'She's breathing,' Jason said to me, almost hyperventilating as he jumped in the back seat. Li was more composed. In fact, he set the secret in motion. That's my memory of it anyway. We probably all have different versions of that night. But seeing as we've vowed to never talk about it again, I can't be entirely sure what their memories of that night are. But I definitely remember Li suggesting we drive off; leave her.

So we did. Li turned the car around, headed back towards Drimnagh.

Each of us silent for the whole half-hour drive. We even turned the car radio off. It was the most silent silence I've ever heard.

'Here y'are,' Jason says, plonking the three pints in front of us.

'Cheers,' I say, holding my pint glass up.

We clink. Again.

'Now,' Jason says, looking at Li as he sits himself into the chair between us. 'What've ye got to tell us, buddy?'

I like this guy. He's polite enough to include me in the conversation, but also loyal enough to his girlfriend to indicate he has no interest in me. We've shared a couple of anecdotes, a few laughs. But he's mentioned his fiancée to me twice already. If he was interested in pursuing me, he'd have kept his relationship schtum. He's a good guy; cute, honest, funny. His fiancée is a lucky girl.

'Can I get you one back before we leave?' he asks.

'Oh no, thank you. I owed you that for spilling your pint,' I reply.

He waves his hand.

'Ah… let me get you one back.'

He motions to the barman.

'Glass of red for the girl please.'

'And a couple of pints?' the barman asks.

'Nah, sorry – we have to head off now,' Niall says back to him.

Shit.

'Are you eh… are you leaving now?' I say.

'Yeah – we've to meet another mate.'

'Well, I'm only going to have that one you ordered me if you're having one,' I say, finishing off my wine. He looks at his friend, then back at me.

'G'wan… two pints of Miller as well,' he shouts over to the barman.

Great – he's staying. I've got to work harder on him. Everything seems very positive so far, but I don't have enough information. Not yet anyway.

'So, what is it you do?' his friend asks me. 'Lemme guess, you're a model?'

I sniff a laugh out through my nose. Quite a few people take that guess with me. Perhaps they're right in some way, but only if they use the past tense.

My modelling career basically involved multiple meetings, eight five-minute TV appearances, and sixteen catwalks – some of them in front of about eight people. That was it. I spent most of my twenty months as a model being peered at by casting agents and hearing the word 'no' over and over again. No wonder I became an introvert. People with positive mind-sets certainly don't work in an industry plagued by rejection. You think I'd have been well prepared for it. I had an older sister who had been through the ringer before me, who could pass on appropriate advice. But Amanda almost seemed embarrassed by the fact that her job wasn't as glamorous as her younger sister assumed it was. She didn't want to ruin the fantasy for me. Not once did she ever say anything negative about her work – not to me anyway.

My agent – Anne Ray – was a good confidant. I got lucky there. I'd heard horror stories about other agents. She did her job perfectly and was completely transparent and trustworthy. She always got me in front of the right people. But I couldn't close the deal. I'd say I was recruited for about two per cent of the jobs I'd present myself for. It was Anne's idea for me to visit Patrick Clavin. She even paid half of the fee. She felt my commercial face would benefit from his work; that he could put a portfolio together for me that would define what path I should take in the industry. He was a lovely man, Patrick. I felt at ease with him straight away.

Even though he'd shot a thousand models before me, he wasn't boring company at all. He was personable, asked me about me, not about work. He'd heard of my sister, had never shot her though. He was very sympathetic when I told him of her plight.

'You are very beautiful, very commercial,' he told me. 'But so too are ninety-five of the last one hundred girls I've shot.'

I'd heard this loads of times and had already begun to realise my looks didn't really help me at all in this industry. Casting agents aren't looking for pretty faces, they're looking for unusual faces.

'Have you thought about glamour?'

I sighed, almost rudely.

'It's been mentioned,' I said. 'Anne has said it to me a few times, but I just... it's just not why I wanted to be a model.'

'I totally understand,' said Patrick. 'Look, the money is good. And it's all about hotness. In the glamour industry, all that's required is good looks. You certainly tick that box.'

I chewed on my lip, trying to let on to Patrick that I was thinking about his proposal. But the truth was, I'd already thought about it; already decided glamour modelling wasn't for me. I couldn't imagine my dad opening up a magazine to see me smiling back at him, my arms folded under my bare breasts.

Patrick rang Anne, had her on speakerphone for about twenty minutes as the three of us discussed the prospect. Patrick cut a deal with Anne; said he would destroy his negatives, that he'd send digital versions of the photos to her and insisted she would be the only one who held copies. So I agreed. I took off my clothes, changed into some sexy lingerie he had in storage, then let him take some risqué shots – some of them nude. Nothing too graphic. Everything was nicely lit; sexy, classy and I certainly didn't feel as uncomfortable as I feared I would. But I knew these photos would never see the light of day; that I'd have a conversation with Anne the next time I was speaking to her and tell her I didn't want them to be sent out to anyone. And she kept her word; took it with her to her grave two years ago. Anne Ray was always honest with me. It's actually a must-have trait in the fashion industry. Everyone's honest with everyone. Too honest, I would say. I worked with Patrick again, trying to perfect a commercial portfolio for myself, but it didn't get me anywhere. There are just too many commercial girls in this world.

I tell Niall and his friend a brief synopsis of the truth. I *had* been a model – tried it out for a couple of years. Got nowhere. Neither him nor his mate could believe it.

'But I see models all the time in ads and stuff that aren't half as good lookin' as you,' Niall says.

I thank him for the compliment, touch his arm as I am doing so and pause to see if he will reciprocate my approach.

'Yeah sure, if it was just about looks, my fiancée cudda been a model too,' he says. That's so cute. Too cute in fact. I'm almost feeling a bit neglected here. I would be hurt if rejection wasn't my actual aim.

I watch Niall drain down the last of his pint of Miller, trying to work out whether or not I had enough information on him. I think I do.

'Claire, it has been a pleasure meeting you,' he says, holding out his hand for me to shake. And I do shake it, as if we're professionals who have just ended a work meeting. Niall has no idea I'm the only one working right now.

'Yeah – I enjoyed our little chat,' I say. 'And you too, Martin.'

I hold my hand out for his mate to shake and suddenly they are on their way, heading for the exit. Before they've reached the door, I have the phone to my ear.

'Hey Sabrina,' says Lorna answering. 'Have you completed the job?'

'Three Heinekens,' I say to the barman as Zach and Li take a seat. I get the sense this could be one of those shitty nights where we let Zach's mood dictate everything. Though that could all change depending on what Li has to tell us. It can't be anything to do with The Secret. Li's been the best at brushing that under the carpet. In fact, I'm pretty sure it plays less on his mind than it does mine and Zach's. Li's the nicest bloke I know. But he can be cold and calculated when he needs to be.

'First round is on us, Jason,' the barman says after placing the three pints on the bar and winking at me. 'For that goal against Holland.'

I thank him, almost apologetically, then plonk my arse onto the seat between my two best mates.

'Slainté,' Zach says as we clink glasses for about the eighth time tonight. And we've only had a couple of drinks. It's just so rare that the three of us get out these days that we can't help toasting each other. We're not toasting much. Just the fact that we're in a pub. It's such a rarity these days.

I know it's my fault, I'm the one who moved away, who got a career that meant I had to be disciplined – but I don't think anyone's complaining. I sometimes wonder how our friendships would have gone if I hadn't moved to England. Perhaps we'd have all pissed each other off by now. We probably wouldn't be such good friends if we'd spent every single weekend of the last twenty years doing what we're doing now: drinking beer and talking shit.

'Now, what've ye got to tell us, buddy?' I say, turning to Li.

He picks up his mobile phone, scrolls through it then turns the screen towards me and Zach.

'Fuckin' hell – yes! Congratulations mate,' I say after my eyes focus to take in the photo.

'I've ordered it online. It's gonna arrive next Wednesday.'

'She'll be fuckin' delighted,' says Zach. 'How ye gonna do it?'

'Well, we're going to Lanzarote next month aren't we – I'm gonna do it there.'

'Hold on, you're gonna get engaged in Lanza-fuckin-rote?' Zach asks.

'Y'know, on the beach when the sun goes down or is coming up, or something romantic like that.'

'Don't mind him, Li,' I say pulling my best mate in for a hug. 'Why would you take tips on romance from this fuckin' eejit, huh?'

The three of us hold each other in a bit of a huddle. We're good like

65

that, good at noting milestone moments in each of our lives. When we want to be, we can be right in the moment, all of our stresses and strains miles away; The Secret all but forgotten. But these moments happen way too infrequently these days.

'And I want you as best man,' Li says after releasing us from the huddle. 'And you as groomsman, Zach.'

We don't answer, not verbally anyway. We just reform the huddle and soak in the moment again.

'Bottle of champagne,' I shout out to the barman. 'Most expensive one you have.'

I walk up to the bar, a smile wide on my face. I'm so happy for Li. And for Niamh. They're an ideal couple. Perfect for each other. They're both so headstrong – it makes me a little jealous actually. I don't think anybody would have thought when we were younger that by the time we all got into our thirties, Li would be the only one who had his shit sorted out.

'A thousand and ninety-nine euro,' the barman says, holding up a black bottle. I can make out the word Krug-something or other on it.

'T'fuck,' I say. 'Over a grand?'

'You said the dearest one.'

I stare over at Li, watch him smile as wide as he can while Zach ribs him again for planning on getting engaged in Lanzarote.

'Fuck it, go on,' I say, handing over my debit card.

Li deserves it. I had two reservations when I left for England; one was that I would be leaving my little brother Eric behind. I knew he looked up to me, would miss me terribly, and two; I would be leaving Li behind. For the exact same reasons.

Playing for Cherry Orchard put me in front of the world's most influential scouts. I'd heard rumours that head scouts from Manchester United, Arsenal and Celtic were looking at me, but that's all they were – *rumours*. Besides, I wasn't the only good player on the pitch. At the level I was playing at with the Orchard, every one of the twenty-two players on the pitch at any one time had something special about them. I'd often walk out of the dressing room after a match, hoping a scout would call after me and offer me a trial. But that's not how it happened. I was hanging around a street corner with Li and Zach one Tuesday evening when my dad shouted my name out from the hall door of our house. I thought I was in trouble, until I got closer to my old man and could sense he was trying to stifle a smile.

'This fella wants to talk to you,' he said, motioning to the living room.

'Jason Kenny, how are you?' the stranger boomed out as if he was an actor on a stage. 'I'm Billy Kirby – Everton football club.' I stared at my old man. He wasn't stifling his smile anymore.

'Here we are, boys,' I shout out, getting back to the table with the black bottle of whatever-it-is and three flutes. 'Let's get this into us.'

I pour each of us a glass, hold mine up for our ninth clink of the night, but one of significance; so much so that I think it deserves a little speech.

'I'm so proud of you, Li, and proud of Niamh too. Here's to many, many years of happiness and eh... loyalty,' I say, meeting Zach's eye. He laughs. He knows he shows absolutely no loyalty to Tina. Doesn't hide that fact from anyone, except for her, of course. 'Congratulations man.'

We each clink glasses and take a sip.

'Uugh,' says Li as Zach makes a face, almost gurning with disdain at what he's just poured into his mouth. I'm certain my face is mirroring his.

Wow – a fucking grand for this piss.

I scroll through my phone, pull up the picture of the engagement ring I've ordered for Niamh, then twist the screen around so it faces both Jason and Zach. I dart my eyes between both of their faces, waiting on the penny to drop.

'Fuckin' hell – yes! Congratulations mate,' Jason says, his mouth wide open.

'I've ordered it online. It's gonna arrive next Wednesday.'

'She'll be fuckin' delighted,' says Zach. 'How are ye gonna do it?'

'Well, we're going to Lanzarote next month aren't we, gonna do it there.'

'Hold on, you're gonna get engaged in Lanza-fuckin-rote?'

Typical Zach. He can't let me have my moment without taking the piss somehow. But I know he's delighted for me. I tell them I'll ask Niamh on the beach at sunset, or sunrise, then Jason drags me in for a hug. I hook my arm around Zach and bring him into the huddle too. I'm such a lucky bastard. Two great mates and a girlfriend who's going to be mine forever. If she says 'yes' of course. Though I'm pretty certain she will. She loves me as much as I love her.

'Don't mind him, Li,' Jason says. 'Why would you take tips on romance from this fuckin' eejit?'

I stare up at them both.

'And I want you as best man,' I say to Jason, 'and you as groomsman,' to Zach.

They both grab me in to repeat the hug, the three of us soaking in the news.

'Bottle of champagne,' Jason calls out over my shoulder to the barman.

'So where we gonna have the stag?' Zach asks after Jason runs to the bar. 'Should probably go to Kiev, I heard the birds there are fuckin amazing.'

'Was thinking of something a little quieter,' I tell him. 'Out to the west coast; Galway, Kerry maybe.'

'T'fuck!' he says, before sipping on his beer. 'What are we supposed to do, fuck some traveller birds on a stag?'

Zach has never noted mine and Jason's loyalties to our girlfriends. He always includes us in his plans for cheating, as if it relieves some of the guilt from within him. A bit like The Secret.

The story circulated in the news for two full days; in both the newspapers and on the tele. Caitlin Tyrell was only nine years old at the time. Her dad had trusted her to go to the chipper as a late night treat. It was only a five-minute walk from her house, the only hurdle being the road she had to cross. And then we came along. Fuckin' eejits.

Bizarrely, the newspapers reported the police were on the lookout for a red saloon car. A car matching that description had been noted as speeding nearby around the time we hit Caitlin. That piece of information, given to the Gardaí by a witness walking their dog, was all the cops had to go on. And it was all they did go on. We got away with it. In the eyes of the law anyway – we certainly didn't escape the guilt. Well, I didn't anyway.

'I'm so proud of you, Li, and proud of Niamh too,' Jason says, after passing around a flute of champagne to each of us. 'Here's to many, many years of happiness and eh... loyalty – congratulations, my man.'

We each clink flutes.

'Uugh,' I say, almost spitting the drink back out. 'That's disgusting!'

Zach just rests his flute back on the table, squelches up his face to show how much he hated what he's just tasted. Jason follows suit.

'I just paid over a grand for that,' he says.

Zach and I burst out laughing.

'Fuck it, let's get outta here,' Zach says. 'Let's go celebrate in style. Pick up some chicks.'

'Where we off to?' Jason asks, standing up.

'Coppers?'

The three of us look at each other, nod our approval, then head out the door.

'I'm bringing this piss with me,' Jason says, picking up the bottle of champagne.

He strolls out of the pub behind us, slurping from the neck of the bottle, then passes it to me. It tastes just as revolting from the bottle as it did from the flute – like fizzy dishwater.

The three of us saunter up Aungier Street, passing the bottle between each other. I'm certain each time it comes back to me, none of the champagne is missing. The other two must be doing the same as I am, pretending to drink from it.

I'm delighted the night has turned around. Zach had threatened to turn it into a bit of a messy evening with trying to cop off with that Sabrina girl, but he's in much better form now – singing football songs with his two arms held wide over his head.

I was looking forward to tonight, couldn't wait to tell them both that I had just ordered an engagement ring for Niamh. She has no idea. Only five people know now; me, Jason, Zach and my mam and Jinny. They both helped me look online for the perfect ring that would suit Niamh's finger.

Mam insisted Niamh would like a Number Nine cut stone, similar to the one Dad bought her. So we settled on a white gold version of a Number Nine cut. It cost me nine hundred and ninety quid – the most expensive thing I've ever bought.

I'm going to ring Niamh's dad in a few weeks' time, bring him for a pint down his local, do the decent thing and ask for his permission to marry his daughter. It's all planned out, except what I'm actually going to say to Niamh when I ask her. I want to say something meaningful, from the heart. Ensure it's the best moment of her life.

We turn on to Harcourt Street, Zach still chanting some sort of nonsense. He's probably improvising. He used to do that as a kid; make up chants about himself and ask me to sing them on the sidelines of the Bosco's matches. I think he was deadly serious, though you never quite know with Zach.

'Scuse me,' the bouncer says holding his hand to Zach's chest. 'Think you might have had a few too many.'

'He's with me,' Jason says, stepping forward.

'Ah, Jason Kenny! How are ye, my man? Listen, you'll have to get rid of the bottle, or finish it outside, then come in.'

'Here y'go, love,' Zach says, passing the bottle to a group of girls walking by. They take it from him, laughing their heads off.

'Copper Face Jacks mutha fuckers!' he screams out, smiling at the bouncer as he passes him by. Jason looks back at me and rolls his eyes.

Then we follow Zach inside the club.

◆

NUMBER FIVE LETS OUT A YAWN; doesn't even think to try to hide it. She's not tired, just bored. She isn't the only one. Number One hasn't been doing a good enough job as Head Juror. Not because he fails to reign in the arguments, but because he lacks authority.

He has been going through the night in chronological order, yet despite the jury being almost two hours in to their deliberations, they are only ninety minutes through the night in question. The numbers don't add up.

'It's insignificant,' Number Five whispers to Number Six as Brian repeats his argument for the third time. She didn't mean for anybody else to hear her, but she wasn't as discreet as she'd hoped to be.

'Sorry Number Five,' interjects Number One. 'What was that?'

Number Five lets out a deep breath, stares at Number Six for support and when none is forthcoming decides to speak her truth.

'Isn't it kinda insignificant? I mean we've been arguing this for almost half-an-hour alone. So what if she did have nude photos taken six years ago, so what if she didn't. What does it have to do with her possibly being raped years later?'

'Patrick Clavin is a character witness,' Number Twelve spits out. 'He is suggesting that not only is Sabrina Doyle interested in sexy images but she is also a liar.'

'Whoa, hold on there,' croaks Number Eleven. 'Clavin is not suggesting anything of the sort. He just gave a contrasting account about his work with Sabrina than she gave – that's all. Having said that, his testimony is significant in some ways. I believe Clavin, I think Sabrina did do nude shots and is too embarrassed to admit to them.'

'Well, we've had a deep enough discussion about it,' says Number One, bouncing his paperwork off the table again. 'I think it's fair to say most jurors agree with the testimony of the character witness. But that's all it is – a slight on Sabrina's character, not a certain indication that she was or wasn't raped.'

'It isn't insignificant, of course not,' says Number Twelve, 'but I guess we can all calculate just how significant it is in our own judgement.'

Number Twelve is doing his best to remain patient. He's normally smug, arrogant. Is already certain that the rest of the jury will eventually swing around to his way of thinking: *not guilty*. Twelve's real name is Dave Barry, a thirty-seven-year-old insurance broker from Inchicore in Dublin. He's happy enough with his nine-to-fiver, content with the bang-on average €38,000-per-year salary he accumulates. Has figured out a way to make it work for him, his fiancée of ten years and their now eleven-year-old daughter Molly. He could do better – certainly has the intelligence to carve out an enviable career for himself – but chooses not to. He's fine as he is. He complains about life, but is happy to complain. Number Twelve was initially intrigued about being called up for jury duty; his excitement growing when he realised he would be involved in the Jason Kenny case. He lied during the jury selection process: said he didn't know who Jason Kenny was. He wasn't the only one.

'Should we have another verdict vote now?' Brian offers to the table.

'You and bloody voting!' Number Three calls out, slapping at the arm rests of her wheelchair.

'Let's just hold off,' says Number Twelve. 'Maybe we can have one in another hour... see how our talks go before lunch.'

There is no protocol when it comes to juries having verdict votes during their deliberations. Some juries, like this one, start with a verdict vote. Some like to dive straight into their arguments, starting with the main points of the trial. This jury decided to discuss the night in chronological order, which is not an unusual tact when it comes to rape trials. Because these type of rapes tend to follow a similar pattern of victim-meeting-accused, victim-not-liking-accused-as-much-as-accused-likes-victim, victim-and-accused-ending-up-in-same-place, victim-taking-advantage-of-accused, it makes sense for jurors to examine the night in order. Though it's no surprise that the most significant debate lays heavily in the back end of the deliberations. The whole trial boils down to whether or not the jurors feel consent was or was not given during the sexual encounters both parties admit occurred sometime between midnight and half-past midnight during the night in question. Quite often a juror will have a very set verdict in their mind that they arrive at during a rape trial... until it comes to the final argument. Then, they can easily be persuaded they had it wrong all along. The truth is, during final arguments, gut instinct can easily be eroded.

'Well, let's move on to something that *can't* be considered insignificant then,' Number One says, without prompt this time. 'The defence's key argument, I guess, is that Sabrina knew who Jason Kenny was and sought him out for sex. I guess their strongest argument is that they believe she followed the men all the way to Copper Face Jacks. Now, we have solid evidence at this point that backs up their claims.'

Number One presses at a button on the conference table just in front of his Head Juror's chair.

'Can we see the CCTV footage of Harcourt Street, please?' he says into the speaker beside the button. The TV screen on the wall blinks on again.

'Okay... yes, this is the footage of Jason, Zach and Li all entering Copper Face Jacks at exactly eight-forty p.m.,' he says pointing towards the tiny white digits in the corner the screen.

'Can we have the footage of Sabrina at eight forty-one on Harcourt Street?' Number One says, pressing down on the button on the table again. The screen blinks off. When it blinks back on, there is no mistaking the woman strolling past Iveagh Gardens, a mere five-minutes' walk from the nightclub the men had just entered. Even though the footage is grainy, Sabrina's white jumpsuit sticks out like a sore thumb in the centre of the screen.

'So as you can see, around about the same time the men are entering the club, Sabrina is close by having left the Hairy Lemon pub a good half-an-hour earlier,' Number One says.

'The one thing that bothers me about this,' says Number Twelve getting up off his chair, 'is that Iveagh Gardens, where she is walking right here,' he points at the screen, 'is past Copper Face Jacks. So she actually walked *past* the club. Not only that, this isn't the only time she walks in this direction. CCTV footage has her here about fifteen minutes later, right?'

'Yep, at eight fifty-six, she made the same trip,' Brian says, checking his notes. 'She practically walked around the block. She must have been waiting for them, then followed them into the club. She was after Jason in this inshtance, I've no doubt about that.'

'Can we totally rule out coincidence?' Number Three poses.

'A coincidence that they ended up in the same nightclub after being in the same pub some ten minutes' walk away?' Number Nine responds, raising an eyebrow.

'Copper Face Jacks is a well-known club in Dublin, probably the most well-known. If you are on that side of town, and you fancy going to a club, then Coppers is the most likely destination.'

'Not when there's a nightclub directly across from the Hairy Lemon where they'd all been. Break For The Border. If she just fancied a dance, which is the reason she gave for going to Coppers in her testimony, why not go for a dance in Break For The Border... why walk all the way up Harcourt Street – *alone*, let's not forget – just to end up in the same place as the three men she'd already been talking to, one she already admits to kissing?'

Number Nine hates bringing up this argument, because she feels so sorry for Sabrina. But this is the one part of the night in question that irks her the most. It stopped her from voting guilty in the earlier verdict vote even though she really wanted to. But she's certain Sabrina followed the three men into Coppers; is starting to get swayed towards not guilty after putting her hand up as undecided earlier on.

'I agree with you,' Number One says. 'I find her testimony here very brittle. It can't be just a coincidence. Plus, we kinda have proof here, right? She was walking around in circles... she was killing time. Surely she was just waiting on the men to settle in the club.'

Sabrina had testified that she often attended Copper Face Jacks – sometimes with her former boyfriend, the odd time alone. One bouncer even testified at the trial that he knew Sabrina's face to see in the club, if not her name. He said she used to go there with her boyfriend, that she always stood out to him because she was so much better looking than her other half. He did admit though that he hadn't seen her in there for 'quite some time' before the night in question. His testimony was the only crack of light Sabrina's legal team could cling to in this argument. They tried to suggest that visiting Copper Face Jacks wasn't unusual for Sabrina Doyle. Her own testimony on the stand, which did add up to what she had told police when she first reported the rape claim, was that she wanted to take in some fresh air after downing 'a few red wines' in the Hairy Lemon and just as she was walking around Iveagh Gardens, she thought "to hell with it, I'll go into Coppers for a dance, before going home". No matter how innocent she looked on the stand, passing off her bumping back into the three men in Copper Face Jacks as "mere coincidence" was difficult for each juror to buy.

There was one moment within the trial that helped bridge the coincidence theory somewhat though. Li never took the stand during the trial; a position most defendants take when faced with a rape charge. It's just too risky for them to put themselves in the position of being pelted with questions from the prosecution who are obviously intent on trying to trip them up. In Ireland – unlike most other European countries – juries are instructed that they must not draw any inference whatsoever about a defendant's decision not to take the stand. Despite this, Jason and Zach argued against the wishes of their defence team, both opting to give evidence. They wanted to put their side of the story across to the jury. During their time on the stand, the prosecution asked them both if they had told Sabrina they were going to Copper Face Jacks. Both admitted they hadn't. It meant the 'coincidence' argument could not be ruled out entirely. After all, if Sabrina didn't know where the three men were going when they left the Hairy Lemon, and she couldn't possibly have seen them entering – given her location at the time – then how could she have followed them in there?

'It's true that Sabrina couldn't have seen them entering Copper Face Jacks, right?' Number One says pointing to the screen again. It was a rhetorical question. He knew the answer. Everybody did. 'Because we know she was on the other side of Iveagh Gardens when they went in. So either she knew they were going in there, or – as she puts it – it was merely a coincidence that they all ended up in the same club.'

'Do you reckon Li told her where they were going?' asks Number Seven.

'You'd think if he did tell her, then he would have taken the stand to confirm this,' answers Number Twelve, sitting back in his chair and combing his fingers through his thinning hair in frustration. 'Listen, I know I'm in the not guilty camp and have made my feelings on this known. But just everybody for one second... look at the evidence here. We have to admit that it looks very likely she somehow caught wind that the men were in Coppers and she followed them in there. We can't know for certain, but the CCTV footage at the very least paints a picture of a woman who seems a bit on edge. She walks around in circles for twenty minutes before going inside the club. This doesn't look good for her. I'm as certain as I can be, without full knowledge, that she followed them in there. I know it doesn't suit my overall verdict, but I believe Sabrina Doyle is lying in this instance.'

20:40
Zach

I turn around, notice a gaggle of birds walking past the entrance of Copper Face Jacks and hand them the bottle of champers.

'Copper Face Jacks mutha fuckers!' I scream out as I pass the bouncer and head in to the club. Fuck you, dude. I'm with Jason Kenny.

You have to readjust your eyes when you walk into Coppers, even this early in the night. The place is only open a few minutes but it's always dark; the low ceilings and lack of windows giving it a bit of a claustrophobic feel.

It's not packed – not yet anyway – but there must be fifty or sixty people in here already. I kinda love Coppers. It's cheesy as fuck, but everyone always has a good time in this place.

It has the reputation of being the place to go if you wanna cop off with someone. Ye normally get birds from down the sticks coming up to Dublin just for a night in Coppers – in the hope that they can snare some bloke from the capital. And I've been that Dublin bloke for a load of those birds. I'm happy to do my bit. Give them what they want. I'll certainly be happy to do that tonight. I'm dyin' for me hole. I mean, I can get it off Tina whenever I want, but it's just not the same, is it? Having sex with someone who's supposed to have sex with you just isn't sexy at all. Having to talk someone into sex, filling them with the bullshit that will help dampen their panties... now that's a proper fuckin' turn on.

I take every face in as I head towards the bar. I haven't seen the perfect girl – not yet. But it's early. The night is young. I turn around, find the other two are yards behind me. I don't know what takes them so long. They're always chatting, always in each other's ears. I've often wondered if they discuss The Secret behind my back. They probably assume I'm the strongest out of the three of us, that I've handled it all fine. But I do think about it – every now and then. Especially when I'm lying in bed, unable to sleep. The pictures of Caitlin Tyrell that I saw in the newspapers all those years ago can sometimes talk to me. She sometimes calls out in pain.

I thought Li got over it all pretty quickly to be honest. Especially as he was the one who was driving. I often think it's just his secret and that me and Jason are helping him keep it from everyone else. But I'd do anything for Jason and for Li. I'm never envious of them. People think I got pissed off with Jason because he became a pro and I didn't, but that's bullshit.

He knocked on my door one Wednesday morning slightly earlier than normal before we headed off to school. Told me he had something important to tell me. I was surprised he had agreed to go to Everton. I tried to talk him into waiting until Man United or Liverpool came knocking, but I couldn't blame him. Course I couldn't. I probably would have jumped on that deal myself if it came my way.

Me and Li had just finished our Leaving Cert a few months before Jason made his first-team debut. Li had already made up his mind, years ago. He wanted to study marketing at Rathmines College. I really didn't have any plans... well aside from turning pro. But, as I was approaching eighteen, I knew that wasn't going to happen for me. I even trialled for a couple of League of Ireland clubs. Both St Patrick's Athletic and Shelbourne agreed to let me train with them, but neither offered me a contract. By the time I trialled for them my heart had already decided it wasn't in the game anymore, though. My passion for the sport had gone, even if my ability hadn't.

I didn't know what to do with my life after school. I thought about following my brothers to different corners of the world, but I didn't wanna miss out on Jason's journey. I wanted to be with him as he made a name for himself.

He didn't want me living in England with him, though – felt it would be a distraction for him to have me or Li with him all the time. That pissed me off a little, especially after all I'd done for Jason over the years. But I could kinda understand it. When it comes to football, Jason has total dedication, total discipline. He even had that when he was ten years old playing for the Bosco.

I tried a couple of different jobs. I worked in a paint factory in Walkinstown for a few months before getting bored. Then I tried my hand at a bit of security, but that was a load of me bollocks. I left that one after ten days. I'd spend most of my time in the local pubs, spending whatever money I could cobble together on pints of Heineken. It didn't take long for me to give in to everything I had been warned to steer clear of from the time we were in school. The Drimnagh gangs are notorious around Ireland – everyone knows about them because they're plastered on the front pages of the Sunday tabloids every other week. I was determined not to get involved. I wanted to prove to everyone who thought I'd easily get tangled up in the gangs that I was stronger than they thought I was. But I couldn't help it.

It wasn't just the money that attracted me to working for Alan Keating. It was the fact that I actually had somethin' to do – a reason to get out of bed in the mornings.

'Shots, shots, shots,' I chant as Li and Jason finally catch up with me at the bar.

'Not fuckin' tequila,' Jason moans as he reaches for his wallet.

'What then?'

'Get those Baby Guinness things,' he says, 'they're not so harsh.'

'Three Baby Guinness,' I shout to the barman. It sounds like such a shite name for a shot. Shots are supposed to be a proper drink, a drink for grown-ups. They shouldn't have the name 'baby' in them at all. It sounds like a pussy's drink. But I have to agree with Jason – they do travel down the throat well.

'Okay boys,' Jason calls out as the barman places the three shots in front of us. 'Let's get the night truly started. Are we ready?'

Jason hovers his debit card over the reader until it beeps, places it back in his wallet, then hands each of us a tiny shot glass.

'One, two three... go.'

We throw the shot into our mouths, crease our face up at the taste of Sambuca hitting the back of our throats. Then we begin to nod our head to the beat of the music and head towards the dance floor.

I lean against a lamppost, scrolling through my phone and glancing up at the entrance to the kebab shop every twenty-seconds or so. It's starting to get cold. I should have brought a light jacket to go over the jumpsuit.

I tug at the V again, not because I'm wary of one of my breasts falling out, but because goose bumps are popping up right through my cleavage. I take a look at the digits on the top of my screen. 20:45. The night is young. People are buzzing around town; some arguing over what bar they should go to next. I spot a couple outside Break For The Border snuggling into each other. It makes me think of Jason Kenny, not that he's been far from my mind over the past hour anyway. I click into the internet browser on my phone and type his name into *Google*. Jaysus, he looked a lot more hand-some tonight than he does when he's on the pitch. He actually looks alright in half of the photos on Google, not so cute in the other half. It seems to me as if he's grown into himself, has grown into his looks as he's aged. Ginger guys do tend to get more handsome the older they get. His hair is less orange in the more recent pics, more a dark shade of auburn. Plus, the beard he has now is brown – it offsets the ginger. I like him. A lot. Such a shame I rushed back inside when I got the text message from Lorna. I don't normally have much to get excited about; hooking up with a celeb is certainly a good night out for me. Getting his phone number and meeting up with him for a date would have been even better.

I click into his *Wikipedia* page, try to work out how big a deal he is. He's played for both Everton and Sunderland. Whatever that means. I've heard of both teams at least, so it can't be that bad. He's made four hundred and ten appearances for Everton, two hundred and eighty-eight for Sunderland. Has sixty-two Ireland caps. But only scored three goals. Maybe he's not that good. He grew up in Drimnagh, was born in 1983. He's exactly ten years older than me. It even mentions here that he is a devout Christian. It's the only blemish I can find. That and the fact that if we had kids together, they could end up with orange hair.

As I'm scrolling through his page, I look up again, to the entrance of the Kebab shop. They're coming out, both holding a plastic bowl filled with chips. They turn left, on to Aungier Street. I place my phone back into my bag and follow. Slowly. I don't want them to notice me. I'll have to stay a distance behind them because I stick out like a sore thumb in this bloody white suit. I guess it wasn't a good choice for loads of different reasons.

As I turn on to Aungier Street I notice a picture of Nadia Forde smiling back at me. She's lovely, Nadia. Has done so well for herself. But I often wonder what made her stand out over me. She seemed to be the model who landed most of the jobs I auditioned for.

I never really gave up modelling. I guess it gave me up. Anne always held out hope that things would pick up for me, but she used to send me for cheap marketing jobs just so I could earn some money. The jobs were petty tacky. I'd stand at food festivals or car festivals and hand out fliers for about eight hours a day. Or worse, I'd have to wear some poxy fancy-dress costume to interact with kids. I don't mind kids, hope to have three myself one day. But the job of having to pretend to be happy and upbeat for eight hours consecutively was a serious stretch for me.

By the time I turned twenty-one, marketing was pretty much my full-time job. Anne called me into her office one day, said she had to let me go from her books; that I was wasting my money handing her over fifteen per cent for shit marketing jobs I could easily get for myself without her help. I thanked her profusely for all she had done for me over the few years I was with her. Made her promise once again that the nude photos I did with Patrick Clavin would never see the light of day. I knew they wouldn't. I regretted doing that shoot as soon as it was over. Even though Patrick was lovely and even though I trusted Anne implicitly, I was hugely uncomfortable that those images existed somewhere.

I stay about a hundred yards behind the two of them, stopping anytime they slowed down. I've no idea where they're off to. Hopefully they're heading home. But I know for a fact that they landed in the Hairy Lemon about an hour ago and had two pints with me. They can't be calling it a night. They must be off somewhere else. Lorna told me I didn't have enough information on Niall Stevens yet; that I must get some concrete evidence one way or the other for the job to conclude. It's not the first time she's made me do this. It's the main aim of the job. I know I haven't nailed it; not yet anyway. Just because Niall mentioned his fiancée to me a couple of times doesn't mean much. I haven't justified the money Lorna is paying me. But I will. I'll give her the information she needs as soon as Niall and his mate decide where they're going next.

They turn on to Harcourt Street, my old territory. It's where Eddie used to bring me all the time. He was obsessed with this area of town. In fact, we met there; in the beer garden of Diceys. I do some calculations in my head. That would have been four years ago last month. Jaysus. Time does fly, even when you're not having fun.

Niall and his mate walk past Diceys and I immediately know where they're heading for. I cross over to the other side of the street and watch as the bouncer stops them for a quick chat before allowing them in.

Fucking Copper Face Jacks. Typical. It must be a couple of years since I've last been in there. I bet it hasn't changed. But I can't follow them straight in. That would look too suspicious. So I take a walk, decide I'll do a few laps of Iveagh Gardens and give it about fifteen, maybe twenty minutes before I pop in. Then I'll get the job done. At this rate I could be in bed before ten o'clock tonight. Perfect!

Zach's the only one with natural rhythm out of the three of us. But it never really stops any of us. We take to the dance floor every time we're out – throwing shapes, most likely off beat. Well, I certainly do. I've never been able to dance. Never know what to do, other than flail my arms and stomp my feet. Jason has some moves, but most of the time he looks pretty awkward. We don't give a shit though. Once Jason's on a dance floor, the sharks circle. Suddenly there are dozens of people around us. Celebs are a DJ's dream. They get the party started.

I like Coppers. Always have fun when I'm here; not that I'm here that often anymore. Not since I met Niamh. Not because she doesn't like me to go out, but because I'd genuinely rather stay in. Throwing back shots and downing pints of beer just doesn't seem like an ideal way to spend a night anymore. That's what you're supposed to do in your twenties, not your thirties. I should be curled up on a sofa watching Netflix with Niamh, having an early night so we can go to Homebase with fresh heads in the morning. That's the stage of life I'm at right now. And I'm happy with it. *Very* happy with it.

I stare over at Zach, watch him body pop and assume the life I live would be hell on earth for him. He's the same age as Jason and me, but he doesn't agree that you have to slow the social life down as you get older. He's just as hungry for it now as he was when we were twenty-one. I doubt he's ever been to Homebase. Certainly not with Tina. He doesn't go anywhere with his wife. I very rarely see them together. They met when they were eighteen, both still immature. I'm sure that immaturity still lives in their relationship. They can't shake off the mentality they had with each other when they first met. I know Tina can't be that easy to live with, but she deserves better than Zach. He treats her like shit. I was thirty-two when I first met Niamh, she had just turned thirty. We were both mature, both knew what we wanted in life by the time we hooked up. That's why our relationship works.

I was scrolling through Tinder one evening, as was becoming the norm back then, swiped right when I saw her profile, then kept scrolling, swiping right on other profiles too. But she got back to me within the hour and suddenly we were arranging a date. I probably swiped right on about a hundred profiles on Tinder over the course of six months. Only two ever arranged a date with me. The first girl I met was called Felicity. She didn't look anything like her profile picture – still, we had a good night out and she promised she'd ring me during the week to arrange a second date. That call never came.

I was genuinely beginning to think I'd never have a girlfriend; felt Irish girls just didn't fancy the Korean look. But it was never about looks between me and Niamh. I was slightly put off by her weight when we met for that first date, but after about ten minutes I just didn't give a shit. We were wrapped up in each other's company, immediately opening up to each other as if we'd been best pals for decades.

A week later, on our third date, we were both muttering those three special words to each other. It just felt right. I did love her. Now I'm totally besotted – not just with her, but with us. We are a great couple. And I love the fact that we're both each other's first real partner. We both suffered the same awkwardness through our twenties when it came to trying to find somebody to settle down with. We share so much in common.

At first we were amazed that we liked the same type of music, that we gorged on the same TV box sets. But over the years, we've learned that that's not what 'having things in common' is truly about. Our politics align. We're both huge liberals. Feel the world has to pull together, not drift apart. We were dumbfounded that Donald Trump got into the White House on the promise of building a wall between Mexico and America. And we were even more flabbergasted that the majority of people in the UK felt it was necessary for them to draw a border between their shitty little island and the rest of Europe. I can never understand anyone who thinks the world should separate. Neither does Niamh. And it was through these types of beliefs that helped us fall head over heels with each other. I genuinely don't know what I would do without her. If I lost her, I think I'd just end it; jump off a bridge or tie a noose around my neck. My life wouldn't be worth living without her. Which is why I'm going to tie her to me permanently. I can't wait to open the box, crouch down on one knee and ask her to be my wife. I just need to figure out what I'm going to say. I want it to be super romantic. Maybe Zach's right. Perhaps getting engaged in Lanzarote is a bit cheesy. Niamh deserves better. I'll have to think it through; come up with something that will blow her mind.

'Shot, shot, shot,' Zach yells into my ear. 'Your round, homeboy.'

I smile at him, walk myself off the dance floor towards the bar. I don't mind doing shots. They're certainly a lot easier on the gut than beer. Though I know I'm going to regret the shots in the morning. Especially when I've got to get up at eight to trek out to Homebase.

Niamh wants a new dining table for the apartment. I'm not sure how she's going to reconfigure the whole room to fit a dining table in, but she insists us having breakfast, lunch and dinner in front of the TV isn't doing her waistline any favours. She's a heavy girl – there's no disputing that – but I love her just the way she is. Though if Niamh wants a dining table, a dining table she will get.

'Baby Guinness,' I say to the barman, holding three fingers aloft.

Before the shot glasses are put in front of me, the two boys are by my side.

'Shots, shots, shots.'

'I gave eh... yer ma a shot,' I say back. It's met with the usual straight faces; no laughter, dead eyes. I can never quite nail a 'yer ma' joke.

The three of us bounce up and down on the dance floor, not giving a shit. It looks like we've started a tsunami – loads more join us, bopping away to Rihanna's vocals destroying another great Calvin Harris track.

I only really do this once a year these days. Normally in the first week of June – just after the season has finished and I fly home to Dublin to hang out with these two idiots. I'm chuffed Li decided to share his news with us. It's totally changed the dynamic of the night. All three of us are buzzing.

I watch Zach whisper into Li's ear and then Li leaves the dance floor. I didn't quite hear what he said, but I'm pretty sure he repeated the word 'shots' three times over, informing Li it was his round.

He takes his wallet from the back pocket of his jeans as he makes his way to the bar. I wonder how he's doing financially, especially with a wedding to plan soon. I could help him out, offer to pay for part of the day – but only if he wants me to.

It's quite odd being flush with cash. You never quite know where to draw the line of generosity. I walked into the Marble Arch – our local boozer in Drimnagh – after I'd signed my first big contract with Everton and offered to buy everyone in the place a round. A few people thanked me, but some barked over to me that I was being a show-off. You can't win. So I don't do anything like that anymore.

I've helped Li and Zach out a few times, but I don't really offer money for fear of looking like I'm being condescending. If they want me, if they want money, they know where I am. Not that I'm going to have money for long. The days of earning thousands of pounds a week have come to an end. I've a good few quid in the bank, a few property investments dotted around Britain. But there's no way I'm as rich as most people assume I am. People think all Premier League footballers are on hundreds of thousands a week. That's bollocks. Only a very small handful earn those amounts – the top guys; three or four players at the biggest clubs.

The biggest contract I ever signed was for twenty-eight grand a week. I was on that for four years at Everton. The tax man ate a lot of it for me, but I still had more money than I could spend. It seems like heaven from the outset, playing football and getting paid for it, but I preferred the days when all I was interested in doing was playing football. Playing for the Bosco, or for Cherry Orchard or even for Everton's youth teams gave me a lot more satisfaction than playing in the first team.

I leave the two lads at the bar, tell them I'm dying for a piss. I really wish pubs and clubs had VIP loos. The most awkward thing about being a celeb is getting approached while you're taking a leak. It probably happens nine times out of ten when I'm in public places. I think lads assume the toilet is a sanctuary where we can all be as one. I never can quite wrap my head around it. I've had hands held out to me for shaking while I'm holding my dick, have had people take photos of me at the urinal too. One bloke even asked me to sign his own dick once, holding out a marker pen. I told him I could sign 'Jay' but that was about all I could fit.

'Jason Kenny, ye legend ye!' somebody says, grabbing at my shoulders as I try to ensure my dick is spraying in to the urinal. 'How are things goin', mate? Still at Sunderland, yeah?'

I just nod my head. I don't even look at him. I don't want to be staring at blokes when I'm holding my dick.

'They're gone a bit shit, aren't they?'

Cheeky fuck!

'Who do you play for?' I ask, again without looking up.

'Me? I just play for me local team – St Eithne's out in Cabra.'

'Eithne'... never heard of them!' I say, zipping up and grinning.

I walk out without washing my hands. Couldn't be arsed entertaining that ass hole.

And that's when I see her. On the stairs.

I spot him leaning against the wall, talking to his mate. So I inch closer to them, but don't approach. I'll let him spot me; that'll look less suspicious.

Lorna's instructions are still ringing in my ear: "get a definite yes or no." I already know it's going to be a 'no'– I've had that impression from the off. Yet it's still not definite, not certain. And I don't get paid for uncertainty. It needs to be a red light or a green light; amber won't do.

I hate having to do this in clubs. They're way too noisy. Especially in here. I don't know why Coppers is noisier than all other clubs, probably because the ceilings are so low; the whole space seems to be condensed. I circle the ring atop my glass of non-alcoholic red as I wait on Niall to notice the coincidence; that somehow I've ended up in the same nightclub as him and his friend Martin.

'Heya love,' some spotty fella says to me.

'I'm waiting on my boyfriend,' I tell him before he's even asked me a question. He just walks on by. I wish I could carry the confidence I have when I'm working into the real world. This job is certainly edging me in the right direction though. It's made me realise I should have more fun; have more courage. I check the time on my phone. 21:06. If he doesn't notice me soon, the goal of ending up in bed by ten o'clock is going to be impossible. Fuck it. I don't have the time to wait. Well... that's not strictly true, I *do* have the time – I've nothing else to do – but I don't have the patience to wait. I pace towards the two of them.

'Niall! Martin!' I say, all high-pitched.

'Ah, how-a-ya, Claire,' Niall says, embracing me with a quick hug. I get the same from Martin before a silence settles between the three of us. They both stare at me, awkwardly. They're not taking this as a coincidence. They know I followed them here.

'Listen,' I say sighing and holding my eyes closed. 'I never do this, so I'm sorry for being so blunt but eh... is there any chance I could eh... is there any chance you and I...'

'Jee,' Niall says, getting the message without me actually saying much. 'I'm flattered. Three years ago, hell yeah. But now?' he shakes his head. 'I'm loved up, Claire.'

'It's okay, it's okay. I just thought... ye know... you only have one life – I liked you, thought I'd just go all balls out and ask.'

I laugh awkwardly as Niall drags me in for another quick hug.

'Your fiancée's a lucky woman,' I whisper into his ear, before turning on my heels.

They don't call me back. Fine by me. My job is done. I have a red light for Lorna. A definite 'no'. I remove my phone from my bag as I walk up the stairs that lead to the exit and then I pause, just to text Lorna the update. That's when I hear my name being yelled over the music.

'Jaysus, what are you doing here?' I ask after turning around. My heart rate rises, in that excited way it does when the boy you fancied in secondary school decides to talk to you in the corridor.

'Eh... dancing,' he says. 'That's what you'd normally come to a club to do. What are you doing here if you're not dancing?'

'Ah... I just popped my head in for old time's sake as I was walking by. I used to come here... for years. I've decimated that dance floor plenty of times,' I say. 'But I'm on my way home. I fancy an early night.'

'C'mon,' he says, holding his hand out for me to take. 'Come have one with us before you go. We're celebrating.'

I don't get an opportunity to ask what they're celebrating. By the time he has taken me back down the few steps I'd walked up, the music is so dominating that he'd barely be able to hear me anyway. We stroll across the dance floor, my heart thumping. I genuinely haven't felt this way since I was a kid. I certainly didn't feel this way when I first met Eddie. In fact, there were no butterflies at all, no excitement. I just decided to go out with him because I thought it'd be convenient.

Eddie's a friend of my cousin's. I assumed he was a genuine guy, and at that stage that was all I wanted – somebody I could trust. Somebody I met generically, not some twat who approached me in a club. I didn't really fancy Eddie, he certainly wasn't my type, and I still can't quite work out why we went out with each other for three years. I think I was just getting desperate. I felt embarrassed about being a twenty-one-year-old who had never had a boyfriend. I used to tell people I was single by choice; that I didn't want to be in a relationship. It was easy for people to buy that line from me. I was good looking and guys approached me all the time. Only I knew I was lying. Only I knew that I actually struggled to find a boyfriend and that I had wanted one for years.

'HEY!' the Asian guy shouts in my ear. The other one – the bald one – hugs me; not a half-arsed hug like Niall and Martin offered me, but a proper squeeze. He holds me for probably eight seconds too long. He seems awfully pleased to see me. He mumbles something into my ear. I'm not sure what he's saying, can't make it out, so I just nod my head and laugh.

'SHOTS! SHOTS! SHOTS!' Jason chants. The other two join in and suddenly I find myself being pulled to the bar by all three of them. I check my phone for the time again as we wait on the barman. 21:19. I definitely won't be home before ten now. Fuck it! Might as well have some fun.

What's the worst that could happen?

NUMBER SEVEN FILLS her glass with water again. It hasn't gone unnoticed that she uses the facilities more than anyone else. She's bored by proceedings, feels that every argument is dragging on for fifteen minutes more than necessary. Too many jurors are too keen to get the last word in. It means points are getting repeated for emphasis. And emphasis only.

To stop her eyes rolling, Number Seven opts to get up off her seat and make her way to the water dispenser. Number Four follows her – he, too, sick of listening to Brian and Number One re-establishing arguments they've already raised.

'Those two'd do yer head in,' he whispers into Number Seven's ear.

'You do my head in,' she whispers back. He bumps off her, hip-to-hip. Number Six cops it, shakes her head with disdain. She hates these two flirting with each other, yet she can't keep her eyes off them when they're together.

'It's a bit too weird innit... y'know that she was walking around in circles, then just followed them into Coppers,' Number Four says to Number Seven as he scuttles in front of her to fill his own glass.

'Yeah – but it's just... I can't get away from the fact that she didn't see them go into Coppers. And nobody told her that's where they were going. I really don't know what to make of this argument. Anyway... the most important thing is what happened in the hotel later. If she was or was not pursuing Jason all night... it still didn't call for her being raped, right?'

Number Four shrugs his shoulders, then sucks his lips. He's been baffled by all of the different arguments. His mind seems to be getting swayed depending on who's talking, yet he still remains genuinely undecided on his overall verdict.

'You two shouldn't be talking about the trial away from the conference table,' Number Eight says, raising his voice as he twists his head to look over his shoulder. The room falls silent.

'Oh... no, we were just talking about the water,' Number Four says, holding his glass up to his fellow jurors.

'That's a lie. I heard you mentioning the hotel and whether or not she had been raped by the end of the night.'

'Okay... listen,' Number Four says, looking agitated as he makes his way back to his chair. 'I was just asking Number Seven if she would like a fresh cup of tea instead of a glass of water and then we very briefly just said that it will be interesting when we get to the discussions about what happened at midnight in the hotel room. Honestly.' He holds his hand up in apology, palm out. Number Four is an experienced liar. Is known among his mates as a bit of a bullshitter.

'We should only discussh the trial at the table, that's a very strict rule,' Brian stresses by banging his fist on top of the table.

'Yeah... okay,' says Number Seven as she takes her seat. 'Calm down. We're sorry. It was a five-second conversation. Nothing else was said. I promise.'

There are strict rules when it comes to serving on a jury. The case you are examining can't even be discussed with your loved ones once you go back home. It's a rule that is pretty much broken in almost every circumstance, though. Jurors don't necessarily go into every detail – they keep names out of it for the most part – but they do discuss the trials with their spouses, siblings, parents and friends. Of course they do.

Under Irish law, a former jury member can go to prison for discussing the trial they examined publicly after the fact. But even though the rule is regularly broken, that specific law has never needed to be enforced. It's nigh on impossible for even the most honourable person to keep all of the juicy details bottled up inside. It's tough being a juror overall, more mentally challenging than the majority of people assume it is. Some people detest the thought of being a juror, some revel in it. But nobody can really foretell just what the experience will be like – especially if you are tasked with examining such a high profile case as this one. It's a lottery – not just the trial you are chosen to examine, but whether or not you'll ever be called for jury duty in your lifetime.

Every Irish citizen aged eighteen or upwards, whose name appears on the register of electors within Dail Eireann, is eligible for duty. There are categories of people who are ineligible: lawyers, Gardaí, members of the defence forces. Some are excusable, such as priests, medics, students. Those over the age of sixty-five are excusable too, but Number Six waived her right; was keen to get involved. Anybody, of any adult age, any class and with any range of intelligence can decide the fate of the most complex of cases. And therein lies the biggest problem of the judicial system: everyday people just don't understand law.

Gardaí could spend years piecing together a serious crime, such as murder – for example – only for twelve regular Joes and Josephines to dismiss most of their investigation simply because the nuances of the case went over their heads. The make-up of a jury is a mixed bag – you don't know what you're going to get. It was difficult for the lawyers on both sides to find adequate numbers for this trial. Out of the ninety-eight people summoned for jury duty ahead of selection, seventy-nine confessed to knowing who Jason Kenny was. That meant they couldn't be eligible to serve on this jury. It left both the prosecution and defence lawyers having to narrow to twelve jurors from a tiny pool of nineteen. Still, they ended up with a diverse range of individuals.

The average age of this jury is forty – which happens to be the exact average age of juries in Ireland.

At twenty-two, Number Seven is the youngest juror by some six years over Number Five. Number Six is the oldest at sixty-eight; Number Eight the next eldest – a full decade younger, though he genuinely looks like the oldest in the room. Number Eight's real name is Gerry Considine. He'll be fifty-nine next week. He has never really had a career, just hopped from job-to-job over the course of three decades. At the moment he works as a security guard at Independent House on Talbot Street. He presses a button, lets people in and out of the building. He's huge. Six foot, four inches tall; weighs nineteen stone. The weight is mostly in his belly. He looks unhealthy, as if a heart attack is just around the corner. But his regular check-ups at his local doctors' surgery in East Wall – an inner-city suburb of Dublin –confirm all is good on the inside. Gerry's the other juror – aside from Number Twelve – who lied in order to be selected. He knew who Jason Kenny was prior to being called for jury duty. Is actually quite a big football fan. Number Eight raised his hand as 'undecided' earlier, but has had a strong inkling all the way through the trial the three men are not guilty. Although he feels Sabrina is a very eloquent and attractive girl, there was something about her that he couldn't quite put his finger on. The defence's tactic of painting Sabrina as cunning and untrustworthy had a massive impact on Number Eight. He isn't the only one swayed by their narrative.

'Is it perhaps time for a verdict vote?' Brian offers up.

His suggestion is met with a couple of audible sighs, but he has a point. The jurors have just discussed one of the main arguments of the trial; was or was not Sabrina fixated on sleeping with Jason Kenny that night? Did she seek him out?

Her appearance at Copper Face Jacks – innocent and coincidental as it was – had a huge bearing on most jurors' mind-sets. Sabrina, out of respect – not only for her job, but for her client – couldn't bring herself to admit she was following another man to Copper Face Jacks at any stage of the investigation. She didn't divulge this to the Gardaí when they initially questioned her about her claim, nor did she fill her own lawyers in on this key piece of information during any of their multiple meetings over the past eighteen months. She knew she didn't have a good enough reason for turning up at Coppers otherwise, but hoped the jury would believe her insistence that it was an honest coincidence; that she just fancied a dance and by strange synchronicity ended up in the same club as the three men she had been talking to earlier.

It was wise that she never mentioned Niall Stevens during any of the investigation, though. Had Stevens been called as a witness, he would have testified that she blatantly came on to him that night. It would have ruined her case. In fact, the case wouldn't even have made it to court had Stevens been questioned by Gardaí. But the Gardaí weren't looking for him, because nobody mentioned him. The defence lawyers weren't seeking another man as part of their own investigation either. They genuinely believed Sabrina followed Jason, Zach and Li to Copper Face Jacks because the three men themselves remain quite adamant that she had.

Niall Stevens is totally unaware of his involvement in such a fateful evening. He hasn't forgotten about the hot girl in the white jumpsuit who made a pass at him a year and a half ago, but he has no idea whatsoever that she is Ms X – the girl entangled in the major rape trial that has engulfed the nation.

So many details of Sabrina Doyle, even down to what she was wearing on the night in question, have been shared in court, but can't be reported in the media. There are strict rules when it comes to the victim's identity. She can't be named. The professional media never cross this line, but it's impossible to stop anonymous idiots from sharing pictures of her, outing her, on social media.

As for Jason, around half of the country have figured out he's the big-name international footballer on trial, yet he still can't be named by journalists for legal reasons. All defendants, famous or not, have a right to anonymity in major criminal cases; their names will only be reported in the media if the jury find them guilty. If this incident occurred north of the border, all three men would be named in the press. The Irish legal system prefers to protect those accused from public humiliation. In Britain, the accused would be named, the general public even allowed inside the courtroom should they wish to attend the trial.

'Why don't we use the paper slips?' Brian says, stretching to grab the box from the middle of the table.

There are no strict rules on how jurors conduct their verdict votes. But pens and cut-out slips of paper are left in the room for them to conduct secret ballots should they deem it necessary at any point. Using this method, now, contradicts Brian's earlier reasoning for having constant verdict votes. He had said that it would be beneficial for every juror to know where every other juror stood throughout the course of the deliberations. Using the secret ballot method means the jury aren't going to gain that knowledge. Still, nobody questions him. They're all up for a secret ballot; feel it would hurry proceedings, feel they won't necessarily have to explain themselves in detail – they just need to scribble one of three things; guilty, not guilty or undecided on a slip of paper. Brian shuffles around the room behind each juror's chair, tossing a slip of paper and a pen in front of them.

Number One then decides to stand, feeling a need to show awareness of his responsibilities.

'Okay, so this is straightforward,' Number One says, holding his slip of paper and pen up to the jurors, as if he was a teacher about to give instruction.

'Yes, we get it,' says Number Eight.

Number One sits back down, his face slightly brushed with embarrassment. Number Five cups her piece of paper as she writes down her verdict, as if she's doing an exam she doesn't want others to copy from. It's rather pointless – everybody is aware she is firmly in the guilty camp. She has made no secret of that fact.

'Okay, so just fold your paper twice and put it back in the box,' Number One says after scribbling 'guilty' on his. He holds out his piece of paper, the verdict facing him, and genuinely folds it twice as if showing his fellow jurors what folding is. This instruction would be patronising, only nobody glances up at him. They're too busy scribbling. When they're done, they toss their verdict votes into the box; some folded twice, some only folded once, one not folded at all.

Number One glances around the room, notices everybody's slip of paper is now inside, but still asks anyway.

'Is that everybody in?' he says.

'Yep,' rasps Number Twelve. 'Get counting, head boy.'

Number One slides the box onto his lap, out of the sight of everybody except the two jurors seated next to him. He slips the first piece of paper out, looks at it, then places it face down in front of him; then repeats this action another eleven times. When the box is empty, Number One has three small piles of papers on the table. He already knows the result but decides to count again, trying to emphasise to his fellow jurors just how seriously he is taking his role.

'Okay, I have a result,' he finally says after drawing in a large breath for the sake of creating a bit of drama. 'Three guilty... six not guilty... three undecided.'

Sabrina seems reluctant to join the lads on the dance floor. That suits me; gives me a break without having to stand alone. We watch the other two bounce around to some remix of a shite Drake song and then we smile at each other. She really is beautiful – top to toe. Not my type though. I always assume good-looking girls are hard to live with. They're normally insecure. You just don't know what you're going to get with a looker.

I've seen Jason with quite a few girls who have been plastered on magazine covers and the like and every single one of them proved to be a headache for him. They start off all nicey-nicey, but after a few weeks their true colours come out. They'd moan at him for wanting to watch something on TV rather than paying them attention, or they'd crack up if they ever saw him talking to another girl.

That's why I love Niamh so much. It really is a case of what you see is what you get with her. We've never argued, never had a fight. We're totally open and honest with each other one-hundred per cent of the time. It's quite odd. I always felt inferior to my two best mates. Zach got the looks and the confidence, Jason got the talent and with that, the celebrity. I got nothing. Yet I'm the only one who has ever found true love out of the three of us.

I've no doubt that I'm happier than those two, though they certainly look happy now. They're like two happy spas bouncing around a tiny dance floor as if it's their last night on earth. It's amazing what a few shots of Baby Guinness can do for your mood. I'm glad, because I had a fear when Sabrina showed up in here that it might cause a rift between Zach and Jason. But it hasn't. Not yet anyway. Zach's tried to pull Sabrina up for a dance a couple of times, but she ain't budging. My guess is she's too self-conscious to dance, which is odd, given that she told us she only came in here to have a quick dance before she headed home. Though none of us really bought that. She followed us here. She must have.

'Let's play favourites,' she shouts into my ear.

'Favourites?'

'Yeah,' she says, leaning closer. 'It's a good way to get to know each other, especially in this noise. I say something, you tell me what your favourite of that is.'

I look at her and smile. I think I get it.

'Movie?' she shouts.

'Eh... *Goodfellas*.'

She smiles, nods her head.

'You?' I shout back at her.

'The Notebook.'

'Oh – I love that too,' I say back, noting how camp that actually sounds when said so loudly. But I do love it. Me and Niamh. We musta watched it about a dozen times.

'Song?' Sabrina shouts.

I think about it, stew her question over in my mind.

'*Do I Wanna Know* – Arctic Monkeys.'

'Yes!' she says, holding her hand up for me to high five. 'I love the Arctic Monkeys.'

'TV show?'

'Stranger Things. Addicted to it.'

She peels away from me, her mouth slightly ajar, her face folding back into a smile. She high fives me again. Seems like we're into the exact same things. She grabs me in for a hug.

I notice the time on the digital clock behind the bar over her shoulder as we hug. 21:39. Not too bad. We've been out for just over a couple of hours now. Three pints of Heineken and three Baby Guinness shots down me. Things could have been a lot worse. It's not unlike me to be puking into a toilet bowl after being out with Jason and Zach for a couple of hours. At this rate, I'll be fit and raring to go to Homebase in the morning.

We'll be visiting there quite a lot over the next few months. Me and Niamh have a whole life to plan for. Literally. I woke up a couple of weeks ago, one lazy Sunday morning, to hear her whistling. I'd never heard her whistle before. Didn't know what the hell was going on. I staggered down-stairs, watched her frying up some sausages and rashers and knew instantly that she was in a great mood.

'What's up with you?' I asked her.

She just turned to me, beamed a huge smile and continued whistling.

'Niamh?'

'Just take a seat, sweetheart,' she said. 'Breakfast's nearly ready.'

I sat on our coach, in just my boxer shorts, and turned on the TV. There's normally a whole load of politics shite on every Sunday, so I switched over to the sports channel, hoping to see Jason in a bit of action. Though it's rare that the highlights of his games make broadcast anymore. Sunderland were rock bottom of the Championship at this stage, their rele-gation to League One all but confirmed. They're just not significant anymore.

'Hey, turn off the tele,' Niamh said as she entered the living room. She handed me a tray with a mountain of breakfast on it, then retreated to the kitchen and came back with a tray of her own.

'You woke up hungry, I gather?'

'I woke up happy,' she said. 'Now eat up!'

I did as I was told; Niamh and I staring at each other as we stuffed our faces. She couldn't stop the smile from beaming on her face. I knew she was excited, assumed it had something to do with buying something in Homebase later that day. When we'd finished breakfast, she took my tray from my lap, placed both my tray and hers on the carpet and then pulled a white stick from the pocket of her dressing-gown. I took it off her, stared at the blue cross on it, then beamed a smile right back into her face. I'm still as giddy about that now as I was in that moment.

'Book?' she shouts.

I gurn my face, hold my hand up.

'Eh, don't really read that much,' I say to her. She frowns; looks disappointed in that answer. Such a shame. We'd just learned we had so much in common. I can't believe a girl can be this down to earth *and* this good looking.

She leans towards my ear, is about to tell me what her favourite book is when Zach arrives between us. Instead of trying to drag her to the dance floor this time, he drags her aside. Shit! I've a feeling the awkwardness I was dreading is about to erupt.

'Fancy another drink?' Jason asks me as Sabrina and Zach stroll away.

'Sure.'

We both walk towards the bar in silence. It was only after he ordered two pints of Heineken that I posed the question.

'You not worried he's gonna fuck things up with her?'

'Nah. She followed us here for me,' Jason says.

'Yeah, but he'll get pissed off, won't he? I'm more worried about him fucking our night up, than anything.'

Jason shrugs his shoulders, hands the barman his debit card and then clinks my glass.

'We'll see how he handles it,' Jason says as we stare over at both of them on the other side of the club. Zach places his hand on the small of Sabrina's back and leads her up the stairs. I take Jason in, out of the corner of my eye.

'Where the hell they going?' I ask. He doesn't answer. He just stares at the stairs until they're out of sight. I take him in again. I know Jason. I know every single look he can possibly adopt on his face. He looks worried.

Bollocks.

I've got a bad feeling about this.

I love that I'm a better dancer than Jason. I've always had better rhythm than him, better balance. It's why I was a more natural footballer than he'll ever be.

But I know that people are only dancin' round us because of him. Celebrity really does fascinate the regular Joe. But I'm not gonna let his celebrity beat me to that Sabrina bird. She's amazin'. My eyes nearly popped out of me head when I saw her come over to us again. I'm delighted she followed us here. I guess she came for Jason, but she'll be leavin' with me. She's playing hard to get at the moment, though. Won't get on the dance floor with me. Maybe I should take her aside, have a chat with her; let her know I'm interested. I'm sure I can charm that jumpsuit right off her by the end of the night.

'C'mere for a sec,' I say into her ear as I grab her hand. I don't even look back at Jason; assume he'll be all right with it. He can score any bird in this club he wants.

I walk her over to the stairs, away from the blast of the speakers.

'So... what brought you here; wasn't me was it?' I say.

'Sorry?' she shouts back at me, turning her face so that her ear inches towards my face.

'Did you come here lookin' for me?' I shout.

She looks confused. I don't think she caught the humour in my question.

'We can't really talk here,' I say. 'Let's pop outside for a minute.'

I don't even think of Tina when I'm chattin' up other birds. I think all the guilt I could ever feel was used up on The Secret. Even when it comes to sellin' drugs, helping fund gangland crime, I feel no guilt whatsoever. I just get the impression that life is too damn short for feeling that way.

Alan Keating first asked me to sell drugs for him when I bumped into him in the toilets in my local boozer. I'd been hanging around him and his associates for a couple of months, keen for company more than anything else. He broke it down for me really easily; said if I could shift fifty grams of coke for him every week, I'd end up pocketing a grand for myself. I couldn't say no to that. The most I'd ever earned in a week was four hundred euros, and that was doing shitty security shifts. Selling drugs is an easy gig. All I had to do was pick up the merch from Keating's associate out in Blanchardstown, build up some leads and literally swap small bags of coke for large wads of cash.

For the first few weeks I only brought in about two grand, my cut being fifteen per cent. But I pretty soon got the hang of it and within two months I was earning the grand a week Keating had promised I would. He's alright Keating, if you're on the good side of him. But I know things about him that would keep most people up at night.

It's funny. Most of the tabloids know exactly what Keating gets up to, but he always keeps his nose clean. The cops have nothin' on him. He's been one of Ireland's most notorious gangsters for a couple of decades, yet he hasn't spent any time behind bars. I sorta respect him. I don't envy him, not like I envy Jason. But I respect him.

Though getting involved with him was not how I'd hoped my life would go. Word started to get around that I was entangled in the Keating gang, but I denied it to anyone who brought it up with me. Li must've asked me about it a hundred times. He kept catching wind that I was hangin' around with that lot. I just told him that we all happened to drink in the same pub and that was that.

I was initially worried he'd tell Jason. And if Jason found out, he'd freak out. He was always adamant that we'd steer clear of the gangs in Drimnagh. It was driven into him by his parents. I agreed; promised him a thousand times I wouldn't get involved. But it's difficult when you have fuck all else to do. Especially when your best mate is away in England livin' out your dream.

I started to do a bit of coke myself, just to pass the time. I began skimming off the top of the stuff I was supposed to be sellin' for Keating; assumed I wouldn't get caught. But I couldn't have been more wrong. When it comes to shifting cocaine, every single granule is practically accounted for.

'You've been stealing from me,' Keating said, staring through me one evening. I stuttered some awful excuse back at him.

'Don't worry about it, kid,' he said. 'I'll let you away with it... on one condition. You're mates with Jason Kenny, right? I wanna meet him.'

I take all of her in after we've stepped outside. She really is a fuckin' cracker. A proper ten. Definitely out of my league. But I don't give a shit. I'll try it on with whoever I happen to think is the hottest bird in the place. And nobody's gonna be hotter than Sabrina – not tonight anyway.

'So, what were you saying?' she says, making me refocus after we step outside.

'I was just askin' if you came to Coppers lookin' for me?'

She makes a gurning face. My fault. The line didn't come out the way I intended it to. It was supposed to be banter. Comedy is all in the timing; I didn't get the timing right with that one.

'I just fancied a dance,' she says, filling the silence. 'I didn't know you guys were in here.'

'No... I'm... eh... I was just eh... kiddin',' I say. Jesus. A girl's never had me this tongue-tied before.

'So... are you good friends with Jason?' she asks.

Bollocks! She's too into him. This is gonna take a whole lotta charm to win her over to my side.

'Yeah – we're best mates. Have been since we were kids. He eh... he could have any woman he wants in there,' I say, nodding back to the club.

'I'm sure he could,' she says, putting her hands on her hips and nodding. I swallow hard; think about giving up the ghost until I notice two rickshaws parked up at the footpath a few yards down from the club entrance.

'Hey... ever taken a rickshaw ride around Dublin?' I ask.

She looks over her shoulder. Laughs.

'Can't say I have, no.'

'C'mon then.'

I grab her hand and begin to run down the few steps towards the footpath.

'What? No... I... I—'

'C'mon, it'll be fun!'

He's just bought me two drinks; a shot of Baby Guinness that all three of us downed before I'd barely said hello to each of them, and then a glass of red, which I'm still holding as he throws himself around the dance floor in front of me.

It seems quite bizarre that he can't dance. I would have thought a professional sportsman would have had at least some sort of natural rhythm. He seems to miss the beat every time he jumps... or claps... or does any type of movement. It'd probably be embarrassing if it wasn't for the fact that everybody is surrounding him, as if he's brilliant – as if he's Justin Timberlake or something. His moves look awkward, but they're kind of endearing in a way. He's not taking himself too seriously, has a smile practically tattooed across his face.

I just stand at the edge of the dance floor, trying to get to know Li a little better. Perhaps if you want to impress a guy, it's good to impress his mates first. I drift away in the Drake song that's booming out, imagine myself as a footballer's wife. A WAG. I picture the lifestyle: the cars, the swimming pool, the big house. I've never wanted much, am not that interested in money, really. But my thoughts are floating away, like a loose buoy in the ocean. Maybe I deserve all those luxuries, to compensate for all the shit I've been though over the years. That'd certainly infuriate Eddie... if he knew I was dating a footballer. It'd sting like hell. I'd love it.

He wasn't all bad, Eddie. Just at the end. We started off like any other couple, dating in restaurants, bars, clubs. We used to come here a lot actually. But that all died off after about six months. Suddenly, we were just sitting in, watching crap on TV, barely talking. We had nothing to say anyway; we were bored of each other. He started going out himself, leaving me to watch the crap TV alone. I should have known then; should have known he wasn't for me. But I stayed with him – just because I didn't want to be single. Not again. I can understand why women stay in bad relationships. A bad relationship is only bad to them. But being single looks bad to everybody. I'd probably still be with Eddie if I hadn't, by chance, bumped into Lorna a couple of years ago. I wonder how much better Jason is compared to Eddie. Maybe all blokes are the same. And he's a footballer after all... that probably makes things even worse. He can score any girl, any night. The thought of this stops my buoy from drifting any further out to sea. Suddenly the big house, the swimming pool and the fancy cars disappear from my mind. Why was I even thinking that far ahead in the first place? I had barely introduced myself to him when he had his tongue down my throat, opening his jeans so I could wank him off. I sigh. A deep loud sigh; disappointed in myself for getting carried away. Then I turn to Li, realise I've gone quiet on him, that I have forgotten we were in the middle of getting to know each other.

'Book?' I ask him.

'Eh, don't really read that much,' he says, disappointing me. I read constantly, sometimes consuming three books at the same time. I look at him with mock disappointment etched on my face.

'C'mere for a sec,' Zach says, butting in between me and my new best buddy.

He leads me towards the stairs. It's quieter here, but not much. He tries to say something else to me, but I can barely hear him.

'We can't really talk here. Let's pop outside for a minute,' he shouts while pointing up the stairs. I look over my shoulder, towards Jason. He's just followed Li to the bar, barely noticing me walking off with his mate. I silently tut, then follow Zach up the steps, playing over in my mind whether or not I should just go home.

'So, what were you saying?' I ask when we get outside.

'I was just asking if you came to Coppers lookin for me?'

What the hell is he talking about? He can't be serious...

'I just fancied a dance,' I say. 'I didn't know you guys were in here.'

'No... I'm...eh... I was just eh... kidding,' he says. Wow. If that was him kidding, this guy ain't gonna make it as a stand-up comedian, that's for sure.

'So... are you good friends with Jason?' I ask, trying to suss whether or not Jason is actually into me.

'Yeah – we're best mates. Have been since we were kids. He eh... he could have any woman he wants in there,' he tells me. My heart sinks. I know what he's trying to allude to. Jason's not interested. Maybe this guy's just trying to get his famous mate's cast offs. I'm sure that happens all the time. I check the time on my phone again. 21:54. I should probably get a taxi – call it a night.

'Hey... ever taken a rickshaw ride around Dublin?' he asks, his face beaming like a kid at Christmas.

'Can't say I have, no.'

He grabs my hand, jumps down the three concrete steps onto the footpath and leads me towards one of the rickshaws lined up on the pavement.

'What? No... I... I.'

'C'mon, it'll be fun!'

I remain silent, hop on the back of the rickshaw, then laugh at him when I notice his big grin. You'd swear he was a ten-year-old after being allowed on his first roller coaster.

'Where d'yis wanna go?' the guy cycling the rickshaw asks us.

Zach looks at me. I'd like to say, 'My house in Drumcondra if your legs can take you that far'. But I don't. I remain silent as I try to figure out in my head what the hell I'm doing.

'Just around town,' Zach says. 'About fifteen minutes' worth. How much is it?'

'Fifteen minutes around town, eh... twenty quid.'

'Cool – let's go, mate!'

I've never been on one of these before; don't know why the hell I'm on one now. But here I am, sitting on an uncomfortable wooden bench while some poor young fella cycles as fast as he can to bring us nowhere in particular. I don't wanna be here. Not just because it's uncomfortable on my ass, but because it's uncomfortable in general. I'm pretty sure Zach is about to come on to me. How can I tell him I'm not interested, that I was only hanging around because I liked his best mate? His famous mate. Though maybe he's used to it. Maybe he won't mind being told that.

'Are you a magician?' he asks, turning to face me.

'Huh?'

'Are you a magician? Because every time I look at you everybody else disappears.'

I laugh. Properly laugh. Not because his line is funny. But because it's so *not* funny. I've had guys come on to me before, but not as if they're reading Christmas cracker jokes.

'Was your da a boxer?' he says, 'because damn! You're a knockout.'

I laugh again, almost snorting into my hand as I hold it to my face out of embarrassment for him. Zach sure is funny; just not in the way he thinks he is.

I love these tunes; could bounce around the dance floor to this shit all night. Though in truth, I'd love to be doing nothing more than kissing Sabrina right now. But I'm trying to play it cool with her; feel I probably pushed things a little too far when we first met in the Hairy Lemon earlier. Perhaps I don't need to be this stand off-ish given that she's followed me here, but I'll just refrain from being all over her a little more; give her the impression I'm not desperate. She is cute. *Very* cute. But it's not just that. There's a connection. I can't quite put my finger on it. But I have a feeling – or probably a hope more than anything – that something could come of this. And I need this. I need a bit of fortune back in my life. Maybe I'll give it another couple of songs, then I'll drag her aside, try to have a quiet word with her. Try to get to know her.

Bollocks.

I watch as Zach acts before me, taking her aside, walking her towards the stairs. He can be such a selfish cunt sometimes. I stop dancing, walk towards Li and ask him if he fancies another drink.

'You not worried he's gonna fuck things up with her?' he asks me.

'Nah. She followed me here,' I say. I'm trying to remain calm. But I am a little pissed off. Sabrina's way out of Zach's league but I wouldn't put it past him pulling her. He's pulled out of his league loadsa times before.

'Yeah, but he'll get antsy won't he, if she tells him she's already been with you? I'm more worried for him fucking our night up than anything,' Li says.

'We'll see how he handles it,' I reply as I watch them head up the stairs, hoping that she stares back at me. She doesn't.

'Where the hell are they going?' Li asks. I don't answer.

'Two Heinekens,' I say turning to the barman.

Tonight's the first night I've drank alcohol in almost a year. I stayed off it all season. Was doing my best to have my contract renewed. I'm not sure anyone at the club noticed, to be honest. The club's a fucking mess. Top to bottom.

I only enjoyed my first season at Sunderland, after that it turned into a cluster fuck. We've been relegated in each of the last two years, from the glamour of the Premier League down to the averageness of League One. I miss my days at Everton; miss the thrill of a proper Merseyside Derby, the excitement of being on the television almost every week.

Sunderland offered Everton eighteen million for me in the summer of

2014. I had another offer; could have gone to Crystal Palace. I wish now that I had. But at the time, Sunderland looked in better shape than them... felt I was going to a club with aspirations. I was thirty-one at the time, had a feeling it would be my last major contract. They were paying me twenty grand a week, until we were relegated to the Championship and that was halved. I know things could have been worse – a lot worse. But it's difficult to transition from significance into insignificance.

If I had never made it, never played in the Premier League, I wouldn't be depressed now. But because I did make it, because I was somebody, the crash back to reality has been hard to take in. Such is life, I suppose. There's not much I'd change looking back. Maybe a few things. I'd have signed for Palace over Sunderland for one, would definitely have worked harder at keeping Jessica. Oh yeah – and I certainly wouldn't have let Li drive the car that night. I never forgot her face, never forgot her name.

I've searched for that name all over the internet, but I haven't found her. I'd say I think about Caitlin Tyrell as much as I think about my own dad. Practically every day. Certainly every time I'm praying.

'Cheers,' Li says as we clink glasses again. 'She'll be back in looking for you in a few minutes – don't worry about it.'

We stay at the bar, in the quiet, staring out at the crowds of people. This place is starting to get pretty packed. I think of a technique my therapist often recommends to me – 'think of the positive'. I don't really have much positivity going on in my own life, but Li's news is reason enough for me to be upbeat. I should be really happy for him. I guess he's the only one out of the three of us who's truly happy, who has managed to get practically everything he's ever wanted.

'I'm so proud of you, Li,' I say, nudging his shoulder. 'You're gonna be a great husband. Niamh's a lucky girl to have you, and you're lucky to have her.'

He smiles; a big wide grin that has a ripple effect on me. Suddenly I'm smiling – even if it is someone else's happiness that's doing it for me. I play over the possibility in my head of opening up to Li; finally telling him I've been depressed for two years... that I'm really unhappy... that I have no contract for next season... that my career is over. But I don't want to ruin his excitement. Instead, I grab him in for a hug.

'I love you, man.'

'I love you too.'

I can see tears form in his eyes when I release him.

'I eh... nah,' he shakes his head.

'What?'

'I can't.'

'Ye can't what?' I ask.

'I can't tell you... well I really shouldn't tell you...'

'You can tell me anything,' I say, grabbing onto his shoulder.

'Niamh will kill me. It's early. She's only two months—'

'Yesss!' I say, picking him up and spinning him around. 'Oh man – whatever about being a great husband, you're definitely going to be a great father!'

And I mean it. He will be.

He's been such a great older brother to Jinny. Nobody cares more about other people than Li. If anyone had've pointed out the nerdy Korean kid in primary school and told me he'd be the person I'd be most envious of in the whole world in thirty years' time I would have thought they were fucking insane.

But it's true. Li is living a life I could only wish for.

THE AMBIENCE in the room heightened somewhat after the secret ballot result was revealed; most of the jurors beginning to feel eerily optimistic that a final verdict is just around the corner. The pace of discussions has picked up somewhat. Everyone – even Brian and Number One – seem to be giving their opinions in bullet-point bursts, keen to move the debates on as swiftly as possible. Though in truth, the secret ballot vote hasn't made as massive an adjustment from their initial vote as they feel it has.

There was certainly a shift towards not guilty, especially in comparison to the earlier vote. But had they taken the time to think through the latest vote in more detail, rather than rush into the next discussion, they would have realised they weren't really speeding towards a final decision at all. Three undecided out of twelve is still a lot of votes to play for – exactly one-quarter in fact. And if those undecided were persuaded into the *guilty* camp, then all matters would be tied: six each. The old adage of 'it ain't over till the fat lady sings' is a well-worn saying in legal circles. It has even been known that eleven:one ratios have been overturned by jurors, albeit very rare. So the six not guilty, three guilty and three undecided result of the secret ballot means relatively little in terms of reaching conclusion.

The judge set these twelve off to find a unanimous decision; that is *all* twelve jurors must agree on the same verdict, as is the norm in every case of this magnitude. Some judges may call jurors back, as early as five or six hours into deliberations – though most likely after a couple of days – to let them know he or she will take an eleven:one vote ratio, maybe even a ten:two.

Judge Delia McCormick – who presided over the Sabrina Doyle versus Jason Kenny, Zach Brophy and Li Xiang trial – has a reputation for being quite patient with her jurors. She's likely to not want to see them for at least another few days. Though this is certainly the most high profile case she has ever presided over and it's conceivable that she, too, is feeling pressure like she's never felt it before.

She did, to her credit, handle the whole trial particularly well. She was fair, yet stern, with both sides of the courtroom. The defence may have received a slightly harsher time of it – more of her raised eyebrows, more of her quick, snappy retorts – than the prosecution, but that was only because they were more experienced lawyers when dealing with cases of this magnitude. They knew just how far to push a judge.

Still, Sabrina's lawyer – Jonathan Ryan – didn't have a free ride of it. McCormick kept him in check, was as short and snappy with the young buck as she was with the more experienced lawyers on occasion. Ryan tried all the original tricks everybody would recommend to a victim. He insisted Sabrina dressed demurely in the courtroom. Most days her hair was tied back into a simple ponytail. She always wore a skirted suit, all of them a dark shade. No make up. Ryan told her to try to look as vacant as she possibly could in the courtroom when witnesses were giving evidence. He wanted her to look like the every girl as much as possible.

'Don't react. To anything.'

He said that to her over and over again, stressing the point on days he felt she may get particularly emotional.

He was delighted with her performance on the stand, though that was a self-congratulatory pat on the back more than anything. He coached her. His predictions about what questions would arrive from the defence were on the money. Her rehearsed answers were delivered with the expressionless face and tone he had drilled into her.

Judge McCormick would have been aware that Sabrina's answers were rehearsed. Three jurors – Number Twelve, Number Ten and Number Nine – clocked that some answers came across as scripted too, but most jurors just didn't even consider the possibility.

Truth is, these rehearsed answers paint no sign of guilt on her part. Both Jason's and Zach's testimonies were rehearsed to some extent too. Though there was one real moment from Li when he broke down at the desk during a break in proceedings while informing his lawyers that he had lost his fiancée, Niamh, and full access to his ten-month-old daughter, Sally, because of these accusations. Aside from that, the boys were always on script. A lawyer wouldn't be doing their job properly if they didn't pre-script answers for any questions they could foresee coming their client's way. It's part and parcel of the system. For lawyers, each case is like a game – a game they are intent on winning. And in order to win that game, they'll take *any* advantage they can get.

Sabrina was – understandably – stressed about her cross-examination. In rape trials, it can often seem as if it is the victim who's on trial. She felt her whole life was being examined. Sabrina was accused of stalking Jason Kenny on the night in question, accused of heavy drinking, accused of being fame hungry and accused of being a nude glamour model desperate for attention. One tabloid ran with the headline 'Ms X is Ms XXX' after Patrick Clavin's testimony. And yet Sabrina is supposed to be the victim in this case. No wonder a large number of rape victims are reluctant to report their attackers.

Jason, Zach and Li's defence lawyers did all they could to paint Sabrina in a negative light. They also aimed to make her appear hesitant on the stand. If defence lawyers are successful in making a complainant seem hesitant, then it can go a long way to breathing a feeling of reasonable doubt in the jurors' minds.

Although the defence team are considered to be among the best in their field, they were disappointed overall with their cross examination of Sabrina Doyle. Perhaps they thought she would be an easy target, but she somehow, from somewhere, found an inner-strength when she was on the stand.

When Gerd Bracken – the defence team's lead lawyer – ended his interrogation of Sabrina by whipping off his glasses and moving intimidatingly towards the stand, raising his voice: 'I suggest to you, Sabrina Doyle, that this is *not* a case of non-consensual sexual relations, but a case of consensual sexual relations with three men that you subsequently regretted, isn't that right?' she looked him square in the eye and replied 'I said no, I said no, I said no – not subsequently, but *while* I was being raped.'

Although she gripped a handful of tissues throughout the two days the defence lawyers cross-examined her, she didn't have to use them to wipe away any tears. She was impressive up there; had a steely determination to get through the test without giving the three defendants – or indeed their legal team who she had grown to despise – any satisfaction whatsoever. She wanted to portray herself as a strong woman when she was up there. And she did.

'Well that's true,' Number Ten says, 'you can look at it both ways.' She was agreeing with a point Number One had just raised about Jason's character. Discussions were heating up; the secret ballot result changing the gears of the conversation. 'Jason Kenny is far from squeaky clean. He may have made a success of himself, but he's no saint.'

The jurors had moved on, were now at the beginning stages of a discussion about the three character witnesses that were called to give testimony about Jason Kenny.

Clara Groves, a sixty-three-year-old founder of a charity called YouKnight – set up in in Dublin in 1978 to support disabled people – testified that Jason was not only generous with his money, but with his time too.

'For the purposes of this trial, I actually went through all of my notes and counted up the hours Jason has given to us over the years,' she testified. 'He became an ambassador for YouKnight in December 2009, still is to this day. He has, according to my calculations, given up almost six hundred hours to help us. He's over and back to Dublin as much as he can be to offer support. Has travelled to America with us too, just to see some of our beneficiaries live out their dreams. And that's on top of the seventy-eight thousand pounds he has personally donated within that time frame too. He's an amazing, caring man. We have a couple of celebrities who are ambassadors of YouKnight, but nobody gives more than Jason.'

Former Ireland international coach Mick Dempsey also backed up Jason's character on the stand, the highlight of his testimony suggesting 'Jason is the kindest footballer of all of the footballers I've worked with – over three hundred of them. He's deeply religious, and it shows in his character. He's very humble, very caring.'

It had been reported in the newspapers that former Ireland captains Robbie Keane and Richard Dunne would also act as character witnesses for the high-profile accused, but while the defence did certainly make initial plans to contact these famous names, this route was never going to be taken. It wouldn't have been wise for Keane and Dunne to put themselves on display like that. Their reputations would have been damaged by a guilty verdict had they testified.

The truth is, they were never officially approached. The newspapers caught wind of something small and blew it all out of proportion. They splashed with 'Keane and Dunne to give evidence' headlines. It was sensationalised bullshit. And the journalists who reported it knew it.

Despite Clara Groves's and Mick Dempsey's positive accounts of their dealings with Jason Kenny, it was the testimony of a prosecution witness – a Mr Frank Keville – that made the biggest impact on the jury.

Keville is a freelance crime journalist, courted by all major newspapers in Ireland. He never considers any of the contracts offered to him though, preferring freelancing. He makes much more money that way, selling to the highest bidder. His bravery as a journalist and a photographer has been lauded by those in the Dail on occasions. He's been in a wheelchair for six years after one gang's assassination attempt on him failed. And even since then, he has proven he has no fear inside his bones. Keville makes his money trying to expose Dublin gangland criminals, stalking them in an attempt to catch them in precarious situations. The tabloids love to run a story about criminals partying it up; living a luxurious life on money made underground. These stories both intrigue and disgust readers in equal measure. Keville knows what the mass population wants; certainly knows what editors want.

'I have no doubt whatsoever that Jason Kenny and indeed Zach Brophy are good friends – an associate, I would say – of Alan Keating,' Keville said on the stand.

Alan Keating is one of – if not *the* – most notorious gangsters in Ireland. It was fully explained to the jurors who Keating is, not that they needed telling or reminding.

Keville had photographed Jason and Zach with Keating and other members of his gang on five separate occasions. These pictures appeared in both the *Irish Daily Star* and *Sunday World* over a four-year period. Not much was made of them at the time. Jason was from Drimnagh; same place a lot of gangland members are from. Painting Jason as a criminal, or as a criminal by proxy, didn't ring true with the population of Ireland. They just figured Jason and Keating had friends in common, that the newspapers were just sensationalising. But Keville's testimony didn't seem sensationalised at all. The jury hung on his every word.

'Jason and Zach have not only been good friends with Keating for a few years, they both knew this man from a very young age. They grew up in Keating's shadow. Some in Drimnagh say Jason would have been a gangster had it not been for football. I don't believe being a footballer took him away from gangland crime – it's still a part of his life.'

Keville wasn't making things up for the sake of it. He genuinely believed Jason was involved with Keating's racketing and smuggling; had been told this by a few insiders. It was the insiders feeding him the information who were wrong. They sensationalised the story. They said Jason was part of Keating's gang because they knew it would make a good article, and that – as a result – they would get more money from Keville for passing on such juicy information.

'Frank Keville is a very decent man,' says Number One. 'Somebody we should believe. He has nothing to lose; is hardly making stories up for the sake of it. And look, he has photographs to prove his testimony.'

'Yep, this guy has evidence,' Number Five follows up.

'Hold on,' says Brian. 'A photograph is not evidensh that Jason Kenny is a gangster. And it certainly isn't evidensh that he is a rapist.'

'No, but it proves that he hangs around with gangsters, that he probably hangs around with rapists,' Number Five retorts.

'Ah for crying out loud! Who said Keating and these gangland criminal are rapists? Surely they're just into trafficking drugs, laundering money,' Number Twelve argues, his face turning red.

'Criminals are criminals. Probably into every sort of crime,' Number Five says.

'That makes no fuckin sense—'

'Hold on, hold on,' Number One says, standing up. 'Can we calm things a bit?' He sits back down, bumps his paperwork off the table again.

'Frank Keville is a character witness,' he says, steadying his tone. 'His job on the stand was to give us an understanding of Jason Kenny and Zach Brophy's personalities. I think it's fair that we can deduce Jason and Zach are no saints, given Keville's testimony. No, it doesn't confirm to us that Jason and Zach and Li raped Sabrina, but it does confirm to us that Jason and Zach can't be fully trusted. Remember... the police statements say that Jason denied all involvement with Keating, yet Keville was able to provide us with proof that they – at the very least – socialise with each other.'

One photograph that appeared on the front page of the *Sunday World* in 2011 – when Jason Kenny was at the peak of his career – portrayed Jason laughing with his left arm wrapped around Alan Keating in an inner-city Dublin pub. Zach was also in the photo. It had a huge impact on some jurors, particularly those who felt the three men were guilty of rape. It gave their verdict validation; painting Jason and Zach as scumbags. Not even Clara Groves' or Mick Dempsey's glowing testimonies about Jason – which followed Keville's testimony – could smooth over that massive bump.

'I, one-hundred per cent, believe Frank Keville,' says Number Five.

'Me too,' Number Six follows up.

'And me,' Number Three says, readjusting her wheelchair so she can be more face on with Number One – the juror she was aiming her feelings at. Number Three was now being swung back towards a guilty verdict having changed her initial 'guilty' call in the first vote to 'undecided' in the secret ballot.

'I believe him too,' says Number Four, speaking on this subject for the first time. 'And I know he's just a character witness; he wasn't talking about the rape or anything like that, just giving us details on Jason and Zach's background... what sort of shit they're into. But... I don't know how to say this without sounding a bit stupid. I kinda forgot about his testimony a bit until we brought it up in this room. Now that we're talking about it, it seems like one of the most intriguing parts of the trial, yet twenty minutes ago, it barely registered with me.'

'Well that's why we are given this time in the jury room – to thrash out everything we heard, to highlight it all,' says Number Ten. 'And I agree with you. Keville's testimony has rung more true in this jury room, on reflection. I guess reading it in black and white has had a bit more impact. It's really making me question Jason Kenny's character.'

'Agreed. I have to admit, I don't like Zach and I'm not really sure about Jason,' says Number Four. Maybe there's something really dark about him. He's holding secrets. Probably feels entitled because he's both a footballer and a gangster. He might even think he's invincible, certainly will if he's found not guilty by us.'

Number Four's mind was racing. He was never quite sure what way he was leaning, every new discussion pulling him in a different direction.

Number Four's real name is Clive Suttie, a thirty-nine-year-old from Donabate in north Dublin. He's a manager for a finance and insurance firm called Fullams. He's likable, but has the maturity levels of somebody ten years his junior. It's why he keeps following Number Seven to the water dispenser; still has a tendency to believe that stalking a girl is the best way to get her into bed. He is really starting to get bored by the deliberations, but is still intrigued and is enjoying the responsibility he has been handed. Though he is slightly growing annoyed by the fact that his mind seems to be changing on a whim. Overall, he's undecided; is not sure how this is all going to pan out. He has an inkling the jury may be hung after a few days of deliberating. He can't see how Brian and Number One, for starters, are ever going to agree on a verdict, let alone everyone else in the room.

And if he's right – if the jury are still hung after the judge's patience wears thin – the case will be dismissed. Jason, Zach and Li will walk out of the court free men. Even if the vast majority of jurors think they're guilty.

She's still laughing – hasn't stopped – as the rickshaw guy races off Grafton Street, turning right at Stephen's Green to make his way back towards Coppers.

I've used a couple of cheesy lines – not my normal approach – but they seemed to have worked. Though I'm still not sure if she's into me or into Jason more. I decide to stop with the cheesiness; cut to the chase.

'Your eyes are amazin',' I say. She doesn't answer. Just stares at me, purses her lips in mock embarrassment before turning away. I'm sure she's heard that line a million times before.

'I've a feelin' me and you are gonna hook up tonight,' I say.

'What?' she says, turning to me again.

'Yeah... I'm not saying that we're gonna hook up right now, but at some stage tonight.'

I smile. Her mouth just falls open. Then she looks the other way again.

I'm not sure how to take that. Maybe she's thinkin' about telling me that my prediction is not gonna happen in any way shape or form. Or maybe she's contemplating it; wondering if she should be pursuing me now, not Jason.

I allow the silence to remain between us. I've done most of the talkin' anyway for the past ten or fifteen minutes. All she's done is laugh. We're about five minutes away from the club. I needed to let her know what I was thinking. Needed to do it before we got back, before she ran into Jason's arms. I did the right thing, no matter how awkward I feel right now.

Tina's face threatens to pop into my head but I don't let it. Fuck that. She bores me. We're just set in our ways. Our relationship is a necessity, because we have two kids, but it's boring. I know it and she knows it. She doesn't mind me going to the pub all the time, doesn't mind me going to clubs. She's probably aware I cheat on her, but she's willing to turn a blind eye, just to keep the family together.

I don't like being a parent. Have never been afraid to admit that. Once the kids came along, all the doors to my life closed. It meant I could never follow my brothers to other corners of the world; could never make life choices that I'd like to have had the option to make. Freedom becomes a thing of the past once you become a parent. It sucks. Plus, kids are annoying as hell. Who the fuck wants a poxy little six-year-old snotty-nosed high-pitched idiot running around their house anyway?

I'm pretty certain that lads only have kids because women talk them into it. And women only have kids because they feel that's what they're supposed to do. If anyone thinks it through properly, like *really* thinks the whole thing through, the world's population would be a helluva lot smaller.

'You got any kids?' I ask. The silence has been going on too long.

'Me? No!' she says. 'You?'

I shake my head. Stare up at the night sky as our rickshaw guy approaches Harcourt Street.

'Y'know what... you can leave us here,' I say, handing a twenty euro note to him over his shoulder. Poor fella. I can't believe he cycled around town with us two on his back for a quarter of an hour for the sake of a bloody score. I help Sabrina off the rickshaw by taking her hand. I almost pull her into me as she gets off, but I'm not quite getting the vibe that that's what she wants. She's hard to read. Maybe I came on too strong by suggesting we were gonna get it on tonight. I should have just continued with the cheesy lines. She was enjoying them.

It's starting to get cold. If I had a jacket I'd take it off, throw it around her shoulders, start playing the gentleman card. I can change my game up depending on the circumstances. I initially thought this bird was just up for a laugh, but maybe she needs a bit more maturity.

'My eh... my mam's unwell,' I say as we slowly walk towards Coppers.

'Oh, I'm so sorry to hear that,' she says.

'Yeah – Alzheimer's. Barely knows who I am anymore. Sometimes she thinks I'm her husband... once she thought I was her father.'

I notice her stare at me as I slump my hands into my jeans pocket. I probably should have been an actor. My ma's fine. Nothing wrong with her. Has the sharpest mind I know.

'Once... when I visited her in the hospital, she jumped out of the bed, wrapped her arms around me and tried to kiss me on the mouth. Started calling me Frank – my dad's name. I had to leave the room, didn't stop crying for about half-an-hour. It's tough going. I'm all she has. And I'm there every day for her. I go up to have lunch with her in the hospital and stay for about three hours at a time.'

'That's so sweet,' she says. 'And is your boss okay with that? What is it you do for work?'

'I eh... I run my own business. A digital tech company. We're doin' very well. Well, we were doin' very well. With me taking time off work, the business has suffered. But family before profit right?'

She purses her lips at me again but this time in a sweet way, not in the pitiful way she pursed her lips at me ten minutes ago. I pause when we get to the entrance of Coppers, swirling my foot in a circular motion around the pathway.

'It's tough, y'know. It was always me and Mam. The two of us together. Now I just feel like I'm on my own. I'd never known what loneliness was until my mam started to forget who I was.'

She reaches out with both her hands, grabs me in for a hug. I can feel her tits press against my chest. I'm a fuckin' genius. I always know how to play it with birds. Always know how to read the game. Just like I did as a footballer.

'I'm really sorry you're going through this,' she says. 'But... y'know what? It doesn't mean you have to stop living your own life, right? Your mother would want you to get on with it; would want you to be happy.' She leans off me. Stares into my eyes. 'C'mon, let's go back inside. Let's get you back on that dance floor.'

I can't help it. I lean in. Lips first.

'Bottle of champagne,' I shout to the barman. 'Most expensive one you have.'

'No, will ye bleeding stop,' says Li. 'Stop buying champagne, man – none of us enjoy it. What are you like?'

I just laugh. Out loud. Then I drag him in for another hug. A long one. So long, I even have time to wave the barman away from us over Li's shoulder as he shows me another black bottle of champers. Probably the exact same piss I spent a grand on earlier.

'That kid is going to be one lucky little shit having a dad like you,' I say. And I mean it. I never lie. I may hold the truth back a lot. But I never lie.

'Thanks,' Li says, pulling back from the hug, staring into my face.

He can tell I'm tearing up.

'Jeez... I'm not the only one to have a kid. Zach's got two you know? Why the tears?'

'I just... I'm just so happy for you,' I say, as I wipe my eyes. 'And...' I pause. I'm not sure what to say. I can't pour it all out. Not here. Not when Li can barely hear what I'm saying anyway over the loud music. I just hold a finger to each temple and let everything sink in. 'I'm just not having a good time of it lately,' I spit out. 'But fuck it, your news has perked me right up. So... you're gonna be a husband *and* a dad next year huh... unbelievable!'

'Yeah – but keep it a secret, okay? Niamh doesn't want anyone to know. Not until she's past the three-month mark. Start of August, that's when we're telling everyone. 'Sure you'll be back in Newcastle by then, right? What date does the new season kick off?'

I pinch at my temples again. Close my eyes.

'Jason... Jason, what's wrong, mate?'

'I've no contract, Li. I'm done. It's over.'

I've been dreading telling anyone this. Mainly because I have no idea what I'm going to do. My agent has tried to pimp me around to other League One clubs, even League Two clubs. The consensus seems to be that I'm past it. The only way I can make money now is through celebrity appearances. But fuck that! Or I could do what Zach does – sell drugs. He thinks I don't know. But of course I do. I've known for years. He came to me one day, palms up in apology.

'Don't overreact, but I've been... I've been hanging around Alan Keating and that lot for the past while,' he said. It wasn't a surprise to me. Li had filled me in, told me those were the rumours doing the rounds in Drimnagh.

'I kinda got myself into a bit of trouble... it's fine. Nothing's gonna happen to me. But eh... Alan, he eh... he wants to meet you. Just to have drinks with you. That's it.'

I could have punched him in the face. It was one thing getting himself caught up in that sort of mess, but dragging me into it was close to unforgiveable. But there's a bond between the three of us that means we never fall out, never fight. We're devoted to each other, no matter how much of a prick Zach can be at times. I guess it all stems back to The Secret. We'll always have each other's backs no matter the circumstances.

'He's just a fan of yours. Would like to hang out, that's all.'

So I did. I hung out with Alan Keating and his cronies. I still kinda do, every now and then. Just to keep the peace. I'm in no danger. They just enjoy the fact that they can hang out with a professional footballer. It makes them all feel a bit more significant. I have a couple of pints with them when I'm back in Dublin and have arranged a few match tickets for them every now and then. They've always been cool with me. Treat me well. But didn't the newspapers get hold of pictures that were taken of us hanging out; splashed them across the front pages of their fucking papers.

'Kenny And Keating: Best Buddies' was the headline in one. I wanted to sue the arse off them but there was nothing to sue for. The article didn't libel me, it didn't really say anything, other than insinuate I was hanging around with Ireland's most notorious crime lord. Which is exactly what I *was* doing.

I didn't react, didn't even release a statement acknowledging the article. I just let it slide. It was the talk of the town for a few days before the nation moved on to talking about something else. I'm sure it's damaged my reputation somewhat. But it's a good job I scored that jammy goal against Holland all those years back. It's kept me relevant. If it wasn't for that goal, I'd just be another washed up footballer nobody gives two shits about.

'What do you mean no contract? Sunderland are letting you go? You're their best player for fuck sake.'

Li looks shocked. His mouth is practically hanging open.

'New manager, new ideas,' I say, still holding my temples.

'What are you gonna do?'

I shake my head. I don't know the answer to Li's question. I've played that question over and over in my head almost every hour for the past couple of months, but I genuinely haven't come to a conclusion.

'I'm just... I'm falling apart,' I say, almost crying.

Li grabs a hold of me. Steadies me.

'Jason, tell me what I can do to help. Anything. I'd do anything for you, mate.'

'You're all I have.'

'You need somebody else, Jason. You need to find someone to settle down with. Hey – what about this Sabrina girl, you seem into her. And she's lovely. I get on great with her. Why not give it a proper go? Not just a one-night thing, ask her out... see what can come of it.'

I shrug my shoulders. I get his line of thinking. It aligns with mine. That's exactly what I've been stewing on for most of the night. Well, from the moment I first saw her. She could be the one for me, could be exactly what my life is missing.

'Y'know what? Let's fuck off to Newcastle,' Li says. 'You're always at your most comfortable in your own home. C'mon, fuck it, Jason. The four of us. Me, you, Zach, Sabrina. Show her what you're all about.'

'Newcastle? Tonight? Sure I only came home yesterday.'

'Yeah – but to hell with it. Look around you. Fuck this shit. Let's go on an adventure. I'm with you. Show Sabrina your gaff, show her what she could have if she was to hook up with you.'

He's talking shite. Must be the Baby Guinness. But without even thinking it through I find myself taking my phone from my jeans pocket and clicking into the Ryanair app.

I've only ever seen Jason cry at his dad's funeral. I know these are supposed to be happy tears. But I sense he's not just crying because I told him I'm going to be a dad. There's something else going on. I can always tell with Jason. I know he's depressed, has been for the last couple of years.

'I've no contract, Li. I'm done. It's over.'

Wow. I didn't see that coming. I can't believe Sunderland don't want to keep him on. He's been the only one trying over the past couple of seasons. He gives his all to that club.

'New manager, new ideas,' he tells me as he stares down at his feet. He's embarrassed telling me this. Feels as if he's letting us all down. He's so sensitive. He wears the weight of our expectation on his shoulders. Always has done.

'What are you gonna do?' I ask him.

He continues to stare at his feet – pinching his temples as if he's trying to massage his troubles away.

'I'm just... I'm falling apart,' he says as the tears begin to fall down his face. I hold him in to me, so nobody else can see him crying.

'Jason, tell me what I can do to help. Anything. I'd do *anything* for you, mate.'

'You're all I have,' he sobs.

'You need somebody else, Jason, you need to find someone to settle down with... Hey – what about this Sabrina girl, you seem into her. And she's lovely. I get on great with her. Why not y'know... give it a proper go. Not just a one-night thing, ask her out... see what can come of it.'

I'm not just feeding him this line to help him feel instantly better. Jason needs somebody. He needs a partner; a reason to get up every morning. He needs his Niamh.

Maybe this Sabrina girl is it. I know he could have any other girl in this nightclub, but I've seen the way he looks at Sabrina. I sensed his frustration when she walked up the stairs with Zach. I knew his heart was cracking a bit.

'Y'know what? Let's fuck off to Newcastle. You're always at your happiest in the comfort of your own home. C'mon, fuck it, Jason. The four of us. Me, you, Zach, Sabrina. Show her what you're all about.'

I don't know why I offer that as a remedy. I'm trying to think of ways he can impress the girl he's into.

'Newcastle? Tonight? Sure I only came home yesterday.'

'Yeah – but to hell with it. Look around you. Fuck this shit. Let's go on an adventure. I'm with you. Show Sabrina your gaff, show her what she could have if she was to hook up with you.'

He shakes his head, but I watch as he takes his phone out of his pocket and clicks into the Ryanair app.

'There's a flight at eleven thirty-five,' he says, sucking up his tears. 'What's that... an hour and a half from now? Think we could make it?'

I nod my head and smile, but I'm not that enthused at all. I'm supposed to go to bloody Homebase with Niamh in the morning. She won't be happy if I tell her I'm in Newcastle. But she'll understand in time. She knows I'd do anything for Jason and Zach. Has actually mentioned to me a few times that she adores how loyal I am to my two best mates. It's one of the reasons she fell in love with me. It makes her feel certain that I'd never hurt her. She trusts me and I trust her. One hundred per cent. She's the only one I've ever told about The Secret. I couldn't help it. Couldn't bear to keep anything from her. I guess that's true love.

'Sweetie, I have something to tell you that I'm ashamed of – but no matter what, you have to promise you'll keep it a secret,' I said to her as we were lying in bed one night.

She took it well, just as I imagined she would. She kept repeating that we were young and dumb and didn't know any better. She held me close, wiped my tears; made me a big fry up the next morning. We haven't mentioned it since.

I'd already known I wanted to spend my life with her, but her handling of the biggest secret I will ever have confirmed it for me. I started to look for engagement rings online the next day. I had no idea how expensive they were. I thought of asking Jason for a loan but knew deep in my heart that there was nothing romantic about that. So I saved; put a hundred euro aside every month for a whole year until I could afford the ring I had picked out. I hope she likes it. I can't wait to ask her to marry me; can't wait to be a dad.

I'm the luckiest mother fucker alive. If only I could help Jason and Zach to be as happy as I am. But maybe none of us deserve to be happy. After all, we did ruin a young girl's life. Perhaps karma already caught up with them, and is just around the corner waiting to pounce on me.

'Fuck it!' Jason says. 'It's booked. Four flights. She's gonna think I'm a fuckin' psycho, isn't she?'

I laugh, not knowing what to make of it all. But I know I must be positive. This was my suggestion after all.

'I think she'll think it's romantic,' I say. But I don't know what to believe. 'Won't we need our passports though?' I say, sipping from my beer.

Jason shakes his head.

'Nah.. just once you have photo ID you can catch a flight from Ireland to UK, right?'

I shrug my shoulders.

'Think so, yeah. We'll see what she says when they get back. So what exactly happened between you two at the Hairy Lemon anyway?' I ask.

'I asked her to go outside, couldn't help myself. I pushed her up against the wall, started snogging the face off her. Then I bloody unzipped my jeans, asked her to stick her hand inside.'

I cringe. I've known Jason to be this up front before, but only with girls who give off the impression that that's exactly what they're after – Jason's dick.

'And...?'

'Well she did, started jerking me for a while. But I felt guilty immediately. Couldn't understand why I was being so disrespectful to a girl I actually liked.'

I blow out my lips, almost making a fart sound. Jason just laughs. At least I've cheered him up a bit.

Then I notice the eyes almost pop out of his head. I turn around to see what he's staring at and catch her walking back down the steps, Zach lagging behind.

'How the fuck are you gonna tell her you've just booked her a flight to Newcastle?'

I laugh as I ask this.

Jason repeats what I'd just done moments ago – blows out his lips and shrugs his shoulders.

'I've no fuckin idea, mate.'

He's a nice guy – I'm sure of it – but he didn't half make me cringe throughout the entirety of that rickshaw ride. It was a cute attempt at trying to chat me up; certainly a new experience for me. Nobody's ever tried to charm me that way before. But I did want to get off the rickshaw as soon as I got on it. It was blatant what was happening. He used every trick in the book. He started off with some God-awful cheesy lines I'm sure he read somewhere in a list online, and then opted to be all confident and cocky as if that's what would win me over. When none of that worked, he gave me the sob story about his mother. It's endearing that he looks after her, that he has a big heart. But I'm just not into him. Even if I wasn't into Jason, there's not a chance I'd hook up with Zach. He's just not my type in any way. He's too laddish, too immature, too short.

I'm beginning to feel the discomfort dissipating as if we both agree that nothing's going to happen, that we can both just be friends. But that's the moment he decides to lean in for a kiss.

'Oi,' I say laughing, trying to lighten the tension so he doesn't get offended. But I feel I owe it to be straight with him; to be honest with him after he just opened up to me. 'I'm sorry, Zach but... y'know. I'm kinda... I'm into Jason.'

I watch his chin fall to his chest. I reach out my finger and pick his chin back up so that he's looking at me.

'I'm sure you'll make a wonderful girl happy some day,' I say. 'But it's not me. I'm sorry.'

He smiles back, then motions that we should just head back inside.

I've no idea whether Jason is into me or not, so it's a bit of a gamble going back in here. I'm half tempted to go home, but intrigue has a hold of me. I'll probably walk in to see Jason pinning another girl up against the wall, his tongue circling her mouth just like it was circling mine a few hours ago. He probably has no intentions of getting to know me any further, but fuck it – I'll give it a go. I keep reminding myself that I need to lighten up, that I need more fun in my life. Let's see what Jason's intentions really are. If he isn't interested, I can just head home, which is what I was about to do anyway until he dragged me over for a drink with his mates. It'll be no loss either way. In half-an-hours' time I'm either gonna be hooking back up with a celebrity or I'll be on my way home in a taxi. Win-win either way. Though I certainly know which win I'd prefer. Which is exactly why I find myself walking back down the stairs of Copper Face Jacks.

Any other time I've come in here, I've been with Eddie. I never quite understood why he used to bring me to this place. We'd spend most of our time standing at the edge of the dance floor, drink in hand, watching everybody else have a good time. He took himself way too seriously to dance. And that's actually part of the reason I've chanced coming back in. I watched Jason dance earlier on – or attempting to dance. I love that he doesn't take himself too seriously. I love that he's the total opposite of Eddie in that respect. Though maybe he's just as much of an untrustworthy bastard. I don't know for certain how many times Eddie cheated on me, but I do know he would have fucked Lorna one night when she came on to him. She reported to me that his exact words were 'fuck yeah!' when she suggested bringing him back to her place. I wasn't surprised when she told me. I just packed up my stuff, wrote him a note and closed the door behind me. He tried ringing me about ten times a day over the next week; even called up to my parents' house with a bunch of flowers. My dad told him where to go. I haven't seen or heard from him since.

I stare at his face, just to gauge his reaction as he notices me and Zach walking towards him and Li. His smile makes my stomach flip. I need to calm down. I shouldn't be getting this excited, this carried away. But then again, love – or lust as it most probably is – isn't really an emotion you can control.

'Drink?' Jason asks.

'Sure. Red wine please,' I reply. Zach doesn't say anything. He just scratches his head, looking awkward, almost embarrassed. I wonder if Jason knew what Zach was about to do and it makes my heart race again. Maybe they're all in it together. But as Jason grabs my hand and leads me towards the bar, my paranoia subsides. I can't believe he is having such an effect on me. My emotions have been up and down all night.

'Where've you two been then?' he asks, as he rests his forearms on the bar.

'Oh, lovely Zach took me out for a rickshaw ride.'

'A fuckin rickshaw ride? – the old romantic.'

I squint at him, trying to understand what the fuck is going on. He pulls me in close, talks into my ear.

'Don't mind Zach. He just tries it on with any girl he thinks is pretty. I haven't told him you and I had kissed.'

He leans back to gauge my reaction. I just squint again.

'Listen, I like you. I do. Really like you. Don't let Zach's cheesiness put you off me. I'm nothing like him. We're best mates, but total opposites.'

I bite my bottom lip, just to stop my mouth from smiling as wide as it wants to.

'I hope your lines are better than his,' I say.

Jason laughs out loud, then leans back in to my ear.

'You gotta tell me one of the lines he said to you.'

I try to think back. I remember them being explicitly cheesy, yet can't remember any of them word-for-word.

'Oh something like 'is your dad a boxer, because you are a knockout.'

We both burst out laughing; so loud that the couple standing next to us at the bar stop talking just to stare.

'Ah Jason Kenny,' the fella says, holding his hand out. 'Ye bloody legend!'

I play with my hair, try to keep calm. But I'm excited. I've always wondered what it would be like to go out with someone famous; someone other people look up to. I just stand back and watch as the fella stands with his arm wrapped around Jason while his girlfriend takes a photo of them together. When they're done, I lean in to Jason – just to let everyone know he's with me. Jee... I am changing. I am lightening up. Maybe Jason is Mr Right for me. I've never felt this comfortable in any man's company before. It's so strange – we've only known each other for about ten minutes.

'So... can you beat that?' I ask him as he leans back on the bar.

'Beat what?'

'Is your dad a boxer?'

We laugh again. Almost in sync.

'I think I can,' he says.

I raise my eyebrows, signal to him that I'm ready to hear what he has to offer.

'Well, let me ask you this first: what are your plans tomorrow?'

Wow; now that is a good opening line. He's already talking about the future. Our future.

'I eh...' I say, swiping strands of my hair away from my eyes. 'I don't have any plans tomorrow.'

'And eh.. do you have any photo ID on you tonight?'

'Huh?' I say, wrinkling my brow.

'Do you have photo ID with you?'

'Yeah... why?' I ask, really slowly.

'Good,' he says. 'We're flying to Newcastle tonight and you're coming with us.'

◆

A LIGHT KNOCK rattles the door. Number Nine – being nearest to the door – stands up, takes three steps and opens it. The other jurors can't see the face on the other side of the door, just the paperwork being handed over to their peer.

'Thanks a mill,' Number Nine says, offering the young man dressed in black a polite smile.

She strolls back over to the table and stretches across it to hand Number One the notes.

'Okay, here we go,' he says, licking his finger and then flicking through the three sheets.

'It was about half-way through his testimony,' says Number Twelve, trying to be helpful.

'Hang on,' Number One says, before humming to himself as he tries to speed-read through the pages. 'Got it.'

He sits more upright, both elbows now resting on the table. '"They were laughing and joking all the time",' he reads. '"They looked like boyfriend and girlfriend" – and then Mr Ryan asks: "Yes, but that was just your assumption, right? That they were boyfriend and girlfriend?" – Scott answers, "Yes, of course – my assumption. That's what I even told police when they interviewed me. I thought they were boyfriend and girlfriend, found out much later – when the investigation was going on – that they weren't." Ryan then asks: "You told Gardaí that even though you assumed they were boyfriend and girlfriend you thought she – and I quote – "wore

138

the trousers", yes?" Okay – and this is the sentence we're looking for... Scott then answered: "she was in control, laughing, joking. I can't remember what they were saying, but I got the impression she was having more fun than him. She was doing all the laughing".'

'Ah, so – *"she was having more fun than him, she was doing all the laughing"* – I knew it was something like that,' Number Twelve says. 'So... what does this tell us?'

'Well, it contradicts her testimony, doesn't it?' Brian says. 'Sabrina said she was trying to get Zach away from her, that he kinda made her go onto the rickshaw; that all she wanted to do was go back to the club.'

The jury room falls silent. Each juror trying to soak in the opposing testimonies of Sabrina and an eye-witness called by the defence – a Mr Donagh Scott. Scott was only eighteen when he pulled up in his rickshaw outside Copper Face Jacks at ten-forty on the night in question, to be met by Sabrina and Zach running towards him.

Scott testified on the stand that it was indeed Zach who called to him first, that he didn't notice whether Sabrina was reluctant to get on the rickshaw or not. But he did testify that she seemed more than comfortable when she was taking the ride.

'She wasn't just comfortable, she was enjoying herself, I thought,' Scott said on the stand. 'I remember her laughing and joking.'

He admitted he remembered Zach and Sabrina clearly from that night, because he thought the girl was 'particularly attractive'. He remembered thinking Zach had 'done well for himself'.

'This Donagh guy isn't the first witness to contradict statements made by Sabrina. The photographer Patrick Clavin, Donagh now – and obviously the other two; Jason and Zach – they *all* contradict almost everything she has said. She is the common denominator here... perhaps she is just a consistent liar?'

'Well of course Jason and Zach would contradict what Sabrina is saying. She believes she was raped, they don't believe they raped her. Of course they have opposite views – that's bleedin obvious,' Number Five says.

'Yesh, but Patrick Clavin the photographer and Donagh Scott – they're both independent witnesses. I mean they don't need to lie, do they? They don't gain anything,' Brian says, offering up his opinion for the first time in two minutes, an unusually quiet break for him.

'Well, we could say the same about the journalist guy that testified against Jason and Zach – what's his name again?

'Frank Keville,' says Number One.

'Yes, Mr Keville – he is an independent witness too and he has differences of opinions to Jason Kenny and Zach Brophy. Does that make them consistent liars too? And... for the record, this Donagh Scott guy – nice as he is – his testimony is kinda pointless, isn't it? It's all assumption. If he *assumed* Sabrina and Zach were boyfriend and girlfriend – and we know for a fact that that assumption was wrong – then maybe all of his assumptions are wrong. Maybe his assumption that Sabrina was enjoying the rickshaw ride has been wrong all along too.'

'Yeah – that is a point Sabrina's lawyer raised in court. How valid is this guy's testimony anyway?' asks Number Six.

'Well, if the judge allowed it, it's valid. He was an eye-witness in the middle of the night in question. We have to take on board what he said.'

Scott's testimony didn't do the prosecution any favours. It painted Sabrina in a bad light, suggesting she was flirting up a storm with Zach. If any jury member felt it was accurate that she was flirting with both Zach and Jason during the night in question, then it enhances the argument that the intercourse that took place later in the hotel room was consensual.

'I just... I can't,' Number Four rubs his face with his palm. 'My mind keeps changing. I keep feeling sorry for Sabrina, thinking these men raped her, then the next minute I think she's just a liar.'

'Everybody,' Brian says, rotating both his arms as if he is a preacher addressing his congregation, 'we keep falling into the trap of making ashumptions, opinions. It's not about what we feel. We can't pass judgement based on how we feel. We need to go by the evidensh.'

'Change the record, Brian,' Number Five says.

'It needs re-emphasi—'

'Hold on,' Number Twelve says, interrupting Brian's comeback. 'Brian is right. We take each piece of evidence at its merit. Here,' he says pointing at the sheets of paper in his hands, 'we have an eye-witness testifying that Sabrina wasn't uncomfortable on that rickshaw, okay? We have to put that in our pocket and move on. It is evidence that perhaps suggests Sabrina isn't always truthful.'

'Well, we could put it in our pocket – as you say – as evidence that doesn't paint Sabrina in a good light. But I will put it in my pocket as evidence I won't consider too strongly,' Number Eleven says.

It's been a while since Number Eleven voluntarily offered her thoughts.

'Donagh Scott's testimony is all based on assumption,' she continues. 'He doesn't know how Sabrina was feeling. He can't have known. Yes, we should all put it in our pocket as evidence, but not necessarily how you see it, Number Twelve. How we individually see it – and that may be differently. We all have our own perception on this.'

Number Eleven's starting to grow in confidence as deliberations drag on. She, too, sick of listening to the same voices over and over again.

Number Eleven has had a strong feeling that the three men raped Sabrina. She was particularly disturbed by the doctor's evidence towards the end of the trial.

Doctor Dermot Johnson examined Sabrina two days after the alleged rape, testifying on the stand that Sabrina had suffered an internal cut on the night in question. But he also emphasised that this type of cut can appear as a result of consensual sex, not just forced sex.

Even so, Number Eleven was appalled by his testimony. The images Sabrina's lawyer showed in court of similar internal cuts, tattooed Number Eleven's mind. From the moment Doctor Johnson left the stand, Number Eleven was convinced Jason, Zach and Li raped Sabrina.

Number Eleven is a forty-one-year-old mother of three from Tallaght called Magdelena Andris. She's been a resident in Dublin her whole life after her parents emigrated from their home city of Saldus in Latvia back in 1973. She is highly creative – works as a graphic designer for a popular digital company called ebow in the centre of Dublin – but lacks in other areas. She can't piece all of the evidence together bit-by-bit like some jurors do. She can only see the bigger picture. It's the way most creatives brains work. The doctor's testimony, although not supposed to be taken as any proof of rape whatsoever, has been making her decision for her. She is firmly in the guilty camp. Hasn't wavered.

'Let's move on,' says Number One. We can all take Donagh Scott's evidence as we see fit. There are differences of opinions, but that's why we're here – to argue this case. We are getting to the key part of the night – the decision to go to the airport. What do we make of this?'

Number One turns to his nemesis, Brian, as he asks this. It's a gesture of goodwill. He is beginning to feel their spat needs mending if he is to eventually persuade everybody to agree with him and find the three men guilty.

'Oh me?' asks Brian a little taken aback. 'I think it'sh quite telling that Sabrina was up for something. She was certainly up for flying to Newcastle, right?'

'Doesn't mean she was up for sex with all three men?' Number Three says, tapping her fingers against the armrest of her wheelchair.

'True,' replies Brian. 'But I'm just stating a fact. Sabrina admitting she was keen to go to Newcastle with the three men does shay a lot, don't you think? She was certainly comfortable in their company at that stage.'

Sabrina *had* admitted to police during their investigation, as well as on the stand during the trial, that she had fallen for Jason in Copper Face Jacks and hoped a relationship might form between the two of them. When Jason suggested all four of them fly to Newcastle, and back to his house for the night, she felt accepting this invitation would help her get to know him more. She said she liked Li, thought he was a nice man: "harmless" was an adjective she used. But admitted that Zach "kinda unnerved me a little bit". She said she wished at the time that it was just her and Jason who were flying back to Newcastle. Either way, she felt comfortable enough in all three men's company to take them up on their offer; felt she had got to know them somewhat. The possibility of being raped never entered her mind.

It's estimated by the Rape Crisis Network that in eighty-five per cent of rape cases, the victim is known to the accused. This particular case is a grey area when it comes to that statistic. Sabrina barely knew each of the three men she was accusing of rape; had met them only five hours previous to the incident. Although she admits to being "comfortable enough" in their presence, this case would be added to the statistic of the fifteen per cent of rape cases where the victim does not know the accused. It's unusual that random rapes occur. Most sex crimes are premeditated, normally by a family member or a friend of the victim. In fact, most rapes aren't necessarily motivated by attraction, but more so by opportunity and a lust for power men crave over women. This case was slightly more unusual than a regular rape trial. Especially so, given that there was a major celebrity involved.

'So, Sabrina admitted that she fancied Jason by this point and was quite intrigued when he suggested they all fly to Newcastle, back to his house for a party,' says Number One. 'What was she thinking?'

'Eh... that she was going back to a footballer's house for a party,' replies Brian.

'And would that be a decision most women would take? I mean, I find that hard to believe—'

'I can't speak on behalf of 'most women' but I do think a lot of women would be interested in an invite back to a celebrity's house,' Number Eleven says, interrupting Brian.

A ripple of argument races around the table. Most jurors feel Sabrina's position here was justifiable; that it certainly didn't point to any agreement to having sex with all three men. Her lawyer justified her statements on this when he cross-examined Jason and Zach; made sure both men admitted on the stand that no talk of sex had occurred at this stage of the evening and that everybody was in agreement that they would just fly to Newcastle to have some fun. Despite this, Number One was adamant that Sabrina's actions at this point in the night were incredibly suspicious.

'I think she knew what she was up to here,' he says. 'She knew something kinky was going on. She meets a guy one night and a few hours later she decides to go back to his house? C'mon guys... what sensible girl would do that?'

'I would,' Number Eleven admits. 'In fact, I have done that.'

'Me too,' says Number Five.

The jury room falls silent, except for the sound of some jurors shuffling in their chairs.

I take a peek at my phone as Li turns to face us, arguing that there is no way we can make the flight. And if we do, photo ID may not be enough to get us on board.

'It's ten to eleven,' I say. 'The flight's taking off in just over half-an-hour, right?'

Jason nods his head.

'Yeah – we should be boarding now,' Li says.

'Shut up, Li, relax will ya – we'll get there,' groans Zach.

I turn my head, just to look out the window as we speed up the N1. If I got out of the taxi now, I'd only have about a twenty-minute walk to the comfort of my own bed.

'Guys, we're supposed to be boarding around now, and we're a fifteen minute drive from the airport, we still have to go through security, walk to the gate... I don't think we'll make it,' Li says, still staring over his shoulder at the three of us in the back seat. I'm on the left side of Jason, Zach to his right.

'Let's just see...' Jason says. Then the taxi falls silent.

I try to soak in what's going on. I'm practically by-passing my neighbourhood to head to the airport, in order to catch a flight to Newcastle – what am I doing? I have no plans for the weekend, won't be letting anybody down – but this is a little crazy, especially for me. Maybe I'm coming across as desperate. I've observed girls being desperate before and it's really cringeworthy. I've seen models practically sell their souls to get ahead in life. I never thought I'd be one of them. Not in a million years.

I close my eyes, rest my head back on the chair and think my actions through again. I'm trying to comprehend whether going to Newcastle or not will make Jason fall for me. If I go, I've got his attention. But if I ask the taxi man to pull over now, to let me out, that's it, isn't it? I'll never see Jason again. He assured me we'd get time alone once we got to his place, that his house was so big that the other lads would most likely just crash out in the cinema room while we got to know each other a little better. I assume sex is on his mind. Why wouldn't it be? I've already tugged at his penis. I think I will have sex with him. It could be my first step on the ladder of me trying to lighten up. I've only ever had sex with two men before. That's quite disappointing, especially for someone who looks like me. I have men come on to me all the time, but barely give any of them more than a polite smile and a shrug of my shoulders. I don't intend on being slutty, but maybe I should adopt a bit more of a personality. Become more outgoing. More fun. Begin to live the life I want to live, not the one that I live in fear of other people judging me. When am I ever gonna get a chance to have sex with a celebrity anyway?

My head starts to spin. The angel on my shoulder is urging me to retreat into the quiet little hermit I've always been – the person I don't want to be anymore. The devil on my shoulder is telling me I am the complete opposite of that; young, free, single. Up for fun. Up for the craic. I'm pretty sure nine out of ten girls in this situation would have sex with Jason Kenny. Why can't I be one of those nine? For once. But mostly I want to be with Jason Kenny because... well, I want to be with Jason Kenny. Not just tonight, but beyond tonight. I know I'm attracted to his fame, to his lifestyle, but why shouldn't I be? If that is part of who he is then I'm entitled to be attracted to it. But if I want Jason Kenny long-term, what should I do short-term? What should I do tonight? Play hard to get? Doesn't that make me that one out of ten who doesn't have sex with the celebrity... the frigid? Doesn't that just make me the Sabrina bloody Doyle I don't want to be?

I open my eyes, lift my head from the back of the chair and look at him. He stares back, smiles then rests his hand on my knee. A wave of warmth washes through my stomach. That's made my mind up for me. I'm really into this guy. Fuck it. I check my phone again, then sit more upright.

'Okay, it's almost eleven. We'll probably get to the airport at a quarter past. If there are no queues at security, which there probably won't be this time of night, we could get to the departure gate around half-past, twenty-to twelve at the latest. If the flight is slightly delayed, we can make it.'

'That's the girl,' says Zach, holding a hand up for me to high five. 'You really are up for this, huh?' he says. 'Ye know Jason has a swimming pool? Ye like to swim?'

I just laugh, probably because I'm excited by the notion that my next boyfriend could genuinely have a bloody swimming pool in his own home.

'I do like to swim, yeah,' I reply. 'Pity you didn't give me time to go home and get my swimming gear.'

'Ah, we don't use swimming gear. It's all skinny dipping in Jason's gaff,' says Zach. 'It's a strict rule.'

I try to imagine what Jason's house is like. I remember actually being impressed by Eddie's house, and that was because it was a three-bed semi-detached. I bet Jason's is ten times bigger.

Eddie would have liked me to have been his house slave. He was happy for me to give up modelling. Happy for me to clean his kitchen, hoover his floors, iron his shirts. It was never going to happen. I think that's why we started to have rows actually. I was never going to fit in with his idea of a picture-perfect girlfriend. He courted that old-fashioned, traditional relationship. I was way past that. I wanted my own independence. He tried to downplay my career, insisted I wasn't a model – just a marketing puppet. He knew how to hurt me; knew what buttons to push. I still maintain that I only went out with him because I was desperate. Before him, I only ever had one boyfriend. And perhaps labelling Stuart a 'boyfriend' is pushing it. We only hooked up a few times over the course of about a month when I was nineteen.

Stu was a model, too. We met on a shoot, decided to go out for lunch together during a break in our day. I lost my virginity to him a week later. Never told him he was popping my cherry. I was too embarrassed to admit that I was a virgin at that age. We had sex another three times before his phone calls stalled. He never explained to me that he was dumping me, we just never saw each other again. I didn't have sex with anyone else until I met Eddie two-and-a-half years later. I didn't miss it, certainly didn't pine for intercourse. Stuart's penis was quite big, quite painful. It wasn't until I met Eddie that I actually enjoyed sex for the first time. He was a lot smaller than Stu. A lot more comfortable inside me. But after doing it non-stop for the first four months, our sex life took a nose-dive. I didn't realise until about two years later that he must have been getting it elsewhere during all that time. I started to miss the sex and genuinely only started to masturbate for the first time when I was twenty-three. Still do so on a regular basis. I'm often envious of people who have great sex lives. When you look at porn on the Internet, people are into all sorts of quirky stuff. I've never quite worked out what gives me my kicks. When I lie back and play with myself, I'm normally thinking of a rugged, handsome man lying on top of me. I'm sure that's boring to most other people – straight missionary sex – but it's kind of all I know. Maybe it's not just my mind that needs opening, maybe my legs need it too. I begin to wonder what positions me and Jason will do it in tonight.

This was a great idea. There's only one chick. But what a fuckin' chick she is.

Normally when we go back to Jason's gaff, there's a gaggle of birds with us. He's probably not up for sharin' Sabrina, but I'll see what I can do.

We've never shared the same bird on the same night, but I know Jason's well aware of a bit of roasting. It's ripe in football. I've read about it count-less times in the tabloids – four or five players sharing the same bird at the same time. Jason's always maintained his innocence in that regard; claims he's never been a part of any gang banging. But let's see if I can change his mind tonight. It'll be a bit weird fuckin' a bird in front of me mate, but things could be worse. I could be at home, lying beside Tina with a limp dick – which is practically what I do six nights a week anyway.

I don't hate Tina. I just hate the boredom of our relationship. It's tedious. I'm no good with routine – and a wife and kids is all about routine, especially if you want it to work perfectly. It's not as if I don't want to remain with Tina for the rest of my life, or that I don't want to be a great dad. I do. I just don't want that to be my entire life.

Li turns around from the passenger seat, but I don't give him time to moan again.

'Relax will ya? For crying out loud. Just turn around and keep your fingers crossed.'

He does. He stares out the windscreen as we turn onto the airport road. I think we'll make the flight. They're always running a bit behind. My problem is – though I haven't said it out loud – that I think you now need a passport to fly from Ireland to the UK. I don't think any old photo ID works these days. It used to. But I think they stopped that a couple of years ago. Fuck it. It'll be an adventure anyway.

'Have you rung Niamh yet?' I ask Li. I'm guessin' he's secretly hoping we don't make the flight so he can have a lie in with his bird in the morning. So much has happened tonight, I almost forgot he's told us she's going to be his fiancée soon.

'No, I'll call her once we get to the airport,' he says. 'What about you? You let Tina know?'

I stare at him, crease my brow. He doesn't get it.

'Who's Tina?' Sabrina asks. The taxi falls silent. Jason turns to me, knows I must have been feeding Sabrina's head full of shit when I took her for that rickshaw ride.

'Me eh... me wife,' I admit.

'You're married? Wow!' Sabrina laughs. 'Wedding ring in the pocket is it?'

'I don't wear one,' I tell her. 'Never have.'

'That's interesting. I could have sworn you were trying to come on to me earlier... remember... on the rickshaw... You eh... asked if my dad was a boxer?'

Jason giggles.

Fuckin' bitch. She's trying to embarrass me in front of my mates. I'm gonna hurt her when I fuck her later. She'll be walkin' funny in the morning. I'll make sure of it.

I actually haven't had a bit of strange pussy in a few weeks. That can happen. I can go a while without pickin' some bird up. But hangin around with Keating and his lot can normally clean up any dry spells for me.

They're all mad into prostitutes. Keating even has a few on his payroll. Sex with prostitutes is a bit of a last resort for me though. I don't enjoy it as much. Not sure how anyone can get satisfaction from having sex with someone who doesn't necessarily want to have sex with them. If a girl is fuckin you for the pay, not for the enjoyment, then where's the thrill in that?

I hooked up with a tiny little Scottish hooker last summer who made me wash my dick in front of her before we had sex. That was a load of me bollix. I couldn't enjoy the session we had. Not after that. Even when I came, I produced a retarded amount of cum. Just a spit that dribbled down my shaft. It looked a bit pathetic; almost embarrassing.

Hookers just don't do it for me. I can never quite figure out why they do it for anyone. Same as rapists. Where is the fun in having sex with someone who doesn't want it as much as you? If the pussy is dry, how is a man supposed to enjoy it? And trust me, I've fucked dry pussy lotsa times. Tina's. She just seems incapable of getting wet these days.

Our sex life is shit. When I get horny, I jump on board. It's either that or have a wank. Sometimes I opt for the wank, but more often than not I call Tina upstairs, ask her to lie on the bed and do her duty. But it's not that enjoyable. The best part of sex is convincing somebody to have sex with you. Talking them into it. That's how I get my kicks – that moment when they finally give in, finally give me the go-ahead to fuck them. That's the real thrill of sex for me. Pulling birds is the main event. I'll have my work cut out for me pulling tonight. But I'm up for the challenge.

I look over at her. She winks at me. I'm not sure if that's finally a sign that she's up for it with me or whether or not she's just cooling tensions because she knows she just tried to embarrass me.

The driver takes us up the ramp of the airport slip road, over the speed bumps and finally comes to a stop.

'Forty-two euro,' the taxi man says. Jason looks at me. I look at Li.

'Do you take card?' Jason says, breaking the silence.

'Course I don't take card,' the taxi man says, his foreign accent thick and condescending. 'It is a taxi.'

'I've no cash,' Jason says.

'Nobody has cash these days,' I say, just before I notice Sabrina reach inside her bag.

'Here's fifty,' keep the change,' she says to the taxi man, before opening her door. We all follow her out.

'Don't worry about it, Jason can pay me back,' she says as all four of us run towards the entrance.

'It's almost twenty-past,' Li cries racing inside, heading straight towards the security gates. 'Bollocks!'

We look at what he's pointing at. There's quite a queue at security. It's not huge, but this'll take at least ten minutes to get through.

'Fuck it,' says Jason. 'Let's try it anyway. We might get lucky; certainly if the flight is delayed.

He scrolls through his phone, walks towards the first security gate and swipes his way through. Then he hands the phone back to Sabrina.

'Scan this here, sweetie,' he says, 'then pass the phone back to the lads.'

There are only two security gates open. Both of them have a queue of maybe twenty people. We won't be getting through here in a hurry. I check the Dublin airport app on my phone, it informs me the flight is due to leave on time. We're not going to make it.

'Don't mind that shit,' Zach says to me when I share the bad news. 'Those apps are bollocks. They don't update them often enough. We'll be fine.'

I don't share his optimism but I decide to call Niamh anyway, let her know I won't be home tonight. She's used to me spending some time in Newcastle with Jason, has even been over with me once or twice to his place. But I've never rung her on a whim and told her I'm imminently taking a flight.

I step away from the queue as the tone rings.

'Hello,' she says, sounding groggy. She must have already crashed out.

'Hey babe,' I tell her. 'Listen, Jason isn't having a good time of it. Remember I told you I thought he was suffering a bit of depression?'

'Huh huh,' she says. I can hear the rustling of our duvet. She must be sitting up in the bed, anticipating bad news.

'Well... it's true. He opened up to me tonight. I suggested he head home, back to Newcastle, back to his house where he's most comfortable. And eh... I'm going with him. Me and Zach. We're just going to stay with him for the night.'

'You're flying out to Newcastle tonight?'

'Yeah. He needs us, Niamh. I don't know everything, but when I find out exactly what the cause of his depression is, I'll let you know. Either way, I'll be back with you tomorrow. Probably tomorrow evening sometime.'

She pauses. I know she's thinking of our plans to spend some of our hard-earned dough in Homebase in the morning. But she won't mention that. I know she won't. She's way too selfless.

'Okay, hun. What has he said so far... what's wrong?'

'Well... I think it's his career. I think Sunderland are letting him go. No other club seem that interested in signing him. That, coupled with Jessica finishing things with him last year, he's just... he's just... he cried on my shoulder tonight, Niamh. Haven't seen him cry apart from the day of his dad's funeral.'

'Oooh,' she says, 'give him a big hug from me, won't ya, hun?'

'Course I will. And… we'll do Homebase maybe on Sunday instead, is that okay?'

'Don't worry about that. You get Jason smiling again.'

That's why I'm marrying this girl. She's so understanding. I can imagine Zach trying to make the same phone call to Tina… letting her know he's queuing up for a flight to Newcastle on a whim. She'd go ape shit. She just doesn't trust him. And I don't blame her.

I hang up the call and re-join the lads and Sabrina in the queue. It's moving slowly. I can't understand how people get this so wrong. Why do they have to be repeatedly told that liquids must go in a clear plastic bag? Why do they have to be retold that laptops and iPads have to go in separate trays? It's all sign-posted around this place, yet some travellers only realise what they're supposed to do once they get to the top of the queue. I love that scene in *Up in the Air* where George Clooney's character is teaching Anna Kendrick's character how to travel. He suggests queuing behind Asian people at security checks because they always travel light, and always pay attention to the rules. It's one sure-fire way to get through security quicker, but we don't have that luxury here. We just have two queue options, and both are filled with half-drunk Irish people. I guess we're half-drunk Irish people too, but we've no baggage; no liquids to put in plastic bags, no laptops or iPads that need placing in separate trays. As soon as it's our turn, we'll fly through security – but it's the waiting that's paining me. I check my phone again. 11:25. We're supposed to have boarded by now. I don't think there's a chance in hell we'll make this flight. But I don't want to say that to the lads. Not again. I've been moaning about our chances of catching this flight all through the taxi journey here. I could sense they were all getting irritated by me.

I stand behind the three of them and keep my mouth shut. I'm kind of miffed that Jason is playing it so coolly with Sabrina. The whole idea of this trip is to get him excited about her. She's so open and genuine – would be a good steady influence on him if it worked out. But he seems to be treating her like another mate of his. The three of them are just laughing and joking. He should be all over her, letting her know that he's really into her. Maybe he's playing it cool on purpose – trying to treat her differently to how he treats any other girl he picks up on a Friday night.

At least he's laughing. He seems to be a far cry from the Jason who was crying on my shoulder an hour ago. I let out a big sigh as another passenger at the front of the queue has to be called back to take his bloody belt off. What the fuck am I doing here? I just want to be at home. Would love to be curled up, spooning my girlfriend right now.

I take my phone from my pocket again, flick through my pictures. I bring up a photo of Niamh and pinch at my screen so I can zoom right into her face, to catch her beauty. I know most men wouldn't find her attractive, but I can make out every perfection on her face when I do this. I fancy her as much now as I did when I first fell in love with her three years ago.

I flick to the image of the engagement ring I've ordered for her and it sends a spark of excitement through my stomach. I can't wait to make her mine forever.

I can tell Li is agitated. I'm not sure if it's because he thinks we're going to miss the flight or whether it's down to the fact that he's going to miss Niamh tonight. He's the last one through. Typical that the alarm would go off as he walks under the security gate. Myself, Zach and Sabrina stand back, watch him get patted down and when the security guard finally waves him on, the four of us race as quickly as we can through Duty Free, slaloming around the aisles as we go.

We all come to a stop at a large screen when we reach the other side. I spot the flight we're on first.

'There,' I say. 'The six-ninety flight. Gate one-one-seven.'

'It says 'closing',' Li screeches, before we all sprint off again.

'We'll be fine.'

It's a good job we've got no baggage with us. The airport is fairly empty, but I can sense everybody in here staring at us as we leap over cases and seats, pelting through the departure lounges as if our lives depend on it.

If somebody caught this on video, I'm pretty sure it would make the news. 'Kenny Races Through Airport'. It's a nothing story. But I've been part of nothing stories plenty of times. I think the most needless headline I've ever read about myself was 'Kenny Queues For Burger'. Somebody spotted me ordering at a food truck in Newcastle's city centre during a random mid-week lunch time. And that was it. That was the story. A man ordering lunch. That's modern media. Everybody and anybody can be a journalist. They just need to use that little mobile device they have in their pocket and if they get an image of a celebrity doing anything, the media will lap it up. Journalism well and truly has gone to the dogs. Anything can be posted as news these days, passed off as fact when it isn't true whatsoever. It's how Donald Trump got into the White House, how fuckwits like Boris Johnson, Michael Gove and Nigel Farage managed to persuade people in Britain to leave the EU. All lies. And the main problem is that most people are just too fucking dumb to see through the lies. I'm definitely depressed about not having my contract renewed at Sunderland. But the one shining light about no longer being a pro footballer will be the fact that I'm no longer newsworthy. Knowing that I can queue up for a burger without being paranoid that I might be making a headline will be a nice little victory for me.

'Down here,' Li says, pointing at steps. The bloody Ryanair flights always take off from the back arse of every airport. That company are too miserable with their money to spend on the nearer gates to depart from.

The four of us shuffle down the steps and when we arrive at gate 117 we're met by nobody. It's empty. Totally derelict. The only thing left here is a wheelchair that somebody must have taken to the departure gate. I hate seeing wheelchairs or disabled signs. They make me think of Caitlin Tyrell.

When I couldn't find any trace of Caitlin online, I decided to pay a visit to a charity who dealt with people who had been left disabled by car accidents. YouKnight they were called. I visited their headquarters without invitation one day. Just so it would remove some guilt from my mind-set. The charity is run by a bunch of saints; folk who give up their time for those in need. Nobody earns a cent for the work they do with people in need. I walked in, had no meeting booked or anything, just strolled towards a woman sitting at a random desk at the front of the dilapidated building.

'I'm eh... here to just take a look around,' I said. 'I'm interested in maybe helping out if I can.'

'Sure, we'd love that,' the woman said. 'I'll call down Clara and she'd be happy to have a word with you.'

I sat on a chair as she made a phone call and took in my surroundings. It looked like a community centre, slightly run down, but with a lot of love attempting to cover over the cracks. There were paintings and drawings from patients dotted across the walls. Photographs of their faces, too. I wanted to believe one of the patients was called Caitlin. But I never found her.

'Hi, can I help you?' a woman said to my back.

'Oh – hi,' I replied turning around. 'You must be Clara...'

I saw her face light up.

'Jason Kenny. Wow – what are you doing here?' she said, holding her hand out for me to shake.

'I eh... I read about what you guys do and I want to help out.' I put my hand inside my jacket, pulled out an envelope from my pocket.

'I'm hoping you might take this for starters.'

I watched Clara's face as she opened the envelope and pulled out the cheque. She lit up.

'Are we late... did we miss the flight to Newcastle?' I ask the first person we come across.

'Eh...' she scratches her head. 'I can get you on. Quickly though.'

She holds her hand towards me.

'Passport,' she says.

'We eh.. don't have passports, but you take regular ID, right?' I say.

She shakes her head.

'We haven't done that for a few years now. You need a passport to travel by air, even to Britain.'

Bollocks!

I sigh. A deep loud sigh, muffled by my hands spread across my face.

Then we all look to our feet and hobble off to sit on the horribly uncomfortable steel chairs.

'I need to go to the loo,' I say after a while.

I peel my back up, vertebrae by vertebrae, and head for the stairs.

'Hold up,' Zach shouts, jogging after me. 'I need a piss meself.'

We both plod up the steps and when we reach the top, Zach holds a hand across my chest.

'Hey, let's book a hotel room across the way,' he says.

'Okay...' I reply without really thinking it through. 'Eh... what do we need a hotel for?'

'C'mon man.' Zach steps in front of me. 'We're both banging that bird tonight. I don't care if it's in your gaff in Newcastle or the Airport B&B. She's too hot to not bang. We're not letting this opportunity go.'

I squint my eyes at him. Try to make out whether he's being serious or not. I don't say a word. I just study his face.

'C'mon man, you're a fuckin' footballer. This is what footballers do. They play football and fuck hot birds. How many times have I talked to you about a roasting, huh? Here's the perfect opportunity. She's mad for it.'

'She's not mad for it, she's—'

'She's willing to take a flight with three strange blokes to Newcastle for fuck sake. She's practically got her tits out all night... her nipples are fighting to stay inside that jumpsuit she's wearing. She followed us to Coppers. She has 'mad for it' written all over her.'

I'm still staring at Zach's face, still squinting.

'She's already kissed you, right?' he says, not relenting. 'Already kissed me. She's probably down there sucking the face off Li as we speak.'

'Hold on. She *kissed* you?'

'Course she did. Was all over me on that rickshaw. She's up for it, man. I'm tellin' ye. C'mon – we owe each other this, Jason. You're a pro footballer. I've always had a hard on for roasting some young one. I get mad jealous when I read about footballers doing this all the time. You know all I wanted was to be a footballer... I've missed out on all these opportunities. C'mon man... ye know what this would mean to me.'

I lean my head back against the wall. What Zach is saying is just noise. I'm barely listening to his bullshit anyway. I'm used to zoning out on him. He doesn't see women as human beings... just as sex toys. It's nothing new. It's not the first time he's mentioned roasting to me. And it won't be the first time I turn down his offer either. But all I'm playing over and over in my head is an image of Sabrina kissing him. My heart feels heavy. I thought she was different; thought she was genuinely into me. I was even thinking I wouldn't have sex with her tonight. That it'd be more romantic if I just got to know her. I was hoping we would just curl up, watch a movie together in my cinema room. Maybe have a few snogs under a blanket. But that's all out the window now. She has no intentions of getting to know me. Zach's right. She's only after one thing. I fuckin' hate being a celebrity.

I let out a sigh, zone back in to hear Zach still talking about fucking roastings.

'Here mate, give us your phone,' he says. 'You go have a piss, I'll book a hotel room nearby.'

I let out a loud sigh, clench both of my fists until my knuckles turn white. Then I release them slowly, finger by finger.

'It's okay,' I say, grabbing at my phone. 'I'll book it.'

◆

NUMBER FIVE'S silently hoping her face isn't turning red as she coughs into her hand, aware all eyes are on her.

She sits more upright, eyeballs Number One and repeats what she'd said for emphasis.

'Yeah – I have gone home with guys after meeting them that night. I think most women – definitely of my age or whatever – would say the same. It doesn't always lead to sex and I certainly wasn't just going home with them for sex. But y'know... y'know...' She begins to stutter.

'Absolutely,' Number Eleven says, backing Number Five up. 'Social-ising in these days is a lot different to what it was a generation ago. Both myself and Number Five have admitted to going back to guys' houses after meeting them that night, and that's just two girls out of seven in this room. I don't—'

Number Seven holds her hand up, stopping Number Eleven in her tracks.

All jurors turn towards her.

'Listen, I wouldn't say this to most people... but I feel I need to say it here. I've done the same; have gone back to a man's apartment after meeting him that night. Like Number Five said, it wasn't necessarily for sex... I just... I just wanted the night to continue. I have a feeling Sabrina did the same thing here. I don't think we should judge her just for wanting to go to Jason's home. Agreeing to go to his house is not an agreement for sex.'

The jury room falls silent, save for the sound of a couple of jurors swallowing hard. The arguments are not only getting heated, they are getting personal too.

Brian tap claps his hands, in appreciation of the three jury members speaking their truth, though most view it as him seeking attention again.

'Okay...' Number One says, killing the silence. He shuffles his paperwork, wondering where they should go next with their deliberations. 'Ah yes,' he says, 'the taxi driver who drove them to the airport... what did we make of his testimo—?'

'Inshignificant,' Brian spits out before Number One has finished the question. 'Well, inshignificant in terms of he didn't really add much, did he? He jusht said that he drove them to the airport.'

'I agree with Brian,' Number Five says, generating stares from around the table. It was the first time Number Five had agreed with anything Brian had said. 'All this fella said was that Li sat in the front, Jason, Zach and Sabrina in the back and that there were no signals of discomfort or anything. I didn't see his testimony as helpful in any way.'

'Yeah – I'm surprised the judge allowed it,' says Number One. 'I mean what did it do for either side?'

'Well, the defence tried their best to make him say Sabrina was comfortable, right?' Number Seven says. 'But yeah... it doesn't add anything to the case because Sabrina admits herself that she was quite comfortable at this stage.'

'I guess the judge just wanted the testimony of all those who interacted with the four of them throughout the night; thought it would benefit us. The rickshaw guy testified, the taxi man who brought them to the airport... the taxi man who then dropped them from the airport to the hotel... I guess his testimony was kinda insignificant too, huh?'

A nod of heads circulates the table.

Trevor Coyne – a fifty-two-year-old taxi driver for over two decades – also testified, despite only driving the three men and Sabrina for less than five minutes from one side of the airport to the other. He described Zach as being 'snappy' and 'a little hostile' but aside from that offered nothing of significance during his time on the stand. In rape cases – especially ones like this where there is an admission of sex from both sides, but a discrepancy over whether or not it was consensual – evidence is hard to come by. Judge McCormick was trying to give the jurors an overall picture of the night in question, by allowing the rickshaw driver and taxi drivers to give accounts of their time spent with all four players.

Delia McCormick has thirteen years' experience of presiding over trials. This has been her tenth rape trial to judge. In eight of those trials, the defendant – or defendants – were found to be not guilty. Rape is one of the most difficult crimes to earn a conviction in. In fact rape is one of the most difficult crimes to even make it to trial. This trial barely made it because evidence is practically scarce. This whole case relies heavily on the statements of witnesses. And even at that, there are zero witnesses to the actual crime itself. Except, of course, for the four people involved; three of whom offer almost the exact same account of the specific half-an-hour – between midnight and half-past midnight on the night in question during which the claimant claims she was raped – while her account is, obviously, in stark contrast to theirs. 'The odd one out' as defence lawyer Gerd Bracken suggested during his closing argument.

The only hard evidence offered to the court was that delivered by Dr Dermot Johnson – the doctor Sabrina visited two days after the incident. He professed that the internal cut Sabrina suffered was 'certainly as a result of rough intercourse', backing Sabrina's claim. Though under cross examination, Dr Johnson was forced to admit that cuts like the one found inside Sabrina can occur as a result of consensual sex. He did suggest on the stand that this type of cut wouldn't occur if intercourse was being enjoyed by the claimant, but this vital piece of expert evidence washed over the jurors.

'If Ms Doyle,' he said on the stand, 'was a full participant in the intercourse and – as a result – was producing cervical fluid, this cut would likely not have occurred.' He was trying to state, in his opinion, that this cut was the result of non-consensual sex; that Sabrina's vagina must have been dry in order to be cut. But every time Number Eleven – the only juror affected by the doctor's testimony – tried to bring this up, she was shut down.

'If the cut can happen in consensual sex then it's insignificant isn't it?' Number Twelve had said, his arms out almost in apology. All of the other jurors agreed with him on this. They agreed to wash over Dr Johnson's testimony; felt the defence lawyer's counter argument overshadowed it.

'So, given your expertise, Doctor Johnson, can you inform the jury that these cuts can – and indeed *do* – occur from consensual intercourse?' Gerd Bracken asked.

Dr Johnson, being the noble and honest man he is, nodded his head, moved closer to the microphone and said 'yes'.

That was enough for the jurors to forget the main point he was trying to make; that Sabrina mustn't have been producing 'cervical fluid' during the intercourse. Had he not been so technical with his phraseology, this argument might have rung more true with more jurors than just Number Eleven. Had Sabrina's lawyer highlighted this part of the doctor's testimony by describing it in layman's terms, using words such as 'cum', or 'wet' or 'moist' then the jurors would have considered it more readily. As it was, Dr Johnson's testimony – which Judge McCormick felt was pivotal in the trial – was far from pivotal in the minds of eleven of the twelve jurors.

'It seems it's all we have to go on, innit?' says Number Three. 'Just random people's words. How are we supposed to convict these three men when we have such little evidence to use against them?'

'It'sh what I've been saying all along,' Brian says, his face gurning into a smug grin. 'There jusht isn't enough evidensh to convict.'

Number Three taps her fingers against her wheelchair armrest again, then takes in a loud breath through her nostrils.

'But how do prosecutors provide evidence in a case like this? How is a girl who has been raped supposed to get a conviction against those who raped her when they all agree that sex did indeed take place? The argument is consensual or not consensual isn't it? But how are we supposed to know?'

The room falls silent again. Some jurors shake their heads. The speed in which their discussion turned once they felt they were on their way to a verdict has stalled. There's been more silences in the past fifteen minutes than there had been for the entirety of the three-hours of deliberating before that.

'I just... I just,' Number Three says, pushing a finger to her eyeball, forcing the tear that threatened to fall from it back inside. 'I know we're not supposed to let our own personal feelings dictate our argument, but I can't help but think that if Sabrina was raped – and I think she was – we can't let these men get away with it. It's our job to deliver justice.'

'That'sh not true,' says Brian. 'It's the judge's job to deliver jushtice. Our job is to weigh up the arguments. That's all.'

Number Three snorts in an attempt to suck back up the tear that has now begun to fall down her cheek.

'I think I have to change my mind,' she says. 'I have to go from guilty to not guilty. I thought all along that I'd decide guilty, because I believe in my heart that Sabrina was raped. Well...' she says, holding up her palm before steadying her breathing, 'I believe that Sabrina feels she was raped. That, I genuinely believe. The three men might not think it was rape, but she certainly does.'

Then the tears come quicker. She holds her entire face in the palms of her hands and begins to sob.

Number Three's emotions reverberate around the table. She wasn't supposed to be the one to crack. She had proven to other jurors that she was strong minded, probably because she was weak in body.

Number Three's real name is Caitlin Tyrell. She's just turned thirty. She's been in a wheelchair since three months before her tenth birthday when she was run over by a car a mere ninety-metres from her home in

Howth, County Dublin. It was a hit and run; the driver never caught. She underwent almost three years of rehab before she was allowed home full-time. Since then she has gone on to live a happy life. She works as a receptionist at a health club in Dublin's city centre and recently got engaged to a man who suffered a similar tragedy to herself; he too wheelchair bound for life. She had felt, from the very outset, that all three men in this case were guilty; she just damned the lack of evidence, so much so that she was now beginning to change her mind.

The tears currently rolling down her face have nothing to do with Sabrina – as most jurors assume they do. She is crying because she has just – in the past few moments – realised that she *has* to find all three men not guilty of this charge, even though she doesn't want to. Her head is over-ruling her heart. And that's exactly how it should be when you sit on a jury.

Despite Number Three's realisation, she is hopeful that an argument can be raised that will help her change her mind once more. But she's not confident of that. She's been through everything in her head countless times... she doesn't think such an argument exists. Her tears are tears of frustration, tears of guilt almost. She wants to see Jason, Zach and Li go down.

Number Eleven rubs Number Three's back and offers a sympathetic turning down of her lips.

'I know how you feel,' she whispers into her ear.

'This is difficult for all of us,' Number One says, standing up. 'None of us could have predicted just how emotional this would be. I almost feel like crying myself sometimes. In fact I've found myself wiping my eyes when I'm in bed at night these past few days as the trial culminated... but I guess we need to try to push emotion aside for now and give full focus to our mission: debating the arguments raised in this case and eventually coming to a verdict.'

Number Three sniffs and nods frantically at the same time, to agree with Number One's sentiment. She sweeps the palm of her right hand across her face, removing any moisture left and then smiles up at the Head Juror.

'I guess,' he says to her, 'when this is all finished, we'll all be crying. This will bear a heavy scar on all of us.'

A succession of tuts are heard around the table; not tuts of irritation, but tuts of sorrow.

'The hotel,' Number One then says before sitting down and re-adjusting his glasses.

Brian interrupts him.

'Yesh... the hotel. It's one thing that Sabrina wanted to go to Newcashtle, to maybe see how the other half lived, to witness the luxuries a professional footballer possesses... but why go to a hotel room with three strangers, a hotel room that ish only twenty minutes from her own home?'

Number One coughs, then answers Brian's point.

'It's interesting that that is your take from the whole hotel room thingy,' he says. 'My take on it is different. As the prosecution lawyer mentioned a few times in court, why the hell did Jason only book one hotel room, when all three men were coming back to it with Sabrina? Talk about evidence, there's evidence right there that there was collusion from the three men about group sex.'

'That's not evidensh,' Brian says raising his voice, dissipating the emotional sentiment that existed in the room moments prior. The arguments were well and truly back underway. 'There is no evidensh of collusion there at all.'

'If he only booked one hotel room, what does that say?'

'That he booked one hotel room,' Brian says, his voice still louder than it needs to be. It was almost as if he was taking Number One's point as a personal attack.

'Listen,' Number One says, rising from his seat again, looking down at Brian. 'It is reasonable for us to believe that there were discussions in the airport by the three men that alluded to them all having sex with Sabrina. If there wasn't... why did he only book the one room?'

'He booked a suite. The defence lawyers showed us the picturesh of the suite. There was more than enough room for four people to shleep there that night.'

'There was only one fuckin bed, Brian!' Number One snaps back, shouting louder than his nemesis had just moments ago.

'Calm down!' Number Three says. 'We are arguing the case, not arguing egos here.' The rest of the jurors look to her, not at Brian nor Number One, to continue the debate.

'This was an argument raised by Sabrina's lawyer because he felt it was significant,' she says. 'It is certainly worth us arguing, but not in these tones. I suggest you sit down, Number One – and I suggest both of you refrain from raising your voices so much.'

Number Three pats down the shoulders of her blazer, readjusts her lapels and then places both of her hands, palms down, on to the armrests of her wheelchair.

'At the airport, Jason booked the Merchant Penthouse Suite for all four of them. The prosecution and defence raise different arguments for this... it's our job to straighten out those arguments. Let's do this sensibly and maturely. It might change people's minds in here... my mind has already been changed and it may even change again, so this is really important. Let's calm down and ask the very obvious question here.' She looks around the table, her head swivelling right, then left. 'Number Four, let's start with you. Do you believe Jason booked the hotel suite so that all three of the men could have sex with Sabrina?'

Number Four sucks in some air, then twists his bum into a more comfortable seating position.

'My opinion on that is...' he pauses, staring into space to consider his answer. 'My opinion on that is—'

A knock at the door interrupts him. Number Nine rises from her seat and pulls at the door. The jurors look at her as she nods her head at the young man dressed in black before turning to them.

'Lunch is ready,' she says.

All that bloody running and we didn't even have the right ID.

I don't know whether I'm happy about this or not. The whole trip was supposed to be about Jason anyway – a mission to get him to cheer up. But maybe it's just best that he asks Sabrina for her phone number and they try to get to know each other another time. There's no need to try and get her to fall in love with him tonight. I was just trying to think of ways to keep him feeling positive. It almost broke my heart, hearing him sob on my shoulder in Coppers earlier.

I glance over at him. I don't know whether he's back to feeling down or whether or not he's just jaded after we ran here. Each of the four of us are sprawled out on a steel chair in the departure lounge opposite the gate we were supposed to depart from. He shouldn't be jaded, I guess. He is a professional athlete after all. Maybe he *is* feeling down again... depressed. He's awfully quiet for someone who's supposed to be trying to impress this girl. I'll get into his ear in a minute. If anyone can cheer him up, it's me. I'll tell him to play it cool with Sabrina, that I was wrong to suggest he should rush things tonight with her.

'I need to go to the loo,' Jason says.

Zach gets up almost immediately after him. I wouldn't mind joining them, wouldn't mind having a go at trying to alleviate the tension in Jason. But I'm too tired. I need a couple of minutes to get my breath back. I haven't run that far or that fast in... actually I don't think I've ever run that far or that fast. And all for nothing.

'Tired?' Sabrina asks, turning her head to face me as the other two ramble up the steps. She's slouched just as much as I am in her chair.

'Bollixed,' I reply while letting out a deep breath.

'Me too. Who would have thought I'd ever be in such a rush to go to bloody Newcastle?'

I laugh. It's not the first time she's made me laugh tonight. She's strangely funny for someone so attractive. That combination rarely marries. I assume that if you're good looking you must be a bit more reserved. More self-conscious. Sabrina was certainly quieter in the first part of the night when we met her, but she's opened up since. Maybe it's the wine. She seems to have come out of her shell as she's got to know us. And I think she likes me; she's comfortable with me.

She stood joking and laughing with me at the edge of the dance floor when we were in Coppers and snapped at both of the lads when they were taking the piss out of me on the taxi ride here. She's lovely. I can certainly see what Jason sees in her. She seems to have it all. I hope it works out between her and Jason. Would like Sabrina to be a part of our lives. I know I've only known her for a few hours, but I think I'd actually miss her if I never saw her again.

'Well, you were right all along,' she says to me.

'Huh?'

'You kept telling everyone that we wouldn't get on that flight.'

'Oh yeah,' I say letting a sniffle of laughter come out of my nose. I finally sit more upright. Sabrina does the same. But we both just stare ahead. Too tired to move any more than sitting up.

'I'm so happy for you.'

'For me?' I say, turning to face her.

'Yeah. Getting engaged. That's such amazing news. Niamh's a lucky girl. You're gonna make her so happy.'

'Thank you,' I say, studying her face, wondering why she's so perfect in every possible way. She must have flaws. Can't be this ideal. Surely perfect women don't actually exist. You can't have it all. You can't have the personality to match the looks.

'How you going to do it – how are you going to ask her?' she asks.

'Well,' I pause before letting another laugh sniffle out from my nose. 'I was originally going to ask her when we go on holiday next month. We're going to Lanzarote.'

Sabrina lets a little squeal seep from the back of her throat.

'That would be so romantic. Over dinner, when the sun is going down or something like that?' she says smiling at me.

'Yeah... that's... that's *exactly* how I was imaging it,' I say. 'It's just eh... Zach thought that was a bit cheesy.'

'Zach?' she says, resting her forearms on her knees. She turns her face to look at me. 'Zach who does nothing but cheat on his poor wife is trying to tell you how to treat yours?'

I laugh and begin to play with my fingers out of discomfort. I don't know why Sabrina is making me feel this way. I'm starting to think I might actually fancy her. That's nuts. I haven't fancied anyone since I met Niamh. I haven't even had a celebrity crush.

'You're right, I suppose,' I say.

'No – *you're* right. You do it whatever way you want. Just make sure it's a special memory for Niamh. That should be your main aim.'

I smile at her, soak in her beauty. Then shake my thoughts away. I imagine Niamh curled up in our bed at home. Our baby growing inside her. Maybe it's time I joined her back there.

I check the time on my iPhone. 11:31. If I get a taxi from outside the airport I could be home by midnight. I won't wake Niamh or anything. But I can just squeeze up against her. Spoon her. Place my hand on her swelling belly.

Sabrina takes me out of my thought by placing her hand on my knee.

'You're a good man, Li. You've got it all. Guys wanna look like Zach or maybe they wanna have the celebrity like Jason, but ye know what? All a girl really wants is somebody who's nice. Who's trustworthy. Who's genuine. I kinda... I envy Niamh.'

She's staring into my eyes as she's saying this. I feel my dick wake up. It removes itself from slouching on my balls, as if its alarm clock has just gone off. I stand up immediately, turn my back on her and pace across the floor.

'Thank you,' I say back over my shoulder before I shake my head again, removing the guilty thoughts from my mind. I pace towards the window, see my reflection staring back at me.

'Where are those two?' I ask, trying to change the subject.

'Hmmm,' Sabrina mumbles before walking towards the edge of the steps. She stares up them. The airport is eerily quiet. 'Wonder what they're up to?'

She begins to walk up the steps, but just as she rests her hand on the bannister we can hear them. Well, not necessarily both of them. Zach more so.

'Whoop,' he calls out, running down the steps. He rushes at Sabrina, almost pulling her over in a sort of wrestling move. I think it's his idea of a hug. 'C'mon, you two, we're going over to the Merchant Hotel for drinks. Jason's sorted it.'

I walk closer to my reflection, then let out a big sigh that fogs up the window. Balls. I really don't wanna do that. I just wanna go home.

He's so adorable. I bet he's totally devoted to Niamh; wouldn't even dream of cheating on her. She's lucky. I tell him that. I'm glad I can open up to him, that I can pay people compliments without feeling self-conscious. I'm starting to come out of my shell tonight. Being around these three has really helped me. They're a good remedy for somebody with a slice of depression.

I lean over to Li, just to let him know how proud I am of him, even though I've only known him for a few hours. It's almost as if he feels like a little brother to me.

'You're a good man, Li,' I say, honestly as I can. 'You've got it all. Guys wanna look like Zach or maybe they wanna have the celebrity like Jason, but ye know what? All a girl wants is somebody like you. Somebody who's nice. Who's trustworthy. Who's genuine. I kinda... I envy Niamh.'

I think my straightforwardness has unnerved him a little. I'm not sure he's used to compliments. He gets up from his chair, paces towards the other side of the room. He's probably wishing he was back home with his soon-to-be fiancée.

The entire departure lounge falls silent again. Just the sound of Li's footsteps brushing off the shiny floor producing hardly any noise at all.

'Where are those two?' I ask before getting up off my chair and heading towards the steps. I'm about to climb them in search of Jason when I hear the two of them coming towards me. When Zach sees me, he runs down the steps, yelling. He practically lands on top of me as if we're celebrating a lottery win or something.

'C'mon, you two, we're going over to the Merchant Hotel for drinks. Jason's sorted it.'

I stare at Jason over Zach's shoulder as he plods down the stairs. He doesn't seem to be as excited about this as Zach is. In fact, he barely looks at me, he just offers me a strained smile without our eyes meeting.

'Yeah – c'mon, we'll go over for a few drinks. I have this deadly suite we can all crash in,' he says.

I swallow hard. Not sure how to take it. Is that just confirmation that I'm going to have sex with him? Shouldn't I be a little upset that he booked a hotel room without even asking me? I'm not sure how I'm supposed to feel; how I'm supposed to play this.

I think Zach notices my hesitation more than Jason.

'Fuck it, Sabrina, c'mon. They do some lovely cocktails over there. Let's have a few of them, let's make a night of it, huh?'

I just nod my head. But I'm still a bit hesitant. Unsure.

'Ye know what... I think I might just go home,' Li says as he walks towards us.

'Well, if you're going home, I'm going home too,' I say. And I mean it. I need Li to come with us to the hotel. Somebody needs to keep Zach company if me and Jason are to get down to business.

'Whoa, whoa, whoa,' says Zach, holding his arms out. 'You're both coming over. We're having a few drinks each... if you all wanna go home after that, I'll order you a taxi each, but c'mon – were having fun, right?'

He grins wide. I'm not sure why he's so excited about a couple of extra drinks.

I look at Jason, wondering why he's quiet in comparison. Maybe he's wondering if he's coming on too strong by booking a hotel room. I bet that's why he's asked Zach to reveal the news... as if it was all Zach's decision, not his. That's kinda cute. I think. I walk over to Jason, just to let him know he shouldn't be feeling guilty. I'll let him know I'm up for it. That I want to have sex with him.

'Come on, Li, we'll both go over, have a cocktail and a bit more of a laugh. It's early days, right? Not even midnight,' I say.

I smile at Jason. He smiles back. Then I wrap both my arms around his waist and lean in to him.

'Relax,' I whisper into his ear. 'Everything's going to be okay. You don't have to feel any guilt. I'm up for this. I'm eh... actually quite horny.'

It's the naughtiest thing I've ever whispered to anyone. But I feel like I'm a different person tonight. It's probably the excitement of hooking up with a celebrity. I hope that's not too strong; hope Jason is up for sex just as much as I am. He must be. He practically had me pulling him off after meeting him for two minutes earlier on.

'You really are a filthy little bitch, aren't you?' he says, cupping my ear.

I giggle. I feel so happy. In about an hour's time I'm going to be having sex with somebody who people have posters of in their bedrooms. This is going to be one of the best nights of my life. It already is. I genuinely think I've found not just a future boyfriend, but two new best friends too.

I've never really had male friends before. I've always assumed any guy who wants to talk to me is talking to me because I'm attractive. I certainly didn't have any male friends when I went out with Eddie. He wouldn't even let me talk to *his* friends. That's how jealous he was. His paranoia must've rubbed off on me. After about six months of being convinced he was cheating on me, I found a company online who would confirm it for me: Honest Entrapment. For two thousand euro they would have an attractive girl come on to my boyfriend and send a full report of his reaction to me. I met with Lorna one Tuesday morning and by Friday she was all dressed up, ready to coincidentally bump into Eddie when he was out with his mates in Tallaght. I called to her small offices in Rathfarnham the following Monday for my report. I wasn't surprised. Not one bit. Lorna is gorgeous. She may not be as naturally pretty as I am, but she's definitely sexy. Long blonde hair, bright green eyes. She always wears roaring red lipstick. It makes her look like a magazine model. But like me, she never made it into the magazine pages as a model. She had just as much of a stressful time of it in that industry as I had.

'I flirted with him from the outset, played it a little cool, then turned up the heat. When I suggested he come back to my place, his exact words were "fuck yeah",' she told me. She reached out a hand to mine. Held it. I didn't need the comforting she was offering. I knew there was no chance in hell he would turn down an offer of sex from another woman. I just wanted clarification. A definite reason to dump him. Which is what I did later that day.

'Go on then, I'll go over for an hour or two,' Li says. I beam a big smile, then walk towards him and offer him a hug of his own.

'Okay then, boys – let's go,' I say as I lead them all up the steps. I really am starting to like the new me.

She walks towards me, smiles, then wraps both of her arms around my waist –seconds after she did the exact same thing to Zach.

'Relax,' she whispers into my ear. 'Everything's going to be okay. Lighten up. I'm up for this. I'm eh...' she leans in closer to my ear, 'actually quite horny.'

Wow. I really thought she was a genuinely nice girl. I can't believe I had almost fallen for her; almost visualising a future for the two of us. I'm such a fucking idiot. I should know this by now. No hot girl wants a future with me. They just want a night. A thrill. A story for their friends.

'You really are a filthy little bitch, aren't you?' I whisper back. And I mean it. She is. It's such a shame. She really doesn't need to be like this. I wasn't even planning on having sex with her. I wanted to play it cool. Play it slow.

I stare down at her as she snuggles into my shoulder, then my eyes gaze down the length of the V in her jumpsuit and decide I can't turn this offer down, no matter how hurt I'm feeling right now. This'll be nothing new for me – fucking a hot girl while depressed. It's what I've been doing every weekend for the past year, ever since Jessica left me.

I look over at Zach as Sabrina releases her bear hug. He winks at me. He's such a little shite. But I love him. I don't know what I'd be like if it wasn't for Zach and Li. I'd probably be suicidal. They are the only two blokes on the planet who make me genuinely laugh. I mean, I laugh all the time in the dressing-room. But I'm not genuinely laughing. I'm just laughing because that's what I'm supposed to do.

Dressing-rooms are full of men who have never really grown up. Millionaires who think it's funny to put glue in their mate's shampoo, or who think it's funny to cut the toes out of a mate's socks. I probably thought those things were funny the first time they happened. But it's been the same shit jokes for the past fifteen years now. I'm bored by it all.

I'm devastated by the fact that my time as a footballer is at an end, but I'll only miss the buzz of playing in front of tens of thousands of fans every week. I won't miss the dressing-room, won't miss the ladishness.

I took my first coaching badges a couple of years ago, but I didn't progress further than that. I knew even then that I didn't want to be involved in football once I retired from playing. Punditry is an option. I do talk a good game; have been on the RTÉ panel a couple of times. But punditry is genuinely full of bullshit. The truth is, there are no experts looking in from the outside of football. No observer of the game can ever truly know what a manager's intention is when he sets out his team. And that's why every opinion a pundit throws out there is literally nonsensical. Players talk about this all the time in the dressing-room; we cringe listening to pundits pretend to know what they're talking about.

I want out of the sport altogether; think I might work in charities. It's probably my calling. It's probably what God wants me to do. Maybe we were meant to hit Caitlin that night.

I watch Sabrina laugh and joke with Li as the four of us stroll up the steps, in search of the exit. I am disappointed, but I think I'm mostly annoyed; annoyed at myself for falling for her. I should have known. Then I notice Zach looking at me. He winks again. Little shite! His cheeky winking is starting to turn a light bulb on over my head. Why the fuck do I believe him? Why have I bought the line that she snogged him? *Yes*, I know she hugged him as soon as he ran down the stairs, and *yes* she did go missing from Coppers with him for about twenty minutes or so. But she told me he came on to her and she denied his advances. Why do I believe him over her? He fucking lies on a regular basis.

But he wouldn't lie to me. Would he? Not his best mate. Surely.

As the four of us stroll through the deserted airport I begin to play all of my time spent with Sabrina over in my head. I'm trying to work her out. Then I let out a sigh. If she hadn't made it so blatantly clear to me that she wanted sex, I could have bought the nice-girl persona.

I rub my face with the palm of my hand. This is always the way my body informs me that I'm feeling depressed. Maybe I should cancel this whole hotel room thing; ask Sabrina out on a date next week. Get to really know her.

I take my phone out of my pocket, log into my Facebook account and search for Sabrina Doyle, hoping I might get some insight on her. There are dozens of Sabrina Doyles. None of them look like her.

'Ah, here we are, here's a way out,' she says. I watch as she wraps her arm around Li and leads him through the door. What the fuck is she playing at? Is she up for fucking all of us? Is this what she's after? Three dicks? It couldn't be. She just likes Li as a friend, surely.

'Hey,' I say, calling after her. 'My phone's just died. Can I have a quick look at yours? Just want to check in on my emails to make sure the hotel reservation came through.'

She goes into her handbag and takes out her phone.

'Sure,' she says thumbing in her passcode. 'Here you go.'

I haven't really thought this through. I'm just trying to get a sense of who she is. She doesn't have the Facebook app. Doesn't seem to have any social media apps at all. So I check her text messages; bring up the last one she sent.

Asked Niall out straight if he would be interested in going home with me tonight. Red light on this one, Lorna. He genuinely wasn't interested. I'll give you a full run down in the morning.

That was two hours ago. Who the fuck is this chick?

We pace out of the departure lounge lookin' like the oddest gang of misfits on the planet.

I've no idea how this is going to go down. She's defo more into Jason than me, but when we get her into that hotel room, we'll get her up for it. No better man than me to convince a girl to let me inside her.

I've never had a threesome before. Have often fantasised about having one, but there's normally two pussies and one dick in those fantasies, not the other way around. But this is what life should be like for a footballer. Jason should be well up for this. I'm not sure why he's gone all quiet and mopey since they wouldn't let us on the flight. Maybe he's just nervous at the thought of having sex while I'm in the room. But we'll be fine. It's not like we're gonna force her into sex or anything like that. We'll just talk her into it. She probably won't need much talkin' into it anyway – she's going to have sex with two blokes; one of them a professional footballer, it should be every girl's fantasy for fuck sake.

We spot a short line of taxis as soon as we get outside and hop in the first one. Li, as usual, gets in the front. This time Sabrina sits in the middle of the back seat, between me and Jason. It seems exciting to me, but everything falls kinda quiet after we tell the taxi man where we're going. The Merchant Hotel is only a two or three-minute drive, the opposite side of the car park.

'Are you eh... Jason Kenny?' the taxi man asks, staring into his rear-view mirror.

'That's me,' Jason replies.

'Jaysus, Sunderland are gone to the dogs, aren't they?'

Most people who meet Jason like to mention the goal he scored against Holland, but the odd one or two can be ignorant bastards.

'They're still a professional football club, mate,' I reply. 'Playing ball for them sure as hell beats driving around in a taxi.'

'Ah jaysus, I was just sayin—'

'It's alright,' Jason says, relieving the tension. 'And you're right, they have gone to the dogs.'

'Can you not get a move? Back up to the Championship again, or even the Premier League. You were never the fastest, maybe you can still play Premier League,' the taxi man says.

Jason forces out a laugh.

'My Premier League days are long gone.'

'Sorry,' the taxi man says again. 'I didn't mean anything bad by that... it's just y'know yourself. Two relegations in two years for Sunderland. They used to be such a great club. I'm a big footie fan meself.... You eh... you don't play for Ireland anymore, no?'

'No, retired from international ball there about three years ago,' Jason says. 'Thought it might prolong the club game for me... not sure it worked.'

They're still ping-ponging football talk to one another when the car comes to a halt.

'Here y'are, lads... there's seven euro on the meter, but it's on me,' the taxi man says. 'If you can sign this for me.'

Jason leans over to sign a small slip of paper the taxi man pulled from somewhere while the rest of us climb out of the car. I stare at Sabrina's ass as she shuffles out ahead of me. I can't believe I'm gonna fuck her later. She'll defo be the most attractive bird I've ever pulled.

Jason follows us into the lobby and then heads straight for the reception desk. I stand back with Li and Sabrina, wondering how all of this is going to play out. It probably would've been better if we'd just let Li go home when he said he wanted to. It'd be beneficial if he was out of the way for this.

I let a loud breath seep out of my nostrils. I'm not sure whether I'm more excited or nervous for what's about to happen. I'll be mortified if it turns out Jason has a bigger dick than me. But God couldn't have been that kind to him. Surely he didn't get the breaks in football and the bigger cock. Not that I believe in God. Jason's the only deluded one out of us in that regard. But I don't even think he does believe in that bullshit. He's just been conditioned to follow through with his faith. His whole family are religious. His ma and his younger brother still go to mass every Sunday. I often say it's quite the coincidence that they all ended up believing in the same God. Out of the three thousand or so Gods that humans have invented, it's quite the coincidence that every member of the same family believes in the same one. It has to be conditioning. People only believe in Gods for one of two reasons, one; conditioning – their faith is decided by their family before they're even born or two; they're desperate. Only desperate people who are looking for direction in life, looking for friends, end up believing in that type of bullshit. I can't wrap my head around why anybody would want to lie to themselves. It's all a bit nuts to me. All I know is that I've got one life to live, then I'll be worm food. Which is why I'm gonna make the most of the time I have. It's why I don't mind hangin' out with Keating and his cronies. And it's why I don't mind fuckin as many women as I can.

'Alright guys, the Merchant suite, top floor,' Jason says, swingin' a key card at us. We all walk slowly towards the lift. I pick up a menu from the reception desk as we go.

'Here, what cocktails do you wanna order?' I say, handing it to Sabrina.

Li practically rests his chin on her shoulder as he looks at the menu. Jason presses the number twelve on the elevator and suddenly we are rising high.

'Oh, that has loads of ice in it, must be like a Slush Puppie. I'll have one of them; a Mango Margarita,' Li says. 'That'll go down well.'

'Yer ma goes down well,' I say, holding my fist out. Li and Jason bump me, Sabrina just eyeballs me and mocks a head shake.

'Me too. I'll have one of those as well,' she says.

'Fuck it,' I say, 'we'll order four. Jason... you up for one, yeah?'

Silence.

'Jason?'

'Huh?' he says, snapping out of his daydream. He must be feeling the same way I am. Half excited, half shittin' himself. He's probably wondering if my dick is gonna be bigger than his.

'Do you want a Mango Margarita like the rest of us?'

He nods his head, laughs a little. Then he walks out of the lift, leading us down a wide corridor towards the suite. Li makes a phone call to the reception as we stroll along the corridor and orders the four cocktails.

'Here we are,' Jason says, swiping his key over the reader by the door.

I allow the three of them to go in ahead of me. I wanna see Sabrina's face when she notices we've only booked one room.

'Oh wow,' she says, entering. 'This really is stunning.'

I watch as she takes in the lounge, follow her as she makes her way to the tiny kitchenette and then towards the flowers before she takes a sniff of them.

Then she walks through the double doors that lead to the large bedroom. She doesn't react. Doesn't say anything apart from purring at how amazing the suite is. She isn't put out at all by the fact that there's only one bed. My palms begin to moisten. Fuckin' deadly! This bitch really is up for this.

◆

THERE'S NOT much of an aesthetic difference between this room and the one they'd spent the previous three and a half hours in.

This one's slightly larger, and certainly more dimly lit. They don't have that big bright lamp shining down on them – just a regular bulb that doesn't offer as much of an unflattering glare. It's a more hollow room, too – the voices almost echo around it. The walls are still painted a clean white and the carpet is the same bright red that seems to lie behind every door in this building.

The young man dressed in all black paces quietly around the table, stopping at each juror to stretch over them and fill their glass with ice water. The table is more rectangular than the one in the jury room; five seats on each side, one then at each end. Brian, of course, sat in one of these as if he was the head of the family. Number Ten, who sat in the other, offered her chair to Number One – as Head Juror – but he waved away her invite, insisting it didn't matter where he was seated during lunch.

The young man dressed in all black pauses in the doorway after he's finished filling each of their glasses, then asks the jurors if they have any questions. Each of them shake their heads.

'Lunch will be served in the next few minutes,' the young man dressed in black then tells them before he opens the door and walks out, shutting it tight behind him. The turning of the latch echoes off the walls, almost like the clanging sound of a prison cell being locked. The room falls silent, save for the subtle sound of a few jurors sipping on their water.

'Okay,' Number One finally says, 'the judge said it is dependent on us whether or not we'd like to continue deliberations over lunch. I propose we do, but if the majority feels as if they'd like to take a break for the next hour, I totally understand.'

His fellow jurors all look around the room, most nodding their head in unison.

'So will we do a vote?' Brian asks.

Number Five tuts – loudly – but nobody responds to her, they just stare at their Head Juror for instruction.

'Hands up,' he says, 'if you would like to continue deliberations over lunch?'

Eight hands fly up, followed by another hesitant two. Only Number Four and Number Five keep their hands down. They both fancy taking a legitimate break; Number Five because she is lazy, Number Four because he knows that if deliberations are to continue, he will be called on first. After all, the jurors were seeking his opinion on the fact that Jason only booked one hotel room when they were interrupted by the lunch call.

'Ten:two,' Number One says, calling out the result. 'Majority rules. We *will* continue deliberations. So... we were discussing the hotel, right? Number Four, you were about to give your opinion on why Jason only booked one room. Would you like to begin the discussion?'

Number Four rubs one of his eyes, buying himself another couple of seconds to think through his opinion. It didn't help that he had the two-minute walk through a maze of corridors to consider his answer before he found himself in this position, because his mind kept changing. His answer to this question didn't match with his verdict overall. He was now beginning to feel that the men should be acquitted, that they didn't rape Sabrina Doyle. But he couldn't justify the booking of only one hotel room based on this verdict.

'I eh... I think Jason ordered one hotel room because they all felt as if group sex was what was gonna happen,' he says really slowly, as if he didn't want to say it at all. When the room stays silent and all eyes remain fixed on him, he feels pressured into elaborating. 'I eh... just don't see any other reason for it. One bed? They must have known what was going to happen at this stage. But...' he says, sitting more upright, 'maybe Sabrina knew at this stage, too. Maybe they discussed group sex, all four of them, at the airport.'

'That's total speculation,' Number Five says. 'Nobody, not Jason or Li or Zach or Sabrina mentioned group sex was discussed at the airport. So you've just made that up.'

'I'm just—' Number Four was about to answer but his words were being drowned out by arguments reverberating around the whole table. Almost everybody was talking, nobody listening.

'Hold on!' Number One says loudly, slamming the palm of his hand onto the table, causing the cutlery to zing with vibration. 'Can we all just settle down?' The room falls into line immediately. 'It's a good point Number Five has raised. Nobody has testified that group sex was ever mentioned at the airport, yet only one bedroom was booked. I mean... this seems really iffy.'

Another ripple of murmurings arise, but Number One holds his hand up to stop it and then stretches his index finger out, pointing it at Number Ten. 'Sorry guys, one at a time. Number Ten – you speak up.'

'I just wonder if at this particular time in the night Jason was just booking the room for him and Sabrina to spend the night in, that the other two just went along for the cocktails but were supposed to leave when the party died down or whatever. I find it hard to believe that he just booked one bed for all four of them to sleep in. I don't think the room was booked for all of them to spend the night there. They failed to get to Newcastle, so they decided to continue the party in the Merchant Suite... maybe the idea was that Zach and Li would get a taxi home or whatever at some point in the night. And y'know... one thing led to another and...'

'And what?' Number Five asks.

'And all three men had sex with Sabrina.'

'Yeah but with her consent or not?' Number Twelve poses.

'Well that's the big question isn't it?' Number Ten says. 'Sabrina insists she said "no", the boys insist that word never came out of her mouth.'

This whole trial boils down to whether or not the jurors believed Sabrina tried to stop the men from having intercourse with her. The defence team tried to argue that everybody consented to group sex; probably agreed upon because of the amount of alcohol that had been consumed by all involved. Gerd Bracken said that Jason, Zach and Li had drunk five or six pints of Heineken each, had three shots of Baby Guinness and then sipped on a cocktail when they got to the Merchant Hotel. He held both his hands up in the court, right in front of the jury and said, 'Yes, my clients are willing to admit they were intoxicated to some extent that evening, they are honest, hard-working men. They want to tell you the truth... and yes, they consumed a lot of alcohol during the night in question. Unlike Sabrina Doyle,' he said, turning to face the claimant. 'She says she wasn't really intoxicated because she mostly drank non-alcoholic wine throughout the evening. But it is a fact that Jason bought Sabrina four glasses of red wine – *alcoholic* red wine – two Baby Guinness shots and a Mango Margarita cocktail. Sabrina Doyle wasn't as sober during the night in question as she would try to lead you to believe,' he continued. 'She consumed, that we know of – there could have been more – twelve units of alcohol. The men also consumed twelve units of alcohol. Each of them were relatively as intoxicated as each other. Sabrina Doyle was not as sober as she would like to lead you to believe.'

Bracken was telling the truth. Given that wine contains more alcohol than lager, even though Sabrina had fewer drinks, she consumed just as much alcohol. Though he did sensationalise Sabrina's testimony. She didn't argue that she was sober during her time on the stand, she just insisted that she drank a mixture of non-alcoholic wine and alcoholic wine. She testified she "may have been drunk, but didn't necessarily feel drunk," during the night in question.

It was an argument Bracken spent too much time on; the jury weren't swayed by it at all.

'So...' Number One says, 'we had a strong movement towards not guilty in our last vote. Are we saying that this argument, about there being only one bed, will lean us back the other way?'

'Doesn't change my mind,' says Number Twelve.

'Me neither,' says Brian. 'There just ishn't enough evidensh.'

Number Six coughs into her wrinkled hand. It's the only noise she's made in about an hour. It makes everybody turn to her; interpreting her cough as her preparation to finally speak. She picks up her glass of water as everybody looks at her, takes a long sip, swirls the water around her mouth and then lets out a gasp.

'I just would like to know... eh... how does the topic of group sex come up? I know I am from a different generation, but is group sex something that is a regular occurrence these days?'

She turns to face Number Seven, not because she is aware that Number Seven is a bit slutty, but because there are only two people in the room who are particularly young looking, and she opted for Number Seven over Number Five, simply because she doesn't fully trust the latter.

'Well... no. I agree that our generation is a little more forthcoming when it comes to sex, but I agree with you, Number Six – I don't know how the topic of group sex would ever raise its head,' Number Seven says. 'How does a guy ask a girl if she would like to have sex, not just with him, but with his two friends, too?'

The jury stew on this notion, each of them playing it over in their heads when they are interrupted by the door unlocking and then re-opening. The young man dressed in all black wheels in a large trolley, then stands to attention.

'These are the chicken dishes,' he says. 'Can you raise your hand if you ordered chicken?'

He then places a dish in front of those whose hands are stretched towards the dim light bulb, before leaving the room again.

'Has anyone, for inshtance...' Brian says before hesitating. He knows he is heading into controversial territory. 'Eh... I know some of you have been very kind to be forthright with your own experienshes, but has anybody here ever... y'know... eh.' Brian blushes, scratches the side of his head before continuing, 'anyone ever participated in group sex?'

The door opens again.

'These are the beef dishes. Can anyone who ordered beef now raise their hand?'

The young man dressed in all black then rounds the table, placing plates in front of those who now have their hand in the air. He then tilts his head forward in a bow as he stands at the top of the table before wheeling his trolley back out and closing the door behind him.

'Can you pass the salt?' Number Five says to Number Eleven. Number Eleven reaches across the table, grabs at the shaker and then passes it along the line.

'The chicken's nice today,' Number Three says.

'Yeah... nicer than it was yesterday, isn't it? Sauce is more sweet or something, isn't it?' says Number Seven.

'I have,' says Number Nine.

Number One stares at her and raises his eyebrows as he takes a bite of his lunch.

'I mean, I have eh... I have had group sex,' she says.

The sound of forks being placed back down on plates clangs around the room.

All eyes turn to Number Nine. She just stares down at her lap, her fork still holding a bite-sized chunk of beef in its prongs.

'And... for the record, we did discuss it beforehand. My eh... husband and his friend eh... Mike... we just...'

Number Nine's real name is Valerie Kinsella, a thirty-six-year-old factory operative who lived most of her life in Co Wexford before moving up to Clondalkin in Dublin two years ago to find employment. She dyes her hair platinum, packs her face with make-up. Her whole look screams insecurity, because that's exactly what she is: insecure. But she's nice; doesn't wallow in self pity; is happy to concede that she's not perfect and never will be. Though she does try to look as perfect as she can; or certainly what she perceives to be 'perfect'. She's actually had threesomes quite a number of times; but is only recalling the first time she did it to her fellow jurors. She doesn't want to come across as too slutty. Though she doesn't regard herself as a slut at all; she and her husband just have a more exciting sex life than most. However, she feels she owes the jury some sort of truth here. Is aware that consensual group sex is a real possibility with regards to the night in question. She believes Sabrina did have sex with all three and then perhaps regretted it the next morning upon reflection. She's believed this from quite an early stage during the trial because she has seen it happen before. She once had sex with a friend of hers and her husband, only for her friend to never speak to her again out of sheer guilt. She genuinely believes Sabrina may have suffered the same – or similar – post-sex shame.

'My husband and I got talking and we discussed what we'd like in the bedroom and so he asked his friend and...' she sighs, stops talking, feels she has shared enough. She wants to get across the fact that – in her experience – threesomes *are* discussed before they occur. They don't just happen by chance.

'Thank you so much for sharing your truth with us,' Number Twelve says. Number One's mouth is slightly ajar, others just eyeball each other or look down at their dinner.

'So... you feel as if the idea of everybody having sex during the night in question would have been discussed, it didn't just happen?' Number Twelve says directly to Number Nine.

She nods her head, then finally bites the beef she'd been holding on her fork for the past two minutes.

'From my experience, yes,' she says, her mouth full.

'I always assumed she was having sex with Jason and then the others just walked into the room, took it upon themselves to get involved,' Number Seven says, 'but its just my own theory. I can't imagine a discussion where Sabrina is asked if she would have sex with all three men and she just agreed to it. I think she was having sex with Jason, then either got caught up in the moment and had sex with the other two... or...'

'Or what?' Number Four asks.

'Or they all took advantage of her, raped her.'

'Why didn't she scream the house down?' Number Four asks, putting his fork aside. 'If she was raped, why wasn't she screaming "no"? That's one thing I can't get right in my head.'

'When girls are being raped, they go numb,' Number Five says.

'And do you know that for a fact?' Number Four asks.

'No!' she snaps back. 'I think I read that somewhere,' she says.

'You *think* you read it shomewhere?' Brian rhetorically asks in a conde-scending tone, almost huffing out a laugh.

Not many around the table were buying Number Five's argument. But she was right. Studies have found that victims of rape are more likely to fall silent during the ordeal rather than fight against their attackers. They can fall limp, waiting on the ordeal to be over and done with. This reaction, albeit quite sensible in a way, goes a long way to blurring the lines between consensual and non-consensual sex. If a victim isn't saying 'no', how is the attacker supposed to understand their reluctance? Of course, another argument can – and often does – ignite from this: if a victim hasn't given consent, why is an attacker having sex with them in the first place?

This is just another element that makes rape cases as convoluted as any criminal case can be. Except, in this trial specifically, the claimant insists she said "no". She admits she didn't scream the hotel room down, admits she didn't fight strongly against her attackers, but is adamant that she said "no". Sabrina claims she said it "at least three times" when one of the three men was penetrating her from behind "while the others looked on". All three men deny this. They say the word "no" never came out of her mouth.

The reporting of this specific part of the trial has led to one of the hashtags that has gone viral over the past couple of weeks via social media: #SheSaidNo. In fact both #MeToo and #SheSaidNo have trended every day of the past fortnight on Twitter in Ireland. Women's voices are echoing around the hills and valleys of the entire nation as this trial dominates the media. The jury aren't aware of this; they all agreed not to check any news during the entirety of their service. But they were made aware of some of the protestors who swamped the entry to Dublin's Criminal Courts over the past two days as both sides delivered their final argument and it became apparent that the jury would soon be deliberating their verdict. Each of the jurors heard the chant 'She Said No' as they were escorted through the back door of the courts earlier this morning. Judge McCormick informed them that they needed to blank out any protests they had overheard, and re-established to them that they were the only ones who could make a proper judgement; that those protesting were not privy to the facts of this case like they were.

'Uuuugh,' Number One says as he rubs at his face. 'No. Such a simple word. Two letters. I guess this is what it all boils down to, isn't it? We've been arguing for...' he hesitates, twists his left wrist, 'almost four hours now. Arguments over who approached who first; did Sabrina give Jason a handjob; did Sabrina follow the men to Copper Face Jacks; why decide to go to Newcastle; why book one hotel room; who looked uncomfortable in the taxis... lots of different arguments. And while all those arguments and points are important in us understanding what happened that night, our judgement essentially boils down to what happened in that hotel room, doesn't it?'

'Yep,' Number Seven says, the 'p' of the word popping out of her mouth. 'What I wouldn't give to have been a fly on the wall in the hotel suite that night.'

Jason swipes the keycard over the reader of the door and it instantly unlocks. He pushes at it, walks in ahead of me.

Wow.

I guess this is how the other half live. When I stay in hotels, I barely have enough space in the rooms to walk either side of the bed. But I can't even see the bed in this place yet. There's a huge plasma screen on the wall, facing two lush grey sofas. A bar area. A kitchen. The smell of the fresh tulips is subtle, yet it's the overpowering scent. The hotel rooms I normally stay in are damp, musty. I walk towards the tulips standing in a gorgeous Waterford crystal vase on a desk on the far side of the room near the big window, take in all of their freshness through my nose, then read the message attached.

'Welcome to the Merchant Penthouse Suite. Enjoy your stay.'

I watch as Jason walks towards a huge wooden door, almost the entire width of the room before he slides it open. The bedroom. It looks so cosy, densely lit. Almost romantic. I walk towards the room and as I do, I can feel Zach staring at me. He's still into me, there's no doubt about that. He probably envisages getting into this bed with me, but that's not going to happen. This room is for me and Jason. Zach and Li can sort themselves out.

There is such a peaceful presence in the whole suite; the quiet, the subtle lighting, the smell of the flowers. An excited twinge twists in my stomach. I'm not excited about the sex, I'm excited about the prospective lifestyle I could be living if I become Jason's girlfriend. Jaysus, even Jason's wife. Imagine. Mrs Sabrina Kenny.

I shake my head. I can't get too far ahead of myself. In fact I'm still trying to figure out if he's on the same page as me tonight, let alone years down the line. I thought he was a while ago, but he keeps turning from hot to cold. I strain my eyes towards him, trying to read his thoughts without making it obvious I'm checking him out. I watch as he runs his hand over the bed sheets, watch as he walks out of the bedroom towards the sofas, watch as he lounges down into one of them and grabs at the TV remote control. Only then does he look at me. He winks. Then turns away. I'm pretty sure his coldness is calculated. He's trying to play it cool, trying to not come on to me too heavily, too eagerly. He intrigues me. His cold isn't like Eddie's cold. When Eddie was in bad humour, it was transparent. He didn't hide it. He held no intrigue for me whatsoever. I didn't feel any sort of loss after I'd dumped him. I only felt excited. Not just because I was starting a new life without him, but because I was starting a new professional life. My new job took up all of my time. Eddie was pretty much forgotten within a week of me telling him it was all over. Once Lorna filled me in on her entrapment of Eddie, she offered me a job.

'I need a hot brunette,' she told me. 'I've got to know you well over the past few weeks and genuinely feel you could be an asset to the business.'

I didn't know what to say. I didn't think I'd have the nerve to carry out the work. But I accepted her offer later that day for the simple reason that I felt it would be more exciting than handing out discount vouchers which was all my work seemed to consist of those days. Besides, the money on offer was too good to turn down. I've made thirty-eight thousand euro since starting with Lorna in the space of fifteen months. I'd never come even close to earning that amount as a model or in marketing. It's not a life-changing amount, but it's consistent and it's fulfilling.

I've carried out seventeen entrapment cases for her, including Niall tonight, and my statistics lie at ten green lights, seven red lights. I've had to break ten women's hearts with my findings. I, rather pretentiously, assumed no man would turn down the advances of somebody who looked like me, or indeed Lorna. But that's not the case at all; some men are genuinely faithful to their other halves. And I think that's what gives me the most fulfilment in my job. The knowledge that great men do exist. Somewhere.

It's weird – I get my kicks out of being turned down, rejected. I almost fist pumped the air earlier when Niall told me he was 'loved up'. I'm actually looking forward to writing up my report for Lorna tomorrow, ahead of meeting his fiancée on Monday evening to pass on the positive news. She'll be delighted. And I'll be delighted for her. She's a lucky girl.

Li motions over to Jason to turn down the volume on the TV as he walks to the door.

'Just in here,' he says to the waiter, 'leave them on the table.'

The waiter places a large circular tray – on which sits four yellow-coloured iced Margaritas – on top of the coffee table in front of Jason and then stands up, staring straight ahead.

'Oh,' Jason says, patting down the pockets of his trousers. 'We eh... don't carry cash on us, can you add a tip to the bill?'

I intervene, pulling my purse out of my bag, retrieving a tenner from it.

'Here you are... forget adding it to the bill.'

The young man smiles at me, folds the ten euro note neatly into his waistcoat pocket and leaves us to it. As soon as he's gone, Jason re-highers the volume on the TV, then picks up one of the glasses.

'To the boys,' he says.

Both Li and Zach reach for glasses of their own, before I move between them and pick up mine.

'And Sabrina,' Li says as we all clink.

'Yeah, and Sabrina,' Jason says, before staring over the rim of his glass at me while he downs his first sip. He looks menacingly at me. Maybe he's trying to be sexy; trying to motion to me that he's ready for action. He's not being presumptuous. I have told him, after all, that I'm horny, that I'm up for this.

I look behind me, eyeball the bedroom and then look back at him. He smiles at me; gets the gist. A wave of excitement runs itself down my spine. I can't believe I'm going to have sex with a celebrity.

I stroll into the room, and head straight for one of the big grey couches in front of me. I could actually spread out on it at this stage, lift me legs up, lie my head down, fall asleep. But I'm actually looking forward to the cocktails we ordered. That was the only reason I came here. I think.

I watch Sabrina as she walks around the room, taking it all in. She's probably never been in a suite this impressive before. I wonder what her life has been like; her family, her upbringing, her career. She's really cool, really attractive. It'd be quite unfortunate if she hasn't had these type of luxuries before, but I get the impression she hasn't. She's practically purring as she takes in the entire suite. I guess just because you've got the looks, doesn't mean you also get the luck.

Which is quite funny. It seems as if she has everything, yet I bet she's not as happy in life as my Niamh. And poor Niamh, even I have to admit it, didn't get the luck when it comes to looks. But that just goes to show. All these things we worry about as kids such as what we look like to other people it means sweet fuck all in the grand scheme of things. The main goal of life should be maintaining a level of happiness. But we seem to relate happiness in a bizarre way. If you looked at Jason from a distance, you would assume he has everything: fame, wealth, adoration – yet he's the most miserable man I know. Sabrina looks as if God personally designed her, yet there's a sadness behind her eyes. Then take me and Niamh; we've no money at all – just a very basic income that affords us a small flat in Drimnagh – and we certainly weren't personally designed by any God, yet we are as giddy and as happy as any people we know. I don't think there is any correlation with the things we equate to happiness with actual happiness.

There's a knock on the door. I swing my legs off the couch and go to answer it. A young man in a white shirt enters and places the tray with four cocktails on it onto the glass coffee table. Jason tells him he should add the tip to the entire bill, but Sabrina intervenes, handing him a tenner. Before the young man leaves I already have my cocktail in my hand. It looks just like I'd hoped it would – a large glass of slushed ice.

'To the boys,' Jason says holding out his glass.

'And Sabrina,' I say, before clinking. I stare at her, wait on her to acknowledge the fact that I included her in our little gang, but she's too busy eyeballing Jason. Now that we're in the hotel room, I get the impression she's ready to forget the fact that me and Zach are even here. That's fine by me. If they want to go into the bedroom and fuck, I'm okay sipping on my cocktail out here.

I pick up the TV remote and turn the volume even higher than Jason did on the music channels. I assume this will distract me. Yet I can't help but turn my eyes to Sabrina every now and then. I'm beginning to feel really guilty. I haven't fancied anyone else since I met Niamh. Yet here I am, weeks after finding out the love of my life is pregnant and just weeks before I'm about to ask her to marry me, getting distracted by a hot brunette in a white jumpsuit.

I decide to pick up my phone and flick through pictures of my girlfriend while I sip on my cocktail. This'll help ease the guilt.

Niamh's got the same colour hair as Sabrina. Only Niamh's isn't natural. She dyes her hair dark brown because she hates her mousy natural colour. But hair colour is the only thing they share in common. Niamh's a lot shorter than Sabrina. She's certainly a lot wider. I'm pretty sure a hundred out of a hundred blokes would pick Sabrina over Niamh. But as I stare at pictures of my soon-to-be fiancée I know just who I'd pick. Sabrina might have the tight waistline, the perfect skin and a sheen of light running right down her cleavage. But I bet she's not as easy to live with as my Niamh is. Niamh never argues, never creates any sort of rifts between us. There is no such thing as drama in my life.

As I flick through my photos, the guilt seems to be dissipating. My body begins to fill with relief. I was genuinely getting worried how much I was beginning to fancy this girl. I almost felt as if I was going behind Niamh's back just looking at her. It was a weird, dark feeling that I don't ever want to creep up on me again. When I ask Niamh to marry me next month; that's it. I want one of those marriages where the man doesn't even look at another woman. I'm going to be faithful to her for the rest of our lives.

I begin to cheer up and start singing along to the Little Mix song playing on the TV as I throw the straw out of my glass and begin to swig down my cocktail. Jesus, I wish I had been drinking these all night. They are a million times more refreshing than a pint of bloody beer. I begin to rock my hips back and forth wondering whether it's the alcohol in this Margarita that's making me feel so good or the release of the guilt I had been feeling for fancying Sabrina. Then I watch as Jason takes Sabrina by the hand and walks her towards the bedroom. Suddenly I stop dancing, stop singing. The good feeling engulfing me suddenly dies and I find myself back on the couch, placing my straw back in my glass and stretching out my feet so I can fall back into a slouched position. Jesus... I think I feel jealous.

Jason

Zach has been trying to create a party atmosphere. As soon as we got in, he paced around the room, looking for signs of whether or not Sabrina is interested in a threesome and then decided to turn on MTV, blaring it as loud as the remote control would allow him to. Maybe he wants to get us all up dancing, hoping that will lead into the bedroom.

I'm not sure how I'm feeling. It's unusual I would read a girl wrong like this. I'm not sure why I assumed Sabrina was different to the rest of them. Perhaps it was Li. He seemed to oversell her to me; telling me that if I showed her my house in Newcastle that she'd eventually fall for me. I'm beginning to think that Li is more fixated on Sabrina than me and Zach are. At this stage, all Zach and I want from her is a bit of pleasure. Li seems to want to befriend her, to make her part of our lives. After the text I just read on her phone, I've no interest in ever seeing Sabrina again. She's here for one reason and one reason only. It's such a shame she's a slut, she really doesn't need to be.

I watch her as she sips on her cocktail. Jesus, she really is gorgeous. Perfect looking I would say; head-to-toe perfect. I can't find a flaw in her appearance. The only flaw I found was in her phone. If she hadn't whispered that into my ear about half-an-hour ago when we were back in the airport, I wouldn't be feeling so low right now. It's hugely frustrating but I find myself in a position no different to any other night out. Some hot girl wants to bang me, and I ain't gonna say no. I've had this assumption in my head for the past year or so that sex will relieve me of my pain. But I'm not sure I even enjoy sex anymore. I don't think I've enjoyed sex since I last made love to Jessica.

I know I felt down – depressed – long before she and I finished, but it wasn't really strong in those days. I didn't mope around like I do now. I was only down because the football I was playing was quite shite and the club I was playing for seemed to lack any ambition. If Jessica had stayed with me, had have supported me through it, I think I'd be fine by now. But we finished things around about the same time Sunderland were refusing to negotiate a new contract with me. I knew I was losing my girlfriend and my career at the same time.

I tried to make up for my miserableness by donating more to YouKnight and hanging around with some of their patrons. But it didn't really fix my head. I have no idea how I feel. Or why I feel. I don't know whether the

197

guilt of us hitting Caitlin all those years ago is the reason my head is fucked up.

Bizarrely, my life didn't become any worse for almost killing her. In fact it rapidly improved in the years straight after. I lived out my dreams, became a rich man in the process. Only now, as my life is slowing down and I am waking from that dream, am I starting to suffer from all of the guilt football had steered me away from. I always thanked God for looking after me following The Secret, but I'm beginning to think now that God barely even knows I exist. He has seven billion people to look after on earth. Why was I ever so arrogant to believe he was looking down on me? I was arrogant to genuinely believe that he not only let me get away with almost killing Caitlin and running away, but also allowed me to become a professional footballer thereafter.

I pick up the crucifix from my chest, stare at it and then sneer. I genuinely don't know what to believe anymore. I've never been more confused in my entire life. I swig at my cocktail, then place the glass back down and gurn at its bitterness. Sabrina catches my eye. I play the words she whispered into my ear back at the airport.

I'm up for this. I'm horny.

I feel my dick twitch a bit. Fuck it. There's no way I'm turning my back on her. I'm not going to deny myself the chance to have sex with a perfect looking girl just because she didn't turn out to be as innocent as I first assumed she was. I'm going to peel that jumpsuit off her, have her bounce up and down on me until I shoot a load. I know I'll feel like shit straight after it, as I do every time I have a one-night stand, but I'll enjoy it while it lasts. I think I will anyway. Though I'm wary of Zach. I want to have Sabrina to myself, at least until I'm done. If she's up for having sex with him after she's had sex with me, fine. I genuinely won't care. But I'm not interested in the whole threesome thing.

I fake-laugh at Zach and Li jumping around the hotel room, attempting to get some sort of party started. While they're distracted, I walk towards Sabrina, take her by the hand and lead her to the bedroom.

'You said you were horny, right?' I say as I turn around and sweep the doors shut.

Yes! I thought I was the only one in partyin' mood. But Li lifts his lazy ass from the couch and begins to sing and dance; shouting out the wrong lyrics as he normally does when he's in good humour.

Jason's barely said a word since we got here. I think he's nervous about the threesome. I wonder if he's nervous about the actual act of the threesome or whether it's because he doesn't know how to raise the subject with Sabrina. I often wonder how these roasting sessions normally play out among footballers. Do they ask girls straight out if they want as many dicks as they can fit in, or does it all happen naturally? Does one guy start having sex with a girl and the rest just join in when they feel like it?

Jason's probably playing the same shit out in his head. But you'd think he'd know more about this than I do. He hangs around footballers on a regular basis. He has to know how these things go down. I'm well aware he hasn't taken part on any roastings before, but he must have heard a hundred stories in the dressing-room.

I don't take my eyes off him as he walks towards Sabrina, takes her by the hand and leads her into the bedroom. Then I stare over at Li, assume we'll just keep the party going while Jason fills Sabrina in on what's gonna happen. But Li's already given up.

He plonks himself back down on the sofa, staring through the television, not necessarily at it.

'C'mon Li,' I scream over at him. 'Give me more of them dance moves!'

He doesn't answer me, he just continues to stare into space.

I pick up the remote, turn the volume down on the TV and then plonk myself beside him. I'll play it cool; give Sabrina and Jason a few minutes before I go in.

'Penny for 'em,' I say to Li.

'Huh?' he says,

'Penny for your thoughts, mate.'

'Ah,' he says while trying to sit back upright. 'I don't know. Bit of a weird night, isn't it?'

I just nod my head; half-wondering what's going on behind those closed doors, half-wondering what the hell Li is going on about. He can be quite innocent and naïve, can Li. I bet he doesn't know what's going on.

'It was supposed to be a night where the three of us catch up, but it seems as if the whole night became about her,' he says, nodding his head towards the bedroom door.

'Our nights out always become about women,' I say, elbowing his shoulder.

'Aren't we all a bit old for that shit now, though?' he says. 'I mean you're married, I'm getting married. We're all in our mid-thirties now... it just seems a little... I don't know, juvenile. I really wanted to have a good night with my two best mates, share my good news. I feel like my news has just been sorta... I don't know... almost forgotten about.'

Jesus. I've never known Li to be the self-pitying type. I don't recall him ever making the conversation about him. This is the sort of deep shite Jason normally comes out with. Me, me, me. Sad, sad, sad. Li is normally the one that shakes this sort of shite from Jason. Maybe I got it wrong. Maybe Li understands exactly what's going on here. And maybe he doesn't agree with it – thinks we're pushing things a bit too far.

'I'm going to be a daddy,' he says, looking up at me.

'What?'

'Yeah, Niamh's only two months in. She's due in the new year.'

'Man!' I say as I get to my feet. I hold out my hand for him to shake, then I fall back on top of him, squeezing him as hard as I can.

'I'm so happy for you, Li. You're going to be a great dad.' And I mean it. He will be. There's no doubt about that. 'So, you're gonna be a married man with a kid next year huh?'

He smiles at me. But it's a weak smile.

'What's up with you the last hour or so... why ye so glum, Li?'

He sighs, then shrugs his shoulders.

'Maybe I'm just tired. Maybe I should just go home to Niamh. I should have gone home straight from the airport. Probably shouldn't have even gone to the airport, that was a shite idea. How did I get so drunk to even think we could get to England using our bloody driving licenses?'

He puffs out a fake-laugh.

'Hold on, it was *your* idea to go to Newcastle?' I ask.

'I was just tryna cheer Jason up. He said he wanted to impress Sabrina, so I suggested going back to his place, showing her everything he has to offer.'

I stare at Li, then scratch at the stubble under my chin.

'But... she's not that into him.'

'Huh?' he says, twisting his head to stare at the closed bedroom door. 'Looks to me as if she's pretty into him right now.'

'Nah man, she's just interested in sex. She's gaggin' for it. I'm gonna fuck her meself.'

Li looks at me, then refocuses his eyes as if he can't believe quite what he's looking at.

'Yeah, she's up for it,' I say. 'She told me, told Jason. That's why Jason booked the room, she's up for a threesome.'

'Bollocks,' he says, his jaw slightly open.

'Honestly,' I say as I get up from the sofa again.

'Doesn't make any sense. Why did she insist I come back to the hotel room too, then? She said she wouldn't come here if I didn't.'

I walk towards the bedroom door, as if I'm desperate to prove Li wrong.

'Maybe she wants your little Korean dick too,' I say before I slide the bedroom doors open and step inside.

Jason grabs at my hand without even looking at me and leads me towards the bedroom. My stomach turns itself over. I know that's down to nerves, but there's also some excitement wrapped up in there somewhere. I'm about to have sex with a celebrity.

'You said you were horny, right?' he whispers to me as he sweeps the doors shut. The noise of Li and Zach singing along to Little Mix is instantly drowned out.

'Eh... yeah,' I say, biting at my bottom lip in an attempt to look sexy. Then I swallow. Hard. That's particularly unsexy, I'm sure. But I couldn't help it. The nerves are getting the better of me.

'Let's get it done then,' Jason says.

'Done?' I ask.

'Yeah... lets have sex,' he says as he moves closer to me, placing a hand around the back of my neck and pulling me in for a kiss. And I do kiss him, take his tongue into my mouth as I stew over what he's just said. Then I pull away from him.

'Get it *done*... as in get it done and over with?'

He stares at me, then squints his eyes to look past me.

'I eh... didn't mean it like that, but you eh... you said you were horny, that you wanted to have sex with me... so, here I am, here you are and here,' he says patting at the duvet cover, 'is a bed.'

Then he kisses me again. I don't pull away. I let his tongue circle my mouth again as it dawns on me that I'm nothing special to Jason Kenny whatsoever. I'm just his Friday night girl for this week. I should have known all along. What was I thinking? Why the hell did I think I'd mean anything to him?

I swing him around, then release from the kiss and push him onto the bed. I genuinely flick my thoughts between jumping on top of him and turning around and opening the door to leave. His smile makes my mind up for me. I deserve a bit of fun. I need to stop being a prude. A celebrity is lying on a bed waiting on me to have sex with him. Why am I even hesitating? I owe myself this. I owe the devil on my shoulder this little victory. Only two dicks in my twenty-five years? That's quite sad. In fact, it's worse than quite sad. It's pathetic.

I place a knee either side of Jason's hips and straddle him, bending down to take his tongue back into my mouth. Suddenly, he's tugging at the zip on the back of my jumpsuit. The shoulders of my suit release and I actually feel a bit of relief as my boobs pop out. They'd been threatening to do that all night. I no longer have to pull at the V to make sure they're tucked in. They're out there now. Free. And they're all yours, Jason Kenny. He doesn't hesitate. He snuggles his face in between them, proving no man, not even one who must get it on a regular basis, has any patience when it comes to tits.

I try to shake my head of any niggling thoughts. I just want to be in the moment. I want to enjoy it. I don't need to overthink it. I don't need to worry whether Jason and I will ever see each other again. Though I'm pretty certain we won't. I guess he's made himself clear. I'm the girl he has chosen to have sex with tonight. I may as well try to enjoy it. Though I have to say, I feel a little disappointed when I unbutton his shirt and place my hands onto his torso in search of the six-pack I assumed any professional athlete would have. But he just has a regular hairy belly. It's nothing special. It's not quite as fat as Eddie's but it's a far cry from the chiselled athletic body I had assumed I'd be grappling with tonight. I shake my head again... I'm such an idiot for overthinking. I genuinely feel that's why I don't enjoy my life. I'm never *in the moment*. Even during the most special times in my life, I'm always too concerned about what others are thinking; about what this means for my future; my reputation. I'm sure the years I spent being judged as a model have affected my whole outlook on life. I always assume I'm being judged, being talked about. I'm too self-conscious. That's why I take myself too seriously; why I don't have enough fun, enough sex.

I suck in through my teeth as I feel a pinch, but the pain doesn't last too long. Literally just one second. Now that Jason is grinding slowly from behind me, it feels right. His is probably the most perfect fit out of the three I've had inside me. Men seem to be obsessed with size. From my experience now, of having three different sizes altogether, average length is what's best.

I force out a little groan, just to let him know I'm enjoying it, but I'm wary of being too loud. I don't want to alert Zach and Li from their little party. Though I'm sure they know what we're up to. They're not stupid. I'm enjoying this, enjoying the fact that I'm being a bit slutty; that I have lightened up; that I'm being taken from behind by a guy I just met a few hours ago. I don't feel any guilt, in fact quite the opposite. I think I'm actually proud of myself. I don't think I've ever been this excited. I laugh as Jason continues to thrust inside me; a laugh aimed at myself. It's the first time I've ever appreciated a bold decision that I've made. I feel myself getting wetter. Enjoying every moment.

Then the door slides open. It's Zach.

'Can I join in?' he asks. I just stare at him. I don't know why I'm not disgusted. Don't know why I haven't rolled over, pulled the duvet up to hide my naked body. I haven't said a word in response by the time he walks closer to me.

'Sabrina... do you mind if I join in?' he repeats.

I look over my shoulder, at Jason. He shrugs.

A threesome? Jesus. I'd literally be doubling the amount of penises I've had in my entire life in just one night. Isn't this supposed to be a lot of girls' fantasies? Is it supposed to be mine?

I bite at my bottom lip again, stare down at the mattress and then back up at Zach.

♦

THE YOUNG MAN dressed in all black is assisted by a young woman dressed in the same attire as he removes all remnants of lunch from the table. When they're done, the young man dressed in all black turns to the jurors and offers a slight bow again before he and his colleague shuffle out the door, shutting it tight behind them.

The jury members, left alone for the first time in ten minutes, don't immediately return to their deliberations. Number Eleven is discussing *Game of Thrones* episodes with Number Ten. Brian and Number Twelve are locked in a political debate about the state of the education system. Number Seven and Number Four are talking about their own lives. Number Five, Number Three, Number Nine and Number Eight are discussing the court system, deliberately avoiding any mention of the specific trial they are all currently serving on. Number Six has just been tuning in and out of each of the conversations happening around her as she chews the inside of her cheek. She's starting to get tired. They have been deliberating for four hours and fifteen minutes now, including their discussions through lunch, and it all seems to be getting on top of her.

Number Six's real name Cynthia Lafferty, a sixty-eight year old from Crumlin in Dublin. She was relishing being called for jury duty, even though she could have been excused on account of her age. She's almost addicted to American crime shows; felt being on a jury would be just like being an extra in an episode of *Law and Order*. Number Six has been a widow for six years; her husband Arthur finally failing to uphold his diet of fry-ups and pints of Guinness, collapsed to a massive heart attack right in front of her one Friday morning. She has two middle-aged sons who call on her more regularly than they did prior to their father's passing, but it doesn't make up for the loss. She's excited to be involved in this case – it gives her something to do – but she's been more than happy to keep herself to herself. She's been content to watch what's going on around her. As if it was on a screen. She remains in the guilty camp, though recent arguments, particularly over lunch, have led to her feeling that she's just not up to date with modern generations. She's beginning to think group sex is a phenomenon she just doesn't – and never will – understand. She thought Sabrina was the innocent party because no woman in their right mind would willingly have sex with three men in one night, but her belief has been shaken by her realisation that she can't fully comprehend Sabrina; that she can't fully comprehend the modern twenty-something. They are a far cry from the twenty-somethings Number Six knew when she was twenty-something.

The separate conversations hush when the young man dressed in all black re-enters the room.

'Now, I will lead you back to the jury room,' he says, pointing his full hand towards the door he'd just walked through. Each of the jurors pick up their notes, shuffle towards the door and then out on to the first corridor. They remain silent as they turn two corners before finding themselves inside their deliberation sanctuary again. Each of them sit back down in the exact same seat they'd occupied prior to lunch. It was akin to the habit they subconsciously adopted in the courtroom; every day the jurors sat in the same seat they had done from day one, even though that wasn't a necessity.

The young man dressed in all black lightly clears his throat to court everybody's attention and then speaks up.

'It is now two-ten p.m.,' he says. 'Deliberations will continue until four p.m. today unless a unanimous verdict is reached. If not, I will be back at four p.m. to dismiss you from deliberations for the day and escort you elsewhere. If that is the case, you will all reconvene here at nine-thirty a.m. tomorrow. Does anybody have any questions?'

Number Five raises her hand and the young man dressed in all black nods at her.

'Is the judge expecting us to deliver a verdict today?'

Brian tuts, then answers her question before the young man dressed in all black has a chance to.

'Of course not,' he says. 'This young man ishn't here to answer on behalf of the judge. He's jusht talking about our itinerary; when we finish, when we restart tomorrow. He'sh not here to answer questions like that.'

Number Five swings her jaw, just about stopping herself from retaliating to Brian's condescending tone.

There are no strict time limits on jury deliberations when it comes to these kind of trials. A lot of rape verdicts are delivered within a matter of hours by jurors, but other deliberations can go on for days should the case be specifically complex. The Sabrina Doyle versus Jason Kenny, Zach Brophy and Li Xiang trial does have it's own perplexities, but it is far from as convoluted as some rape trials can get. The three defendants' lawyers will see an early verdict as a positive; as they will assume that the jury came to a quick resolution of innocence on their clients' behalf. But the time for such optimism will be just about passing them by at this stage. Both sides will be now stewing over the likely reality that the jury will not deliver a verdict today.

Gerd Bracken – and his team of defence lawyers – as well as Jonathan Ryan would have been aware that the jury requested to watch the CCTV footage of Jason and Sabrina exiting and then re-entering the Hairy Lemon either side of the 'handjob' argument as well as sought the transcripts of rickshaw rider Donagh Scott's testimony this morning. These jury actions could be seen as a positive for the defence, but Bracken is way too experienced in his field to get carried away by such thoughts. He's been through this rigmarole many times before. He'll only know the juror's decisions as soon as they walk back into the courtroom. His tell-tale sign is that jurors who are about to reveal an innocent verdict to the court normally look to the defendants upon re-entering the jury dock, while a jury about to reveal a guilty verdict will shy away from looking at the defendants.

'So... inside the hotel suite,' Number One says after the young man dressed in all black closes the door behind him and leaves them to it. 'I mean... what can we say? We know for a fact that all three men had intercourse with Sabrina, so the big question is; did she give consent?'

'Sorry,' that'sh not the argument at all,' Brian says. 'The argument ish not whether she gave consent, but did she specifically *not* give consent.'

'Huh?' Number Five says, overemphasising her word as if she's a stroppy teenager, her face all contorted. 'Wha' you talkin' bout?'

'There'sh a considerable difference between offering consent and specifically not offering consent,' Brian says.

'He's right,' Number Twelve says, backing up the politician. 'Nobody specifically seeks consent, do they? I mean, when we're having sex, we don't stop kissing and then ask the person if it's okay if we have sex with them, do we? We just... ye know... go with the flow.'

Number Five's face is still contorted. She doesn't fully comprehend what both men are trying to explain to her.

Number Six turns to Number Five and offers a sympathetic pursing of the lips.

'What Brian and Number Twelve are trying to say is, our argument is not whether Sabrina said "yes" to sex, it's whether or not she said "no" to sex. She didn't have to vocalise her consent. She had to vocalise a lack of consent.'

Number Five turns out her bottom lip, then nods her head slowly.

'But... I mean, how do we do that?' she says.

'That'sh exactly it,' Brian says. 'That's what I've been shaying all along. We can not and will not know what happened in that hotel suite; we simply haven't been offered any evidensh whatsoever that proves beyond all reashonable doubt that Sabrina said "no".'

Number Five understood most of what Brian was saying to her, but he lost her with his use of that fucking phrase 'reasonable doubt' again.

'We can all take a guess at what happened next. But none of us can know for certain and that is why we have to find the men not guilty,' Number Twelve says, his face sporting a look that could only be described as smug.

'But you've been not guilty from the start,' Number Five says. 'You're just driving your own opinion onto others and—'

'I've been not guilty from the start, Number Five,' Number Twelve says, raising his voice over hers, 'because I knew all along that it all came down to this; the fact that none of us in this room knows what happened in that hotel suite and that the prosecution didn't do enough to convince us that their version of events happened beyond reasonable doubt. It's Sabrina's word against theirs. And listen, I feel sorry for Sabrina. I do. But we can't lock three men up for ten years each just because we feel sorry for someone.'

He was right, albeit on the high side with his projection of a possible prison sentence. Jason, Zach and Li are most likely to face somewhere between five-to-ten years behind bars if this jury deliver a guilty verdict. Seven years is the average stretch handed down to a rapist in Ireland, a number that has been ever-so-slightly increasing over the past decade. With all three men on trial now aged thirty-five, it was certainly conceivable that they wouldn't be free men for their fortieth birthdays should they be found to be guilty of this charge. If it is a case that they're found guilty, it will be Judge Delia McCormick's decision on how much time they will serve. Her reputation points to her being a judge who tends to land somewhere just over the average; if she was to go that way in this case, she would be likely to sentence all three men to eight years in prison, even though they have all had clean criminal records up until this point in their lives.

'Let's discuss what happened in the hotel room, rather than just dismiss it out of hand, Number Twelve,' Number Eleven says calmly. Number

Twelve holds up his hands in agreement and then looks towards the Head Juror.

'So the defendants claim that group sex wasn't discussed at all... that Jason and Sabrina began to have sex and then Sabrina became open to the other two men joining in, that's right isn't it?' the Head Juror offers to the table.

'Well, yesh, in summary,' says Brian.

'Do we perhaps need a transcript of Jason and Zach's testimonies to make sure we get this right?' Number One offers up.

Number Ten barks the loudest "yes" in the room, bringing all eyes towards her. 'Let's get the transcript of Sabrina's testimony as well. If we're going to analyse this case as best we can, I think we'll be doing ourselves a service by having their words in front of us. Get twelve copies of each.'

Nobody around the table opposes this course of action. Number One reaches for the button in front of him on the table and as he requests the specific transcripts based around activities in the hotel room, Number Twelve brings up a piece of Jason's testimony that rang true to him during the trial to Number Ten who is sitting next to him. He waits until Number One has finished with his request to the court's assistant and then raises his point to the whole table.

'One thing that stuck out to me from Jason's time on the stand about what exactly happened in the hotel room was when he said something like "Sabrina is a lovely girl, I don't know why she is making this claim, but she only made it in the aftermath".'

'Yep,' Brian says, 'Aftermath is definitely a word he said on the shtand. I have that written in my notes here. He says Sabrina never made a claim of rape there and then. She must have only come up with the notion that she was raped after she left the room.'

'Yes,' I remember him saying that,' says Number Eleven. 'But I also remember her saying she said "no" three times.'

Rumbles of debate strike up from all sides of the table. Number One has to stand, hold his hand in the air and ask for silence. He then lets out a deep breath and sits back down just as a knock rattles on the door.

Number Nine gets up, answers the door again and takes the paperwork from the young man dressed in all black. She flicks through it as she paces the three steps back towards her seat and then stretches to hand them over to Number One.

Number One licks his thumb, then walks around the table, peeling off pages from the bundle and placing them in front of each juror. When he's done, he sits back down, clears his throat and then stares around the room.

'Whose testimony shall we start with?' he asks.

'Start with Sabrina,' Number Five says.

Number One nods his head, shuffles his paperwork until he finds Sabrina's typed script and then speed reads quietly through it.

'Okay, so if we start half-way down the page here... let me see, the fourth paragraph on the first page of Sabrina's testimony where it says "Jason took me by the hand..." – does everybody see that?'

The jurors muffle a yes and then Number One looks across the table.

'Would you like to read it, Number Eleven?' he offers. Number Eleven nods, then clears her throat.

'"Jason took me by the hand and led me to the bedroom. I had a feeling what he was after, but I didn't stop him. I didn't say 'no' – not at this point. As I already said, I fancied Jason initially. We began to kiss on the bed and he took off my suit and began to fondle my breasts before we started to make love".'

Sabrina had told the police initially that she had had consensual sex with Jason before all three men ended up having non-consensual sex with her.

'"Then Zach walked into the room and started to touch me and I felt really uncomfortable. I wasn't sure what he was doing. I didn't want him to touch me. I wanted to tell him to go away, to leave me and Jason alone but... I don't know what came over me. He wanted to kiss me and I told him no. But suddenly he was up on the bed, was having sex with me while Jason just stood there and watched and I told him, I said 'no'. But nobody did anything. And then Li came in and did the same. I said 'no', I said 'no' three times. At least three times. But one of them just grabbed my hair, shoved my face into the mattress and continued to have sex with me. By the end I didn't know who was having sex with me when or even how many times any of them had sex with me, it all turned into a blur... but I know – I swear to you – I said no, I said no many times. It was hurting me. I hated it. Every minute of it. I just wanted them to stop".'

Number Eleven stops reading and looks up at the table, her eyes moist, as if what she's just read were her own words.

'Thank you for reading that, Number Eleven,' Number One says. 'So – Sabrina explicitly says she said 'no' and said that word 'at least three times'. Do we need to analyse anything she specifically says here?'

'Under cross-examination, didn't Bracken really push her on the argument that all three men were never in the room; no group sex really took part, that she had sex with the three men separately?' Number Eight asks.

'Yes, he did. And Sabrina stood firm. She never froze or hesitated on the stand, even though he did his best to push her buttons. But we can discuss the cross examinations in a second. Let's just look at her exact testimony of what she said occurred. Do we need to analyse anything specifically that she said here?'

'We only need to analyse the fact that her words aren't consistent to what Jason and Zach said on the stand – that's essentially what we're looking into,' Number Twelve says.

'True,' says Number One. 'So do you mind reading Jason's statement there...'

Number One shuffles through his paperwork again, but Brian beats him to it.

'Fifth paragraph down, where he says he shtarted to make love to Sabrina.'

'Yes... thank you, Brian,' says Number One, before raising his eyebrows towards Number Twelve.

'Okay,' Number Twelve says before taking a deep breath. '"I was making love to Sabrina when Zach walked into the bedroom. Sabrina wasn't shocked. She looked up at him and he genuinely asked if it was okay if he joined in. I mean... I wasn't happy about it. I didn't say anything, but Sabrina nodded her head. I thought it was a bit odd, this had never happened to me before. I was also a little bit disappointed. So when Zach started to make love to her, I snuck out of the room. I didn't stand there and watch as she says I did. And then me and Li just watched tele for a few minutes, before Li went to the bedroom. And... I don't know what happened. I wasn't there. But I didn't hear anyone screaming 'no' or shouting 'no'. Sabrina made love to all of us that night. I don't believe she felt at any point in the night that she was raped. I think she only came to that conclusion the next day. Sabrina is a lovely girl so I don't know why she is making this claim, but she only made it in the aftermath. I'm certain of that".'

'This is my take on it,' Number Eight says. 'Always has been. I think Sabrina only felt she was raped after the fact. She went home, thought it all through and felt a bit guilty about what happened, then rang the police.'

A slight ripple of argument threatens to erupt but Number Twelve puts an end to it within seconds.

'Let's just read Zach's version and then I think it might be an appropriate time after that for us all to get our points across,' he says.

'Yes, in fact after we read this, it may be an appropriate time for us to have a verdict vote,' Number One says.

His idea was met with a nodding of heads around the table.

'Okay... so let's read Zach's statement from the time he walked into the bedroom.'

00:05

Jason

I reach around Sabrina's back and fumble until I find the zip. Within seconds I'm snuggling in between her tits, licking at that sheen that runs right through her cleavage; something I'd been looking forward to doing all night. It was all so tempting, on show like that. I'm horny, but I'm also really disappointed – sad almost.

I'm not necessarily angry with her. I'm angry with myself.

I can't understand how I can continue to be this gullible; this stupid. I've been a celebrity for seventeen years. I should know that women aren't interested in me... not the real me.

As I'm pulling her jumpsuit off, I make a mental note to book a session with my therapist as soon as I get home. So much for having a break back in Dublin to sort my head out. Right now I feel as low as I ever have. Still, my depression doesn't seem to affect my dick.

I turn Sabrina around, into my favourite position and without any fore-play at all, I enter her. This is nothing new. When girls make it obvious to me that they're interested in one thing, what's the point in wasting time on foreplay? The only time I got engaged in that sorta thing was with Jessica. I actually used to even enjoy foreplay with her. I miss her so much. I know we argued a lot, especially towards the end, but Jesus, I'd give anything to be having an argument with her right now if it meant she'd still be in my bed when I wake up in the morning. I think it's worse to be lonely when you have lots of money. I have so much to share with someone, but nobody to share it with. When I wake up in my house in Newcastle, I can almost hear the silence. The gaff is so big that I rattle around in it. It dismays me that people equate money to happiness. It's just not the case at all. Mo' money, mo' problems is definitely accurate. Well, it is for me anyway. I hate that my friends think I should just go out and find a girlfriend, as if it's easier for me than it is for anyone else. Surely it's harder for me than the regular Joe. Tonight's a great example of that. I thought I'd met somebody interested in me, not just my celebrity. But I couldn't have been more wrong. All she's wanted was this. Me inside her. Even my therapist's advice doesn't ring true a lot of the time. I bet he'll say to me that I should have embraced the fact that Sabrina was interested in me because I am a celebrity. But that line just doesn't bridge any of my depression. It never has. My therapist isn't a celebrity, so how can he know exactly how I feel? I really can't find anybody on my level that I can talk to.

There's no way I can confide in other footballers. We just don't commu-

213

nicate like that. Imagine me strolling up to one of my teammates and telling him I had to fuck this hot bird because she wanted me to, but all I really wanted to do was to roll over on the bed, play with her hair and get to know her more. I'd be laughed out of the dressing-room.

I'm not so down that I've considered suicide – I'd be too afraid to hurt my mam and my little brother that way. But, sometimes I do feel as if it's the only way out of this miserableness.

I feel a tear roll down my face, so remove a hand from Sabrina's waist to wipe it away. Then I notice my crucifix bounce up and down on my chest as I continue to thrust in and out of her. I pick it up, stare at it for a second, then let it go, squeeze my eyes shut and force another tear out. I really am pathetic; fucking a hot girl from behind while crying. This would be the lowest of the low if I hadn't already been here before.... doing the exact same thing; tearing up while having sex.

I'm not even sure whether she's enjoying this – she's very quiet for somebody being thrusted into, especially as she had told me she was looking forward to this.

I reach back down, and grab at one of her breasts to see if that makes either me or her enjoy this any more than we currently are when the door slides open. I'm not surprised to see Zach standing there, asking Sabrina if it's okay if he joins in. My dick immediately goes soft inside her. She looks back at me, as if to ask me if it's all right. I barely react. I just shrug my shoulders. I'm more intrigued to find out if she's up for this, if she's as dirty and as slutty as I assume she is from reading her text message earlier.

She doesn't say anything as Zach moves closer. I remove myself from her, and just kneel back on the bed as Zach inches even closer, almost touching Sabrina. She still hasn't said a word. Zach looks at me, then back at her. This is getting awkward. *Really* awkward. In fact, it's her making it awkward, her silence that is filling the room with suspense.

The only sound that breaks the silence is Zach unzipping his jeans. He whips his T-shirt off and flings it to the ground. I think he assumes he's being sexy. I can barely watch this. I'm so not up for a threesome. It doesn't interest me in any way. My dick is soft anyway. No way it's gonna get hard again, specially not with Zach in the room. I balk back in the bed as Zach moves in to kiss Sabrina. I don't feel jealous, just uncomfortable.

'No... no,' she says, 'no kissing.'

Zach smiles up at me. I think he's taken that as a signal that she just wants to fuck. As he inches closer, I throw my legs over the side of the bed and stand up. I can barely watch. Then Zach climbs onto the bed, knee by knee and almost crouches into the position I was seconds ago.

I tip-toe out of the open doors. I think I want to throw up.

214

I feel Jason go limp inside me. I'm not surprised. Your best friend walking in on you having sex is hardly recipe for a thrill. Though I assume this isn't their first rodeo together. I'm probably just another girl on a long list that they've doubled up on. They probably do this most weekends.

I try to think it through, but my mind is muddled. Am I supposed to say 'yes'? Am I supposed to want a threesome? Is that what most girls fantasise about? It's certainly not anything I've fantasised about. But what would I know? My sex life is about as limited as any twenty-five-year-olds could be, I'm sure. Maybe this is my ultimate test: do I want to be more light-hearted and fun, or do I want to remain the same old boring Sabrina Doyle?

I still haven't answered when Jason slips himself out of me as Zach unzips his jeans and slips them – and his T-shirt – off. I collapse my hips onto the bed and rub my hands over my face. When I lift my gaze up, Zach's face is coming towards mine. I balk.

'No... no, no kissing,' I say before I plant my face back down into the mattress. That's the second time he's tried to kiss me tonight. The second time I've swung my mouth away from his. I mean he's kind of handsome, I guess. Probably handsome to most girls. But I don't find him attractive at all. I certainly don't want to kiss him. I wish he'd go away, leave me and Jason to it. I was enjoying what we were getting up to. But within seconds of me refusing to kiss him, I feel him behind me, playing with me. I guess he took my 'no kissing' as a come on of sorts. Then again, I still haven't said 'no' to the question he asked two minutes ago. *Can I join in?* I still don't know why I haven't answered when I feel him insert his fingers inside me. Maybe I'm just in shock. Or maybe the little devil on my shoulder is winning out; wanting me to be more sexually active, wanting me to be the opposite of who I am.

I keep my face down, decide to be a bit more open and maybe go with it. But I can't bear to look behind me. Not necessarily at what Zach's up to, but more because I don't want to see Jason. I'm so pissed off with him. I genuinely thought I meant something to him earlier in the night. But now he's just standing there, watching as his best friend tries to please me from behind. I'm not sure if he even is pleasing me. I'm still a little wet, but I'm certain that's just the remnants of the excitement I had when Jason was making love to me. If this is supposed to be their big fantasy – a threesome – why has Jason just stopped? Why aren't we all in it together? I shake my head, decide to stop overthinking it. I can't enjoy this if I'm overthinking. I squeeze my eyes shut, shove my face firmer into the mattress and try to think of things that normally excite me.

When I masturbate, I normally imagine a rugged, handsome, tattooed man pleasing me. So that's what I imagine now. A David Beckham-type; muscular, strong arms wrapped around me, whispering sexily in my ear, telling me he wants me to cum. I can feel myself getting a little wetter. It's got nothing to do with whatever Zach is doing back there. I'm not sure what he's up to, but I try to blank him from my mind. It's not him behind me. It's my tattooed, muscular hunk. Only I don't think my hunk would be pinching me and hurting me as much. I suck the pain away through my teeth and get back to my daydream; my fantasy. I want to try and enjoy being a bit slutty for once, somebody who's not frigid. C'mon Sabrina – enjoy this. You deserve it. Two penises in one night.

I allow myself a little smile. The devil on my shoulder will be so happy I'm giving in. I might regret this in the morning, but for now I owe it to myself to have some fun.

Jason steps off the bed and stands aside, almost inviting me to go ahead and get stuck in.

I'm not sure how this is supposed to play out. If this is a threesome, shouldn't Jason still be on the bed? Shouldn't we be doing what I've seen done in loadsa porn movies? Shouldn't Jason have his dick in her pussy, maybe I should have my dick in her mouth? Maybe she shouldn't be just lying there with her ass in the air. Maybe she should be sitting up, pleasuring both of us at the same time.

I guess none of us know what we're doin'. None of us have ever been on this rodeo before. Sabrina is on the bed, me and Jason off it. So much for a roasting.

I stare at my best mate, but he's just gazing down at his feet. I don't deliberately look straight at it, but I can sense through my peripheral vision that his dick has gone soft. I'm not sure he's up for this. Maybe I should take the lead. This threesome was my idea after all.

I climb up behind Sabrina, one knee at a time while I begin to tug away at my dick. The atmosphere is a little too weird. I can't seem to get it up. It won't stand to attention. Which is really weird. One of the hottest girls I've ever seen is lying in front of me, fully naked, her ass in the air, but I just can't seem to get my mindset right.

I watch as Jason shuffles out of the room, tip-toeing quietly as if we're all asleep. I initially wanted a threesome, wanted group sex, just to try it for the sake of trying it. But now that he's leaving the scene, I feel a bit of relief wash over me. Sabrina and I can just get on with it. I'm about to have sex with a bird that looks like a fuckin' glamour model.

I cast my eyes down the back of her neck, her spine, her ass, the backs of her thighs – just in search of a blemish, maybe even a freckle. Nothing. She genuinely looks as if she stepped out of my TV from one of those *PrettyLittleThings* commercials or somethin'.

So why the fuck isn't my dick hard?

I continue to tug away, tickling at my balls in an attempt to turn myself on, but it's just not happening. I decide to play with Sabrina, maybe turning her on will turn me. I'm not great with foreplay, rarely use it with Tina. Our sex life consists of me saying I want it and her just giving it to me in whatever position I fancy. When we first started going out, we'd spend ages in the bedroom, finding out what each other's fantasies were. But now we just try to get it over with as soon as possible. Our sex life is basically an assisted wank for me. That's basically it. When I cum, we're done. I'm good at getting sex, but not necessarily good at sex itself. I don't need to be. What can I say? I'm a lazy, selfish fucker. But I want to try to turn Sabrina on. She deserves to enjoy this as much as I do.

I start by rubbing my fingers gently against her inner thighs for a few seconds, hoping that will get her groaning. But she's still quiet, still face down on the bed. She's a little wet, a little slippy down there, so I allow my finger to enter her. Still no groans of satisfaction. I enter another finger and begin to thrust them in and out. It feels weird. Not her insides, but the whole atmosphere. I can only hear the muffled beat of the music Li is playing in the other room. It's all very eerie.

I try to imagine what Sabrina must be thinking. She said she was up for this. Why is she just lyin' there, saying nothing? Maybe she's not as slutty as she led us to believe.

I stare down at her, willing myself to get hard as I take in her perfect skin, but... nothing. My dick falls even limper in my hand. I try to force it inside her, still limp, hoping my fingers can guide the way. Once I'm inside her, I'll harden up, we'll get this going. We could both be cumming soon, cumming together. But it's not working. I can't get myself in. This has never happened to me before. I'm so glad Jason left the room. I'd be mortified if he knew I couldn't get it up for a hottie like this. It's unnerving me that she's so quiet. Maybe she just doesn't want this. Maybe she's going to regret all of this in the morning.

'Are you okay?' I ask her. She doesn't move a muscle, not even a nod of her head. She didn't say 'yes', though she also didn't say 'no'. So I try again, try rubbing my dick on the back of her legs, hoping the smoothness of her skin turns me on, turns me on enough to get hard; hard enough for me to slip inside her.

NUMBER EIGHT HOLDS his hand to his mouth, clears his throat rather noisily and then begins to read Zach's testimony.

'"I walked into the room because it was clear to me that Sabrina had wanted more than just straight sex with one of us that night. She had flirted with both me and Jason through most of the night. And Li. She got on really well with Li. Probably got on better with him than anyone. We didn't discuss sex, but the fact that she came into the hotel, with just one bed, and went straight to it with Jason led me to believe that my suspicions were right all along. So after they were in there for a while, I popped into the bedroom and asked her out straight. I asked if it was okay if I joined in. I asked her, one hundred per cent. I just said 'would it be okay if I joined in?' She looked at me like in a really sexy kinda way, then she nodded her head. So, I just did... I joined in. I got on the bed, no real eh... what's-the-word... eh foreplay, yeah, foreplay, nothing like that. I just started having sex with her. She was kinda face down on the bed, but she was enjoying it. We both were. At no point did she say the word 'no'. I swear. I swear. We probably only had sex for... I don't know, it wasn't much longer than five or six minutes. It was the first time I'd ever had sex with the same girl as somebody else in the same night and it just didn't feel right so I... y'know didn't cum, like. I just stopped".'

Number Eight looks up, awaits a response.

'What was it Zach said about Jason being in the room at the same time?' Number Three asks as she scans through the page.

'It doesn't say it here, but he was pushed on that in cross-examination.

Jonathan Ryan asked him if he ever felt uncomfortable having sex in a bedroom alone with a girl before and when he replied 'no', Ryan asked him why he felt uncomfortable this time,' Number One said.

'Yeah and before he was given time to answer Ryan said something like: "I put it to you that you felt uncomfortable and didn't climax because your friend was in the room looking at you performing sex with Sabrina, isn't that right?" but Zach just denied it,' Number Twelve says.

His summoning up was pretty accurate. Jonathan Ryan was intent on tripping both Jason and Zach up in cross, trying to get them to admit, albeit through a slip up, that there was more than one man in the room at any point while acts of sex were being carried out; much like Sabrina testified had happened, which totally opposed the men's account. While Zach hesitated and stuttered quite a lot on the stand – and came across as lacking in any kind of sympathy, unlike Jason – Ryan still didn't catch him out quite as he would have hoped.

It was a dangerous game for Jason and Zach to play, putting themselves on the stand and open to cross-examination, but they managed to get through it. It couldn't be said that they passed the test with flying colours, but they passed nonetheless. The media reported Zach's testimony as being quite 'insensitive', noting his lack of sympathy and all but painting him as guilty – well, as much as they legally could. The reporting of his testimony spiked the #SheSaidNo social media movement. The day after his testimony – which was the day the national newspapers reported it – #SheSaidNo was posted 113,068 times in Ireland alone. A national record for any hashtag used in one day by quite some distance. There was no doubt about it; in the eyes of the general public, all three men were guilty of this crime. Yet the public only had scraps of evidence that could legally be reported to base their views on, which were – more often than not – sensationalised by the print media.

'Lishten,' Brian says, standing up. 'I know we're going to do a verdict vote now, but I jusht want to suggest that we should discard the option of 'undecided' this time. It'sh not an option the judge has necessarily given us. We can go guilty or not guilty, so maybe they're the only two options we should use. And I'd just like to add that in order to vote guilty, you have to be certain beyond reashonable doubt that the three men raped Sabrina. That's all I want to shay.' He holds both his palms towards his fellow jurors as he sits back down.

For once, Number Five doesn't react to Brian's lecture. She sits in silence and contemplates the vote ahead, just like everybody else around her. Number One removes the box from the middle of the table and proceeds to walk around the back of each juror, placing a pen and a slip of paper in front of each of them.

'Okay,' he says, returning to his chair and standing behind it. 'I agree with Brian's suggestion tha—'

'Bout time you agreed with him on something,' Number Eight says. It raises a chuckle around the room, cutting at the tension.

'Well, I don't think it'll be the last time I agree with him today, I must say,' Number One says, only to be met with 'ahhhhs' from each corner of the table. Number One was practically admitting that he was about to change his vote. At least that's what everybody was assuming.

'Calm down, calm down,' he says. 'I agree with Brian that we should all only have two options now. Guilty or not guilty. When you are done writing down one of those two verdicts, please fold your slip of paper in two, like this,' he says, showing them a run through of how to fold paper again, 'and then place it back into the box.'

He shoves the box into the middle of the table and then sits back down. The room falls deathly silent. Most jurors immediately begin to write. Number Three, Number Eight, Number Nine and Number Four stew on their thoughts, the latter twisting the top of his pen back and forth as he stares into space. Folded slips of paper are being tossed into the box and by the time Number Three, Number Eight and Number Nine have finally finished, Number Four is still contemplating his vote.

'Take your time,' Number One says, when he notices Number Four is the only juror not to have delivered a slip of paper yet.

'Don't rush him!' Number Five says.

'I'm not rushing him. I wasn't being sarcastic. I was being serious. Take your time, Number Four. This is as important a decision as you will likely ever make.'

Number Four groans, then fills each of his cheeks with air, before letting it all rasp out through his lips.

'Fuck it,' he says. 'I gotta do it. I don't want to... but I gotta write this.' He scribbles down his verdict, doesn't fold his piece of paper, he just flicks it towards the box, missing it by inches and then holds his head in his hands and folds himself forward, leaning on the table as if it's nap time.

'I didn't like doing that,' he mumbles into his own armpits. Number Seven reaches out a hand to the back of his neck, offers him a subtle massage as Number One begins his count.

'This is so tough,' Number Seven says tutting. 'Tough on us all. I never would have thought being a juror would make me so... depressed, I guess.'

Number Four rises from his slouched position, reaches out his two hands to hug Number Seven. They hold each other until Number One declares he has a result.

'Okay guys. A significant shift,' he says. 'Nine not guilty; three guilty.'

Almost every juror strains their eyeballs around the table. They're all asking themselves the same question, but nobody dare ask it aloud. Not yet anyway. Brian was finding it hardest to hold it in; the question poised to dive off the tip off his tongue. Yet part of him was feeling more relieved than annoyed. He felt things were finally heading in the right direction; the direction he had argued for from the very beginning.

Though at this stage in a trial, after four hours and forty minutes of deliberations, he didn't need to be that smug. Leads of nine:three had been won over before, and will be won over again in this room. There was still a chance that it would be won over today.

'Who are the three that voted *guilty*?' Brian just blurts out. He couldn't hold it in any longer.

'That was a secret ballot,' Number Five snaps back at him.

'Well I know you're one for a start. I don't think this needs to be a secret anymore. We need to openly discuss this. Who are the other two?'

'Whoa, whoa, whoa,' Number One says, standing up again. 'Let's calm down. Please.' He sighs, rubbing each of his eyes with the thumb and index finger of his right hand and then says, 'I agree with Brian again here. There is no need for this to be a secret. It needs discussing. After all we have discussed over the past four hours or whatever it is, who now genuinely thinks that we should convict Jason, Zach and Li?' he asks, then sits down.

Number Five raises her hand. Number Three lets a sigh force its way out of her nostrils and then raises her hand too. It was quickly followed by Number Eleven's. Not quite the three ladies who had opted for 'not guilty' in the very first verdict vote, but almost. Number Three and Number Five haven't wavered from guilty, Number Eleven has gone from undecided to guilty – the only juror who has fallen that way. Number Six, who had been guilty in the original verdict vote, had now had a total change of heart. She figured she couldn't base her opinion on her own experiences, that she'd never understand the modern twenty-something and had come to the conclusion that it's absolutely possible in this day and age that a pretty young girl like Sabrina would offer her body up to be used by three men she met one night.

'Okay,' Number One says. 'I guess my fair question to you three is, why do you think it has been proven beyond reasonable doubt that these three men raped Sabrina Doyle?'

The three women look towards each other, none of them keen to speak first.

'Listen, it's my opinion that you all dismissed the internal cut too soon', Number Eleven finally says. 'I think the cut points to beyond reasonable doubt that Sabrina was forced into a situation she didn't want to be in.'

'No but that—' Number Twelve starts to say, but he's cut short.

'Shhh,' Number One says, 'let Number Eleven make her argument.'

'We saw the pictures of all those cuts that Doctor Johnson showed us. I know they weren't pictures of Sabrina's cuts, but similar cuts and they just have to be the result of... I don't know... forced sex. I can't get away from that. It's strong evidence for me. I'm not sure why we haven't discussed this in more detail around this table. We seemed to dismiss it a bit.'

She stops talking and purses her quivering lips.

'Okay, well if you don't mind me replying to that,' Brian says. 'It's jusht that although Doctor Johnson said that in his opinion Sabrina's cut was likely to be from forced penetration, he did alsho admit on the stand that these cuts can occur in consensual sex too. He also said they happen more regularly than anyone knows because most females don't get checked after consensual sex, do they? These checks are only really carried out for those who have been raped or are claiming rape.'

'Despite what he said,' Number Eleven says, almost getting animated now, 'he still concluded that in his expert opinion Sabrina's cut was from the result of forced penetration.' She raises her eyebrows at Brian, shrugs her shoulder.

'I understand what you are shaying and I really appreciate your point—'

'She's dead right,' Number Five chimes up with. 'I'm with her. Ye can't argue against a doctor's opinion anyway, can ye?'

Number One stands up again, holds both of his hands out and brings them down slowly; his way of reducing the tension that's threatening to erupt. It works. The room falls silent again.

'We appreciate you making your arguments, ladies. What about you, Number Three? Would you like to tell us why you feel the men should be found guilty?'

Number Three scratches her fingernails against her left temple and then stares down at the wheels of her chair.

'If I'm being honest – and I obviously need to be one hundred per cent honest – I opted for guilty because I knew almost everybody else... I could sense it... was going to vote not guilty and I eh... I just want the discussion to continue. I feel... I feel Sabrina is owed more than the time we've spent here. Maybe we should all sleep on this, come back to it tomorrow. We're only four and three quarters of an hour in, trying to break down a trial that lasted five weeks... it just doesn't seem fair to her... it's not fair on Sabrina.'

Her eyes don't leave the wheels of her chair as she speaks.

'So you voted guilty to hold off a unanimous decision?' Number Twelve asks her, his tone calm.

'If I'm being honest, yes... yes I did.'

'Okay... but if I can ask you, what do you *genuinely* think the verdict should be based on the evidence we discussed?'

She looks up from her wheels, takes in a few faces.

'Based on what we've discussed, it would be...' she hesitates, shakes her head, almost as if she's disagreeing with herself. '...eh... it would have to be *not* guilty. I don't think the case was proven, but I'd like for us to give it more time.'

An intake of breath can be heard from both sides of the table.

'Well I'm sticking with guilty,' Number Five chimes in with, shifting what had been a mature tone. 'I agree with Number Eleven that the cut is huge and points to guilt and I also know in my own heart, deep inside my soul, that these men are guilty. So I'm not changing me mind. I told yous earlier I wouldn't change.' She shrugs her shoulder towards the centre of the table.

Number One speaks up. 'Well, we all appreciate everybody's opinion here. I guess the one thing we need to discuss, given where we are now, is the doctor's evidence about the cut as that seems to be the dispute here. That is – I guess it's fair to say – what is stopping us from making a unanimous decision. Shall I eh... call it in, request the doctor's testimony?'

'Yesh ring it in,' says Brian. 'But if you don't mind me saying in the meantime while we wait on Number One to make that call, I think one thing we should make fully clear here is that Gerd Bracken didn't overly push Doctor Johnson on the stand for a particular reashon. I believe that once he got the doctor to admit that these cuts can occur in both consensual and non-consensual acts of penetration it meant he felt he did enough here. It gave us reasonable doubt. And that means we can't really convict based on this piece of evidensh alone. The defence really won with Doctor Johnson.'

'He still said that in his expert opinion that this cut was likely from forced sex,' Number Eleven says.

'You're right, he did. But he could only offer opinion, he couldn't say for sure. And then Bracken of course got him to basically admit to us – to the whole court – that this cut *could* have been from consensual sex, so he did almost contradict himself on the stand.'

The jurors quieten down when a knock is heard at the door. Number Nine rises to answer it, takes the paperwork from the young man dressed in all black and then hands it over to Number One.

'Hmmm,' Number One mumbles as he flicks through the notes. 'It's only one page of testimony, he wasn't on the stand for long.'

'That's quite telling,' says Number Twelve.

'In what way is that telling?' Number Eleven asks.

'I don't believe that even Jonathan Ryan felt Doctor Johnson's testimony was enough for a conviction. I think he was a witness who could help their cause, but he knew that Doctor Johnson would also testify that these cuts occur in both consensual *and* non-consensual sex. I don't believe anybody thinks this was as big a deal as we are making it now. I appreciate,' he says holding his hand up, 'that Number Eleven feels it *is* a big deal, and for that reason we are discussing it, but...'

He tails off, begins to read through the testimony like everybody else seems to be around him.

'Here,' calls out Number One. 'See here, paragraph three. He was asked about these types of cuts and he said they only occur when there is "no or little cervical fluid being produced by the female". The cut is confirmation that Sabrina wasn't producing these types of fluids and therefore wasn't turned on.'

'Yeah, so doesn't that make forced penetration more likely, if she wasn't turned on... wasn't enjoying the sex?' Number Eleven asks.

'Yeah – but look, he was asked that specifically by Bracken. He was asked if it was true that a woman wouldn't necessarily be producing cervical fluid even in consensual sex, and when the doctor replied "yes", Bracken then said, "so, just to clarify, these cuts do quite often appear in females during consensual sex?" and the doctor said "yes". This,' he says, turning his page over to face his fellow jurors, 'gives us reasonable doubt. We can *not* convict based on this testimony. The prosecution didn't win this witness. Doctor Johnson didn't prove rape. I'm sorry... I am. I wish we had more definitive evidence for everybody to stew over, but we didn't discuss Doctor Johnson's evidence in fine detail because we knew it sort of evened out the playing field. It doesn't give us grounds to find these men guilty beyond reasonable doubt. Does that help change your mind?' He directs his question towards Number Eleven.

Number Eleven can't hold in her emotions. Snot and tears began to fall down her face. She pulls both of her jumper's sleeves on to the palms of her hands and begins to wipe across her nose. As she does, she nods her head.

'Yes,' she sniffs when she removes her hands. 'You're right. It's not enough... not enough to convict.'

'So ... are you saying you are now changing your verdict?'

She continues sniffing, then nods her head again.

'Not guilty,' she whispers.

'I'm not guilty too,' Number Three says, slapping her palms against the armrests of her wheelchair.

An audible intake of breath is heard around the table, then everybody's face turns towards Number Five.

'I'm not changin' me mind,' she says.

'Number Five!' Number Eight shouts out. But he's quickly hushed.

'If you don't mind me shaying,' Brian pipes up as he flicks through his notes. 'I scribbled down the judge's final directions to us here, the speech she gave us this morning before she set us off on deliberations... I just think this will sum it up for you, Number Five. Do you mind if I read it to you?'

Number Five just nods her head, her face still showing signs of hostility. But inside she was shaking; was wondering how she was going to wriggle out of the situation she was finding herself in. She wanted to vote guilty based on the fact that she just happened to believe Sabrina over the three men in question, but she also knew that the backbone of her argument relating to 'gut feeling' and 'opinion' wouldn't get her anywhere.

Number Five's real name is Teresa Brennan, a twenty-seven-year-old shopping centre shelf-stacker from Coolock in north Dublin. She's normally cocky, even though she doesn't have the look to carry it off. She's tiny – only five foot one – has mousy brown hair and a face filled with freckles. She had to adopt an argumentative manner from a young age to stave off bullies at school. By the time she'd completed her Leaving Cert the adopted person- ality had become a permanent fixture. It's a shame she feels the need to constantly rebel, but that's what her personality has evolved into. She could have been a much more amenable person. Much more likeable. She's been in the guilty camp from the outset, took an instant dislike to the three men, but particularly Zach. She hated him as soon as she clapped eyes on him, feels he has the word guilty tattooed across his oversized forehead. Her temperament makes her come across as rash, hence the amount of times she's been shut down by fellow jurors during these deliberations. But she's starting to melt; the hard exterior she adopted as a kid in school is dissi- pating in this room.

Brian begins to read from his notes. 'The judge said to us, "your only task is to decide whether the prosecution has made you certain of the defen- dants' guilt. Do not allow yourshelves to be distracted from that task, do not allow yourshelves to be dishtracted by unproven opinion, do not allow your- shelves to be dishtracted by opinions you may have heard outside of this courtroom or the jury room, do not allow yourselves to be dishtracted by your own gender, by your own experiences, by anything other than the evidensh provided in this very courtroom over the past five weeks". Number Five – Judge McCormick was telling us that there wasn't enough evidensh.

Just as I've been saying from the very start. She's telling us we can't decide this trial based on our own gut feelings. She was bashically telling us that we should be looking towards a not guilty verdict. The prosecution did not prove this case. I'm sorry. I am. I wish there was more to go on, but there simply isn't any evidensh.'

Number Five hangs her head.

'Number Five, at some point the judge will come back and let us know that eleven-to-one is enough for a verdict, so you hanging out is not—'

'Why don't we just hang on till tomorrow like Number Three said... all sleep on it?' Number Five offers up. 'We need to—'

'No,' Number Three says, reaching down to her wheels, moving her chair backwards to get out from under the table and then pushing forwards towards Number Five. When she rolls up beside her, she reaches a hand out to hold one of hers.

'I'm sorry, Number Five,' she says, tears rolling down her face. 'Like you, I believe these three men raped Sabrina. I'd like to see them behind bars. But our job is to look at the evidence and there simply isn't enough evidence for us to reach a guilty verdict.'

Number Five begins to sob, then stretches across the wheelchair to grab at Number Three, holding her in a tight embrace. She nods her head on Number Three's shoulder and whispers.

'Okay. Okay.'

'So that'sh it, is it? We're all not guilty?' asks Brian.

A slow tsunami of heads nod around the table.

'Not guilty, Number Five?' Number One asks, his tone sombre.

She releases herself from Number Three's hug and lets out a deep breath, spraying some of her tears on to the table.

'Not guilty.'

Everybody soaks in the reality; the room falling silent, but for the sound of Number Three and Number Five sucking up their tears.

'Shall I ring it in?' Number One asks, breaking the silence.

'Ring it in,' says Number Twelve.

Number One holds down the button and takes a deep breath.

'The jury have reached a unanimous verdict,' he says.

00:25
Sabrina

I'm wondering why I'm breathing so calmly when inside I feel flames are starting to ignite. I can hear my breaths reverberate from my nose onto the mattress and then back into my ears. I'm getting annoyed by the fact that I can't get my train of thought on to the right track. I should either be enjoying this, or... totally incensed. But I'm neither. I'm just tired, sinking my head further into the mattress while Zach attempts to turn me on. Why am I being so indecisive? Maybe I'm not cut out for being the easy-going, fun Sabrina. Maybe I'm supposed to be dull, supposed to be frigid.

'You okay?' Zach asks. I take a moment to think about his question, but I actually don't know the answer. Both the angel and the devil on my shoulder have gone quiet. I think I'd be too embarrassed to say 'no' at this point anyway. So I just say nothing, keeping my face firm against the mattress. Jason enters my mind. I wonder how he is feeling as he stands back and watches his best mate try to have sex with me. But I can't look behind, can't even bring myself to raise my nose from this bed. I feel Zach rub himself between my legs. He's all warm, clammy. This is far from sexy. None of it feels right. I'm supposed to be turned on – I'm anything but. Then he enters me. I think it's his penis. Could be his fingers. It's not a nice sensation... quite rough actually, but I turn my face sideways just to give my nose more space to breathe through, resting my right ear on the mattress instead.

'You're so hot,' Zach says as he writhers around behind me. I don't answer him. He groans. I'm not sure whether it's with satisfaction or out of frustration. Maybe he's not enjoying this either. Threesomes are bullshit. Well this one is anyway. I certainly won't be having another one in a hurry. My whole sex life has been shit. I'm beginning to think sex is the most over-rated and sensationalised act humans bang on about. Or maybe it's just me... after all, I am the common denominator in my shitty sex life. I am the only one who's been there with all three men I've let inside me. Or four. It's four now, I guess. Two tonight. Wow. I wonder when that will sink in for real. Four penises. All of different length, girth, and all these sizes have been vastly overrated. I haven't really enjoyed any penis that has entered me. Not really. Sex with Eddie was all right at the start, but it soon got boring. Maybe I'm the boring one. Maybe I should get up off my face, turn around, pull Jason and Zach on to their backs and jump on top of them, one at a time. Ride them like a cowgirl. Be a proper dirty little slut. But I actually have no interest in having sex with any of them. Not any more. My mojo is gone. All I want to do is go home, curl up into my bed and fall asleep. Maybe I'll wake up in the morning and regret this. Or maybe I'll wake up and feel disappointed that I didn't give it my best shot. It's really annoying me that I don't know how I feel, how I should feel, how I will feel.

I want to say 'no'. I want to repeat the word fifty times. Tell Zach to get away from me, tell him and Jason to get out of the room, that I need time to myself. But the word won't come out. I can hear myself say it, over and over again. But I know it's only inside my head, nobody else can hear it.

Then Zach takes me out of my thought by letting out a loud groan. I'm pretty sure it's out of frustration more than anything. He's not groaning in ecstasy. He's not even inside me anymore. No part of his body is. I think he's just kneeling back on the bed, panting– letting out sharp, heavy breaths.

'You're amazing,' he says, then he pats me on the back as if I'm a little pony he's just been on for a ride around. I let out a deep sigh – the only significant sound I've made in the past twenty minutes. I look up when the music grows louder. The door's swiped open again. I manage to move my head to look behind and make out Li's silhouette. I wrap one arm around my breasts so he can't see them; hold my other hand down by my crotch. But aside from that, I can't move. I know my ass is still hovering above the mattress, my knees, head and shoulders still sunken into it.

Then I feel him crawl up on to the bed, changing positions with Zach.

This can't be happening. Li's not going to have sex with me. Is he? We get on with each other like brother and sister. This can't be right. I hear myself scream 'no' inside my head. Then I feel him enter me. What the fuck is going on?

I raise my head fully from the mattress for the first time and stare back at Li. His glasses have steamed up, he's thrusting into me as quickly as he can. It's not hurting me, in fact I seem to have moistened somewhat. But I know I'm not turned on. I know I don't want this. I take a deep breath and brace myself to say the word that has been circulating in my head for the past five minutes. I don't know why it won't come out. I shake my head. But I don't think he can see me. My breathing gets quicker, then sharper. Speak for fuck sake, Sabrina. Speak. Say it. Say it!

'No, no, no!' I scream.

There's something not quite right about tonight. Both myself and Jason are flat out on a sofa each; neither of us talking. We're just drowning in the shite music blaring from the TV.

I can't believe Jason gave up on Sabrina, allowed Zach to take control. For somebody who's been a huge success as a professional athlete, he really can be such an easy pushover at times. Especially when it comes to Zach.

I imagine what Zach's up to now. Probably getting an amazing blowjob from one of the most beautiful women I've ever seen. I was starting to get jealous when Jason took her into the bedroom about twenty minutes ago, but I'm not jealous now. I'm just frustrated; frustrated with Jason, frustrated with Zach, *definitely* frustrated with Sabrina. She seemed like such a nice girl. I can't believe she's just another slut. The world seems to be full of them these days.

I should have just gone home when we left the airport and curled up in bed beside Niamh. I was actually looking forward to going to Homebase in the morning. Maybe we still can. We got to get that paint for the bathroom.

Jesus. I really am getting old – worrying about the state of our little apartment. Can't believe I'm going to be a dad soon, going to be a married man not that long after. I'm so lucky. But I'm aware of my luck, so that's okay. I don't live with any guilt that I've managed to find everything I've ever wanted in life. I've got a decent job, an adorable family, great mates, an amazing girlfriend. There's nothing I would change about my life. And I know there are not a lot of people who could genuinely say that.

I stare over at Jason. I know he certainly couldn't say that. He's definitely depressed. His eyes are closed, but I know by the way he's slouched on that couch that he's crying inside. Maybe we all just need to get the fuck out of here. Get Jason home. I'll call into his mam's tomorrow afternoon when I'm back from Homebase. Have a proper heart-to-heart with him then.

I drop my feet to the ground and muster enough energy to get myself to a standing position, stretching and yawning when I'm finally upright. There's no noise coming from the bedroom. I step closer to it, try to gauge if Sabrina and Zach are finished. I think they are. I'll tell them we're checking out, heading home.

But when I slide the door open I see Sabrina in doggy position, her skin as perfect as any models' I've ever seen. It looks as if Zach has just finished. He's steadily getting himself to a standing position after popping his cock back inside his boxer shorts. It's not a smile he shoots in my direction, it's more of a gurn. Then he taps me on the shoulder as he passes me and makes his way towards Jason. I don't look at him because I can't keep my eyes off Sabrina's ass. I've never seen anything like it.

I start rubbing at myself, my dick standing to attention. She hasn't moved. Maybe she's waiting on me. I look behind me at the boys, then back at Sabrina. I wonder if I owe myself this – my last hurrah before I get married. But before I've stewed the thought fully around my head, I'm on the bed, my dick in my hand. I'm not even sure when I pulled down my zip. And now I'm inside her. I can't believe it. I never thought I'd have sex with somebody this hot. It feels so good. I want to take a snap shot of this moment, so I can play it over and over in my head for the rest of my life. Though I can't really see Sabrina's beautiful face.

She raises her head from the bed. She's panting. She really is enjoying this. What a dirty slut. Three dicks she's had tonight and is still gagging for more. Or is she? I watch her shake her head. Her breaths becoming sharper.

Then she snaps her face back towards me.

'No, no, no!' she shouts back.

I twist her hair around my hand and grip it tightly. Then I force her face back down on to the mattress and hold it there while I continue to thrust in and out of her.

'Shh,' I whisper. 'Keep quiet. I won't be long.'

THE END

- It is believed, though it can't be proven, that in ninety-two per cent of rape cases reported to police, the claimant is *not* lying.

- However, despite that, only *eighteen per cent* of rape trials ever end in a guilty verdict.

FIND OUT WHAT HAPPENED TO THESE CHARACTERS NEXT...

Watch an exclusive interview with author David B. Lyons in which he discusses this story in finer detail and explains what may have happened to the characters following the trial.

To watch, just click here:
https://www.subscribepage.com/shesaid

BOOK II

THE CURIOUS CASE
OF FAITH & GRACE

You won't know what to make of the Tiddle twins…

For my favourite sister...

Debra

✝

Grace pinched her tongue between her teeth and lifted a knee towards her chest. Then she stamped down as hard as she could.

The squelch was so loud and gross that it caused Clive to twist his head in disgust. He stood upright, strode towards his daughter and picked her up by the underarms.

'What have you done?' he shouted, spraying spittle into her face.

She didn't answer. She was too busy trying to squeeze tears from her eyes.

Clive dropped his gaze beneath his daughter's dangling feet, then baulked.

The sight was gross; the frog now a splattered mixture of green and purple slimy mounds. He knew only half of the frog was on that path; the other half likely stuck to the bottom of his daughter's shoe.

Clive placed Grace down, ensuring she missed the mess, then ordered her to take off her shoes before following him in to the kitchen.

She continued to force out the tears as she unbuckled her shoes, only pausing when she noticed Faith pull the net curtains of the living room window across to stick her tongue out at her. Grace sucked up the wet snot that was about to run onto her top lip, then shrugged a shoulder towards her twin. Faith laughed, but she wasn't sure why she was laughing exactly. It might have been because Grace had just splattered the frog to death – or perhaps it was just funny to see Daddy all up in a rage.

The twins had only just turned four years of age then, but splattering that frog to nothing remains Grace's earliest memory. It's not so much the punishment she got from her old man that sticks in her mind. It's that noise. That squelch. She can still hear it today – seven years on. And she can still feel that sensation under her foot no matter what shoes she's wearing on any given day. There was something strangely satisfying about that squelch.

Clive and the twins had just been to Phoenix Park earlier that morning to catch some pinkeens from the Doggy Pond. And when the frog hopped up on the bank next to them, both Faith and Grace insisted in unison that they take it home and treat it like a pet. So they did. Except they didn't – treat it like a pet, that is. Grace killed it within half an hour of them arriving back at their bungalow.

'You will spend the next hour kneeling and praying to our Lord – asking him to forgive you, do you understand?' Clive said, staring down at the top of his daughter's head. She was minute by comparison, wiping her eyes in front of his crotch. 'Well... let me hear you,' he said.

She sucked more wet up her nose, then looked around herself in the hope of catching her sister's eye. But Faith was out of sight – hiding behind their bedroom door, and peering through the crack.

Grace slowly placed each of her knees – one at a time – onto the carpet, brought the two palms of her hands together, and stared up at the giant crucifix hanging from the wall.

'Dear Almighty Lord Jesus, please forgive me for killing Grebit. It was a accident. I was just walking in the garden and—'

'Don't you dare! Don't you dare!' Clive grunted. He adjusted his footing so he was standing even more dominant over his daughter. 'If you attempt to lie to our Lord Jesus Christ, you will end up in Hell. Do you understand, Grace Tiddle?'

Grace and Faith had been made well aware of Heaven and Hell ever since consciousness. Religion was driven into them from day one; Clive and Dorothy hovering above their cribs as soon as they were born to chant prayers at them.

Grace, her face blotchy from all of the rubbing, opened one eye to stare at up her father's tall frame, then closed it quickly again when she noticed him peering down over his rotund belly at her.

'Okay. Jesus... I stamped on Grebit, but I am so sorry. Please forgive me. I want to go to Heaven, not Hell. I want to be with you. Not burning. I will never kill another frog again. I pwomise.'

Clive snorted, then stepped over his daughter.

'One hour. Keep asking for forgiveness. If I hear you stop, you will be given further punishment.'

Then he headed into the kitchen for his usual mid-morning nap. He'd sit at the squared table, his back against the wall, and close his eyes for half an hour before getting back on with his day. He got up early, did Clive Tiddle.

Always at five a.m. He'd have breakfast, plan his sermons, then do a spot of gardening before taking his little kitchen snooze. He'd follow that pattern almost every morning. But not on Saturdays. Because that was when he'd skip the gardening to spend time with the twins. Which is why the three of them had ventured out to the Doggy Pond that morning. Though Clive would much rather have been doing gardening. He loved gardening. Probably because he had the look to carry it off. He was massive; six-foot, five inches tall, and he almost always wore a gilet – autumnal in colour – over a plaid shirt. His sandy hair was greying but the straw-orange moustache that covered his top lip hadn't lost any of its colour. The hairs of his 'tache hung over his mouth in a thick, stunted length when he talked, like the bristles of a broom. He looked much older than his years – at least a decade older. So did Dorothy. It wasn't that their skin was particularly weathered, worn or wrinkled. It was more to do with how they dressed. And acted. They were both old-fashioned. Frumpy.

'...and I pwomise I will take good care of everything my mammy and daddy buy for me, like dolls and rosemary beads and other things...'

'Psst.'

Grace held her eyes closed firmer to rid herself of her sister's distraction.

'Psst.'

Then she sighed, opened one eye again and peered over her shoulder.

'Go 'way,' she said.

Faith was standing in the doorway, giggling.

'You killed Grebit.'

'Shh... Daddy will be cross at both of us. Go away. I need to pray. For an hour, Daddy said.'

'That was naughty.'

'Shhh.'

Faith continued to giggle, holding her hand to her mouth. She often giggled by means of communication. Faith – second born by twenty minutes – developed slower than her sister from the outset. Grace instantly fell into line; abiding by the routine Clive and Dorothy had put in place for their twins. But Faith could never handle it. She would often be awake when she was supposed to be asleep, asleep when she was supposed to be awake. And she would talk when she was supposed to be quiet, then fall mute if anybody ever asked her a question. She might've been ever-so-slightly prettier than her sister – though there's really not much in it; they're identical, save for the fact that Grace has a small freckle under her left eye and a slightly wider nose – but in terms of intellect, Grace has always been atop that podium.

'I can't hear you!' Clive's voice boomed from the kitchen.

'...and our Lord Jesus Christ,' Grace raised her voice, 'to whom I owe my

life, I promise to always abide by your teachings and to read the Bible every night.'

She wasn't sure what she was saying exactly. She was just repeating phrases and sentences she'd heard time and time again – either in church, or at home.

She loved her daddy. And her mammy. Both twins did. Their parents gave them everything they had ever needed; a comfy bed to sleep in at night; a church in which to pray; food; sweets – on special occasions. And a big back garden in which a one-hundred year old huge oak tree stood that they would run around all day, every day if their parents allowed them to. The Tiddles' house itself wasn't huge. It was of decent size. A three-bed detached bungalow on the foothills of the Dublin mountains. But that bungalow was placed inside seven acres of land; a small split garden to the front where Clive would prune his rosebushes, water his plants and mow his lawn every Saturday. And to the back, a rough expanse of green field that seemed to travel as far as the horizon.

Dorothy was actually a stricter parent than her husband but Clive did possess a stern growl every now and then that would rush dread into the twins. Grace knew well that he would be furious with her if she stamped on that frog. But she just couldn't help herself. Kneeling down in front of the crucifix would be worth the satisfying sensation of splattering Grebit into the garden path. Or so she thought. Five minutes in, she was beginning to get itchy. She kept lifting her knees – one at a time – towards her chest so she could scratch at them for a little relief while she continued praying.

'Whatcha doing there, love?' Dorothy said, coming out of her own bedroom, a basket of washing gripped tight to her hip.

'I eh... Daddy told me to pray for an hour because...'

'An hour? Because what, love?'

Dorothy's brow sunk. And her big brown eyes bore into the back of her daughter's head.

'I, eh... I stood on the frog.'

'Oh Mary, mother of God,' Dorothy said, blessing herself with her free hand. 'Did you kill it?'

Grace swallowed, then slowly nodded.

Dorothy blessed herself again and whispered something towards the ceiling.

'Silly girl,' she hissed when she looked back down. Then she trotted across the hallway, the basket of washing still stuck to her hip, and into the kitchen. She didn't notice Faith hiding behind the twins' bedroom door as she stormed past.

'Uuugh,' Grace said into her hands when she heard her mother strike up the conversation about Grebit with Clive.

And then Faith giggled from behind her. Again.

'Hail Mary, full of Grace, the Lord be with you...'

Grace turned to see her twin walking towards her.

'You're better off doing prayers we know, rather than just saying sorry to Jesus all the time,' Faith whispered as she knelt beside her. 'It helps the time go quicker.'

Grace beamed a smile at Faith, and then both of them closed their eyes tight and began chanting a Hail Mary in unison.

Even though Faith was slow to learn, she never had any problem rattling off prayers. Both of the twins had been chanting Hail Marys and Our Fathers since they were two years old. It was as if prayers took priority in their development. They needed to learn prayers first, before they could learn anything else.

Though it seemed apt for Clive and Dorothy that their babies would be immersed in prayer. After all, it was prayers that brought the twins into the world.

It took seventeen years of trying for the Tiddles to fall pregnant. And when a blue cross finally appeared on one of the hundreds of white sticks Dorothy had peed on over those years, they immediately fell to their knees and thanked the Lord Jesus Christ. Not the science that led to them undergoing a dozen rounds of IVF.

They were abuzz with their miracle.

And that was before they had learned they were getting two at once.

ALICE

I've mastered the art of stifling yawns. The trick is to let the yawn manifest itself at the back of the throat while keeping your lips sealed together, then allowing the air to slowly and quietly seep out through the nostrils. It makes my eyes water every time I do it, and I'm certain that if anybody was staring at me they would be able to tell I was stifling a yawn. But nobody's staring at me. At least I hope not anyway. But best I don't gape my mouth open like a hippo in case I'm seen to be finding this tiresome. It's not boring – far from it. It's fascinating, really. But the silences are long and plentiful. Way too plentiful.

I twist my left wrist a little and strain my eyes down. 4:21 p.m. The judge seems to be wrapping everything up. I should be home around five-ish again today.

I find myself glancing up at them as the judge continues to rattle on. I can't help it. If anybody *was* staring at me through the course of this trial, they'd have noticed me do this plenty of times. I just find them so intriguing to look at. Identical. And charged with the most horrendous crimes possible. Imagine bludgeoning both of your parents to death; repeatedly stabbing them with a kitchen knife until they gasped their last breath. I don't know whether they're more cute or more creepy looking to be honest. I've never made up my mind on that. There *has* to be some dark stuff going on behind those big brown eyes, though. I bet that's why I can't stop looking up at them; I'm trying to find that darkness – to justify the verdict I have come to. I'm certain they're guilty... no doubt about it.

The judge stares up over the rim of her glasses at the twelve of us and coughs politely into her fist. It's her regular cue, to let us know she's about to address us directly.

'Members of the jury,' she says. 'I know this has been a tiring and testing two weeks for you all. We have now heard from the last of the witnesses in this case and you will no longer be offered any further evidence. Tomorrow we will hear final arguments from both the defence and the prosecution, after which I will release you to deliberate your verdict.'

Some of my fellow jurors sit face on, nodding back at Judge Delia McCormick, others glance around sheepishly at their peers. I can't keep my eyes off the twins. I've desperately wanted to witness how Faith and Grace have reacted to each and every word spoken during this trial, even if it was only a case of the judge addressing us jurors as a matter of protocol. Grace glances straight at me, meets my eye. It's not the first time she's done this over the past fortnight, but this is the first time I don't blink my gaze away. I stare straight back at her until Imogen – one of her defence lawyers – leans over to whisper something into her ear and our moment is gone. I've often played around with the theory that it was perhaps just Grace who killed Clive and Dorothy. Maybe Faith had nothing to do with it. She's too quiet. Too... what's-the-word... lacking. As if she wouldn't have the where-withal to kill. Though I've read that can be a common trait amongst murderers.

The jurors to my right stand and suddenly I'm standing too, without me hearing the judge dismiss us. Then we do what we usually do – walk to the side door in two straight lines of six, cloaked in total silence. We've done this every day for the past two weeks, but it always feels uncomfortably awkward; as if the whole world's eyes are bearing into us.

It's relaxing though, to hear everybody's breathing return to normal as soon as we reach the corridor. We must all hold our breaths longer than usual when we're seated in that dock.

'Gee, looks like we'll be starting to deliberate tomorrow,' the obese guy says, turning to me.

I turn my lips downwards in mock dread.

'I know, we've... we've a lot to discuss,' I say.

He nods his chins at me and then uncomfortably places the palm of his hand on to my left shoulder.

'I can't wait to see which way each of the jurors have been swayed, can you, Alice?'

I really want to shrug his hand away. But I'm more polite than that. So I answer his question while he's still touching me.

'It'll be interesting alright. I think I know which way I'm going to vote already. Do you?'

He raises an eyebrow, then looks about himself before leaning closer to me.

'We're not supposed to discuss this without the other jurors... but,' he looks about himself again, 'not guilty.'

Not guilty. Who else does he think did it?

'What about you?' he says, inching his face even closer to me, his breath stinking in a sickly warm way.

I shake my head while subtly blowing away the stench.

'I'm undecided,' I say.

I'm not undecided – not at all. I'm certain they did it. But I just don't want to explain myself to him, not with his nose just inches from mine.

'Okay, okay... listen up, members of the jury,' the young woman dressed in all black calls out while clapping her hands. Obese Guy leans away from me, and I inhale again. 'Your day is over. You are all free to return home. May I remind you that it is vitally important you stay away from any news items about this court case, regardless of the medium. Please do not listen to any TV news channels which may discuss this trial, nor radio stations. Please do not read any newspapers. Stay away from your mobile phones and computers so as not to be influenced in your deliberations by anything that may occur outside of these courts.'

She feeds us this script every afternoon before we leave. As she does, I look around at my fellow jurors to try to read their reaction to it. I'd love to ask each of them if they have broken any of these rules. I bet they have. I find it impossible to stay off my phone.

'How long will final arguments take?' the blonde with the bad acne asks, interrupting the young woman dressed in all black.

'Well, that's impossible to say. Different trials call for different levels of argument and it will be totally dependent on what each of the legal teams have planned.'

'But is it safe to say we will begin deliberating tomorrow?' the young woman with the braces asks.

The young woman dressed in all black clicks her tongue against the top palate of her mouth while slowly swaying her head from side to side.

'I would guess so,' she finally answers. 'Final arguments shouldn't take up the whole day. Just don't quote me on that. But, eh... I can see you beginning your deliberations tomorrow, yes.' She offers a sterile smile. 'Now... as I was just about to say, you will each need to be here by nine a.m. tomorrow. Court will resume at 9:30 a.m. Does anybody have any further questions?'

I observe the shaking heads before me and then without waiting, the young woman dressed in all black steps aside and we are all free to go.

As soon as the fresh air hits us, we each politely mumble a goodbye to each other – and then we're gone. Mostly in different directions. Two of us – me and the middle-aged woman with long red hair whose name I *think* is Sinead – pace towards the taxi rank outside the entrance to Phoenix Park.

'Go on, you first,' she says to me in her posh Dublin accent.

'Are you sure? You were here before me,' I say, smiling back at her.

'No, go on. I got the first taxi yesterday. Your turn to go first today.'

I tilt my head at her. She's posh. But she seems lovely. We've had this kind of exchange almost every evening; me insisting she takes the first taxi, her then reciprocating the following day. But that's been the extent of our conversations. I'd love to ask her about the trial, about what she thinks of Faith and Grace. I've often wondered if I should ask her where she lives, for if we were heading in the same direction we could share a taxi, and then during that taxi ride we could have a right ol' yarn about the trial. But all of that is frowned upon. Legally. We're not supposed to discuss the trial until all twelve of us are in a room together, seated around a table. It's just the gossip in me that wants to break the rules. I'm too impatient. Though there's not long to wait now. Tomorrow we'll all be finally sitting around that table.

She smiles her lovely teeth at me as I wave out of the side window and then suddenly I'm off. On my way back home. Back to my sanctuary where I can forget about the trial for the evening and concentrate on my family, save for the odd time I visit the loo with my phone and inevitably hop on to Twitter to search for tweets on the Child X and Child Y trial.

I can tell my husband has been a little put out by me being on this jury, but he doesn't huff and puff. Ever. He's way too nice to huff and puff. I married well. *Extremely* well. Noel may not be anything close to a George Clooney look alike. But he's a sweetheart. Genuinely the nicest person I have ever met in my life. I say that all the time. And I don't mean it in any sort of cheesy way; the way most married wives would describe their husbands. I actually mean it. Noel Sheridan is as genuine and nice as humans come. Certainly any human I've ever come across anyway. He has treated me the way every woman dreams of being treated; with respect. And he's as good a dad as he is a husband. Zoe and Alfie's relationship with Noel is what gives me most satisfaction in life. I can't wait to get home to them; tell them the jury will be starting deliberations tomorrow and that our household should finally be returning to normal. This could be all over by tomorrow. I'm sure most of the jurors feel the same way I do: guilty. It's odd the obese guy told me he is going to vote not guilty, but perhaps the rest of us are all singing from the same hymn sheet. All twelve of us are supposed to agree. Though I've read that Judge McCormick can come back to us at any time if a verdict hasn't been reached to tell us that a ten:two ratio in favour of any particular verdict would be enough to put an end to the trial.

As the taxi crosses the bridge over the River Liffey, I swipe my phone from my pocket and tap into Facebook. I don't know why my thumb automatically goes to the Facebook app... but it does. Because I'm pretty sure I actually hate Facebook.

There doesn't seem to be much going on. Annie Clavin posting up more pictures of her grandkids. Cute. I tap a like on that one. Jessica Murphy posting more pictures of her lunches. Not cute. Scroll. Davey Lynch posting more political bullshit as if he thinks anybody is paying attention. Scroll.

'Rough day?'

I glance up and smile into the rearview mirror.

'No. No. Not at all. Just tiring.'

The taxi man cocks his head.

'Not you on trial is it?' he says, grinning.

'Gee, no. I'm, eh... I'm a juror on a case.'

'Ahh,' he says. 'Then I better not probe any further.'

I laugh out loud. A fake laugh. But enough to put an end to the conversation so I can return to Facebook.

Michelle Dewey showing off her wealth by posting up pictures of her perfect home. Again. I like Michelle. In the flesh Michelle. But Facebook Michelle's a bit of a bitch.

'It's not the... eh... you're not a juror on that Child X and Child Y case, are ye?' I look up into the rearview mirror again and silently sigh through my nose. 'Ah no. Don't tell me. You can't tell me. Don't mind me,' he says, waving his hand in the air.

I offer a wide smile and as I do, my phone vibrates in my hand. A text message. From a strange number.

I open it and then crease my brow. That looks familiar. A still of what I'm certain is the same wallpaper they use in the bedrooms of the Hilton Hotel.

And immediately my heart drops.

I press at the play arrow and without pause I hear my heavy panting. Followed swiftly by my loud squeals of ecstasy.

Holy fuck!

I thumb at the pause button and then look up into the rearview mirror. The taxi man must be pretending he didn't hear that. But he had to have. That was loud. *I* was loud.

I mute the sound on my phone, press the play button again and stare at myself, my eyes rolled back in euphoria as Emmet pounds at me from behind.

Who the fuck sent me this?

DAY ONE

I jarred my forearm into his throat, forcing him to look up at me. He was only a kid; greasy skin, a poor attempt at a moustache and gelled down flat hair.

'Empty your pockets.'

'Alright, alright,' he shrugged.

I released my grip and took a tiny step back to give him room to unzip his coat. What a giveaway; a long coat on a hot summer's day.

'Careful,' I said, eyeballing him as he reached for his inside pocket.

He tutted, then held a balled fist towards me. I placed my palm under his and he dropped about a dozen light bags into it. Pills. I could tell by the weight.

'I know you've got more,' I said.

He shoved his hand into his opposite inside pocket with a scoff and then dropped a few more bags into my other palm. Heavier. Weed.

I leaned closer to him, almost nose-to-nose.

'That's everything, I swear,' he said. 'Go on. Search me.' He stretched his arms out wide.

I took two further steps back so I could peer up and down the full stretch of laneway.

'I believe ye,' I said, curling both of my hands into a ball. Then I stared into his spotty little face. 'How old are you?'

'Fifteen.'

'Fifteen...' I shook my head. 'You could get eight years for carrying this around with you. That's more than half of the life you've lived already... think about that.'

He didn't say anything. He just stared down at his expensive trainers. They always wear expensive trainers. And brand new ones almost every time, too. I've often joked that sports stores must have more drug money running through their tills than all the dealers in Ireland combined.

'Off you go,' I said, cocking my head.

His brow dropped and his bottom lip hung out.

'You're not... you're not going to...'

I shook my head. And he ran – not a jog, a sprint – to the end of the laneway, skidding to a fall as he tried to turn the corner.

I pushed a laugh out of my nose before I opened my hands. Six quarter bags of weed and about twelve wraps of what looked like that pink MDMA shit that was doing the rounds back then.

I waddled straight over to the big bin at the end of the laneway and lifted the lid. Then I baulked backwards as a butterfly – a giant of a butterfly – flapped its way towards me and perched itself on the edge of the bin. It frightened the shite out of me. I stared it at, noticed it had four wings, and two heads. I'd never seen anything like it before. Then it just flew directly upwards and lost itself in the glare of the sun. I puffed out a laugh, then dropped the bags of pills into the bin and slammed the lid closed.

It was hot that whole week; the sun unusually high in the sky. So I rested my hand on top of the car when I got back to it and took a good look around me – just to take a breather after chasing that spotty little shit down the laneway. It always looks stunning around this neck of the woods when the sun is shining; the green in the Dublin mountains seems to turn luminous.

After I got in and turned the ignition, I pushed at the cassette tape, feeding it into the radio and, after a weird clicking sound, the piano of Billy Joel started to play. I U-turned to head for home; to give Sheila the little surprise I had gotten for her when my other radio started to spit at me, just as I was about to sing along. I immediately stabbed a finger at the eject button of the cassette tape, then grabbed at my radio.

'Say again,' I said, squinting into the sun.

'BA99, can you hear me?'

'Yes. I can hear you loud and clear.'

'BA99, there has been an emergency call to the St Benedict's Bungalow which is at the end of Barry Lane.' I squinted even more. 'You there, BA99?'

'Yes. Yes. It's eh... St Benedict's Bungalow? Isn't that the church people... the eh... Tiddles?'

'I'm not sure, Detective. I don't know the address. And I've not been made aware of any names. There's been a, eh... homicide called in. A double homicide.'

I skidded the car into another U-turn, placing the radio on the passenger seat, and when the car was back straight on the road I picked the receiver up again.

'Children or adults?'

'I'm unsure, Detective. Are you on it?'

'Two minutes from the scene.'

I whistled a sigh through my lips after I placed the radio back on its cradle. It's a maze of windy roads that lead to Barry Lane. But I didn't have to make too many of those turns. I was only a mile and a half away.

I swerved into a line of gravel that splits an otherwise perfectly-maintained garden. And as I did, little Johnny came to greet me, puffing out his cheeks. He looked pale. As if he was about to throw up.

'Jesus, Quayle,' he said before I was fully out of the car. 'I'm sorry to blaspheme... especially here.' He looked around himself, then back at me. I thought he was going to pass out. 'Two bodies. Cut up. Cut right up. Sliced, I would say.'

I held my eyes closed and shook my head.

'Adults?' Johnny nodded. 'They've two twin girls, right? Little ones.'

'They're nine, yeah,' Johnny replied, looking down the length of his tie. 'They're in the, eh... sitting room now... with Sully.'

I scrunched up my face, then we both turned and headed for the front door. As soon as I stepped inside the hallway, the large crucifix hanging on the back wall took my attention, even though in my peripherals I could already make out a body laying just inside the kitchen door frame. When I took my gaze away from the crucifix and finally looked to the body, I immediately knew it was him.

'Clive Tiddle,' I said, almost in a whisper.

'You know him, Detective?' one of the paramedics kneeling beside the body asked.

I shook my head as I stood over the body and counted twelve stab wounds.

'I just know of him; he runs that church at the community centre.'

The two paramedics mumbled to each other, something about their realisation of this being 'the church family'. But I wasn't paying much attention. I was bending over the wife's body, counting the stab wounds in her. Seven.

'Dorothy Tiddle,' I said whilst staring into her eyes. They were still wide open.

'You, eh... wanna talk to the twins?' Johnny said.

I sucked a cold breath in through the gaps in my teeth and stood back upright.

'Sure.'

The paramedics pursed their lips at me as I walked past them, to follow Johnny back down the hallway and into the living room. That's when I saw them for the first time. They were both wearing floral-patterned dresses which seemed to disappear into the floral-patterned couch they were sitting on. Sully was next to them.

I noted they weren't crying. Not then.

Sully cocked her head up when she noticed me and then stood.

'Detective Quayle, this is Faith and Grace Tiddle,' she said. 'They're both nine years old – and about fifteen minutes ago, Grace here called 999 to report... eh, what it is we have found here today.'

I dropped myself to a one knee lunge. For some reason. I'm not sure why. Perhaps to match them for height. But I felt uncomfortable immediately.

'Faith... Grace,' I said as softly as I could.

'I'm Grace,' the one on the left said, 'and she's Faith.'

I reached a hand towards Grace and she looked at it before gripping it. Then, almost immediately, she started crying. And so did Faith.

I didn't know what to say.

I looked over both shoulders to see Johnny and Sully gazing down at me. Then I turned back to the twins and reached a hand to Faith.

'I know you are both shocked right now and... and... grieving, but I think it's really important that you tell us everything you have seen today, so that we can catch the people who... who did this.'

Grace sniffled up the end of her crying. And then Faith did the exact same thing. It was eerie how they started crying and ended crying right in sync with one another.

'So... can you please tell me how you discovered... how you discovered... whatever it is you discovered?' I asked.

Faith turned to Grace.

'We were at dance class,' Grace said, and then she swallowed. 'We go to a dance class every Saturday at Ms Claire's. And when we got back we walked into the kitchen to get a glass of water and...'

Grace paused. And looked at her sister.

'We found Mommy and Daddy with lots of blood. They are dead. We know they are. They are not breathing,' Faith said. And then she started to sob again. And so, too, did Grace.

I held my eyes closed and said, 'I'm sorry.' Again.

I didn't know what else to say.

'Did you see anything else, any*body* else?' I asked.

They shook their heads in unison.

'Has, eh... has anything gone missing from the house that you've noticed?'

They both shook their heads again.

'It doesn't look like a robbery, Detective Quayle,' Sully said, whispering over my shoulder. 'No sign of a break-in. Though the back kitchen door wasn't locked.'

'Was the kitchen door open when you found your parents?' I asked the twins.

Faith turned to Grace again.

'No. I don't think so,' Grace said.

'Well, let me put it this way... have you – or you, Faith – closed the back kitchen door since you came home from dance class?'

Their two heads shook again.

I stood back up from my lunge and turned to eyeball both Johnny and Sully, then I cocked my head subtly for them to follow me into the hallway.

'Looks like somebody just stabbed the parents to death and then...' Sully whispered to me as soon as we were out of earshot.

'What?' I whispered back. 'They just came in the back kitchen door, stabbed two people to death and then left through the back kitchen door.... closing it behind them?'

Sully shrugged as an answer to my question. So I stared at Johnny. And he shrugged too, his face still sickly pale.

I began to walk away from them, slowly. It was like a corridor of a hallway; two doors on either side of it. One of the doors had a mini blackboard hanging from it, that had the names "Faith & Grace" scribbled across it.

I twisted at the handle of that door, took one step inside and then back out. I did the same at the next three doors; one a bathroom, one a spare bedroom and another which was Clive and Dorothy's bedroom. It had an oversized bed in it, with a framed photograph of a white Jesus above the bedposts, staring back at me. When I stepped out of that room I turned to the large crucifix on the back wall for a while before I heard a shuffling behind me.

'Y'okay, Quayle?'

'This is fucking mental,' I whispered back to Johnny. 'I've had a look in each room. All the windows are closed. Are you certain the only way in and out of here is through that back kitchen door?'

'We were only here a few of minutes before you, Quayle... But, eh... I checked all the windows too, and had a look at the front door. It locks from the outside.'

'Jesus,' I said, staring at the man himself nailed to a large cross right in front of me.

'This is gonna be some case, Quayle,' Johnny says. 'Have you ever done anything like this before? Where are you even gonna start?'

I placed my hands on my hips, my eyes still glued to the blue eyes of the white Jesus. And then I sighed.

'I have no bloody idea, mate.'

✝

Clive Tiddle spent almost every single one of his school days being bullied. His height didn't intimidate the other boys at all. He was extraordinarily tall but he was gangly and thin with it back then. Awkward looking, it would be fair to say. Between his appearance and his surname, he never really stood a chance in his teens.

In primary school they called him 'Lanky' just because he towered above the rest of them and that was the default slagging in school for whoever was the tallest. He didn't really mind that name. But by the time he got to secondary school he'd been christened 'Tiddly Wanks' – a cryptic nickname that was a play on his surname, mixed with a well-known board game and a huge slice of immaturity. That nickname did get him down, literally. His shoulders slumped and he became very insular through his mid-teens. But it didn't get him down as much as being called 'Gombeen' did. That's the nickname he was stuck with for the last three years of secondary. Nobody in school could ever remember quite where that nickname originated from, and nobody ever figured out that it made absolutely no sense whatsoever, but boy did it stick. Even years after Clive had graduated, he would still hear the odd 'Gombeen' being shouted at him from across the street. He was an outcast; as out there as outcasts can find themselves. He had no friends. And a family who never seemed to notice – nor care – that he had no friends.

He didn't lick his aloofness from a stone, though. His parents were similar. Well, his father more so. Brian Tiddle worked on the rigs in the north of the Irish Sea and would be gone for more months than he was home while Clive and his sister Janet were growing up. His mother had quite a few jobs over the years; from working at the local dry cleaners to packing boxes at a factory on the outskirts of the city. She often worked two jobs at once. It meant Clive and Janet rarely spent time with their parents; though it wasn't a huge concern – they were both wise enough to look after themselves. And they did. They looked after themselves – not each other. They stayed as far apart from each other as you can in a small three-bedroom terraced house. It wasn't that they hated each other or would wind each other up; it was just a case of that's what the Tiddles did – they looked after themselves.

Not having a friend certainly led Clive to assuming a girlfriend was well out of the question when he was growing up. He wasn't wrong – he didn't get a sniff of the opposite sex. But that all changed when he literally bumped into Dorothy Wyatt on a random Tuesday evening. He was rounding the corner of George's Street whilst looking behind himself and crashed into a girl he couldn't stop obsessing over for the next week.

'It's my fault, I should have been looking where I was going,' she said, all embarrassed and coy. 'I'm running late to catch my bus, s'why I was in so much of a hurry.'

He smiled at her, soaking in her large brown eyes.

'No... don't be silly. It was my fault,' he said.

She touched his shoulder – an actual touch – and then turned on her heels and paced away.

He visited the scene of that chance meeting every evening for the next week, at the exact same time. Until, the following Tuesday, he looked up from staring at his shoes and there she was... squinting at him.

'You!' she said, pointing.

'Oh,' he mocked surprise and then held out his hand – a gesture he'd rehearsed.

'My name is Clive. Clive Tiddle,' he said.

'Tiddle? That's a name that'd make you laugh.'

She actually did laugh when she said that. And he tried to mirror her, only his laugh sounded fake. The joke was far from original for him.

'Dorothy Wyatt,' she said, placing her hand loosely inside his and allowing him to shake it.

Dorothy had just finished a class. She was doing a night course in Accountancy at Dublin Business School; studying because she was starting to fret she may need a career given that no member of the opposite sex had shown much interest in her. That's painful for anyone when they're heading towards thirty, but certainly so if you live within a strong Christian family, given that it's quite uncommon for Christians to go unmatched. Everybody is always fixing folk up through different 'family' contacts in the church. 'Oh, y'know Linda Brady's son... he's single' – that kinda thing is rampant among 'families' of faith. It was rare for a churchgoer to reach their late twenties without getting married. And if that was the case, the major worry was that they might end up with somebody who doesn't believe. That's mostly why Dorothy's father didn't mind when she approached him with the idea of doing a night course in Dublin Business School. He'd rather his daughter have an actual career – even though it wasn't ideal for a church woman to have a career – than to marry outside of their faith.

Dorothy hadn't been bullied as much as Clive had been at school. Though her faith didn't exactly make her Little Miss Popular either. She wasn't hated, but she was certainly considered odd; given that she used to mention Jesus Christ's name in conversation way more than any teenager wanted to hear it.

She got through school mostly unscathed, considering. Though she was happy to finish her Leaving Cert because it gave her more time to spend with her mother and her aunties. She always felt she was a bit too mature for the girls at school, much preferring the company of those the generation above her. Not many would have considered Dorothy pretty, even though she had round chocolate-brown eyes, because her style reflected that of somebody much older; choosing to wear floral patterned summer dresses with lace collars almost every day as if she was living in a previous century. But Clive did indeed find her pretty. In fact, he thought she looked even prettier the second night he 'bumped' into her. It was the eye-contact. Nobody had ever held his stare while talking to him before.

He walked her to her stop that night and by the time her bus arrived had plucked up enough courage to ask her on a date.

'Sure,' she beamed at him. Then she turned to wave the bus to a stop before snapping her head back at Clive. 'Oh...' she said, 'you are Catholic, aren't you?'

His gaze flicked downwards, to the crucifix hanging from a thin chain around her neck, and then he nodded confidently.

'Course, yeah,' he said.

He wasn't lying. Not technically. He had been christened and so his registration on the census all through his life confirmed him as a Catholic. Though he hadn't been to church for over a decade; not since his school required him to go. But his lack of church experience never became an issue because he fit right in with Dorothy and her church 'family' from day one. He really began to feel, quite early on, that he hadn't just found himself a girl-friend when he bumped into Dorothy Wyatt, he'd found himself a whole new life.

As soon as he met Dorothy's mother and father he went about pleasing them in any way he could. He even started to dress like Dorothy's father;

never quite realising over the years that the reason Noah Wyatt dressed in gilets and plaid shirts was because he was a keen flyfisherman. Clive never flyfished in his life, because he couldn't swim. Nor could he do boats. But he dressed like a flyfisherman every day for the rest of his life after meeting Noah for the first time. New life. New look.

Clive and Dorothy married in the spring of 1995 in front of three hundred and fifty guests – a lot of whom they had never even met. 'Course you can bring your cousin,' is the way invitations are handled for mass Christian weddings. The more the merrier. As long, of course, as the guest was Catholic. No point bringing an atheist along. They just think we're all crazy.

That's not to say the wedding was totally starved of sceptics. Clive's parents and Janet were in attendance. They hated the day though, constantly rolling their eyes every time the name Jesus Christ was brought up – almost as if it was his special day and not necessarily the bride and groom's. It was the last day the Tiddles ever spent together, though. Clive would lose both his parents not long after he and Dorothy wed. His father collapsed with a massive heart attack as his mother was undergoing cancer treatment. She died three months after him. Both aged fifty-two. The same age Clive would be when he'd meet his death.

Clive and Dorothy couldn't wait to begin trying for a family. In fact, they literally didn't wait. They did it for the first time on their wedding evening, not night. They left their reception not long after their beef dinners and headed straight to the bridal bed to much wolf-whistling from their 'family'.

'We'll get better at it,' Clive said as he lay beside his bride after their first attempt. And they did get better. Not necessarily in a sexual way. Just in a practical way. They figured out when the best times were to try to conceive and they read manuals on what positions could prove best for conception. Dorothy particularly liked doggy-style. But despite their studious approach to baby making, nothing ever seemed to work for them. They were always disappointed when Dorothy would inevitably receive her period cramps each month. Yet deep down she was convinced that this was all part of the plan – that Jesus would deliver them what they wanted in time. But one year fell into two and then four years seemed to become five years really quickly. Then it was a decade... and more.

Visits to the Rotunda Hospital for tests didn't really get to the heart of the problem. It couldn't be determined who was at fault. Clive's sperm counts were mostly high, but quite often inconsistent. And Dorothy's ovulations weren't particularly predictable. But the specialists couldn't pin-point exactly why it hadn't happened for them, given that they had been trying so much, for so long. As they rounded the bend into their forties, they decided they had to go the IVF route... that perhaps Jesus was leading them that way.

It was an expensive way he was leading them, if indeed he was leading them at all; certainly expensive if you try it twelve times which is what the Tiddles did over the course of a ten-year period. Until one day Dorothy peed on a stick... and finally that blue cross that she'd only ever seen in her daydreams appeared before her eyes like a miracle. Three months later they'd learn that it was a double miracle.

'This one's Faith. And this one's Grace,' Clive would say, introducing his bundles of joy for the first time to 'family' members. 'We wanted their names to reflect our gratefulness to our Lord Jesus Christ.'

ALICE

I grip the top of Mrs Balfe's garden wall as I lower to my hunkers and try to force the bile from the back of my throat. But nothing comes. Just a horrible retching sound. I spit. And then hold a hand to my mouth to mop at it.

After I steady my breaths, I reach into my jacket pocket and take out my phone again. My fingers quiver as they hover over the screen. But I manage to press into the text message again. I don't know why, though. It's not going away. Maybe I should ring whoever this is back; ask how the fuck they got their hands on my video. I hover my finger over the number, then instantly feel a need to clasp my hand to my mouth again, dropping my phone to the concrete. The bile retches from me, splashing just outside Mrs Balfe's garden gate. Jesus. If she saw me here like this the whole neighbourhood would know about it by the end of the evening.

I hold my eyes closed and try to breathe steadily before I press my hand against Mrs Balfe's wall to help guide me back to a standing position. Then I pick up my phone and check the message again... It's still there.

Maybe I should ring Emmet. See if he knows what the hell this is about. He can't have anything to do with it, though... surely? Can he? Course not. Jesus. My brain is frying.

I click into my contacts and without hesitation press at Emmet's number.

'Hey,' he answers.

'Emmet – listen,' I say and then I breathe out a long, shameful sigh. 'You need to be honest with me, you hear me?'

'Alice... you okay?'

'Emmet,' I sigh again, 'do you – or do you not – have a recording of that... that...'

'What? The me and you video? No. Course not. I've told you a hundred times. You made me promise that you'd be the only one to ever have the video. That's why you agreed to... y'know... do it.'

I scratch furiously at the side of my hair, then begin to yank at it. I know he doesn't have a copy of the video. We recorded it on my phone. I saved it. Then hid it in a draft email so I could be the only one to ever watch it.

'Alice? What's up? You sure you're okay? Why you asking about the vid—'

'I'm just... eh... I'm just being paranoid,' I say, pulling my hair tighter. 'That's all. Just... just one of those days.'

'You sure?'

'I'm fine. Fine. Just... y'know I'm serving on this bloody trial and the pressure... and – don't mind me. I'll see you soon, right? Next Friday we're doing that night at the Hilton.'

'Yeah... yeah. Looking forward to it. But I think I'll probably be seeing you—'

'Okay, bye, bye, bye,' I say, hanging up.

Of course Emmet doesn't have anything to do with this. Why would he?

My weight gives way and I'm back to my hunkers again; my breathing growing sharp. I can't cope. I seriously can't cope with this. Somebody knows about the video. Somebody *has* the fucking video!

I spit again; the last remnants of the bile that was swimming in my mouth and then groan as I push against the wall to get back to a standing position. Again. I've been like a fucking yo-yo here.

I have to find out who has this video. I need to know what they plan on doing with it.

I begin to text the number back. Then tut and delete it. I rewrite another text. And delete that too. What the fuck am I supposed to ask? There's just too many questions. I shake my head, and as I do I just jab my thumb at the number and bring the phone to my ear. My heart rate rises with each ringing tone.

'So you decided to ring, not text,' a voice says. It's a woman. A woman's distorted voice.

'Who the hell is this?' I ask.

'Calm down, Alice... Then listen *very* carefully, okay? I will send this video to your husband's phone unless you do as I say.'

'What... what...' I circle the pathway outside Mrs Balfe's house, my hair tightly twisted around my fist.

'It is your job to ensure the twins are not found guilty. If they are, I'm gonna text this video straight to your loved ones with one push of a button.'

'What... this is all about the trial? Who is this? How did you get my video?'

'Oh Alice. That wasn't very difficult. The draft folder of your emails? Tut, tut.'

'Hold on... what... you hacked my phone? What do you want me to do? I can't... I can't...' I stop pacing when I hear her laugh back at me. 'How the hell do you expect me to convince eleven other jurors to vote not guilty, that's... that's...' I whisper-shout into the phone.

'Oh Alice. It's more simple than you think,' she says. 'You don't need to convince eleven jurors... just two.'

I stop pacing and squint.

'Two?'

'Anything but a guilty verdict and I will destroy this phone. And everything that's on it will go away. All I need is a hung jury. If you and two others hold out and don't vote guilty, the trial collapses. And your life is spared.'

I pause.

Everything pauses.

My voice.

Her voice.

My breathing.

My squinting.

My hair-pulling.

'So I need to... I need to...' I stutter.

'You know exactly what you need to do, Alice.'

Then she hangs up.

And I drop to my fucking hunkers again. Spitting. But spitting out nothing. Not even saliva. My mouth's gone all dry.

I knew I shouldn't have recorded that bloody video. I just... I just wanted it to masturbate to. Me and Emmet only get to meet up once every month... or even two months, sometimes. It's not easy. And because I was finding the whole experience so thrilling and... horny, I asked if I could record a video of us together, just so I could get my own kicks out of it in my alone time. I thought it was safe, locked away in a hidden folder in my email account. I'm a fucking idiot.

'Everything alright, Alice?'

I look up, and when I see her I release the grip on my hair.

'Evening, Mrs Balfe,' I say, beaming a fake grin in her direction. 'Just having one of those days, y'know?'

She stares back at me from her front door, her eyes narrow, her brow sunken, her arms crossed under her fat boobs. She's eighty-two now, Mrs Balfe – our neighbourhood's chief curtain twitcher.

'I, eh... gotta get home. Noel will have dinner almost ready,' I say.

She doesn't respond. She just stares at me, as if she's never seen me before. Maybe she's finally going senile. I hope she is anyway; well... I certainly hope she didn't see me panic attacking outside her home.

I pocket my phone and stroll on as my mind begins to swirl again. It must be that Gerd Bracken fucker. He's a slimeball. He must have something to do with this. That's why he always wins his cases – the bastard must be blackmailing jurors all the time. Though it can't be him. It's a woman. Maybe it's that Imogen one who works with him – though I can't imagine that. She's as quiet as a mouse.

I chew on my bottom lip and try to think of all the women who have been involved in this case – wondering who benefits the most from the Tiddle twins being acquitted.

By the time any of my thoughts have made sense I'm at my hall door; my key already inside the keyhole. I pause and take a deep breath. Noel will be home. With Alfie. Noel's been getting off work early for the past couple of weeks while I've been in court, just so somebody's here when our son gets in from school. I let the breath slowly seep out of my nostrils and then I turn the key and finally walk myself inside.

'Hey, Alfie,' I say when I see my son half way up the stairs. 'How was your day at school?'

'Fine,' he says with a grunt. I'm used to it. It's how kids his age communicate when they're asked questions they don't want to answer. I went through it all with Zoe. It's not easy.

'Hey love,' Noel says, sidling up to me while wringing his hands in a kitchen towel. He kisses me on the cheek, then pulls at the lapel of my coat, taking it from me. 'How did you get on today?'

'Grand. Grand. Eh... yeah, grand.' I say.

I look at him. And his face immediately creases.

'Jesus, you okay?' he says. 'You look like you've seen a ghost.' I open my mouth to say something, but nothing comes out. And suddenly my knees collapse and I'm on all fours. Just like I am in that bloody video. 'Sweetie... Alice...'

I can hear Noel. I just can't bloody answer him. The oak floorboards in our hallway are spinning and I need them to slow down before I can even try to settle myself to open my mouth.

He reaches under my stomach and lifts me to a kneeling position.

'You're white,' he says, placing a hand on my forehead. He blows out his cheeks. 'No temperature, but maybe you should take a lie down. Here, let me help you to the sofa.'

I shake my head. And as I do I feel my cheeks fill.

The bile roars out of me, slapping onto the floorboards.

'Mam, mam, what's wrong?'

Alfie runs back down the stairs. I try to smile up at him, but when I do, I feel more bile reach my throat. I managed to swallow it down though, then swipe at my chin with my forearm, mopping up the streams of spit that were hanging from it.

'She's okay, Alfie,' Noel says. 'Here son, take her arm and help her to the sofa.'

'Ye know what,' I say, blinking my eyes so that I can refocus. 'Just take me to bed. I wanna go to bed.'

Noel steadies me by leaning into me and taking my weight. Then he leads me up the stairs without asking any further questions.

When we reach our room he perches me carefully on to the edge of the bed.

'It's nothing, Noel,' I say, holding my hand to my face. 'Just a bloody ham dinner I had for lunch at the courts, I think. A little bit of food poisoning is all.'

He kneels down in front of me so he can stare up into my face.

'It can't be food poisoning, sweetie,' he says. 'You haven't thrown up any food. Just bile. That's your stomach lining splashed all about our hallway.' He places his palm on my forehead again. 'Still no temperature.'

I kick off my shoes and lie back.

'It's just this bloody trial,' I say to him, a burst of emotion forcing its way out from the middle of my face. Tears. Snot. The lot. 'It's so much pressure. So much pressure.'

He lies beside me, rubs at my arm.

'Oh sweetie,' he says. 'I'm so sorry you have to go through this. Must be almost over now, though?'

I sniff.

'Last witness was called today. It's closing arguments in the morning and then... then it's up to us.'

'Ah... so that's all this is... it's just a bit of anxiety floating around in your little tummy,' he says, rubbing around my navel. 'You have a big decision to make tomorrow. That's all this is.'

I turn to face him and stare into his eyes. I haven't stared into his eyes from this close in ages. Probably years. I love him. So much. So, so much.

'You're right. Just a bit of anxiety. I'm sorry.'

'Don't be sorry,' he says. 'I'm gonna go clean up the hallway. You, eh...

you get yourself some rest. Call out for me when you need me. Do you think you'll come down for dinner in an hour or so?'

I suck in through my teeth and shake my head.

'Not sure, Noel. Think I'll just, eh... think I'll just play it by ear. I don't feel up for eating.'

He holds his hands to his hips, creasing that sorrowful look at me again.

'Okay. Get some rest, sweetie. Big day tomorrow. It's just, eh... Zoe rang earlier. Her and Emmet are coming over for dinner.'

—

DAY ONE

Even the sound of the gravel crunching under the wheels of a car didn't take my gaze from that white face. I'm not sure how long I'd been staring at it for or even why I was staring at it; perhaps I was willing Jesus to tell me what he had witnessed inside that house that morning.

'Quayle,' Johnny shouted from the doorway, 'Tallaght are here.'

I puffed a long, loud sigh out through my nostrils, then formed my fists into a ball and stormed down the hallway – as if I was on a mission.

'This is *my* investigation, Tunstead,' I said as soon as my shoes touched the gravel. He creased his eyebrows at me, glanced at his partner, Lowe, and then sniggered.

'Wow, calm down, Quayle,' he said. 'Jeez... have some respect. I doubt the bodies have even cooled yet and you've already got twisty knickers.'

I looked at Johnny as he stood alongside me, then back at the two detectives.

'Two bodies, adults,' I said, softening my tone. 'I'm certain I know their names. Clive and Dorothy Tiddle. They run the church around here.'

'Cause of death?'

'Stabbings. Multiple of them.'

Tunstead and Lowe exchanged another glance.

'Sign of a break in?' Tunstead asked, struggling to remove a notepad from his back trousers pocket. His suits are always way too skinny for detective attire. Not that I'm an old prude or anything. It's just this prick thinks he's acting in a movie; skinny suits, skinny tie, shiny shoes – a thick head full of Brylcreemed black hair.

'Listen, I'm in charge here, Tunstead,' I said, stepping closer to him and placing my hand over his notepad.

'Relax Quayle,' he said. 'I'm only taking some notes. Listen... I get it. This is your patch. We're just here to assist. Support.'

I looked to Lowe, and she nodded her head at me.

'No,' I sighed out of my mouth. 'No sign of a break-in. But the, eh... back kitchen door was unlocked.'

'Was it open when you got here?'

'Nope,' Johnny piped up, popping the p sound out of his mouth. 'The twins say the kitchen door wasn't opened when they found the bodies.'

'Twins?' Lowe said, shifting her stance on the gravel.

'Two nine-year-old girls,' I said.

'Did they ring it in?'

I nod.

'So, eh...' Tunstead took a step closer to me and leaned his nose towards my ear. 'It's not the twins who killed them, is it?'

'Pfft... course not,' I said, almost laughing. And suddenly I could feel all three of them staring at me. As if I'd just said something outrageous. 'No. No. Course not,' I repeated. 'They're only nine, for crying out loud.'

Tunstead scribbled something on his notepad, then cocked his head at Lowe before turning back to me.

'Well,' he said, 'let's have a look then, shall we? You got some gloves? Foot protectors?' I stared straight into his eyes before I felt a need to look at my shoes. 'Jesus Christ, Quayle.' A cringe churned inside my stomach.

'I didn't have gloves with me,' I said. 'All I did was take a look in the kitchen at the bodies, then checked for any sign of a break in. That's all. I'll make sure it's all reported in the log book. It'll be fine.'

'Make sure that's logged, Quayle,' Lowe said, nodding at me, a pinch of sympathy etched in her expression. She's nice, Lowe. At least I think she is. Too nice to be working with that prick anyway. But sometimes even she looks at me like I don't know what I'm doing – and I've been on the force close to two decades longer than she has.

Tunstead walked to the back of his car to pop the boot, then carried back four plastic packages. Gloves. And foot protectors. He handed a pack of each to Lowe, and then me and Johnny stood there in an awkward silence as they both slipped them on.

'How long are SOCO gonna take to get here?' Tunstead asked as he snapped on his second foot protector.

I swallowed, then stared at Johnny.

'Eh... shall I ring them now, Quayle?' Johnny asked, looking confused.

'Yes, yes! Of course. Quick as you can,' I barked back at him.

I could feel Lowe and Tunstead glare at me with disappointment again.

'SOCO will have gloves and protectors for you when they get here,' Tunstead said. 'Don't go inside that house again until you're wearing them. I don't want you contaminating the murder scene.'

'That's my murder scene,' I said, almost too loud. Maybe even so loud the twins might have heard me.

'Well, get your arse in to your murder scene as soon as you get the right gear on, yeah?'

I held a clenched fist to my mouth as Tunstead and Lowe stepped inside the bungalow. I was cringing that I hadn't thought to ring SOCO as soon as I got there. I just wasn't used to taking control. I should have been taking action – not staring at that bloody crucifix. It wasn't as if I hadn't been at a murder scene before. I had. Lots of them. It's just I'd never been the lead detective at a murder scene. Murders just don't happen around here. It's just too quiet... too remote... too peaceful. I'd been at murder scenes in other jurisdictions. Especially in Tallaght. But I was normally the one assisting those two pricks who had just entered my murder scene. It had never been the other way around.

'SOCO will be about half an hour,' Johnny said, pocketing his phone and walking back towards me. I liked Johnny from the moment he joined our station. He'd only been there about a year before the Tiddle case. It was just me, him, Fairweather and one other uniform – Sully – working from the station then. Rathcoole was always being rumoured to be facing closure. Not a lot happened around our area, and as a result our funding was constantly culled. We hung in, though. A small station on a small budget, looking after the small communities dotted around the foothills of the Dublin mountains.

'Shit, we'll need to get Sully out,' I whispered to Johnny. 'She's no gloves or foot protectors on in there either.'

'But, eh...' Johnny paused and began to tug at his ear, 'who'll stay with the twins?' I didn't answer him; I just stared up into the cloudless sky. As if the answers to the thousands of questions that were circulating my head were just going to rain themselves down on me. 'Quayle...' Johnny took a step towards me. 'You sure you're okay with this? Why don't you let Tunstead and Lowe run the case. They've a lot more exper—'

'Fuck no,' I said to him. 'This is our case. Our station's jurisdiction. It's up to us to find who did this.'

Johnny thinned his lips and nodded his head.

'And we will, Quayle,' he said. 'I'm with you all the way, boss.' He looked over his shoulder, then back at me. 'So, eh... what'll I do? Do you want me to take Sully out? Surely we should have somebody with the twins at all times. The shock they must be under—'

'Bring them outside with Sully,' I said, rolling my shoulders, feeling as if I'd finally made my first decision of the case. I made an instant pact with myself there and then that I would always make the twins' welfare my priority. 'We need to get somebody here to look after them. Who in the force looks after child welfare... who do we ring for that?'

Johnny pushed his chin into his neck and shrugged.

'Haven't you got one of those smart phones?' I said. 'Look it up. Who should we ring?'

As he removed his phone from his trouser pocket again, I mirrored him and stared at my screen, wondering whether or not I should ring Fairweather. I knew she was on the golf course. That was nothing new. I always liked Fairweather. She took me under her wing when I joined Rathcoole Station and we worked closely together for twenty-five years; keeping the streets of Rathcoole and the surrounding mountainside free of crime, save for the odd drug deal and car theft. She semi-retired the year prior to the Tiddle murders and by that stage spent more time on the fairways of the K Club than she did at the station. I was always fearful of when she would fully retire because I didn't fancy running the station all by myself. I liked my working life just as it was. Well... just as it was before I answered the call to the Tiddle's bungalow that morning.

I turned when I heard footsteps shuffling behind me. It was them. Moving in unison like two dolls that had just come to life. It was such a surreal moment, because I could see Tunstead behind them bent over the body of their father.

I got down to my hunkers and held out a hand to each of them just as Johnny and Sully joined us outside. Grace grabbed a hand first. Then Faith. I stared at them, right into their big brown eyes; shifting my gaze from one to the other.

'I'm so sorry,' I said. Again. And then, from behind me, I heard the crunch of gravel under wheels. I turned to see a large white van; a big-ass aerial on its roof. It skidded to a stop behind my car. And then two men clambered out; one with a camera balancing on his shoulder, the other wide-eyed and almost excited looking. As if murder was a drug to him.

'Sully,' I said, 'get the twins in the back of my car. We need to get them out of here now!'

ALICE

I stab my finger at the elevator button, then step back and wait.

'Morning,' the redhead says, startling me.

'Morning,' I say back. 'Sorry... I'm away with the fairies here.'

She smiles her lovely teeth at me.

'Why wouldn't you be?' she says. 'I'm the same. This trial is...' she shakes her head, '...I was awake most the night thinking about it.'

I snort out a laugh.

'Oh, me too. Me too.'

I actually spent fifteen hours in my bed last night and still didn't get any sleep. At all. I went to bed at twenty past five straight after I puked all over the floorboards in our hall and stayed there until seven o'clock this morning when my alarm finally beeped. I was sitting up by that time, staring at the digits; waiting on 6:59 to turn into 7:00 so I could justify getting myself out of bed.

I glance at Red Head out of the corner of my eye as we ride up the elevator in silence. I wonder what verdict she has going on inside her head; perhaps I can convince her she should vote not guilty. That was specifically what consumed most of my thoughts when I was awake in bed last night: which jurors I can convince easiest. The obese guy already told me he would vote not guilty, so I only need to convince one other, providing he doesn't change his mind of course. Red Head is definitely an option for me. So is the guy with the ridiculously high quiff. And maybe the short girl with the braces. They're the youngest, so probably the most naïve and impressionable. But hopefully I don't need to influence or convince anyone. Maybe two or more are going to vote not guilty anyway.

I can't even begin to imagine how Noel would react if he found out me and Emmet have been having sex. His whole life would just deflate. He'd evaporate into a heartbroken mess. I know he would. I can't be quite so certain how Zoe would react. I tortured myself trying to wonder if I'd ever have a relationship with my daughter again if she saw that video. Though that specific torture has been going on a lot longer than just last night. It's been with me ever since me and Emmet started our fling. I couldn't help it. I just couldn't. He's so... so well-built. Like one of those Dreamboys or whatever they're called. A six pack and all. When was I ever gonna be taken from behind by a hottie with a six pack? That was not the kind of offer I'd ever gotten. Not even when I was eighteen. No hot guy ever wanted me. None of the rugby players at my school even gave me a second glance. And now I have a semi-pro rugby player giving me orgasms I would never have had my whole life had he not started dating my daughter a year and a half ago.

I didn't think anything of it when I first met him. I certainly never thought I wanted to fuck him. Or that I wanted him to fuck me. Of course I didn't. He was my daughter's new boyfriend. All I was concerned with then was whether or not he was polite. That's all any parent looks for in their offspring's partner. Having an affair never crossed my mind. Ever. I was totally faithful to Noel. Until... until that first night. I just couldn't help myself. I still can't. Even last night, when I heard Emmet coming up our stairs to go to the bathroom, my body tingled. I was hoping he'd poke his head around my door, ask me how I was. Give me a quick kiss. But he didn't. He washed his hands, went straight back down to have dinner with the rest of my family. Probably for the best, though. Zoe came into me twice. Just to hold her hand against my forehead and give me assurances that all will be okay once this trial is finally over.

'Oh, we're going in already,' Red Head says, nudging me.

I look up, see the young woman dressed in all black opening the door to the courtroom, and suddenly we're all filing inside one-by-one, enveloped in that awkward silence yet again.

I form a diamond with my fingers on my lap as soon as I sit down and bow my head a little. This has become a routine. A ritual. I never know where else to look. But as soon as the door on the far side of the room clangs open, my head shoots up. I can't help it. Grace walks in first, followed by Faith; both of their faces void of expression. Just as they are every day. They plonk themselves into the same seats they always occupy: Grace next to Gerd Bracken's assistant Imogen, Faith on the far side of her sister. Imogen whispers to Grace every now and then through parts of the trial. But Faith never says anything. Not a word.

'All rise,' a voice shouts.

And the whole court gets to its feet to welcome Judge Delia McCormick in the most formal way imaginable. I wonder if she feels awkward coming in and out of this courtroom drowned in that awkward silence like I do.

She peers up over her glasses at the benches in front of her when she sits.

'The court will hear final arguments.'

And that's it. That's all she says.

After the long silence that follows, Jonathan Ryan, who's done quite a decent job as lead prosecutor even though he must be only in his late twenties, clears his throat nervously, then strolls ever-so-slowly towards us. I'm certain he's staring straight at me.

'Ladies and gentlemen of the jury,' he says. His head swivels up and down the two rows of jurors, taking each of us in. 'I am under no doubt that Faith and Grace Tiddle murdered their parents Clive and Dorothy Tiddle in cold blood on the morning of the day dated fifteenth of August, coming close to two years ago now. And you should be under no doubt too.'

I look over his shoulder at Gerd Bracken, hoping – *wishing* – that his closing argument trumps whatever the hell Jonathan Ryan is about to produce here.

'You are lucky – as jurors,' he says, taking one step back from us and beginning to gesture with his hands, 'because this is a very straight-forward trial in terms of judgement. Yes, it has been chilling and I'm aware that a lot of the content would have been difficult for you to digest over these past two weeks. But in terms of arriving at a verdict... this couldn't be simpler.'

I whisper 'shit' to myself, then stare up the row of faces to my right. The woman with the overly big bust catches my eye and squints at me – so I flick my gaze swiftly back to Jonathan Ryan.

'You don't have to be a legal expert or indeed a crime scene expert to understand the facts of this case. There was zero evidence. Zer–ro,' he says, rolling his 'r'. 'None. Nada. Not a thing. Not a strand of evidence, that suggests somebody else entered that house on the day in question to kill Clive and Dorothy. Somebody inside that house carried out that murder. Only somebody from inside that house could have done this. And, as you have heard through expert witnesses, only somebody of miniature stature could have done this. Unless, of course, you believe the sensational story the defence have tried to spin. That a Hollywood movie-esque contract killer arrived in Rathcoole, broke into the Tiddle house unnoticed, stabbed two people to death in the manner in which a child – or children – would stab somebody. And then left. Without leaving a trace of their own DNA – or *any* evidence whatsoever. Not a trace. Pufff…. gone.' He gestures an imaginary disappearance with the flick of his fingers. 'And even if you believe that somebody so intelligent and stealth-like and genius at killing people without leaving a spickle of evidence could exist and wanted to target Clive and Dorothy, do we really think that *genius* would forget to bring a weapon with him – that he just happened to use a knife from the Tiddles' kitchen?'

He puffs out a silent snigger. Then he takes a step back towards the desk he had spent most of the trial sitting at and perches his bum onto the corner of it, staring up at us, his arms folded.

I find myself looking around the room during his rehearsed silence. I wonder if the bitch who's blackmailing me is in here. I glare at the defence table first. Gerd and Imogen. Maybe they hired somebody to hack my phone. It was definitely a girl I spoke to last night, so it's not him himself. And it couldn't be Imogen. She's just too… quiet… too fragile-looking. She looks like a female Harry Potter; round glasses, pale, oval-shaped face. I shake my head a little then look into the gallery at the glum faces in the crowd. The court has been full every day of this trial. I look at Kelly McAllister and then at Janet Petersen, wondering if they're the ones who got their hands on the recording of me and Emmet. I guess they might benefit from the twins getting off in some way. But would they even have the means to do this? Would they even know what hacking a phone is? I shake my head more firmly this time, trying to get rid of my thoughts. I shouldn't be playing detective. It doesn't really matter who it is. What matters is that I convince the people sitting beside me here to let these twins go.

'…The defence will attempt to tell you the girls couldn't have done this. That nine-year-old girls couldn't be so cool and so calculated as to strut off to dance class minutes after killing their parents, acting as if nothing happened. But this is simply not true. Claire Barry, their dance teacher, clearly said when sitting in that witness stand in front of you, that Faith was "particularly quiet" that day. That the defendant was acting out of sorts.'

I sniff my nose at this a little. Faith is always quiet. From what I can make out anyway. I'll convince the jurors that this part of the prosecution's argument is bullshit.

'It's normally the little things; the little things, members of the jury, that ensure guilty people are convicted. When Grace Tiddle dialled 999, she didn't even sound upset that her parents had been killed. When Detective Denis Quayle attended the scene minutes later, neither of the girls were crying. They went and had a McDonald's… *a McDonald's*! Imagine that? You find your parents stabbed to death, lying in pools of blood, and then you go out and have a Happy Meal. Those are the types of 'little things' that will convict a guilty person. But this trial isn't even about the little things. You – members of the jury – don't have a tough decision to make. Your decision doesn't even need to come down to the little things. You've been a lucky enough jury to have big things to discuss. Such as the fact that there is simply no evidence that anybody else was inside that house that day; that the Tiddles were killed at the hands of a child or children; that the Tiddles were killed with a weapon from inside their own home. A home in which only four people live.'

He leans up off his table and takes a couple of steps towards us again.

'Let me repeat something I said there again, members of the jury... There is *no evidence* that anybody else was inside that house that day. Clive and Dorothy Tiddle were killed *inside* their own home, by somebody already *inside* their own home, who used a weapon – a kitchen knife – from *inside* their own home.'

I swallow and then strain my eyes to look up the row of faces to my right again. 'Let me ask you this, members of the jury,' Jonathan Ryan continues. 'Which tale is more likely to be true? That a Hollywood movie-type hit-man crept into the Dublin mountains one day to murder two innocent church-goers in cold blood without bringing a weapon and then left without leaving so much as a jot of DNA or evidence, or...' he tilts his head, puffs out a tiny snigger. I hope the other jurors are finding this as arrogant as I am. I don't think it's going to do him any favours. He wasn't like this during the trial. 'Or two kids, who finally came of age to realise the abuse they were receiving at the hands of their parents—'

'I object!' Gerd Bracken stands to his feet, his balled fist slamming onto the desk in front of him.

Judge McCormick brings down her gavel, and then... silence.

'Mr Bracken, you are an experienced enough lawyer to know you do not get to object during final arguments.'

'But, Your Honour, he cannot stand there and just lie like that. The prosecution brought miniscule evidence to suggest Faith and Grace suffered any sort of abuse at the hands of their parents.'

Judge McCormick knocks her gavel against her table again, then turns to Jonathan Ryan.

'Mr Ryan, I would ask you to be very careful with your use of language in your final arguments.'

'Your Honour,' Ryan says, almost bowing at her. 'What I was basically getting at... members of the jury,' he says, turning back to us, 'is... are you more likely to believe that a made-up Hollywood creation swept into Rathcoole to murder two innocent people, or that a set of twins who had religion bombarded at them from day one of their lives finally rebelled by putting an end to that bombardment? When all reason and all common sense and all logic is considered in this case then – you will have to agree with me, members of the jury – only one version of those two events could possibly be true.' He steps forward and grips the bench in front of the first row of jurors. 'It is a fact that Faith and Grace Tiddle killed their parents. It is now your job – and your responsibility – to confirm them guilty of that crime.'

He turns to the judge, almost bows again and then strolls back towards his seat.

Is that it? Five minutes telling us stuff he already said during the trial. I thought it'd be longer than that. Though I'm not quite sure what I expected... a PowerPoint presentation or something? I thought a final argument would be a lot more detailed than a small summary.

Though what he said was quite convincing. Jesus... I wonder what all the other jurors are thinking right now after that. I'd definitely find the twins guilty. No doubt about it at all. What Jonathan Ryan said makes perfect sense. Nobody else could have done this.

Bracken needs to nail his closing argument now. He needs to trump Ryan's. It's not just Faith and Grace's lives that depend on it. Mine does too.

'Mr Bracken,' the judge calls out.

Bracken stands, opens the single button of his suit jacket as he walks out from behind his table and then grins at us.

'Ladies and gentlemen of the jury...'

DAY ONE–DAY TWO

I knew she was in bed as soon as I turned onto our street. There were no lights on downstairs.

I checked my watch as I strolled up our garden path and noted it was five to twelve. The last minutes of the day. And what a day it was!

As soon as I got inside, I shuffled out of my blazer, hung it on the bannisters and made my way up to her.

'You're ever so late,' she called out before I had even made it to the top of the stairs. I smiled. The first smile I'd smiled since I began listening to Billy Joel just before my Garda radio spat at me.

'You won't believe the day I've had.' I held a hand against our wardrobe for balance as I kicked off my shoes. Then I loosened the belt of my jeans, for a little relief, before bouncing up on the bed beside her. She placed the book she was reading onto her lap and leaned a little towards me, just so I could kiss her forehead.

'Go on,' she said.

'Well, first things first... as always,' I said, grabbing her hand. 'How have you been today?'

'Never mind me,' she replied, gripping my hand tighter. 'I've had a day like all the rest of my days recently. You, clearly, haven't. Why are you getting home at darn-near midnight... somebody get killed?' I scrunched up my face, and as I did she removed her hand from my grasp and held it to her mouth. 'Oh no, somebody did get killed...'

I sat more upright in bed and turned to face her.

'Two people actually. D'you know the couple who have the twin girls... they run the church in the middle of the mountains?'

She squinted, her head shaking ever so slightly.

'Have they a silly name?'

I nodded.

'Yeah. Tiddle.'

'That's right... It's not them who were killed... was it?'

'Afraid so. The parents. Both stabbed to death inside their own home.'

Sheila covered her bottom lip with her top lip.

'How old are they?' she asked.

'We found out he was fifty-two – Clive Tiddle. The wife, Dorothy, she was fifty. I thought they were much older, but...' I shrug. 'I guess the twins are only nine, so—'

'Jeez, how are they... the twins?' Sheila asked.

'They're fine... well, physically anyway. They weren't part of the attack. They were at a dance class when it happened. Came home just after midday and found their parents lying there... in the kitchen. Lots of blood. Pools of it.'

Sheila leaned a little closer to me.

'You think *they* did it... the twins?' she asked.

'Not you as well.'

She crinkled her nose up at me.

'No, no. I'm just... just...'

'You're reading too many of those books,' I said, slapping at the paper-back on her lap. 'Starting to think you're a detective yourself, huh?'

She smiled. I love it so much when she smiles – even if it's just a sorrowful smile like that one was. She was producing a lot of sorrowful smiles back then. But at least it was better than no smiles at all, which is the state she had been in for the nine months prior.

'But you, eh... you did verify that they were at a dance class, right?' she asked.

'Course I did. They were at dance class between eleven and midday. Their dance teacher confirmed it.'

'Sweet Jesus. That's some case,' Sheila said.

'Yeah, a case I'm lead detective on,' I spat out. 'It happened on our patch.'

She rubbed at my arm as if she was congratulating me, then offered me another one of those sorrowful smiles.

'You'll nail it,' she said, holding a hand to her mouth to cover a yawn.

'Hey,' I said, swinging my legs over the side of the bed. 'I almost forgot, the day that was in it. I, eh... picked you up a little something this morning.'

I hopped off the bed, paced across the landing and then headed down the stairs to snatch at my blazer . I took the small bags from my inside pocket and tossed the blazer aside when I got back into the bedroom.

'Here you are, my lovely.' I threw the bags of weed to her lap and jumped back on the bed.

Sheila made on 'O' shape with her mouth.

'Six quarter bags... That's about two months' worth, right?' she asked.

I winked at her.

'How did you get your hands on this?' she said as she opened up one of the small bags to take a sniff.

'Ah...' I waved my hand, knowing she wouldn't ask again.

'Thank you.'

'Do you wanna do some now?'

She took another sniff from the bag and then shook her head.

'No. Thanks. I'll take some in the morning. With a nice cup of tea.'

She pinched each of the quarter bags from her lap and then dropped them beside the lamp on her bedside table. I love looking at the profile of my wife in that kind of dim light. It makes her look like her old self. When she was more beautiful.

'So where are the twins now?' she asked, turning back to me.

'It was a crazy day,' I said before I blew out my cheeks. 'The media turned up before the Scene of Crime Officers. We had to get the twins out of there as soon as possible. I didn't know where to bring them. We brought them to the station, then... we ended up in McDonald's.'

'McDonald's?' Sheila made a face at me.

'It's just... they were hungry.' My heart dropped a little. Even my wife seemed to be questioning everything I'd done in the case up until that point. 'It's alright now, though,' I said. 'Tusla arrived at about three p.m. They sorted the twins out.'

'Tusla?'

'A specialist child welfare agency. That's what they do... look after kids who are subjects of crime.'

'How are they, though – the twins? They must be inconsolable.'

'They seem fine one minute. Then they start crying the next. It's a little bit spooky. Once one cries, the other follows. And when she stops the other one does the exact same thing. As if their batteries get switched off at the same time. You can't help but feel for them though. They're... they're...' I hesitate.

Sheila shrugged at me. 'They're what?'

'Cute, I guess. Two little cuties. They're only nine and... Jeez, can you imagine finding your parents stabbed to death at that age?' I patted at

Sheila's knee and then kissed her forehead again. 'Sorry, love. Not the kinda news you want to hear right before you fall asleep.' She yawned again. 'Go on. Knock off your lamp. I'm going to go downstairs, see if I can let my mind unwind.'

I was as excited by the case as I was frightened by it as I sat at our kitchen table, my hands clasped atop of it, my mind whirring. I knew this story would be all over the news the following morning and was already starting to worry that the press would come down hard on me; that I'd be under pressure, under scrutiny. I'd already made some bad fuck ups even though the case was barely half a day old. I couldn't believe I traipsed into a crime scene without gloves or protectors on. And I couldn't believe I forgot to call SOCO straight away. Or Tusla. Though I didn't even know who Tusla were before Johnny checked it on his smart phone. And then I went and brought them to bloody McDonald's. Jesus. McDonald's! It just seemed like the right thing to do at the time. They were hungry. I was hungry. Johnny said he was peckish, too. And I thought it'd be better for them to be out and about, rather than sitting in our pokey little police station while we waited on Tusla. I didn't think it'd be such a big deal; certainly didn't think the press would get hold of it.

ALICE

Bracken's a sleazeball. No doubt about that. There's been an arrogance emanating from him that has bordered on cringeworthy throughout the entirety of this trial. But he seems to have softened his face for his closing argument – is tilting his head a little, squinting at us as if we're twelve teeny-tiny puppy dogs.

'What Mr Ryan here has just shared with you is pure fabrication. A weak prosecution argument, if I may be so bold.' He steps towards us. 'Your only options aren't whether Faith and Grace did this, or some Hollywood movie-esque contract killer did it. That's absurd. And quite a fictionalised analysis of a very real tragedy. Does Mr Ryan genuinely believe that two nine-year-old girls, who loved their parents so much and who were about to go on a dream family holiday, killed those parents for a reason he has only ever speculated about? Then these nine-year-olds just hopped off to go to a dance lesson as if nothing happened? Arrived home from that lesson, rang the police and have – for the past twenty months – manage to hide that dark secret from the many experts who work in the police force, who work in child welfare and who work in law? Talk about a Hollywood tale... that's a Hollywood tale right there, ladies and gentlemen. I don't think Mr Ryan does genuinely believe what he preached here this morning. It just happens to be his job to try to make *you* believe it. That's all. That's all his closing argument was – Mr Ryan simply doing his job.'

Bracken places his hands in his pockets, as if this is a breeze for him. And as he does I feel adrenaline spinwash inside my stomach. Go on, Bracken. Nail it!

'Faith and Grace didn't murder anyone,' he says. 'I have spent twenty months getting to know them. Trust me. They are not murderers. They are sweet little girls who are still grieving the loss of both of their parents. Mr Ryan is right in one way, though. He says the facts of this case are simple. I agree. I do. They are. Just not the "facts" he shared with you.' Bracken does that air-quotes thingy with his fingers. 'Put in front of you over the past fort-night – ladies and gentlemen – was a case in which the lead detective is on record admitting that he *doesn't* think the defendants are guilty. Let me say that again… the *lead* detective – Detective Denis Quayle, twenty-five years on the force – is on record as saying he doesn't believe Faith and Grace had anything to do with this double homicide. His own words – said directly to me and recorded on my tape were, "You can take it from me, Mr Bracken – the twins didn't have anything to do with this." But besides that little fact that I would like you to keep in your minds as you consider your verdict, the biggest factor you, as jurors, need to consider before it leads you to acquit-ting these innocent girls is that this court – that prosecution,' he points at Ryan, 'did not provide any evidence whatsoever beyond doubt that my defendants are guilty. There is plenty of doubt about the case they have brought to this court. There is *doubt* whether or not the investigation was handled correctly. There is *doubt* that Faith and Grace had any motive whatsoever to carry out this crime. There is *doubt* about the contents of that safe. There is *doubt* that Faith and Grace even had the wherewithal to act out this level of crime.'

He steps closer to us.

'And when there is doubt – jury members – it is your job to acquit. You know – as much as I do, as much as anybody inside this courtroom here today knows – we simply do not have the answers to this case. The answers to this case were not proven in front of you over the past two weeks. We don't know the answer as to why Clive and Dorothy had so much cash. We don't know the answer as to why anybody would want them dead. We don't know the answer to where the murder weapon is. And without all of the answers – jury members – it would be remiss of you to find Faith and Grace guilty. Thank you.'

He returns to his seat swiftly. I'm shocked. I thought closing arguments would last most of the day. I flick my wrist. 10:21 a.m. That's it? Are we going to start deliberating right now?

The whole courtroom falls silent except for the sound of shuffling as Judge McCormick sifts through her paperwork. Maybe lawyers don't want to bombard a jury with too much during closing arguments. They just want to sell us the verdict they want us to buy. I guess both Ryan and Bracken did that equally well in the few short minutes they tried to sell to us. But I don't believe Bracken for one minute. I've no doubt those twins are hiding some sort of crazy behind their eyes. They definitely did this. I just need to convince these people sitting beside me that they didn't.

'Okay, members of the jury,' Judge McCormick says, staring over her glasses at us. 'You have now heard all of the evidence, all of the witness statements and all of the arguments of this trial. You will hear no more, though you can – of course – request transcripts of any aspect of the trial during your deliberations. Before I give you some orders and release you to begin those deliberations, I want to say something to you.' She removes her glasses and rests them on the desk in front of her before staring back up at us. 'I want to thank each of you for your service during this trial. In all my years as a judge I have never been involved in a case quite like this one. It was not easy for my experienced ear to hear some of the facts of this case and so I am certain it was not easy for you to hear some of the facts of this case. It has been a mentally tough two weeks for you all, I'm sure. On behalf of the legal and judicial arm of our nation... thank you. Your job, now, is to come to a unanimous verdict based only – *only* – on the evidence you heard in this courtroom.' She bounces the butt of her paperwork off the desk. 'I now dismiss you to begin your arguments.'

I'm the last of the jurors to stand. And then we all shuffle out, one-by-one in that awkward bloody silence again, to be met by the young woman dressed all in black. She leads us down a long corridor and then stops at a door – a door just like every other inside these modern courts – then removes a large bunch of keys from her pocket and unlocks it. The young guy with the quiff sits to one side of me at the conference table. Red Head sits on the other. Again. I notice then that all of the jurors seem to have taken the same seats they took when we were first in this room two weeks ago, discussing who our Head Juror should be. I was tempted to put myself forward for it, but chickened out at the last minute. Only Obese Guy and the rough looking guy with the scar across his forehead put their hands up. Men. They have so much more confidence than us women. Or arrogance. I'm not quite sure what it is. I could kick myself now for not putting myself forward. I would have had a lot more sway and influence if I was Head Juror. Though I probably wouldn't have won the secret ballot for the position. Not against Scarhead. He trounced Obese Guy eleven to one. Obese Guy must've been the only person to vote for himself.

'Okay,' Scarhead says when we've all settled around the large oval table. 'Well... that was an intense couple of weeks. Don't know about you all, but I've been dying to find out what you think about this case. I don't know how I've stopped myself from asking you about it every day in those bloody corridors.'

'Me too,' I burst out of my mouth. A few turn to face me, some with smiles of agreement, some with a hint of impatience because I talked over the Head Juror mere seconds in to him opening deliberations. I hold my hand up in apology, then signal for Scarhead to continue. 'So, eh...' he says, looking around the faces. 'Where'll we start? I looked online to see how these types of thing are supposed to be dealt with but, eh... there is no manual, I have come to realise. Every case is different. Every deliberation is different. All I can gather is that we have to come to one of two conclusions... we need to come to a unanimous conclusion that finds Faith and Grace either guilty... or not guilty.'

'Well,' I say loudly. The jurors all turn to face me. Again. 'That's not strictly true. It doesn't have to be a case of us definitely getting a unanimous verdict. We could be a hung jury. Easily. Not all of us have to agree. If we don't, we shouldn't beat ourselves up about it.'

'That's true. I believe the judge might come back and take a vote of ten to two either way if she wishes,' Red Head next to me says. I turn to her. And smile.

'You're right,' I say. 'That can happen. And may happen. But I would just like to say that we shouldn't beat ourselves up even if we don't come to a ten:two agreement in some way. If people are unsure or undecided, that's perfectly okay.'

I can feel Scarhead stare at me. I've taken control of his deliberations.

'I know... eh... sorry, what's your name again?' he asks.

I look back up at him.

'Alice.'

None of us really exchanged names throughout the course of the trial. In truth, we rarely got a chance to speak to each other. Once, early on in the trial, Obese Guy leaned in to me in the corridors and asked for my name. And so too did Red Head. I asked for their names too, out of politeness, but I didn't log them in the memory bank. I'm just no good with names. There are badges that we could fill out and stick to our chests during the deliberations, but nobody has brought up that option. Besides, I'm fine not knowing. Though now everybody knows *my* name, because I'm the only one who has been asked for it at the table. And it hits me. Maybe somebody in here is the one blackmailing me. Maybe somebody in this room has hacked my phone. I pivot my head to take in each of the six other women around this conference table, then shake my head. No. Course it's nobody in here. Why would it be a bloody juror? I think I'm starting to go a bit crazy.

'You're right, Alice,' Scarhead says. 'But perhaps we should at least aim for getting a majority decision or a unanimous decision. After all... that is our job here.'

I nod at him.

'Why don't we see if we have a majority one way or another already?' I propose. 'I think we'd benefit from an early verdict vote... just to see where everybody stands.'

'Good idea,' Red Head says, rubbing at the arm of my blouse. 'The trial is fresh in our minds right now. Fresher than it'll ever be. Why don't we find out how each of the jurors feel? Instinctively. I mean, we've all been dying to find out what's going on inside each of our heads, haven't we?'

Nobody objects. A few nod their heads and, as they do, Scarhead stands up.

'Right... yeah, okay. I agree. We'll just go around the table. This is obviously not a final verdict vote... just an indication of how we feel instinctively following the trial.'

Perfect. I'll know what the playing field is like within a matter of seconds. I'll know which jurors I have on my side, and which ones I might need to work on. I need at least two other people in this room to help save my life. And Zoe's. And Noel's. They don't deserve any of the shit that will hit them if this jury return a guilty verdict.

'Why don't we start with you then, Alice?' Scarhead says, sitting back down. 'In terms of instinct only: do you think the twins are guilty or not guilty?'

'Not guilty,' I spit out of my mouth, leaving no pause between his asking of the question and my answering of it.

'Okay, okay,' he nods again. 'I like it. No hesitation. Maybe we should all do that. Next...' he says. Red Head looks up at him.

'Not guilty,' she says. And as soon as she does I feel a bubble of excitement form in my stomach.

'Next.'

'Guilty.'

'Guilty'

'One hundred per cent guilty,' the blonde with the acne scars says.

Holy shit.

'Guilty.'

'Guilty,' Scarhead says when it comes around to him.

Bollocks.

'Not guilty,' Obese Guy says. I nod. He's definitely on my side. He won't waver. I'll make sure he doesn't.

'Guilty.'

'No doubt they're guilty,' the guy with the thick-rimmed glasses says.

'Guilty.'

'Not guilty. Not yet anyway,' says the last juror – the young guy with the stupidly-high quiff. 'There's a long way to go. And I could be convinced they're guilty, but for now, it's too early for me to commit to that.'

I try to do a quick count in my head... but seem to have lost track.

'Eight guilty, four not guilty,' Scarhead says, answering my maths problem for me. Shit. I've only got three on my side from the outset. I need to make sure two of them don't change their minds while we're in here. And sure that idiot with the stupidly-high quiff has already admitted he could easily be persuaded into the guilty camp.

I've got Red Head, Obese Guy and Quiff Boy here to work with. Four. Four of twelve. Jesus. It would be only three of twelve voting not guilty if I actually voted how I wanted to vote. These deliberations would be practically over before they'd even begun. My stomach turns itself over and my hands instantly begin to sweat. This is not good. I've wanted to know all the way through this trial what the other jurors were thinking. And now I finally know. The majority in this room, like me, think the twins did it. That would have been great news yesterday morning. But now it's a fucking nightmare. My actual, genuine nightmare coming true.

I stand up, hold a palm to my forehead, then suddenly find myself on all fours, panting heavy breaths into the squared patterns on the carpet.

DAY TWO

I was really groggy the next morning; had no idea how much sleep I'd managed to catch. Only about one hour, though. Maybe two. Max.

I showered, put on my crispest white shirt, my favourite navy blazer and a pair of jeans before I joined my wife at the kitchen table, sitting on the same seat I'd spent hours numbing my bum on the night previous.

'You're going to nail this,' she said to me exhaling cannabis vapour towards our ceiling. I grabbed my toast on the go, kissed my wife's forehead, then drove to the station and waited – and waited – for Fairweather to arrive. She was supposed to meet me at eight a.m., but didn't arrive till gone half nine.

Fairweather was as supportive as my wife was that I could nail the case. Though she did let me know on quite a few occasions that I hadn't handled anything of this magnitude before. Tallaght Station had been on to her numerous times since the murders, demanding they run the case. But Fairweather stayed strong; told them they could count on me.

In that meeting, on that early morning of day two, she looked me straight in the eye and asked if I was as suspicious as she was about the twins.

'It's not the twins,' I said almost laughing with the absurdity of it all. 'I spent most of yesterday with them. They are not killers. No way.'

Fairweather cancelled her game of golf that day but she didn't accompany me on my investigation. She stayed at the station, handling the multitude of questions coming her way not just from the media, but practically the entire community. Everybody wanted to know what had gone on. I was adamant I wouldn't stop until I had the answer for them. Though I was still kinda cringing about a couple of the mis-steps I'd taken on day one.

Fairweather wasn't that concerned that I approached the scene without protectors on, nor that I took my time ringing SOCO and Tusla. But she was somewhat baffled that me and Johnny took the twins to McDonald's. I still don't get the furore over that. They were hungry, for Christ's sake.

I rang SOCO as I drove to the church, just to get an update on when they'd be able to deliver results for me. The next day, they said, though they did give me a little insight during that call; informed me that there was certainly nothing obvious found that pointed in any direction. They said whoever did this was very careful not to leave any evidence whatsoever.

I was surprised how many people had packed into the church that morning. Though it's not technically a church; it's a community centre. A basketball net hangs above the stage and the straight lines of a basketball court are still taped over the pale floorboards. Though they did do their best to dim the lighting to mainly candlelight and decorate the walls with framed biblical paintings. More white Jesuses.

The congregation were a mix of not only generations, but cultures. From teenagers to those close to retirement. And from pale skin to black skin. But every face was drawn with the same sombre expression. Some looked as if they'd been crying non-stop since they'd heard the news.

Kelly McAllister did most of the speaking. She looked me straight in the eye, made me promise that I'd find out who killed their leaders. I found it odd that these people saw Clive and Dorothy Tiddle as the people who should be worshipped. They were so frumpy and ordinary.

I stood on the stage to make a little speech, to calm each of the church-goers down as best I could. I promised I wouldn't rest until the killer was put behind bars.

My phone vibrated a few times while I was in that church. Tunstead was desperate to get hold of me. But I wasn't giving in to him. My main focus was the investigation. He and Lowe could wait.

I spoke with so many people in the church that morning individually – over sixty of them. I wanted to know if they were aware of any people who didn't like the Tiddles. I learned there had been whispers of unrest around some residents of Rathcoole; complaining that the church seemed to be taking over the mountainside. The Tiddles were bringing people in from all corners of the globe to the local area every Sunday – but nobody I spoke to in the church seemed to believe that complaining stretched beyond anything other than a slither of unconscious racism. One name kept coming up, though. Repeatedly.

Tommo Nevin had let it be known in no uncertain terms that he didn't want 'darkies' strolling the laneways of the Dublin mountains.

'He's not the nicest man I've ever come across,' Kelly told me. 'But I don't believe he's a killer.'

She was in a state of shock the whole time I was there, shaking her head constantly as if she couldn't quite fathom what had gone on.

'Well, if it wasn't Tommo Nevin,' I said to her, 'who else could it be?'

She looked up at me, through the tears in her eyes, and shrugged ever so slowly.

I placed a hand to her shoulder.

'You look after these people,' I said, nodding towards the grieving parishioners around us, 'and I'll look after the investigation.'

I gave her a long hug, then left them all to it to grieve for the loss of their leaders.

The sun almost blinded me when I finally pushed open the double doors and stepped outside.

'Get anything useful in there?' a voice said from beyond the glare.

I held a hand above my eyes as a visor. Tunstead was wearing another skin-tight suit – this one tanned brown. Lowe had on a light, navy blazer, like me. But she matched hers with pants. Not jeans.

'Y'know,' I said, leaning against my car, 'people around this neck of the woods didn't like the Tiddle family. Mainly because they were bringing foreigners up here. Some folk don't like seeing dark brown faces among the bright green fields.'

Lowe stuck out her bottom lip and placed her hands into her pants pockets.

'Anybody in particular?' she said.

'Yep. A Tommo Nevin. Apparently he had it out with Clive Tiddle a couple of months ago. Didn't hide his racism either, from what I understand.'

'Tommo Nevin's not a murderer,' Tunstead said, sniggering at me like a prick. 'He's just an old-school man with old-school views.'

I turned to Lowe.

'Well, I'm gonna go talk to him now. See what he was up to yesterday. What are you guys—'

'Quayle, we need to talk to the twins,' Tunstead interrupted. 'There's a whole load of questions they need to answer. Let's get them to the scene and have them walk us through what happened when they got home from their dance class yesterday. We could end this case today.'

I scoffed.

'You think it was the twins?' Tunstead and Lowe looked at each other.

It always irritated me when they did that right in front of me. As if I couldn't bloody see them. 'Well, you're wrong. It wasn't them. It couldn't have been them.'

'They had time to do it, then go to dance class, then come home and ring 999,' Tunstead said. 'They bought themselves an alibi by going to dance class, but it's not going to prove enough.'

'What... and then they just lied to the paramedics, lied to uniformed cops, lied to us detectives, lied to Tusla and have been able to hold in the fact that they killed their parents in cold blood ever since? You saw them yesterday. You think they're capable of that much calculation?' I asked.

Tunstead shifted his standing position.

'That's why we need to talk to them... we gotta find out what they know,' he said. 'It's been almost twenty-four hours since they called in the homicides and they haven't been questioned thoroughly.'

'Well, I'm off to interview Tommo Nevin first,' I told him. 'Then I'm going to visit the twins at Tusla.'

'Quayle,' Lowe said, taking a step towards me. 'Let's start with the twins. Please. Arrange for Tusla to bring them out to the scene. Me, you and Tunstead can meet them there and... look, you can lead the questioning. This is your investigation, after all. We just want to assist you. Support you. But I agree with Tunstead... we need to start with the twins. Find out what happened at the scene... then we can start elaborating on other theories.'

The three of us barely said a word to each other as we stood on the Tiddles' gravelled drive, waiting on the twins to arrive. Though I spent most of the time internally kicking myself for giving in to Tunstead's request. It was only because Lowe approached me in such a nice way that I decided Tommo Nevin could wait till later. Besides, I hadn't seen Faith and Grace since I handed them over to Tusla the evening before, and I was keen to see how they were holding up.

They weren't crying when they got out of the car. But they looked as if they had been. I strolled towards them, bent down and squeezed them both with a one-armed hug.

'I'm so sorry to do this to you,' I said. 'But as I told you yesterday, I am going to find out who did this to your mammy and daddy and I just need some help from you, okay?'

Grace looked as if she was about to sob, but she managed to hold it back.

'But... but we don't know who did it... we don't know anything,' she said.

I rubbed her back.

'Everything will be okay,' I said. 'But there could be something, anything that you may be able to tell me and the other two detectives over there, that will help us find out who did this. So just tell us everything you know, no matter how small you think it is. Okay?'

Grace nodded her head and rubbed her eye at the same time, and then Faith mirrored her movements almost perfectly.

I stood back up, then motioned for them to walk towards Tunstead and Lowe.

'Thanks for getting them here on such short notice,' I whispered to the two Tusla staff who had been introduced to me as Joe and Dinah the previous evening. 'How've they been?'

Joe blew out his cheeks.

'Okay,' he said. 'Considering.'

Dinah leaned towards me.

'Are they suspects, Detective Quayle?' she whispered.

I shook my head.

'No. No. Not at all. This looks like a professional job. Whoever did this knew what they were doing. We just need the girls to walk the scene, see if they can come up with something – *anything* – that'll help us out.'

They both looked at each other and shrugged.

'Okay, Detective,' Joe said.

'What... not you guys as well. Do you think they did it?'

'Ohhh.' Dinah held both of her palms towards me. 'That's not for us to say. That's your job.'

I squinted, then glanced over my shoulder to see Lowe and Tunstead spark up conversation with the twins and decided I had to join them.

The bungalow was really cold when we walked inside. Bizarrely cold. As if we had just walked outside from being inside.

'I'll lead,' I whispered to Tunstead. He took one step back, then waved his hand down the hallway.

I strolled to the end of the hall where Faith and Grace had stopped in front of the giant crucifix, and crouched down to my hunkers.

'Okay, Faith and Grace,' I said, slowly. 'Can you tell me what happened the moment you arrived home from dance class at about 12:15 yesterday afternoon?'

Faith looked at Grace. And as soon as she did Grace started to cry. Not a sob. A full-on howl. And without any haste, Faith followed suit.

✝

The 'family' members of Clive and Dorothy's church, which had expanded to well beyond five hundred people by the time Faith and Grace arrived, were equally as intrigued as they were infatuated by the twins when they were born.

They were undoubtedly cute; their little button noses complemented either side by the same large chocolate brown eyes their mother had. There was often, in their very early days, a queue of people lined up the aisle of the community centre all waiting to coo at them in their double pram. Clive and Dorothy would stand on the stage during those processions, basking in their miracles. Even folk from the neighbourhood who had never set foot inside the church prior to their arrival popped along to offer cards and gifts. Both parents were high as kites; for the first three weeks anyway. But Faith's refusal to sleep when everybody else was trying to sleep soon increased tensions. Even Clive, who had never so much as raised his voice in all the time he'd been with Dorothy, began to fume. Though he'd do so as quietly as he could; gurgling his frustrations in the back of his throat while Dorothy would try to rock Faith back to sleep. It was always Dorothy's responsibility to get up in the night to whisper lullabies to Faith – the job of the mother. Adapting quickly to the tiny progresses humanity makes doesn't seem to come naturally to believers of faith – any faith.

Dorothy didn't mind getting up anyway; never even thought to suggest that Clive's sleep should be ruined to see to their daughter. Dorothy was tired, but not overly-tired – could still function. Which was just as well, as their growing church needed her as much as the twins did. Both Clive and Dorothy *had done incredibly well from starting out as regular parishioners at St Bene-dict's Church at the bottom of the Dublin mountains as soon as they moved into the area, to running the whole parish eighteen years later. Through their struggles to conceive, the Tiddles decided their calling must be to preach God's message rather than parent. So... they immersed themselves even further in their local church. Though they were pretty much the only ones who did. By the mid-nineties, when Clive and Dorothy moved into the area, the traditional church had had its day – certainly in Dublin. The Irish capital was by then abuzz with new money and becoming way too liberal to be both-ering itself with two-thousand year old books. The attendance in churches in Ireland dropped by over one thousand percent in 1995 compared to the figures from the decade previous. And St Benedict's Church was one of the old-school churches that suffered. It suffered gravely, in fact. The numbers attending any of the regular Sunday sermons was practically making its way to single figures. So they cut down from four Masses each Sunday to three... and then two, until they were eventually only running one sermon at eleven a.m. each Sunday. And even that one sermon was in danger of hitting single figures for attendance.*

The parish priest at the time was Fr Frank Munro. He was just beyond middle-aged but still brightly and filled with character – as well as Guinness – when he died. He adored the Tiddles because they did their utmost for the church. They started as regular parishioners attending services, to helping to bring up the offerings, then passing out Holy Communion and eventually even reading gospels. They inched their way onto the altar over the years and became a key part of the church's mechanism.

They were probably the closest people in the world to Fr Frank as he withered from life. He didn't know he had a tumour pulsing at the side of his brain. It must have been growing for at least two years prior to diagnosis, the professor at Tallaght Hospital had told him. He died ten weeks later. Gone. Just like that.

A lack of newly-ordained priests, by now down to just one per year in the country, made filling the vacancy at St Benedict's Church impossible. In the end the Catholic church chose to close it down, which was an unusual posi-tion for them to ever take. The feeling was that the church-goers in that specific small area of the Dublin mountains were a dying breed, and the statistics of Mass attendances over the previous decade had firmly illustrated that. The church building, over three-hundred years old, still sits high in the Dublin mountains, but the natural habitat around it has overgrown, making it look like something out of a graphic novel.

Clive had kept the church going initially after Fr Munro had passed by giving sermons. But only because a few parishioners begged him to. He immediately loved it; standing on that altar with everybody listening to what he had to say. It was the total opposite of what he had been used to his whole life.

'We have to keep this church going,' he would often repeat to Dorothy.

She agreed; but couldn't see how it was even possible. Clive wasn't ordained – the Catholic church would not allow it. And they didn't.

But their insistence on closing the church down didn't deter Clive from his longing to be on an altar, preaching. He approached the local community centre and asked if they could give him use of their facilities for two hours each Sunday afternoon. And they agreed.

By that stage he hadn't even thought about money. Though, out of pure traditionalism and instinct, they did pass around a collection basket during their first Mass. Two hundred and forty pounds they took in – and there was only thirty-one people in attendance.

Clive wasn't sure what he was supposed to do with the cash. But he didn't hesitate in quitting his job as a customer service rep for Eircom to become a full-time preacher.

The numbers attending Clive's sermons were rising even before the twins came along, but their birth gave it a huge shot in the arm. It was mainly to do with how cute they were; that and the fact the story often told was that they were conceived by miracle at the hands of Jesus Christ. They were always dressed to the nines – in perfect Sunday wear, even on a regular Tuesday morning. They wore ribbons in their hair consistently and they always adorned a floral summer dress – just like their mother. And her mother before her.

It was incongruous that Clive ended up becoming a church leader though. When he first started dating Dorothy and was introduced to her extended 'family', he instinctively went along with playing the role of a Christian. He knew the answers to almost all the questions. School had saw to that. Bible was the first thing studied every morning at the Christian Brothers Schools in Ireland when he was growing up – and prayers were rostered to be said at least twice a day. He knew the parables, knew the Ten Commandments, knew the rough outline of the story of Jesus' life. So he fit in straight away; nodding away in agreement with everybody's ideologies. But he was lying to everyone as much as he was lying to himself. Believing in a God who created the world a few thousand years ago made absolutely no logical sense to him. But going along with that narrative afforded him a life, afforded him friends, an extended family, a wife, God-damn it! And as a result he became so convincing in his role as a man of God that he almost convinced himself.

Though the lie he was living, as influential as it was in shaping who he was, was really the only negative trait Clive Tiddle possessed. Yes, he was an odd man to look at; almost stand-offish given that he was so tall and had a rotund belly that ensured it was difficult to ever literally get close to him. But all of the 'family' found him really sincere and genuinely polite. Possessing those two traits were particularly important to Clive. Because he was bullied at school, all he'd ever yearned for was for people to be sincere and polite to each other. So he spoke sincerely and politely to everyone who ever crossed his path.

Except for one man, on one occasion. A local fella by the name of Tommo Nevin.

ALICE

'Here,' Obese Guy says, taking my hands and bringing them towards the sink. 'Let the cold water run over your wrists... it'll help you wake up.'

'Oh my God, I'm so embarrassed,' I say, eyeballing myself in the mirror as he twists my wrists left and right under the running water.

'Don't be a silly woman,' he says. 'We're all feeling the stresses and strains of this trial. It's not just you. I barely slept a wink last night.'

I look at his reflection, and when he catches my eye I whisper a "thank you" to him.

Then he turns and whips three sheets of paper towel from the plastic dispenser hanging on the wall before taking my hands again. He pats down my wrists for me, like I'm a four-year-old girl, and as he is doing so the bathroom door opens and the redhead peers around it.

'You okay, Alice?' she whispers, taking a step inside and then closing the door quietly behind herself.

'Embarrassed.'

'Don't be silly,' she says.

'That's what I said,' Obese Guy says.

Red Head approaches me and holds me in a light embrace. I hug her back, even though Obese Guy wasn't quite finished drying me off. It'll probably leave a wet stain on the back of her top, but I feel as if I need this hug.

It hits me as I'm resting my chin on her shoulder that I may not be the only juror being blackmailed. These two in here are also not guilty voters. Maybe one of them is being blackmailed too. Or both. It could be both. I release my hold on Red Head, and stare into her pale face.

'You sure you're okay?' she asks again.

I nod, because I feel I may cry if I open my mouth.

'Why don't we take a seat at the table... when we get into the delibera-tions you'll probably feel yourself again,' Obese Guy says. I look to him and nod again, and suddenly Red Head is linking my arm and leading me out of the bathroom and towards my seat at the far end of the jurors' table. The silence in the room is really awkward, even more so than it is when I'm walking in and out of that courtroom.

I huff an embarrassed laugh across the table when I sit, and then raise a hand.

'Apologies everybody,' I say.

'Don't be silly,' Scarhead says. And then both Red Head and Obese Guy say, "That's what I said" in unison.

'We, eh... didn't discuss anything while you were in the bathroom, Alice,' Scarhead says. 'So the last we all discussed was the result, just before you, eh... fell. The result was eight jurors voted guilty, four jurors voted not guilty. I guess that gives us all a good understanding of where everybody stands. It's a platform for us to begin our arguments, I guess. Though I'm sure minds can and indeed will change as we strive towards a unanimous verdict.'

I sit back in the chair and try to breathe as steadily as I possibly can, to give my panic room to pass through.

'I'll start... I just find them undoubtedly cold,' Scarhead says. 'They are the oddest girls I have ever laid my eyes on and I am convinced they killed their parents. I think their defence team did a great job, and why wouldn't they? Bracken is about the best and most expensive defence lawyer in the country. But he didn't do enough to convince me. And if *he* couldn't do enough, nobody could have.'

'Hold on a minute,' I say, 'it is not our job to judge the lawyers. What you are saying—'

'That is *exactly* our job,' the man with the thick-rimmed glasses says, interrupting me. 'Our job is to judge how the defence did and how the pros-ecution did. Our job is to determine whether or not the defence team did a good enough job suggesting Faith and Grace are innocent. Or whether the prosecution did a good enough job to convince us that they are guilty.'

I want to argue back with him, but I agree with him so much that I'm not sure where to even begin debating against that.

'Nothing was proven. They're innocent,' is all I can muster up.

'I disagree with you,' the elderly woman with the oversized bust says. 'They are cold and creepy. And, let's be honest, they had the time to do it. They planned this. They stabbed their parents to death just before heading out to use that dance class as an alibi, and then they came back and rang the police. They thought they were being clever. But they didn't realise forensics would be able to determine an exact time of death.'

'But forensics didn't specify an exact time,' Red Head pipes up. 'They said it could have been any time between ten-thirty and eleven.'

'Yes, which tells us the twins *could* have done it. They didn't leave their house until about ten forty-five... they arrived at dance class at ten fifty-five. That gave them time to do it.'

'No, no!' I slam a hand to the table. 'It only gives them a very narrow window. These kids can't be as calculated as you are suggesting.'

'They fuckin' are,' the man with the thick-rimmed glasses says.

'Hey, no need for that kind of language,' Obese Guy says. And then everybody begins to talk over each other.

Jesus Christ. This is exhausting. And we're only about ten minutes into deliberations. I just need to hold on to my not guilty verdict and make sure at least two other people do, too. Red Head and Obese Guy seem to be supporting my arguments already. Hopefully they're as stubborn as I am and hold out until the judge determines our time is up and declares us hung.

I can't imagine how my life would change if I got home this evening to find Noel and Zoe had watched that video. I stab my fingernails into my palms and cringe. I'm a fucking idiot.

It was all because of Alex and Lyndsey's wedding. Me and Emmet were both drunk. He stopped me in the corridor as I was making my way to my hotel room, where I knew Noel would be snoring his head off.

'You looked absolutely gorgeous today, Alice,' Emmet said, his tie all loose around his neck. He was swaying a little. And slurring. But I still took it as a huge compliment. Especially coming from him. A twenty-three-year-old with shoulders practically the width of the corridor. He leaned in to kiss me, and I moved away.

'What are you doing?' I gasped. He apologised. And apologised. And then apologised some more before he slumped his way back to the bedroom he was sharing with my daughter. Two days later he texted me to meet him for a coffee. He wanted to explain himself and apologise even further. Which is exactly what he did. I could see the sorrow etched on his face as he told me he *did* find me attractive but that he was so glad nothing had happened because he couldn't live with himself if he hurt Zoe.

I left the café that day almost buzzing. I hadn't been paid so many compliments in years... not since me and Noel started dating. I couldn't stop thinking about Emmet after that. And then two weeks later he called around to see Zoe when she wasn't in, and we ended up sitting across from each other at the kitchen table. We were just shooting the breeze, talking shite, when he rested his hand on my knee. And I instantly got wet. *Instantly*. I could feel the juices practically foaming inside of me.

I kissed him. Leaned forward, threw my tongue in his mouth and we made out, grinding up against each other on our kitchen counter tops until I realised Zoe might walk through that door any minute. And so I got up, put my coat on and went for a walk to nowhere. I had to calm my whole body down.

That night, after Noel went to bed, I played with myself on our sofa, imagining what it would feel like to have Emmet make love to me. As soon as my orgasms were over, I felt really bad. Guilty.

The following day Emmet rang, told me he couldn't stop thinking about me and asked if I would be interested in meeting him at the Hilton Hotel that weekend. I said "no" at first, even shouted at him for leading me on. But five minutes later I rang back, told him he should wear that tight-fitted white shirt he looked so buff in at Alex and Lyndsey's wedding and that I'd see him at eight p.m. on the Friday.

The sex was mind-altering. Better than I'd ever had by miles. Better than I ever will have. I came nine times that night. *Nine!* My whole body shook so hard, it took minutes for it to actually stop. I was just lying there in a sweat, my hand over my face, my mouth grinning from ear to ear.

I have lived, ever since, balancing the highs of those orgasms with the lows of the guilt.

'Alice!' I look up, and notice everybody has turned to face me.

'Sorry. Was away with the fairies there.'

'We were discussing McDonald's, getting everybody's view on it,' Red Head says.

'Oh,' I say, readjusting my seating position. 'Eh... McDonald's... well, as in, eh....'

'Alice, you really need to be paying attention to everybody's points.' Scarhead is talking down to me. Literally. He is stood at the top of the table, peering at me with his eyebrows dipped. 'We've all shared our opinion on the twins eating a McDonald's three hours after they found their parents lying in pools of blood. What is your take on it?'

I shift my seating position again, stare at Red Head who offers me a sympathetic smile, and then slowly lean both of my forearms, one at a time, on to the table.

'It's not as if they just headed off for a McDonald's, is it?' I said. 'The detective and an officer took them there because there was no food for them at the station – and they were hungry.'

'I agree with you, Alice,' Thick-rimmed Glasses says. 'Detective Quayle has been the main problem with this case from the very beginning.'

I shake my head.

'No, that's not what I'm saying. What I mean is... I don't think he's the problem at all. I believe he is the only one who has had this right from the get-go. What if he is right and we all put two innocent children behind bars for the rest of their lives? Think about it. He doesn't truly believe that Faith and Grace killed their parents. And he was the lead detective on the entire case!'

DAY TWO

It took a glass of Ribena each, an ice-pop and a dozen hugs from Joe and Dinah before the twins finally settled down.

Dinah and Joe suggested abandoning the walk-through there and then, to which I agreed. But Lowe talked me around. She said the sooner we did this, the sooner we'd find whoever it was that murdered Clive and Dorothy – and that it was imperative we did it while everything was as fresh as it could be in the twins' minds.

I started by apologising to Faith and Grace. Again. Then I asked about their welfare; how they were getting on at Tusla. They shrugged and nodded their heads. I had to inform them that we were trying to track down their Aunt Janet. Johnny had found out she was their closest living relative. Clive's sister. She was living in Carrickmacross in Monaghan; had moved there over twenty years ago. But she was proving difficult to get hold of.

When the twins had finally settled I asked them to talk me through exactly what happened when they arrived home from dance class the previous afternoon. Without prompt, Grace hopped off the sofa and beckoned Faith into the hallway. They walked to the front door, and me, Tunstead, Lowe and Joe and Dinah looked on as they opened it.

Then they turned to us and Grace sighed.

'We came in and shut the door like this,' she said. Then she slammed the door behind them both. 'We were really thirsty from dancing and so we walked straight into the kitchen to get a drink.'

She strolled past us, towards the kitchen, Faith following.

'Was the kitchen door open when you came in?' Tunstead asked.

The twins paused... hesitated, until Faith looked at Grace.

'Yes. Open,' Grace confirmed.

'Okay,' Tunstead said. 'So, really as soon as you opened that hall door, you would have seen your father's body, isn't that right?'

I flicked my hand at Tunstead, signalling for him to hush. He didn't react – he just stared back at Faith and Grace, waiting for their answer.

'I, eh... saw it when I got to about here,' Grace said, circling her foot on the carpet a few yards short of the kitchen door.

'And you, Faith?' Tunstead said.

She circled her foot in the exact same place as her sister without saying a word.

'And then what?' Lowe asked, in a much more calm manner than her partner had been firing off his questions.

'Then we... we looked inside and saw Mammy and Daddy were lying there with blood all over them.'

'Okay, and tell us more,' Lowe said. I was getting a little peeved that I wasn't the one in control. Tunstead and Lowe were doing all the questioning. But I didn't say anything. Because I was fascinated. I wanted to know the answers to all of the questions they were asking too.

'We didn't stay in here long, we just went out to the hall and rang—'

'Actually,' Lowe said, lowering down to her hunkers. 'I would like Faith to answer this question for me. Faith... what happened next, sweetheart?'

Faith looked at Grace, then at Lowe.

'Then we rang 999,' she said, as she rubbed her eye.

'The back kitchen door was not locked,' I said. 'Is this unusual?'

'It's always unlocked,' Grace said. I nodded at Tunstead when she said this but he didn't seem to notice.

'See this right here?' Tunstead said, picking up the knife block. 'We believe the knife missing from here is the weapon that was used to kill your parents.' He pointed at an empty slit, then swiped another knife from the block and held it up, twisting it ever so slightly.

'Alright, alright,' I said, stepping in. 'That's enough questioning in here,' I said.

I ordered them all to follow me to the living room where we sat the twins on the sofa. I asked them to talk us through their morning routine of the day previous; specifically in the lead up to what happened before they left for dance class. Grace answered most of my questions, but I did use the tactic Lowe had used earlier by asking Faith to specifically chip in every now and then. I felt really guilty questioning the two of them. It didn't feel right. Every part of me was sorrowful. They had literally become orphans in the most horrific manner possible just twenty-four hours prior. And here we were demanding answers of them; not letting them grieve.

They said they had their usual breakfast at about eight-thirty a.m. that morning. Grace was able to tell me what each of them had eaten. Then she said both her and Faith played in their bedroom for an hour or so while Clive and Dorothy spoke in the kitchen.

'So you didn't see your parents for an hour during that morning?' Tunstead chipped in with. 'Do you know if they were definitely alive by the time you left for dance class?'

Grace started to cry. Faith followed. And I made a face at Tunstead again, making sure he noticed my annoyance this time. After the Tusla guys had consoled the twins with a light rub to the back, Grace confirmed that her parents were definitely alive when they left at ten forty-five, because they had kissed them goodbye.

When the Tusla guys suggested we put an end to the questions after that one was answered with a further sob, I agreed. I could tell Tunstead was a little pissed off with me, but Lowe had a quiet word with him and minutes later the twins and Joe and Dinah were skidding the tyres of their minivan off the gravel.

'What's your gut telling you now, Quayle?' Tunstead asked.

'I feel guilty,' I told him. 'Those poor girls. It's a sin to bring them here... questioning them like that.'

He glared at me.

'You don't think they did it?' he asked.

'Detective work isn't about thinking, it's about knowing,' I said. I actually said that instinctively. But it sounded good. As if it should be a quote framed on a wall in a Garda station.

I'm sure he and Lowe shared one of those stares they always share, but I didn't take the time to notice. Because I had turned to walk back down the hallway.

'The kitchen door was always unlocked and we know that there was a man in the community who had a problem with the family,' I said back over my shoulder. 'We need to explore Tommo Nevin.'

'Jesus, Quayle,' Tunstead said as his designer shoes clacked after me. 'You seriously don't think there's anything creepy about those twins?'

'Karl,' Lowe said, grabbing at Tunstead's sleeve.

He sucked in a deep breath.

'You follow Tommo Nevin if you want,' he said, 'we're going to follow up other lines.'

'Well you need to tell me what lines you are following. I'm in charge of this investigation. And I don't want you two going off gallivanting—'

'Quayle. Why don't you just let us take control here... this is a massive case.'

'No,' I spat back at him.

He flared his nostrils. The prick.

'Right,' he said, 'I'm going to take a look in the bedrooms.'

After he'd entered the first bedroom, Lowe followed me to the end of the hallway; where we both stood staring at the white Jesus.

'When you, eh...' she said, 'when you spoke to the church people this morning, what did they say about the twins?'

'They said their hearts went out to them and that they were praying for them.'

'No,' she said, taking a step closer to me, 'that's not what I mean exactly. I assume you asked their opinion on the twins.' I looked at her, then back at the crucifix. 'You didn't ask that question, huh?' she said.

I didn't answer her. I just stared at Jesus' blue eyes.

'Hey!' Tunstead shouted, cutting through the awkwardness of my silence. Both myself and Lowe paced into Clive and Dorothy's bedroom, where he was knelt down in the corner, lifting up a square of floorboards. 'A safe,' he said. 'A pretty big one. I wonder what the hell's in here.'

Lowe looked at me.

'Okay, Quayle,' she said, 'why don't you order somebody to come and have a look at this safe. Whatever's inside it could be of big importance. Then go question Tommo Nevin and follow your gut.'

'What are you guys going to do?' I asked.

'Well, we're going to speak to SOCO, see if they can get a hurry on. This investigation is all over the news, so I'm sure somebody in the higher echelons can put a word in so we can get those results as quickly as possible. Let's get this investigation motoring.'

'I'll do that,' I said. 'I'll make that call to SOCO.'

'Quayle,' Lowe said. She walked right up to me, placed her hand on my arm.

'You are the Detective Inspector of Rathcoole Garda Station. And you are in control of this investigation. We get that. We are here to support you. This is a huge case. A massive case. And even when cases aren't this big, me and Tunstead have each other to lean on to solve them as best we can. Together. But at Rathcoole, there's just you. You are the only DI from your station. You need to lean on us. If you try to tackle this all on your own, you'll go crazy.' She smiled at me. 'You've things to do. Important things. Let us ring SOCO, we have contacts there and we'll get this hurried up. We'll tell them to ring you first, with whatever they find.'

It was unusual Lowe would talk to me like this. With respect. I relented, by nodding my head and replicating Lowe's touch by placing my palm on her arm. Then Tunstead stepped forward.

'Lowe and I have ordered a sweep of the area, we are on the lookout for one of these knives.' He held the kitchen knife aloft; had been holding it all the while questioning Faith and Grace. The prick. 'And I've asked SOCO to take all of the twins' clothes in for analysing.'

'Now hold on!' I shouted.

Lowe patted her hand against my arm.

'Quayle, listen... listen. These are the most practical procedures. This goes without saying.'

'Well, wait until I order the procedures,' I replied. My frustration was flaring up again.

'We *were* waiting,' Tunstead said before he swivelled and walked back up the hallway.

It was Lowe's touch that stopped me from pacing after him. Though I didn't really have much to argue. I knew they were right.

'Come on, Quayle – you know this,' Lowe said. 'It's rule one-o-one: the first suspects are always the ones who find the bodies.'

ALICE

A debate ripples around the table. It seems as if Detective Quayle has split us right down the middle. Some jurors are praising him; saying he did the right thing in looking after the children's welfare first and foremost whilst he continued to investigate. Some – especially Scarhead – are slamming him; saying it was totally ludicrous that he would bring them for a McDonald's just hours after their parents had been murdered. I couldn't understand that argument so much. Then again, had my phone not been hacked and my relationships with my husband and daughter not at stake, I'd definitely be siding with them; demanding that Quayle didn't know what the hell he was doing and that everybody should vote the same as me – guilty as charged.

I want to go to the bathroom again, run the cold water onto my wrists so that my head stops spinning and my palms stop sweating. But I can't. It's not that long since I was last in there, holding up the deliberations so I could take care of myself like a fucking diva. I'm wary everybody already thinks I'm the snowflake in the room; the one who collapsed. The one who keeps tuning out of the discussions. But I guess I've got to stop caring what everybody else thinks of me. I need to show some strength here. I have to have a voice in this room. Otherwise I'm screwed.

'Shut up!' I shout, slamming my hands to the table. 'You are all going round and round in circles, can you please just stop?' I hold two fingertips to my temple as the ripples of chatter drop to a dead silence. I'm aware everybody is staring at me. Again. Even though I haven't fully looked up. 'Listen,' I say, steadying myself by placing a palm to my beating heart, 'we are not here to judge Detective Quayle... we are here to judge Faith and Grace. And I am certain, and my mind will not change on this... there was not enough proof put before us that tells us *without doubt* that they are guilty of this crime.'

'There's loads of proof,' Scarhead says. 'There is no forensics that suggests anybody else entered that house that morning. Only the victims and the two defendants. There is also the fact that the knife used to kill Clive and Dorothy was a knife that was in the Tiddle kitchen, and has since gone missing. Only somebody from inside that house could have taken that knife.'

'Now hold on,' Red Head says. I have a feeling she is going to be my hero. 'A missing knife is not proof. If the knife was found... now that would be proof. But nobody found a knife, did they? There was nothing that links Faith and Grace directly to the murders. Besides, we know that the back door to that kitchen was unlocked. Somebody conceivably could have come in, taken that knife, stabbed Clive and Dorothy and left.'

Scarhead sniffs a patronising snigger from his nose.

'Without leaving a trace?'

Red Head parts her lips, then interlocks her fingers atop the table.

'Well... we don't know. In the same way we don't know for a fact that it was Faith and Grace who killed them. This trial needs to be proven beyond all doubt and jurors are going to have a difficult time arguing against all of the doubt that has cropped up in this case.'

Another ripple of debate sparks from one side of the table to the other. Like ping-pong. Scarhead is the loudest; arguing that trials rarely prove anything indisputably, and that's why there is a need for jurors. But I can't listen to all these voices at once, so I tune out again, eyeballing the bathroom door and wishing my wrists were being soothed by cold water.

'There was no blood,' I say under my breath while everyone is arguing. 'There was no blood.' Louder this time.

'Huh?' Red Head says, turning to me.

'Not on any of the twins' clothes, not on their skin. Isn't that proof enough that it couldn't have been them?' The table falls silent again, all tuning in to my growing volume. 'Right?' I say, my eyes lighting up. 'Police checked all of the twins' clothes; no traces of their parents' blood. The dance teacher... what was her name?'

'Claire,' Red Head confirms.

'Yeah, yeah... Claire. She testified that she didn't see any blood on the twins' hands that day.'

'Yeah but...' Thick-rimmed Glasses says. 'But if they had time to kill their parents before they left for dance class, then they had time to wash their hands. It wouldn't have taken long.'

'And what... dumped their clothes, dumped the knife... they did all this before they hopped off to do a bit of ballet?' I say.

Scarhead bounces the paperwork he has in front of him off the table.

'Alice, if the twins planned this murder – and that's what the prosecution believes because they wanted to use dance class as their alibi – then yes... they would have got rid of the knife, got rid of the clothes they were wearing, washed their hands and went to dance class...'

'I don't believe for one second that two nine-year-olds would be capable of that much calculation,' I lie. I lie because I genuinely feel as if Faith and Grace *are* capable of that much calculation. They are cold. They are evil. I have felt that way about them since I first heard about this case. I'm actually surprised that there are three other jurors sitting around this table who think otherwise. It's obvious they did it. Evidence or no evidence.

'You are saying, Alice, that Ms Claire's testimony suggests that the twins didn't do it because she said she didn't see blood on their hands? Because that's not the biggest take from her time on the stand.' The old woman with the overly big bust has decided it's her turn to have a go at me. 'What I take from her testimony is the fact that she feels these twins *did* do this. She says they were acting weird that day.'

'No she didn't,' I say, snapping back. 'All she said was that Faith was particularly quiet. But sure, as the defence team said, Faith is *always* quiet.'

'Y'know what?' Scarhead says as he stands to attention. 'Claire Barry is a key witness in this case and we are right to be arguing her testimony. But there seems to be disagreement about what she said on the stand.' He rubs at the long scar on his forehead with the tip of his index finger. 'I suggest we ask the court for the transcripts of her testimony, do we all agree?'

I don't answer him. But I don't have to. Because the rest of the jury have answered for me; all of them nodding their heads.

'Great idea,' Big Bust says. And then suddenly our deliberations have paused again while Scarhead pushes at a button on the table to speak with the court assistant, requesting twelve copies of the transcripts.

I sip from my glass of water, noticing that my hands haven't quite stopped shaking. Red Head stares at me, but I don't look back. I just place my glass down, then stand up and take advantage of the small break in deliberations to visit the bathroom. Again.

I stare at myself in the mirror as soon as I've locked the door behind me. I look terrible. As if bags have just decided to form under my eyes in the past few hours. Then I turn on the tap and allow the cold water to flow over my wrists again.

'Hello... you okay in there?' I pause. Then turn off the tap. It's the redhead. I know her voice.

I shake my hands dry then walk over to the door and welcome her inside.

'How are you feeling?' she asks, looking genuinely concerned. I scratch at my head, unsure how I can handle this conversation.

'Grand,' I say. 'It's just... it's just the pressure. The tension. I've so much going on.'

She rubs at my arm.

'I understand. We all feel the same. We all just seem to be arguing with each other, don't we? We don't seem to be making any progress. Is it, eh... just me, or do you think the Head Juror is doing a poor job?'

'Who, Scarhead?' I say, and then I hold my hand over my mouth.

She laughs. Not a big laugh. A polite giggle.

'Got nicknames for us all, have you?' she asks. I shake my head, then mouth an apology. Jesus... I'm coming across like a proper bitch. 'He just doesn't have a good rein on the table, does he? He's letting everybody talk over each other. I wish I had put myself forward to be Head Juror. It's always the bloody men, isn't it?'

'Yes!' I say. 'I was thinking the same. I should have put my hand up too. We'd have handled this a lot better.'

She rubs my arm again.

'I know we're not supposed to talk about our deliberations without the others all present, but... you really believe they're not guilty?' she asks me.

I slap my hand on top of hers and hold it firm against my arm.

'I do,' I reply. And in that moment I immediately get the sense that she's in the same boat as I am. She *has* to be getting blackmailed too.

'Do you?' I ask, whispering.

She sniffs up her nose.

'I don't know what to believe exactly,' she says. 'I just think we – as a jury – owe it to the twins and everyone involved in this case to argue this out in as much detail as we can. I hope they aren't found guilty. They really shouldn't...' she shakes her head. 'Kids being tried in Dublin's Criminal Courts... it's not right. They should have been tried as children in a children's court.'

I stand there staring into her eyes, my hand still clasped on top of hers.

'Yeah, you're right,' is all I can say.

She tilts her chin to her chest and stares at me. I want to ask her out straight if somebody texted her her dirtiest secret last night and is blackmailing her to ensure a not guilty verdict. I wonder what her secret is. Probably an affair as well. Though she's no ring. Must be something else. Maybe she's fucking her boss. Or maybe she's a high-class hooker or something. I don't know.

'Remember I said to you that I've so much going through my mind?' I say, ready to open up to her. She nods. And as she does, I take a deep breath. 'Well it's just, eh... it's just—'

Knuckles rattle against the door.

'Ladies, I really need to use the loo.'

DAY TWO

He looked like trouble the moment I laid eyes on him. The faded tattoos of Chinese symbols on his knuckles and an in-flight swift on the side of his hand gave that away. It was hugely ironic that he would be a racist piece of shit, yet thought nothing of it to brand himself with a foreign language for the rest of his life.

'Whatcha want?' he grunted.

He looked old, weathered. About seventy, with tightly-shaved hair that was so short and so white that it glistened.

I held my badge in front of his face.

'Mr Nevin, I'd like to speak to you about the double homicide of Clive and Dorothy Tiddle.'

Nevin opened his door further, giving me space to walk in, and as I did he tutted.

'Tragic, that is,' he said. 'I hope you don't think I did it.'

His house was tiny. A small two up, two down in a tight cul-de sac estate at the foothill of the mountains.

'Just making inquiries,' I said.

He led me to his sitting room which was mostly taken up by an over-sized TV screen.

'Clive and Dorothy invited many strange people to that church of theirs... I guess...' he shrugged.

'You guess what, Mr Nevin?'

'Well, I guess something like this was bound to happen, wasn't it?'

I stared him up and down.

'You mean their deaths were "bound to happen"... as in you knew they were going to happen?'

He shook his head and delivered a slimey snigger from the side of his mouth.

'No, no, that's not what I'm saying at all, Detective. All's I'm sayin' is they hung around with enough dodgy people that I'm really not as surprised as everybody else in this town seems to be.'

I asked if I could sit, and when he signalled that I should with a wave of his hand, he sat too. On the sofa opposite me.

'Funny you say they hung around with "dodgy people", as that's the reason I'm here, Mr Nevin. I've heard that you had an issue with the types of people Clive and Dorothy invited to their church.'

He sniggered. Again.

'Is that what's bein' said?' He rubbed at the stubble on his chin, then leaned forward, his forearms on his knees. 'Detective, I am not a racist. I am not... what's the word... the one beginning with X?' He clicked his fingers.

'Xenophobic?'

'That's the one. I'm not xenophobic either.'

'Well, that's not what I have heard, Mr Nevin. I have been informed you had a problem with the colour of some of the churchgoers' skin.'

He reproduced his snigger; same puff of laughter from the side of his mouth.

'I don't care about the colour of their skin. I care about where I live. You don't get many nicer areas in Dublin than this one. I've lived here all me life. I like the quiet. I like the people. We just need to keep it that way.'

I sat forward.

'As in, you just want white people walking these narrow country lanes?'

'There y'go again, Detective. Making it all about skin colour.'

'You call the churchgoers "darkies" – that's what I've heard. "Darkies". What are you referring to when you call them "darkies"? The colour of their shoes?'

'I only used that phrase to explain them. To describe them. So people know who I'm talkin' about.'

'So it is about skin colour,' I said.

He stood up.

'Whatever, Detective. Either way, look where hanging around with different skin colours got Tiddle and his Mrs, eh? A first-class ticket to Heaven.'

My phone buzzed in my pocket. But I wasn't to be distracted.

'You think one of the churchgoers did it?' I asked.

'Course they did. It was hardly anyone who lives around here now was it? When is anybody killed around this neck of the woods? Can't remember a murder around here in my lifetime.'

He opened his sitting room door, inviting me to leave. I could tell he was starting to feel uncomfortable.

'Nice tatts,' I said as I stood and made my way towards him. 'Mind if I...' I held my hands out, and after a slight pause he formed two balls of fists and then held them up. The swallow on the outside of his left hand was blue, but it had practically faded into an outline. And the Chinese symbols, I'm sure, were meant to be black, but were now a tired-looking cracked charcoal.

'What do they mean?'

'War,' he replied, flexing his left fist. 'And peace,' he said.

I grinned.

'Clever,' I said, gripping both of his fists so I could stare at them more closely. Then I turned his hands over and asked him to open them.

It was a good gut instinct.

'Mr Nevin, where did you get this cut from?' I asked.

It was a fresh wound, about four centimetres in length, inside his right palm.

'Doing the lawn,' he said. Then he looked at me all funny. 'So you *do* think I did it?'

'I'm just following all lines of enquiries, Nevin.'

'Well, are you arresting me because I have a cut on my hand, Detective?'

I paused and then shook my head before I reached inside my blazer pocket for my notepad. As soon as I took it out he placed his hand on top of it. 'No need for that, Detective. If you aren't arresting me, your time here is up. Send my sympathies to those two young girls they have. Though in my opinion, I'm pretty sure their pain is actually just ending now.'

'Sorry?' I squinted at him.

'No more cult shit for them to go through. They can grow up to be normal. As regular as you can be after finding your parents dead, I guess. But I bet any money in the world that their lives will end up better now than the shitty ones they would've had playing apostles.'

I leaned closer to him.

'You're not the nicest of men, are you, Nevin?'

He sniggered that horrible snigger again, then reached for the handle of his front door and yanked it open.

'Bye, Detective,' he said.

I was fuming when I stepped outside, but the air helped me to slowly breathe it down.

I had missed calls from both Fairweather and Tunstead while I was in there. So I jabbed my finger at Fairweather's name when I got back into the car.

'Hey, boss,' I said.

Silence. I always knew she was going to deliver bad news when she started with silence.

'Quayle... Laurence Ashe has been on to me. He wants Tallaght to take over the investigation. Thinks it's too big for us to handle.'

'I'm right on top of this, Fairweather,' I said. 'It hasn't even been two days; we've not even heard from SOCO yet. I'm pretty sure that as soon as we get results back from the lab, we'll know exactly where we stand.'

There was another silence.

'They seem to think they know who did it. They're leaning towards the twins... and they feel your questioning of them this morning was too... too "protective", they said.'

'Listen. I circled a knuckle around my temple. 'They are two nine-year-old girls who just lost their parents. There is no need for us to start throwing accusations at them, especially when I have another lead... somebody Clive Tiddle had a strong falling out with.'

'What are you talking about?'

'A Tommo Nevin. He's a racist piece of shit. He didn't like the Tiddles overcrowding the area with immigrants. I've literally just pulled away from his house now... fucker is hiding something. And get this... he had a nasty scratch on the palm of his right hand.'

Fairweather fell silent again. And as she did I slapped at my steering wheel. I wasn't frustrated with Fairweather. I never have been. I was pissed off with Tunstead. The prick had been telling me he and Lowe were willing to support me, but they must have been going behind my back and bitching to their boss about how I was handling the case.

'Interesting,' Fairweather finally said. 'But, eh... Ashe is wondering why you haven't yet corroborated the twins' story? They say they were at dance class when the murder happened. And I know two Tallaght Detectives spoke to the dance teacher and she confirmed that they were there between eleven and twelve that afternoon. But why have you not spoken to her yourself yet?'

I rubbed my knuckle deeper into my temple.

'I'm gonna speak to Claire Barry now,' I said. 'I'm not that far from the dance studio. I'll be able to rule out the fact that the twins seemed distracted when they were dancing on Saturday morning.'

'Ms Claire already confirmed to Tallaght that Faith was particularly silent during that lesson. That's what Ashe told me.'

I sighed. A deep sigh.

'See... this is what happens when cops like Ashe make accusations when in truth they don't know the personnel involved in the case. Faith is *always* quiet. She's practically mute.'

'Well, Detectives Tunstead and Lowe seem to think the twins—'

'Fuck Tunstead and Lowe!' I shouted. 'They are the ones supporting *me* in this case. And I'd appreciate support from you, too.'

'Of course. Of course,' she said. 'I'll have words with Ashe and let him know you are confident you can see this investigation through.'

I looked up at the sky through my windscreen and hocked a frustrated grunt at it.

'Listen, Fairweather,' I said. 'I'm sorry. I shouldn't be shouting at you. I'm on this. I've got it.'

By the time we'd hung up, I was already at the gate of the new-built hut that sat on the edge of the mountains about a mile away from the Tiddle bungalow.

I walked up to it, noticed the cheap signage that read 'CDC Dance Studio' and pressed at the buzzer.

Claire was lovely. Pretty. Tall. And slim. Very slim. With long, long hair that went all the way down past her bum. She held an extremely sorrowful, pale gaze all the way through my meeting with her; was shaking almost.

'Ms Claire, I believe you told a colleague of mine that Faith was particularly quiet on Saturday during her class. Faith is always quiet, is she not?'

'Oh Detective Quayle, I don't know what to believe. I've barely slept a wink since I heard the news. I just keep thinking back to how the twins were in my class on Saturday. It's hard to take in that two killers may have been doing ballet and tap just over there minutes after stabbing their parents to death.'

'Hold on... is that what you believe? That Faith and Grace are capable of this?'

'Oh... I don't know what to believe...'

I held my hand to hers. Just to stop it from shaking.

'How long have you known Faith and Grace?' I asked.

'They've been coming to my studio for over two years.'

I pulled the chair I was sitting on slightly closer to Claire.

'And knowing them for over two years, do you believe they are capable of murder?'

Claire raised her shoulders towards her ears.

'The Tiddle family... y'know... they're just... they're just...' She paused and pursed her lips at me.

'Go on, Claire.'

'I don't want to be one of those anti-religious types. People are free to believe what they want to believe. But I always found all four of them quite... *odd*. There's always been something strange about that family.'

'So you knew Clive and Dorothy, too?'

She held a shaking hand to her face.

'One or the other used to drop the girls off to begin with. Then the girls started coming to class by themselves.'

'And you've always found the twins odd, too?'

'Just different. They don't pal around or even talk to the other girls. They just sneak off into a corner during break times and whisper to each other.'

I sat back in my chair.

'I find them odd, too, Claire, I must admit. But being odd or believing in a God doesn't make you a killer.' She began to sob, so I leaned forward and gripped her hand again. 'Claire... don't allow their uniqueness to cloud your judgement. I just want to know what time Faith and Grace showed up here on Saturday, and what time they left at.'

She looked at me with her glazed eyes and nodded again.

'Yeah, yeah. They got here at about five to twelve, as they always do. Left when the class was over, as they always do. They were certainly here alright... they were here for the full hour.'

'Then it couldn't have been them, could it?'

She sniffed up her nose.

'So Clive and Dorothy were killed while the twins were here?' she asked.

I tapped my fingers against the back of her hand, unaware of the exact answer to her question. Early indications had been the deceased weren't long dead by the time I arrived. But we still hadn't heard from the coroner on the exact time of death.

'We think so,' I said, just to dampen her sobs.

She was too nice to be this upset.

I had more missed calls while I spoke to Claire, but didn't check them until I got back to my car. I immediately assumed a lot of them were Tunstead... again. But they weren't. They were mostly from my wife.

I pressed at her name.

'Denis, Denis.' Sheila sounded panicky, out of breath. 'Come home. Quick. I–I—' Then the line went dead.

ALICE

Scarhead picks up the sheets of paper in front of him, then clears his throat.

"'Yes, it is true. I did tell the policeman that I thought Faith was particularly quiet in class that day. But it wasn't just her quietness... I don't know. She seemed a little dazed, though I have to say, she danced for the full hour of that class.'" Scarhead looks up at us, then continues reading.

"'But on reflection, I just can't quite put my finger on it. I've thought about that day, that dance class, a thousand times at least in the two years or whatever it's been and I just...'"

'She shook her head saying that,' Red Head pipes up.

'Yep,' I say, agreeing with her. 'It was like she wanted to say Faith was quiet that day, but the more and more she's thought about it over the months, she's not sure what she believes exactly.'

Acne Girl, who normally disagrees with me, nods her head.

'Yeah, that's the impression I get from her, too. Claire Barry's testimony was kinda... what's the word... indifferent. It didn't make me believe the twins were guilty at all.'

'So what did, then?' I ask.

'Now hold on here,' Scarhead pipes up. 'We're not quizzing jurors on their reasons for their verdict vote earlier, we are discussing the testimony of an important witness here. Claire Barry spent the next hour in the company of Faith and Grace right after they killed their parents and—'

'That's only if you think they killed them,' I say, as snappy as I possibly can.

I was gaining confidence. Finally sitting upright, finally arguing my side.

Nobody seemed to pay me any attention when Red Head and I walked back out of the toilet. I was glad of that. Because it meant they hadn't been talking about me when I was gone. As soon as we sat down beside each other, Scarhead began to read the testimony he had requested from the court. I felt sorry for Claire Barry when she was on the stand. She looked stressed, as if she had been worried sick about her day in court every day for the past twenty months. She constantly sipped from the glass of water in front of her, asking the court clerk for a refill every ten minutes or so. Her hand shook every time she took the glass to her mouth for the full hour and a half she was on that stand. It was almost as if she was the one on trial.

'And then Bracken said to her,' Scarhead continues, '"So you say Faith is always quiet in class, yes?"'

'"Yes."'

'"And you say Faith danced for the full hour of this class... does she always dance for the full hour in your classes?"'

'"Yes."'

'"Well, then... I'm wondering what the difference is... if Faith is always quiet in your class, and Faith is always dancing in your class, what was the difference between this Saturday and every other Saturday? I suggest, Ms Barry, that when you were asked by police if the twins had acted strange in your class on the Saturday in question, you said Faith was quiet, because she *was* quiet. But I put it to you that on reflection you have realised that what you said to the police wasn't out of the ordinary at all. That is all, Your Honour."'

'Yeah, he sounded really smarmy the way he ended his questioning of her so abruptly,' Thick-rimmed Glasses says. I agree with him. He did. Bracken oozes smarmy. I didn't think his questioning of Claire Barry went that well for the defence at all to be honest. He came across as if he was bullying her, trying to convince her that she was confused. He didn't let her answer his last point, he just flung an accusation at her and then told the judge he was done.

'True,' the old woman with the oversized bust says. 'I think the whole court liked Claire. And by undermining her, Mr Bracken lost that particular battle.'

'It's not a battle,' I say. And then all eyes turn back to me. 'Listen,' I say, easing the potential tension. 'It's true to say that Claire Barry should have been a great witness for the prosecution. Her witness statement was one of the main reasons the detectives were focused on the twins in the first place.

Part of my problem is that the detectives didn't really look into any other suspects.'

'It's not our job to play detective,' Thick-rimmed Glasses says.

'I know that... I know... it's just that it's our job to either suggest that the twins did this beyond all reasonable doubt, or simply that it wasn't proven beyond reasonable doubt. And even here... Claire's testimony...' I say, pointing at the sheets of paper in front of me. 'It offers nothing definite, just like all the other evidence offers nothing definite. That's why we need to find Faith and Grace not guilty. The case simply wasn't proven.'

The entire table falls silent. I must have struck a chord. That was my best moment so far.

'Hmmm,' the young girl with the braces says, nodding her head.

'You, eh... you seem to be wavering now,' Red Head says to her.

It's exactly what I had been thinking.

'No, she's not wavering. We all know the twins did this—'

'Hold on!' Red Head says, interrupting the man with the thick-rimmed glasses. 'How are you feeling now, Lisa?'

Lisa. The girl with the braces' name. Doesn't matter that I've just learned her name. I won't remember it. I sit closer, leaning my arms onto the table, willing her to say she's going to change her mind, that she wants to vote not guilty.

'Truth is, I'm pretty certain in my heart of hearts they did this,' she says. *Shit!* 'But, I kind of agree with you and, eh... Alice.' I smile at her. 'I don't think the prosecution really proved the case.'

'Well if you think they did it, then you must find them guilty,' Scarhead says, and then the table goes off on one again. Everybody talking. Nobody listening.

'Hold on! Hold on!' Acne Girl shouts. She's usually mute. Which is why her shouting shuts everyone up instantly. 'I believe they did it too,' she says quietly. 'I – *one-hundred percent* – believe they did it. It doesn't matter to me if Faith was particularly quiet or regular quiet in that dance class, because I am sure that they are cold and calculated enough to dance their little asses off as if nothing had happened that morning. They had the time to do it, too. I know there was a huge argument over timelines. But let's face facts on that. Clive and Dorothy could have been stabbed between ten-thirty and ten forty-five – which is before the twins left the house. They're guilty.'

'But sure, Clive and Dorothy could easily have been killed between ten forty-five and eleven,' Red Head says. 'The experts said it was any time between ten-thirty and eleven. So, just as easily as the twins could have done it before they left, somebody else also could have done it after the twins left. Timing doesn't win the argument here, either way.'

Scarhead groans into his hands.

'Jeez,' he says. 'The argument is: did the twins have time to do it? Yes, is the answer. They had time. Simple as.'

Red Head looks at me, as if I am the one armed with the rebuttal to what Scarhead has just said. I'm not, though. He's right. The timing issue comes down to 'could the twins conceivably have had time to do this?' And they could. Conceivably.

'Well, I don't believe they did it,' is all I can say. 'Ye know what... we left something out of the verdict vote we had earlier.' I don't know how I got here. I think I just wanted to change the subject. Or maybe it's because the girl with the braces is on my mind. She sounded like she might be wavering. 'We never made *undecided* an option. We just said guilty or not guilty. I bet some people in here are undecided. Would you all mind...' I say, looking sheepishly around the table at them all, 'if I asked you to put up your hand if you are undecided with your verdict.'

Scarhead tuts. But nobody else says anything. And then the young guy with the high quiff who voted not guilty earlier sticks his hand in the air. Bollocks. This is backfiring on me. I've lost one from my team. But then the girl with the braces reluctantly raises an open palm too. Half-arsedly.

'What does this prove?' Scarhead says.

'Not much,' I reply. 'I wanted the vote to be just and true. We never gave an option for undecided and it is a legitimate stance for any of us to take right now.'

He huffs. Like only one of those blokes who hates it when a woman stands up for herself huffs.

'It's okay,' I whisper to the girl with the braces. 'You can put your hand down now.'

Everybody turns to Scarhead, wondering where he is going to lead us next. He coughs, then sifts through his paperwork.

'We could, eh...'

A knock at the door saves him from his awkwardness. Red Head beats me to it, getting up first and answering it. I watch her nod her head before she turns to us.

'Lunch time,' she says.

Some don't even hesitate. They're on their feet. Though I have to admit, I'm eager to get to that dining room myself. Arguing does work up an appetite.

Braces is the last to leave the room. I hold back at the door, and wait for her.

'Hey,' I say, offering my brightest smile. 'I eh... hope you don't feel as if I put you on the spot asking about undecided jurors.'

'No, no. Not at all,' she says, 'I mean, I'm here for my voice and my opinion, so I gotta speak up. Thank you for allowing me to have a say.'

I place my hand on the small of her back as we walk the maze of corridors.

'You really are undecided, huh? Ye know, if you have any doubt at all, you gotta go with not guilty.'

'I know... I know, it's jus—'

'I mean, I'm sorry, I don't wanna tell you what to do...' I'm whispering now because we've just caught up with the others, all standing in a line outside the dining room door. The young woman dressed all in black unlocks it with her overly big bunch of keys and then we all head inside.

'I don't think you're telling me what to do,' she whispers back to me. 'It's just I've thought all the way through this that they were guilty. In fact, every witness who took that stand seems to think they did it.'

'Not really,' I whisper back really quietly as we take our seats across from each other at the end of the table. It's not like the table from the Jury Room. It's more rectangular, more restaurant-like. 'Detective Quayle didn't think they were guilty, now did he? And he was lead detective on the case.'

Her eyes squint and then her head starts to nod. I think the penny might be dropping with her. I'm doing well at this.

'Perhaps you're right,' she says.

I lean closer to her. Give her my best puppy dog eyes.

'Lisa, think about it, you can not—'

'Hey, you two...' Scarhead shouts down from the top of the table. 'Hope you're not discussing the trial.'

I grin a fake smile at him and shake my head.

'We weren't,' I lie.

'Good. Because I was about to suggest we don't discuss the trial at all. Let's give ourselves a break. To enjoy some lunch. Don't know about you all, but I'm starving.'

The young woman dressed in all black places a plate of ham and mash in front of me, then stretches across to place one in front of Braces. Our eyes meet through the steam of our lunch, and then everything goes quiet.

✝

The two hundred and forty pounds Clive and Dorothy took in the collection basket at their very first Mass would be – by quite some margin – the least amount they would ever take in.

Even before Faith and Grace were born, their weekly pull was averaging over the one thousand euro mark. Following the arrival of the twins, that amount instantly doubled, then trebled as Clive really got to grips with marketing his sermons. He had long since given up trying to convince Dubliners that the answers to all the questions they ever wanted to ask lay somewhere within the book he would preach from. Dublin folk had taken too long as it was finally catching their breath after the suffocation brought to them by the Catholic church. They had only just woken up – and weren't remotely interested in falling back asleep.

So Clive had a brainwave. He recruited immigrants; foreigners, lost souls he could find in the city centre. He bought a bus, had somebody brand the side of it with stickers that consisted of a crucifix and the title "The New St Benedict's Church" and then set about recruiting loners in the city. He promised them tea and Jammy Dodger biscuits – which he always delivered – as well as an ear. It was everything these lost souls had ever wanted.

Over the years the Tiddles welcomed over ten thousand people to their church. Christian folk like to come and go. A lot of believers are actually much more liberal than their reputations suggest. They like to travel and often just kip on other 'family' members' sofas – anywhere in the world – as a means of getting around. It's a bohemian, non-conventional way of living. That's one of the most redeeming features of the communities that grow from churches – they really feel as if they are all in it together. The community centre actually packed one thousand people into the large room Clive and Dorothy had converted into a church in one day. It was for the double christening of Faith and Grace. Some folk even flew from so far as Melbourne to attend.

Even Aunt Janet – Clive's sister – and her husband, Uncle Eoin, turned up. She was irked that she wasn't a Godparent, but her complaints fell on deaf ears.

'I'm the only blood relative you've got!' she snapped at Clive. He barely responded, but to say he wanted people who believed in God to actually be Godparents. He never even thought to consider Janet. In fact, he was loath to even invite her and her husband as he knew they would both turn up in tracksuits. They were never out of tracksuits.

The Godparents to Grace were married couple Corey and Dana Calisis who Clive and Dorothy were really close with at the time, but who had since moved back to California. Faith's Godparents were Paul Doughtery – an Irish guy who was influential in helping Clive and Dorothy set up their church after successfully setting up his own in the outskirts of Cork, and Kelly McAllister – a young Scottish lady who had been one of the early recruits of Clive and Dorothy as they went searching in the city. She practically married herself to The New St Benedict's Church as soon as she walked inside that community centre.

They took in almost one hundred thousand euro on the day of the twins' christening; each invitee told not to bother with presents, that a church donation would be most appreciated. The average donation was a hundred euro; offered up by quite a lot of people who couldn't really afford to offer up that much cash. They genuinely didn't mind though; it was another liberal trait of churchgoers. Money wasn't such a big deal. God would provide no matter what.

The twins were three months old when they were christened and so tiny that they almost looked as if they were drowning in their dresses and bows. Dorothy had handmade their gowns; silk-white meringue-style with lace collars and cuffs; complemented by huge white and pink striped bows that were actually bigger than the babies' heads.

Even by this stage it was obvious that the twins had different personalities. Grace was an extrovert, always trying to create noise, to seek attention. Faith was already in her own world; quite often asleep when there were crowds around so as not to receive any attention whatsoever. Often she would just lie there, not necessarily with her eyes closed, but with them rolled to the back of her head.

Grace was such an attention-seeker early in her life that Clive felt a need to put a stop to it. Even when she was just a toddler she would ask too many questions; was full of wonderment. Sometimes she would even stump Clive or Dorothy with questions about the Bible. And out of fear of her doing so in public, Clive sat her down and informed her of her responsibilities and role within the family. Even though he loved her – adored her – and gave her the attention she was seeking most of the time, he couldn't risk her ever being such an extrovert that she would question all of the beliefs he had spent years convincing himself he needed to believe.

'So why don't you just be a bit more like Faith,' he said to her when she was just three years of age. 'Quiet.'

He was so convincing to his daughter – as he always was – that she practically became the opposite of the person she naturally was. She fell into the role of being an introvert; only speaking when being spoken to. It wasn't as if the twins were always quiet. They would converse constantly when alone. Grace would do all of the asking; Faith would make all the decisions.

'What will we do today, Faith, wanna play teddy bears on the rug?'

'What colour bow shall we wear in our hairs today, Faith?'

'Shall we go to the bathroom and do pee-pee now, Faith?'

Grace offered up all of the questions; Faith would stand there, sometimes rolling her eyes to the back of her head in consideration, and would then make the decision.

They were thick as thieves as soon as they were born and didn't mind being stared at in church. It was all they knew. Daddy would help out churchgoers with some wise words and counselling during the week, in between writing his sermons, and Mammy would bake fresh Jammy Dodgers and make tea for anyone, whoever visited the community centre. She was practically there full-time and began acting as Clive's sidekick – being a counsellor of sorts. She was very good at what she did, Dorothy. She would always convince folk that their worries were mainly superfluous. After all, 'this is part of God's plan' is a hell of an ace card to have up your sleeve when you are trying to counsel people. Any grievance anybody could possibly ever have would be temporarily settled and calmed by a visit to Dorothy. She would often contradict herself, but she had learned how to talk her way out of any situation. Besides, she was lovely; a real honest woman who genuinely had everybody's best interests at heart. She might not have looked like the nicest and most friendly person in the world – her hooked nose and dated, short hair not particularly appealing – but she did have a kind heart. And kind eyes. Though when it came to the money being generated by the church, her generosity somehow seemed to evaporate. It wasn't that she actually wanted to hide the money from everyone or even steal it in any way; it was *genuinely a case that she didn't actually know what to do with it. Neither of them did.*

Dorothy was a little sterner with the twins, certainly in comparison to Clive. It would often be her who handed down punishments or who raised a voice at them. But it was never anything bad. A shouted 'Girls!' if she heard them practising their tap-dancing too loudly in the kitchen or a 'What are you two up to now!?' if she thought they were talking too much in their bedrooms. She never hit them. Never even considered it. Her punishments consisted of the twins having to do extra chores around the house – or, more often than not, a lengthy prayer session. She pretty much raised the twins how she was raised: stern, fair and smothered in traditionalisms... as well, of course, as old-fashioned floral dresses and oversized hair bows.

In truth it was mainly Grace who found herself on her knees praying as a course of discipline; she was always the loudest. Not necessarily with her voice, as Clive had well and truly stemmed that, but with almost everything else she did. She couldn't help it. Although both girls were slight and light, Grace running around the house would sound like a refrigerator falling down a staircase; whereas Faith moved with such considered carefulness that often Clive and Dorothy wouldn't even hear her entering a room.

Faith did, one day, get into a lot of trouble for not listening to her father. He had been trying to tell her that her dinner was almost ready and that she needed to come to the kitchen. But she didn't hear him. She was too busy zoning out, doing that thing she does when she rolls her eyes to the back of her head.

'I called your name five times!' Clive snapped.

Faith turned out her bottom lip as an offer of apology. But she was sent to her bedroom to pray for twenty minutes nonetheless, ensuring the dinner she would eventually eat afterwards would be cold.

'Why do you do that... the eye thing?' Grace asked her that night. Faith squinted at her sister, and tilted her head. 'Y'know... the eye thing,' Grace said, and then she rolled her eyes into the back of her head to show her sister what she meant.

Faith's brow pointed downwards. She was truly confused

'What do you mean?' she asked.

'Well...' Grace threw the covers off her legs and sat on the edge of her bed. 'Sometimes you're praying and stuff... and then you just go all quiet and....' She rolled her eyes again to the back of her head.

'Oh, do I?' Faith said, grinning. 'I guess that's when I'm listening.'

'Listening?' Grace said. 'Listening to what?'

'To him,' Faith replied. 'To Jesus.'

DAY TWO–DAY THREE

I must have paced the corridor a thousand times before the door finally snatched open.

As soon as it did, the rate of my heart slowed, because the first thing I saw was the doctor smiling at me.

Sheila was sitting up in the bed and although she looked paler than normal, she seemed to be back to herself: giving out to me.

'You should've gone back to work, Denis,' she said. 'Y'know he's working on the big case you are reading about in the papers every day, Doctor. He's lead detective.'

The doctor formed an "O" shape with his mouth.

'The, eh... religious family up in the Dublin mountains? What a strange one that is. Anywhere near to finding out who did it?'

I shook my head.

'Sorry Doctor... you know as much as I do about confidentiality in the workplace.'

'Of course,' he said, almost embarrassed that he asked in the first place. 'Anyway... Sheila has recovered remarkably well in the past couple of hours. She was just too dehydrated. That's all. We've run some tests and we should have the results back soon. But seems to me as if she's been starving herself of water. Two litres. Every day. It's very important.'

I inched closer to the bed and pursed my lips at her.

'So... what kind of tests did you run?' I asked the doctor, whilst still staring at my wife.

'It's nothing to worry about. More routine than anything. I wanted to run another ultrasound to the stomach. Just to monitor the tumour.'

'Think you'll have any results tonight?' I asked.

'Earliest will be first thing in the morning,' the doc replied. Then he stepped closer to the bed too. The opposite side of it to me. 'Sheila is adamant she will not undergo any more chemotherapy... said the two of you have spoken at length about this.'

I grabbed my wife's hand and brought it to my mouth to kiss her knuckles.

'Never again, Doctor. She's never felt worse than she did during those months. It was fading her away.'

'Well, we're mightily impressed how healthy she's keeping. Without any medication for the past few months, she seems more than reasonably healthy.'

'It's the weed, Doc,' Sheila said, laughing. I glared at her, my eyebrows dipped. 'Oh, it's okay, Denis.' She waved her hand. 'Everything said in this room is just between the three of us, isn't it, Doc?' She didn't wait for him to reply. 'I've been vaping some cannabis. And I've... I've never felt better. Well, not since I was young anyway. It's a miracle plant. It hasn't only put an end to the cramps in my stomach, it's stopped the misery in my head, too. I'm never in a bad mood. Not anymore. I love it. In fact... I'm gonna send Denis home to pick up my vaporiser so I can have a puff out in that garden there.' She nodded out of the ward window, to the decking below.

The doctor held his clipboard close to his chest, then smiled out of one side of his mouth.

'We've been hearing some eye-opening research on cannabis,' he said. 'But I'm, eh... I'm no expert on it. Far as I know it's still illegal here.' Then he touched Sheila's shoulder and looked at me. 'Detective.' He nodded and made his way to the doorway, where he paused and turned back. 'I've informed Sheila we'll be keeping her in overnight. We want to keep her hooked up to the intravenous so she can rehydrate.' Then he smiled at us both and pulled the door closed.

I turned to my wife as soon as he was gone, my eyebrows dipping again.

'Relax, Denis,' she said. 'You heard him yourself. He's only heard good stuff about the research that's going on.'

I leaned in, kissed her forehead and then sat in one of those uncomfortable blue plastic chairs for the next two hours, telling her all about my day.

We were only disturbed once. By Fairweather. Ringing to tell me the media were constantly on to her looking for an update on the case, and she felt she could no longer palm them off. She insisted I held a press conference the next morning; just to get them out of her hair. So I agreed. Even though I hadn't a clue what I could – or even should – tell them yet.

She also informed me that Aunt Janet had been tracked down and would be making her way to Dublin in the coming days. Johnny, who had contacted her, said she hadn't been very specific on when she would make the trip, nor did she seem to be in any rush.

'She sounds weird. And cold,' Sheila said when I filled her in. 'Ye think *she* did it?'

I laughed. Told her again she needed to stop living inside one of her novels.

I did go home. To pick up the vaporiser. Then I escorted her downstairs, into the vacant garden decking that was reserved for smokers, and stared at her in the moonlight as she exhaled vapour. The weed always has an immediate effect on her mood; her lips turn upwards and her eyes widen. Just like old times. It was cold that night, but we stayed outside on that wooden decking for over an hour and shot the breeze; about the case, about her illness, about the fact that we never had kids, about travelling the world. That topic was bound to come up any time we spoke at length. We love Tuscany. And Florida. We often go to Florida. But just for two weeks a year. Like normal people. Sheila always had dreams of me retiring and us having the freedom to travel. Though that was before she was diagnosed with stomach cancer. Like most folk tend to do, we stupidly planned that the best years of our lives would be for a time a lot of people don't actually get to see.

It was gone one a.m. when I finally crawled into bed that night. Though I still couldn't sleep. There was too much to think about. Clive and Dorothy. Faith and Grace. Tommo Nevin. Claire Barry. But I was mostly tossing and turning with thoughts about my wife's results; fearful the doctor was going to inform us that it's chemo or bust. I didn't want to watch her fade away again.

My biggest fear, ever since I met Sheila, has always been losing her. And I really thought I was going to at the start of that year. She looked awful. Her hair and eyebrows had disappeared and I could almost fully grasp her whole waist with my two hands. But she gained some weight and grew her hair back as soon as she decided to come off the chemo. And her mood picked up. That's because when we went online to find the best alternatives to chemotherapy in order to reduce the size of a cancerous tumour, cannabis kept screaming at us as the answer.

It was Tunstead who woke me up. Constantly ringing. He rang four times between seven a.m. and seven-thirty. But when I eventually sat up in bed, I rang Sheila rather than him.

She was adamant that she would be coming home later that morning, once she got the intravenous out of her arm. She didn't seem as worried about the results as I was; had long since given up caring about how much time she had left. Her mantra had been "quality, not quantity," ever since she sucked in her first hit of cannabis.

'Right, you're doing this at the church, you all set?' Fairweather said to me as soon as I arrived at the station.

'Doing what?' I asked.

'Your press conference.'

'Press conference?' my voice went all high-pitched. 'I just thought you wanted me to release a statement or something.'

Fairweather looked at me, displaying *my* confusion on *her* face. Then she shrugged her shoulders.

'It's a press conference, Quayle,' she said. 'And it starts in twenty minutes, so you need to get your ass over there.'

'Alright... alright...' I said. 'Let's get going then.'

She shook her head.

'I've, eh... I've an eight-thirty tee time.'

I didn't respond; didn't even bother to laugh. Or sigh. I just swiped my keys from my desk and headed for my car. It didn't surprise me that Fairweather didn't disrupt her plans while this investigation was going on. This case was the last thing she wanted. She was used to the quiet life... yearned for the quiet life. I knew she was going to retire once this was over. She couldn't risk her routine being put out like this again. I reckoned Fairweather did more work in those five days than she had done in the two decades I was working with her prior to them. And yet she still fitted in two rounds of eighteen holes.

'Do you not answer your fuckin' calls?' Tunstead barely waited for me to open my car door when I pulled into the community centre car park.

'Relax, Tunstead. I have more important things going on than making sure I get back to you without hesitating.'

He was about to fume back at me, but Lowe rubbed his arm, calmed him down.

'I was wondering if you wanted me to take this press conference. I've done a dozen of these—'

'I know what I'm doing,' I snapped. I didn't. Not at all. In fact, I really wanted to accept his offer, especially after I'd walked into the church to see an ocean of TV cameras. But I didn't. Because I didn't want him to think I thought he was a better cop than me.

'Just don't use anybody's names. Except the deceased. If you mention Grace and Faith by name, you will damage any case we bring to the courts.

They are too young to be named. Don't reduce the chances of us getting a verdict.'

I stared at him, then at Lowe.

'You two still think it was them, don't you?' I tutted. Then I walked down the aisle of the church, and pursed my lips in sorrow at a crying Kelly McAllister before taking my seat at a makeshift table just in front of the stage.

My heart rate definitely rose. I could feel it. Then I went and spilled the jug of water over the table when I tried to pick it up to pour myself a glass. My hands were too sweaty. It just dropped. Then smashed. And the water splashed everywhere.

It took a tiny army of people to come to my rescue before everything was set up and ready to go again. I could see one of the journalist's impatience growing; her director yelling into her ear.

As soon as everything was set back up, she was the first to speak.

'So, Detective Quayle, can you read your statement out before answering some of our questions?'

'Sorry,' I said. 'A statement?'

She stared at me, then at the journalist beside her.

'We were told you would have a statement to make on the double homicide of Clive and Dorothy Tiddle, Detective. The nation is waiting. We are live...'

ALICE

Scarhead made the decision to not discuss the trial without even consulting the rest of us. He just proclaimed that we'd all benefit from giving our minds a rest by enjoying some food. In fairness, I think everybody around the table agreed with him, because nobody questioned his proclamation.

So the twelve of us talked about ourselves instead over lunch; the guy with the thick-rimmed glasses welcoming us all to open up a bit about our livelihoods – asking us about our jobs. We listened to each other as we chewed on our ham. Everybody seemed different over lunch. More relaxed. More themselves. Even Scarhead showed some redeeming qualities. I wouldn't have put him down as a hairdresser. Though after he'd told us he ran his own unisex salon in north county Dublin I did, for the first time, notice he does have a particularly trendy cropped do himself. I hadn't looked at it. My eyes never went above that scar.

The girl with the braces – who I constantly tried to make eye contact with across the lunch table for nothing more than to purse my lips at her and let her know that I've got her back – is an insurance consultant in Fullams Accountancy. Red Head owns her own architectural firm, and she lectures on architecture part-time at Trinity College. Impressive. Quiff Guy is a student, but he's also the lead singer in a band. Sinono, they're called. He said they get thousands of hits on Instagram every day... whatever that means.

I told them I work in catering. Which I do. But I kinda egged myself up a bit; saying I provide for high-end corporate events. I don't really. I provide for the odd party here and there, picking up business through word of mouth. I don't have to work. Not really. Noel's job brings in enough for the entire house to run like clockwork. But I didn't want to be a housewife. I always assumed I'd have a career. That I'd be a chef; working in some super cool restaurant. Maybe even open a restaurant of my own. But ambitions like that are hard to fulfil if you're a woman, and almost definitely if you are a woman who wants a family.

My diploma is in culinary arts. I knew what I wanted to do as soon as I left school. And straight from college I got a job in a cute little restaurant in Malahide. The commute was a bit of a bitch, but I enjoyed the heat of the kitchen and stayed there for four years until just after I'd met and fallen in love with Noel. Even then he was bringing in close to a hundred grand a year. So he constantly asked me why was I bothering to travel all the way to the coast every day to earn myself a measly few quid. And I guess when I fell pregnant with Zoe it just made sense that I would never go back. I had a baby to raise, after all. Between Zoe and the absolute struggle we went through to have Alfie, I set up my own sideline business: Sheridan Catering. Just to stave off the tag of 'housewife' more than anything. I provide for friends' and family's parties. But that's essentially all I do. Every now and then. Whenever the phone rings.

I don't resent Noel in any way for having the high-flying career while I twiddle my thumbs for most hours of the day. I've just come to realise that that's how it is for women. We always get the shitty end of the stick. But I guess it's just as well we get it – could you imagine the fucking headache it would be for all of humanity if it was men who got the shitty end of the stick?

Scarhead took his time figuring out where we should take our deliberations when we settled back around the jurors' table after lunch – shuffling his paperwork around, trying to appear as if he knew what he was doing.

After a few prompts and inputs from others around the table he eventually decided we should continue to deliberate Detective Quayle's testimony. I guess it made sense. We seemed divided right down the middle on how Quayle handled the investigation from the get-go.

Quayle was an odd one. I kinda liked him. He smiled up at us all when he was on the stand and even bowed to us gently after he was done. But I would certainly question whether or not he is a decent detective. He looked too timid, too nice, to deal with such serious matters. Though maybe the stereotype of a detective being a bit of a wise-guy smartarse is only down to the glorification of that profession on TV. I think it was Quayle's moustache that made him look friendly; he kept playing with it, spreading it out with his thumb and forefinger before he answered most questions put to him.

'I think that he looked a little awkward in that press conference the defence team played for us, but that's the only reason anybody is questioning whether or not he did a good job,' says the old woman with the oversized bust.

She, like me, seems to have a soft spot for Quayle.

'It wasn't just the bumbling press conference, was it though? He went on record with Faith and Grace's lawyer a couple of days later and said that the twins didn't do it. Then he arrested them and is now not sure whether they did or didn't do it.' Thick-rimmed Glasses was speaking, tightening the knot Quayle seemed to get himself entangled up in through the course of the entire investigation. The detective refused to say on the stand whether or not he felt the twins were guilty. Yet he was the one who went on record a couple of times admitting he didn't think they did it. And that was before he arrested them five days after the murders. He called out to Janet Petersen's house – where Faith and Grace had ended up following the death of their parents – and placed them both under arrest for double homicide. Then he retired from the job. He just said he had enough of it and left. He was asked, on the stand, whether or not he received a handsome pay-off for his twenty-five years of service. But he refused to answer that too, backed by the judge who agreed the answer to that line of questioning was redundant. Quayle was a witness for the prosecution but it was really hard to determine whose side he was on exactly. I think that's why he fascinated us jurors. And probably why our minds were split on his testimony.

He had said, and we all heard it played over and over again in court, at the press conference he did two days after the murders that there was 'just one suspect' in the case. And then we heard a voice recording of him talking to Gerd Bracken two nights after that, insisting the twins were not the main suspects. Yet, he arrested them a little over twenty-four hours later. No wonder we were all confused by his investigation; no wonder we were spending so long discussing him.

My take on it is that those above Quayle knew the twins were guilty from the off, but he wanted to protect them initially. Probably because he's just a nice guy. But I don't believe he doesn't think they did it. He must know they did it. Because they did do it. They had to have done it. I really wish he had have answered that question in court, because it would have made a huge difference in this jury room. I'm pretty sure Quayle's reluctance to admit the twins are guilty is the reason Red Head and Obese Guy can justify their not guilty verdict. I'm sure it's why the other jurors think I'm holding on to my not guilty verdict too. But it's not. I'm only holding on to mine because some bitch has the recording of me fucking my daughter's boyfriend.

'I don't think he believes they did it,' I say when I'm finally asked for my opinion. 'He didn't believe they did it straight after the killings, didn't think they did it while he was investigating the case and I don't believe he thinks they did it now.'

'You don't know that for certain,' Scarhead says.

'Listen,' I reply to him, 'if he thought they did it, he would have just said so on the stand. He would have just said "I arrested them because I think they're guilty." But ye know why he didn't say that? Ye know why he wouldn't answer that question in court? Because he didn't want to let his former colleagues down. Out of respect, he didn't want to step on the prosecution's arguments.'

'It's such a shame he retired straight after the case,' Thick-rimmed Glasses says. 'If he was still a cop, he would have *had* to admit he thought they did it.'

Thick-rimmed Glasses is right with what he's saying. Quayle retiring straight after this case added a huge dollop of intrigue that otherwise shouldn't have any intrigue at all. It should be simple. Faith and Grace are evil and they killed their parents in cold blood. End of. But Quayle's missteps along his investigation offer a sliver of doubt to this case – and that gives us three who are voting not guilty justification for our stance.

'We could talk about how Quayle handled this investigation all day... but as I've said before, he's not the one on trial,' Scarhead says.

'I disagree,' I say. 'I think Detective Quayle is the absolute key in this trial. He investigated the case and is hesitant to say the twins did it. In fact, all he is ever on record as saying is that they *didn't* do it.'

'He was surely on record when he arrested them. So by arresting them he is admitting he believes they did it. He hardly arrested two nine-year-old girls, as they were at the time, thinking they were innocent'

'Uuuugh... we're gonna go round and round in circles talking about this guy.' Thick-rimmed Glasses is starting to flare beetroot red, flapping his arms in the air and reeling back in his chair. 'Why don't we look at more evidence, rather than just trying to second-guess witnesses all the time. Can we look at the cold, hard facts of this case... so that we can all surely come to the same obvious conclusion, here? The twins did this, right. The evidence says—'

'The evidence says fuck all,' I say. A few gasps are heard around the table. I don't know why. I'm not the first to swear in this room today. Nobody gasped before when Scarhead swore.

'Well... what about the stab wounds?' Thick-rimmed Glasses says. And then I reel back in my chair, because the stab wounds are the most significant aspect of this trial. They literally point to the twins being guilty.

DAY THREE

I stormed out of the church furious.

Not embarrassed.

Not mortified.

Not ashamed.

Just furious. Why the hell didn't Fairweather warn me I'd to read out a statement?

I slapped both hands to my face when I got back into the car.

Maybe I should have let Tunstead handle the bloody press conference.

I just rattled off some nonsense about the time of the death being "approximately eleven a.m. on Saturday, the 15th of August", then I suggested we are zoning in on a suspect. When another reporter asked me if I was talking about "a sole suspect, not two?" I immediately knew what he was getting at.

'Just a suspect, at the moment,' I said as sternly as I could, then I called for the "next question".

I couldn't wait to get out of there. When there was a slight hesitation after the fifth question, I just stood up and declared that I needed to get back to work on the case.

I didn't look anyone in the eye as I traipsed through the crowd of photographers and journalists and then down the long aisle of the church.

'Fairweather, that was live,' I grunted down the phone as I pulled out of the church car park. She didn't say anything. 'Did you watch? Did I make a fool of myself?'

'I... I... no, I didn't know it would go out live. I wasn't sure what to expect to be honest—'

'You're the bloody station chief, you should have told me what to expect.'

There was a silence for more seconds than there needed to be whilst I cringed inside. Then I heard a golf ball being struck on the other end of the line.

'But... listen, Quayle,' she said, 'Tallaght said you wouldn't be able to lead this case and I was adamant that you wouldn't put a foot wrong. This is the second time you've snapped at me. There are crossed-wires, clearly. But that's because we are a small operation. We don't have the resources and the experiences like the detectives in Tallaght do. Are you sure you don't just want to pass this over?'

I deep sighed into the phone.

'I'm onto something here,' I said. 'I just wouldn't mind a bit more support.'

There was another silence while I imagined her looking around the golf course.

'I'll get back to the station,' she said. 'But I want you to know; I'm all for giving this to Tallaght.'

I thanked her, hung up and then checked who had been miss-calling me while I was talking to Fairweather. I'd heard two different beeps and was hoping at least one of them was from the hospital.

But both missed calls were from the same strange number.

I stabbed my finger at the callback option and held the phone to my ear.

'Hello, Sana Patel,' a voice answered. I knew the name. She's SOCO.

'Patel. It's Detective Inspector Quayle.'

'I have the results you were looking for, Quayle,' she said. 'Not sure you're going to be thrilled. Not much to go on, I'm afraid. The Tiddles were killed with a knife from their own kitchen. One knife out of a set of six is missing from the scene. It fits the murder weapon perfectly. Whoever murdered this couple took that knife from its block, stabbed both deceased multiple times and left. Clive was stabbed thirteen times; three times in the chest, nine times in the torso and once in the upper left thigh. The fatal stab wound was one made to his heart. I believe it was the first stabbing. Dorothy died slower. She was stabbed seven times, all in the lower torso. A stab wound to her liver is likely the cause of her death. But she likely bled out for up to an hour.'

I rubbed at my temple to help absorb everything Patel was saying.

'Any DNA left? Any leads as to what sort of profile we're looking at here?'

'That's the weird thing, Quayle,' she said. 'The killer came and left without leaving a drop of DNA. Whoever did this knew what they were doing. Small. Definitely small. Or certainly whoever killed Dorothy was small. The stab wounds, they're not only low. But delicate. Two inches in depth.'

'Small... as in... you think it's the twins, too?'

'Oh I'm not making any judgements,' she said. 'That's your job. But I will say small doesn't mean kids, per se. It could easily be a short adult. Five foot, three inches max, I would say. Though this is only a light theory. And a very early theory at that. I should also add, though it's very difficult to know for certain, but it's likely Clive Tiddle was asleep when attacked. First two stab wounds were to his chest, around the heart. Then they were all lower after that. He likely woke, tried to stand and was then downed.'

'Interesting... but that's it?' I asked. 'No DNA at all?'

I could hear her suck a breath in through her teeth.

'It's unusual, but not unheard of.'

I gurned.

'What about the time of the killings?'

'I could conclude a half-hour window. When I first examined the bodies it was six p.m. I could determine there and then that Clive likely died somewhere between ten-thirty and eleven. Dorothy sometime later, somewhere between eleven and twelve.'

I squinted, doing the maths. These timings narrowed down the twins' likely involvement to just fifteen minutes. They left the house at ten forty-five to go to dance class, arriving at ten fifty-five. If the murders happened at the earliest possible time – ten-thirty – that means they could only have had a fifteen-minute window. It wasn't them. It couldn't have been them.

'Let me ask you this, Patel,' I said, 'when DNA is absent at a scene, what does that normally tell you?'

'Well,' she said, before pausing. 'It's rare. But it guarantees to mean one of two things: either somebody whose DNA would already be at the scene is the killer... Or...' she paused. Hesitated.

'Or what?'

'Or... somebody who knew exactly what they were doing carried out the murder.'

I had finished the call by the time I'd reached Sheila's ward, then, after I'd hung up, I paused in the doorway, just as I was about to push it open. I could hear her lecturing the doctor.

'Go on, Doc,' she said. 'Tell me... how many people do you think died in the world since the turn of the century because of alcohol?'

He chuckled.

'Oh, I don't know, Mrs Quayle... hundreds of thousands.'

'Millions. Three and a quarter million to be exact. Isn't that a staggering number? And here... tell me, how many people do you think died since the turn of the century due to pharmaceutical drugs; pain killers, that kinda thing?'

I had to stifle my laughter. I knew this argument off by heart. She says it to almost everybody we ever meet. And now she was lecturing a bloody doctor about it of all people.

'No idea,' the doctor said.

'Over two million.' The doctor whistled in surprise. Then chuckled again. 'And last question,' she said. 'How many people do you think have died since the turn of the century from taking cannabis?' I observed the doctor through the crack in the door. He shrugged both his shoulders. 'Go on, have a guess,' Sheila pushed him. And then I pushed the door open to save him.

'Zero!' I said.

'Exactly,' Sheila smiled at me. 'Zero since the start of this century,' she continued. 'Zero since the start of any century. Nobody has ever died from cannabis intake. It's impossible. And yet that's the one that's illegal. Mad, isn't it?'

I walked over to her and kissed her forehead.

'It sure is, sweetheart,' I said to her. 'You seem in good spirits.'

She was sitting up in bed, her arm free from the intravenous, her smile wide.

'Do you wanna tell him, or will I, Doc?' she said.

'Oh, that news is all yours,' the doctor replied. He matched her smile.

'From a Brussel sprout to a garden pea,' she said to me. I must have looked confused. 'My tumour,' she followed up with.

'Huh?' I said, turning to the doctor.

'That's the metaphor I used,' he said. 'The tumour, it's... it has decreased by about sixty per cent. From the size of a small Brussel sprout when we last measured it three months ago, to a garden pea today.' He pinched two fingers together to show me how small a garden pea is.

Sheila sang along to the radio all the way home, to songs she didn't know the words to. Then I left her on the couch to watch an old Robert Redford movie while I raced back to the station.

Fairweather looked sombre when I got to her; sad almost.

She cocked her head, subtly, towards her office. And I followed her in to see Tunstead staring at me. The prick. As well as another man with a very serious expression etched on his face who was sitting in Fairweather's chair.

'You haven't been easy to track down today, Quayle,' he said.

'Quayle, this is Tallaght station chief Laurence Ashe,' Fairweather said to me. I eyeballed Tunstead, who was leaning his back against the wall as I shook Ashe's hand.

Then we both sat down and he leaned closer to me.

'I'm gonna cut to the chase,' Ashe said. 'We're taking you off the case, Quayle.'

ALICE

'Yeah... the stab wounds absolutely scream guilty to me,' Braces says.

I remain reeled back in my chair as heads nod around me.

'The one thing that really stood out to me was not so much the fact that most of the stab wounds were in the lower and middle torso of both victims, but the lack of depth of the stab wounds. Whoever stabbed Clive and Dorothy was short, most likely weak. Five centimetres... is that right, that was the deepest stab wound? Most of them just two or three centimetres?'

'Yeah... that's what everybody agreed on; the crime scene investigation, the defendants' expert's findings, and the prosecution experts' findings,' Scarhead says.

'Yep, but that's about all they did agree on,' Red Head says. She's really great at pushing back against anything the guilty mob are offering up.

I dart my eyes at her, but leave her to this argument. I don't want to speak up. The stab wounds argument is an impossible one for us to win.

'Okay... well, let's go through it,' Scarhead says, taking the reins. 'So, your point, Lisa, isn't it?' he asks Braces Girl. She nods her head. 'Are you saying the depth of the stab wounds is what mainly leads you to believe Faith and Grace are guilty?'

She stares down at the table in front of her, then begins to slowly nod her head.

'Yeah, I think that is the clincher for me. That and the fact that Clive was likely asleep when he was killed, even though the expert couldn't say for certain.... wouldn't the twins perhaps know if he took a nap on a Saturday at mid-morning? So those kinda things as well as all the psych reports on the girls make me think they're guilty. Everybody seems to find the twins quite odd, don't they? Aunt Janet. Kelly McAllister. As well as Joe O'Beirne and Dinah Dore who worked at Tusla. Claire Barry, the dance teacher. Nobody painted a glowing report of the twins; that's always said a lot to me.'

''Cept for Denis Quayle,' Red Head pipes up. Pushing back again.

There's a slight pause in the proceedings, as everybody soaks up Quayle again... Then they all turn to Scarhead.

'Well, let's stay on the stab wounds while we are discussing them. We all now have a copy of the testimonies given by Doctor Barry O'Hanlon and Professor Eleanor Kane in front of us.'

It was agreed by all of us that we should order these as soon as the issue of the stab wounds arose. Even I agreed. When the last thing I wanted to do was go through these testimonies. I felt one side of these theories absolutely plausible, the other – argued by the defence – was pretty much fantastical. I don't want to argue for the fantastical... it'd make me look ridiculous. But I guess I'm going to have to.

'I'll read some of Doctor O'Hanlon's testimony first,' Scarhead says. 'So, eh this is when prosecution lawyer Jonathan Ryan asked him, "The Crime Scene Investigation team initially reckoned these stabbings were made by somebody five foot, three inches in height and then they came back on that and insisted what they meant was *at most* the killer or killers were five foot, three. Your findings are somewhat a little different, are they not?", "Inches different,"' O'Hanlon said.' "We believe the attacker to likely be four foot, nine inches to five foot, one inch."'

Scarhead looked up at us when he read that out. We were all aware both twins were exactly four foot, nine. It was repeated to us numerous times during the trial; especially when it came to the evidence surrounding the stab wounds.

'And then, Ryan asked, "And the depth of the wounds themselves, Doctor O'Hanlon, what did they inform you?", "Well, I don't want to say the word weak. That's not it exactly. Two, three, four up to five centimetres deep is not a weak stab wound. They are stab wounds directed to damage or kill. Especially given that they were all around vital organs... but... my genuine understanding of the impact and locations of these stab wounds points to a child... or children."'

'That is when Bracken objected,' Thick-rimmed Glasses says.

'And the judge agreed with him,' Braces Girl offers up.

I sit forward and eyeball her a bit. I wonder what she's thinking now. If I can get her over to the not guilty camp, I'd be in a strong position. That'd be four. But she keeps bloody changing her mind. And this argument isn't going to change her mind the way I want it to be changed. I open my mouth to reply to her, but I'm beaten to it by Scarhead.

'Well, that's the golden nugget of the case, is it not?' he says. 'One of the experts is saying children definitely did this.'

'Hold on... he didn't say *definitely*, let's just be clear,' Red Head says. 'He just said his examinations point to the attackers being children. Nothing *definite* about it. Besides, he wasn't the only expert talking about stab wounds, was he?'

She was referring to the defence's expert witness – Eleanor Kane; a professor of Forensic Science at the Coombe Lab. Blonde, sharp bob cut, attractive, impressively confident and one hell of a talker. Except for one little thing. She was talking shit.

'Well, shall I read from Professor Eleanor Kane's testimony?' Scarhead asks. And everybody nods their head. Including me.

'"The stab wounds would not necessarily have come from a child,"' Scarhead reads and suddenly I'm sitting upright again. Even though I know this is all bollocks. '"There is a known disguised stabbing technique favoured among street criminals – it's an old underground Martial Arts Technique called the Mikna Sqay. It's when somebody disguises the fact that they have a knife right up until they stab, piercingly in-and-out, in-and-out repeatedly and in very swift fashion in the lower body, landing in all the major organs down there. The stab wounds suffered by both Clive Tiddle and Dorothy Tiddle hold all the hallmarks of an expert assassin."'

I hear a couple of dismissive huffs, around the table; quiet ones, puffed lightly through nostrils.

'I mean... what do we say to that? An expert assassin?' Most faces turn to Red Head, probably because she's the most vocal of our not guilty camp. The party of three. And a half. If you count the one undecided.

'All that says to me,' Red Head says, glancing towards me as she sharply sits up in her seat, 'is that it can't be considered a fact that this was children.'

'Ah come on!' Scarhead says. And then arguments spark across the table again. This is doing my head in.

'Hey!' I say. Loudly. Cutting through the noise. I hate this part. When everybody turns to me. 'It is not our job to play detective here. But Clive and Dorothy Tiddle were not regular Joes, were they? They were quite strange. They raised quite strange children. In a strange way. They lived very strange lives.'

'They ran a church, Alice, not a cult,' Thick-rimmed Glasses says.

'What's the difference?' I shrug my shoulders as a ripple of groans come at me. 'Okay, okay... okay,' I say, literally cutting at the air with a swipe of my hand. 'I'm just saying that the Tiddles are not like us... they have many,

many friends; acquaintances from all corners of the world, built up over many years. I don't want to say anything more than that, other than to let it be known as a fact that they knew people, lots of people from all different walks of life. And we must bear that in mind... they weren't normal.'

'So what... you think one of these many people they met in their lives came back to kill them?'

'That's not what I'm saying at all,' I answer back. 'It's just when you think about the contents of what was found in that safe.... it's just not normal. They had what the rest of us would call secrets. The expert assassin theory, if that's what it is – or the Hollywood movie hit-man theory as Jonathan Ryan called it in court... is it really as farfetched as the other theory on offer?'

A flurry of answers all at once fly at me, but Scarhead shushes them.

'Well, you raise the contents of the safe there, which is fair enough,' he says. 'And we will get back to that. But don't you think it's absolutely unbelievable that somebody – some hit man as you say – came into Rathcoole, up the mountains, past dozens of houses along the roads and not one person saw a thing. Not one person that day saw a strange man or woman coming or going. And not a jot of evidence proves that anybody was in that house that morning; other than all four Tiddles. I mean... come on... you can't really believe this, can you?'

'I didn't say I believe it,' I reply. 'I'm just saying that it's not implausible, and if it's not implausible then there is doubt in the other theory. There is doubt that it could only have been children, there is doubt that it was Faith and Grace. And when there is doubt, you gotta acquit.'

'Very good,' Red Head says, rubbing at my arm.

Everybody else falls silent. I bloody nailed it. I actually turned that around. I went from losing what was clearly the prosecution's greatest weapon – the stab wounds – and turned it into a win. At least I think I did.

I look up at Braces. It's hard to read how she's reacted to that. She's just sitting there, nonplussed, staring back up at Scarhead as he decides where to take our deliberations next.

'Well, I guess it's a case that the prosecution have their side and the defence have theirs, right?' he says.

'Well,' Red Head replies, 'I think you'll find that is what a trial actually is.'

She gets a snigger from Quiff. I wonder where Quiff's head is at. He was on my side earlier, but he seemed to be swinging the other way. I'd rather have Braces on our side than him anyway. Me. Her. The Red Head and Obese Guy. That seems to me like it would stay strong. We could easily hold out for a hung jury.

The door rattles again, and as it does I look at my watch. It's just gone half-four. Jeez... that afternoon flew in. I guess we got some arguing done. I certainly did. I'm proud of myself.

I turn my shoulder and see the young woman dressed in all black entering.

'Judge Delia McCormick would like to ask if you are near an agreeable verdict?' she asks.

'Eh...' Scarhead hesitates, rubbing at his scar. 'What do we think, guys?'

'No. Jeez. We are not, no!' I say, really snappy. 'There's no agreement at all. We had an earlier verdict vote... four people said not guilty, then this young man,' I say, pointing at Quiff Guy. 'And this young girl,' pointing at Braces Girl, 'are still undecided. So no...'

'Are you?' Scarhead says, looking at both of them. 'Undecided?'

'I, eh... I'm not sure,' Braces says. 'So yes. Undecided, I guess. I'd like to think it through in my head... and then come back tomorrow, argue it out some more.'

'And you?' Scarhead asks Quiff.

'I'd like more time too... but have to say, the Hollywood hit-man thing, it's just so difficult to buy—'

'Alright, alright,' I say. 'No need to enter into deliberations with this lady in the room. Let's just answer the judge's question. No,' I say, turning to the young woman dressed in all black, 'we are not close to an agreeable verdict.'

She looks over to Scarhead, awaiting confirmation from the Head Juror.

'Not very close, no,' he says.

'Okay, I will let her know, though I am sure I will return to you in moments.'

She scurries out of the room, closing the door tight behind her.

'I'm sorry,' I say, holding my palm out to Quiff Guy. I was a little short with him there, cutting him right off. But it was ludicrous to even discuss whether or not we are close to an agreement. We're nowhere near it.

I look over at Red Head as everybody shuffles in their chairs and I'm certain she nods a nod of approval at me.

I'm about to spark up small talk with her when the door rattles again.

'Ladies and gentlemen of the jury,' the young woman dressed all in black says really formally. 'You have been dismissed for the day. The court will ask you to return at nine a.m. tomorrow to reconvene your deliberations. We thank you for your time and service to these courts.'

We're all standing in the doorway of the court's side entrance within seconds, the cold hitting us as soon as the door opens.

I walk slowly behind Red Head, unsure whether or not it's appropriate to talk to her now that we've opened up lines of communication, albeit in the company of all the others. But we don't say a word as we cross the road towards the taxi rank, not until we reach the first car and she turns to me.

'You're first today,' she says.

'No. No. I got the first one yesterday. It's you today.'

'Oh yeah.' She laughs. And then she purses her lips at me.

'You seem to be feeling much better this afternoon, Alice.' she says. 'You were really socking it to them there at the end.'

I laugh this time. And then I take one step closer to her.

'You adamant they're not guilty?' I ask.

'We, eh...' she looks up and down the street. 'We really shouldn't discuss it out here.'

I shake my head.

'No. Sorry. My bad. Please... go on. You grab that taxi. I'll see you in the morning. Try to sleep well.'

'You too,' she says.

I hold up my hand in a wave before I spin on my heels and head for the second taxi.

I've barely finished telling the driver where to take me when my phone buzzes in my blazer's breast pocket.

I squint at the number on the screen and as I do my stomach flips itself over.

'Hello,' I say, my voice shaking.

'What's been going on inside that jury room... tell me!' the distorted voice yells.

DAY THREE

I eyeballed all three of them. Ashe. Then Tunstead. Then Fairweather. She just twitched her wrists helplessly at me.

'You can't throw me off this case,' I said.

'Quayle, you do not have the experience—'

'This has nothing to do with experience,' I said, crossing my arms at my chest.

'Of course it has,' Tunstead said from behind me. The prick.

'So you have lots of experience in this, do you, Tunstead?' I said, turning to him. 'Double homicides in the Dublin mountains. Religious family. Twin girls, who you think are the main suspects. You have lots of experience with that type of case specifically, do you?'

'That's not what we mean,' Ashe said. 'And,' he interrupts me as soon as my mouth opens to respond, 'the twins *are* the main suspects.'

I threw my hands in the air.

'It's not your call,' I said. 'This crime happened in the mountains, on St Benedict's Road. That's our jurisdiction.'

'Christ Quayle,' Tunstead said. 'Jurisdictions? This isn't the 1990s anymore. We are all the one force, we all lean on each other. Especially in cases of this magnitude.'

'I *am* leaning on other members of the force,' I replied, irritated. 'Johnny and Sully are out talking to all of the neighbours and anyone who frequents the area. You and Lowe and a number of other officers are leading a search of the bungalow's grounds and all areas around it. There are twenty-eight uniforms overall helping in that search. The force *is* in use, doing a great job. But it's doing a great job under my orders.'

'Well, they won't be under your orders anymore,' Ashe said.

'You have no right to remove me as lead detective. It happened in my jurisdiction, as much as Tunstead here doesn't want to believe jurisdictions are actually a thing anymore. I was first at the scene. I am very familiar with the entire area of the mountains. It's my case, no matter what way anybody looks at it.'

Ashe sniffed his nose, then peered over my shoulder at Fairweather. She didn't say anything. That disappointed me. I really wanted her to stick up for me. For us. For our station. Though I shouldn't have been surprised. I knew she would much rather do without the pressure of all this. It would suit her if we handed it over. I didn't see it as pressure. I never felt any pressure. I just saw it as a case I needed to solve. It happened in the mountains, to people I am tasked with protecting. I wasn't going to give this case up to feed egos.

'Quayle, I'm going to give this to you straight... I like you. I do. I think you've been a mighty fine detective for Rathcoole Garda Station.' I knew that was a slight, as much as he tried to finely wrap it up in a compliment. *For Rathcoole Garda Station...* as he feels arresting folk for petty crime or drug dealing is about the peak of my limit as an investigator. 'But this murder happened a little over forty-eight hours ago now, right?' I looked around myself, then nodded my head. 'In those forty-eight hours or so, it has become apparent that there are two suspects in this case. Yet they have been under the guidance of Tusla since four p.m. on Saturday afternoon and have only been released once to visit the scene, where you questioned them.'

'I don't agree that they are the only suspect—'

He held a finger up to silence me.

'But your questioning of them was so delicate, it bordered on babysitting.' I leaned back in my chair and gasped. 'When you are questioning a suspect, it is your job to find out what they know, not find out how they are.'

'I just want to stop you there,' I said, pointing a finger just as he had. 'I know this case more than anyone. I was first on the scene and I have spent the most amount of time with Faith and Grace.'

'Yeah, at McDonald's,' Tunstead said. I held my eyes closed briefly to let the disdain wash over me.

'They are two orphans now,' I said. 'Two young girls who lost both their parents in cold blood two days ago. We know where they are. They are in Tusla's care. And from what I understand, they are getting fantastic counselling there. They are grieving and getting the best support they possibly can. While they are grieving, I am investigating the case to rule out any other line of enquiry.'

Ashe scratched at his chin.

'Tunstead tells me you are looking at some bizarre racism angle because Clive Tiddle once had a shouting match with some old geezer.'

I sigh and then look back at Fairweather for support.

She hesitated before taking a step towards us.

'You and I, Ashe,' she says, 'are equals. I insist Detective Quayle remains on the case. You want your station in charge, I want mine...'

She shrugged her shoulders. And Ashe sighed. Then, after leaning back in his chair and twiddling his fingers, he shot back up and swiped at the phone on Fairweather's desk.

'We'll call the Assistant Commissioner, he'll decide who takes the lead.'

I stood up, and as I walked to the door I eyeballed Tunstead just to shake my head at him. Then I strolled straight to the cooler to pour myself a plastic cup of water. I was sipping from it as the ringing sounded from the Fairweather's speakerphone.

'Hello, Assistant Commissioner Riordan,' Ashe said as soon as the ringing tone stopped. I strolled back into Fairweather's office, still sipping on my water. 'This is Detective Superintendent Laurence Ashe. I am here with fellow Detective Superintendent Brigit Fairweather, Detective Inspector Denis Quayle, both of Rathcoole Garda Station. And one of my own Detective Inspectors – Karl Tunstead. We are at a, eh... a bit of a standstill over who should run this Tiddle case.'

'Well, whose jurisdiction is it, Rathcoole's right?'

I eyeballed Tunstead. But he pretended not to notice me.

'Well, with all due respect, sir. That is correct. The crime happened at the foot of the mountains. But as you know, sir, Rathcoole Garda Station is a small outfit. Just four employees and they are not used to dealing with crimes of this, eh... magnitude.'

I tilted my chin ever so slightly forward towards the phone in anticipation of Riordan's response.

'Yes, well. I expect Rathcoole are leading the investigation with the full support of Tallaght. The support of the whole force.'

'Yes... well that is supposed to be the case,' Ashe said. He looked at me out of the corner of his eye and began to play with his fingers. 'It's just that my best Detective Inspectors – Detectives Tunstead and Lowe – they are reporting to me that lead detective Quayle is letting his ego get in the way. He is keeping them at a distance.'

'What!' I crushed the plastic cup in my hand and then spun on my heels to face Tunstead. 'You what?'

'Now calm down, Quayle,' he said, backing into the wall. 'All's I – we, me and Lowe – said was that we needed to be more involved in this case. We need to know what you are doing... where you are going. We need access to the suspects and you're blocking us from doing what we need to do. Anytime I ring you I can't get through. You're not answering...'

I huffed and shook my head. The prick!

'Sir,' I said, turning towards the phone. 'Detective Tunstead has a narrow mind in this case. He is solely focused on two suspects in particular.'

'Yeah – the twins, right?' Riordan said.

'Yes,' I replied, just as my own phone began to ring in my pocket.

'Well, isn't Tunstead right though? That's who all the evidence points to. Shouldn't this be an open and shut case?'

'Well, the twins haven't said much, sir,' Tunstead said, stepping forward. 'Because Quayle here won't let us speak to them. He doesn't believe it was the twins.'

'Huh?' Riordan said.

'That's nonsense, sir. Tunstead and Lowe accompanied me to question the twins at the scene of the crime. So please take what this detective says with a pinch of salt.'

'Jesus, can you all calm down!' the phone spat out. 'You are dealing with the biggest case this country has seen in years, don't make me take you all off it. Do you hear me? Grow up. The lot of you!'

The whole office fell silent.

'You don't have another suspect, Quayle, right?' Riordan asked.

'Actually, sir...' I tossed the crushed cup into the bin under Fairweather's desk, then leaned my hands either side of the phone. 'The deceased had rows with one neighbour in particular who lived at the very bottom of the Dublin mountains. It was race related. The Tiddles ran a church and invited a lot of immigrants to that church. They had a small bus that they used to pick people up in and bring them out to the mountains every Sunday. They'd stay for the entire day, coming and going to Rathcoole village. Well, one particular neighbour – a Mr Tommo Nevin – didn't like this. He had a run-in with Clive Tiddle about it.'

'What kind of run-in?' Riordan asked.

'Well, a shouting match. A back and forth. Witnessed by others.'

'That's it?' Riordan said. 'They shouted at each other and now you believe he broke into their house without being noticed and stabbed both husband and wife to death?'

'Well...' I stood back upright and stared down at my shoes. 'I don't have everything figured out yet, sir. But at least I have motive. Tunstead and

Lowe have no motive. There is no reason whatsoever to suggest the twins would want their parents dead. Everyone says they were a close family.'

'Everyone says the twins are weird,' Tunstead said.

'Oh shut up, you two... acting like children,' the phone spat at us again. My phone rang in my pocket in the resulting silence.

'Ain't you going to answer that?' Ashe asked me. 'You are lead detective on the biggest case in the country. You may need to find out who's trying to contact you.'

I took my phone out and then stabbed my finger at the green button before walking back towards the water cooler.

'Hello.'

'Detective Denis Quayle, this is Robin Deutch of Golden Locksmiths. You asked us to ring you as soon as we managed to open the safe found at crime scene 82033. St Benedict's Bungalow. I believe, eh... it's the Tiddle case.'

'Yes, yes, yes,' I said.

'Detective Quayle, we managed to open the safe almost an hour ago and—'

'Almost an hour ago, what took you so long ringing me?' I asked.

'Well, Detective, we eh... we had to count it all.'

'Count it?'

'Money.'

'Money?'

'Four hundred and forty thousand in used notes.'

I swivelled back into the office and stared at everyone inside. Then I paced towards Fairweather's desk.

'Say that again, Robin,' I said after I'd pressed at my speakerphone button.

'We found four hundred and forty thousand euros in used notes in the Tiddle safe. And, eh... holiday tickets. For Disneyland, Florida. That's the entirety of the contents. The safe was practically packed with cash.'

I looked at Fairweather and offered her a tiny wink. Then I eyeballed Tunstead and Ashe, a grin stretching across my mouth.

'I told you this wasn't the twins,' I said.

'This doesn't change much,' Tunstead piped up.

'Oh, it changes a lot. Know many people with nearly half a million in used notes hiding in their bedroom floorboards, Tunstead? Looks as if the Tiddles weren't quite as squeaky clean as everybody thinks they were.'

I turned to Fairweather's desk, placed a hand either side of the phone again, and bent forward.

'Sir, I had been sniffing around other theories for these past two days. I knew something wasn't quite right. I implore you to make the right decision and maintain me as lead detective in this case. I am no rookie. I have been in the police force for over twenty-five years. I have an exemplary record... isn't that right, Fairweather?' I said, turning to my boss and then waving her towards the phone.

She took a step forward.

'That's right, sir. Detective Quayle's a fantastic member of the force.'

I winked at her again, and then held my breath.

'You guys have such little experience in this kind of case,' Riordan said. It fell silent until we heard the sound of him popping his lips on the other end of the line.

'Quayle, you're gonna involve Tallaght Garda Station in the case, give them rights access, fill them in on everything you do...okay? You're all working on this together. You need to be a team. We don't need any wannabe-heroes here. We need this case solved as quickly as we can solve it.'

I looked back at Tunstead.

'Of course, sir. Once I am the lead detective and they are following my orders, I am happy to oblige.'

'Well either way, I'm going to determine what the next move is on this case. We'll look into the contents of the safe in time, but I want the twins formally interviewed as a matter of urgency. Everyone I speak to says this was the twins. They should have been leaned on straight away. Yourself and the two detectives from Tallaght need to get on that as soon as you possibly can. Do we have a deal?'

'Deal,' I said.

'Well then, Quayle, you've bought yourself forty-eight hours. You don't make an arrest by Wednesday lunch-time, I'm handing this over to Tallaght!'

✝

As the success of *The New St Benedict's Church* grew, so too did Clive and Dorothy's work load. It actually got out of hand at one point – too many sermons to write, too many parishioners to console, too much money to count – that they decided between them that they needed an assistant.

Kelly McAllister wasn't necessarily the obvious choice, given that she had tendencies, but she had been with the church the longest out of the entire 'family' and both Clive and Dorothy had developed a soft spot for her.

When Dorothy had first recruited Kelly – finding her begging for money on the trams; skinny, spotty, greasy-haired and famished – she instantly knew she could transform her. Though she never would have envisioned Kelly would eventually become their closest confidante. Nobody would have. Kelly had strong issues around addiction. She relied on alcohol, drugs and – on the rare occasions she had cash in her pocket – gambling. It's why she left Glasgow in the first place. She threw all her wages up the wall; betting on anything from televised horse racing to side wagers with neighbours about who would be the next person in their community to die. She couldn't help it; gambling gave her a reason for being. It raised her endorphins as much as the drugs did.

Soon after she'd been let go from her job as a waitress in Clydebank for consistent lateness, she took a ferry to Antrim, which was followed by a long bus ride to Dublin. Just to get away from her old life. She had been living most nights on the streets of the Irish capital for almost a year before a woman with a hooked nose and large brown eyes sidled up to her on a tram one day.

'Jesus will repent all your sins,' the woman said. 'Fancy a hot cup of tea and a Jammy Dodger?'

Dorothy took a shine to Kelly instantly; felt befriended by the melodic lilt of her Glaswegian accent. She ensured Kelly got lodgings, calling on an array of folk who attended the church to sort her out with a spare bed or a couch if and when they could. There was always a welcome mat at the door of these people's homes. Feeling refreshed in life, Kelly began to turn up almost daily at the community centre. She'd often find Clive or Dorothy running through some paperwork for the coming Sunday's sermon or perhaps hosting a counselling session with one of the 'family'. And pretty soon after those daily drop-bys she was right in the middle of that 'family', chanting hymns and songs towards the makeshift altar with her hands in the air during sermons. She loved every minute of it, and within two months had come completely off the drugs; though the alcohol and gambling not so much.

By the time the twins came along, Kelly was a key member of the church; often taking up collections or assisting Clive by handing him different microphones on the stage. Even though she was by then a very good confidante of the Tiddles, she was still genuinely gobsmacked when she was asked to be Godmother to one of the newborns. She is officially Faith's Godmother, but she was insistent she would love them both equally. Though those early visions she had of spoiling two little sweet girls never really came to fruition. Yes, she held them when they were babies, and quite often babysat. But by the time they were two and three years of age – when they were beginning to communicate with others – they seemed to fall mute and were quite awkward for her to be around. Any time Kelly tried to talk to them, they could barely understand her thick accent anyway. So she just admired them from afar like everybody else did. She'd wave at them when she'd see them at the community centre – or at the Tiddle home – and make a tiny bit of small-talk that wouldn't be reciprocated. And that was about it. There were no hugs, no kisses. Just waves, from about six feet away. She thought them odd, but she never said a cross word about them to anyone.

Although Kelly's mind-set changed under the tutorship of the Tiddles, her body never did. Even in her mid-forties, she had the shape of a ten year-old boy. She's barely five foot tall and has the waistline of a standard shop-front mannequin. No bust, no hips, no ass. Her hair is always held back tight by a scrunchy, though she does go to the effort of applying mascara; the only make up she ever wears, save for a big day at the church such as a wedding or a christening when she might also apply some lipstick.

She had been part of the 'family' for over almost eighteen years when Clive first leaned in to kiss her. She had no idea it was coming. He just inched his face down to hers and pressed his lips to her mouth – then he leaned away and held a finger to his lips to shush her.

'Jesus put us in this place,' he said. And then he leaned back in; his lips ajar, his tongue poised.

Clive hadn't been looking to have an affair; family, for him, was always priority – both his immediate family and his church family. But Kelly had sort of grown into a more mature woman at that point and he was genuinely getting the distinct impression she was courting a come-on from him. He felt she'd hold hugs with him a little too long, or that whenever she was supposed to kiss his cheek, she would press her lips ever so close to his mouth. This wasn't actually the case at all; that was how Kelly began to greet everybody as she grew in confidence as her status in the church progressed. The first day Clive noticed her lips went dangerously close to his, he hesitated and leaned away from the embrace in shock. He masturbated thinking about Kelly that night, and a lot of nights afterwards for the next three months. Until he finally picked up the courage to act on his desires.

The first night he leaned in to kiss her properly they made love behind the stage of the church; him thrusting into her from behind with his trousers around his ankles, his gilet and plaid shirt still on.

Guilt often niggled at Clive, but by this stage he was now a minor celebrity amongst his own people and felt as if he was owed this extra gift in life. Kelly genuinely saw the affair as her duty; though she enjoyed the orgasms – had never really had proper adult sex before.

Dorothy was the right mix of too busy and too naïve to notice that the two people she saw the most throughout the day were actually riding each other when she wasn't looking. Clive would often make excuses that he was giving sermons in other churches around the country when he'd usually be shacked up in a city-centre hotel having sex with Kelly.

'Listening to who?' Grace said, squinting back at her sister.

'Him. Jesus.'

'Jesus?' Grace placed her hand over her mouth. 'Why do you listen to him?'

Faith looked confused.

'Because we're supposed to talk to Jesus.'

'Yes, silly,' Grace said, giggling. 'But we talk to him, he doesn't talk to us.'

The confusion didn't dissipate from Faith's face. And then they both fell silent as they perched on the edge of their twin beds and faced each other.

'Faith...' Grace finally said, scratching at her temple. 'Does Jesus speak to you?'

Faith tilted her head again, then shook it slowly from side to side.

'No. Course not,' she replied. Grace giggled, but Faith – who normally mirrors her sister's emotions; whether laughing or crying, or huffing in anger – kept her lips turned down. 'He doesn't talk. He just kinda... sends me signs.'

'Huh?' Grace said.

Faith looked at her sister.

'He sends me signs.'

'He what?'

'He, eh... sends me signs. He would leave the light on in the bathroom, or something on the floor. Or something would knock off the cabinet in the living room... signs.'

Grace gasped.

'Signs... what do you mean? He, he... hold on!' Grace swallowed, then inched closer to her sister and placed her hands on her shoulders. 'You know when I killed Grebit last week, what did Jesus say about that? What sign did he send you, because I've been... I've been...' Faith shrugged her shoulders as Grace tried to find her words. 'You mean you didn't ask him?' Grace said, sounding disappointed.

'I don't... I don't ask questions. He just—'

'Well ask him now, ask him now. I want to know what he thinks of me killing Grebit. I want to know if I am going to go to Heaven or Hell... please... please, Faith. Ask him. Do it for me.'

ALICE

Noel's been perched on the edge of our bed for the past five minutes, brushing a hand gently up and down my thigh.

'Are you sure, sweetie?' he says. Again.

'Of course,' I reply, smiling. 'I've told you a thousand times. I'm fine. I feel much better than I did last night. Don't put yourself out. This case might be all over tomorrow. We can get back to normal. You go have fun.'

He leans in and kisses my nose.

'Love you,' he says.

Then he stands up and *finally* leaves the bedroom. I hear him jog lightly down the stairs and scoop up his car keys from the hall table before the front door swings open and then clangs shut behind him.

I sit more upright, my back against the rail of our bed and finger-tap the screen of my phone back to life. I told her I'd ring back at seven forty-five. It's two minutes past that time now. When she rang earlier, demanding to know what happened in the jury room, I had to whisper down the line to her that I was in the back of a taxi. She insisted I ring her as soon as I got home, but I told her I wouldn't be alone until about quarter-to-eight... because that's when my husband leaves every Thursday evening to partici- pate in a quiz night down our local pub. She paused. For ages. Then agreed.

I'm not strictly alone. Alfie's here, playing computer games in the back room downstairs. It's where he spends way too much of his time. I know we really shouldn't let him play those things for so many hours, but it keeps him quiet. And isn't that the goal of every parent in the world: quiet. I love my kids. To death. I really do. But I've been a mother for over twenty-three years now. It's been a long old stretch. It just didn't seem to ever stop for me... not when there's a nine-year age gap between them. It took us two years of trying naturally, six years of IVF and four miscarriages before we had a successful pregnancy with Alfie. He was our little miracle. But by this stage I don't mind admitting that I wish he was at the age Zoe is now; where he is about to move out. That'd be nice. I think me and Noel deserve some peace and quiet. It'd be lovely to not *have* to mother every day. Zoe's practically moved out by now. Although not officially. She stays over with Emmet most nights of the week. He shares an inner-city apartment at the IFSC with a guy he works with. Most of her wardrobe is in that flat. So I guess she's almost gone.

I finally pluck up the courage to press at the number on my phone, then tentatively hold it to my ear.

'You said you'd ring at quarter to... you're three minutes late!' she barks, answering before one tone had even rung out.

'I had to wait on my husband to go out,' I say. I hear the shake in my voice as I say that. I promised myself earlier that I'd be strong during this phone call. That didn't last long.

'Just get to it. What happened in that jury room today?'

'Well... eh... what do you want to know exactly?' I ask.

'Tell me where the verdict is heading?'

I take a deep breath.

'Probably to a hung jury,' I say. I'm sure I hear a hint of a 'yes' through her exhale, but I just continue to fill her in. 'We had a verdict vote at the start of our deliberations and it came out eight guilty, four not guilty. It seemed to be pretty much the same by the end of the day, except one person who earlier said not guilty has changed his mind and I'm pretty sure one girl who said guilty is about to change her mind. She told me at the end of the day she was now undecided.'

'Okay... Tell me which jurors are not guilty.'

'Well, me – obviously.' I say. 'The redheaded girl.'

'Sinead Gormley.'

'Oh, you know the names?'

'Course I know the names,' she says.

I dip my brow, my mind whirring. Whoever this is must have hacked into every one of the jurors' phones, tried to get dirt on them all. Maybe I'm the only one they found dirt on. But the redhead is arguing just as adamantly as I have been... I bet they have something on her too.

'And, eh... you know the big guy, the fat one with the grey hair?' I say.

'Gerry McDonagh,' she says.

'Eh yeah, him... and, ehm, the young girl with the braces.'

'Lisa Glennon.'

'Yeah, Lisa. Well, she is the one who told me she was now undecided.'

'Interesting,' the distorted voice says, then I hear her click her tongue off the top pallet of her mouth. 'You, Sinead, Gerry and Lisa. Not what I had in mind, but...' She pauses again. I think she's taking notes. 'How watertight do you think the four jurors are who are saying not guilty, then?'

'Well, Lisa is not watertight because she initially voted guilty, then the arguments started to change her mind. Especially because me and the redhead were going on and on about there just not being enough evidence. I think me and the redhead will hold out.'

'And Gerry... the fat guy?'

'I think he'll hold out too,' I say.

'That's all you need, Alice. Keep those two on your side and you will get out of this whole mess. Just make sure at least three of you hang on. The judge will end up accepting a ten:two vote, probably at some stage tomorrow. So make it your job to ensure those guys hang on. If you don't... you know what'll happen. That's a very compromising position you tried there with your daughter's boyfriend. Right from behind. A pounding, I would call it. Surely your husband would just throw up if he saw that video,' she says.

I hold my eyes closed, an attempt to simmer down the boiling of my blood.

'Who else are you playing this game with?' I hiss.

'Sorry?'

'Who else are you blackmailing? The redhead?'

'You're the only one,' she replies.

I don't believe her.

'Really? The redhead, surely. She's as adamant as I am that the twins are not guilty.'

'You're the only one, Alice. It's all up to you.'

'Why do I not believe you?'

She sniggers out a laugh.

'Alice, do you think most women go around sleeping with their daughter's boyfriends? Of course I don't have dirt on anybody else. You're the only slut sitting around that jury table.'

I hold my eyes closed again.

I really don't want to lose it with her. I just need to concentrate on how best I can keep this jury hung. Then this whole bullshit will be in the past. I can't fuckin' wait for it to be all over. Jesus. The Tiddle case. Feels like it's been in my life forever.

I lied to the judge. I'm certain I wasn't the only juror who did. Nobody could have let that story pass them by. Course I read about the Tiddles when they were all over the news. Everyone was talking about the strange double homicide in the Dublin mountains. The twins were only known as Child X and Y in the newspapers and on TV as they couldn't be named for legal reasons. But it's been more about them than it has been about Clive and Dorothy. They had initially been arrested for a few hours three days into the investigation before being let out with an apology, but then they were re-arrested two days later. And it's been pretty much in the news relentlessly ever since. It took the guts of two years for the case to get to court.

Because Faith and Grace were only nine, early reports said they may never face a big trial – something to do with the Children's Act in 2001 or something. There was a lot of legal to-ing and fro-ing, which got even further complicated when Gerd Bracken took over the twins' case; no doubt driven by the mass exposure it would bring to his brand. He wasn't successful in keeping this trial from the courts though; eventually it was decided Faith and Grace would face a jury in Dublin's Criminal Courts – to be tried in much the same way an adult would under such circumstances. Faith and Grace remain only the third and fourth children respectively to ever be tried as adults in the history of the Irish court system. I know everything about the case. Because I read all about it as it was happening.

I was pretty chuffed when I was called for jury duty. I know most people think it's a pain in the ass to get that letter in the post. But I immediately felt it'd be a week away from organising a friend of a friend's fiftieth or sixtieth birthday snacks. I fancied the break from the norm. Though I had no idea I'd be on this bloody trial – one of the biggest in the history of the state. The whole country's been glued to this.

When Judge Delia McCormick looked us jurors square in the eyes at the beginning of this trial and asked us if we followed the Child X and Y case in the media over the past couple of years, I held her stare and shook my head.

'No, Your Honour. Nothing,' I said. And about half an hour later I was the second to be given a juror's chair. The days were long and the silences were plenty, but the trial itself was fascinating in so many ways... I was really enjoying it. Right up until this psycho bitch texted me yesterday.

'Listen,' I say. 'I'm going to do my best for you... I'll make sure both the redhead and the fat guy keep their not guilty verdict. But please – I beg you – don't send that video to my husband... to my daughter. No matter what happens. They don't deserve this.'

'No, but perhaps you do,' she says. 'Now you listen to me, Alice. This isn't a fucking negotiation. You make sure it's a not guilty verdict, or Noel and Zoe get sent that video. Simple as that. You either win. Or you lose. And you stand to lose everything.'

I hold the phone away from my ear and reel my head backwards. Then I snap the phone back to my ear.

'I would benefit from knowing if the redhead is part of the deal. Do you have dirt on her too? Is she with me on this?'

'She's not fuckin' part of any deal, Alice. Don't make me repeat myself. It's only you. It's only up to you.'

A tear falls from my eye, surprising me. I didn't know I was close to crying.

'Okay,' I say. 'I'll do my best. It's all I can do.'

'Maybe I can help you a bit. What arguments are you, Sinead and Gerry using to defend your not guilty verdicts?'

'Evidence, mainly. Or the lack of evidence. There is nothing concrete about this at all... That's what we keep saying.'

'Good. Good,' she says. 'But you should also argue the money.'

'The money?'

'Yeah... the safe. It brings doubt into the equation and doubt gives a legitimate reason for a juror to hold out. The Tiddles had almost half a million euros in used notes in their bedroom, it shines a light on different possibilities. That brings doubt, enough reasonable doubt to acquit.'

'Does it really?' I say. I kinda dismissed the money argument as soon as it was brought up at trial. Admittedly I was nailed on finding the twins guilty by that point, but still... stealing money or saving money or whatever it was the Tiddles were doing with so many used notes wasn't strong enough evidence for me to change my mind. Faith and Grace did this. I've no doubt about that at all.

'Of course it does. Well... as much as doubt gets in this case.'

'Hold on... you think they're guilty, don't you?'

She laughs.

'It doesn't matter one jot what I think. I'm not on the jury. The truth of the matter is, if you press the money argument you stand the best chance of having a legitimate reasoning for holding on to your not guilty vote. Just keep pushing back on every juror who is demanding they are guilty. Keep pushing, pushing, pushing. Hold on... and at some point the judge will deem you hung.'

I nod my head, soaking in what she's saying.

'Okay,' I whisper down the line as another tear falls.

Then the dead tone sounds.

DAY THREE

Tunstead wanted Tusla to escort the twins to the police station, but I was insistent I would do it. I fancied a little time with the two of them before we officially sat them down; felt I owed it to them to treat them like children before we started to treat them like suspects.

'I'll take them in my car, you guys follow,' I said to Joe and Dinah as we were leaving the Tusla premises. They had to be present for the interview. Which suited me. Anything that could dilute the Tallaght detectives' influence on the twins.

Faith and Grace were offered legal assistance, but they suggested having Dinah and Joe was adequate enough for them. After all, I had promised them they were only being brought in for a routine interview.

I tried to make them feel as relaxed as possible as I drove them to Rathcoole Garda Station. I asked them about their dance lessons. About their favourite popstars. About what they watch on TV. They didn't have much to say. Not just because they were naturally quiet, not to mention in the thick of the grieving process, but because they didn't have answers. They didn't have a favourite popstar and they didn't have a preferred TV show. Because they didn't listen to music. Nor watch TV, except for the odd cartoon.

'What about Mickey Mouse, Minnie Mouse, that sort of thing? You like them?' I asked.

I stared in my rearview mirror, to gauge Grace's reaction. She stuck out her bottom lip and squinted.

'Disney?' she asked.

'Uh-huh, Mickey and Minnie are the king and queen of Disney,' I say. 'You eh... like Disney?'

'It's a dream. Our dream. Isn't it, Faith?' Grace nudged her sister, then nodded her head before she met my eyes in the rearview mirror.

'Did you know you were, eh...' I paused, uncertain how to phrase exactly what I wanted to ask, 'you were going on holiday to Disneyland?'

I stared at both of their reflections for their reaction. Grace looked up at Faith and I am certain I noticed her clench her jaw. They didn't reply. Not with words.

'Girls, did you know your mother and father had booked tickets for a holiday to Disneyland in Florida?'

No answer. Both of them looked away from each other and stared out of their respective windows. Then I noticed Grace brush a tear away from her eye with one finger.

So I indicated, slowed the car to a stop and turned to them.

'Faith. Grace. You are going to be asked questions in the police station. And you're going to need to be more vocal. You need to speak. It is the only way we will ever find out who did this to your mother and father. Please don't be silent when the other detectives and I speak with you. Be open. Honest. Do it for your mother and father. Tell us everything you know.'

They both looked towards me, but their faces were blank of expression. No tears. No words. It was no wonder everybody found them odd. My heart went out to them.

'It will help you if you tell the detectives that you knew you were about to go on holiday; that you knew about the trip to Florida,' I said.

Grace stared at me.

'We did know,' she said. 'Daddy surprised us with that a few weeks ago. We were really excited about it.' Then she started to cry. Hysterically. She reached out a hand to grab at Faith's arm. And then Faith started crying too. I waved my hand side-to-side in apology and waited for them to calm down. When they eventually did, I turned the key in the ignition and we were back on our way.

I had insisted the questioning go on inside Fairweather's office, rather than one of the two tiny interview rooms in Rathcoole Station. Fairweather's office wasn't big by any means – about the size of a single bedroom, mostly taken up by a small oak desk parked in the middle of it – but it was the largest room in the whole station. It was so tight with us all huddled around that oak desk that all of our knees were practically touching.

I led the way – apologising once again for the twins' loss and letting them know that their welfare was of our highest priority. I tried to read from their body language whether or not they understood that they were suspects, but their body language seemed to say as much as their mouths did.

'It has been brought to our attention by experts that the incident in which your parents were murdered occurred sometime between ten-thirty and eleven o'clock on Saturday morning,' I said, pursing my lips at them. Grace stared back at me, stony faced. Faith just kept her gaze on the carved edges of Fairweather's desk. 'That means it is probable that your parents were murdered at a time when you were in your house. You say you didn't leave until ten forty-five to go to your dance lesson with Ms Claire. Correct?' Grace glanced at the two Tusla employees and then back at me before she nodded. 'But, eh... it couldn't be the case now, now could it, that your parents were dead before you left, because you say you kissed them goodbye before going to dance class...'

Grace nodded again.

'Faith?' Lowe asked, her voice delicate.

Faith took her stare up from the table towards Lowe and then gently nodded.

'Speak. Please.' Lowe softened her face and leaned herself closer to Faith.

'We kissed them goodbye,' Faith said, in a whisper.

I felt so sorry for her. I didn't want her – nor Grace – to be in this situation. I was pained for them. Genuinely. None of this felt right.

'Okay...' Tunstead said, trying to ease some of the tension that had become apparent as Lowe tried to coax something from Faith. 'You both kissed your parents goodbye, left your home at ten forty-five and then got to dance class which is a little less than a mile from where you live, at approximately ten fifty-five. And when you got there and went through your lesson... ballet, I believe...'

Grace looked at Tunstead.

'We do ballet and tap,' she said.

Tunstead swallowed.

'It's just that your dance teacher Ms Claire, she tells us you, Faith, were particularly quiet in the lesson that day.'

'Faith is always quiet,' Grace replied.

'Yeah, she's always quiet,' I said. Tunstead and Lowe turned to glare at me, but I pretended not to notice and looked to Dinah and Joe instead. 'I've spent time with Faith these past few days and I've barely got a word out of her.'

Faith glanced up at me slowly and even though she didn't say anything, I could sense she wanted to meet my eye.

'Ms Claire knows you are usually quiet,' Tunstead said turning to Faith, 'but she said you were *particularly* quiet that day. Did you sense something was wrong at home, perhaps?'

That was a good question, in fairness to the prick. It gave the twins an opportunity to account for the "weirdness" everybody was suggesting they had adopted ever since the murders.

Grace shook her head. And then Faith mirrored her.

'Let's move on for a second then,' Tunstead said. 'I'm wondering if your parents had anything planned for the family that you are aware of.' Grace shrugged her shoulders. 'Any days out... holidays perhaps?'

Then Faith looked back up at me again, before turning to her sister.

'Florida,' she whispered.

'Huh?' Tunstead inched his ear closer to the twins.

'Florida,' Grace said. 'Mammy and Daddy had booked a holiday. We are going to Disneyland in Florida.'

Tunstead scratched the back of his neck, then stood up.

'Ye know what... Grace... we would like you to stay here with Detective Quayle and Joe. Dinah, if you wouldn't mind accompanying myself and Detective Lowe into another room with Faith, we can complete our line of questioning separately. Then we can get you two back to the Tusla premises as soon as possible.'

Faith and Grace both looked to me. As if I was going to plead with Tunstead that they shouldn't be separated. I wanted to speak up for them... but couldn't find much cause for complaint. It made sense that two suspects under any circumstance be questioned separately. So, instead, I nodded my head.

And then Tunstead, Lowe and Dinah stood up and waited until Grace nudged at Faith and Faith finally and reluctantly decided to leave with them.

'When will we get to go back to Tusla?' Grace asked me as soon as they had all left.

'Soon,' I said. 'I promise.' Then I turned to Joe and sucked on my lips. I wasn't sure what to ask next, where to take this.

'Grace, you know you may not be able to return to Tusla for too long, right? You know Aunt Janet is on her way to Dublin soon.'

Grace's brow uncreased.

'Are we going to have to live with Aunt Janet?' she asked.

'Well...' I paused to look at Joe. He offered nothing. Not because he didn't want to. But because he knew his job was to stay as neutral as possible.

'We'll see...' I eventually said.

A silence fell on the room. It was an awkward silence. I wasn't quite sure how Joe was feeling about all of this. Nor Dinah, for that matter. Tusla staff really were playing a blinder at keeping quiet. Their jobs, after all, were not to play judge and jury, but to maintain the welfare of these children as best they could.

'Why is nobody out there looking for the person who killed Mammy and Daddy?' Grace said, ending the silence

'Well...' I replied, 'there are people out looking for clues in and around where you live. Plenty of police officers. Dozens of them.'

'But you are the main detective. And these other two... Detective Lowe and Detective Tunstead... why are you all just in here, talking with me and Faith? Shouldn't you be doing... something else?'

I took in a deep breath.

'The issue seems to be, Grace,' I said, edging my face closer to her, 'that the team who study the scenes of crimes haven't found any trace of evidence that anybody else entered your kitchen during the morning of the murders. There was no DNA left at the scene.' Grace scrunched her mouth up again. 'DNA – it's evidence that suggests somebody was in the kitchen. There is some historic DNA, from you, Faith, your mother and father of course.'

'And Kelly?'

'Huh?'

'Kelly. Kelly is always in our kitchen. She comes in the back door, leaves by the back door.'

I leaned forward.

'Kelly McAllister? The young Scottish lady who helps run the church?'

Grace nodded her head. But before I could follow up with another question, the door to Fairweather's office swung open, and in stomped Tunstead.

'Grace Tiddle, we are placing you under arrest for the murder of your parents Clive and Dorothy Tiddle.'

✝

Grace was growing in frustration with her twin's inability to fetch an answer to her question.

'But can't you ask him one more time?' Grace pleaded.

She had been worried about killing that frog ever since it happened; genuinely frightened it might be a big enough sin to damn her to Hell for all of eternity.

'It doesn't work like that,' Faith said. 'He doesn't talk to me like that.'

The twins were still sat beside each other, perched on the edge of Faith's bed; Grace's face still sunken.

'Then how do you know he's talking to you if he doesn't talk to you?' she asked. Faith shrugged. 'Is it Jesus or God who talks to you?' Faith turned to face her sister. 'What's the difference actually?' Grace asked. 'Is Jesus God? Daddy has said that, hasn't he? But then... I thought... isn't Jesus God's son?'

Faith curled down her mouth and turned her bottom lip out.

'Oh yeah...' she said, nodding slowly.

'Is it a man's voice when he speaks to you?' Grace asked. Her seventh question in the space of ten seconds; all but one of them not answered.

'I've told you... I don't hear his voice,' Faith said.

And then they both just sat there for ages, saying nothing while staring around their neat bedroom.

'But can you,' Grace broke the silence, 'ask him again... please? I just want to know if killing a frog means... means...'

'You're not going to go to Hell,' Faith said. 'Cos you follow Jesus – and it *says in the Bible that Jesus always forgives. What's the verse Daddy always says, "Be kind to one another..."'*

'"Be kind to one another, tenderhearted, forgiving one another, as God in Christ forgave you,"' Grace said.

'Yeah, 'sactly.'

'What, so... God will definitely forgive me for killing Grebit?'

'Yeah,' Faith said.

And then Grace got down on her knees and clasped her hands together.

'Lord Jesus Christ,' she said, squeezing her eyes shut. 'I am sorry for killing Grebit and thank you for forgiving me for doing it.'

Then she opened her eyes and slapped Faith on the thigh.

'Right, let's play with our dolls. Which one do you want to play with?' she said.

The guilt of killing the frog dissipated somewhat for Grace after that little chat, but it darted to the forefront of her mind three years later when she was told she'd have to give a priest her first confession prior to making her Holy Communion.

'Dear Father,' she said to Fr Michael – the local priest at Rathcoole Church, 'this is my first confession.'

The priest pulled back the curtain inside his confession box and smiled at the tiny seven-year-old sitting in front of him.

'I welcome you to the practice; it will cleanse your soul. And your name is...' he said, his country accent thick.

'Grace. Grace Tiddle, Father.'

'Ah yes... one of the Tiddle twins. You are a girl of strong faith, I believe.'

'Oh, that I am, Father.'

'Well, what is it you wish to confess, my dear?'

'Eh...' She swung her legs back and forth under the wooden bench she was sat upon. 'I want to confess to lying to my mammy and daddy.'

'Hmm... mmm,' the priest murmured.

'I told them I was sick one time when I didn't want to go to dance class and I wasn't sick. I was just tired.' The priest cleared his throat. 'Is that bad, Father... that I lied?'

'Jesus will forgive you, my dear. You should say three Hail Marys in sorrow.'

The priest reached for the curtain.

'Eh... I have one more confession, Father,' Grace said, her legs swinging even quicker now.

'Yes, my dear?' Fr Michael said.

'I killed a frog.'

'A what?'

'A frog. I squashed it with my shoe?'

'You stamped a frog to death?'

Fr Michael's face contorted.

'And I know it says in the commandments... it says Thou Shall Not Kill. But... but... I, eh... I don't know why I did it. I was only four at the time. And it is just a frog though right, and doesn't Thou Shall Not Kill actually mean humans? I think it means just humans. Does it, Father? Does it just mean humans?'

'Well, er...' Fr Michael held a fist to his mouth, to disguise his twitching grin. 'Twenty Hail Marys.'

'Twenty?'

'Yes, twenty.'

'And Jesus will forgive me because my sister says that Jesus will forgive anything. Does he... does he forgive anything?'

The priest tweaked at the curtain again.

'Well, I'm afraid I must move this on, I have dozens of you Holy Communion boys and girls to see today.'

Grace stood up, and was so small the priest could only see the tip of her bow through his window frame.

'Twenty three Hail Marys in total for me, Father, yes? And all is forgiven?'

The priest widened his grin.

'Yes my dear, twenty-three Hail Marys.'

It took Grace less than ten minutes to fire out the Hail Marys. It was a nothing punishment for her. She was made to do six times that by her dad while kneeling in front of their crucifix just after she'd killed the frog anyway. And now surely all was officially forgiven. Because that was an actual confession. To an actual priest. In an actual church.

The twins made their Holy Communion the Saturday following their first confessions. The problem with them being dressed as cute as pie practically every day of their lives was that when it came to their Holy Communion, they were dressed decidedly average in comparison to everybody else. They were still cute. As cute as any seven-year-old in a bride's dress can possibly look. But so was every one of their peers that day.

Though they still had a great time of it. And both collected over a thousand euros each. They just kept receiving card after card – mostly with pictures of angelic young girls on the front – and every time they opened one either a one-hundred-euro note or a fifty-euro note would fall out.

Poor Aunt Janet was cringing when the girls were opening her and Eoin's card because they knew the blue notes they put inside were going to make them look cheap. Still, the twins looked up and thanked Janet and

Eoin with as much authenticity and conviction as they thanked everybody else.

Their Holy Communion was only the fifth time they'd ever met their Aunt Janet. She had long since moved to Monaghan – years before they were born – and yet they had never been to visit that county in all their seven and a half years. They only saw her on the odd occasion she would visit Dublin; perhaps for a family funeral, or – on this occasion – a Holy Communion. The twins were confused about Janet; never quite realising why she wasn't part of their church family. Neither Clive nor Dorothy had ever brought up the reality that outside their 'family' there were people who didn't actually take what was written in the Bible quite so literally. Janet and Eoin, though, weren't all that different from those who attended The New St Benedict's Church. They were down and outs, and lonely too. Neither of them held down a job in Monaghan; preferring to live off benefits. They certainly weren't living their best lives; but they still didn't reach low enough to seek refuge in any church – let alone the Tiddle church. Janet resented Clive for becoming all holy because she never thought for one minute that he believed any of that stuff. She'd often try to strike up the argument with him, but he would douse it pretty quickly.

The night of the twins' Holy Communion was the first time they'd ever spent in proper conversation with their Aunt Janet and Uncle Eoin. They were yawning by eight p.m. and so Dorothy suggested Janet and Eoin bring the twins back to the bungalow while she, Clive and Kelly cleaned up after the long day of celebrations.

'Did yis have a good day?' Janet asked as the four of them slowly walked back up the winding roads that led to the Tiddle bungalow.

'The best,' Grace said.

'And you... Faith?' Eoin asked.

Faith didn't move a muscle in her face. She just continued to walk, her eyes rolled back in her head.

'Oh, she's praying,' Grace said. 'She does that. Well, she's not really praying... she's listening.'

Eoin turned to stare at his wife and as he did so Janet stiffened her nose at him, disguising her laugh. Then she tried to change the subject to something that didn't give her the heebie jeebies.

Dorothy didn't erupt when she came home just gone midnight to see the twins still up talking to Janet and Eoin; she just stared at the clock, then raised an eyebrow at them before they jumped up. They raced each other to their bedroom, calling out a goodnight to Janet and Eoin, then they climbed out of their white dresses and in to their patterned pyjamas before they both knelt down to pray.

Dorothy had come home alone because Clive suggested he'd stay behind to do some editing on the sermon he was to offer his 'family' the following day. He was lying. He didn't do any paperwork. Instead, he spent the next hour and half fucking Kelly. Mostly from behind.

They were pretty much at it every week then; whenever Clive was in the humour and he could come up with an excuse to Dorothy that his needs lay elsewhere. Kelly had long since stopped enjoying the sex, but she sure was still loving the attention she was getting from the leader of her church. His predominance was still very much an attraction for her; as if she was getting fucked by the most popular guy at school. The fact that he was an awkwardly tall chap with a rotund belly and a bristle-like moustache with blotchy pink skin wasn't of much importance. What was important was that lots of people wanted his attention. And he was giving it to her.

Dorothy hadn't a clue. Not an iota of a clue. She trusted her husband too much. Trusted Kelly, too.

At this stage, Clive's responsibilities in the church involved the sermons and the counselling of 'family'. Dorothy's input, meanwhile, in to those two areas receded as the church evolved. She became more interested in the accounts; how much each sermon would cost; how much petrol they could put in the bus to bring members of the family to and from the community centre; how much they needed to pay the community centre for rental of the space. Though in truth she didn't have to worry about any of that – because the spend was so insignificant when compared to what was actually coming in. She had to tell Clive one day that they'd need to start hiding the cash somewhere, because so much of it was pouring in. They had always agreed they couldn't use a bank – they had absolutely no paperwork to back up having such large amounts of cash. So they had a large safe installed within the floorboards of their bedroom and began to pack it full of used notes. It took them four years to earn their first one-hundred thousand euro, but less than half that time to earn their second one-hundred thousand. And then the money just wouldn't stop.

Dorothy kept the sums well hidden, though Kelly would ask the odd question here and there about the collections, especially on occasions she would see Dorothy leafing through notes in the office. But she never stumped Dorothy so much as she did the day she suggested the Tiddles must have a huge safe in their house to hold all of those notes. She was genuinely trying to be humorous. It was a quick quip, not meant to cause any offence.

But Dorothy froze in disdain for a moment before she continued to leaf through the notes.

'Mind your own fucking business, Kelly,' she snapped. And that was the start of their falling out.

ALICE

'Morning.'

Obese Guy greets me with a wide smile as soon as I turn onto the corridor us jurors gather in every morning. I look up the line of them and realise I'm the last one to arrive. Again.

'Good night's sleep?' he asks.

'Eh... yeah,' I reply, nodding. Lying.

And then it goes silent between us for way too long. Because all we really want to talk about – all we have in common – is the case. But we can't. Because the twelve of us can only discuss it when we're all together.

When I look down the line of jurors again I notice everybody is in the same boat; afraid to talk to one another. All eleven of them are resting their backs against the wall, until I notice the front few lean off and it causes a domino effect down the line. The young woman dressed all in black must have just opened the door.

We file in one by one, the shuffling of our feet off the blue carpet the only sound that can be heard until Red Head sees me heading for my usual seat next to her and greets me with an overly-familiar welcome, hugging me with one arm.

'How are ya?' she says. 'Sleep well?'

Everyone seems obsessed with how I slept? Maybe I look like shit.

I offer her a thin smile.

'Not really,' I say. Being honest.

I did sleep for a few hours, but on and off. I kept tossing and turning, playing the arguments on repeat over and over in my head, playing the responses I would give to jurors who were demanding the twins were guilty, playing Noel's face on repeat as he watched the video of me and Emmet fucking. Like proper full on fucking. Me being drilled from behind like a slut.

'Me neither,' she says. And then she sits down. And I do the same. Just in time for Scarhead to bark his first order of the day.

'I am just going to open by saying that when I reflected on my performance as Head Juror yesterday I was disappointed. I feel I can do a better job. But that means I need to have more of a rein on proceedings.' Red Head looks back at me, sucking her lips and raising her eyebrows. I really wanna know what her game is. 'Now, I know we have an idea of how everybody was thinking when we left this room yesterday. So I don't propose we do a verdict vote right now... not until we have discussed the case in more detail. We've a long day ahead of us. And I suggest we really kick into the arguments. There are vital parts of this case that we didn't even discuss yesterday.' A few heads nod around the table. 'The safe,' he continues. 'Most of the witnesses. The confession.'

Red Head puffs out a snigger.

'The safe is interesting,' I say. Because that is the argument I rehearsed the most while I was tossing and turning. The bitch on the phone said the money offers reason for doubt.

'I agree,' Scarhead says, placing his forearms on to the table and leaning forward. 'I'm up for opening our deliberations about what was found in the Tiddles' bedroom safe. Is that a fair place to start day two of our deliberations? Anyone have any objections to that?' He looks down at his notes as mumbles of 'yeses' float around the table. 'The contents of the safe was one of the early points raised by the defendants, but did it *really* tell us much?' Scarhead asks.

Two jurors try to talk over each other – Red Head, who seems awfully keen to race out of the traps, and the old woman with the oversized bust.

'Actually, hold on,' Scarhead shouts over them, waving his hand in the air. 'I said I was going to be a better Head Juror, so rather than just throw questions out there, I want to aim them at individuals, so we all get a chance to talk. Eh... Sinead,' he says, turning to the redhead. 'Please... you first. You were quite vocal in your support for a not guilty verdict yesterday, does the money found in the safe play a huge part in that?'

'Not just the money. But the tickets.'

'Really?' Thick-rimmed Glasses says, poking in his first oar of the day.

'Yeah – why would two nine-year-old girls kill their parents on the eve of going on their dream holiday?'

'It was hardly the eve of the holiday,' Scarhead bats straight back at her.

'The holiday was seven weeks away. That is the ultimate time of buzz for a kid going on holiday. The countdown to the holiday itself. Especially this kind of holiday. They'd never been anywhere else like it before. They only ever holidayed in Ireland. Their excitement would have been huge.'

'But do we believe they even knew about the holiday?' Thick-rimmed Glasses asks.

'Yeah... well, they said they did.'

'*They* said they did?' Scarhead raises his eyebrows to a ridiculously high level.

'Hold on. The question was put to them – we all heard the tape of the interview – by Detective.... what was his name, the handsome one?'

'Detective Tunstead,' I say. My second words of the day.

Red Head looks at me, smiles and then stares back at Scarhead.

'Yeah... Tunstead. When he asked her about a holiday, Grace mentioned Disneyland. She knew about this holiday. The twins knew. Why would they kill their par—'

'Hang on,' Scarhead says. 'I don't think it mattered one jot whether these two knew about the holiday or not. They killed their parents. I can't believe we have people in this room who listened to that entire trial and heard everything every witness had to say, and despite that they are *still* saying not guilty.'

'The holiday is absolutely worth arguing about,' Red Head snaps back.

'I agree,' I say, sitting forward, cutting through the tension that was threatening to flare so early into the morning. We're only about four minutes in. It seems to me everybody prepared their arsenals overnight, and they're all ready to fire. '*Everything* found in that safe is of huge importance.' Then I cough. Giving myself a vital second to locate the monologue I tried to store to memory last night. 'From a legal point of view, if we here in this room are to find Faith and Grace guilty of this charge, then we must do so without any reasonable doubt, okay?' Heads nod back at me. 'Well, the money drops us all in the reasonable doubt camp.' I shake my hand to the middle of the table waving away anyone who was even thinking of responding so swiftly to that – all part of my rehearsal. 'Because the money opens up the possibility of a motive lying elsewhere. And whilst it is not our job to determine *who* or *what* that motive is or even *how* it came about, we do have to consider the contents of the safe as part of our evidence. And the money found in that safe informs all of us that we don't know the full story of the Tiddle family; especially what Clive and Dorothy were up to.'

'Ah... for crying out loud, they were just Jesus freaks,' Scarhead says. 'They were collecting money every week. That's where all the cash came from.'

'Five hundred grand?' Red Head says, all high-pitched.

'Hold on. Hold on. Hold on,' I say, waving my hand again. 'I wasn't finished yet. I just want to say that once there is doubt about a particular piece of the jigsaw, then all the playing pieces must come down.'

Scarhead scrunches up his face.

'That doesn't even make sense,' he says. That's not exactly the reaction I thought I was going to get at the end of my prepared speech. When I rehearsed it last night, I imagined the whole of the jury table nodding back at me and turning their lips downwards. Impressed.

'Jigsaw pieces falling down? Jigsaws don't fall down,' Scarhead says.

'Huh?' I offer back to him. And then I think through what he's saying. And I feel like a fucking idiot. How the hell did I get that muddled up? I must have rehearsed that phrase twenty times over and over to myself last night – and genuinely thought it was impressive every time.

A spark of debate ignites again. But Scarhead silences it by leaning himself across the table and yelling.

'I don't think the safe holds anything of significance,' Oversized Bust says, ending the silence Scarhead's yell created. 'I mean... it's interesting. But didn't we all know the Tiddle family were a little bit...' she wires her index finger around her temple. 'Everyone who testified in the trial said they were an odd family. Clive's sister Janet says they were strange. Claire Barry the dance teacher. The neighbours. Even their best friend Kelly McAllister admitted to them being different...'

'So?' Red Head says.

'Well, doesn't them having all the church money inside a safe in their house only reaffirm that? That they are different to all of us. They run a church. Money comes through that church. They take it all in... They don't use banks. It's not a traditional—'

'It offers up another motive, that's all we have to understand,' I say interrupting her, trying to reaffirm my point, even though I totally agree with everything she is saying. No matter what angle you look at this trial from, one thing's for certain – the Tiddles are one hell of a strange bunch. 'And if we can agree that it does open the door of even the smallest possibility of another motive, then it gives us legitimate reason to acquit Faith and Grace.'

'You don't really believe they're not guilty, do you?' Thick-rimmed Glasses leans forward to look towards me. He's actually looking at me as if he's disgusted. 'You are just looking to get them off on some technicality, aren't you?'

'I'm trying to do my job properly,' I reply. 'If we are to find Faith and Grace guilty of this crime, then we must be able to swear to do so beyond all reasonable doubt. The Tiddles having that much money in their house offers reasonable doubt.'

'But it doesn't,' Scarhead says. 'It only tells us that Clive and Dorothy were running a church. And pocketing the money. Tell ya what... let me put it to the table by show of hands. Does the contents of what was found in the safe change anybody's mind in terms of what you were thinking yesterday?'

I hold my breath in anticipation of anybody changing their mind over this. Because I worked bloody hard on that argument...

But everybody stays still. Every fucking one. I convinced nobody.

'Okay... well then perhaps we can—'

'The argument about the safe hasn't changed my mind,' Braces interrupts Scarhead. 'But I should say, seeing as you asked, that my mind was changed overnight.' I begin to fidget with my fingers. I spent part of my night wondering about Braces. 'I know I voted guilty yesterday and by the end of the day I said I was undecided... well, I had a good think last night and I wanna say...' She holds a silence for way too long. As if she's revealing the winner of The fucking X Factor. 'I am going back to my original verdict. I think they are definitely guilty.'

Bollocks!

Red Head looks back at me. Then leans in and whispers, 'You argued that well...' I smile back at her. But I feel gutted. I thought I was going to nail it with that little speech, but instead of gaining people to our side, we lost one to the guilty camp. My head begins to spin again. And my hands are getting moist. It's only me, Red Head and Obese Guy now. Jesus. This is close. We've got to hold on. We have to be strong.

'Okay, well, eh... thanks for letting us know you had a good think about it last night and finally came to a settled decision,' Scarhead says, offering Braces a grin.

'Another thing,' he says, before puffing out a pretentious laugh, 'that we didn't really mention yesterday was Faith's confession. Now... Detectives Tunstead and Lowe are on record, in more ways than one, of saying Faith confessed to these murders.'

Red Head laughs. Out loud.

'The confession is a crazy argument,' she says. 'Faith didn't confess to jack shit.'

DAY FOUR

I was furious. Fuming.

I spent most of that night in a stand-off with Tunstead and Lowe – one I didn't win. It was an outrage. A fucking "confession" they called it. We rang Ashe and argued it out over the phone. He decided the twins should spend the night in two separate holding cells with a lawyer called to meet with them the next morning. He said he would reassess as soon as he could get Riordan to view the tape of Tunstead and Lowe's four-minute interview with Faith. I was slapping my hands against the walls of Fairweather's office, snapping at both Tunstead and Lowe. I'd never acted like that before; had never had reason to. The fury was overwhelming. I only managed to calm down when I got home and listened to my wife's light snore as I lay next to her in bed.

Tunstead arrested them on silence. *Silence* – that was his feckin' reasoning. He and Lowe claimed Faith nodded her head when she was asked outright if she had anything to do with their parents' murders. I watched the tape of their interview, over and over that night. Close to a hundred times. Faith stayed absolutely silent when Tunstead asked her that question, then her forehead slightly tipped forward. It was scandalous.

The footage was grainy and black and white – that's how outdated Rathcoole Station's security system was – but you could clearly see Tunstead get a little over excited as soon as Faith's head took the slightest dip. 'For the record, Faith just nodded her head,' he said, excitedly. And then he repeated the question twice to her. He got no further response, so decided to arrest her there and then. And without further hesitation, he stormed out of that room and into my interview room to arrest Grace.

'I promise you she nodded her head,' Tunstead argued with me. 'The footage doesn't do it justice, but you can see... you can see the nod.'

Lowe agreed with him. Dinah – who was also in the room when they were interviewing Faith – said she wasn't looking at the twin when she made the apparent gesture.

I sat up in the bed that night and replayed the footage in my head again and again until I eventually fell asleep.

It was a heavy sleep my alarm woke me from at seven a.m. the next morning but I darted out of bed, my mind immediately alert. I headed straight for the station; in the same clothes as the day before and without a breakfast. Again.

Johnny was there, waiting on me so he could finish his shift. He, along with twenty-four other uniforms – and some volunteers – had spent much of the night combing the areas within a two mile radius of the Tiddle bungalow. After I got an update from Johnny, I popped in to the holding cells to speak with the twins. I kept apologising and let them know I was doing my best to get them back... back to wherever it was they were supposed to go back to. I'd often wondered where they'd end up. They could hardly live in Tusla forever. Though their alternative options didn't sound particularly appealing. Clive's sister Janet, who was taking her time reacting to her brother and sister-in-law's tragic murder, didn't exactly seem like the nurturing type. I'd checked their records in the system. They'd both been arrested for petty crimes over the years. Nothing major. Shoplifting. Minor fraud, where Eoin scammed three hundred euros from door-to-door collections using a fake charity laminate. He never spent time behind bars; just community service – painting fences for two weeks. Kelly had had one arrest to her name. A drunk and disorderly. In and out of the cell in one night, she was. All in all, it hardly seemed like the ideal environment for two grieving girls to be living amongst.

I did wonder if those connected to the church would take Faith and Grace on. I thought initially Kelly McAllister might end up with them. From everybody I questioned during the investigation, it seemed she was the closest to the family; certainly closer than Janet and Eoin. The Tiddles ran quite the church – between four and five hundred devoted followers attending every Sunday sermon. It was a hell of an operation. And Kelly McAllister was at the top of that organisation. She was the Tiddle's left-hand woman. She and Clive and Dorothy spent day-in and day-out with each other. Though when Quayle had spoken to Kelly, he got the distinct impression she wasn't exactly enamoured by the twins. She asked how they were, constantly. But she didn't go to Tusla to meet them; certainly didn't suggest she would take care of them.

As soon as I heard Fairweather's familiar footsteps at the door of the station I raced out to meet her.

'Have you seen this tape?' I snapped.

'Ashe sent it to me last night,' she replied.

I shrugged my shoulders at her. She knew what I meant; knew I was furious she didn't return any of my calls.

'Quayle... you and I go back twenty-five years together. I adore you. You are like family to me.' She looked down. 'Everyone is saying they did it. Nobody knows what psychological condition these girls have, but we need to get tests done on them. They could be psychotic in some capacity. Clive and Dorothy... they were killed with knife wounds consistent with those delivered by somebody of the twins' height and strength and—'

'Uuuuugh,' I grunted, interrupting her.

My blood was about to boil over. I thought if I was going to get support from anyone it would be her.

'Look Quayle,' she said. 'Everybody wants to get this case right. Ashe is absolutely certain that the arrest is fully warranted and I've been led to believe Riordan is going to agree with him this morning, officially. I've heard he has viewed the tape and feels we must do our job and take these girls in. He is due to ring me first thing this morning to confirm. It's why I'm in so early.'

I held my hand to my forehead and just stared back at my boss. Then she shrugged *her* shoulder.

'The girls have been appointed counsel. A Mr Phelim O'Brien. It was all arranged last night.'

O'Brien wasn't a run-of-the-mill defence counsel lawyer. He was from a decent firm – Costello and Lynam. The best man in Dublin Tusla could organise for the twins at such short notice. He ended up coming to their rescue that morning; proving to be more than a match for Riordan in a phone conversation we were all in on. Ashe, Tunstead and Lowe as well as Fairweather and me were standing around a speakerphone inside Fairweather's pokey office, my toes constantly tapping in frustration.

'It is a nod of the head,' O'Brien said, 'no doubt. But a nod of the head is not an affirmative answer to Detective Tunstead's question. Faith is a child lacking a huge amount of confidence. She repeatedly looks downwards when asked a question. And I know that having only spent ten minutes with her before this phone call. You know and I know there will be a diagnosis for this child. Perhaps both children.'

And that was that. The twins were out of their holding cells within half an hour. And I was feeling pretty smug.

I thought O'Brien was great. I've often wondered how differently he would have handled Faith and Grace's trial had Gerd Bracken not jumped on it for the exposure.

Johnny and Sully contacted me soon after the twins were released and told me Aunt Janet was due in Dublin later that afternoon.

I met her for the first time at Tusla. She had been asked to visit the children as soon as she arrived from Monaghan. She was dressed in a tracksuit and her hair was matted to her head; unlikely washed in quite a few days. Maybe weeks. And her eyes looked heavy; worn from what looked like a tough life.

She was a strange sort; but in a different way. She looked like she didn't have any direction in life. Perhaps she needed to belong to Clive and Dorothy's church, but when I asked her if she too was a woman of faith while we were alone in Tusla, she produced a sarcastic snort.

It wasn't a surprise that she was odd. Isn't that what they say about all the Tiddles – that they're odd. Though her name wasn't Tiddle anymore. It was Petersen. She'd married a Monaghan man twenty years prior after meeting him at a former friend's hen party. They lived in a tiny flat on the edge of a town that reached pretty much to the Northern Irish border. She told me that she barely saw nor heard from Clive practically her whole life. They might meet up at the odd Christmas and almost certainly at a family funeral. She insisted it wasn't Clive's dedication to the church that drove them apart; it was that she always felt him to be different to her.

'We never felt like brother and sister,' she said before she curled a stick of gum into her mouth. 'Not even when we were kids. And I think when he went to the church, that was kinda the feather that broke the camel's back for us. Because he was looking for a new family, and I guess I was kinda happy to let him find a new family. I feel sorry for him. And Dorothy. I do. I never hated them. I just didn't love them. That's all. That's not a crime.'

She slowly counted in her head when I asked her how many times she had met the twins. 'About eight or nine,' was the answer she came up with. Pretty much once a year.

'When's the last time you saw the twins?'

'I think it was their Holy Communion a couple of years ago.'

'And you haven't spoken with them since?'

'A few phone calls. They liked to call me. But not that many.'

'What's your impression of the twins?'

She sat back in her chair.

'Bit odd, aren't they? I mean... why wouldn't they be? Being raised inside a church. No chance of being normal, had they?'

I pursed my lips at her and nodded my head.

'I believe you were in Dublin two days prior to the murders. You didn't see your family then?'

She shook her head.

'Very rarely popped by to see Clive when I'm in Dublin. I'd see some friends, do some shopping on Henry Street... that's about it.'

'Well, I have to inform you, Janet. You are Faith and Grace's next of kin,' I said.

She didn't react. She just sat there; almost nonplussed, twisting at her hooped earrings.

'Of course. They can move in with me and Eoin,' she said '...if they've nowhere else to go.'

The twins weren't hesitant to leave Tusla with her. But they didn't exactly seem in a rush to get out of there either. Though, as Johnny repeatedly said to me, they never seemed to feel any way about anything.

I waved at the twins as they were driven away. Only Grace noticed me – she wiggled a goodbye with her baby finger.

I'd watched Tunstead and Lowe's interview with Faith so many times, I had almost forgotten about my own interview with Grace. So I turned on my heels, settled into the monitor room at Rathcoole Garda Station and pressed play on the tape of my short interview.

From the high angle of the recording, Grace looked even smaller than she really was, sat back into one of Fairweather's oversized office chairs.

'Kelly,' she said. And my nose inched closer to the monitor.

'Huh?' I replied to her on the tape.

'Kelly. Kelly is always in our kitchen. She comes in the back door, leaves by the back door.'

I stopped the recording, sat there in silence for a while, then snatched at my blazer and headed for the door.

'Where you off to, Quayle?' Fairweather called out as I passed her.

I didn't answer. I sprint-walked to my car, hopped inside and drove straight to the community centre.

ALICE

We watched the footage on loop. Probably twenty to twenty-five times – Tunstead asking the question, Faith's head slightly dipping as an answer.

When this was shown in court for the first time I was adamant she was admitting to everything; she literally tilted her forehead forward to answer 'yes' to a direct question.

'She's just looking down. That's no confession,' I say.

'It isn't so much that it's a confession,' Thick-rimmed Glasses says, 'it's her natural reaction to being asked the question. She and Grace had obviously sworn each other to secrecy over this; that they wouldn't admit anything to anyone. And my God are they good at it... even to today they are denying everything. But here...' he says, standing up and jamming his finger onto the screen hanging on the wall of the jury room, 'she let her guard slip.'

'So you are saying she let her guard slip for one millisecond of this whole debacle ... yet for the past two years, she managed to keep her guard up? What you're saying doesn't make sense. This is not a confession.'

I look around the table and shake my head.

'C'mon, Alice, she nodded,' Scarhead says.

'She dipped her head, afraid to answer the question, just like she's afraid to answer any question. If you asked Faith Tiddle what her favourite colour was, she'd dip her head. She is not a communicator. There should have been a bloody investigation into why these guards thought it was okay to interview the twins separately without any legal representation.'

'They had the Tusla reps with them. It was legitimate.'

'That's not legal representation!'

I was handling this as well as I could. Faith slipped up for a second, almost fell out of character. She nodded when Tunstead asked her if she had anything to do with the murders as a natural reaction. Then she froze. I'm certain of it.

'Listen,' Red Head says, cutting through the tension that's threatening to flare. 'Regardless of what you think happened or didn't happen in that interview with Faith, the fact of the matter is we cannot convict based on that nod of her head. It's not evidence. It is not a smoking gun. It is a frightened nine-year-old girl who had just lost her parents, and just been separated from her twin sister – her other half – for the first time since they'd lost her parents. For the first time ever, probably. She was frightened and confused. I – like Alice here – think it's an absolute disgrace that the cops were allowed to interview in this manner. I urge you all to not consider this... this *confession* as you all call it as reason enough to find these girls guilty. In no way is this a confession. As I said earlier, it really is jack shit.'

'But the judge allowed this tape in court, Sinead... he wants us to deliberate it. He wants us to consider it as part of the evidence,' Thick-rimmed Glasses says.

'I think I'd even be shy being interviewed by Detective Tunstead, right? What is he... six foot four, handsome like a movie star,' I say.

'What's what he looks like got to do with it?' Scarhead replies.

'Well... because to a shy girl of nine years of age who has only ever been in communication with her mam and dad and twin sister her whole life, she must have felt all kinds of intimidation sat opposite him. I mean... I know I would and I'm a grown woman.'

'Ah come on. Faith had experience of being at church gatherings every week... she didn't just deal with her direct family. She had new people to meet all the time. Hundreds of them. You're just making excuses for her now—'

'Hold on... hold on,' the woman with the big bust says. 'I'm with you.' She points at Scarhead. 'But this lady has a point too.' She curls her finger to me. 'There is no question, as Gerd Bracken argued during the trial, that Faith suffers with levels of anxiety... what was it he called it?'

'Social anxiety disorder,' Red Head says.

'Yes. Well... we can all agree from seeing her at the trial that she is not a girl who likes to communicate. I don't even remember seeing her talk to Grace, just a nod of the head and the odd whisper in the entire two weeks. Have to say... I am certain these girls are guilty of this crime and I won't be changing my verdict. But I think we should, in this instance, agree that Faith suffers with some kind of disorder and to argue that the twins *defi-*

nitely did this because Faith slightly nodded her head is being unfair to justice. We have now watched that tape I don't know how many times... we have gone around in circles arguing what is on that footage and we are getting nowhere.'

The room falls silent. It's always awkward when it falls silent, even though it falls silent quite a lot. It's just a case of jurors allowing a realisation to seep in.

'You're right,' Acne Girl replies to Big Bust. 'Perhaps we shouldn't fixate on the actual video footage of the interview... what about this Detective... what's his name again... the tall handsome one?'

'Tunstead,' I said.

'Yeah... Tunstead, perhaps we'd serve our time better discussing his testimony rather than obsessing about this tape. He did say a few interesting things on the stand. He came across a hell of a lot better than that Quayle guy.'

'That's not fair,' Red Head says. 'Why is everyone so keen to belittle Detective Quayle? As far as I can make out, he was the most caring person involved in this case; he had everybody's best interests at heart right from the beginning.'

'Not this again,' Scarhead says. 'We've argued about Quayle. We've argued how he investigated this. We've argued his testimony. Let's move on. Otherwise we're going to get nowhere. We're going around in circles. I agree with this gentleman. Let's discuss Detective Tunstead... an interesting man, I found.'

'I trust him,' Braces says. And immediately after she does so, I tut. I feel like I've totally lost her now. She swayed yesterday. But today she's right back in the guilty camp. Firmly back in it. 'He just came across as very precise. As if he was in total control. He believes the girls did it. Is adamant.'

'I, personally, thought he was a little bit sleazy,' Obese Guy says.

'Me too,' I say. Even though I didn't think that at all. Tunstead *is* like a movie star; he has real presence – is very fanciable. I believed every word that came out of his mouth. 'He came across as someone who has way too high an opinion of himself. You can't trust people like that.'

'Jesus Christ. We can't even agree on the personality of a bloody witness,' Thick-rimmed Glasses says. 'As a twelve, we don't agree on anything, do we? We all have different opinions on every bleedin' aspect of this trial. Not just whether the twins are guilty or not, but whether Quayle is a good detective, whether Tunstead is a good detective. I'm just getting sick to the back teeth of this back and forth, arguing about stuff that isn't even relevant. Did the fuckin' twins kill their parents or not... that is all we have to answer to. Not whether Tunstead was handsome or sleazy. Christ!'

He covers his face with his hands, pushing his glasses upwards. Probably because he was aware he was turning beetroot red. I totally get his frustration. We have been spending way too much time going off on tangents we really don't need to be going off on. Though the tangents are suiting me. Holding out is key.

'I'm sorry,' I say. 'But our job is to argue all aspects of this case. We're not going to deliberate such a long trial in such a short amount of time.'

'Please can we just end this today?' Thick-rimmed Glasses pleads, taking off his glasses and rubbing at his eyes. 'The last thing we need is us all coming back here next week.'

He isn't the only juror hoping we can end this before the weekend started. A few others nod their heads and mumble in agreement with him.

The fact that it is a Friday is playing on their minds. It has been playing on mine too. If we don't conclude our verdict today, there is a really big chance we will all be back here next Monday morning, sitting around this table again, arguing nonsensical aspects of the trial. My mind is focusing, however, on something that I am hoping may come to fruition.

'Perhaps the judge won't have us back next week,' I say. 'If we don't come to an agreed verdict by the end of the day, maybe she'll declare a hung jury.'

'Ye think so?' Quiff asks me.

'It's possible. We'll have been arguing for practically two whole days... Judge McCormick might feel that's enough.'

'But sure, she hasn't even come back to us yet to say she'd take less than a unanimous verdict. I don't think she's close to putting an end to these deliberations as you may hope, Alice,' Scarhead says.

'Listen,' Big Bust intervenes. 'Why don't we all see where we're at right this minute? Things may have changed for jurors over the course of this morning's deliberations. I know a couple of jurors were swaying in their verdicts yesterday afternoon. Do you think we should have another vote?'

'I guess that makes sense,' Scarhead says. 'Perhaps we're closer to a verdict than we realise.'

'I don't think so,' I say. And then a huff of groans sound out from different seats. They all hate me. Me and Red Head and Obese Guy. Because we're the ones stopping them from returning to normality.

'Right, let's have a vote,' Scarhead says. 'By a show of hands.' I rub my sweating palms up and down my thighs as he speaks. 'Those whose verdict is not guilty, can you raise your hand?'

My hand and Red Head's hand shoot up. Then we both slightly lean forward to look down the line of heads on our side of the table and notice

Obese Guy raise his hand. I glance to my left. Towards Quiff and Braces. But they remain still. It's not really a surprise.

'And those whose verdict is guilty, can you please raise your hands?'

All of the remaining jurors hold their hands aloft. Except for Quiff. He's still motionless.

'Sorry young man,' Scarhead says to him. 'You, eh...'

'I'm undecided,' Quiff says.

Thick-rimmed Glasses audibly puffs out his cheeks, making a loud fart-like sound. But he's not the only one who has shown a touch of exhaustion at what Quiff has just said, others reel themselves back in their chair and wash their hands over their faces.

They're all beginning to think what I've been thinking.

We're gonna be a hung jury.

DAY FOUR

A sense of déjá vu hit me as soon as I pushed open the double doors to the church. All heads turned to face me – just as they had done when I'd pushed those doors open two days prior.

I took two steps into the awkward silence, then paused and clasped my hands.

Ever so slowly, Kelly eventually stepped down from the makeshift altar and click-clacked her way up the long aisle to approach me. She moved so slowly that it was genuinely creepy; like something from a horror movie – her stumpy high-heels slapping off the floorboards of the basketball court.

'G'd afternoon, Detective Quayle,' she said in her sweet Glaswegian purr. 'Have ya more news fo' us?'

I took a step and leaned my cheek towards her ear.

'I, eh... I was hoping to talk to you... alone,' I whispered. I leaned back to observe her face. She just turned her lips downwards and nodded her head.

'Well... am in the middle of a Mass dedicated to the memories of our leaders, Can you wait till I'm finished?' she said.

I looked up at the multiple rows of faces still staring back at me.

'Sure.'

Kelly touched me on my shoulder, then turned on her heels and walked slowly – *painfully* slowly – back to the stage. When everybody's eyes followed the click-clacking of her shoes, I snuck myself on to a chair in the back row and then listened as Kelly bullshitted her congregation in the sweetest of Scottish lilts.

The gist of her nonsense was about how God had a plan for Clive and Dorothy and that they were taken from this earth, in this way, for a purpose.

It unnerved me a little that the praying all focused on the two dead Tiddles; not necessarily the two who were still alive. But it didn't shock me. It's hard to be shocked by anything these staunch believers say anyway. So much of their beliefs are contradictory. If they truly believed God had a plan and that Clive and Dorothy were in a happier place... why the hell were they all dabbing at their eyes with tissues?

'Why, eh... why no mention of Faith and Grace?' I asked Kelly as soon as she led me into the back office, behind the stage, once her eulogy was over. It was the first question I nailed her with – she had barely closed the door behind us when I asked it.

She stared at me, then fidgeted with her fingers.

'I did mention Faith and Grace, Detective,' she said.

'Barely. You said you were praying for them, that you know God has a plan for them... actually... lemme ask you this, what do you mean by that exactly?'

She sat down, then motioned her hand to the chair opposite hers, across from a desk strewn with paperwork.

I took the seat, then leaned forward... letting her know I was still awaiting an answer to the question I'd posed.

'Do you want me to explain to you how we here in this church believe the world works, Detective, s'that what yer askin'?' she says.

'I'm asking a simpler question than that, Kelly. You said you knew God had a plan for Faith and Grace.... what is this plan?'

She leaned forward, mirroring my two elbows on the desk and smiled.

'God has a plan fo' us all, Detective.'

I pinched the bridge of my nose and silently sighed.

'I don't need a sermon, with all due respect, Kelly, on your beliefs. I just need you to let me know what you think God has planned for the twins.'

She sat back and clasped her hands.

'I don't know,' she said.

'But you just told everyone out there you knew God had a plan.'

'Yes, but what that plan is I don't know. We are not privy to God's—'

I held my hand up to stop her going on and on about absolutely nothing.

'Did you or did you not reluctantly mention Faith and Grace in your sermon because you believe they had something to do with Clive and Dorothy's murders?' I asked. Getting to the point. She fidgeted again, looking down at her clasped fingers. 'They are not the only suspects,' I said. She shot a look up at me.

'But they've been arrested for the murders, right? It's been all over the newspapers, Detective. We all... all of us here... we all know who Child X and Y are.'

'I'm sorry to inform you that that was a miscommunication between one of our detectives and one of the twins.'

Her face contorted.

'Huh? So... they've bin let out?' Her Scottish lilt went even more high pitched.

'Yes.' They have been brought to the home of Janet Petersen – Clive's sister.' Kelly looked to her hands again. 'Do, eh... do you know Janet?' I asked.

'Yes, well.... I've met her a few times.' She sat back upright. 'Who, eh... who else are your suspects, Detective?'

I tilted my head

'I'm sorry, Kelly. I can't divulge that information.'

'It was the twins!' she said, her face still, her eyes wide. She was glaring at me as if she was willing herself to not blink.

'Kelly, with all due respect—'

'It said in the papers the stab wounds were by the hands of children.'

'Don't believe all you read in the papers, Kelly,' I said. 'The stab wounds may not necessarily have come from children. They came from somebody short.'

She creased her face at me again.

'They are short, Detective. Of course it was them. Who else could it be?'

I fell silent; not because I didn't want to answer her, but because I wanted to study how straight she was being with me. I wanted her to know that when I said the word 'short' that I was staring straight at her petite little features. She didn't baulk though, nor give anything away.

'How much do you know about the running of this place, from a business point of view?' I asked.

'Detective... it was the twins. There is no conspiracy to be had here.'

'What if I told you,' I said, tilting forward, 'that half a million euros in used notes were found in Clive and Dorothy's bedroom?'

She looked down at the table first, then her mouth slightly parted. I knew right then and there she was about to lie to me.

'I don't know anythin' about no money,' she said.

'Really?'

'Really,' she said.

'Why are you so certain the twins did this?' I asked.

'Well... given everythin' we've heard. It's not just the newspapers. Some of your uniformed officers have been very good to us... calling in here each day to keep us up to date with the case.'

'No. No. Hold on,' I said, shaking my finger at her. 'I don't want to know what the newspapers told you or what police officers have told you. I want to know why *you* are saying the twins did it.'

Kelly held her eyes closed for a brief moment. And when she opened them, they were glistened with forming tears.

'Because Faith and Grace... well... eh... well, they're just... they've always been really strange. Creepy,' she says.

'That's tough judgement,' I said to her, 'coming from a Christian.'

'Och... It's just that I know the twins. *We* know the twins,' she said nodding over my shoulder, back out to her 'family' in the church.

'And?' I said.

'And... like I said, we'd all agree that the twins have just always been a bit odd.'

'Odd as in serial killer odd?' I asked.

She grimaced and shook her head at the same time.

'That's not what I'm saying.'

'What about the money, Kelly? Why don't you leave the detective work of trying to determine who the killer is and help the enquiries by answering straightforward questions? Clive and Dorothy Tiddle had half a million euros in used notes inside a safe in their bedroom. Why?'

'I... I.... I don't know,' she said. 'I am...' she paused.

'Surprised?' I said. I was beginning to enjoy this. It was so rare I ever got to lead the questioning on a suspect in a case like this. I was convinced I was doing great at getting under Kelly's skin. Then again, perhaps a five-foot, high-pitched Scottish lass isn't exactly difficult opposition.

'Surprised? At the amount, yes. That they had money... no.'

'So you knew they had big money?'

'I knew nothing.... that's the truth,' she said. 'I just suspected that they 'ad money. They were very generous. I got so many gifts from them... lots of us did.'

'Where do you suspect their money came from?' I asked.

'Well... here,' she said.

'Half a million?'

She thinned her lips.

'Like I said, I'm surprised with the amount...'

'Me too,' I said.

'You knew the business of the church inside out, did you not, Ms McAllister?'

'I.... I... I think I'm going to need to speak with my lawyer,' she said.

Bingo!

'Ms McAllister, you are not under caution in any way. I am here, asking you questions as a witness. You knew the family better than most... better than anyone, given what I understand. I am simply trying to solve the case of—'

'I am no longer gonnae answer any of ya questions, Detective. If you wish to continue to interview me, I will insist on the presence of legal representation.'

I held my hands up and dipped my head.

'Kelly, I will leave you in peace,' I said, 'if you will just do me and the investigation a good turn by answering one more question.'

She flicked her eyes up to meet mine, but didn't say anything.

'Where were you between half past ten and midday last Saturday, the fifteenth of August?'

She huffed a tiny laugh at me.

'You think I'm a suspect?' she asked.

'It's a simple question, Ms McAllister.'

She looked all around herself, down at her clasped hands, then left, then right.

'Saturdays are my days off. The only day off I have each week. I was... where I normally am on a Saturday afternoon. Home for the morning before I went to the, eh... I was in The Velvet Inn. Watching the horse racin'.'

'You were in the pub that early in the day?' I asked.

'You said one more question, Detective.'

I grinned.

'Like I say... I'm sorry for your losses, Ms McAllister. I'll leave you to it.'

I stood up, nodded my head at her and walked out of her office, past the stage and down the aisle; my head down so as not to make eye contact with any of the congregation who all seemed eager to talk to me. I paced as swiftly as I could without coming across as rude, my mind whirring. Something wasn't adding up. Kelly seemed very defensive; hesitant to answer some of my questions. Though it wasn't my questions that seemed to be irking me. It was one of her answers.

The Velvet Inn. That's where Tommo Nevin drinks.

Clive sharply stood up – his matted-with-sweat hairy belly hanging over his y-fronts – and rested both of his hands on his hips.

'What are you talking about?' he hissed, his tone curt, sharp.

They were both standing either side of a double bed in one of the city-centre's Ibis Hotel rooms. Even though The New St Benedict's Church was bringing in over ten thousand euro a week in collections, Clive never got out of the habit of using cheap hotels for his rendezvous with Kelly.

She puffed out her cheeks and looked down at her toes.

'I'm talkin' 'bout us... being more together. Committin' to each other.'

Clive squinted at her, his bottom jaw hanging open in shock.

'You want me to... you want to...'

'Leave Dorothy!'

Clive's mouth popped as it snapped shut. Then he sat on the edge of the bed with his back to Kelly and washed a hand over his face.

'Don't be a silly woman!' he said.

'Clive—'

'Don't be a silly woman, Kelly!' he snapped, turning around. He got on to his knees on the bed and gripped both of her biceps. 'Why would you ask such a thing you silly, silly woman. You need to... you need to repent for asking such things—'

'You've been having sex with me for o'er fifteen years, Clive. Dorothy is... Look, Dorothy is old. She's getting cranky in her old age. You guys barely speak. She doesn't speak with me anymore. She sits in the office all day countin' money and you... well, you're either meetin' members of the family *or saying a Mass. And when you're not doing either of those things you're having sex with me. Your marriage is nothin' anymore. Leave her. I need someone to wake up with in the mornings... I'm forty-two now...'*

Clive's grip squeezed tight around her biceps. Then he began to shake her.

'You will repent for what you have just said. You seek the forgiveness of not only our Lord Jesus, but me also – your man. "I do not permit a woman to teach or to exercise authority over a man; rather, she is to remain silent".' Clive heavy-breathed as he spat the Bible verse at her. 'Never let this thought cross your mind again, Kelly. Listen to me carefully... if this does cross your mind, you will need to find another family.'

Kelly's eyes had already been filling with tears, but as she nodded her head in response – Clive's fingers still tight around her biceps – one finally fell.

'Okay,' she said, slapping the streaming tear away with her palm.

And then she quietly slipped on the clothes she had worn to the hotel the night before and left the room, closing the door carefully behind herself.

Kelly wasn't entirely sure why she made that proposal to Clive that morning. She was feeling isolated, frustrated. And that led to her eventually snapping at him by asking him to leave his wife... even though that wasn't exactly what she wanted herself. Her relationship with Dorothy had soured after she was sworn at. And soon after that Kelly's role within the church was diluted; she was certainly never allowed in the office where the money was being counted again. And other 'family' members were beginning to get picked over her for some routine duties that she had been responsible for over many years. The only time she really spent with the Tiddles was on Sundays, at the sermon. Just like everybody else.

She turned back to the drink for comfort. And the gambling. She was actually drunk the day Tommo Nevin cornered Clive outside the community centre one Friday evening. Though the confrontation – as soon as it got heated – sobered her up somewhat.

'We don't want none of those kind around here, no more,' Nevin shouted.

'What do you mean those kind?' Clive replied, as calmly as he could; trying to ease the tension that had already become apparent.

'This is Ireland, Tiddle. A beautiful part of the country. Let's keep it Irish.'

Nevin took an intimidating step towards Clive after saying that. But Clive held his ground and smiled through the bristles of his thick moustache.

'You're correct. It is Ireland,' he said.

'Well then, stop bringing them darkies up this neck of the woods. They're everywhere. They're in the bloody Spar doing groceries, hanging around the

410

cafés. I even saw two of them in the pub the other day. The neighbours didn't mind them going to your church, Tiddle, but they're all drawing a line now. Nobody wants them hanging around the mountains.'

Clive interlinked his fingers and placed them on his bulging belly.

'Darkies? Are you referring to their skin; for I see dark skin as not a problem at all. Dark souls... ah now, that is a different matter altogether. And I fear it is a dark soul you may possess, my dear neighbour. Fancy a talk up in my office? We do cups of tea and Jammy Dodg—'

'Don't you fucking dare try to preach to me, you deluded gombeen,' Nevin said, taking one more step towards Clive in an attempt to match him for stature. But his chest only reached to Clive's navel and a moment of awkwardness grew over them both. Kelly, who had been standing watching the confrontation in silence, noticed Nevin curl his fists into a ball and then ran towards them.

'Stop it, stop it, you two,' she said, getting between them and stretching her arms out wide.

Nevin eventually backed away, smirking out of the side of his mouth, and left to walk back down the winding roads that led to the tiny terraced estate he lived in at the bottom of the mountains. Clive didn't even take the time to consider thanking Kelly for her input, and instead huffed and puffed his way back inside the community centre all hot and bothered because somebody had the audacity to talk to him that way. It gave him flashbacks to school; flashbacks he hadn't had in decades.

Kelly had actually known Tommo Nevin's face. He drank in the same pub she had been frequenting since she'd turned back to the booze. She was aware of his first name and the fact that he seemed like an old-school Jack the Lad, though she barely took much notice of him, nor his mates as they'd sit at the bar and rip the piss out of each other. She was too consumed with the horse racing on the screen in front of her every time she went in to The Velvet Inn. Though she did begin to take a bit more notice of Tommo after his confrontation with Clive. She'd often peer over her glass of vodka and coke to stare at him in between races. He was old – almost seventy – but she began to imagine him fucking her; gripping her hair with his tattooed fist and yanking it as hard as he could while he thrusted in and out of her. It was the power of a man that turned Kelly on. Clive had practically convinced her of that. The confrontation Nevin had with Clive that day in the community centre car park had actually made her hot under the collar because somebody was questioning a man she had never seen questioned before.

She would never fuck him. Of course not. He'd probably die of a heart attack if he was to fuck Kelly how she was imagining it in her daydreams. But she liked to fantasise about it. And did so often.

The twins had heard rumours of the confrontation, but as was usually the case, they bit their tongues and didn't ask any questions.

They were too busy doing their own thing anyway, and by this stage and age were much preferring their own company than any congregating with their 'family'. Not that they'd lost their passion for all things Jesus; it was just that they could be themselves when they were in their own company and preferred it that way. The novelty of seeing their daddy speak to a large room full of people had long since worn off. But then again, so too had the novelty of the twins themselves. They just weren't as much of a draw as they used to be, given that a lot of their cuteness had been lost as their bodies stretched. So their staying inside their bedroom most of the time kind of suited everybody. Not that they'd ever miss the Sunday sermon. No chance. They just stopped hanging around the community centre after school to watch 'family' members come and go without so much as holding a polite conversation with them. Staying home was much more enjoyable; much more pleasurable for them.

'What you doing?' Grace asked Faith when she saw her stretching to her tippy toes to turn at the tap.

'Just watering the plants for Daddy.'

'You? Why?'

'Jesus told me to.'

'Oh...' Grace said.

'I saw a picture of flowers being watered in a magazine and I know it was Jesus telling me that the flowers must be thirsty... and look.' Faith walked out of the bathroom carefully carrying a heavy can of water with both hands, and led Grace to the flowerbed at the front of the house. 'They're all dry. Daddy never lets them get this dry. And then I find a magazine at the bottom of our garden about watering plants and... so...'

Grace tilted her head back.

'So that's how he contacts you, that's how he talks to you? Pictures in a magazine?'

Faith shrugged.

'He just talks to me how he talks to me; different ways for different things.'

'So, not through magazine pictures then?'

Faith shook her head.

'No. That's the first time he's done it through a magazine.'

Grace held a knuckle to her left temple and rolled it around. She was massaging herself; had got a little excited thinking Faith had finally revealed the code. But now she was back to being confused about how Faith and Jesus communicated as she had ever been.

Grace was never jealous that Faith had a direct line to Jesus. She felt if Faith had it, then so did she. Because they came as a pair. It would just go through Faith first and then eventually to her.

She would often look for signs herself, Grace. But it never worked for her. Her lateral thinking was much more advanced than her sister's. What wasn't advanced was her understanding that her sister wasn't as clever as she was.

Grace would take long baths, close her eyes tight and pray to Jesus to drop something inside her head. But it never worked. Or she would kneel down and pray for over an hour at times in the community centre, her eyes fixed on a burning candle wick, begging Jesus to blow it out, just to let her knew he was listening. Or she would stare out her bedroom window, into the long fields that stretched beyond the back of the bungalow, hoping the stars in the night sky would spell out a sign to her. She was actually doing just that at the unusual time of two a.m. one morning when she saw Clive dragging a heavy-looking black plastic bag across the field. He left it at the foot of the oak tree and then walked back to help Dorothy carry a small step-ladder to the same location.

Grace rubbed her eyes.

Then she watched as Clive climbed the ladder and fidgeted with a thick branch until a large hole opened up in the trunk. The branch just seemed to spring open, like a special effect in a movie. Then he dropped the bag inside the hole, crunched the branch closed and climbed back down the ladder.

DAY FOUR

The sun had almost disappeared by the time I was strolling up his tiny garden path.

I rattled on the door as hard as I could, not stopping until, through the frosted glass, I could see his blurry figure making his way towards me.

He fake-laughed when he opened the door.

'What are ye accusing me of today, Detective? The disappearance of Betsy Blake?'

Then he produced that horrible side-mouthed grin.

'Mr Nevin, may I?' I motioned over his shoulder and, after a pause, he stepped aside.

'I'm in the middle of me tea,' he said.

When I walked into his living room a plate of unfinished lasagne was sitting on the sofa; an episode of EastEnders paused on the television.

'Wouldn't have put you down as a soap fan, Nevin,' I said.

He shrugged his shoulders.

'Your problem seems to be that you judge books by their covers, Quayle,' he said.

Then he motioned his hand to the worn leather armchair adjacent to where he was eating and nodded.

I took out my notepad before I sat.

'Mr Nevin, when I spoke to you two days ago you discussed, briefly, with me the issue you had with Clive and Dorothy Tiddle bringing immigrants to this neck of the woods for sermons; can you give me more detail on the specific issue you had?'

He shook his head.

'I don't have an issue with them coming to their sermons or to pray or do whatever nonsense it is they do in that community centre. If they wanna come to the community centre and get down on bended knee and talk to the stars... fine by me. That's not the problem I had with Tiddle.' He shivered. Like a bad actor. 'I actually can't believe they're dead. It's eh.... It's...'

'If you can stay on track, Mr Nevin,' I said.

'My problem isn't them coming to do what they wanted to do; my problem is that they don't just go to their church and go home. They stay around the area... shopping, going to the pubs, talking to the neighbours...'

'You have a problem with them talking to other people?'

'Ah, but they don't talk normal, do they? It's preaching. Going around telling folk that God is in their hearts... fuck right off, ye get me?'

'So you *do* have a problem with their religion... I thought your problem was the colour of people's skin?'

He scratched at the back of his head, then picked up his plate and began forking lasagne into his mouth.

'It's not a racist thing, it's just...' he said, chewing, 'it's the silly accents, the differences in people. We don't need that around here.'

'And you think not wanting people here because they have funny accents is *not* racist?'

'Listen, call it what you want, Detective. This is a quiet little town filled with Irish people – Irish people for centuries – and we want to keep it that way.'

'We?'

He swallowed. Picked up another forkful.

'Well... me and whoever else... I know there are other people around here who feel the same as I do. They'd just never say it out loud. I was the only one to confront Tiddle. And that's why you're here, isn't it? Because I was the only one who had the balls to tell him we didn't want that kind round here. But that's as far as I went... I had words with him. I didn't – for Christ sake! – have anything to do with him being killed.' His voice tensed. 'Anyway, I thought you had the killers locked up... their kids did it, right? Probably sick of their parents going on and on about religion. What were they... nine, the papers said? Yeah, probably just grown up enough to realise their parents had them locked inside a cult.'

'The kids didn't do it,' I said.

He looked up at me, and one of his eyebrows raised.

'What, so the newspapers have it all wrong – this Child X and Y thing is a load of bollocks, is it?'

'It was a misunderstanding. Child X and Y were brought in for routine questioning... they were not arrested.'

'Every newspaper reported they were arrested, Quayle. Is this how much you've fucked up this investigation already?' He sniggered out of the side of his mouth again. 'You're arresting their children one minute, coming to me the next.'

I wasn't put out by him laughing at me. I knew I was about to put him up against the ropes. I still had big punches to hit him with.

'Do you think the Tiddle family were worth much money?' I asked him. He scoffed.

'Probably. Aren't all these religious freaks collecting big dosh? It's the only reason they're in it, right? See those big players in America with their super churches... rolling around in money they are. And they don't pay tax... did ye know that? Not a penny.'

'So you *are* aware the Tiddle family may have had some money?'

'Listen. I don't know nothin' about the Tiddle family, other than they run the church and bring foreigners to this neck of the woods. Yes, I had a row with Clive Tiddle – but don't even think about treating me as a suspect in this murder. You'll be barking up the wrong tree.'

'It's my job to bark up all the trees, Mr Nevin. I've spoken to many people around the mountain side, and those who visit the church. Do you know the only person who ever had a problem with the Tiddles seems to be you?'

'Obviously not, Quayle. Somebody else must have had more of a problem with them than I did, huh?'

'Well, let me put it to you this way, Mr Nevin,' I said. 'You had a problem with the Tiddle family bringing immigrants to the church. You unloaded a racist tirade at Clive Tiddle on the twelfth of June this year. And you have just admitted that you felt the Tiddle family had money.'

He did that stupid snigger thing again.

'You're just making this up as you're going along, Quayle, aren't ya? You don't know what you're doing.'

'You've already fucked up, Mr Nevin – and you are totally unaware of it.'

He dipped his chin into his chest and stared at me.

'Are you gonna tell me how I fucked up?' he asked before burping.

'When I was here two days ago, Mr Nevin, you told me you never heard of Kelly McAllister.'

He made a funny face at me, as if he was squelching up his nose. More proof of his bad acting.

My phone buzzed in my pocket, but I didn't want to take my gaze away from Nevin's scrunched up face.

'Is she the little Scottish lady—'

'Ah... you do know her? So you lied to me the first time I asked you that question...'

My phone buzzed again. It was a text. From Fairweather.

Ring me now!

I held a finger up to Nevin.

'Gimme one sec.'

I pushed at the green button and strolled into Nevin's square hallway.

'Ever hear of Gerd Bracken?' Fairweather said as soon as I held the phone to my ear.

'Course,' I said. And in the silence between me saying that and Fairweather speaking, I knew what she was getting at. The hungry bastard of a lawyer was attaching himself to the twins. Sleazy fecker. The biggest defence lawyer in Dublin – a man as desperate for attention as he is for money.

'You're joking me,' I said.

'Nope. He's out in Janet Petersen's house right now, talking to the twins. He's asked to speak with you as a matter of urgency.'

I peeked back inside at Nevin who was slouching on his sofa, the plate of lasagne now resting on his belly.

'Okay – I'll get myself out there asap,' I said. Then I hung up and called out.

'I'll be back, Nevin.'

He fake-laughed loudly as I stormed out of his house, slamming the door shut behind me.

Bracken looked just as slimy and tanned in real life as he did on TV. I almost baulked backwards when he stretched his hand towards me to introduce himself, his tan was that orange.

'Grace and Faith tell me you have been the only officer they feel they can trust,' Bracken said when we all sat down around the Petersen's round kitchen table. There was me, Janet and her husband Eoin, as well as Bracken's assistant lawyer – a quiet girl called Imogen. She just stared down at the papers in front of her the whole time, taking notes while Bracken threw questions at me. The twins sat in the living room on their own watching cartoon after cartoon.

'Regardless of whether or not Faith and Grace say you have been great with them, ultimately – as lead detective on this case, Detective Quayle – it is your responsibility that they were wrongfully arrested last night. As soon as I heard about their arrest – and the reason for it – I picked up my phone and made sure I was attached to this case. I've taken over from Phelim O'Brien – and now you must answer to me.'

I felt instantly intimidated, though I was well aware Detective/Defence Lawyer relationships were supposed to work the other way around. But he just seemed to ooze control. Somehow.

'Hold on one second,' I said. But I was immediately interrupted by the louder voice.

'No, you hold on, Detective. I have watched the footage of Faith's interview with Detectives Tunstead and Lowe. How could you allow this to happen? How could you allow two innocent girls to be questioned in a police station without appropriate legal counsel?'

'They had members of Tusla with them... they were offered legal counsel, they said they were fine with Dinah and Joe.'

He tutted at me, then flicked over his paperwork.

'Have you any idea, Detective Quayle, how much damage arresting two innocent nine-year-old girls could have on their mind-sets for the rest of their lives? They have just found their mother's and father's bodies in pools of blood inside their own home, they are right in the middle of the grieving process and then you go and arrest them and keep them locked up in a holding cell overnight...'

'I didn't arrest them!' I said.

'You are the lead detective are you not? This is your case is it not?'

I looked around at the faces staring at me; Janet's face was long and jaded looking. Eoin didn't show much emotion at all, he just sat there with his arms folded. There was no noise from Imogen, except for the sweeping of her pen on paper. When I looked up at Bracken again, his eyebrow was raised – he was still waiting on an answer to his question.

'Listen,' I said holding my palms outwards. 'I *am* in control of this investigation. In fact, when I got the call to come here to meet you I was in the midst of interviewing a suspect who had had issues with the Tiddle family.'

Bracken leaned back in his chair.

'Ah...' he said, turning his bottom lip downwards. 'So you *are* doing other work on this case...'

'I obviously can not divulge any information to you, Mr Bracken.'

'I don't need any more information than you've already given me, Detective Quayle... except perhaps for an answer to one more question.' He leaned forward. 'Sir,' he said, 'do you believe my clients are guilty of this crime?'

'No,' I said, holding his stare. 'You can take it from me, Mr Bracken – the twins didn't have anything to do with this.'

ALICE

I kept eyeballing Quiff across the table, hoping he'd meet my stare – give me some indication that he was going to sway back over to our not guilty camp.

The poor youngfella looked confused. Pained almost. He didn't know what to do; was being dragged by his mind from pillar to post. Yesterday morning he voted not guilty, then changed to guilty by the end of the day. This morning he's being swayed back again; is now undecided. That's great. The more confused he is, the longer he's likely to hold out. And that's what this is all about. Holding out; holding out until the judge's patience wears thin.

I try to put an age on Quiff; he's older than my Zoe but probably only by about four or five years. I'd imagine he's somewhere in his late twenties. I look down the line of heads on my side of the table as deliberations continue around me, and stare at Obese Guy. He wasn't particularly quick to raise his hand to acknowledge his not guilty verdict in the last vote. I hope he's not being swayed. Though I don't think he will be. He seemed adamant the twins were not guilty – even told me so before deliberations began. Red Head won't be swayed either. She seems really intelligent. Her mind is made up. Besides, I've a feeling she might be getting blackmailed too. I'm feeling positive the three of us will hold out.

Then, when this trial is over and done with and the judge declares us a hung jury, I'm going to tell Emmet I can't see him anymore; that our affair has to stop. I'll miss it, of course. The orgasms are just so bloody divine... but they can't be worth it. I'll just have to remember them... play with myself a bit more as I think about Emmet to rid myself of the addiction. I just can't risk Noel and Zoe ever finding out. I was stupid and naïve to even start the affair in the first place. The more I think of it, the more I feel this bitch – whoever she is; the one blackmailing me – has actually done me the world of good. I needed this scare; needed a good reason to finish things with Emmet.

'Right-ee-o,' Scarhead says. 'It seems as if we're at a bit of a stalemate.'

'We're going to be a hung jury,' I say, probably a little too exuberantly.

'Calm down, Alice,' Thick-rimmed Glasses says. I hate that everybody in here knows my name. It feels wrong. Creepy. I wish they'd all done what I'd done; not even bother to remember anyone's name. 'We're only half-way through our second day of deliberation. The judge will be expecting us to argue for a lot longer than this.'

'Oh, I don't know. Alice might be right,' Scarhead says, agreeing with me for the very first time. 'Juries don't deliberate for too long. Maybe two days, perhaps three at most. But given that this is a Friday, I wouldn't be surprised if the judge declared us hung by the end of the day, rather than take everybody back to court on Monday. Unless, of course, we can convince you three... and you of course, Cal,' he says, looking at Quiff, 'that this case *has* been proven beyond doubt.'

'I don't think so,' I say.

He purses his lips at me.

'Are you sure, Alice... there is no way you can be convinced of the twins' guilt?' I, ever so slowly, shake my head back at him whilst holding his stare. Then he turns to Red Head. 'What about you, Sinead?'

She lets out a small moan; a pained moan.

'It's just. It's so wrong to have two children who look so vulnerable be in court like this. It doesn't sit right with me. But aside from that, I have to agree with Alice. I'm not sure this trial proved beyond all doubt that Faith and Grace did this. And we owe it to the twins, we owe it to Clive and Dorothy. And the church. And all their friends. The detectives. We owe it to *everybody* involved in this case to argue it out as much as we can.'

Scarhead looks disappointed in that answer. Perhaps he doesn't like the idea of more arguing. So he turns to Obese Guy.

'And you, Gerry?'

Gerry sucks his lips.

'The case hasn't been proven.'

'Jeez, well, who else do you think killed them, then?' Thick-rimmed Glasses says. He seems to be the one whose patience is stretched the furthest. 'Well... anybody got any other theory?'

'Our job isn't to decide who killed Clive and Dorothy – it's to deliberate whether or not Faith and Grace did it,' Red Head says.

'What about that little Scottish lady?' Obese Guy offers up.

'Huh?' Scarhead replies.

'Kelly, isn't it? The pretty-ish one who runs the church.'

'What – you think she killed the Tiddles? You playing detective now, Gerry?'

Gerry wobbles his chins.

'No... no... I'm just saying that the trial we just witnessed over the past weeks ended with two arguments, didn't it? Either Faith and Grace did it, or a professional hit man – someone clever enough to not leave a trace of themselves – did it.'

Scarhead shrugs his shoulders.

'You mean the Hollywood movie contract killer theory?' he says.

'Well... I guess if you are to buy into the theory of a contract killer doing it, then we'd have to assess who would have hired a contract killer.'

'And you think Kelly McAllister hired a contract killer?'

Scarhead laughs and Obese Guy looks up the line of faces to meet my stare. I just glance down to my lap.

'Eh... I guess she stood to benefit from Clive and Dorothy being out of the picture?' he says, shrugging.

'What the fuck?' Thick-rimmed Glasses says, rubbing at his face again.

'She took over the church, right?' Obese Guy says. 'Runs it all on her own now. She even testified to that when she was on the stand as a character witness. She also seemed dismissive of Faith and Grace, especially for somebody who is a woman of God. She was quite accusatory for someone who had known them their whole life.'

'Exactly,' Scarhead says.

'Exactly what?'

'Well, she knows them as well as anybody, and even *she* is convinced they did it.'

'Well, she probably would say that, wouldn't she... especially if she has something to hide?'

Thick-rimmed Glasses slaps both of his hands to the table and heaves himself to his feet. 'This is getting outrageous now,' he says. 'You are going off into the woods with your theories here. Are we really all going to sit around this table and let these two little murderers get away with this, just because you are more keen to play detective than to do the job you have actually been asked to do? I suggest we get back to talking about—'

He's silenced by a rattle of knuckles on the door, then plops himself back on to his chair as Red Head goes to answer it.

'Lunch time,' she says, looking over her shoulder at the rest of us. A collective sigh sounds from all corners of the table. Literally relief all around.

We all file out of the jury room like obedient students though, as if most of us hadn't, just seconds ago, had our fists balled up in frustration; our blood pumping.

'Psst... toilet break?' I whisper out of the side of my mouth to Red Head as we begin to stroll down the corridor.

She stares at me for a little too long without answering, then whispers, 'Sure.'

We excuse ourselves before heading into the dining-room, the young woman dressed in all black nodding at our request to visit the toilet.

I blow a raspberry out through my lips and place my hands on my hips as soon as the door swings closed behind us.

'You okay, Alice?' Red Head asks.

'We've got to hold on.'

'Calm down, Alice. You just need to stay strong with your beliefs. Just don't get bullied. Don't let them rile you up.'

'I won't. I won't,' I say, my hands still on my hips. 'I'm so worried.'

She holds a hand to my elbow and grips it.

'You really haven't handled the pressure of this trial well, have you? Do you normally suffer with levels of anxiety?'

I shake my head. And almost sob out a cry as I do so. I want to ask her if she's being blackmailed too. It would make such a difference to know the two of us are in this together. If we are, then it's only a matter of convincing Obese Guy and all will be okay. I dab at my eye, to stop the tear from falling and then swallow.

'Anything going on outside the court that has caused you any... any other pressure this week?' I ask.

She stares away from me for a second, glancing at the door of one of the cubicles, then her eyes dart back to mine.

'No. Why?'

'Oh... don't mind me. You seem, like me, to be quite stressed by this too.' That's a lie. She doesn't seem fazed or stressed by this at all. In fact, she has taken this in her stride better than anybody else around that table. 'It's just... I've just got this other thing going on as well... and it seems like double the pressure and... agggh,' I say, shaking my head and laughing out loud. In the echo of the tiled bathroom it actually sounds as if I'm at the start of a bloody mental breakdown. 'No, it's just...' I compose myself. 'I wondered if you are feeling as stressed as I am.'

She shakes her head.

'I'm not saying this trial hasn't been stressful, or bloody frustrating more than anything else, but other than that....'

She leaves her sentence hanging there, perhaps hoping I'll just pick it up. Or maybe hoping I'll just shut the hell up and lead us to the dining room. After all, neither of us have actually used the loo since we came in here. I just rattled off question after question to her as soon as the door was closed. Yet I haven't actually asked her what I want to ask her. How am I even supposed to approach the subject of blackmail without giving the game away?

'I hope you stay strong in the jury room, I know I will,' is all I can muster. But then again, I guess that's all I really want to know; that's all this boils down to.

'I will be strong. To my convictions.'

'Those poor twins,' I say. Her eyes dart to the cubicle door again. 'You do believe the twins, right? You don't actually think they could have done this?'

She shifts her heels, steadying herself on the tiles.

'You really wanna know what I believe?' she asks, meeting my eye again. 'I know we weren't supposed to follow the case in the media in order to get on this jury, but I... I mean you couldn't miss the magnitude of this case. Who could?' she says.

'Yeah... course, me too.'

'I never believed as this case was being dragged through the system that these children should have been tried here. This case should have gone straight to the Children's Court in Smithfield. Instead both sides argued and argued and delayed and delayed this case until they finally ended up here... somehow. It's been a mess. We shouldn't be judging kids this way... at Dublin's Criminal Courts – as if they're adults. It's scandalous. This whole case has been handled terribly from the start. And if we find Faith and Grace guilty, they could end up in prison their whole life.'

'They won't though, surely?' I say.

'No. Well... we don't know what sentence they'd serve. But life in prison is a possibility. And that is why this case should never have been allowed to get this far. To these courts. The state pushed way too far on this. *Way* too far.'

'Wait,' I say, holding my hand up to her again, a penny dropping inside my head. 'You think they did it, don't you?'

The bathroom door sweeps open.

'Ladies, the jurors have something they wish to share with you,' the young woman dressed in all black says to us. We all look at each other awkwardly, and then she leads us back to the dining room where we sit down beside each other in the last two remaining seats at the far end of the table.

'We've been waiting for you two,' Scarhead says, twiddling an envelope with his fingers. 'We didn't want to open it until we were all seated together.'

'It's from the judge,' Big Bust says.

Scarhead rips at the top of the envelope, then scans the contents himself quickly before reading it aloud.

'"Ladies and gentlemen of the jury,"' he says. '"I write to you not to add pressure, but to perhaps relieve some. It has been a testing time for all involved in this trial. And while I understand you cannot take the huge decision that lies in your hands lightly, you have now been deliberating for ten full hours; six yesterday and four this morning. I am therefore – taking into consideration the length of your deliberations – now willing to accept a verdict agreed upon by ten jurors, and not a full unanimous decision. Regards, Judge Delia McCormick."'

Braces, sitting directly across from me, whistles quietly.

'Y'know what?' Thick-rimmed Glasses says. 'You, Cal...' he points his finger at Quiff. 'You've been guilty, not guilty, undecided... may I ask you just for my own peace of mind and in light of the letter the judge just sent us... where do you stand now?'

Quiff sits more upright in his chair.

'I, eh... I always felt they did it. I think they're guilty, it's just...'

'Well, that's that sorted then. You think they're guilty!' Thick-rimmed Glasses waves his hand in the air, like a pretentious snob; except he has thick-rimmed glasses. Pretentiousness looks awkward coming from someone wearing thick-rimmed glasses.

'No... that's not what I'm saying,' Quiff says, readjusting his seating position again. He is literally uncomfortable.

'Hold on, didn't we say we wouldn't discuss the trial over lunch?' Red Head says, coming to Quiff's rescue.

'We won't discuss it. I just want to know where he stands, because then we'll know where everybody stands. And I think, given what the judge has just sent us, it's about time we started making our minds up.'

Quiff coughs.

'I think they're guilty,' he says, his voice almost breaking. 'I guess I was just trying to give them the benefit of the doubt as we argued everything in the jury room, but even though I wanted somebody to give me a good reason to say not guilty, nobody really has. I'm, eh... no. I won't be changing my mind again. It's made up. I wish Faith and Grace all the best of health no matter what happens. And I hope they don't have to spend all their lives behind bars. But, eh... I find them guilty – guilty as charged.'

I groan silently in the back of my throat, then look to my right to meet Red Head's eyes.

'Okay then,' Scarhead says. 'We are now nine guilty to three not guilty. The judge will accept a ten:two verdict. Seems as if we're getting very close.'

DAY FOUR

I was relieved to leave the Petersen house that night.

Bracken is quite intimidating. I guess that's what makes him so successful at what he does. I'd seen him on TV and in the newspapers lots of times; he's probably the only celebrity lawyer in the country – hasn't lost a case in years. He held my stare as he lashed out at me over the twins' arrest the night before. And I just held my hands up in apology and told him I was doing all I could to get this investigation back on track.

I went into the living room before I left to give them both a big hug. Grace muttered a soft "thank you" in to my ear; Faith was too busy staring at the cartoons over my shoulder to even realise I was hugging her.

I took a look at the clock on my dashboard as soon as I got back in the car. It had just gone ten p.m. – the pubs would still be open. As I drove, I counted up the hours I had left to convince Riordan and Ashe that I was on to something – or face being thrown off the case. Fourteen. Not a lot of hours. But I was starting to grow in belief I wouldn't need them all. Kelly and Nevin had already fucked up. I was convinced they were in this together. And I was going to prove it before Riordan's stopwatch reached zero.

'A non-alcoholic beer,' I called out.

When the barman nonchalantly placed a bottle in front of me, I flashed my badge.

'Detective Denis Quayle,' I said.

He looked taken aback at first, then he leaned his forearms on to the bar and bent towards me.

'This about the, eh... Tiddle murders?' he said.

I squinted at him.

'What do you know about the Tiddle murders?'

'As much as everyone else does,' he says pushing up off the bar and flicking his head at another customer. The customer ordered a Guinness and then the barman stepped away from me to pull the pint. He left the Guinness to settle and came back, leaning onto the bar again.

'Who would have thought it... around here?' he says. 'And it's their own kids everyone is saying... that's who Child X and Y are—'

'It wasn't the kids,' I said, slapping my hand on the bar. Then I sighed. And the man waiting on his Guinness stared at me wide-eyed.

'What... so Child X and Y aren't actually *their* kids?' the barman asked, scratching at his hair.

'No... no...' The two of them were glaring at me now. 'It's... listen... I can't divulge anything about the case. I am not here to answer questions. I'm here to ask them. Please...' I motioned to the settling Guinness. Then the barman topped the pint's head and plonked it in front of the customer who handed over the exact change and left us to it.

'What questions would you like to ask, Detective?'

I looked around myself. The bar was busy with chatter; no more prying ears.

'Does a Tommo Nevin frequent this place?' I asked.

'Tommo? You think Tommo killed the Tiddles,' he laughed. 'Because he had that row with the husband that time? Tommo is a fucking looper... or a character is the best way to describe him. But a killer... no – that's crazy talk, Detective.'

'I just asked you a simple question, eh....what's your name?'

'Paul.'

'Well Paul,' I said. 'I wasn't accusing anybody of anything... I just asked you a very simple question.... does Tommo Nevin frequent this bar?'

'Eh, yeah. Tommo's in here three or four times a week, I guess. Loves himself a pint of Heineken.'

'Thank you, Paul,' I said. 'And let me ask you this... does a Kelly McAllister frequent this pub?'

'Kelly... Kelly? Is that the little Scottish one? Pretty she is. But a bit...'

He left his sentence hanging there.

'Yes. Scottish lady. About five foot nothing.'

'She's in here every Saturday, I believe. Is big into the horse racing. Puts on a few bets, sips on vodka and cokes in that corner over there. Wait...' he said, shaking his head a little, 'why you asking about Kelly and Tommo?'

'I need you to tell me if they know each other, Paul.'

'Pffft... no. I mean not that I know of. Tommo sits here,' he says pointing at the bar stools next to where I'm sitting, 'she's always back there, right next to the tele.'

'Have you ever seen them in conversation?' I asked.

Paul shrugged his shoulders.

'Everybody knows everybody in this pub. But... Kelly seems to keep herself to herself as far as I know. I've heard stories of one or two of the lads messing with her, trying it on with her... but that nonsense didn't last long. Lesbian, she is. Did ye know that? That's what she told one of the lads.'

I tilted my head, trying not to act surprised by that.

'But they know of each other, Kelly and Tommo, right?' I said.

Paul folded his arms.

'To be honest, I don't really know. I don't usually work Saturdays. That's the only time that Scottish woman comes in. So I'm not really aware how she mingles with the other punters. Far as I know she just keeps herself to herself.'

'So you weren't here for opening hours last Saturday?' He shook his head. 'Were any of these bar staff?' I asked.

He looked around at the guy and girl pulling pints down the other end of the bar.

'None of us... it's the other shift pattern. Mike, Jamie and Nina would have been in first thing on Saturday.'

I put my Detective badge back in the inside pocket of my blazer.

'Well in that case I'm gonna need to see your CCTV footage from that day,' I said. 'Can I view it on site?'

Paul hadn't a clue how the CCTV worked, but luckily Tracey – his colleague – did. She led me to a small office-cum-stock room at the back of the pub that had a tiny grey – and grainy – monitor in it, sitting on top of three old-school phonebooks. She slipped in a tape labelled with last Saturday's date and I watched the footage play from the time stamped 10:30 a.m. I was certain I was going to find a flaw in Kelly and Tommo's alibis.

The shutters of the pub had barely gone up when Tommo arrived with two other men. It was 10:33 p.m.

'Who are they?' I asked Tracey.

'Tommo in the middle, Matty on the right and that's Chaz – his real name is Dave but they call him Chaz... because of Chaz 'n' Dave...'

I stared over my shoulder at her and her face dropped from smiling to stifling.

Sure enough, Tommo and his mates sat on the stools at the bar Paul had told me they always sit in.

Three more men came in, and after ordering their pints they sat on the far side of the pub. Then another four arrived, followed by a young-enough couple. I bit my lips as I stared at the blinking footage of the front entrance. I wasn't sure if I wanted to see Kelly arrive or not. If she didn't arrive, then her alibi of being at the pub during the murders was blown and I had made a major breakthrough in the case. But if she did arrive, I was desperate to see if her eyes met Tommo Nevin's; certain that if they did then they must have known what was happening in the Tiddle bungalow at this exact time.

It didn't take long. It was exactly 10:48 when her miniature frame strolled through the door. She sidled straight up to the bar and spoke briefly to a bald barman. I leaned forward, my nose close to the screen and stared at her; waiting to see if she looked to her right; made any inkling of an acknowledgement towards Nevin. I was growing in certainty that they were up to something and that they must have been consciously using The Velvet Inn's CCTV as their alibi.

When Kelly grabbed at her drink and made her way to sit down at the back of the pub, right beside the big screen, I was gutted. The footage I was watching was grainy and blinking, but it certainly didn't show any acknowledgement between the two of them.

'Fuck it!' I hissed.

'You okay, Detective?' Tracey asked me.

'Can I, eh... can I take that tape back to the station with me?' I asked her. 'I need to pore over it in more detail...'

She turned her lips downwards and nodded her head.

'I guess so,' she said.

I called Sheila when I was back in the car; told her I'd be home late again. I didn't like her having to go to bed alone for the fourth night in a row, but she wasn't complaining. She never complains. Ever. Sheila doesn't have it in her nature to moan.

I thought I'd be pretty much left alone in the police station; just me with the TV monitors for company. But I knew that wouldn't be the case as soon as I got to the front door. I could hear voices. Mumbled voices coming from Fairweather's office.

I walked in to see Fairweather, Ashe, Tunstead and Riordan all seated around the desk in deep conversation. I knew instantly they were talking about me, because the chatter dropped as soon as I walked in.

Riordan stood up and took a couple of steps towards me.

'Detective Quayle, David Riordan.'

'I know who you are, sir. I've seen you speak at the Garda Ceremony a couple of times.'

He smiled.

'Well, we were just talking about you,' he said.

'No shit!'

He puffed out a rather feminine giggle for such a rough looking man and then pointed his hand to Fairweather's desk; motioning for me to join them.

'Before you start,' I said. 'I'm on to something. I have suspects. I have motive. I have opportunity.' Tunstead tutted. The prick. Everybody else just stared at me. 'Clive Tiddle had a run-in with a local layabout; Thomas Nevin. Nevin was known to be really angry about the Tiddles bringing brown faces to this neck of the woods. And we have witnesses who claim they had a shouting match about eight weeks ago. On top of that, Nevin has a fresh scratch inside his right hand.'

'Nevin isn't a bloody killer, Quayle,' Tunstead said.

I held my index finger to my lips.

'I'm talking now, Tunstead,' I said, then I turned back. 'Kelly McAllister – the little Scottish lady who helps the Tiddles run their church – well, she knows all about the money the Tiddles had in the safe and... guess what? Her and Tommo know each other. They drink in the same pub – The Velvet Inn.'

'Jesus, Quayle. Half of Rathcoole and the surrounding area drink in The Velvet Inn,' Tunstead said.

'Half the folk don't drink in The Velvet Inn... there are four pubs round here, smartarse, how does that even make sense?'

'Okay... then a quarter of the folk around here drink in The Velvet Inn. Two people who drink in the same pub is hardly a coincidence.'

The room fell silent. And I kinda squirmed a little.

'They were after the money in the safe,' I said, trying to compose myself. 'Kelly knows all about how that church is run. She benefits hugely from having Clive and Dorothy out of the picture. When Tommo Nevin had that row with Clive Tiddle, she must have got in contact with Nevin, asked him if—'

'Jesus Christ, Quayle,' Tunstead shouted, screeching his chair backwards and standing up.

'Calm down, Detective Tunstead,' Ashe said.

'Look Quayle,' Riordan offered up in a soft voice; a voice not befitting his face. It was potted with acne scars; his nose looking as if it had been chewed on by a Jack Russell. 'We've been in discussion with Fairweather here. She talks very highly of you.' I looked at Fairweather and pursed my lips at her. 'Says you have been an almost perfect member of the force for twenty-five years. "Best I've ever worked with", were her exact words.'

'Wouldn't take much, she hasn't worked with many,' I said, laughing. 'We've run this station between us since nineteen ninety-five.'

Everybody laughed. Even Tunstead. And as he did, I immediately recognised their laughs as sympathy laughs. My stomach turned itself over. I knew something was going on.

'We think it's time for you to retire,' Riordan said.

'What!' I screeched.

'Detective Quayle. For your brilliant service to the force you will receive your full pension *and* we are going to offer you a pay-off, just a little thank you for all the years you have protected the people of Rathcoole.'

'This is... this is...' I stood up and began to pace the small room.

'Rathcoole station has been under threat of closure, you have been made aware of that. Well... we're shutting it down and stretching Tallaght Station to cover this area. Fairweather has just announced her retirement, similar structure to the one we are offering you. The two uniforms... what are their names?'

'Johnny Gibbons and Olivia Sully,' Fairweather said.

'Yeah... Johnny and Sully. They'll be offered roles in Tallaght station. It's time, Quayle. Rathcoole is barely a police station anymore. It just doesn't have the resources, let alone the personnel. You know that yourself. We're going to let Tallaght's jurisdiction stretch into the mountains.'

'You can not be serious,' I said. 'Fairweather, what is—'

'It's time,' Fairweather said, looking at me. 'C'mon Quayle. The package we're being offered is more than generous. We've worked here way too long. Let's do something else... you can join me on the golf course. You've always threatened to buy a set of clubs. Or, eh... what about all the travelling you've always said you'd do with Sheila?'

I pressed the butt of my palm to my forehead. Hard.

'And, eh....' Riordan coughed into his hand. 'We've also heard from a journalist from the *Irish Daily Star*, he, eh... he's asking about McDonalds. Says he has a witness that places you there with the twins a couple of hours after the murder. That doesn't look great, Quayle.'

I grunted, then took my hand from my forehead.

'You're letting me go in the middle of this case? The biggest case I've ever—'

'It's not the middle of the case,' Riordan said, standing up. 'It's the end. And we're going to let you sew it all up. As a last hurrah.'

I stared at him.

'It was the twins, Quayle,' Ashe said, mirroring Riordan by standing up too. Suddenly everybody but Fairweather was on their feet. 'Tomorrow morning we want you to charge them with double homicide to round up this case. It'll be your last act as a police officer.'

ALICE

My heart rate was definitely rising; practically thumping at my chest. I barely touched my ham; couldn't even stomach the fact that it was even sitting there under my nose for the best part of an hour. I pushed the plate forward and just sat back in my chair, waiting for everybody else to finish.

I literally went into that dining room confident we were going to end up as a hung jury, and left it absolutely petrified that Noel and Zoe were going to see that fucking video.

'Stay strong,' I whispered into Obese Guy's ear as we re-entered the jury room. He looked back at me and nodded once. Then we all sat.

'Right... so... interesting,' Scarhead says when everybody has finally settled. 'We were told that this was a possibility, but the judge has now confirmed it for us. We don't need a unanimous decision, we need a majority of ten; and from what I can gather we have nine in favour of a guilty verdict. Am I right in thinking that... yes? Perhaps raise your hands if your verdict is guilty.'

Nine hands fly up. The fuckers. Quiff is keeping his stare away from mine as he holds his hand aloft. He knows I'm pissed with him.

'So it's just you three,' Scarhead says, nodding to Obese Guy and then looking towards me and Red Head. 'I guess it'd be a good idea to ask you three for your opinion on why you feel the twins should be found not guilty, then perhaps if we could counter your arguments we may get a break-through in all this.'

I didn't answer. But I didn't have to. The nodding of heads from Obese Guy and Red Head did my answering for me.

'Okay... so Gerry, would you like to start? Why do you think Faith and Grace should be found not guilty of these murders?'

Obese Guy slaps his hands onto his enormous belly.

'My opinion on it hasn't really changed,' he says. 'This case hasn't been proved beyond all doubt.'

'Aren't you taking that a bit literally?' Thick-rimmed Glasses says. 'I mean, we can't know with absolute certainty; we can't rewind the clock, go inside the Tiddles' kitchen on August fifteenth two years ago and witness the bloody crime, can we? Beyond reasonable doubt doesn't mean *absolute* proof, it doesn't mean a smoking gun, or a bloodied knife, as it would be in this instance. It just means did the prosecution prove the case? Well, given that the stab wounds came from children, given that the twins had the opportunity and the means to kill Clive and Dorothy. And given that nobody else's DNA – or any evidence whatsoever – was found at the scene... it all adds up to ample proof that the twins did this.'

Obese Guy brings his hands to rest on the table in front of him.

'I... I...'

'He's entitled to see the phrase reasonable doubt in whatever way he wants—'

'Shhh,' Thick-rimmed Glasses hisses at me. 'We will get to you, Alice,' he says. 'We are asking Gerry here for his opinion first.'

I grind my teeth. If Gerry breaks here, I'm screwed.

'I know what you're saying,' Obese Guy says to Thick-rimmed Glasses. 'It's just that in order for me to put those two children behind bars for years, perhaps even the rest of their lives, I would like much stronger proof than that. I'd actually like the bloodied knife. That'd help, wouldn't it? How come the prosecution didn't find that? I am not going to put these girls in prison just because a specialist says the stab wounds came from a child. There are a billion children in the world. And while I know Faith and Grace live with Clive and Dorothy and obviously had the, eh... means as you say... the stab wounds are not enough reason to convict. Do I think the stab wounds came from children? Yes. Do I believe those children were Faith and Grace? Well, it's very likely. But it hasn't been proven to me beyond doubt... so I am sticking to my verdict.'

Scarhead thumbs his scar.

'And is there anything that could sway you the other way?' he asks.

'I just... I just...' Obese Guy shrugs his shoulders. 'I don't think so, no. I'm sorry. I am. I'm sorry to everyone around this table who wants to get home, wants to get their life back to normal. But I am not sending two young girls to prison for decades just because us twelve have been put out for a couple weeks.'

He's argued well. But he hasn't filled me with confidence. I notice Scarhead look at Thick-rimmed Glasses... I think they feel they can win him over. He opened himself up for targeting when he admitted it was *very likely* the twins may have done it. I've no idea how strong he's going to hold. I need to do something. I need to convince Obese Guy.

I become conscious of my breathing, only because I have to. If I don't slow my breaths down I'm going to collapse onto this bloody carpet again. The palms of my hand are much wetter than they were when I did collapse yesterday. I hold my eyes closed and see the video of me being taken behind by Emmet again. And then I see Noel's face. Watching that video. Jesus Christ.

'And you?' Scarhead says. I open my eyes to answer him. Then notice it's not me he directed that question to. It's Red Head.

'Well,' she says, 'I agree with Gerry. The prosecution didn't prove the case to every degree...'

'This is ludicrous saying the prosecution didn't prove the case... what else did you want them to do?' Thick-rimmed Glasses says.

'Stop it,' Big Bust snaps at him. 'I thought we were giving these three a chance to talk.'

'Thank you, Gwen,' Red Head says. 'It's not just that... it's not just that I don't feel everything was proven, I... I genuinely don't believe they should even be here.'

'Huh?' Scarhead says, his brow all creased. 'What you talking about?'

'This is a court for adults. For crimes committed by adults.'

'Well, that's not true is it? Otherwise they wouldn't be here,' Thick-rimmed Glasses says leaning back in his chair all smug. He's becoming a bigger prick with every passing minute of these deliberations.

'They are only the second set of children ever to be tried for murder in these courts in the history of the legal system in Ireland,' Red Head says, in an effort to shut him up. 'And I didn't believe that first case should have been heard here either. Children's brains are only developing. They shouldn't be put behind bars for a considerable amount of time and then spending that time there as an adult for something they did when they were just kids.'

'Whoa, whoa, whoa,' Scarhead says. 'Are you saying you think they did it?'

My heart sinks. And my stomach rolls itself over. I rub at Red Head's arm, hoping she'll turn to me so I can nod my head at her in solidarity. But she doesn't turn back.

'It doesn't matter if I think they killed them or not—'

'Yes it does. Yes it absolutely does,' Thick-rimmed Glasses says. 'That's what your job is. Now it's a very simple question. Do you, or do you not, think the twins did it?'

'Yes.'

'No,' I say. Before I even knew I was going to say it; it just jumped out of my mouth.

I think the gasps coming from the far end of the table, from Scarhead and from Thick-rimmed Glasses, were more audible than my reaction.

Red Head turns to me.

'Don't worry, Alice,' she says. 'This is what's needed. The whole argument needs to be opened up.'

I rub at her arm again. But I get confused as arguments spark around the table.

'Calm down!' Scarhead shouts, shutting everybody to a silence. 'Sinead... let me get this straight. You feel Faith and Grace are guilty of this crime, but you will not find them guilty because you don't like the fact that this case skipped so many legal procedures in order to get the twins *here*... to Dublin's Criminal Courts?'

'But it *is* being held heard here,' Thick-rimmed Glasses says. 'And it isn't your bloody job to say where their case should be held. It's your job to say whether or not you feel Faith and Grace are guilty based on the evidence put in front of you during this trial. And I guess we all know where the evidence leads you. You think they're guilty.'

'I think we should hear from Alice,' Red Head says.

I pat my hand on top of Red Head's which is still gripping on to my bicep.

'I agree,' I say.

'What... that they did it and you are giving us a protest vote against the system?'

'No, no, no,' I say. 'I eh... agree with, eh.... sorry, what's your name again?'

'Gerry,' Obese Guy says, looking offended that I hadn't kept his name in my memory bank.

'Yeah... I agree with Gerry. I don't think the prosecution proved the case beyond reasonable doubt.'

Thick-rimmed Glasses stands up and begins to grip the back of his chair, his fingers whitening.

'There are alternatives,' I say. 'I know it's not our job to play judge or to play detective, but the money found in that safe tells me the Tiddles were not a very legitimate family. Somebody could have known about their money... we can't rule that out.'

'Ah, for fuck sake,' Thick-rimmed Glasses says. 'We're back to this bloody theory, are we? Accusing other people? Well, how the hell do you think Kelly McAllister benefited from killing Clive and Dorothy? She hardly got her hands on that cash at all, did she? The cops found it. So...' He shrugs a shoulder at me.

'Well, she got to run the church, perhaps all the money being generated through the church goes to her now. Or...' I pause. Because what I'm about to say doesn't really have any weight to it. 'Or Clive's sister Janet, who testified. I thought there was something dodgy about her when she was on the stand. She was so dismissive of her brother and sister-in-law. And now she has custody of the twins. Perhaps she feels they will bring her some money. Any idea what kinda money Child X and Y will get for their story once they're out of here?'

'Enough with the fucking conspiracies,' Thick-rimmed Glasses shouts, whipping off his glasses.

The sweat on my palms is getting ridiculous now, it's almost dripping from me. But I don't give a shit how many people shout. I certainly won't be changing my mind. And neither will Red Head. I'm certain of it. Her argument is moral. And moral arguments are as rock solid as arguments get. Besides, I'm still pretty sure she might be getting blackmailed just like I am. I look to Obese Guy. He seems shaken. I can't let him change his mind.

'I need to visit the toilet,' I say.

'Again?' Scarhead says, tutting.

'I just feel a little under the weather like I did yesterday. I suffer with hypertension. I, eh... Gerry,' I say, 'that trick you did for me yesterday with the cold water... could you show me how to do that again?'

Obese Guy wobbles his four chins up and down and then heaves himself from the chair before holding the bathroom door open for me. I purse a thin smile at him as I walk by and when the door closes behind us both we just stand there staring at each other.

'Gerry, please tell me you're not going to change your mind... please,' I whisper to him.

'Alice, I don't know what to think anymore.'

'Gerry! Stay strong.'

'Everyone thinks they did it. Even Sinead thinks they did it and she was saying they were not guilty from the start. And I... well, when she said that it made me really think if I genuinely feel they did it and... even though it wasn't proved beyond doubt, maybe I do believe they did it. I mean... I don't – and I mean no disrespect to you – but I don't believe in any of the other theories. Kelly McAllister? Janet Petersen? Nah,' he says, swaying his chins left and right. 'I don't even believe you believe those theories,' he says.

'Gerry, please. Please,' I say, taking a step towards him. I find myself leaning over his belly, my nose inches from his. 'Don't change your mind, Gerry,' I whisper towards his lips. Oh my God, the smell of his breath is disgusting; it's warm. But I need to do this. My life depends on it.

My lips meet his and I ever so slowly part them.

✝

Grace couldn't wait for them to go out... leave. Her legs were flexing with anxiety under the table.

'Okay darlings, we'll be back in a couple of hours, finish your breakfast,' Dorothy finally said. Then she and Clive shuffled down the hallway and out the door.

Grace turned immediately to her twin.

'Daddy climbed up a tree and hid a bag in the trunk last night.'

Faith looked up, then back down at her cereal bowl. But she immediately believed Grace. Because they both believed instantly and absolutely everything the other one said. She dropped her spoon into her bowl and then the twins raced each other to the back garden. After they'd juggled the stepladder over to the tree with a great deal of difficulty, Faith held the bottom while Grace climbed to the top. She knew what to do, had memorised it after watching Clive the night previous. She climbed onto one branch after stepping off the ladder, then felt for the hole behind the one above it; the one she was sure her father had dropped the bags into. But it was just a normal branch. She was baffled. So she started to feel around the branch, until her finger tips patted their way onto a tiny switch hidden behind a twig. She pressed the switch downwards, then yanked at the branch while trying to keep her footing steady. And the branch popped open; like a petrol cap on a car, leaving a gaping hole in the side of the trunk. Grace inched closer and, standing even more on her tip-toes, peered inside. Plastic bags. Bundles of them. All stuffed full. Maybe fifteen, twenty. There was no way she could ever get down far enough to get to them. If she had have climbed down, there was no way she could get back up.

She turned and informed Faith what she had found and then they both shrugged their shoulders.

'What you think is in them?' Grace asked after she closed the branch tight shut.

'Dunno. You?'

'Secret files maybe?'

'Maybe.'

It was money. All the money coming in through the church. Three years prior Clive and Dorothy had built a secret safe in the floorboards of their bedroom, which could fit a small person inside of it were they to lie down flat. But it didn't take long for that safe to fill up with over five hundred thousand in used notes. That's how much money they were turning over. Clive came up with the ingenious idea of hiding it in the tree when he was outside in the garden literally trying to think of an answer to his dilemma. He was staring up through the branches as he was wondering how he could keep the money in a safe place... and then a grin slowly started to appear on his face. He told Dorothy it was a sign from God. And she believed him. He almost believed himself, in truth. He made the contraption in the space of a month. It was so simple. But it was genius. A real branch that bore into a large hole that had already existed in the side of the tree. It was a ten foot deep natural cavity that fed into the main trunk. He found a branch that he could ensure looked naturally part of the tree and built a mechanism that would pop it open when a tiny switch was flicked. Not in a million years would anybody have thought the branch was fake; even up close to it. You would only ever find the switch to pop open that branch if that's what you were actually looking for. If you didn't know about the tree, you'd never know about the cavity.

Clive was pouring upwards of forty thousand into it every month. Sometimes the collections would come in close to a hundred thousand if they were running a fundraiser. At the point in which they were murdered, the Tiddles had almost five hundred thousand in used notes stacked in their bedroom safe of which they were living off day-to-day. And more than double that amount inside the trunk of that oak tree.

They were both into their fifties before they even sat down to discuss what they wanted to do with the money. Why they even needed it... If they even needed it... What they were actually collecting it for... After all, they weren't even spending any of it. Or rarely anyway. Not on themselves. They'd spend it on the church. Clive would update the bus every year or so. And they evolved the Community Centre into looking more and more like a modern church year on year. They'd spend cash on the latest sound systems; cushioned pews and the odd celebrity speaker.

The Tiddles never went on holiday, nor upgraded their home to anything bigger than the bungalow they were more than settled in. Even though they easily could have. They were literally lying on the money.

Both Clive and Dorothy were too busy collecting the cash that they genuinely never really got around to talking about how to spend it. They'd turned into robots, really; used to living day-to-day, running their 'family'. Thoughts of the future rarely consumed them. They never really thought of the cash as their reward, even though they had been obsessed about collecting it. Their main focus every day was to genuinely help people who were donating to them feel better. And, of course, to preach the word of the Lord Jesus Christ. That was always their main focus; preaching. They had been well and truly zombiefied into their own cult.

When they finally took the time to sit and discuss what to do with the money, they both agreed on a plan within a half an hour. They were going to start giving it back slowly to the people who had given it to them in the first place. They could redistribute the wealth as they saw fit. A few thousand here to Gertrude and Edin who were just about to get married; a few thousand to Brennan and Leanna who were expecting...

They made love the night they agreed to that plan, both feeling giddy from having a weight lift from their shoulders. It was the first time they'd had sex in eight years.

The Tiddles were the happiest they'd been in a long time as they dreamt up scenarios to financially help out their 'family' members. But what they were most excited about was what they had planned for the twins – even though it only put a tiny dent in the spend. As soon as they discussed the concept of holidays, Clive insisted on Florida first. For the girls. So they could have the time of their lives. They agreed to keep the tickets in the safe; and reveal them closer to the time, so they could record it on their phones and allow everybody to see the twins' reaction when they posted it on the church's Facebook page. It was all planned out. They both felt the twins were owed something really special. Clive and Dorothy discussed how much guilt they'd both been feeling having practically left them to look after themselves. And they both agreed they'd like to get closer to them during that holiday. No better place for a family to get closer than in the buzz of Disneyland.

The plan wasn't to give all of the money away. Far from it. Just a few quid to share around here and there, where and when needed. Dorothy was convinced Jesus had brought them to this destination; where they would have a lot of wealth to distribute amongst their 'family' as they saw fit – a bit like a mini Government. Clive genuinely just loved giving. Watching people's faces as they'd open up a gift or a donation from the Tiddles were among the most treasured moments of Clive Tiddle's life. He truly was a giver.

Though he hadn't really given much to Kelly McAllister lately. Not in the way he used to give to her. They'd long since stopped their affair. Clive couldn't risk it. If Kelly was going to go all 'leave your wife for me' on him, he didn't want to know. He was actually quite relieved that he'd lost the stress of the affair as soon as it ended. Though he did miss the sex.

'What we meeting here for?' Kelly said. She was still unsure of them at this point. Dorothy hadn't really spoken to her since swearing at her. And Clive had been distant ever since he'd put a halt to their stay overs at the Ibis Hotel. Kelly had begun to fade into the background and genuinely felt as if she was just one of the regular 'family' members by this stage, not special anymore. Except she was special. To both of the Tiddles. When they sat down to talk about who meant the most to them in their lives as they planned to distribute their wealth, they both felt guilty about how they'd treated Kelly over the previous year.

'We bought it for you,' Clive said.

'Huh?' Kelly looked around herself.

'Well... we put down a large deposit it on it and have arranged a small mortgage for you. It's all yours. This is your home now.'

It was a terraced home in a tiny estate of six houses at the foothill of the mountains. About a twenty-minute walk up the hill to the community centre where she desperately wanted to spend most of the hours of most of her days. It wasn't that far from The Velvet Inn either. Walkable. She genuinely thought Clive and Dorothy had called her to meet them in that strange house to tell her she needed to find another 'family', such was her hurt of having been shunned. The Tiddles spent more money on Kelly than they did on everybody else combined. She was that special to both of them. They wanted to show their appreciation after she'd spent so many years dedicating herself to The New St Benedict's Church. Besides, she needed the stability. She'd never owned her own home; had jumped from one cheap rental flat or bedsit to another since moving to Dublin. On top of that, Clive and Dorothy had become aware that she was spending more time in the pub and they wanted her to get back to being the Kelly they had once sobered up and who was a joy to be around.

Kelly really wanted to ask them where they got the money from to put such a large amount down on a house for her – out of politeness more than anything. But she never did. Because she knew the answer. And she knew it wasn't to be discussed. Never again.

The one family member they didn't give anything to was actually a blood relative. Janet was furious when she found out Clive and Dorothy had bought Kelly McAllister a home. Grace had let it slip over the phone one evening. Janet had kept in contact with the twins ever since their communion night. Not regular contact; just a phone call every other month. But only because she was fascinated by them. The night of their communion had really opened up Janet and Eoin's eyes as to what they considered the delusion of the church. Catching up with the twins was pretty much a source of entertainment for them. It made a change from just watching the soaps while cracking open another cheap six-pack of beers.

'You cheapskate bastard!' Janet roared down the phone to Clive. 'I have nothing, barely two pennies to rub together and you are buying somebody a bloody house!'

'Now calm down,' Clive said to his sister. But Janet was off on one; likely drunk. Or high. Or both. She and Eoin were the types who felt the world owed them something; the type of couple who'd sit on their arse all day and complain that they had nothing to do.

'You're a fucking freak. You're all freaks. In fact... you're more of a freak than the rest of them. Because you don't believe any of that shit. I know it. And you know it.'

Clive held the phone away from his ear. His sister had always been an odd sort, but this level of bitterness and anger was about her peak. He knew why she was so upset. Because the argument was all about money. And Janet and Eoin were scroungers.

Dorothy and Clive had never even considered offering them any finan-cial help. They weren't part of the church. They didn't deserve any riches if they didn't believe in Our Lord Jesus Christ. Even if they had been half-decent at keeping in contact with Faith and Grace over the past couple of years, they were still distant family as far as Clive and Dorothy were concerned. Real family got down on their knees. And they thanked Jesus every day for giving them life. As far as Clive was concerned, Janet wasn't grateful for anything. There was no way she was getting a penny of that money; especially as she hadn't even put a cent into the pot.

The twins were in their bedroom, unaware their father was having a row with his sister over the phone. In fact, they'd become so insular that they seemed to be unaware of almost everything that was going on. They only ever spent time in their bedroom, or at the community centre on Sundays, or quite often walking around their back garden.

Which is what Faith had been doing one afternoon before she raced as fast as she could through the kitchen, down the hallway and into her bedroom; slapping the door shut behind her.

She was panting heavily; disturbing Grace who was sitting up in bed reading passages from her Bible.

'Faith... you okay?' Grace said, dipping her eyebrows and slamming her Holy Book shut.

Faith was still panting. And she was pale. Very pale.

'You're not going to believe this,' she said.

DAY FIVE

Our heads were spinning; both mine and Sheila's. Though for different reasons.

She was reading over the paperwork Riordan had handed to me in a bright-white envelope, while I was sat on the floor of our bedroom, pouring over the CCTV footage on the small television that I'd managed to hook up to an old video recorder.

I watched Kelly sip on her vodka and coke; watched her scrunch up betting slips and toss them on to the table; watched her leave, presumably to visit the bookmakers next door, then come back in to sip on more vodka and coke just in time for the next race to start.

She did all this, practically on loop, for over four hours – up until just gone twenty past two that afternoon. And while she was doing that, Tommo Nevin was joking with his mates as he slugged back pint after pint of lager. Eight pints he sank in all the time Kelly was in that pub. He probably had just as many after I stopped watching the footage. But I didn't watch past the time Kelly left.

The only tiny suspicion I could find in the four hours and twenty minutes of grainy footage that I'd watched occurred just gone midday, when Kelly and Tommo happened to visit the toilets at the same time. After tossing another betting docket onto the table, Kelly got up and made her way to the narrow corridor that led to the ladies room. A minute later, Tommo left his pint on the bar and headed down the same corridor. There was no CCTV camera covering that area of the pub. Tommo came back into the bar before Kelly; rubbing his right hand up and down his shirt. I hope he was drying excess water on his shirt having just washed his hands, but given that he was so quick in there I fear it may probably have been piss. A full minute later Kelly walked into shot. She ordered another vodka and coke without paying anyone around her any attention. Then she sat back down and waited on the next horse race to begin.

'They could have been up to something here,' I said to Sheila.

'Huh?' she replied, looking up from the paperwork.

'Doesn't matter.'

'I don't see any catch in this at all, Denis,' she said. 'One hundred thousand euro redundancy package, plus full pay for the next twenty years... what are you going on about... what catch?'

I sighed, then paused the tape and joined her sitting up in our bed.

'I don't know if there's a catch in the paperwork... it's just the whole thing seems really sneaky. Why now? In the middle of the biggest case I'll ever have...'

'Because this case has just made them realise that Rathcoole Garda Station doesn't have the resources for this type of investigation. They're going to let you tie up the case... arrest the twins. Then you can rub your hands with it all. Then me and you can go do—'

'I can't arrest the twins when I don't think they did anything,' I said.

Sheila rubbed at my shoulder.

'I'm excited about this,' she said. 'We can spend as much time as we want in Tuscany... And we might as well do it while we're young enough and our legs can still carry us up and down the vineyards.'

I leaned in to her to let her hold me and just about managed to stop myself from crying. It wasn't that I was upset about Faith and Grace, or the case in any way. It was the manner in which I was being dealt with. 'Thanks for your service, off ye go now.' Though in truth, the offer was a fair one. *Very* fair.

I fell asleep in my wife's arms that night – the first time in those four nights that I actually had a decent sleep. When my alarm beeped, Sheila turned in the bed.

'Did a night's sleep help you make up your mind?' she asked. I got out of bed and headed for the shower without answering her. I wasn't being rude. She knew what I meant. I didn't have an answer.

I grabbed breakfast on the go; munching on a banana and a cereal bar as I drove to the station. My mind was whirring; but for once it wasn't the dead bodies of Clive and Dorothy Tiddle that were consuming me, nor their cute little twins. It was my wife. Her eyes lit up last night when I showed her that paperwork. It was nice to have her back at the forefront of my thoughts. She'd gone missing from them over the previous days.

'You're here early,' I said to Fairweather. I noticed she was already dressed for the golf course; a pale green polo-buttoned shirt, navy casual slacks.

'Just getting the paperwork in order,' she replied. 'What about you... you signed on the dotted line yet?'

I took a seat opposite her and then pinched the bridge of my nose.

'Oh... I don't know about this, Fairweather,' I said. 'I just have a feeling I'm only being offered this because they don't want me working for the force anymore. They're giving Johnny and Sully new roles... why haven't they offered me and you one?'

'Well because we're old farts – near retirement age we are.'

'Speak for yourself,' I said to her. Fairweather was sixty-two, bang on the average age for a police officer to hang up their handcuffs. I was four years short of that, still firmly set in the routine and security my day job offered me.

'C'mon Quayle. Hasn't Sheila's cancer made you think about what's most important in life? Don't you two want more quality time together, more adventures? You're not getting any younger.'

'It's not that,' I said. 'Of course the money would be good, spending more time with Sheila would be great...'

'Learning how to play golf...'

'Yes... golf,' I said, puffing out a laugh. 'But... but it's not about the advantages this pay-off gives me that I'm worried about. It's *why* they are offering it. That's what I want to know. It feels shallow, feels as if they just don't think I'm a good enough detective. They think I fucked up this case. I didn't. I'm the only one bloody working on it. Five hours I spent watching CCTV footage last night... The whole offer, it doesn't sit right with me. It just makes me feel like shit, to be honest.'

'Quayle... don't be stupid. Take the offer.'

I pinched my nose again, more to stop the tears from falling than anything.

Footsteps shuffled outside Fairweather's door and then knuckles rattled against it.

'Come in,' Fairweather called out.

Ashe entered, his lips pursed at both of us.

'Hope you both slept well,' he said, 'given the circumstances.'

Fairweather entertained him with chit-chat about her acceptance of his retirement offer while I just sat there, pinching the bridge of my nose.

'You ready to visit the twins?' Ashe asked me.

I shook my head.

'I can't... I can't arrest them when I am not certain of their involvement in these murders,' I said. He didn't reply. He just perched his ass on to the corner of Fairweather's desk and folded his arms. 'I was pouring over footage of Tommo Nevin and Kelly McAllister last night. There's something really sneaky about those two...'

'And let me guess, you didn't find anything?' Ashe said. I stared at him, then at Fairweather. 'Faith and Grace are going to be arrested. You don't have to do it, of course. Tunstead can do it. We just thought it'd be nice for you to finalise this case before you retired.'

I stood up and paced the small square of Fairweather's office.

'I just... I can't... Kelly McAllister. There's something up with her. A Christian, a believer who loves to drink vodka and bet on horses during her day off?'

Ashe shook his head.

'You think Christians don't drink... don't have any bad habits? Jesus, Quayle, in my thirty-odd years of dealing with the dodgy people, I've found these Jesus freaks to be the dodgiest of the lot. Anyway...' he says to me, 'what CCTV footage were you pouring over?'

'Kelly McAllister and Tommo Nevin drink in the same pub.' Ashe glanced at Fairweather. 'They know something about these murders.'

'What was the footage of?'

'Them inside the pub, the morning of the killings.'

'And did you see anything of suspicion?' I sighed, then shook my head. 'What time was the footage from?'

'Half ten, around about the time of the killings.'

'Hold on... they were both in the pub at the time of the killings and you think they had something to do with it?'

'I don't know, I don't know,' I said, placing both hands on top of my head and clasping my fingers.

'If they were in the pub while Clive and Dorothy were being stabbed to death then that clears them... why were you watching that CCTV for hours if it is literally their alibi?'

I shrugged my shoulders.

'Maybe they are in it together, maybe they hired somebody to kill Clive and Dorothy while they used The Velvet Inn's CCTV as their alibi.'

Fairweather and Ashe shared another glance.

'Quayle,' Fairweather said, standing up. 'Listen to yourself. Do you really think Kelly McAllister and Tommo Nevin paid a hit-man to kill Clive and Dorothy Tiddle?'

I held my eyes shut when she said that. Because I knew it sounded ridiculous when said out loud.

The cringing didn't leave me, nor the frustration, for the entirety of the drive to Monaghan. Ashe drove in his car. We didn't talk much about the case at first; he just let me reflect on my twenty-five years as an officer; asking about my favourite colleagues over the years, my favourite cases.

When we eventually turned the conversation to the Tiddles, a lot of what he was saying made sense. Gerd Bracken taking over the twins' case spoke volumes. It was a siren that should have sounded for me yesterday. But it didn't. Bracken taking over Faith and Grace's case meant they *needed* defending.

He beamed his bright-white veneers at me again when we finally arrived at the Petersen house. He was a strange looking man, but magnetising in some way. His skin was orange, not light brown or tanned, but dusky orange. Like a Wotsit. Yet despite that, he was handsome in a weird way.

Ashe allowed me to enter the living room first, into the sound of the cartoons.

Grace glanced over at me, then stood up from the sofa. I think she was anticipating another hug. But I remained upright.

Ashe picked up the TV remote control to press at the standby button. And that's when Faith noticed, for the first time, that we were all in the room.

I hunched down to a bended knee position, just as I had the first time I'd met them.

'Faith and Grace,' I said, really slowly. 'I am arresting you on suspicion of the murder of your parents Clive and Dorothy Tiddle.'

ALICE

I can feel him against my stomach. Hard. Clammy. And oddly round. Like a potato. I'm not sure what's worse; his bulge pressing against me or his saliva inside my mouth. I can actually taste his ham lunch.

I pull away from him, and as I do, he brings a fingertip to his mouth to mop up the saliva that's about to drip from his bottom lip.

'Wow, Alice,' he says, grinning at me.

I want to turn around, run into the cubicle and vomit all of the disgust-ingness away. But I can't. So I just stand still. And swallow.

'You, eh... you won't change your mind, Gerry, right?' I say.

He wobbles his chins from side to side, then beams a huge smile at me. And as he does, I glance down at his pants and notice his bulge is still sticking towards me. Jesus, it *is* shaped like a bloody potato.

'Right, well, let's just get out of here and—'

'Whoa,' he says, reaching a hand either side of my waist. 'Let's have another...' His face pushes down to mine and I allow our lips to touch. But I lean back almost instantly.

'Enough, big boy,' I say. 'You need to calm down.' I point at his bulge. He places a hand over it and chuckles like a teenage boy. 'You need to put that away and compose yourself before you get back around that table. We just need to stay strong.'

'But can we... eh... can we do this again?' he says.

I nod.

'Sure... if we win, if we hold out and this is a hung jury, you and I can celebrate in style.' I wink at him.

He chuckles again as I turn to the tap to rinse my hands. I'd rather be rinsing my mouth.

After I've dripped my hands dry, I turn the latch in the door.

'See you out there, big boy,' I whisper.

I leave him standing with his potato boner still stretching towards me, and when I get back to the jury room I purse my lips at the jurors before I sit.

'All better now?' Red Head asks.

'Much better,' I say. Which is the truth. Obese Guy ain't going to change his mind. This jury's going to be hung. I know it.

I stare directly at his crotch as soon as he returns from the bathroom. I think he's still hard. Or maybe he always has that bulge. I wouldn't know. I'd never looked in that area before it started to stab at my stomach while we were kissing. As soon as he sits down he eyeballs me and curls up one side of his mouth. Uuugh. I can't believe I've just let him snog my face off. I feel filthy. As if I wanna take a scrubbing brush to my tongue. But that kiss has pretty much just saved my life. So I need to just suck it the hell up.

'Okay... well are we sure we're all set to continue our deliberations?' Scarhead says. We all nod and then he shuffles his paperwork again. 'Alice, you do look better. Whatever trick it is Gerry has for stopping anxiety, it sure works. Now... please listen, you two,' he says slowly. 'We didn't discuss the trial when you were in the bathroom, I promise. But we did discuss where we should take deliberations next. As you know, we are sitting on a fine line between giving the judge a verdict or not... some jurors feel we should discuss the investigation again, does that sit okay with you two?'

I turn my lips downwards and shrug my shoulders.

'Whatever you guys wanna do,' I say.

Gerry mumbles a 'yes', then eyeballs me again to offer another half-smile. He's revolting.

'Lisa here...' Scarhead says, 'would like to discuss something she thinks is quite significant.'

Braces sits more forward in her chair.

'It's just...' she says, 'don't we all think it's rather strange that everybody who took the stand in this trial feels as if the twins are guilty? From the two representatives of Tusla, the detectives, the stab wound experts, the forensics experts, Kelly McAllister, even the twins' dance teacher Claire Barry. Doesn't this tell us all something? Even people who are close with the twins feel they did it. Anyone investigating the case thinks they did it.'

'Not true,' I say.

'Well... I assume you are talking about Detective Quayle,' Braces says to me.

'Uh-huh,' I say, 'he is on record as telling the girls' own defence lawyer that he didn't think they did it. He practically said it in a press conference too. So you can't go around saying *everybody* involved in the case says they did it, especially when the lead detective himself—'

'He arrested them, for crying out loud, Alice,' Thick-rimmed Glasses says.

I shrug, trying to match the prick with his own level of pretentiousness.

'Please... continue,' Scarhead says to Braces.

'I actually don't think Quayle feels they're innocent. I think he did, initially, think that. During the investigation. But now I believe he thinks they're guilty – but was just too damn proud to admit he was wrong on the stand.'

'It seems to me as if this is arguing second guesses,' Red Head says. 'That's how you think you'll win a guilty verdict?'

'No, it's not that...' Braces seems more intimidated by Red Head's response compared to mine. She shuffles in her chair, then rings her hands.

'Listen, I've already admitted to you that I think the twins are guilty of this crime but that I disagree with how the legal system has handled this case from the beginning,' Red Head says. 'But you're gonna need better arguments than that to win a guilty verdict.'

Thick-rimmed Glasses lets a frustrated gargle erupt from the back of his throat, then tosses the pen he'd been fidgeting with onto the table.

'Do you not understand how stubborn and arrogant you sound, Sinead?' he says before he presses his two palms against his face. When he removes them, he sighs. 'I'm trying not to get too frustrated, I don't want to shout,' he says. 'But we've been the best part of two days deliberating this trial. I'm sure you can appreciate that all of us who are in no doubt that the girls are guilty are rather frustrated by the fact that you agree with us... yet you disagree with the system. Well, we're not here to judge the system. We are only here to judge the case put in front of us. Now, if you continue to suggest that you feel the girls are guilty of this crime, yet you refuse to find them guilty of this crime, I am going to suggest that our Head Juror makes Judge Delia McCormick aware of your opinion. I'd be very interested to see what the judge has to say about that.'

Another eerie silence washes across the table. Red Head looks to me, and I, very nonchalantly, shake my head at her.

'Don't let him bully you,' I whisper, though it isn't a well-disguised whisper. I know he heard me, the whole table could hear me in that silence.

'This is getting like a football match, or American politics,' Scarhead says. 'Everybody taking sides and refusing to acknowledge anything the opposition are saying. It's actually getting quite pedantic and, may I say, immature. From both sides.'

Everybody shuffles in their chairs. I don't give a shit if he thinks I've acted immaturely or pedantically. I just want to save my marriage, save my relationship with my daughter. Jesus, I've even gone to the lengths of snogging that grotesque-looking fat fuck at the other end of the table. Being seen as immature or pedantic is more than fine by me. Once we're a hung jury, I don't give two shits what anybody around this table thinks.

'It's now coming up to half-past three,' Scarhead says, flicking his wrist to glance at his watch. The judge has let us out at four-thirty every day of this trial, so I imagine it'll be the same today. We have one hour left to sort this out... or we come back again on Monday morning.

'Might not have to return,' I say, my arms crossed under my breasts. 'Judge might call a hung jury by the end of proceedings today, this could be all over in an hour.'

Ripples of chatter reverberate around the table. Gerry seems to instantly get into a heated discussion with Big Bust.

'I don't care!' he shouts. 'I won't be changing my mind!'

He looks down at me and nods slightly after arguing his point. And I cringe inside.

'Okay, okay... enough. Enough already,' Red Head shouts above the chatter, shutting everybody up instantly. She places her two hands wide across our side of the table. 'Thank you,' she says as she sits back down. 'If you could all please give me a minute to explain myself. I think you'll find what I have to say somewhat important.' I notice a number of jurors lean forward on the table. I think, although she has been not guilty from the start, they kind of respect Red Head in some way. I guess she's argued every point sensibly and, dare I say it, *maturely* from the beginning. Especially compared to me and Gerry. I've just come off as some mad woman; disruptive and arguing and fainting. And poor Gerry's just come off as the absolute buffoon around the table. 'They are only children,' she says. 'It is totally unfair that their case has made it to these courts. Not only that... the exposure of this case was so magnified and so sensationalised by a media we have been conned into thinking is unbiased. All media outlets in Ireland are biased – biased towards sensationalism. They only care about *a* story; they don't care about *the* story.' Two jurors remove their forearms from the table. 'The twins, in my opinion, were practically convicted by newspaper headlines two years ago. And the media has never let off since.'

'Why are you fixated on the media? We weren't supposed to be privy to anything about this case before it came to court,' Big Bust says.

Red Head shows the palms of her hands.

'C'mon, Ireland's tiny. We all know it. I didn't research the case. I didn't know everything about the case in any detail until I was put on the jury. But did I read headlines and see bulletins on the TV? Yes. How could we escape that?' she says.

I hold my breath and ever so slowly glance around the table.

'Well I didn't read anything. I just maybe heard the odd thing about Child X and Y,' Big Bust says.

'Exactly,' Red Head says. 'That's all I'm saying... that we all knew about Child X and Y in some capacity. We couldn't escape it.'

'It's just you seem to know an awful lot about it, Sinead,' Thick-rimmed Glasses says. 'You have said you even have opinions on what court this case should have been heard at.'

'Well, hold on, let me stop you there,' she says, 'because I think you're going to like what I have to say.'

Red Head places a hand on my arm, grasping my elbow lightly. I look up at Obese Guy and squint my eyes at him. What the fuck does she mean by saying Thick-rimmed Glasses will *like* what she has to say?

'I was so hopeful that this case would get the fair trial and the fair hearing it deserves. For the children. Those poor children. Can you imagine? Nine years of age, your parents have just been killed in cold blood and you are arrested for their murder? Imagine if they didn't do this... just think about that for one second. I came onto this case as balanced and as open-minded as you can be as a juror. I wanted those children to have the fairest of trials. Because this court... it really only should be for adults, no matter the crime. This case needed a fair investigation. From what I understand, it didn't really get one. Not just because Detective Quayle fumbled, but because of how the girls were treated from the off. Arrested, then rear-rested. Questioned initially without actual legal representation. Silly press conferences. Statements made to Gerd Bracken by Detective Quayle the first night they met... No matter what angle you look at it from, the investigation was a circus.'

I form a ball with my fist under the table and punch some air. Relief more than anything. I wasn't sure where she was going with this initially.

'This case also needed a fair trial. But with Gerd Bracken taking over the defence pro bono, just to get the exposure he knew this case would bring him, I've never felt this trial was going to be balanced. He was as likely to sensationalise this trial as much as the media. But thankfully, the case got a fair judge. And, I must say, it also got a fair jury. I was really, really intent, when I was appointed to this trial, to make sure this jury was as fair as it could be. I wanted us to argue every nook and cranny of this case; discuss the investigation, the treatment of the children, the witnesses, the DNA – or lack of it – the timeline... and we did. We argued the shit out of it all until we started to repeat ourselves.'

I place my hand on her knee. And she puts her clammy hand on top of mine.

'No,' I say. Out loud. Something about her touch has really unnerved me.

'I wanted to hold out,' she says.

'No,' I say again. More panicked this time. 'Tell her, Gerry, tell her.'

Gerry bolts upright, finally clocking what's going on.

'No, Sinead,' he says. 'Don't give in.'

'I'm not giving in, Gerry,' she says. 'I had my mind made up the moment this trial finished. I've been holding out. Because I wanted to give our deliberations the best shot. As soon as the trial finished yesterday morning I said to myself that I'd give it until close of play on Friday.'

'No. No. No. Sinead,' I say. I claw at her, gripping her shoulder. 'You're not... are you?'

She nods her head once at me, then turns to the table.

'The twins are guilty. I just wanted to give them the best possible argument they could get – '

'No... No... Gerry, convince her, convince her,' I say. And as soon as I say it I hear myself. I sound like one hell of a desperate bitch. Probably because I am a desperate bitch.

I sit back in my chair, my mouth wide open, my hands flopped to my side.

'So... so you want me to ring it in?' Scarhead asks, in what sounds like slow-motion.

'Well, that's ten:two now, right?' Thick-rimmed Glasses sounds as if he's miles away, talking at us through a tiny tunnel.

'Yeah, let's just confirm it,' Scarhead says. 'Can I have a raise of hands from those whose verdict is now guilty?'

I squeeze my eyes firmly shut, because I can't bring myself to see the number of hands in the air.

TODAY

Sheila nudges me as soon as the jury's door snatches open, and we both immediately sit more upright on our bench.

I'm not sure how to feel sitting here now. Though the cannabis always seems to keep my heart rate at a steady pace and my mind in a happy place. Most experts on the TV this morning were saying that the longer the jury were out, the more likely it was that they would acquit. Me and Sheila spent much of the day talking about it – she disagrees with the experts; is adamant the twins are going down.

None of the twelve jurors look out to the court as they enter; every single one of them keeping their stare straight and focused.

After they're all seated, the door to our left opens and I lean forward, just to get a look at them. Sometimes Grace looks up at me, but not always. And not today.

'All rise,' a call shouts. And then Judge Delia McCormick enters from the back door and strides her way to her throne.

She flicks through some paperwork on the desk, then clears her throat to signal that she needs everyone's attention. Though she didn't need to do that; all eyes were glued to her already, every ear poised.

'I understand you have reached a verdict,' she says, looking over her glasses at the jury.

'We have, Your Honour,' the Head Juror says.

Then Judge McCormick falls silent as she shuffles her paperwork around some more; as if she's teasing us... holding us all in suspense.

I look to Gerd Bracken. He seems nervous. I've never observed him like this before; holding a balled fist to his mouth and gnawing at it.

'I speak to every occupant of this court room,' the judge says, her voice booming. 'Regardless of the jury's findings, I am warning that *any* overreaction to the reading of their verdict will see you held in contempt of this court.'

The courtroom falls silent again; nobody even daring to whisper while Judge McCormick shuffles through her paperwork. Again.

'Okay,' she says, finally. 'Can the Head Juror pass the jury's verdict to the foreperson.'

A young woman dressed all in black takes a sheet of paper from the juror with the scar and then trots her way to the centre of the court-room and unfolds it.

'In the case of the state versus Grace and Faith Tiddle, charged with the double homicide of Clive and Dorothy Tiddle,' she says, 'we, the jury, find both of the accused guilty.'

Gasps are sucked in from all directions around us. But that's it. No overreaction. No screaming. No cheering. No sobbing. Just audible, sharp intakes of breath. Then silence.

I lean more forward to stare down at the crowns of Faith and Grace's heads. They don't move an inch. Not until Bracken's assistant leans towards Grace to whisper something into her ear. And then Grace passes on the message by turning to her sister. Faith's shoulders heave slowly up and down, and then both twins sit still and silent again.

'Told you,' Sheila whispers, nudging her knee against mine.

I spin around to take in the reaction of some of the faces behind me; Kelly McAllister wiping a tear from her eye with a folded handkerchief, and Janet Petersen staring down at her lap before her husband Eoin cups her face to bring it towards his.

'C'mon you, turn around... it's all over now,' Sheila says, placing a hand to my knee.

I face her, kiss her, and as I am doing so, I hear the judge dismissing Faith and Grace from the courtroom. Both of them are handcuffed in front of the gallery – which hadn't been done through this trial even though they spent all of it behind bars – before they're led back out through the side door they had both just entered five minutes ago.

Bracken and his assistant are in animated conversation below me; clearly not happy.

The judge coughs again, silencing the slight murmur of chatter that is threatening to grow in volume.

'I want to thank everybody in this courtroom for their cooperation in what I can at best describe as a unique court case,' she says. 'Thank you to the witnesses who took to the stand for their expertise and honesty,' Sheila nudges her knee against mine again, 'and to both the defence and prosecution teams. There were strong arguments and strong disagreements from both sides of this courtroom, but I am glad to say I feel both the defence and the prosecution behaved in the manner this courtroom demands... Even you, Mr Bracken.' The judge holds her smile closed, but some members of the court chuckle. Bracken just remains still, a fist still held to his mouth. 'But I would most of all like to thank the jury who had the biggest decision of all to make. I am truly grateful you took your time to argue this out – even though I did suggest to you at lunch-time today that a unanimous verdict was not a requirement.'

The judge pauses to glance down at her notes and as she does I hear the door behind me sweep open. I stare back, to see Janet and Eoin sneaking out before the judge has even completed her summoning up.

'I, too, now have a big decision to make,' the judge says. 'I, like you jurors, will not take my decision lightly. I am going to give myself ample time to research and think this through. I note in my diary I have an available date exactly four weeks from now. So that is when I will recall Faith and Grace Tiddle to the courtroom to hand down sentencing. I can ensure you that it will be a sentence pertinent to the courts in which they were tried. But I will take my time to ensure all procedure is followed and that justice is served in the proper manner. This case has been as unique for me as it has been for you all. This day four weeks is May twenty-sixth. Court dismissed.'

Everybody seems to stand at the same time. And suddenly we're all trying to crush our way out of the double doors at the back of the courtroom.

'Think we can get a flight out on Sunday?' Sheila whispers to me as we get enveloped in the crowd.

'I'm sure we can... I need to get my hands on some of that sun cream I like... the spray-on one.'

'Don't worry,' she says. 'I've already bought it. It's packed in the suitcase.'

I'd love to have my mind in Tuscany right now, just as Sheila has. Just as I promised Sheila I would have as soon as this trial was over. But my mind is whirring with the case still, even though we've just heard the full-time whistle. Ever since I retired, myself and Sheila decided we were going to live out our remaining years just as we'd always dreamed we would. Since I took retirement we've begun to split our years into quarters. We spend January to March in Florida. We love it out there. But American policy says we can only stay in the country for up to ninety days a year. So we do. Literally ninety days every time. Then we head off to a rustic villa in Tuscany, only this year that trip was delayed because of the trial. We don't mind. We've lots of years left. Sheila has shown absolutely no signs of illness since she started on the cannabis. She still has a tumour, but it seems to be reducing in size every time it's measured. For the end of the summer – from July to September – we aim to visit a different country each year. Last year we spent most of our time in southern Portugal. This year we plan on going to the south of France. And then from October until the New Year, we stay at home. In Dublin. Some of our friends have said we're crazy coming home for the winter; that if they had our freedom and our money, they'd go somewhere nice and hot for Christmas. We tried that the first year. It doesn't work. It's not supposed to be hot at Christmas. Besides, there is something so warm about Dublin in the winter months.

I relax my shoulders when my wife holds my hand just as the crowd separates before us to make it through the main entrance.

'Excuse me, Detective... eh, *Mr* Quayle, Faith and Grace have requested to speak with you. Do you mind?'

A middle-aged man I'd never laid eyes on before points his whole hand in the opposite direction of the oncoming crowd.

I look at my wife, and she nods her head.

'Sure,' I say. Then I take Sheila by the hand and we begin to slalom through strangers to follow the middle-aged man. Eventually we turn left into a quiet corridor and make our way to the bottom of it, stopping outside a large brown door.

'They're in there, Mr Quayle.'

I stare at the door and shake my head with wonder.

'Thank you, but do you know—'

I stop talking. Because the man has disappeared. It's just me and Sheila. And that brown door. Sheila shrugs her shoulders at me. Then I shrug one of mine back at her before I push gently at the door.

'Won't be long,' I whisper to her.

It's a long, skinny room. Not unlike the corridors we just strolled down. I shuffle quietly towards the familiar frame of Gerd Bracken in the distance perched on a desk, his back to me.

'I could fuckin' kill her,' a lady's voice says.

'Relax, Imogen,' Bracken replies. 'We only had one juror this time... we usually have three or four, that's why we never get beaten. We just didn't get enough jurors with dirt this time.'

'That's my fuckin' record gone up in the smoke,' Imogen says. 'Losing doesn't suit me.'

My eyebrows raise. I can't believe that when this girl eventually speaks, she's full of vulgarity.

'You're not going to send that text are you?'

I stand there, unsure whether or not I should step in on their conversation. I'm not sure what they're talking about. Sounds to me as if they've just found out only one juror voted not guilty; it must have been an eleven-to-one loss.

'Ah... I don't fuckin' know,' Imogen says, snatching at a pen. 'I'll see what mood I'm in when I finish this shit.'

She clicks at the pen and then begins scribbling on some paperwork. Bracken spins off the desk and almost baulks when he sees me.

'Detective Quayle.... I, eh, hope you, eh...' He looks shaken. The fucker's not used to losing.

'Sorry for creeping up on you,' I say. 'I didn't mean to... you, eh... didn't hear me come in and... a man told me the twins requested I drop by.'

Bracken looks over his shoulder at Imogen who has strangely re-transformed into the little bookworm I always assumed she was.

'What, ehm... what did you hear us saying, Detective Quayle?' Bracken asks.

'Not much. You were discussing the jury... you only managed to win over one juror, is that right?'

He laughs. And slaps his hand on the desk.

'That's exactly it,' he says. 'The twins... they are just in here. Officer Coulter!' he calls out.

Another door at the end of this room opens and I hear the click of their shoes before they appear. They're both handcuffed, and both wearing the same expression they have done ever since I first met them almost two years ago. An expression that says absolutely nothing.

'We just wanted to say thanks anyway, Detective Quayle. Thanks for trying.' They say it in unison. As if they've rehearsed it.

I raise an eyebrow at them.

'I wish you both the best,' I say, and then I turn to leave.

'Detective Quayle,' Grace calls after me. I stop, and spin slowly. 'We, eh... we were wondering, because you never said so in the trial. But... did you ever stop believing in us?'

I huff out a small laugh and then move towards her before crouching down to bended knee.

'Course I stopped believing you,' I said. 'It just took me a little longer than everybody else.'

'Hey!' Bracken calls out, placing a palm to my shoulder. 'You will not engage with my clients in that manner—'

'Shut the hell up, Bracken,' I say, shrugging him away from me. 'I've heard enough of your voice over the past two weeks. You lying toad. The truth never seems to leave your lips, does it? I've had more than a lifetime of hearing your voice.'

I turn and pace towards the brown door and when I snatch it open, Sheila's smile stops me in my tracks.

'That was quick,' she says. 'Did they not have much to say?'

I shake my head.

'Not really.' Then I close the door tight behind me and grab at my wife's hand. 'Now, my love,' I say, 'let's go home and see if we can book those flights for Monday, huh?'

ALICE

I peer from the top of our street, resting a hand to Mrs Balfe's garden wall. I'm looking for any unusual movement from my house. Not that I'd expect Noel – if he had been sent the video – to be stomping around the front garden ranting and raving like a madman. Yet for some reason I've been standing here staring at my house for at least five full minutes... just waiting. Pausing. Gazing. Hesitating more than anything, I guess.

I hear a cough and glance over my shoulder.

'Ah hello, Mrs Balfe,' I say.

She smiles her gums at me. A slightly warmer response than I got from her two days ago. Though I guess that time I was keeled over, trying to puke anything out that would come up from my stomach. I'm not sure why that's not what I'm doing right now. Perhaps my stomach's on strike from rolling itself over. Because that's all it's done the past forty-eight hours. Bizarrely enough, after Red Head outed herself as the moral compass of our jury, my stomach, for some reason, stopped spinning. Not sure why. Maybe because there was nothing I could do about it anymore. It was out of my hands from that moment onwards. My life was now all in the hands – or at the finger tips to be more precise – of the bitch who hacked into my phone. All she has to do is tap at her screen once and my life is over.

I've dialled her number ten times since I got out of court about half an hour ago. But her phone's dead. I've also texted twice; both times pleading that she doesn't send the video to Noel or Zoe. I was adamant as I could be in the texts that I had done the best I could; that I was really impressive in arguing for not guilty.

The keys jingle in my shaking hands as I attempt to slot one into the keyhole.

When it finally goes in, I turn the lock, sneak quietly inside and take off my coat to hang it over Noel's on the butt of our bannister. Then I sniff.

Stir fry. Noel's usual Friday evening dinner. Things are running as normal. I let out a grateful breath and then head for the kitchen, passing the shouting voices and guns shooting from Alfie's video games in the back room.

Noel's back is to me as he shuffles at the pan. But he's whistling. So I don't have to see his face to know he's in good form.

'Evening,' I say.

He spins around, his eyes narrow. Then he unties the apron from around his waist and strides over to me. He leans closer, kisses my cheek.

'I heard it on the news... Must have been a tough day,' he says.

'Long,' I reply, sighing.

'Least it's all over now, and those crazy twins are behind bars. You called guilty practically from the start of this trial. I'm proud of you. Sit down... I'll have dinner ready in a few minutes. And a nice bottle of red. Then you can tell me all about it.'

I scan the countertops of our kitchen after he's turned back to the frying pan.

'Where is, eh... where's your phone?' I ask.

He pats at his trousers pockets, then nods towards the hallway.

'Must be still in my jacket,' he says.

He hasn't checked his phone since he got home... that must be an hour or so ago now. Maybe she *has* texted him. Maybe he just hasn't bloody seen it.

'What ye need it for?' he asks as I make my way back towards the hall.

'I thought I had Debra and Paul's number in my phone but it seems to have disappeared. I just want to store it again...'

There's tension music playing from Alfie's game as I walk past... hitting my current state of mind right in the fucking bullseye. I lift my coat and then tug at Noel's, and feel weight in the inside pocket. I grab for the phone and immediately tap into it.

One text message alert.

My shoulders arch up to my ears.

Then I let out a slow exhale.

It's only Shay – Noel's friend from the quiz team... bantering about a question they got wrong last night.

'What you smiling at?' Alfie says, startling me.

'Oh... nothing,' I reply, and then he pulls open the door to the down-stairs toilet, walks inside and slams it shut behind him.

'Alfie!' Noel shouts, startling me again.

I palm his phone into my trouser pocket.

'He's in there,' I say.

'C'mon,' Noel says to me, holding the kitchen door open. 'Dinner's ready.'

I kiss my husband on the lips as I walk by him and then take a seat.

Chicken stir fry in soy sauce. He knows that's my favourite.

Alfie bundles out of the loo and into the kitchen without, I bet, washing his hands. But I'm sick of telling him and am way too tired for that conversation again.

'Another stir fry?' he grunts.

Little shit.

'Why don't you make dinner for us tomorrow instead, huh?' I say. He doesn't answer that. Never does.

Noel pulls out a chair and sits into it, then he pours us both a glass of red.

'Would you rather not talk about it then?' Noel asks.

'Eh...' I shake my head. 'I, eh... the stir fry looks delicious... is this a different soy sauce?'

He laughs. And so do I.

Alfie looks up at us and rolls his eyes.

'Well, even if you don't want to talk about it, I just want to say we're proud of you, aren't we, Alfie?'

'Yes, Ma,' Alfie replies. 'I am... seriously. What ye did, it was, eh... brave.'

I'm taken aback. Alfie hasn't so much as paid me a bit of notice, never mind a compliment, in years.

'Brave? Thank you,' I say, taking a sip of wine.

'How long do you think they'll go to prison for?' Alfie asks.

'Hold on, son... your mother doesn't want to talk—'

'It's okay... it's fine, Noel. It's nice to have you involved in our conversation at dinner, Alfie,' I say, rustling at his hair. 'Truth is, I don't know how long they will have to spend in prison. There's never been anything like this kind of case in Ireland before. Could be twenty years... could be life. I mean, it's unlikely they'll ever be children again, not in the outside world.'

He scrunches up his face and then shovels a forkful of stir fry into his mouth.

'How long do you think they should go to prison for though?' he asks, chewing.

I blow out my lips.

'Life,' I say. 'They don't belong in society, these girls.'

'Wow,' Noel says, laughing with his mouth full.

'Does that sound really harsh?' I say.

He nods his head and as he does, Alfie laughs. And I feel something I haven't felt in way too long. Happy. So I laugh too. Out loud. Until I see the hall door swing open behind Noel and in that instance I am certain my life is about to end. It's Zoe. And she's stomping straight towards me.

'How did you get on, Mam?' she says, holding her arms out to me. I stand up and take her hug, my heart resetting.

'Well... this is nice,' I say. 'All four of us together for dinner, huh?'

'Ah sure I've been thinking about you all day. Especially how ill you looked the other night. Guilty it was, anyway. Just what you wanted. It must have been so tough. I'm proud of you, Mam,' she rubs the blades of my shoulder. And as she does, I laugh out loud. Again.

'Ah, so your dad ordered you both to turn up for dinner this evening and for you to say you were proud of me, huh?'

Alfie's the first to laugh, and then everybody follows.

'We're just here, cos we love you, Mam,' Zoe assures me as she pours herself a glass of red. 'Be nice for you to get back to normal, but I bet you have a story to tell, after all that, don't ya?'

'Oh yeah,' I say. 'Too fucking right I do.'

And everybody laughs again. Alfie particularly loudly. Because I rarely let him hear me swear.

'I'll get you a bowlful,' Noel says to Zoe.

'Lovely stuff, Dad,' she replies. And as she says that, she removes her phone from her jeans pocket and places it on the table beside her wine. I stare at the screen. It's blank. The smile drops from my face and my heart begins to thump. But I don't think it needs to. I really don't believe that bitch is going to text. She would have done it as soon as the case was called in court. Why would she wait?

Zoe teases Alfie about being locked in the downstairs back room, asking what he *really* gets up to in there.

'I hear what boys your age do,' she says, trying to embarrass him. Noel looks at me and grins.

'So how are you feeling now, Mam... overall?' Zoe asks.

I puff out a laugh that is almost a cry, too; my eyes instantly watering.

'I just... I just feel grateful,' I say.

Then Zoe's phone vibrates on the table at the exact same time Noel's buzzes against my thigh. And I know. I know right now in this moment that my life is fucked.

I drop my fork to my bowl as Zoe picks up her phone. And then, as soon as her thumb taps against the screen, I hear it...

My heavy panting.

Followed swiftly by my loud squeals of ecstasy.

✝

'We have to kill Mammy and Daddy,' Faith said, cramming her words in between heavy breaths.

Grace got to her feet and rubbed at both of her eyes.

'Huh?' she said.

Faith first tried to steady her breathing, then her body, by gripping the magazine she was holding in her hands even tighter.

'We have to kill Mammy and Daddy. Jesus needs them. It says so... it says so in this,' she said, throwing the magazine onto her own bed. Grace bent down, picked it up and stared at the two-page spread her sister had left it open on. It was an article about the Menendez brothers – two young men who took the lives of both their parents in cold blood in America.

Grace looked up over the magazine spread and stared at her sister.

'But... but...' Grace stuttered. Then she tossed the magazine back onto her sister's bed. 'But it's just a story in a magazine.'

Faith shook her head.

'No it's not. The magazine was open on that page in our garden. Jesus left it there.'

Grace squinted, then picked up the two-page spread again and cast her finger down the side column.

'But, sure, there's a small article on this page about a butterfly too, one with four wings. A conjoined butterfly it's called; look, it says how rare they are. You sure Jesus is not sending us a message about butterflies?'

Faith shook her head again.

'No. It's about the main story – the killings. Killing parents. He wants us to do it.'

'No he doesn't. He can't. He can't,' Grace said.

Then she chicaned herself around the bed and reached an arm to her sister's shoulder.

'Why would he want us to kill Mammy and Daddy, Faith?'

'Cos maybe he wants them... maybe they're needed in Heaven. With him.'

'But then who'd look after us?'

Faith shrugged. Then she mirrored her sister by placing a hand to Grace's shoulder.

They both stood there for a moment in silence, forehead to forehead.

'Trust in the Lord with all thine heart; and not lean unto thine own understanding. In all thy ways acknowledge Him, and he shall direct paths.'

Faith whispered the verse, practically into Grace's mouth.

Then they both sat slowly down on their own beds, knees up to their chins and tried to talk it through. Twenty minutes later they were on those knees, pleading with Jesus. Begging that if he was asking them to do what they think he was asking them to do, then they'd need another sign. They prayed for the lamplight in their bedroom to flicker; for the conjoined butterfly to flap its wings on the page of the magazine; for a roll of thunder to rumble in the sky; for a knocking sound outside their bedroom window. But nothing happened. Except silence. And stillness.

They were both in the garden the next day, still stewing over the magazine when it appeared from out of nowhere.

Faith stopped dead in her tracks.

Grace fell slowly to her knees. As if she'd been shot in the gut and the realisation of mortality was ever so gradually dawning on her.

They didn't say anything. Not for ages. They just replayed what they'd witnessed again and again... over and over in their minds. It flew over their heads and landed on one of the protruding roots of the oak tree. A butterfly. A conjoined one. Two black and white wings, and two yellow ones with thin red stripes. It stalled there on the root for a short while, looked about itself and then flew upwards through the branches and out of sight.

Grace eventually went back inside without saying a word. But Faith lasted another two hours; frozen in the same spot.

She did eventually follow her sister into the safe haven that was their bedroom. Neither of them came out all night, except to take dinner from the kitchen to eat on their beds.

'We are practising a new prayer,' Faith said. 'Can we eat dinner in our bedroom tonight, please... please?'

They knew they could get away with this sort of thing. All four Tiddles eating dinner at the kitchen table had long since stopped being a routine that must be adhered to.

'Sure,' Dorothy said. 'But don't get any dinner on those bed clothes.'

They took their plates from their mother and then trotted to their bedroom to plan how they would kill her... and their father.

'When are we going to do it?' Grace asked.

Faith chewed on her dinner. And then swallowed before answering.

'Tomorrow.'

'Tomorrow. Why tomorrow?'

Faith took another bite, then shrugged back at her sister.

'We can do it while Daddy's having his Saturday mid-morning nap. Just before we go to dance class.'

Grace looked down at her dinner, before tossing the fork onto the plate and pushing it away from herself.

'How are we going to do it?'

'Knife; one of those big black sharp ones in the kitchen,' Faith said.

'You've been thinking about this.'

'I knew,' Faith said, still chewing. 'I knew as soon as I saw that magazine.'

The day before had been still. Real still; the sun blazing high in the sky as it had done all that week. Faith decided to have a walk in the back garden while Grace was taking a shower. It was lying there next to the bush that ran along the side of the garden. A magazine. Wide open on the two-page spread about the Menendez brothers. She knew instantly it had been sent by Jesus. This was the second time he'd left her a message via magazine. The first magazine she'd found in the back garden – almost two years previous – had actually blown from a neighbour's bin who lived half a mile up the slope that led to the Tiddle bungalow. It was open on a feature about dying plants. And so Faith simply saw to it that she had to water her father's plants. They did need watering – Clive had begun to neglect his hobby as the church evolved into his only obsession. And so Faith saved the plants' lives thanks to Jesus through the medium of magazine. The second magazine – the one with the article about the Menendez brothers killing their parents – had been placed there by Eoin. For a laugh more than anything. When Janet was fuming; literally kicking the walls of her tiny flat all up in a rage about her brother and his 'tight-ass dirty cunt of a wife', Eoin happened to be flicking through the magazine that had come free inside the midweek tabloid newspaper.

'Hey...' he said turning to his wife and snorting out a laugh. 'Why don't you leave that for Faith to find? She might think it's a sign from God and actually do it.'

They were driving to Dublin the next day to see a friend and to do some shopping anyway. Eoin genuinely only brought the magazine for the laugh. To stir some shit. The twins had informed their aunt and uncle, on the night of their Holy Communion, that Jesus communicated with Faith. And since that revelation both Janet and Eoin began to ring the twins every now and then when they were bored and drunk, just to see what crazy Jesus shit they had been up to recently. Faith had told them over the phone once that she'd found a magazine in their garden that had a story in it about saving dying plants, and went on to proudly detail how she managed to bring her father's roses back to life, thanks to Jesus. Janet and Eoin often had to pinch their noses to stop their laughter from being heard down the line during those phone calls.

Janet dismissed the joke of leaving the magazine for the twins to find as 'fucking stupid'. But Eoin still brought it with him for the drive to Dublin because he had nothing else even close to being regarded as fun or exciting to do. And so rather than spend an hour shopping with his wife, he took a drive out to Rathcoole to toss the magazine over the bush that separated the Tiddle's garden from a large expanse of yellow field. He laughed to himself as he did it. Then popped himself back in the car and drove back to the shopping centre; hoping his wife was done with her browsing.

He had nothing to do with the butterfly. Nor did Janet. That, appearing the following day in the Tiddle back garden and flapping its four wings, was pure happenchance.

'Won't we go to Hell... I mean what about Thou Shall Not Kill?' Grace asked.

Faith shook her head.

'Not if Jesus asked us to do it. He'll forgive us.'

'But sure... won't the police know it was us?' Grace said. 'Is Jesus telling us we have to spend our lives in prison?'

Faith shrugged.

'We'll just follow Jesus's plan... wherever it leads us. The police won't have to know it was us. That's why we do it before dance class, because we can tell the police we were at dance class when Mammy and Daddy were killed.'

Grace puffed out her cheeks, but she was still wide-eyed and blood was gushing inside her veins. Faith was much more relaxed. Much more calm. Her face may have been a little on the pale side, but she was taking everything in her stride.

After all, Jesus's plan is what it is; no need to ever feel any emotion about it whatsoever. If he's the one in control, all will be okay.

'We can do this,' Faith said. 'We kill them with the knife, wash our hands real quick, change our clothes, and get to dance class as soon as we can. When we come home, we can ring the police, tell them we found Mammy and Daddy just lying there.'

'Yeah but what do we do with the knife? And the clothes that we use when we kill them? And the magazine? The police will find them all. They'll know it was us.'

'They won't find them,' Faith said.

'Huh?' Grace replied, her fingers fidgeting. 'Where we going to hide them?'

Faith threw her legs over the side of her bed and stood. Then she made her way slowly to their bedroom window and pulled back the curtains; revealing, to her sister, the silhouette of the oak tree as it stood tall in front of a blood orange sky.

The End

Want to discuss what happened to these characters next?

•How long did Faith and Grace get sentenced for?

•What happened after Alice's daughter viewed the video?

•How Denis and Sheila Quayle are getting on in their travels?

Please click the link below to watch an exclusive interview with author David B. Lyons in which he answers all those questions and discusses this book in more detail.

www.subscribepage.com/faithgrace

BOOK III

THE COINCIDENCE

How wide can a coincidence stretch your beliefs?

For Lin

The coincidence that occurs in *The Coincidence*

was inspired by a true story.

3,000 days ago…

'We all here cos o' coincidence.'

Those were the first words Christy ever spoke to Joy. Up until that point in their brief journey together, Joy had been content to just stare down at the filthy shoelaces of her Converse trainers rather than at the intimidating, lanky woman sat across from her.

'Life for everyone is a gift from God, alright… the God o' coincidence,' she continued.

Christy's accent was a marriage of her natural Nigerian husk to a southern Texan drawl. She had learned to speak English by listening to the sermons of Terence Huntcastle; a famed Christian pastor who hailed from Dallas and who ran one of the biggest superchurches in the whole of America. She played his tapes non-stop on a smashed Sony Walkman during her seeking of refuge from Nigeria over twenty-five years ago, and can still rattle off each of those sermons word for word today.

'A one in five hundred million miracle we all are. You're a one in five hundred million miracle, curly-haired girl, you know that?'

Joy slowly lifted her gaze from her shoelaces and met Christy's blood-shot eyes for the first time.

'S'true. When yo dadda made sweet, sweet love to yo momma and orgasmed his ball sack inside her, five hundred million of his little swimmers began a mega race to yo momma's golden egg.' Christy leaned as forward as she could. 'And you know which little swimmer won that one in five hundred million race, curly-haired girl? You. You, Joy Stapleton! You literally are a coincidence. We all are.'

Joy's heart sank. Not because Christy was preaching, but because she had mentioned her name. Though she knew she shouldn't be surprised by that. Her tiny frame, covered by her oversized curly mane would be, by now, unmistakable to anyone in the country. And likely would be for the rest of her life.

That short one-way conversation was pretty much all Christy and Joy shared while the van chicaned its way around the mazed inner city streets of Dublin, until its engine finally died. Then the two front doors of the van opened and slapped shut in unison, before footsteps clacked against concrete. Christy leaned as forward as she could again.

'Yo gon' be fine, Joy. Just keep yo pretty head down.'

'Welcome home, ladies,' the big fat ginger one said, pulling the back doors open, blinding his passengers with the low sun. When he stepped into the van, it sunk under his weight and Joy had to hold her breath to stave off the heavy stench of B.O. as he bent over to free her wrists. Then he exposed the top of his ass crack just inches from her face when he turned to free Christy.

'Step down,' he said, motioning to the bright outside world. It was freezing cold that afternoon, but the sun was still shining low in the sky, highlighting the cloud of Joy's exhalations as she stepped onto the concrete yard.

The tall cranky looking one was waiting for them, standing with her hands on her hips by the back wheel of the van. She and Fatso then led the women towards a grey stone wall that seemed to stretch as wide as the eye could see. There was a small blue wooden door in the middle of the wall that they made their way towards, then Fatso stared up into the CCTV camera hanging above it and, without much pause, the blue door buzzed open. The four of them entered a much smaller concrete yard, though this time the door on the wall opposite wasn't wooden, nor was it small. It was wide. *Very* wide. And made of steel.

Fatso stared again into a camera that hung over it until another buzz sounded. And when the steel door was pushed open, a chorus of screeches immediately echoed from the distance and within that split moment Joy's whole body paused; her feet, her thoughts, her breathing. The screeches were quite literally her worst nightmare coming true.

'Don't mind the noise,' Christy whispered over Joy's shoulder. 'S'not as bad as it sounds.'

'You first,' a voice from the shadows shouted. Joy blinked her eyes, ridding them of the glare of the outside world, before she could make out the figure of a woman standing behind an arched-wooden desk. She trundled over with Fatso still flanked by her side. 'Well, I guess I don't need to ask your name, now do I?' the woman behind the desk said. 'So, let's start with question number two, huh? Date of birth?'

Joy swallowed, tasting the last of her pride as it slid down her throat.

'First of January. 1986.'

'Well, congratulations, Joy. I can confirm you've definitely come to the right place.'

Fatso sniggered, then covered his mouth with his fingers when the woman behind the desk glared at him.

'Empty your pockets. I need all belongings in here,' the woman ordered as she slid a blue tray across the desk.

'I, eh... I don't have anything on me,' Joy replied, stiffening her nose in an attempt to stall the tears.

'Except for this,' Fatso said. He stuffed his chubby fingers into Joy's jeans pocket, fumbling for longer than was necessary before pulling out a photograph. He carelessly skim-threw it into the tray, and the woman behind the desk took a long stare at it before glancing back up at Joy.

'That it?'

'S'all's she's got,' Fatso replied.

'I, eh... I was told I could take that with me,' Joy said, her voice quivering.

The woman clicked her tongue against the roof of her mouth, then picked the photo up and stared longingly at it before handing it back to Joy.

'Okay, but I'm gonna have to take the laces out of those trainers.'

Joy looked down at the filthy laces she had spent the majority of the van ride staring at, then dipped to her hunkers to yank them from her Converse. She had barely dropped them into the tray by the time Fatso was grabbing at her elbow again, guiding her past the wooden desk with a firmer grip than she felt was necessary and leading her towards another steel door. He didn't have to nod at a hanging CCTV camera to open this one. Instead, he pressed one of his chunky fingers to a keypad until the door clicked open. Then he pushed Joy inside with more force than, again, she felt was necessary, before slamming the door shut.

'Ah, well, if it isn't Joy Stapleton,' a sweet voice inside the hollow room said.

Joy spun around to see another one of them standing in front of her, clad – same as 'em all – head to toe in navy. Only this one looked different. She wasn't menacingly grinning, nor furrowing her brow. She actually had kind eyes; eyes not too dissimilar to Joy's best friend Lavinia – or former best friend as she surely was by now.

'Strip!'

'Huh?'

'Strip. It means take off all your clothes.'

'I know what it means.... It's just... what, here? Now? In front of you?'

The woman smiled her kind eyes. And then a long silence settled between them before that kind smile abruptly dropped from her face.

Joy huffed out a sigh, before pulling her arms from the sleeves of her jumper and lifting it over her head, taking her T-shirt with it.

'Everything else,' the woman said, the glint in her eye threatening to return.

Joy reached around and undid the clasp of her bra, revealing her goose-pimple covered breasts before dropping it to the concrete. Then she kicked off her laceless Converse trainers and shimmied her way out of her jeans.

'Lemme see that bush,' the woman said.

After a pause of silence, Joy plucked up enough courage to hook a thumb either side of her knickers before yanking them down.

'Now turn around.'

'Huh?'

'Turn around. And interlink your fingers on top of those lovely curls for me.'

A chill ran down Joy's spine; partly because of the intimidation, but mostly because of the cold. Though as the goosepimples raced their way around her tiny frame, she relented and finally spun to face the back wall, noticing the yellow paint was stained a vomit-inducing shade of brown in each of the corners.

'Now squat.'

'Sorry?'

'Squat. Bend your knees and lower your ass.'

Joy held her eyes closed and then, widening her stance, began to bend her knees – until the steel door clicked open once again and Christy skidded into the room, pushed in with much the same force as Joy had been.

Joy stood back upright immediately, holding one arm across her breasts; her other hand covering her bush.

'Looks like you gettin' all comfortable up in here already, Joy,' Christy said, grinning her stained teeth.

'You start stripping,' the woman in navy ordered her before turning back to Joy. 'And you start squatting.'

So, Joy refaced the wall, placed her hands back on top of her hair and bent her knees, lowering and pushing her ass out as quickly as she could before standing back upright.

'No, no, no,' the woman called out. 'Slower!'

'Hey, you don't think she got somethin' up there, right?' Christy said, cackling. 'She got such a tight lil ass you couldn't fit a tic-tac in that thing. Ma right, sista?'

Joy stiffened her nostrils with irritation, then bent her knees even further before ever-so-slowly lowering her ass as if she was sitting on an imaginary loo.

'See, not even one of those curly pubes fell out,' Christy said as Joy stood back upright.

The woman, ignoring Christy, paced over to Joy, placed a hand to her shoulder and guided her with a forced shove against the stained yellow wall behind her. Then she reached above Joy's head and pulled a gauge down to the top of her curls.

'Five foot, two inches,' she said before biting off the lid of her pen to scribble on her notes. 'Stand up here,' she said, pointing the pen at the weighing scales in the corner.

Joy stepped onto the board while staring over her shoulder at Christy undressing. She took in the back of Christy's long, brown legs and slowly lifted her gaze up the length of her spine till she was staring at her bowed elongated neck. Christy had the physique and posture of a super model. And probably could have been one too had she trod a path in life that hadn't turned her teeth yellow and her eyes red.

'Seven stone, ten,' the woman said. 'I think you'll need to eat a few McDonald's while you're here.'

'Huh?' Joy said, stepping down from the scales. 'We get McDonald's here?'

Both the woman and Christy laughed so loudly that it echoed around the concrete room. And when the woman had decided the joke was no longer funny, she spun around to pull open a steel cabinet door, from which she removed a neatly rolled up grey jumpsuit.

'Here, wear this,' she said, tossing it at Joy. 'It's the smallest one we have.'

'Oh, yo really gonna look like Krusty the Clown now,' Christy said, cackling from the back of her throat again.

When Joy finally smothered herself in the jumpsuit – the sleeves so long it looked as if she had two baby elephant trunks for arms – the woman turned and snatched at a door on the opposite side of the room.

'Way to break your duck, Aidan,' she called out. 'I've got a VIP for you. None other than Joy Stapleton.' Joy peered around the door frame to see who the hell this Aidan was. He looked young. And fresh; his face still producing acne, his forehead void of wrinkles. He was nice looking in the way Dublin men can be nice looking; black hair, pale skin and piercing blue eyes. Eyes that reminded her of Shay's.

'She's Elm House, E-114.'

'E-114, got it,' Aidan said, nodding. He swallowed and then awkwardly stepped aside, welcoming Joy to join him on the steel-grated landing. As soon as she took one step on to the grate, the screeching that had earlier sounded distant raised intimidatingly in volume.

'Oh wait,' Joy said, gasping and spinning back. 'I forgot my photo. I need my photo. It's in my pocket.'

The woman knelt down and felt around Joy's jeans before retrieving the polaroid. She stared at it and paused, before eyeballing Joy.

'Whatever makes you sleep at night,' she said, handing the photo back.

Joy crossed her brow as she snatched at it, then whispered: 'It was a coincidence.'

Then the woman shrugged one shoulder before slamming the door shut just inches from Joy's nose.

Aidan was looking sheepish when Joy turned back around to face him, then he motioned towards a large steel staircase at the far end of the landing.

'Don't worry,' he said, as they took the first step. 'They say the noise isn't as bad as it sounds.'

'Jaysis, it's yer one, innit?' a voice called out when Joy and Aidan had reached the top of the stairs. And then, without pause, a cacophony of wolf whistles echoed, bouncing around the landings both above and below them.

'Ignore them,' Aidan said out of the side of his mouth. Then he stopped in his tracks suddenly, causing Joy to crash into the back of him.

'Sorry,' he said, 'it came on me all of a sudden. E-114. This is you.'

He pushed at the door and stepped aside, inviting Joy to enter first. It wasn't as grim as she had feared it would be; brighter and actually roomier than she had imagined. But she mostly felt relief when she first stepped inside; relief because there was only one bed in there.

'You'll, eh... you'll get three rounds of clothes brought in... so you won't have to wear the jumpsuit all the time,' Aidan informed her as Joy stared into the lidless steel toilet bowl in the back corner of the room. When she turned back around, she met Aidan's blue eyes and he nodded kindly before taking two steps backwards.

'This has to be locked,' he said gripping the door. 'It's just precautionary for the first twenty-four hours. It's what happens when you're high-profile. We'll, eh... we'll bring you some food in the next couple of hours.'

'Can you, eh... get me some sellotape or Blu-Tac or something? I just wanna hang this on the wall beside my bed ... please?'

She held the photograph up and Aidan blinked at it, before slowly nodding.

'Lemme see what I can do,' he said.

Then he took one more step backwards, dragging the door with him and slamming it closed with an echoed clank.

And that was it. She was alone. Finally. Her freedom well and truly taken.

She attempted to look about herself, only there wasn't much to look at. So, she ran her fingers over the thin blue mattress laying on top of her steel-block bed, before opting to perch her ass on to the edge of it.

'Hey,' a voice yelled before loud banging slapped against Joy's steel door. 'I think I know your face from somewhere... or is that just a *coincidence*?'

The cacophony of laughter that followed shook Joy more so than the banging against her door had.

'Yeah, I know who she is,' another voice shouted when the laughter had died to near silence. 'Wasn't she in all the papers for winning Mother of the Year or somethin'?'

The cackles grew in volume, as if all the women outside were competing for the loudest laugh.

To drown the noise out, Joy dropped the photograph on to her thin pillow, then lay her face beside it, wrapping her elbows around her head to smother her ears. Sometimes, when she stares at the photo long enough, she can hear Reese's laugh. And Oscar's giggle.

'Hey, child killer,' a voice roared, before the door received another bout of slapping. 'Don't you dare think you're gonna have an easy time of it in here, ya hear me?'

∴

'Your Honour, my client,' Gerd Bracken says, while remaining seated, 'has spent the last eight years and two months incarcerated in Mountjoy Prison because of nothing more than mere coincidence. A coincidence, I should add, that in the grand scheme of coincidences is not even that coincidental.'

He scoots back his chair, gets to his feet and strolls, slowly, to the middle of the courtroom floor. Judge Delia McCormick peers over the rim of her retro 1950s-style glasses to squint at him, already intrigued. She'd been working up to this trial for months, was staggered it fell into her lap. A retrial – *the* retrial – of the biggest mystery that has plagued the entire nation for well over a decade. She was initially hesitant to take on the role, especially as it was all on her; no fellow judges to debate legal arguments with; no jury to rely on for a verdict. But after careful consideration and painstaking research – not to mention discussion after discussion with both her annoying son, Callum, and her persuasive boss, Eddie – Delia finally accepted the pressure of presiding over the Joy Stapleton retrial. She knew the weight of the world would push hard onto her shoulders, knew the media would sensationalize every word she'd speak, and that the judicial system would scrutinize every move she'd make. But as both Callum and Eddie repeated to her regularly during her dilemma: why become a trial judge if you don't want to preside over the biggest case there's ever been?

So here she finally was; sat in the overly large velvet-cushioned judge's highchair at the back wall of the largest trial room in Dublin's Central Criminal Courts, squinting at Gerd Bracken – a defence lawyer she knew all too well – as he began his opening argument.

'Imagine, if you will for one moment, Your Honour...' Bracken forms a steeple with his fingers and frames them around his navel, 'you call out for your two beautiful young sons, and they never answer back. Two years go by and you are still calling out for them... and they still don't answer. Then a detective knocks on your door one morning, informs you your sons' bodies have been found in wasteland high up in the Dublin mountains.' Bracken shakes his head. 'Sounds like Hell on earth, doesn't it, Your Honour? But imagine that was only half of the story? Imagine six weeks after hearing such devastating news, the same detective knocks to your house again, this time to arrest *you* for the double homicide of your sons. And imagine, eighteen months later, despite the fact that there was *zero* forensic evidence and *zero* eye-witnesses, a jury of twelve find you guilty. And then you are sentenced to two life sentences in prison – unlikely to ever get out. That's a lot for me to ask you to imagine... but I would ask you, Your Honour, to imagine one more thing if you will... imagine this... imagine you were innocent all along?' He allows a silence to wash over the court room as he subtly shakes his head again. 'Your Honour, my client has so far spent over eight years in prison for the most heinous of crimes that she simply did *not* commit. And the only reason she has spent over eight years in prison comes down to mere coincidence. *Coincidence!*'

Bracken kisses his own lips before shaking his head again. Judge Delia doesn't react at all; not to even blink her eyes, which are still peering over the rim of her glasses at the lawyer in the pin-striped suit.

'Your Honour, Joy Stapleton – who may I add is still in the process, many, many years later, of grieving the loss of her sons – has only been convicted of this crime for the simple reason that somebody else out there was wearing the exact same hooded sweat-top to one she happened to own at the time. That's it. That is the *only* reason she was arrested. It is the *only* reason she was convicted. There wasn't one jot of forensic evidence that links Joy to this crime. Not one eye-witness who can link Joy to this crime.' He lowers his voice, and his tone, 'not one credible motive that links Joy to this crime...'

He pauses, then fills his cheeks with air before slowly exhaling; displaying a show of anguish. But this sort of act won't do him any favours. Bracken's melodramatics might work on jurors; in fact, his melodramatics almost *always* work on jurors – he's only lost one trial out of thirty-three over the past ten years. But his melodramatics won't work on Judge Delia. She knows him well; has presided over two major trials he had been the leading defence lawyer on. Still, she has always been professional enough to not allow her own personal feelings on individuals to cloud her judgements. Bracken may well be a sleazeball, he may well love the sound of his own voice and the attention he gets from the media as much as he loves a sunbed, but Delia has evolved an envious ability to shove all of her peripheral thoughts to one side so she can focus solely on the facts of any matter, let alone the matter of a major murder trial.

'Your Honour,' Bracken says, 'I and many, many other people, in and out of the judicial system, have felt, for years, that Joy Stapleton is innocent of this crime. We can't quite understand how or why our judicial system could put a young grieving mother behind bars based on evidence so minimal and so trivial. But I am now glad we have won the opportunity to be here today in front of you at this retrial, so that we can bring, to you, undoubted evidence of this mother's innocence. A cadaver dog, Judge Delia. *The* cadaver dog – a dog named Bunny who helped detectives push their narrative that Joy Stapleton was guilty all those years ago – has since been exposed as not having the adequate training required to determine anything about this case. Bunny, y'see, Your Honour, was said to have found evidence of decomposing bodies in the Stapleton family home back in January of 2009 – mere months after poor Reese Stapleton and Oscar Stapleton were first reported missing. Bunny's findings played a major role in the original trial. But we will bring to you evidence that Bunny didn't know what he was doing all those years back. Because another trial, in London, Your Honour, collapsed four years ago when Bunny's findings in that case were found to be useless... pointless... meaningless... redundant. We will prove to you that Bunny's findings in the original trial concerning Joy Stapleton were just as useless, pointless, meaningless, and redundant. I will also bring forward, Your Honour, a former member of An Garda Siochana who assisted in the original missing persons case of Reese and Oscar Stapleton who will detail to this court that the original investigation got this wrong from the very outset. That's right! A former detective will sit in that seat there,' Bracken points his whole hand to the witness box to the judge's right, 'and tell you that she and everyone else she worked with got this case wrong from the very beginning. I will also bring evidence that the coincidence upon which Joy Stapleton was arrested certainly *was* a coincidence. The girl seen in the CCTV footage wearing a pink hoodie was not Joy Stapleton at all. It couldn't have been. Over the course of this retrial, Your Honour, it will be proven to you that my client did not kill her only two children in November of 2008. Thank you.'

Bracken almost bows – as if he's just nailed one of Shakespeare's most renowned monologues on the stage of The Globe Theatre, before spinning on his heels and walking back to his desk, where he plonks himself next to a sombre-looking Joy.

Judge Delia deflects her gaze and purses her lips at the desk adjacent to theirs.

'Mr Ryan. Your opening statement, please,' she says, before scribbling some notes onto the top sheet of the mountainous paperwork in front of her.

Ryan rises from his chair and clips open the two buttons of his suit jacket before he strolls his way to the centre of the courtroom floor. The courtroom is deathly quiet, despite the fact that not only is it packed inside, but the doors outside of the courts are almost bursting with reporters who couldn't quite get a seat in the arena today.

'Your Honour,' Ryan says, 'Joy Stapleton has spent the last eight years in a cell in Mountjoy Prison for one simple reason. In November 2008, she killed both of her sons – Reese, aged four and Oscar who was eighteen months old – in cold blood. We believe she rendered them unconscious using chloroform, then likely suffocated them to death. She brought them to the Dublin mountains and disposed of their bodies. On the day we believed this happened, we know that Joy Stapleton was wearing a unique pink hooded top. Very unique. So unique in fact, we know Joy to be the only person in Ireland who owns one. Let me say that again. Joy Stapleton is the *only* person in Ireland to own the top that was caught on CCTV footage close to where the bodies were found, on the night we are certain the bodies were buried there. Your Honour... for years, the defendant's argument has always been that this is mere coincidence. But that's hogwash. And we will be able to prove it. The probability of her defence of coincidence is so low, Your Honour, that it simply can*not* be considered coincidence. And I will be able to prove that once and for all in this retrial. I do not wish at any stage to insult the intelligence of this court. But this must be said... In mathematics, two angles that are said to coincide – and note the word *coincide* – fit together perfectly. The word coincidence does not describe luck, or misfortune, Your Honour. The word coincidence describes that which fits together perfectly. We,' he says, looking back to his desk where his assistant Brigit is sitting staring at him, 'will be able to prove to you that Joy Stapleton not only deserves to have spent the last eight years in a prison cell for killing her two young sons, but that she deserves to spend the rest of her life in that prison cell, to see out the double-life sentence that was handed down to her in her original trial.' Ryan takes two steps nearer the judge. 'The detectives during their investigation got this case right. The judge sitting on the original trial called this case right. And the jurors sitting on the original trial called this case right. Your Honour, we're not going to bring witnesses second-guessing the sense of smell of a dog to this court, like the defence team will. We are not going to bring bitter ex-employees of the police force to this court, like the defence team will. We will be putting professionals in that stand; professionals who know this case better than anybody else. And those *professionals* all agree on one thing, Your Honour. And that is, that on the second of November in 2008, Joy Stapleton murdered and then disposed of the bodies of her two baby boys, Oscar and Reese Stapleton.'

It was the door clicking open that woke Joy inside her prison cell for the very first time. She lazily stirred on her plastic blue mattress, then – in stark realisation of where she was – jolted her back against the wall and brought her knees up to her chest. Though much to her relief, somebody outside pulled at her cell door, slapping it back shut.

She panted for breath as she listened to the melee of shuffling feet in the landing outside, and before long that distant screeching that she heard as soon as she had set foot inside the prison the previous evening struck up. She had no idea what time it was, but it sure did seem as if everybody got up and about at the exact same time. Perhaps a prison officer, stationed outside her cell, slammed her door shut. She had been told she wouldn't be mixing with the other prisoners – not for at least twenty-four more hours anyway. And even following that she would be accompanied by an officer everywhere she went.

She spent the majority of her first full day in the exact same spot she had spent her first night – in a foetal position atop that blue plastic mattress. Though there were two breaks – both for half an hour; once in the morning and then again in the afternoon – in the small yard. It allowed her to stretch her legs and breathe in fresher air.

Aidan had joined her for her first half-hour out there, looking as nervous and uncertain of procedure as she was. Yet, somehow, she felt a sense of comfort around him. He had a warmth and was certainly open for conversation. He confided in Joy that the previous day was his first day working as a screw in Mountjoy Prison.

'Your first day as well? And your first job was to take me to my cell… wow, that's a coincidence,' Joy said.

Then she immediately looked down to her feet, as she realised she would for the rest of her life every time she muttered that word.

There were meals each side of the two breaks, too, brought to her cell and left on a flimsy plastic tray atop her flimsy plastic mattress: a breakfast that consisted of toast so dry it may as well have been cardboard, and a reheated microwavable lasagne for lunch that was so congealed it may well have been a stew. The dinner wasn't too bad, though; Indian samosas with fragrant yellow rice. And there were afters too; a large scoop of vanilla ice cream, stabbed with a diamond-shaped wafer.

She had been offered the chance of a shower on three separate occasions, but refused each time. That had always been her biggest fear as she lived through her ordeal. It wasn't the monotony of being holed in a prison cell that frightened Joy. It was the showers.

'There'll be no other prisoners in there,' Mathilda, the female officer who had signed her in at the front desk the previous day, said to her. 'You are being kept from them for the first twenty-four hours.'

'No. I'm okay,' Joy said, sucking up her tears. 'I think I can do without showering for the rest of my life.'

'They all say that... till they start smelling themselves,' Mathilda said. Then she walked out of the cell, slapping the door shut behind her.

Joy lifted her arm above her head and sniffed.

'Okay, okay,' she said, leaping down from her bed and knocking repeatedly at the cell door. 'I'll take one. I'll take my shower now.'

Mathilda chuckled.

'Too late, Stapleton. You had your chance. You'll have to take one with the rest of the girls in the morning. Now why don't you get some sleep. I've a feeling you're gonna need your energy – and your wits about you – tomorrow.'

2,998 days ago...

Her hands were visibly shaking as she reached to take the towel from Mathilda. The prison officer had visited her cell first thing the next morning, as she promised she would, to ensure Joy joined the queue for the showers.

Joy expected 'child killer' shouts as soon as she stepped onto the landing, but the other prisoners were oddly subdued as they brushed past her, probably because it was too early for them to be bothered.

She didn't stand under the water. She just let it fall to her chest, all the while shifting her eyes from side to side, darting glances at the prisoners showering next to her. One of the prisoners met her eye and turned out her bottom lip, accompanying it with a nod. It came across as a sympathetic gesture, but Joy couldn't be sure. It was only when she was dabbing her chest dry with her towel that she was first spoken to.

'I told you we all a coincidence.' Joy looked up to meet the bloodshot eyes of Christy. 'Me 'n' you on the same wing, sista. I think God sent me to protect yo lil ass, huh?'

Joy stood there, naked. And vulnerable. And damp. And cold. Damn cold. The water in the prison's showers never raised to a level beyond lukewarm.

'Hi, Christy,' she said.

And then those drying around her mimicked her.

'Hi, Christy,' they said, their voices mocking and high-pitched.

And almost immediately that horrible cacophony of immature laughter cackled again, sounding even more echoey bouncing off the shower tiles than it did bouncing around the landings.

'Alright, bitches, cut it out,' a middle-aged, flaming red-haired woman, with one foot up against the tiled wall, flossing the towel between the pits of her groins, said. 'If it makes ya feel any better, love, I'm not entirely sure whether you did or whether you did not kill those little kiddies of yours. But I am pretty sure you shouldn't be here. I read all about your trial. I don't think the prosecution offered up enough evidence to send you down. Those jurors, whoever they are, they screwed you, honey.'

'Eh... thanks,' Joy whispered back, before Christy tugged on her shoulder.

'C'mon, get yourself dressed, Joy. We gonna eat some breakfast together.'

They sat on the end of a long bench in the canteen; Christy scoffing her porridge within a matter of seconds, Joy still tonguing spoonfuls of it from side to side in her mouth, her lips turned down in disgust.

'Doesn't all seem so bad in here, now does it?' Christy said, swiping the sleeve of her jump suit across her mouth. 'I know some of 'em been calling you a child killer but I also hear some of 'em say you didn't do it; that you didn't kill yo boys.'

'Seems as if I've split the prisoners...' Joy said before swallowing a mouthful of porridge.

'Split the prisoners, sista? You split the whole darn country. Half the people on the streets saying such a young pretty little thing like you could never do such a thing. Other half think you a stone-cold killer, girl.'

Joy fed herself another spoonful of porridge and allowed it to swirl from cheek to cheek again before swallowing.

'I didn't do it, ye know? That's not me in that CCTV footage. I swear. I've sworn to everybody. I swear to you.'

Christy raised one eyebrow at Joy, then looked around at Mathilda who was standing against the wall next to them – Joy still under guarded supervision when outside of her cell.

'You know you the only person with one of them hooded tops in all of Ireland,' Christy said.

Joy looked down. As she always did when she was lost for a word other than 'coincidence'. Then she changed the subject, by asking Christy about visitation rights. Though she wasn't quite sure if anyone was ever going to visit her. Shay had pretty much refused to believe his wife had murdered their two sons, and even after her arrest had stayed somewhat loyal. But it was noted by everyone in attendance – and certainly by those from the media – that he wasn't present for any of the trial. He had been asked to testify in favour of Joy – to say on the stand that he didn't believe his wife was capable of murdering anyone, let alone their two precious sons. But he stayed away from the court entirely, and indeed cut off any line of communications with his wife. His silence was eating at Joy, even though she knew that there was no chance of them ever getting back together. Not even if she could prove her innocence. Their lives together ended the day Reese and Oscar were first reported missing. There was no chance of them ever going back to where they once were. Despite that, she was hopeful that one day she'd get a tap on the shoulder from one of the prison officers before being told Shay was in the visiting room, waiting for her. Her best friend – or former best friend as she was by now – certainly wasn't coming to visit. Lavinia did appear on the stand, to testify that Joy's personality had changed before her boys were reported missing.

'You think you know who the closest people are in life,' Joy whispered to Christy while pushing her plastic bowl away from under her nose. 'But...' Then she shrugged. Christy nodded, before picking up Joy's bowl and literally digging into her porridge. 'How dare Lavinia testify that I was suffering with depression. I've never suffered with depression. They tested me. I didn't have no post-natal depression.'

'But they tested you two years later, right? After yo boys' bodies were found, not at the time they went missing?'

'You don't believe me?' Joy said.

'E'ryone round here says they innocent, Joy.'

'I *am* innocent!' Joy snapped.

'Calm down, girl. You at risk of losing the only friend you got in the whole world right now.'

Joy unclenched her fists and tilted her head backwards, a groan growling at the back of her throat.

'I'm sorry, Christy. Thanks for... I don't know... thanks for talking to me.'

'Thank *you*, girl,' Christy replied. 'When I do time in here, I normally keep maself to maself. People up in here think I'm all kinds o' crazy. Just me and ma bible when I'm in here normally. S'nice to talk to someone... even if they are a chi—'

Christy stopped herself.

502

'A child killer... is that what you were gonna say?'

'I didn't say that.'

'You were about to.'

'Well, ya know what, girl?' Christy said, leaning forward and resting her fingertips onto Joy's forearm. 'I actually haven't worked you out yet. Ma visions will tell me in time if you guilty or not. They always do.'

'Visions?'

'God talks to me. Lets me know what's what. I pretty much know all the girls in here. See Linda o'er there, the brunette with the short bob? That bitch says she didn't slit her boyfriend's throat. She be lying. I know she did it. I saw visions o' her doin' it.' Joy squinted at the middle-aged woman sat eating a slice of cardboard toast on the far end of their bench, noting she didn't look too dissimilar to Joy's own mother, whom she had sorely missed every day of the past sixteen years. Breast cancer had taken her. Breast cancer that was caught too late. Joy's father was still alive, but he was in a nursing home, aged only fifty-five years, unable to cope with the continued drama that kept unfolding before him. He lost his wife to cancer, his two grandsons to murder and then his daughter to the judicial system in the space of four years. 'And Stella, this one over here, she's down fo' attempted murder. Put a young girl in a coma in a bar one night. Glassed her, then jumped on top o' her and kept punching at her face until all her lights went out. I saw that in a vision too.'

'And what about you? What are you in for?' Joy asked, turning back to face Christy.

'Me?' Christy said. Then she glanced upwards, to eyeball Mathilda over Joy's shoulder. 'They say I held up the petrol station in Glasnevin. My third one they caught me for, they say. I had a sawn-off shotgun, they say. Didn't fire it though. Still got sent down for seven years. Highest sentence I cudda bin given.'

'Seven years?'

'Uh-huh. It's cos I'm black. But I don't like to moan 'bout it. God will see me right in ma next life. Right now, me 'n' Him tryna get me through this one. Seven years for armed robbery... it's a long stretch. Though I bet you with yo double life sentence you prolly think seven years is nuttin, right? But I'm gonna be sixty years of age in seven years. Ma life's clock is tick-tocking away.'

'What about her, the red-headed one?' Joy asked, nodding towards the woman who offered an ounce of sympathy her way whilst floss-drying her under regions in the shower room that morning.

'Oh... That's Nancy Trott. You don't wanna be dealin' with Nancy Trott. You stay well the hell away from that crazy red-headed bitch, ya here me?'

Joy turned back in her seat.

'Why?'

'She nasty. Bitch prolly be raping yo pretty ass right about now if I wasn't here beside ya. With you all tiny and pretty, I bet yo just her type.'

'You serious?' Joy asked, raising an eyebrow. Though just as she did, she noticed Aidan nod his head at her as he stood against the back wall, relieving Mathilda of her duty.

Christy noticed them glancing at each other and did a double-take.

'You fancy that white boy?' she said, a little too loudly.

'Shhh,' Joy hissed, stifling a smile. 'Course not, don't be silly. I'm married.'

Christy tucked her chin into her neck and gurned a face at Joy.

'You are? I don't think the newspapers know whether you married or not. They say yo husband didn't show up to any o' yo trial.'

Joy puffed a small laugh out of her nostrils, then a long silence settled between them before Christy broke it, using the thickest of her Texan drawl.

'Don't know what all y'all see in those skinny ass white boys anyway,' she whispered. 'They so ugly all bright pink 'n' naked. Can you believe I actually escaped a country of big black hunky men to come live here, in sunny Dublin, where all the boys' skin so white sometimes I think I can see right through 'em. But a woman gets horny, don't we? So, fuck skinny ass white boys I do. Though I have to say,' Christy leaned even closer. 'I don't even feel some o' they white dicks when they all up in there, sometimes.'

Joy held her stomach while laughing and reeled back on her bench. But just as she did, somebody grabbed a fistful of her frizzy hair from behind and slammed her nose to the corner of the table.

Delia exhales loudly as she pushes through the door to her office.

She leaves her briefcase, as she always does, resting against the balled leg of her oak desk, removes her robe, which she drops to the floor, and then sits into her padded leather chair; her elbows on her desk, her hands slapped against her cheeks.

It's been a long day, even for her.

Her overall feeling isn't exhaustion though. It's frustration; frustration because the trial hadn't covered as much ground during its opening day as she had hoped it would.

After opening arguments, both sides of the court detoured into an array of legal spats that seemed determined to test the judge's patience. Although the retrial had been granted two full years before it made it to court, the prosecution and defence teams were still, today, discussing minute details from the original trial, arguing whether or not they should be considered by the judge during her retrial deliberations. The paperwork Judge Delia had to contend with for any major trial was often labour-intensive. But for this retrial it had trebled in size; only because parts of the original trial had to be considered, too.

The opening arguments Delia had heard earlier failed to unearth any surprises. Not that opening arguments usually do. Lawyers just like to draw a rough outline of the arguments they will be bringing up in the trial, and very rarely hit a judge or jury with a key twist so early on.

After removing her hands from her cheeks, Delia wiggles her mouse to blink her computer screen to life. And in the time it takes for her old Apple

Mac to refresh, she gazes around her desk – a ritual she isn't even aware she goes through every time she reawakens her computer.

It's a grand old oak desk she gets to look around, worth thousands of euros. Not that she paid for it. It became hers when she inherited this grand office at the back of Dublin's Criminal Courts from her predecessor – Judge Albert Riordan. The office was always densely lit, because the bulb hanging above the desk when Delia first entered was too weak to light the room adequately. But she liked the dimness and the warm ambience it brought to her work environment and so has, for the past nine years, purposely reordered the wrong bulb every time one blows. The dim orange light casts sharp shadows across the old desk; a shadow of the giant computer monitor; shadows from the two cupfuls of pens and pencils that sit beside her computer monitor. And the shadow from the photo frame that stands on the opposite side of her keyboard – framing an image of her and her now deceased husband Ben with their arms wrapped tightly around their only child Callum as they celebrated his graduation from Trinity College back in November, 2008. Although she doesn't like how she, personally, looks in that picture – not with her standing outside the Windmill Pub freezing cold and all hunched up in her winter hat and scarf – the image is as special to her as anything in this life. The flash of a camera. A moment in time captured forever. It's not a special moment to her because the two men in it happen to mean more to her than anything or anybody else; it's special because it's the last image that was ever captured of the McCormicks together. Ben passed away three weeks later, collapsing to a stuttering heart while sat at a conference table in his firm's head office, surrounded by twelve of his colleagues. One tried to revive him after his forehead had slapped to the table, but it was too late. Ben was gone. And has been gone for the past twelve years.

Friends have tried to fix Delia up on dates since she became a widow, but she genuinely isn't interested. She claims she's married to her profession. Besides, she has a man in her life. Callum. He hasn't quite moved out of the family home yet, even though he earns almost a quarter of a million a year and has just turned thirty-five. Despite numerous liaisons with the same sex, Callum is yet to find Mr Right and is way too needy to live alone. Besides, he knows all too well that his mother enjoys having him with her in their family home.

When her ritual of gazing at the items casting shadows on her desk is distracted by her monitor blinking to life, Delia exhales a sigh to reset herself, then begins to tap away at her keyboard. But footsteps cause her to pause pretty much before she has even begun. Then there's a beat of silence before knuckles rattle against the door. She doesn't need to call her visitor in to know who it is. She can always tell by the knock.

'In you come, Eddie,' she shouts.

Her boss grins at her after he's pushed his way through. He's a heavy-set man, is Eddie – over six-foot tall and at least twenty stone in weight. He's just one of those guys who's always been big all over; big shoulders, big hips, big ass. He has worn his greying hair neatly parted to one side in all the time Delia has known him and has immensely bushy eyebrows – shaped like an inverted hairy V.

'Why don't you get a proper light in here, Delia,' he says, staring up at the dim glow above her desk.

'Change the tune, Eddie.'

Eddie closes the office door gingerly, then grips the back of the chair opposite the judge.

'Didn't quite get to open the floor today, huh?'

Delia thins her lips.

'Paperwork and more paperwork. Seemed to me Bracken was trying to delay the day. He kept arguing over the order of the witness list – obsessing about it, truth be told. It was all a nonsense. I think he was trying to delay the beginning of the trial until tomorrow... probably needs more time vetting his witnesses.'

'Wouldn't put it past him. He eh... kept his opening argument pretty close to his chest though, huh? Do ya think he has something up his sleeve? Can't imagine Bunny is his only ace card. A dodgy dog might have been enough to win his client a retrial, but it won't be enough to acquit her.' Delia rubs her fingers across the deep wrinkles of her forehead, then raises an eyebrow across the desk. 'Sorry,' Eddie says. 'It's not my place to say what will or what won't be enough to acquit Joy Stapleton. That power is all in your hands.'

Eddie holds his palms outwards, then scoots himself around and sits into the chair he'd been gripping the back of.

'Defence team didn't say much in opening either, did they?' Delia offers up as she begins clicking at her mouse.

'They don't have much to do, though. As long as they stay firm on why Joy was convicted in the first place, they'll be fine. Onus is all on Bracken to prove Joy shouldn't be behind bars. But he's not gonna be able to do that. I know this is a massive case and the – excuse me for cursing – but the fuckin' media vans outside – did you see 'em?' he asks. 'Never seen so many vans in my life. But truth be known, you don't need to feel a huge amount of pressure on this, Delia. As big a story as it is. This is an open and shut case for you. Take all arguments into consideration and then do what you gotta do...'

'Yes, thanks, Eddie. I do know how to do my job.'

'Course ya do,' he says, chuckling from the back of his throat. 'It's just...'

Delia's breathing pauses, and her fingers hover over her mouse.

'It's just what?' she says, peering over her glasses at him, as if he's one of those chancer lawyers she likes to stare down to exert her dominance. Except she doesn't have dominance in this room. Eddie Taunton does. He's the Chief Justice – is literally responsible for keeping the cogs of the whole judicial arm of the nation turning, and has been doing so for the past twenty years. He has a jovial manner most of the time, but even the most high-profile of figures know he's no pushover. No matter who's in the room, from Supreme Court judges to the President or even the Taoiseach, Eddie Taunton always assumes the role of authority.

'You remember all those years back, I interviewed you for a Supreme Courts Judges Panel chair?' he says.

Delia's hand remains hovering over her mouse, her breath still held.

'Yes,' she says.

'Remember I asked you about this trial in particular... the original Joy Stapleton trial? I knew you'd studied it.'

'Yes.'

'You told me you were sure she did it – that Joy Stapleton was guilty. That the jurors got it right.'

'Yes.' Eddie shrugs. And then Delia finally exhales a long, silent breath through her nostrils before her hand finally rests on to her mouse. 'What are you trying to say, Eddie?'

'I'm not trying to say anything. Just that you believed her to be guilty—'

'This is an entirely different trial, Eddie. What are you trying to suggest?' Judge Delia gasps, then whips off her glasses and leans forward – her eyes wide. 'Eddie, did I get awarded this trial because of an answer I gave to you in an interview seven years ago? Oh my word... that's it, isn't it?' She sits back in her chair and stares up at the dim bulb above her. 'Wow. *You* decided there'd be no jury on this retrial. *You* decided on one judge. *You* decided on me. Eddie... did you set this up because you assumed I'd deliver a guilty verdict?'

'That's not what I've said at all,' Eddie says, holding his hands up. He raises one of his V-shaped bushy eyebrows into a more prominent arch, then creases his chubby cheeks into a grin.

'Eddie... you did, didn't you? You want a guilty verdict. You've played for it?'

'Don't be paranoid, Delia,' he says.

'Why no jury?'

'You know the answer to that quest—'

'Why no jury?'

'Because the whole bloody nation knows about this case. We couldn't get twelve unbiased views. There was never going to be a retrial if a jury couldn't be found.'

'Why me?'

'Delia, forgive me for cursing again, but for fuck sake, we've had these conversations. You were chosen because you're the best bloody judge in the country. Probably one of the best there's ever been. You got chosen on merit.'

Delia squints at her boss, her forehead dipping.

'Eddie, I will be judging this new trial with the freshest of eyes.'

'Course you will. Course you will.'

It comes as no surprise to Delia that Eddie would have preference for a guilty verdict. It'd be less mess for him to clean up as Chief Justice. Delia has been aware for years that Eddie doesn't play every game inside the lines, but surely he wouldn't be so brazen as to ask her out straight to deliver a specific verdict on any trial? Let alone the biggest retrial the country's ever witnessed...

'Well... if... there's nothing of urgency, Eddie, I must get back to...' she points at her computer screen which has by now blinked back off again.

'Sure, sure.' Eddie heaves his large frame out of the chair and rises to his feet. 'Eh...' he scratches at the stubble of his chin. 'You know she did this right? There's no doubt about it all—'

'Eddie—'

'Regardless of what doggy tales or new technology Gerd Bracken brings to this retrial, that's her in that CCTV footage.'

'Eddie!'

Eddie shows her his palms again.

'Alright, alright,' he says. 'I get it. You're the judge.'

Delia grins her teeth and offers him a friendly blinking of the eyes. But Eddie just shakes his head back at her, then he grunts as he pulls open the office door and strolls out.

Delia leans her head back to the top of her chair and puffs out a snort of laughter. Then she wiggles at her mouse again, for her screen to blink back to life, and in the time it does, she stares around her desk again, following her usual routine.

'That was odd,' she whispers to herself.

Joy had been slowly and carefully reintroduced into Elm House; starting with her rejoining the prisoners for lunch in the canteen, flanked by two officers, then being allowed an hour in the games room with the other prisoners, flanked by two officers. And last week she was allowed to take breaks with other prisoners in the yard for the first time – again, flanked by two officers. Each transition passed seemlessly, even if she was shitting herself throughout.

Incredibly, given the force of the smash, her nose hadn't broken. Though it did suffer a severe cut right across the bridge that was only fully healing over now – four months after the attack. The purple and yellow bruising under both of her eyes hadn't relented for well over a month. It was odd that she had been placed in isolation, given that that was the exact same punishment her attacker had received. Stella, her name was – a close associate of Nancy Trott. She was so enraged that Joy had killed her two boys and yet had the audacity to sit in the canteen brazenly laughing with Christy Jabefemi that she waited until the new prison officer relieved Mathilda from her shift of protecting Joy before running over and grabbing Joy by the hair and slamming her face to the corner of the bench.

While Stella's isolation was deemed punishment, Joy's was for her own safety. She resided in a cell that sits between a janitor's storage unit and a prison officer's station on the other end of the gate that leads into Elm House. She spent most of her days in that cell; though she did have the luxury of a TV screen for company with six channels, as well as her own shower. She also had the freedom to go to and from a small yard at certain times of the day that was just on the other side of the janitor's storage unit. After a couple of weeks in, her three rounds of civilian clothes arrived. Three sweatjumpers, three T-Shirts and three comfy pairs of tracksuit bottoms – along with a dozen pairs of underwear and two pairs of trainers. All comfy clothes. And all comfy clothes that finally fit her.

The only people she ever really got to see while she was in isolation were the same two officers she had seen on her first two days on the regular wing of the prison: Mathilda and Aidan. They were both given the boring task of seeing to the lone prisoner as punishment because her attack was deemed their fault. The Governor blamed new recruit Aidan for the attack happening on his watch. But he mostly blamed Mathilda, because she was Aidan's line manager and was supposed to be still training him in. The whole incident was embarrassing for Aidan, though he got over it as time passed. He liked the job of looking after Joy in isolation because it left him with no real mistakes to make. He'd escort her to the yard a few times a day and they'd often sit and talk. He and Mathilda shared eight-hour shifts looking after Joy. Though Mathilda didn't speak much during her shifts, well, certainly not on any personal level. She upgraded her usual stern muteness to a 'Good morning' or an odd 'How are you?' over the months, but the smallest of small talk was about as big as it ever got between the pair of them. Whereas by now Joy had known that Aidan had become a prisoner officer even though his real passion lay in catering and cooking. And he knew that she cheated during her Leaving Cert exams by sneaking notes into the classroom. That was the depth of discussion they had bonded over during those months. She would plead with him to believe her innocence whenever the topic of her sentence arose. But it rarely did, in truth.

It was starting to infuriate Joy that Shay had yet to visit her. Though she could somewhat understand his hesitations. She had spoken to him on the phone, on her first day in isolation after she had been attacked, but she knew by his tone that, although sympathetic and sincere, he was still uncertain and unwilling to commit to her claims of innocence.

The other phone calls she made were reserved for her father. He was a full-time resident in Muckross – a care home for the vulnerable that was situated on the Dublin border. Noel Lansbury was the youngest full-time resident in that home by far, but he took his wife's painfully slow death in the middle of her life so bad that he lost all sense of belonging and began seeking semblances of solace in alcohol. Bottles of it. And then, in the midst of his own depression while slipping into alcoholism, his grandsons went missing two years before his daughter was arrested for their murder. He sunk so low that he was offered a room at Muckross, even though it is essentially a home for elderly folk. The move has worked for him in some respects, though – he has been sober for the past eighteen months anyway. But his life as he had known it has well and truly ended. He didn't make it to Joy's trial, couldn't bring himself to. And despite pleading with his daughter over the phone that he genuinely believed her version of events, Joy has never been quite sure what his true thoughts are.

'Well, if it isn't Annie... "It's a hard knock life, fo' us",' a Texan-Nigerian accent attempted to sing. Joy looked up through her curls to see Christy smiling her yellow teeth at her. 'Welcome back, sista.'

'I'm so scared, Christy,' Joy sobbed immediately. And then Christy grabbed her into a tight embrace, resting her chin atop Joy's curls.

'No need to be scared, come here... sit down, girl.' They entered Joy's cell and both perched on the side of her thin mattress. 'I told ya. That chick

– Stella – who attacked you, she gone, girl. After her isolation, they packed her off to a'other wing. They was thinkin' bout sendin' you to a'other wing, too. But I pleaded with them that I'd look after ya. 'Sides, Nancy Trott put in a good word, too. Said she'll see to it that her girls don't go near you again. She says she didn't put Stella up to attackin' you, but I don't know whether to believe a word that bitch says.'

'But if you don't believe what she says, amn't I still a target?'

'Relax,' a strange prison officer said, poking her face around Joy's cell door. 'The whole wing has been swept clean. You have nothing to worry about. Nobody's out to hurt you.'

Joy contorted her face at Christy, then whispered, 'Who's that?'

'Oh, she the new screw lookin' after you. They took that new guy what's-his-name, off your watch...'

'Aidan!?' Joy shouted. And then she flew out of her cell all up in a rage; marching down the steel staircases of Elm House until she reached the officers' station close to where she had spent the previous four months in isolation. The only person she had struck up any bond with, any relationship with, since she'd been inside was gone. She dropped to her knees outside the officers' station – her heart genuinely pained. But her cries fell on deaf ears.

'Don't worry, sista,' Christy said, gripping Joy in a tight embrace as a crowd of both prisoners and prison officers gathered around them. 'I'm yo best friend. Anything you need. Anything you want, Christy's here... ya hear me?'

Joy sniffled and snotted and coughed and cried... then she looked Christy in the eyes and offered a smile through the stray strands of her frizzy hair.

'Why are you being nice to me? You don't even think I'm innocent, do you, Christy? You said you hadn't worked me out.'

'Christy works everybody out,' one of the prisoners shouted. 'If Christy says you're guilty, you're guilty. If she says you're innocent, you're innocent.'

Some prisoners scoffed and jeered.

'It's true. God speaks to her,' another prisoner shouted. 'You want the truth, Christy Jabefemi will give you the truth.'

For most of the crowd, the drama was over, and they dispersed, content to allow Joy to be sucked into the delusional bible-bashing clique if she so wished.

'Well,' Joy said, wiping at her face. 'Have you worked me out yet... do you believe I'm innocent?'

Christy laughed, then took Joy in for another hug, kissing her on top of her curls.

'I haven't seen a vision for you yet, girl... but if you want, and when you want, I'm happy to give it a try. Just lemme know when yo ready.'

2,859 days ago...

It didn't take Joy long to let Christy know she was ready.

'I want you to believe me... to believe I'm innocent. I need somebody to,' she pleaded.

Since Joy had been in isolation, Christy had won over a small number of prisoners by conducting mind readings and telling fortunes. She had surprised even the most sceptical in the prison with a number of nailed-on predictions. She had even predicted that Joy would be attacked the day before she was actually attacked. She said that's why she was befriending her, because she got a sign from God that Joy needed protecting. Then Christy predicted that some famous public figure would die soon which just so happened to be the night before Whitney Houston took her own life. There was also the time she predicted that Michelle Doherty – a heavily tattooed prisoner in Elm House – would get her love life back on track soon. And lo and behold, two weeks later Michelle's ex-boyfriend Darren visited the prison for the first time in over a year to declare his undying love for her – telling her he wanted them to move in together as soon as she got out.

The cult of Christy was small, but it was growing pretty much week on week, though only because it was a case of either teaming up with the deluded following of insane-but-placid Christy Jabefemi, or teaming up with Nancy Trott and her cohorts of untrustworthy scumbag criminals.

It was no surprise that all of Christy's recently-recruited associates were in attendance to watch her grip both of Joy's wrists across one of the dining room benches, but it was a surprise that Nancy and her gang of cohorts had also joined in. Although Christy's gifts had been put to the test plenty of times before – to some shocking successes and some embarrassing misses – trying to get a read on the most notorious prisoner in the country was being deemed as the ultimate test of sorts. Even prison officers who had, in the secure confines of the prison officers' headquarters, snorted at Christy's claims of being able to see visions, joined the growing crowd in the dining room.

'You are really, deeply, sad.' Christy said.

Then she let go of one of Joy's wrists to hold a hand towards the crowd in an attempt to stifle the sniggers that had already ignited.

'No shit,' one prisoner shouted, and the laughter grew in volume.

'I mean, deeply sad. I can tell you certainly believe you are innocent.'

Another jeer went up, but it was silenced by the shushing that hissed through pockets of the crowd.

'You lived a happy life. In Rathfarnham. You married well. You had two boys. You were really happy. Actually... hold on... your husband was a real success story, wasn't he?'

'Ah here, for fuck sake, can you tell us something my nanny Margaret couldn't fuckin' tell us?' one prisoner snidely snapped. And then an eruption of laughter suffocated the eerie tension that had struck up as soon as Christy had sat down to grab at Joy's wrists.

Eventually, those who were desperate to listen, shushed down the jeers, to the point where only the crashing and clanking of the pots and pans in the kitchen could be heard in the distance.

'You are a Capricorn, my visions are telling me, that right?'

Joy nodded once, her eyes widening.

'Cudda read Joy's date of birth in the papers,' one prisoner whispered to another.

'Well, do you know Joy's date of birth?' the other prisoner responded. Then they both just shrugged their shoulders at each other, and zoned back in.

'And you are an only child, that right, Joy?'

'Uh-huh?' Joy said, the frown on her forehead creasing further.

'And I can tell that you always wanted a career... you were ambitious, right? Until you got married and then you became a housewife... a mother?'

Joy nodded again, and as she did she noticed eyes shifting from side-to-side in the crowd behind Christy.

'Oh... I've got it. I've got it!' Christy said, her Nigerian accent taking over, her volume rising. 'The woman in the pink hooded top... I can see her... I see her.'

There were puffs of laughter produced from pockets of the crowd, but nobody was walking away, not yet anyway. 'And the figure is walking. Walking down the mountains. Her hands are dirty... her fingernails are dirty. I can't see her face. Just the hood. But I am running towards her.'

More jeering fired up. More shushing stemmed it.

'Wait... wait... I'm catching up with her,' Christy said, her breaths growing in sharpness as she gripped Joy's wrists tighter. 'Come here you. Come here you.' She released her grip from Joy, stretched her hand out to grab at nothing and then yanked herself backwards.

'Turn around bitch. Turn around!'

Slam!

Christy slapped her hand on to the bench. And the whole dining room fell silent. Then she opened her eyes. Wide; so wide, Joy could see the blood rings around both the top and bottom of her eyeballs.

'Was it her? Was it Joy?' a voice from the crowd asked.

'Did she do it? Did she murder her boys?'

Christy slapped her hand to the bench once more.

'You didn't do it. It wasn't you under that pink hood.'

A yell of hurrays went up – a few in support of Christy's gift, most mocking – before the crowd disbursed, shaking their heads either in astonishment or in laughter. But some stayed, either to touch Christy in her moment of enlightenment, or to embrace Joy in solidarity.

'Must be awful what you've been through,' one prisoner, whose face Joy hadn't seen before, whispered into her ear.

2,858 days ago…

Joy had been tossing and turning on her bed during the two nights she had been back at Elm House. The mattress she had slept on for the four months she was in isolation had been at least two times thicker than the one in her regular cell.

She was still yawning from a lack of sleep, but leapt out of bed as soon as her cell door clicked open. And, with the two officers assigned to her flanked by her sides, she stormed her way across the landing to push open the door of Christy's cell.

'Mornin, sista,' Christy said, looking up from her bible. 'What can I do ya for?'

Joy stepped inside, leaving the two officers standing by the door.

'I've been tossing and turning all night, Christy… I never asked you yesterday, not with all the excitement that was going on afterwards, but… you say in your vision that you took down the woman's hood so you could make out her face… to see if it was me or not.'

'Uh-huh,' Christy said, placing her bible on her pillow and standing up.

'Well… you were able to tell everyone it wasn't me.'

'Yep. It wasn't you, Joy. You innocent. You didn't kill those boys.'

'Then who did?' Joy asks, fidgeting with her fingers.

'Huh?'

'What did her face look like?'

Christy picked up her plastic bottle and took a large swig from it, swirling the warm water from cheek to cheek. When she finally swallowed, she patted Joy on the shoulder.

'Let's go eat some breakfast, huh?'

They sat on the same bench Joy had been attacked on four months prior, but being attacked wasn't on her mind right now, nor were the two slices of cardboard toast that lay on a plastic plate in front of her.

'C'mon, Christy. Please. Tell me. What did the face look like?'

'I told ya, sister... I don't know the face. I don't know her. I just know she ain't you.'

'Please.' Joy pressed her two palms together. 'Just tell me what she looked like.'

'Listen, I don't see a full face. Just some features. I just saw enough to know she wasn't you. She didn't have big curly hair like you under that pink hood. She had straight hair.'

'What colour?' Joy said, her eyes squinting.

'Brown.'

'And you say you see features, what kind of features?'

Christy tore a slice of Joy's toast in two, then curled one-half of it into her mouth and chewed.

'She had kinda like an oval face. Pale. White. Definitely white. Red lips. Maybe lipstick.'

'She was wearing lipstick?'

'Yeah. Think so,' Christy said. 'Her lips were all bright red.'

'Did you see her eye colour?'

'Brown. I'm sure they were brown.'

Joy gasped, then held a hand to her mouth.

'What is it, sista,' Christy said, stopping chewing, 'you think you know this bitch? You think you know who killed yo boys?'

⁜

Delia licks the tip of her thumb, then flicks through the papers whilst the gallery wait in silence. They'd spent over three hours in this courtroom the previous afternoon following the trial's opening arguments, watching her doing exactly as she is doing now – rifling through paperwork.

'Now then,' she finally says, her voice booming through the microphone. And as it does, everybody in the gallery sits a little more upright in their benches.

The new courtrooms inside Dublin's Criminal Courts contains rows of pews – not unlike a church – in front of which are two benches where the trial lawyers and the defendants sit. Further in front of those two desks, raised higher than any other chair, is where the judge resides, looking down on everybody.

'Mr Gerd Bracken, can the defence please call their first witness?'

'We can indeed, Your Honour,' Bracken says as he stands. 'The defence calls Mr Philip Grimshaw to the stand.'

A shaven-haired man rises from the gallery and strolls solemnly up the thin aisle of scarlet-red carpet before sitting himself into the witness box adjacent to the judge. After his affirmation is completed, Bracken walks his way to the centre of the courtroom floor and clasps his hands.

'Thank you for being here today, Mr Grimshaw,' he says. 'Can you please state your profession for the court?'

'Of course,' Grimshaw says in a thick northern-English accent. 'I am a dog handler. But a specialist dog handler.'

'Okay, but it is fair to say, Mr Grimshaw, that you don't work for the police in your native country, right? You are a freelance dog handler who has, on occasion, been hired by the police force in the UK, is that correct?'

'That is correct, yes.'

'And it is true to say that in early January of 2009, you received a phone call from a detective of An Garda Siochana here in Ireland, requesting your assistance in what was then a missing persons' case? Two boys, Oscar and Reese Stapleton had gone missing and it was suggested you travel to Dublin to help with the investigation.'

'It is true to say that, yes.'

'Now, you testified at Joy Stapleton's original trial that after spending twenty minutes inside the Stapleton family home, your dog Bunny barked which indicated to you that there was a presence of scents associated with decomposing bodies, correct?'

'Eh, well, I can't be certain of the exact words I used. But it should be stated for the record that Bunny made indications, it doesn't have to be a bark. It may have been a sniff and a long pause. But yeah, Bunny gave me an indication that a decomposing body or bodies had been present in an upstairs bedroom of the Stapleton home.'

'So, Bunny doesn't bark... what does he do exactly when he comes across what he thinks are indications to the presence of decomposing bodies?'

'He stays in or around the area. Then sniffs his nose more forcefully... he might bark. Sometimes he barks.'

'So, his reactions are inconsistent – sometimes he barks, sometimes he doesn't?'

'Yeah, that's right.'

'Well then, how do you personally know the difference with any degree of certainty? Does a bark not indicate something different to a non-bark?'

'Well... Bunny is a unique dog, he's retired now actually.'

'Oh, I'm well aware of his retirement, Mr Grimshaw, and we'll get to that in just a second. But let me ask you this question first... Who trained Bunny to become a dog who could sense the presence of decomposing bodies?'

Grimshaw's fair eyebrows drop.

'Well... I did. I train all my dogs.'

'And who trained you, Sir?'

'Who trained me?'

'Yes. Who trained you to train dogs?'

'I, eh... well, I did a course back in Leeds where I'm from in the late-eighties and eh...'

'Yes, Sir. I am aware of the course you took. A dog handling course.

From all accounts, the training you completed didn't exactly teach you how to train dogs to sniff out decomposing bodies, now did it?'

'No.'

'In fact, it taught you how to train your dog to sit, and roll over, and fetch a stick, isn't that correct?'

'Objection, Your Honour, leading the witness,' Jonathan Ryan calls out.

'You may answer the question,' Judge Delia says, nodding her head at Grimshaw.

'It was a lot more than just asking a dog to roll over and sit,' he says.

'But for the record, you never learned or received any qualification in training dogs how to sniff out decomposing bodies, right?'

'I taught myself all of that. I started to help police with some enquiries back in the early nineties and I liked doing that work... so I branched out, started to teach my dogs new tricks.'

Bracken takes two steps backwards, shuffles some paperwork at his desk, then interlinks his fingers around his navel before taking two steps forward again, leading him back to where he began.

'Right, so what we've established is, not only does the dog, Bunny in this case, not have official training in the sensing of decomposing bodies, but his trainer or handler doesn't either, would that be fair to say, Mr Grimshaw?'

'I know for a fact that Bunny can sense decomposing bodies. Bunny has helped out with major investigations over the years—'

'He has, yes. Nine murder investigations; seven in England, one in Scotland and one here in Ireland. It's just that four years ago Bunny's evidence in one trial was questioned, as were your credentials on dog training, and the evidence you brought to that trial was thrown out, wasn't it? And that is the reason we are here at this retrial today, isn't it? Because that evidence was thrown out and it now calls into question all of the trials Bunny has provided evidence for, including the trial of Joy Stapleton. Bunny has been retired since he was dismissed from that trial in London four years ago, hasn't he, Mr Grimshaw?'

'Yes. I have said that already. He's retired.'

'Because his apparent skills have been called into question.'

'I know he is a dog who can—'

'Sir, I am not interested in your opinion. I am interested in the facts. Bunny was dismissed from a high-profile case in London because his skillsets cannot be determined... correct?'

Grimshaw sighs, then sheepishly glances up to Judge Delia before turning back to Bracken.

'Yes, I guess that's what the court said.'

'Okay, well, let me repeat that for the ears of our court again, shall I?

Bunny the dog's particular skillsets *cannot* be determined. We have no way of knowing for certain if Bunny can or cannot sense the presence of decomposing bodies.'

'Nobody knows Bunny better than I—'

'Ah-ah,' Bracken says holding a finger up. 'I didn't ask you a question that time, Mr Grimshaw.' Bracken takes a step towards the witness box and eyeballs the witness. 'Bunny felt he had sensed a decomposing body in a forest near Kent in England in 2016 and you testified on the stand that Bunny had done so. It was, in that same trial, confirmed two weeks later, that Bunny couldn't have sensed these bodies, because these bodies were never in that forest in the first place.'

'Yes but—'

'Ah-ah, still didn't ask a question.'

'Well you better soon get to asking one, Mr Bracken,' Judge Delia says.

Bracken stares at her momentarily, then pivots his face back to Grimshaw.

'Yes or no, Mr Grimshaw – has Bunny been forcibly retired from this line of work because his findings are not scientifically conclusive?'

Grimshaw stares around himself, then relents.

'Officially, yes.'

'And is it true that Bunny provided evidence in the missing persons case of Reese and Oscar Stapleton?'

'Yes.'

'That is all, Your Honour,' Bracken says before he spins on his heels and walks back to his desk.

'Mr Ryan,' Judge Delia calls out as she scribbles some notes onto her paperwork. 'Have you questions for this witness?'

Ryan rises from his chair.

'You are an upstanding member of society, Mr Grimshaw, correct? You've never been in trouble with police? Never even had a misdemeanour? Never been accused of being anything other than just a bit of a loner because you prefer to spend time with dogs rather than humans, right?'

Grimshaw chuckles.

'I guess you could say that, yes.'

'You've never married so therefore have never been unfaithful. But it is true you have the same two best friends that you've had your whole life?'

'Yeah, we met at primary school and have been buddies ever since.'

'So, you are an upstanding member of society who has been faithful and who has never been in trouble for breaking the law. All accurate statements, right?'

Grimshaw nods.

'Yes.'

'You have never, nor never will intend to deceive anybody. All of the work you have done for the police force in the UK and once here in Ireland, it was all done in good faith, yes?'

'Absolutely. I've never tried to deceive anybody in my life.'

'That's all, Your Honour.'

Judge Delia looks over her glasses at Bracken who stands without hesitation.

'Mr Grimshaw. Deception does not always have to be conscious, would you agree with me?'

Grimshaw's eyebrows dip again.

'Sorry... I...'

'It doesn't matter, Mr Grimshaw. You don't need to answer that question. Thank you.'

Bracken sits again and as he does Judge Delia dismisses Grimshaw from the stand with a nod of her head followed by a subtle waving of her hand. Then she rifles through her paperwork in the resulting silence, taking note of Bracken's tactic of disguising a statement wrapped up in a question. She knew he didn't want to ask Grimshaw if he did or didn't think deception was always a conscious act, he just wanted to make a statement to the court that deception doesn't always have to be conscious. She doesn't want to let Bracken get away with snidey mis-steps, but he covers them so well that she really can't condone him for asking an actual question... even if he didn't bother to get an answer for it. There isn't a more experienced defence lawyer in the country than Gerd Bracken. Although Delia knows she would detest the man if she ever had to spend any time with him outside of a courtroom, she has had to admit in the past that she sure is impressed by his skills when inside that courtroom.

'Recess until after lunch-time, perhaps, Your Honour?' Bracken calls out. Delia squints at him. 'Sorry. Our next witness has had trouble with transportation this morning.'

Delia rolls back the sleeve of her robe and takes note of the time on her wrist.

'It's not even midday yet. Seems awfully early for lunch but ehm... yes, court dismissed for two hours. We will all return at one forty-five p.m. sharp.'

Delia wiggles her mouse as soon as she's back at her office desk, and in the time the screen blinks back to life, she has completed her routine of staring at things she is barely noticing; taking in her cupfuls of pens and the framed photograph of her family – smiling at her husband as he smiles back at her.

One of the last smiles he ever smiled. Then, as soon as her hands hover over her keyboard, she hears footsteps outside, followed, annoyingly, by the rap of one knuckle against her door two times.

'Come in, Callum,' she says.

He grins the same grin his father would grin at her when he used to poke his head around her office door.

'So, the dog was dodgy all along?' Callum says. They both offer the same puffed-through-the-nostrils laugh in sync – a habit they have picked up from way too many years of living with each other. 'Doesn't mean anything though does it?'

Delia shakes her head.

'Don't mind that... how was your date last night?'

'Good, actually. He was... what would I say? Genuine. Honest. Didn't seem as if he was full of shit or anything, you know... Nice looking. Nice eyes. Though he needs a beard. His face is a little pasty.' Delia laughs. 'We swapped numbers.'

'What does he do for a living?'

'Listen,' Callum says, smirking. 'You're at the start of the biggest retrial in the history of this country and you wanna talk to me about a guy whose second name I can't even remember.' He cocks his head. 'Go on... tell me. Did the dog testimony have any impact on you?'

Delia removes her glasses, then unclips her pearl earrings and places them carefully to the side of her photo frame.

'It's made an impact. But not a huge one,' she says. 'There were no revelations, were there? Not much we didn't know before today. The dog that sniffed a decomposed body in the Stapleton bedroom all those years ago turns out to be a bit of a fraud. That was pretty apparent in the original trial... to me anyway.'

'Grimshaw was always just a forensic witness fitting the needs of the officers, right?'

'Exactly.'

'But you still think she did it, right?'

'Callum!' Delia barks. 'I am looking at this trial with totally fresh eyes.'

'Course you are, Mum,' he says.

'Y'know, you're not the first one who's dropped by to ask what I'm thinking.'

'Huh?'

'Eddie Taunton... he popped by yesterday. Sounded most suspicious. As if he was leading me towards a guilty verdict.'

'Well, he would want a guilty verdict, wouldn't he? He can't have his whole system come crashing down by admitting we got the Joy Stapleton trial all wrong in the first place. Heads would roll... Lots of them. His would probably be the first to go.'

'Can you imagine the pay-out Joy would get if she was found not guilty after all these years?'

'Tens of millions, right?' Delia turns out her bottom lip and slowly nods her head. 'Taunton couldn't have been leaning on you though, right, Mum? I mean I wouldn't trust him as far as I could throw him, but he's not that dodgy, is he? He wouldn't put pressure on you to deliver a specific verdict, right?'

Delia creases up her nose.

'It was just kind of odd how he spoke to me. He brought up the fact that he asked me about the Stapleton case in an interview years ago. He remembered I was insistent the judge and jury got it right in the original trial; that Joy is guilty of killing her sons. I think that's why I landed this case. He fought for no jury, and one judge. Then he picked me as that one judge, knowing I had once given him a detailed analysis of why the first trial got it right.'

'Jesus. You seriously think he picked you to ensure a guilty verdict?' Callum's eyes narrow, and he sits back in his chair, blowing through his lips. 'He's right in one way though, is Eddie. You're certain she's guilty, aren't you?'

'Callum...'

'Yes! I know... You're looking at this case from fresh eyes. I get it. Of course.' Callum grins. 'So, who's up next after the dog handler?'

'Ehm...' Delia picks up her paperwork and begins to file through it.

'Geez, Mom. How can you be somebody with brains to burn, but no idea how to ever get your paperwork in order?'

'Ah, here, I got it,' she says, removing a sheet from the pile and bringing it to the top. 'Bracken is going to call an ex-detective who was involved in the original case. A Mrs Sandra Gleeson.'

SANDRA GLEESON

I'm not nervous. The opposite in fact. I'm bullish. Determined.

I actually wasn't invited to give evidence at this trial, I offered to do so. As soon as I heard there was going to be a retrial – and that Gerd Bracken would be defending Joy Stapleton – I immediately picked up the phone.

I sheepishly take a peek at Joy as I sit. She hasn't changed. Well, not really. You'd still know it was her. Big bushy curls smothering her tiny features. Though I can tell from here that her skin looks drier, as if she's been parched of fluids for the entire eight years she's been inside. She has one deep lined wrinkle that runs vertical between her eyebrows that wasn't there before. And some of the tips of her curls have faded to grey. Though she's still tiny. Still rake thin. And still unmistakably Joy Stapleton.

'Thank you for being here, Mrs Gleeson,' Bracken says.

'Oh, Sandra, please,' I reply, batting my hand at him.

'Okay... Sandra it is then. The court appreciates and thanks you for your time. Can you state your occupation – and if you don't mind, former occupation – for the record of the court, please?'

'Sure,' I say, repositioning my seating position. 'I work for Integration.'

'Well, you don't just work for Integration, do you?'

'No,' I say, laughing, until I realise this is really not the place, nor the time for my snorty chuckle to be heard. 'I am the founding member of Integration. We are a non-profit organisation whose goals are to ensure immigrants and refugees transition into our societies as seamlessly as possible.'

'Very noble,' Bracken says, nodding. 'And before that?'

'Well before that I was a member of An Garda Siochana. For eight years.

I was a uniformed Garda for four years, then an inspector for two years and a detective for the last two years before turning in my badge.'

'Mind telling the court why you turned in your badge?'

'Sure. I, eh... I didn't feel comfortable. My honest opinion is that the police force is somewhat controlled by what I call systemic fractures. I found, as an investigator, that I was forced to fit my investigations into a certain pattern that was already structured. So, often I found myself having to arrest somebody without true investigation and I felt... well... I felt as if I wasn't doing what I set out to do.'

'Which was?'

'Which was to play a role in society. That's why I wanted to be a police-woman as far back as I can remember. I thought I could help people in our society that way. But that's not what being a member of An Garda Siochana turned out to be.'

'That's interesting. We'll come back to that in a minute or two actually. But for the court, can you firstly detail a case you began investigating back in November of 2008?'

'Well, I assume you are talking about the Oscar and Reese Stapleton case?' I say. We rehearsed that bit. Not that I'm in any way here just to please Gerd Bracken. Truth be known, I don't really like the man. He's a bit slimy. A bit full of himself. But we did talk through what he would ask of me during this trial and I agreed to go along with his script – as long as I was telling the truth. He just wanted to frame the truth in his own pattern. Which is fine by me. He knows what he's doing.

'You assisted Lead Detective Ray De Brun on the Stapleton case, correct?'

'Yes, I did indeed,' I reply. 'But I should stress at this point, that although I am likely to point to some flaws in the investigative practices here in Ireland, I am not here to slander any persons, specifically. The people aren't the problem. The system they work in is the problem. For example, Detective Ray De Brun – as you chose to bring up his name – was a fine detective. And is a fine human being.'

I didn't rehearse that with Bracken. It actually takes him by surprise and he stalls, twitching his fingers. I didn't even plan to say it; it's just that he brought up Ray's name. And I don't wanna go shouting my head off about how flawed the system is and have everyone think I'm defaming Ray. I'm not. I actually like Ray.

'Okay, so you mentioned a flawed system, Sandra. Can you detail that for me?'

'Objection, Your Honour. That's a rather broad question,' the young lawyer on the opposite side of the room calls out.

I look up to Judge Delia who is sucking on her lips, stewing in thought. Her features are hard to read. The eyes behind her 1950s style retro glasses are oval and so dark that it looks as if her pupils are constantly dilated. And she has that cropped brown haircut most women in their sixties seem to have. Though, it's hard to put an age on Judge Delia with any accuracy, but she's got to be around the sixty mark, surely. Or perhaps the hair-do just adds a few years.

'Yes, be more specific in your line of questioning, Mr Bracken,' she eventually says.

'Of course, Your Honour,' Bracken replies, shuffling his frame back around to face me. 'Sandra, you said you felt you were part of a fractured system when you worked for the police force. Can you detail to me how you feel that fractured system played a role in the investigation into Joy Stapleton?'

'Oh, well.' I sit more upright, leaning my forearms onto the small shelf carved around the squared edges of the witness box. 'The Stapleton case, I guess, is a good example of the systemic issues we face with regards policing in this country, because the investigation focused on one suspect from the get-go and then fitted a case entirely around that suspect. Like I say – and I want to repeat this – I don't think the personnel who work in the force are to blame. They – we – we were just following a decades old system that can, in my humble opinion, lead even the best of detectives down the wrong path. My honest opinion is that the system gives investigators tunnel vision. And as I said, I don't blame the individuals, personally. I just believe a lot of detectives suffer with tunnel vision because, ultimately, they are led to believe that success in their line of work is measured by a successful prosecution. But that is so far wide of how success for a detective should be measured. Success for an investigator should be seeking the truth. Bottom line. But that's not what it is. Detectives are measured by the justice system based on whether or not they get a successful prosecution. Detectives are measured by the top end of the police force based on whether or not they get a successful prosecution. And they are measured by their line managers and peers on whether or not they get a successful prosecution. They're even measured by the public by that means too. And it must be said that there is a huge difference between striving to find a successful prosecution, as opposed to striving to find the truth.'

I tap my tongue against my dry pallet, then look to the court assistant and motion a mock sipping to her. I was told there'd be a jug of water in the witness box but there isn't. She nods back at me, then turns and paces out a side door.

'Well, this, coming from an experienced member of the police force is really troubling. Are you saying Joy Stapleton was a suspect right from the get-go and that detectives were solely focused on getting her prosecuted for this crime?'

'Absolutely she was,' I say. 'And because of that, the whole investigation turned into a task of finding out what she did, rather than us being out there and exploring the entire truth of what happened to Oscar and Reese.'

'Can you give us examples of this?'

The court assistant walks back through the side door, holding a paper cup towards me. I mouth a 'thank you' to her as she hands it to me and then take a quick sip, just to wet my whistle.

'Well, detectives felt Joy was suspicious,' I say, 'but there was absolutely zero evidence to suggest she had anything to do with her sons going missing. Of course, because she was a mother who was, at times back then, uncontrollably grieving, investigators had to walk on eggshells around her. Personally, I would have had a preference for looking into other possibilities, cos as far as I was concerned Joy Stapleton was going nowhere. She wasn't getting away from us.'

'So, there were other leads?' Bracken asks.

'Well, in truth, we had nothing to go on. It was like Oscar and Reese just vanished into thin air. So, I wanted to explore all of the thin air. But our investigation seemed to solely narrow onto the grieving mother.'

'Okay, well, if you can give me a specific example of what you call narrowing the investigation...'

'Well, the last witness you had sitting here this morning – Mr Grimshaw... Him and his dog Bunny, right? Our bosses were aware Mr Grimshaw had helped detectives solve murder cases in the UK, so they called him over with his dog to sniff out the Stapleton home. I don't think this was a calculated or conscious deliberate step over the line. I think our bosses genuinely just felt, "How can we prove the mother did this? – let's get sniffer dogs in". So, they searched and searched for a dog handler who they knew had a history of assisting police forces with positive conclusions in this specific regard. They couldn't find one in Ireland, and eventually came to Mr Grimshaw in the UK. And, of course Grimshaw, through his sniffer dog, gave them exactly what they wanted. But truth be known, as you have found out in this court this morning, that is not scientific evidence at all. And I've never believed it to be.'

'Speculation, Your Honour,' the other lawyer yells out.

'Not your place to speculate, Mrs Gleeson,' the judge tells me. 'If you can just answer the direct question please.'

'Well, what I will say is, Bunny the dog's findings – if you want to call them that – weren't enough for an arrest anyway. I was very surprised that *evidence was even allowed in the original trial, to be honest. We knew – or certainly I knew – Mr Grimshaw's credibility was lacking. It amazed me it was allowed into court... but that too, I guess, is a reflection of the court system fitting into a flawed system.'*

'That is more speculation, Your Honour,' the lawyer says, this time slapping his hand to the desk in front of him.

'Mrs Gleeson.' The judge's eyes peer over her glasses at me. *'Your job here is not to speculate, but to answer direct questions. I will not remind you of that again.'*

'Sorry,' I say. Then I turn back to Bracken, cringing a little inside. *'I guess what I mean is the dog coming in is a good example of an investigation following a system, rather than the investigation following the truth. Does that make sense?'*

Bracken interlocks his fingers across his stomach.

'If you could explain that a little more clearly for the court, Sandra.'

'Well, instead of following evidence and letting the evidence lead detectives to a suspect, the detectives already had their suspect and then tried to create the evidence around her. Same with the CCTV footage.'

I take another sip of water, and as I do, I afford myself another quick glance at Joy. She's sitting as still as she can, her fingers forming a fallen steeple on the desk in front of her. She fascinates me. She really does. She's either one of the coldest killers in the history of our nation. Or she has lived one of the most unfortunate and saddest lives in the history of our nation. It doesn't get any more intriguing than that.

'Are you referring to the CCTV of the lady in the pink hooded top?'

'Yes,' I say, before taking another sip of water – though it doesn't seem to be doing anything for the cotton on my tongue. *'When the bodies of Oscar and Reese were found two years after they were reported missing, the investigation didn't turn into "How did these bodies get to this location?" It immediately turned into "How do we link Joy to this location?"'*

What I'm saying is true. About four hours after the bodies had been confirmed as the two Stapleton boys, one detective at our station was rubbing his hands together with glee, shouting 'We're gonna nail her now.' I don't think any of the cops I worked with were nasty, or calculated, or manipulative, even. They were just following the system, without realising how fractured it truly was. Some people just never notice the obvious things that are staring them in the face.

'So, they were actively looking to link Joy to that scene?'

'Exactly. I calculated at the time – because I have been fascinated by this case and this is actually the case that really started to open my eyes into how the system operates – that officers must have viewed over five thousand hours

of CCTV footage. There were two hundred and twenty-eight CCTV cameras at the bottom of the Dublin mountains that recorded footage that night. Some of which still had their footage stored digitally, most didn't. But we still managed to get five thousand hours of footage from different cameras. My problem was they weren't viewing five thousand hours looking for anything suspicious. They were specifically looking for Joy. They wanted to put her near the scene of where the bodies were found.'

'And then what?'

'Then they found those famous three seconds of footage... the footage we've all seen. Where a figure walks by a garden wearing a pink hoodie. And that was that. They felt they had their woman. We knew Joy had been wearing a pink hooded top the day before the boys were reported missing. But as you know, Mr Bracken, this footage is only three seconds long, and we see no face, just a figure in a pink hoodie. And, as was brought up in the original trial as an argument, there was no footage of the woman in the pink hoodie going up the mountain. Only coming down.'

'Sorry... They used three seconds out of five thousand hours as a reason to arrest Joy Stapleton?'

'They did.'

'So, in your expert opinion, detectives fit the whole investigation around their suspect, rather than allowing the investigation to lead them to a suspect, right?'

'Exactly, Mr Bracken. That is the fracture in the system.'

He spins on his heels and points one finger towards the ceiling.

'For the record, this is Sandra Gleeson – an assistant detective working on the investigation into the Oscar and Reese Stapleton case – admitting to us here, under oath, that the investigation was flawed and that my client was a suspect from the get-go. Sandra, the court thank you for your time.'

'Mrs Gleeson,' the other lawyer says, standing up. 'You interviewed for the position of Chief Superintendent in early 2011, correct?'

'That is correct,' I say, before reaching for my glass again. I thought I might get a little breather before cross examination, but it seems to have started before Bracken has even sat down.

'You didn't get that job, did you?'

'No. There was somebody more qualified than me for that position.'

'Seems odd then, that you left the police force nine months later. If you were gunning for a promotion, surely you weren't really that angered by 'the system' as you call it?'

'As I said, I had already made up my mind that the system was flawed.'

'Okay, but that didn't stop you still wanting to be part of that system, did it? You interviewed for a promotion. Are you sure you were not bitter about being overlooked for this position, subsequently left the force and have, ever since, been rather negative about your former bosses?'

I gasp, then slam the paper cup I'm holding onto the shelf in front of me.

'Sir, I left a sixty thousand euro a year job with a fantastic pension and security to earn no wage by running a charity that deals with helping people in society. I wasn't bitter. I was better. I wanted to help people.'

His face drops. Stick that in your pipe and smoke it, young man. You little shit. Trying to trap me. My opinion on the investigative procedures in this country have nothing to do with that Chief Superintendent's position. I never felt I was going to get that role, anyway. Stevie Wood was much more primed for it than I was. He was next in line. I only interviewed for it because that was part of the system too. You were expected to interview... expected to show an eagerness for climbing the ranks.

'You know what, Mrs Gleeson,' the lawyer says, shoving both of his hands into his trouser pockets. 'Let's just get some clarity on the testimony you've given here today, shall we? You are here to testify that in your experience, as a police officer and investigator, the system in which investigators operate in is flawed, right? "Fractured" you called it specifically. You've even said today that you think the judicial system is fractured in some way. Now I'm not disagreeing with you. And I am sure you will find other members of An Garda Siochana and other employees in the judicial system who would agree with you also. But is such testimony really pertinent to this specific case? You happen to be a person who is critical of the system who also happened to work on the Stapleton case, right? So, Mr Bracken rounding you up to testify at this court case kind of gives off the impression that the Stapleton case, specifically, was fractured and that it led to the wrong person being arrested. But that is not what you are here to testify today, is it? You are only here to testify that the system in which you once worked, is, in your opinion, fractured, correct?'

'That is correct, Sir,' I say. 'I am only here to testify that the system is flawed. Not whether or not I think Joy is innocent or guilty. This case – as far as I'm concerned – all comes down to whether or not you believe Joy Stapleton is the lady in that three-seconds of CCTV footage – or whether or not you believe it to be a crazy coincidence.'

'And do you think it's a crazy coincidence, Mrs Gleeson?'

'Objection.' Bracken stands as he shouts, scooting his chair back.

'Your Honour,' the other lawyer says, 'question is pertinent.'

Judge Delia squelches up her mouth then switches her stare from the lawyer to me. But not in time to see me stifle a gasp. I didn't think I'd be asked this directly. Bracken knew I wouldn't guarantee him a positive answer if he asked me on the stand if I thought Joy was guilty or innocent, *because we discussed it and I told him I couldn't be certain that it's not Joy in that footage. But he also told me that Jonathan Ryan wouldn't ask this question either. Because it would be just too darn risky for him. If I say right now that, 'No, I don't think that's Joy Stapleton in that CCTV footage', then I'd blow this case wide open. But if I say I do think it's her, then my testimony here really would and should be regarded as redundant by the judge. I feel my bullishness slip away from me as I wait on her to make her mind up. I hope she doesn't make me answer that question.*

'I'll allow it,' she says. 'I feel that question specifically pertinent to this witness given the testimony she has offered today. You may answer, Mrs Gleeson.'

I look over the rim of the paper cup at Joy as I gulp down the last of my water. She stares back at me, accompanying it with a sombre pursing of her lips. Jesus, I've obsessed about her face for years. Obsessed about this case. It was the case I cut my teeth on as a detective. The case that made me realise the whole system is flawed from top to bottom. I've read every word ever written about this case; have even read the transcripts of the original trial three times. There can't be many people – if anyone – who knows it in more depth than I do. Truth be known, there simply is no evidence that links Joy Stapleton to this crime. By the time the bodies were found, all forensic evidence had long since weathered away. This whole case comes down to those three seconds of CCTV footage – footage I haven't been able to stop thinking about for years. I've even dreamt about it. And in the dream, the hooded figure in the CCTV stops walking, then turns around to stare up to the CCTV camera to wave at me... And yet every time she does, the fecking face is always just a blur. Truth be known, I simply – like everybody else – can't know for certain if it is Joy under that hoodie. Though I have to say, I can see why people find the defence of "coincidence" difficult to swallow.

'Mrs Gleeson, would you like me to repeat the question?' the lawyer asks, growing in impatience as I continue to hide behind my paper cup. 'Do you or do you not think it is just a coincidence that somebody with the exact unique hoodie as Mrs Stapleton happened to be walking close to where her sons' bodies were found on the night we believe them to have been murdered?'

'I'm no expert on coincidences,' I say, taking the cup away from my mouth. 'I have no experience in coincidence. I do, however, have experience in investigative work. And I believe that the investigation that led to Joy Stapleton's arrest was flawed. That's all I'm prepared to testify.'

Joy wobbled herself into the canteen, now flanked – as she had been for the past two months – by only one officer, before pausing. None of her pals were at their usual bench. She glanced around and, sweeping the curls away from her face, placed her palm against her forehead, confused.

'They're all in the kitchen,' one of the elderly prisoners told her.

So, Joy removed her hand from her forehead, offered the back of the elderly woman's head a grateful nod and paced around the back of the counter until she swept open the double doors that led to the kitchen.

They were all gathered around a bench. It was Lizzie who looked up first.

'Oh no, she's here,' she said.

Then the whole group looked up from the bench to see Joy's confused expression heading towards them.

'Surprise!' they yelled in unison, stepping aside and showing Joy the half-iced cake that was slopped onto the bench.

'Congrats, sista,' Christy said, squeezing Joy's shoulder 'We're one year in today. You've come a long way, girl. I'm proud o' ya.'

They ate cake for breakfast, washed down with lukewarm tea, and then Joy sat in the television room with Christy, not only looking backwards about how far they'd come during their year inside together, but looking forwards, to their fight to get Joy's double-life sentence overturned.

It only took Christy to reveal that the visions she saw under that pink hoodie had brown hair, brown eyes and a pale face, before Joy was accusing Lavinia Kirwan of killing her boys. Though her best friend had long been on her radar as a suspect – especially after Lavinia had testified against Joy in the original trial; saying that Joy was suffering mentally in the lead up to the boys' disappearance.

But to make absolutely sure, Joy made Christy go deeper into her visions, to see if a glint of green was in those eyes, like the glint Joy knew Lavinia had in hers; and to see if there was a tiny mole on the side of the figure's neck much like the one Lavinia had. Each time Christy went deeper into her vision, under pleas from Joy, she came back only further determining within Joy's mind that it was indeed her best friend who had murdered Oscar and Reese.

They began the 'Joy Stapleton is Innocent' campaign; a campaign that was supported by about one-third of Elm House, as well as, bizarrely, about one-third of the population outside of the prison's walls.

Although most were sympathetic to Joy's plight, the theory of Lavinia being the killer never really made it past the confines of the prison without being met by derision. Mostly because Lavinia had a rock-solid alibi for the night in question.

By this stage Joy was settling comfortably into prison life, if it weren't for the cold. For some reason she felt colder than the rest of the prisoners, and often wore two sweat tops to wander around the landings of Elm House. She was still being flanked by one prison officer, though most in the wing felt that was largely unnecessary as, by this stage, nobody wanted to harm Joy more so than they wanted to harm any of the other prisoners. Yes, there was a split between Nancy's Cohorts and Christy's Crazies, but physical attacks were pretty much non-existent in Elm House, save for the odd square-up in the games room when somebody felt the rules were being flaunted. Both factions had learned to live together, the only real tension coming when Nancy and Christy happened to confront each other. But they were both prison-wise and aware of their aging years. So, nothing untoward happened between them, bar a tense silence that would eventually be filled. Joy felt uncomfortable by the manner in which Nancy would stare her up and down and lick her lips when Christy wasn't around, but she had long since stopped feeling intimidated.

What didn't leave her, and she was beginning to realise never would for the rest of her life, was the monotony of prison. 'Boredom,' she had come to tell anyone who would listen, 'was the real price convicts paid for their crimes.'

Although the 'Joy is Innocent' campaign had filled many of her weeks and months with some sort of ambition, she was tired and impatient with the lack of progress the campaign was making.

Her lawyers had lauded the efforts of her supporters, but told Joy in no uncertain terms that the courts weren't going to move any quicker for her just because her campaign was earning the attention of the tabloid newspapers. She wasn't entitled to an appeal. And certainly wasn't guaranteed one.

'An appeal in your case would take so long, Joy, you'd be quicker finding new evidence that'd turn the screw on a retrial,' her lawyer told her. 'With the backing and support you have, you could pile the pressure on the system.'

And then he left, never to be seen by Joy again. His time was well and truly up on this case. He had worked with Joy from the early days of her arrest, and was kind, considerate and always professional as he guided her through her original trial. But ultimately, he lost, and she eventually lost him less than a year into her sentence because he just couldn't afford the years it would take to force an appeal through. He knew the system better than anyone; knew he'd be throwing away years of his promising career if he was to stay with this case. He said he'd do the best he could, but Joy hadn't seen nor heard from him for months and she began to realise it was up to her and Christy to get herself out of this mess. Besides, she was never convinced that lawyer truly felt she was innocent anyway. Not like Christy does.

So, with no husband coming to the prison to visit her, and no lawyer now filling her in on her legal rights, Joy only had one hope of a visit – albeit a distant hope, given her father's ill-health. But one day, about ten months in, when she was wiping down the tables in the canteen, Mathilda crept up behind her.

'You got a visitor today, Joy,' she said. 'It's your daddy.'

He looked aged, as if he was fading into a sepia photograph. But he smiled when he saw his tiny daughter walking towards him – the first time she'd seen him genuinely smile since her mother had passed.

They spoke about her case, about her new-found theory that Lavinia may have played a part. Her father entertained the idea, but ultimately didn't seem positive that Joy was likely to turn this mess around. He swore as he held her stare that he believed her innocence, but the inconsistency in his breathing, coupled with the fact that he couldn't maintain his focus on what she was saying for very long, confirmed to Joy that he wasn't up for the fight. She knew she couldn't rely on him to help her.

'Do what you can, kid,' he said. Then he gave her another hug and hobbled his way over to the front desk where Joy watched him struggle to sit into a wheelchair before being pushed out of the prison by a stranger dressed in purple scrubs.

She was saddened to see her father in such ill-health, but a visit was a visit and she skipped her way back to Elm House, the promise of a smile on her lips. The smile, however, didn't last long, not with somebody lurking around the corner.

'You child-killing bitch,' Marian snarled at her. Marian was one of Nancy's cohorts – small but stocky; wide shoulders and thick arms. Joy backed up against the concrete wall and tried to steady her breathing as Marian inched her ugly mug nearer hers. 'You're lucky. If you didn't have Christy Jabefemi by your side most of the time, you'd be in a wheelchair much like I saw your daddy getting into one back at the visitor's hall.'

Then Marian snapped her teeth shut, just inches from Joy's face, and went on her way. The intimidation shook Joy, but by the time she got back to Elm House, everything seemed just as normal as it had been the day before: Christy's Crazies existing alongside Nancy's Cohorts.

She dropped by Christy's cell; not to inform her that she'd just been intimidated by Marian Crosby on the landing below them, but to chat – as if they hadn't spent the last eight months since Joy got out of isolation chatting pretty much every hour they were allowed out of their cells.

'They say a gal on Maple House took her life last night.'

'Really?' Joy asked, her mouth popping open.

'Yep. Used her bed sheets to tie the noose. Ya know, e'rtime I hear of a prisoner hanging, I immediately think they were murdered.'

'Murdered?'

'It's just so easy. I've heard it done befo'. Ya tie the noose, visit the prisoner when they asleep, put the noose around their neck and pull as hard as ya can. But ya gotta get that noose up the top o' the neck, not the bottom, not the middle. The very top. It's not a strangling. It's a hanging. Folk hang from here,' she said, positioning her hand around the edge of her jawline, 'not here,' she said, lowering to the centre of her neck.

'So, you think somebody killed her?'

'Oh, I don't know... I don't know what's going on in Maple House,' Christy said. 'I'm just sayin' e'rtime I hear of a hanging in prisons, I get a little suspish, ya know whaddam sayin'?'

'Who was she?'

'Chick called Audrey. Audrey Murray. Only twenty-eight, that's what I heard. She was in doin' two year for drug dealin'. Now why you wanna go kill yoself when you only in for a couple years?'

Joy shrugged.

'Maybe she didn't enjoy living in the outside world as much as she didn't like living in this inside world.'

'Or maybe, maybe she was just off her head... drugs can do that.'

'Wouldn't know,' Joy says, perching herself on the bed next to Christy.

'You too squeaky clean t'ever do drugs, Joy?'

Joy puffed out a laugh.

'Guess so.'

'Never sniffled a line o' coke ya whole life?'

Joy shook her curls.

'Weed. Ya smoked some dope, right?'

'Haven't actually. I took my first drag of a cigarette when I was fifteen and it choked me so much I swore I'd never smoke again... and I haven't. Wouldn't touch one. What about you?'

'Me?' Christy said, cackling that husky laugh of hers. 'Do I look like I do drugs?'

Joy stared into Christy's bloodshot eyes, then tilted her head slightly, like a puppy dog.

'Yes!'

Christy fell back on to the bed, cackling.

'Yo right. Yo right. I do a lot of drugs outside,' she said, sitting back up. 'Meth. Girl, I love and hate me some meth in equal measure.'

'Meth.' Joy shivered. 'Why?'

'Transforms you. It transforms me anyway. I transform from feeling suicidal just like Audrey Murray, Lord Jesus rest her soul, to making me feel like I can't get enough o' this life.'

'Really? Like an antidepressant?' Joy asked.

Christy put her arm around Joy and squeezed her.

'S'more than that. It's like an alternative world. A world that makes me feel closer to Jesus.'

She intrigued Joy by regaling her greatest hits of misdemeanours she had experienced since she first discovered the effects of methamphetamine some fifteen years prior. And why, whilst she loves being under the influence of the drug, she hates the come down, and constantly has to battle in her mind between living the high of the chemicals coursing through her veins against the low of the aftermath. A big negative, Christy informed Joy, of constantly chasing the high was the fact that it was expensive. And that's why Christy became a thief. She needed money to fund her habit. Which is what kept landing her ass back inside Mountjoy Prison. But while Christy was surviving well inside by using the legal substitute for meth, Desoxyn – which she had administered each day by a medic – she knew that as soon as she was a free woman again, the first thing she'd do was rob somebody so that she could afford the buzz of the real thing.

'I normally suffer in prison. Even with the Desoxyn they give me in here,' Christy said. 'But you, girl, havin' you in here with me, you really helping me survive. Hey... I guess you ma new drug.'

They both cackled; Joy by now having adopted the almost uniformed prison cackle that she found most intimidating in other prisoners when she first arrived.

And it was at the loudest of Joy's laughing, through eyes that were watering, that she saw him appear in the cell's doorway.

'Aidan!' she squealed.

⁞

Delia brings a balled fist to her mouth and yawns into it.

Trials have always been exhausting for her. Not physically, of course – all she does is sit, whether at the trial itself or back here in her dimly lit office. Her exhaustion is purely mental. She once read that there are so many variables to consider when examining a trial of any magnitude, that the muscle strain required to consider them all is the equivalent, to the brain, of running a marathon.

What Delia finds most exhausting of all when judging is the required batting away of her gut. 'Instinct is most annoying for a judge,' she has often repeated over the years. She has had to train herself to not allow her thinking to be clouded in any way by her gut. And yet despite twenty years as a judge – thirty-three years in the judicial system wholly – she still hasn't mastered it.

She uses a technique she read about in a book that details decision-making, called *Mind Fuck*. It involves her scrutinizing every minute detail of a witness's testimony or piece of evidence and then filtering it all into two separate pockets within her brain; one pocket for details of the trial that affect her emotionally. And the other pocket for parts of the trial that fit within proper legal parameters.

The main reason she was yawning into her fist was down to the fact that Sandra Gleeson's testimony was straining this filtering process. Delia definitely noted a slice of solace in the former detective who had spent just over ninety minutes on the stand that afternoon. She could empathise with Sandra when she was complaining of working within the restraints of a fractured system. And because of that, her gut kept screaming that this was a credible witness and must be taken seriously.

After Delia had re-awoken her tired, old computer – following her usual routine of staring around her desk, soaking in the smile of her husband as he wrapped his arm around Callum – the first sentence she typed into her notes was, 'I believe Sandra Gleeson.' But Delia also believed that statement, strong as it looked typed at the top of a blank Word document, held no real significance when considered inside the legal parameters of the system in which she worked. It made absolutely no difference whether or not she believed the witness, because belief without proof is almost akin to redundant in judicial terms. It never matters what a judge or a jury believe, it only matters what can be proven to them.

'What did Sandra Gleeson's testimony prove?' Delia mutters to herself, while dipping her chin into her neck so she can stare down the length of her robe. Delia often does this; speaks to herself, during a deliberation. She believes her outer voice controls her inner voice, as if it refrains her from going outside the lines of her filtering process.

She pauses, and then begins to slowly tip-tap her fingernail against the mouse before she shoots back upright and begins to type.

She proved that when searching for CCTV footage, the investigators were ONLY looking for Joy.

She sits back in her chair and sighs, swiping her glasses up from the bridge of her nose and combing them back into her hair.

'She said there was over five thousand hours' worth of footage searched in the aftermath of the bodies being found... wow!' Delia says to herself. Then she presses the balls of her palms into her eyes and swings ever so subtly from side to side in her chair. 'Five thousand hours....'

This was eye-opening for Delia, even though, right this second, she had her eyes closed. The fact that five thousand hours' worth of CCTV footage had been viewed by investigators was never raised during the original trial. In fact, all that was ever spoken about during that original trial were three seconds out of those five thousand hours. Three measly seconds that end before you can even whisper the question, '*Is that Joy Stapleton?*' to yourself. Three seconds that only show the back of a woman in a pink hoodie walking by a lone, large bungalow owned by a paranoid couple who had a camera installed that peers out onto their modest front lawn. Investigators combed the whole area at the foot of the Dublin mountains looking for CCTV footage – from main roads and private companies – in the aftermath of the boys' bodies being found. One police officer noticed a residential camera during a round of routine questioning and footage from the night in question was requested from the owners of the bungalow. Everything had been stored digitally and so the police received the night-long footage almost immediately.

'Three seconds out of five thousand,' Delia says, sitting back upright. She stretches her fingers, all the while staring around her desk in further thought, filing away her gut instinct as best she could. She likes Sandra Gleeson. Trusts Sandra Gleeson. Can empathise with Sandra Gleeson. But she has to keep reminding herself that none of that matters.

'If they were only looking for Joy in all of that footage,' she whispers, 'then what did they miss?'

She washes a hand over her face, then slaps that same hand to the top of her desk.

'C'mon, Delia,' she says to herself. 'Think!'

Her mind wanders to Gerd Bracken; only because it would fascinate her to know what he would have made of Sandra Gleeson's testimony. He probably doesn't realise how much of an impact her time on the stand has had on the judge. He'll likely have thought Sandra did a good job for him, and that it certainly opened up a crack of doubt. But there's no way he'd have imagined Judge Delia would be so conflicted by what his witness had to say.

Jonathan Ryan, Delia feels, will probably be thinking Sandra's testimony didn't hurt him as he had likely feared it would. Yes, she raised doubt on the legitimacy of the original investigation. But he'll be secretly buoyed by the fact that he held firm in his cross examination. He went balls-out, shocking everybody in the courtroom by asking whether or not she felt the woman in the CCTV footage was or wasn't Joy Stapleton.

But Sandra, to her credit, held firm – and gave as good a non-answer as she possibly could. The way Sandra tackled that question only reaffirmed to Delia that Sandra was both a worthy and a trustworthy witness. She was willing to criticise the manner in which the police scrutinized all of the CCTV footage. But she wasn't willing to criticise the footage itself.

'Everything comes down to those three seconds,' Delia mutters to herself. Though what she was saying wasn't much of a revelation to her. Even when she answered Eddie Taunton's question in that interview all those years ago, Delia had said exactly that.

'The whole entire trial, when you consider it fully, really came down to the CCTV footage,' she had said in the most formal way possible, all suited for her interview in a John Rocha single breasted jacket, complimented by a frilled blouse that bustled together at the collar to form a bow. 'As you know, Mr Taunton, coincident cases are largely problematic for a judge and jury.

But when all is taken into consideration, such as the fact that the pink hooded top in the footage has distinguishable features and is the only one believed to be owned by anyone in Ireland. When you consider the fact that this footage was recorded the night before the boys were reported missing, in a neighbourhood not too far from where the bodies were eventually found. And when you consider that nobody ever came forward to say "That was me in that footage. You can mark me out of your enquiries." Taking all of these *coincidences* into consideration, Mr Taunton, I didn't feel the defence could rely on coincidence as their argument.'

'So, in your professional opinion, the jury got the Stapleton case right?' Taunton asked her.

'I'm certain they did, Sir.'

She couldn't have envisaged, of course, that interview answer would eventually lead to her presiding over the retrial of Joy Stapleton some eight years later.

She begins to tap her finger nail against her mouse again, running through her head whether or not she would answer that question the same way if she were asked it in an interview today; and was beginning to admit to herself that Sandra Gleeson's testimony this afternoon would probably halt her from being so confident in her initial judgement.

She wiggles her mouse, to locate the icon on her screen, then drags it to a folder on her desktop. The computer pauses before flashing an image of a neatly mowed garden at night onto the screen. As white digits tick away in the bottom right corner, a figure walks through the shot, shielded to the waist by a small garden wall – a tiny figure, head down and smothered by a pink hood.

Delia pauses the footage with the figure in the centre of the shot, then inches her nose closer to the screen. She examines the red band around the waist of the hooded top and what appears to be a red string bouncing up from the woman's chest; the exact same trimmings that are on Joy Stapleton's unique hooded top.

A loud ping distracts her from her thoughts, and then a box begins to flash in the top corner of her screen.

An email. From a sender whose address she isn't quite familiar with.

She drags her icon towards the box and clicks on it. And then the computer groans before it flashes another video image on to the screen. Delia presses at the play button and stares at the footage, her eyes widening.

'Oh my... oh my... Oh my fucking God!' she screams. Unusual for Delia. She can't stand swearing. Can never understand why anybody would ever have any use for it, not when there is an infinite amount of words they could use. Her breathing grows in sharpness. Then she stands up and swipes a heavy slap towards the screen of her computer monitor, knocking over her cups of pens and her framed photograph. The frame skids across the desk and falls to the floor. She can hear the glass of the frame smash over the strange grunting sound huffing from her computer's speakers. 'Who the fuck?' Delia says, stretching for her mouse, so she can switch the video off. 'Who the fuck sent me this?'

She bends down, snatches at the smashed photo frame and then immediately brings her thumb to her mouth.

'Mother fuc—' she just about stops herself from swearing again by filling her mouth with her thumb. She sucks on it frantically, then removes it and shakes her entire hand in the air, spraying blood to the floor.

'Judge McCormick.' Knuckles rattle lightly at her door.

'Yes, Aisling?' Delia calls out, before twisting her wrist and looking at her watch.

'You're due back in court now.'

'Yes, thank you. Thank you, Aisling. Coming now,' she says, gripping her thumb tight with her other hand.

'Who the fuck sent me that video?' she whispers.

'Sorry?'

'Oh, don't mind me,' she shouts back to Aisling before she strides towards the door and snatches it open, finding her assistant's eyes furrowed on the other side of it. 'I was talking to myself again.'

'Judge McCormick, are you okay?' Aisling asks.

Delia offers her assistant a fake smile.

'Course I am. Though you couldn't, eh... you couldn't fetch me a plaster, could you? Cut myself on some glass.' She holds her thumb up.

'Ouch... eh... I'm not quite sure where we keep plasters, but I'll take a look in the canteen. There might be a first aid box there. Meanwhile...' Aisling stands aside and waves her hand up the hallway, in the direction of the courtrooms.

'Yes. Yes!' Delia says, nodding her head before she begins to stride forward as fast as she can, kicking her robe with each foot as she goes. She drops the fake smile when she turns onto the next corridor, and as soon as she does, she begins to feel her head spinning. And her stomach. She can't be certain she's not going to vomit. She wants to pause. Wants to catch her breath. But she knows she's already late.

'Who the fuck sent me that?' she murmurs to herself. 'Eddie Taunton. Can't be... can it?'

She brings her hand to her forehead, her gaze fixed to the blurred black and white tiled flooring of the court's corridors as she paces. Though she does look up in time to see the court clerk dressed in all black at the end of the corridor open a door and nod inside it. And before she reaches the clerk to offer another fake smile, Delia hears a voice bellow from behind that door.

'All rise.'

The courtroom is packed again; everybody on their feet to welcome the decision-maker – the only person with any power over the fate of Joy Stapleton. Though Delia is beginning to wonder if she has any power at all now as she sits into her highchair. Her head is still spinning when the court clerk makes a coughing sound, prompting Delia to shake herself from her daze.

'Sorry,' she mutters. Then she stares down at the courtroom, glancing at Joy first, then at Bracken. She offers Jonathan Ryan an almost-friendly nose twitch. Then she flicks her eyes around the room in search of Eddie Taunton. He's not here.

'Mother fucker,' she whispers to herself.

'Sorry, Your Honour?' a court clerk says.

'No... No, I'm sorry. Eh...' She rifles through the paperwork on her desk, before clawing a sheet out from the middle, smudging the top corner of it with a thumbprint of blood. Her hands begin to shake as she holds the sheet. So, she places it back down to the desk in front of her, her hands now hidden from the gallery. 'Mr Bracken, can you, eh...' she fake coughs and burps at the same time; vomit bubbling in the pit of stomach, 'Call your next witness, please.'

'My pleasure, Your Honour,' Bracken says standing up, 'I call to the stand, Monsieur Mathieu Dupont.'

2,371 days ago…

'Joy!' Mathilda shouted.

Joy jumped, holding a palm to her chest, then swivelled.

'Sorry, Mathilda,' she replied. 'I know… I'm supposed to be at school. I'm heading there now.'

'Nope. You're not. You're coming with me.'

'Where?'

'Never mind where. You're coming with me.'

'But I'm about five minutes late for school. I was just having a chat with—'

'Now!' Mathilda said. She didn't roar it. Didn't raise her voice. But her tone cut through. And so, Joy creased her face at Emilie – the prisoner she had been in conversation with – then left her to it to follow Mathilda's rattling keys down the steel steps of Elm House before turning right.

'This isn't the way to school.'

'I told you… you're not going to school.'

'But won't I miss class?'

'You didn't seem that concerned when you were just hanging out at the back of the kitchen with Emilie.'

Joy held her eyes closed and sighed.

She had enrolled in school. Again. After she had spent the first four months of her sentence in isolation following her attack, she decided to do a course when all of the options of how to spend her time on a regular wing were offered to her. The menu wasn't that detailed, in truth. Each prisoner had two basic options: work around the prison, or do a course in the education halls at the far end of the prison. The working options didn't appeal. Joy had never worked in a kitchen before, and even when she was a house-wife and a mother of two, the oven did most of the cooking for her. Gardening wasn't to her liking either. Nor was the washing and cleaning or laundry rooms. So, she decided upon a course in creative writing at the educational facility. Her lack of confidence let her down, however, and after three months she felt she had nothing to offer the class and that was that: she wanted out. She pleaded with the Governor that if he let her out of her course early, she'd do any job at all around the prison, that she didn't mind which one. So, he placed her in the laundry room – the least favoured role generally among the prisoners. Her disdain for that job, which was really only for three hours a day, became evident much quicker than her disdain for producing creative writing did, but her frustrations didn't matter one jot. She would serve in the laundry room for a full year before the Governor would agree to let her choose another means by which to spend her afternoons. So, when that time eventually came around, she chose school again, rather than work. This time a course in Healthy Living was the one she opted for. Not because she was desperate to lose the puppy weight she had gained during her first eighteen months inside, but because that was the course Christy was doing, and they wanted to spend as much time with each other as they possibly could. She'd only started the course a couple of weeks ago, and here she was about to miss the lesson on ripe vegetables because Mathilda was leading her around a maze of landings and through a dozen gates before they ended up deep into the bowels of the prison.

'Never been down here before,' Joy said looking around herself. 'Where we going?'

'I've been told to take you down here cos you got a visitor.'

'A visitor? Me? Down here? Why?'

'That's a helluva lot of questions within one breath, Joy,' Mathilda said. Then her keys stopped jangling, and she spun on her heels. 'Ye gotta wear these.' Mathilda unclipped a pair of handcuffs from her waist belt.

Joy clenched both fists and held her arms out, all the while staring at the yellow door they had stopped outside.

'Who's in there?' she asked.

Mathilda shrugged. Then she turned away from Joy and banged at the yellow door.

'Sir, she's here.'

The door opened and the Governor's large face appeared. He nodded solemnly at Joy and then stood aside. And as he did, Joy saw the piercing blue eyes of her husband for the first time in way too long. Her breathing immediately quickened and her heart thudded. The last time a prison officer told her she had a surprise visit she ended up sitting across from Conor Quinn – a young up and coming lawyer who convinced her he could land her a retrial. She was initially buoyed by his positivity. But after six meetings in the space of five months she was beginning to get irritated, rather than excited, by his visits. It seemed he rarely had an update for her when he did show up, and she was beginning to form an eerie impression that he was meeting with her because he had a crush on her. He wasn't the only one. Joy Stapleton had dozens of admirers, a lot of whom would write to her regularly; to detail their sexual desires. On her first Valentine's Day in prison, Joy Stapleton received over one-hundred cards from strangers.

She was actually a little peeved when, on her second Valentine's Day, in the February just gone, that number had halved. Conor Quinn reminded her of the creepy men who wrote to her regularly. She felt he was content to just be associated with her – to spend time with Ireland's most infamous criminal. She told him the last time she met him that he shouldn't come back until he had made concrete progress towards a retrial. And as a result, she hadn't heard from him for a while and was beginning to realise the inevitable – she truly was going to spend the rest of her life in this godforsaken place. Though that slow realisation didn't depress her as much as she feared it would. She was beginning to feel that she was now a better fit in prison than she would be for the outside world. She wasn't even sure where she would fit in out there anymore. In the real world she'd stand out as the most notorious killer in the whole of the country. In here, she's just another criminal. She barely stands out at all. Not anymore. Not after the furore of her first arriving in Elm House. Though she was beginning to wonder if that furore would spark up again, certainly now that Stella had been brought back to Elm House. It's not as if Stella's arrival was a big shock – she didn't turn up sitting at a desk without warning like her husband just had. The Governor and some of the prison officers had spoken to Joy about Stella's likely return. Joy had told them she held no ill-feeling toward her fellow prisoner and that she wouldn't have a problem if Stella came back to Elm House. But that wasn't true at all. She *did* have a problem with it. A huge problem. Because she was in fear of Stella; in fear of having her face smashed against one of the dining room tables again.

'You sure you're okay with this?' Aidan asked, reading that Joy wasn't as comfortable as she had been letting on when Stella finally returned to the wing.

'I'll be fine,' Joy said to Aidan. 'I've got you, right?'

Aidan smiled at her. As he found himself doing regularly. He'd been back in Elm House just over six months now and spent most of his working hours either pacing the landing outside Joy's cell. Or – when her door finally buzzed open in the mornings – accompanying her to and from the dining room. They shared a similar sense of humour and there was, undoubtedly, a spark between them that didn't go unnoticed. The talk amongst prisoners was that they were riding each other. But they weren't. Even if Joy was often day-dreaming about it.

'What are you doing here?' was the first thing that popped out of her mouth. Hardly welcoming; certainly not considering she had waited over a year and a half to see those blue eyes.

'I, eh... I,' Shay stuttered.

Then the Governor held a hand in front of Joy's chest as she walked through the yellow door to greet her husband.

'Uh-huh,' the Governor said. 'No touching.' He sat Joy in the seat opposite Shay and chained the cuffs she was already wearing to a metal loop under the desk.

'Why are we... why are we here?' Joy asked the Governor while looking around herself.

The Governor stood back upright, all six foot eight inches of him, then clasped his shovel-sized hands together.

'Mr Stapleton contacted me personally about visiting you a couple of weeks ago because he feared his celebrity status would cause somewhat a fuss in the visitor's hall. So, we, eh, we discussed the possibility of him having a private meeting with you and... well, here we are...'

Joy continued to look around herself. The room they were in was no bigger than her cell. And it was swallowed up by two white desks; one of which they were both sitting across from each other at, their faces no more than three feet apart.

The Governor kissed his own lips, then stepped his heavy frame outside and pulled the door tight behind him, though Joy could tell he didn't move from that spot, because she couldn't hear the familiar sweeping of shoes off the concrete floor. She had learned most of the sounds of the prison by now.

Though it was a silence she was hearing as she stared at her husband. Joy wanted so much to be able to move her hands across the desk so she could take his hands in hers. But she wasn't sure how he would react to that.

'Thank you,' she whispered, instead.

He contorted his face by squelching up his mouth, then he reached over and lightly grazed her elbow.

'I'm sorry it's taken so long... I just... I, eh...'

It was unlike Shay to not finish his sentences; to be uncertain of what he was trying to say. She only knew him to be the confident football star she had met and fallen in love with. She stared into his eyes, noticing they weren't quite as aqua as they once were. The stress of losing his two sons, coupled with his wife being sent down for two life sentences had clearly turned those blue eyes grey. He looked jaded. Aged. Far from the pinup he had once been.

'You don't need to explain yourself,' Joy whispered again, because she was aware of the ears just outside the door. It was likely, she felt, that both Mathilda and the Governor were prying. Though she couldn't blame them. The whole nation would love to be a fly on the wall for this meeting. 'I'm glad to see you... even if...' She lifted her arms as high as she could, which wasn't very high at all, before the cuffs clanked against the bottom of the desk.

'Joy,' Shay said, as straight as he could, 'I've had the same questions rolling around in my head for years now...' She unclenched her jaw, and inched herself closer to him. 'Hundreds of fucking questions... thousands even. And... oh, I don't know... I just don't know. I guess I've figured after all this time that this whole nightmare really only boils down to one question. And the only person who knows the answer to that question is you. So here I am... an innocent, broken man asking you to answer one question for me, so that the thousands of questions that fly around my head will finally shut the fuck up. Then maybe... just maybe...'

'Maybe you might get some closure.'

'Closure?' he said out of the corner of his mouth. 'Sleep. Let's start with some sleep. Fuck sake, I haven't had a full night's sleep since the day our boys went missing... I had so many questions that day alone. But the story just kept getting worse and worse...'

'I understand,' Joy said, sniffling up her nose, 'I don't sleep either.'

Shay exhaled a stuttering breath, letting it release in grunting stages, while he bounced his knee incessantly up and down under the desk.

'Well, we are not sleeping for different reasons,' he said. 'The reasons I can't sleep is because I want an answer to a question that you know the answer to... so please, don't compare your lack of sleep to mine.'

Joy swallowed hard. When she walked into this pokey office, she wondered in which tone Shay would speak to her. And even though she had tried to give him her best puppy dog eyes and to paint on her genuine empathy for him, she was aware she had already taken a miss-step, and as a result was getting the curt, abrupt Shay. She didn't know what to say to him. Or even how to say it.

'Sorry,' she whispered. 'This isn't about me. I've missed you. I've missed you so much.' Shay swayed his jaw from side-to-side. 'Have you missed me, Shay?'

'Jesus,' he snapped, raising his voice, 'how the hell am I supposed to know the answer to that? There are a thousand questions forming a queue in my head that are way ahead of that one.'

'Shhh,' Joy hissed over the desk at her husband, 'they're outside, listening.'

Shay held his eyes closed with annoyance, then got to his feet.

'I shouldn't have come... I should have just—'

'Don't go. Please don't go,' Joy begged, squeezing her palms together, the chains clanging against the desk. 'I'll shut up. I won't talk, unless it's to answer that one question you have. Please. Sit down. Talk to me, Shay.'

He pressed his hands against his hips, then, after a pause, relented, sitting back down and producing another long sigh.

'Okay... okay, just get to it, Shay,' he said to himself, rubbing at his face.

He had stayed out of the limelight ever since Joy was arrested, despite multiple pleas for interviews. He had turned down invites from *The Late Late Show* on no fewer than eight occasions and had rejected without too much consideration, a one-million euro advance to write his memoirs by a giant of a publishing company. That wasn't the only publishing deal he had been offered, but it was certainly the most lucrative one. The million-euro offer didn't register much interest though. Money meant nothing to him. Life, it seemed, meant nothing to him. Not anymore. He was too confused and pained to think about anything other than his own confusion and pain.

'When I'm trying to sleep at night,' he spat out, releasing his hands from his face, 'all I hear is that phone call you made to the police, reporting our boys missing. Just your voice on repeat, saying the same thing over and over again. And all that goes on in the forefront of my mind as you are saying these words over and over again is me thinking, *is she acting?*'

'I'm not acting.'

'Shhh,' Shay hissed. 'You said you wouldn't talk.' He steadied his breathing. 'I mean, I can hear it... I can hear the panic in your voice. I hear the panic every time you shout, '*My two sons have been taken!*' I hear it so loud. But I keep asking myself, 'Is she acting panicked? Or is she *genuinely* panicked? Do I even know the woman I was married to at all?' Joy opened her mouth, then relented, her eyes filling with tears. 'But surely you couldn't have been acting for all those years afterwards; not when we were out looking for the boys; not when we started the campaign to find them; not after their bodies were found, right? I mean you just can't have been acting all these years...'

'Is that your question, Shay because, no, I wasn't act—'

'No,' he said, 'that isn't my question. But then again, I seemed to be the last one to know, didn't I? So maybe it's just me. Maybe I didn't know the woman I had married after all. I was the last person to twig that the police were looking at you the whole time. But even when I finally realised they were, and when I got over the shock of it, I still believed you. Because I couldn't believe you had anything to do with killing our boys. That doesn't make any sense.'

'Of course it doesn't,' Joy whispered.

Shay held up his index finger, silencing her again.

'But none of it makes any sense. And then... and then they showed me that CCTV footage.' Joy looked down at the desk, shaking her curls subtly from side to side. 'And I'm pretty sure the first time I saw it, yeah, I recognised that hoodie, but I didn't immediately think, 'that is Joy'. Though it's hard for me to know exactly what I thought the first time I saw it... But what I can tell you, Joy, is that every time I watch that footage now... I see you. Every time. Every damn time I watch it, I see your face under that hood.'

'Shay, you can't believe—'

'Shhh,' Shay hissed again, his cheeks now streaming with tears, his arms stiff by his side. 'I'm just telling you what I think I see, Joy.' He began to sob. 'Not what I know. But I guess, all these questions that fly around my head, about the phone call to the police, about the CCTV footage, about you calling it a coincidence, about the dozens of theories I've read about... they're all nonsense, aren't they? Because no matter what way I think about this, it all comes back to one thing for me. It all comes back to those three seconds of CCTV footage, where a girl wearing a hoodie only you could possibly be wearing walks down a road just a few hundred yards away from where our boys were found.'

Joy leaned closer, placing her forearms on the desk, her chains rattling.

'Let me answer your question, Shay.'

He sniffled up his nose, then wiped a hand over his face, mopping up the wet.

'You always say that it's just a coincidence somebody was wearing that same top; it's no coincidence, is it, Joy? I want you to look me straight in the eye and tell me the absolute truth... You owe me the truth. Is that you in that CCTV footage?'

'No,' she said without hesitating. 'And you have to believe me, Shay. You *have* to believe me.'

He blinked at her, through his tears. Then he stood abruptly, scooting the chair he was sat on towards the back wall.

'Okay...' he said, shrugging his shoulders, 'that is all I came here to ask... so, I, eh... I'm...' he tailed off his muttering as he pulled open the yellow door, exposing both the Governor and Mathilda outside.

'No. Shay,' Joy called out. 'Please.' Shay paused in the door frame, his hand still on the handle of the door, and stared back at his wife, his face blotchy and swollen. 'If you came here to ask me one question... then can you please, *please,* allow me one question of my own... please?'

She gently pressed her thumb into the corners of her eyes, to mop up her tears. Then she was certain she noticed Shay nod, even though he didn't.

'Thank you,' she said, 'all I want to know, Shay, is whether or not you believe me. That's all I want to know. It's all I *need* to know.'

She held her lips tightly closed as she tried to study the muscles in his face. But none of them moved.

'What do you mean believe you?' he spat out, before gulping back more tears. 'Believe you about what in particular? Do I believe you killed our boys?... I genuinely don't know. Do I believe that is you in that CCTV footage?... I genuinely. Don't. Know. I don't know anything. *Anything!*' He punched the yellow door, then he paced out of the pokey office and across the concrete landing.

∴

Delia is so taken by how handsome Mathieu Dupont is, with his jet-black hair, jet-black eyebrows and perfectly chiselled chin smothered in stubble, that his looks seem to have almost diluted her panic attack.

'Mr Dupont, can you state your occupation for the court please?' Bracken asks as soon as the witness has sat.

'Of course, eh,' he says, his French accent thick. 'I, eh... am the PDG – or as you say in Ireland, CEO – of a company we call Provenir.'

'And Provenir is a multi-million euro company that specialises in innovative video engineering, correct?'

'Objection, Your Honour,' Jonathan Ryan shouts. 'What does the value of the witness's company have to do with the relevancy of this trial?'

'Rephrase the question,' Delia says without hesitating, releasing her sweaty hands from her own grip. She stares at her thumb, then lightly squeezes at it, creating a fresh bubble of blood.

'Okay, so Provenir is a successful company, shall we say, that specialises in innovative video engineering, correct?' Bracken asks.

'That is eh... correct. Among other things,' Dupont replies.

'Okay, and isn't it a fact that your company Provenir assisted Pixar on two of their blockbuster Hollywood movies, yes?'

'Oui... yes, we did. We assisted with some communication through email to some of the production company's researchers. We didn't get to go to Hollywood. There was no set.' Dupont laughs. 'We were in communication with Pixar on some specific difficulties they had about perception. That was it. I think it was five emails back and forward... that was it.'

'But your company got a mention in the credits of the movies, correct?'

'Yes.' Dupont laughs again. A husky laugh that sounds as if he might have already smoked a full box of cigarettes this morning.

'You were also a lecturer in Nice, correct – at Nice Sophia Antipolis University?'

'That is correct. Yes. Over the course of maybe eight years.'

'Closer to ten, according to the University itself, Mr Dupont. Nine years and seven months to be precise.'

Dupont laughs his husky smoker's laugh again.

'Was it almost ten years? Wow-wow-wee-wa,' he says. 'My, eh... memory is not so great.'

Bracken smiles back at his witness, showing his veneers. But even he must know that he doesn't come anywhere close to having the best smile in this courtroom. Not today.

Delia gulps, then lightly burps as a pocket of air jumps itself up her throat. She brings her hand to her mouth, then looks about herself, hoping the stenographer didn't hear her almost throw up.

'So, you are a specialist in innovative engineering, and you lectured on this subject for nigh on a decade at a prestigious university in northern France, Mr Dupont. That's very impressive. Thank you for taking the time out of your busy schedule to be with us at this trial today.' Dupont nods back. 'Let me ask you,' Bracken continues, 'upon hearing of the Joy Stapleton case for the very first time when, I believe, a student brought you an analysis of the CCTV footage for his end-of-year assignment, you began to look into the case yourself, correct?'

'I thought it was a very, *very* interesting case, yes.'

'You used your innovative software to try to discover if the woman in that footage could possibly have been Joy Stapleton, correct?'

'That is correct. Well, I first started looking at it with my student – his name is Eric Dupont... no relation.' He smiles a vertical dimple into his stubbled cheek. 'Then I brought it into our studio to take a closer look... eh... intrigued, is the best word to describe it.'

'You were confident you could tell the exact height of the person in that footage... wouldn't that be fair to suggest?'

'Well eh... Mr Bracken,' he says, his accent thickening, 'what I would say is that I felt I could do my best with my best technology to determine the height of the person in the footage.'

'And in brief terms for the court, can you detail how you could do that?'

'Sure I, eh... we – my company, Provenir – developed 3D model software that is able to read persons from still images and determine the exact height of that person.'

'So, that mightn't sound impressive to the courts, because measuring somebody from a photograph or a still seems a little easy...' Bracken holds his hands in front of himself and puffs a laugh. 'But can you tell the court how intricate the measurements must be to determine exact height?'

'Yes. It is not so easy. Because we, each of us, hold so many different heights. Just because my doctor measures me at six foot, three, it does not mean that I am always six foot, three. In fact, I most likely never am six foot, three. Or rarely. I really only am six foot, three when somebody says, Monsieur Dupont, can you stand against that wall so I can measure you? And I think that has only happened to me maybe four or five times in my life. So, most likely and more often than not, I am not six foot, three, even though it is my official height. We all slouch, hunch, bend, lean, pivot... all these things. And, for example, an everyday average height throughout any given day can be up to two whole inches lower than a person's official registered height.'

Delia lightly burps, only this time she envelops it so well that she is certain the stenographer couldn't have heard her. Then the door to her right sweeps open and Aisling walks in, nodding to the judge. She hands her a plaster before sneaking back out in silence. The judge stares up at Bracken as she unpeels the plaster and begins to curl it around her thumb. Then she nods at him, signalling that he should continue.

'So, you took the still of the figure from the CCTV footage, Mr Dupont, then built a 3D model of her and measured her exact height. Is that correct?'

'That is correct, yes.'

'And can you now reveal to the court what the exact height the person is in that footage?'

'One hundred and fifty-four point seven, one five centimetres. Which in your money here in Ireland is exactly five foot, and three quarters of one inch.'

'Five foot, and three quarters of an inch,' Bracken says, nodding his head. 'The defendant here today, Joy Stapleton, Mr Dupont, according to her prison records is five foot, two inches in height. Your finding is that the figure in the CCTV footage is one whole inch and a further quarter inch smaller than that, yes?'

'Yes.'

'That might sound like a tiny measurement to many in this courtroom today, but in your line of work, that's a gulf... correct?'

'What I can say, Mr Bracken, with absolute certainty is that the figure in the CCTV is definitely not five foot, two inches.'

A light gasp is heard at the back of the court and Bracken pauses to allow the effect of it to float through the room.

'And this software you use to determine your exact findings, Mr Dupont, what's it called?'

'Oh... Sonix17, we are not very creative with names,' Dupont says, laughing again, exposing his vertical dimple. Delia almost laughs with him, but in trying to stifle it, she awakens another frog in her throat.

'And Sonix17 was built when?' Bracken continues.

'2017, as the name suggests. I told you we were not very creative with names.'

'2017? Very recently. So, it is fair to say that this technology did not exist in 2012... when Joy Stapleton's original trial took place, correct?'

'Course not, no,' Dupont says, shaking his head.

Delia knew that question was asked just for her benefit – to underline to her that this was brand new information being brought into the legal argument. A retrial can only really be granted if new evidence emerges. This expert's testimony, with new-age technology that couldn't have been used during the original trial, coupled with the fact that Bunny the dog had, since the original trial, been labelled a fraud, was the brand new evidence the defendant was bringing to this court. Delia had known these were the likely trump cards of the defence. But she didn't realised the new technology would be delivered to her in such a convincing and specific manner.

'That is all, Your Honour,' Bracken says, nodding up at Delia. She purses her lips back at him, then squints to the back rows of the gallery. There's still no sign of Taunton. So, she flicks her gaze to her son, then has to hold her eyes closed with frustration to allow the image in the video to wash through her thoughts. She holds her hand firmer to her mouth in anticipation of another burp. But none comes.

'Your Honour, may I?' Jonathan Ryan calls out from his desk.

'Of course, Mr Ryan.'

Ryan rises to his feet, a mysterious smug grin on the corner of his lips. Delia had noted the maturity in his performances during the opening two days of this retrial. This is the third trial she's presided over cases that he has attempted to prosecute. And he seemed, in her eyes, to be getting more assured and more confident each time he appeared in front of her.

'Mr Dupont, thank you for being with us here today,' Ryan says. 'I have found your testimony most interesting, I must say. I also find it wildly inaccurate and I will detail exactly why that is in one moment. But before I do that,' Ryan strides into the middle of the courtroom floor, 'can I just have something clarified, please? When Mr Bracken was questioning you earlier, he suggested your company, Provenir, was a specialist in video engineering.

You answered him by saying "among other things". It is the "other things",' Ryan curls his fingers to denote quote marks, 'that your company *really* specialises in, isn't it? You don't specialise in detailing the height of figures from CCTV footage, correct?'

Dupont laughs again.

'Of course not. We would not be so successful with such a business model.'

'So, what your company really is successful at is developing perceptive-space software for smart phone app manufacturers, correct?'

'Eh... yes. When you say specialise, that is what we really specialise in. That is what makes our company successful. Correct. Working with app developers is pretty much our entire business.'

'Yes. And can I just confirm that when Mr Bracken says you were a lecturer at the University in Nice for ten years. That's not ten years full-time, right? A few times a year you would give lectures on video engineering at the university.'

'Yes. It was three times a year. Each October, January and April.'

'So, thirty lectures in total?'

Dupont laughs.

'It must be... yes.'

'So let me get this straight, Mr Dupont... when Mr Bracken introduces you to the court as somebody who not only specialises in determining the height of somebody through a CCTV still and somebody who has lectured extensively on the subject, that's quite a hyperbolic description, is it not?'

'Hyper...'

'Hyperbolic. An exaggeration?'

'Well, that was Mr Bracken's description,' Dupont sucks the dimple into his cheek again. 'Not mine. I do not consider myself a lecturer. I never have. I liked passing my expertise to students and would have done more hours in the university, but time would not allow, of course.'

'Yes. Well, Mr Bracken has a tendency to be hyperbolic when he feels a witness requires it,' Ryan says, darting a quick glance to the judge.

Delia picks up her gavel and thumps it twice to her desk.

'Mr Ryan,' she yells out. 'I am surprised.' Her eyes grow wide as she stares down at Ryan.

'Sorry, Your Honour,' he says, holding up his two hands and then turning back to the witness. 'Mr Dupont, have you ever met the defendant, Mrs Joy Stapleton?'

'No, no,' Dupont says, shaking his head before signalling to the defendant as if anybody in the courtroom needed her pointed out. 'Today is my first day to see her.'

'So, you, through your software, were able to determine the exact height of a woman you have never met?'

'Well, that is not true. I was not looking to determine if or if not the figure in the footage was Mrs Stapleton. I was just trying to determine the height of the woman in the footage.'

'And you came up with five foot, and three quarters of an inch?'

'Yes.'

'And why do you think that couldn't be Mrs Stapleton?'

'Well... as I said, I was not looking for Mrs Stapleton. I was looking for the exact height of the figure in the footage only.'

'But you testified here today that, and I quote "I can confirm that the figure is not five foot, two." Yes?'

'I did.'

'Where did the figure of five foot, two come from?'

'Well... it came from Mrs Stapleton's prison records, no?'

'Ahhh,' Ryan says. And as he does, Delia gulps, swallowing the threat of another burp. 'Mr Dupont you are a man of exact measurement, are you not?'

'I am. Yes. I guess.'

'Well, do you honestly believe that the measurements taken, probably quite swiftly inside a cold prison medical room with an old stadiometer would in any way be scientifically precise?'

'I did not say that the record of the prison measurement is correct.'

'No, you didn't. Which is why I called your testimony wildly inaccurate at the beginning of my cross examination, Mr Dupont. You may have been measuring against an inaccurate record. We, the prosecution team, tried to retrieve exact measurements of the defendant. We were denied. You admitted under oath here today that this is the first time you have ever seen Mrs Stapleton in the flesh, correct?'

'It is still correct, yes.'

'So, I take it you've never measured her either, right?'

Dupont shakes his head and rubs his fingers across the stubble of his chin.

'No. I have not measured Mrs Stapleton. I live between Nice and Paris. Yesterday was my first time in Dublin in ten years.'

'Because Mr Bracken invited you to be part of this trial... to get you up here to label you successful at this and that, just so your testimony would sound impressive. But if your testimony is all about accuracy, then it fails somewhat if you are comparing to a measurement recorded in a cold prison room by a dodgy stadiometer, does it not?'

'I am not here to—'

'It's okay, Mr Dupont. You don't have to answer that. Because I can tell you that the prison record of Joy Stapleton is not the only record of her height. When Mrs Stapleton was measured by a Doctor Mishia Rasaad in the Coombe Hospital in May 2004, pregnant with her first son, she was measured at five foot, two and a quarter inches. Not five foot, and one quarter inch. When she was measured for a health check-up, five months after giving birth, she was more specifically measured at five foot, one and one-tenth. Then on arrival in prison she was measured at five foot, two, which as you know was marked in a diary. Quite a discrepancy in all those numbers, Mr Dupont, wouldn't you agree? What did Mr Bracken call it earlier, measurements of that ilk are like a gulf to you, right?'

'That doesn't prove the woman in the footage is Mrs Stapleton. None of those measurements you just mentioned are five foot and three quarters of an inch as my software suggests the woman in the CCTV is.'

'No, but what it does suggest, Mr Dupont, is that the measurements you came here to testify against are inaccurate. Wildly inaccurate. Thank you, Your Honour.'

'We thank the witness,' Delia calls out. Then she stands, leaving Dupont looking perplexed that his testimony ended so abruptly and so inconclusively. 'Court dismissed,' Delia follows up with. And as she does, she spins on her heels and dashes down the steps and out the side door as if she's on a mission. The bright white lights of the modern corridor don't help to stem her spinning head. So, she pulls at the neck of her robe, whipping it up over her head and scrunching it up into a ball in her hands as she begins to take sharper breaths.

Then she abruptly halts her power walk, brings the scrunched-up robe to her mouth and vomits into it.

'This way,' Joy said to Carol.

And so Carol followed her. Down the steel steps, across the concrete landing, then into the large space all of the noise seemed to be emanating from.

'Thank you,' Carol shouted over the chatter.

'Don't worry about the noise; all that screeching you hear in prison, it's nothing. Ain't no cats being strangled or hens a-cackling – that's genuinely just the noise of three hundred of us women talking over each other. Loud bunch, aren't we?'

Carol tried to smile, but it came off more like a grimace.

'I, eh… I thought I could ask you because… well… because you're a familiar face, I guess.'

Joy pursed her lips at the new prisoner. She looked just as young and petrified as Joy had been when she'd first arrived in Elm House.

'How long have you been in here now?' Carol asked, as Joy handed her a tray.

'Just coming up to two years.'

'Two years… jeez, is it that long? Can't imagine two years in here… let alone two lifetimes… oh, sorry,' Carol said, holding her hand over her open mouth.

'Don't worry about it. How long a stretch you got?'

'Three months.'

'Three months? For what?'

Carol looked down at the oversized flipflops she was wearing.

'Well… well, it's a bit embarrassing. I tried to skim from my boss. I was running his accounts. Just took a few quid here and there. I didn't think he'd notice. If I fancied a new pair of shoes and I knew I couldn't afford them… I'd just… y'know.'

'Three months for a pair of shoes? Judge musta hated you.'

'Well… it wasn't just one pair of shoes, if you know what I mean. I didn't have a clue how much I'd spent… not until the police came to the office one day. Thirty-six grand I'd spent on myself over the course of eighteen months… Almost double me wages.'

She turned down the corners of her mouth. But Joy was too busy standing on her tip-toes to stare over the kitchen counter to bother listening to Carol's justifications for her crime.

'So, you normally have a choice of three cereals; today it's porridge, Rice Krispies or Corn Flakes. They're not the real deal... cheap knock off versions. But they're alright with a splash of milk. Oh yeah, and then you can have two slices of toast.'

'Ah... okay... this isn't so bad, I guess. I think I'll go for the, eh... Rice Krisp... no, feck it, the Corn Flakes today and I'll—' she looked around. But Joy was gone.

After deciding against cereals, Joy had jumped ahead of the queue and grabbed two slices of buttered toast before heading off to the bench populated by Christy's Crazies.

'Who that bitch?' Christy asked her.

'A nobody. Carol something or other... I was thinking of recruiting her over to our side, but she's only in for three months. Larceny. She's not worth it to us. She'll be gone before we know it.'

They each stared at Carol, all silently taking an in-breath as Nancy Trott sidled up to her, placing a hand to her shoulder.

'See... now she like that kinda gal, does Nancy. Small. Pretty. She love you,' she said to Joy. 'You just lucky I got to you first, sista. We hadn't been in that van together on our first day here, you be gettin' penetrated by those fat, chubby fingers o' hers all night long.'

The gang of Crazies cackled and guffawed at what Christy had just said, even though they well believed her account to be accurate. They weren't sure which one of Nancy's Cohorts Nancy was fingering or being fingered by regularly, probably all of them, but they all knew they would rather be a member of the perceived crazy gang than Nancy's gang – even if it did mean they had to regularly read passages from a bible they knew to be bullshit. It made much more sense to them to pretend to believe in God than be finger raped.

'Okay... okay... let's settle,' Christy said, grabbing the two prisoners next to her by the hand. 'Our Lord Jesus, we thank you for the blessing of these foods you provide for us today and each and every day. May you walk with us and guide us as we continue our journey. We thank you, oh Lord. Amen.'

Then she let go of their hands as the whole bench muttered an 'Amen' in unison, and everybody picked up either a large spoon or a slice of toast and silently got stuck into their breakfasts.

It was during that rather noisy period, when the screeching first strikes up in earnest as the whole wing is finishing breakfast, that Stella hobbled by their table. She stared at them, as she usually does, menacingly, but she wasn't intimidating. Not anymore. Though every time Joy laid eyes on her, she could feel the blunt force to the bridge of her nose, even though that attack had, by now, occurred almost two years ago.

'Ye know, I was thinkin' bout that bitch in ma sleep last night,' Christy said. 'I had a vision. She ain't long for this world. That's what ma vision told me.'

And then all of Christy's Crazies got up from their bench, brought their bowls and plates to the counter and headed back to their cells where they would spend the next hour alone while the prison officers took over the dining room to have breakfast themselves.

At 9:30 a.m., the cells reopened, and then it was off to either work, or school, depending on which road you had chosen. Joy was enjoying the Healthy Foods course she was studying by now, even though she had received a poor grade on her most recent assignment. It wasn't necessarily the course content she was enjoying while she was cooked up in the small education room at the back end of the prison, it was Christy's company. They were two peas in a pod; rarely separated when the cell doors were open.

Joy and Christy would talk openly about Joy's plight; about the fight of an innocent mother spending two life sentences behind bars for the most heinous crime imaginable. The Joy Stapleton is Innocent campaign was going strong; certainly outside the prison. It had snowballed somewhat by social media, though mainstream media rarely covered the cause. They did, when the Joy is Innocent campaign was first founded. But when Joy and Christy started shouting from within the confines of the prison that they had a theory about Joy's former best friend Lavinia Kirwan being the mystery woman in the unique pink hooded top, the cause took a dip in reputation. Lavinia had a solid alibi for the night in question. The woman in the pink hoodie simply couldn't have been her. That fact didn't stop Christy and Joy growing their theory, though. And they would often sit on the bed inside one of their cells and cook up more analysis of Lavinia's possible involvement. But in truth, nobody was listening to them. And especially not Shay. Since his visit five months ago, Joy had heard nothing from her husband. The only update she had been given on his life came via one of the tabloid newspapers, which detailed a story suggesting Shay's hours at his job had been reduced and that he'd been demoted. The newspaper speculated his health had been an issue in the demotion; that he was suffering from constant waves of depression. She thought about writing to him, reaching out after she'd read that story. But despite sitting down with a blank sheet of paper and a pen, she managed no words.

***

2,274 days ago...

It wasn't long after the doors had clicked open, as they do first thing every morning, that the first shriek was heard. It was piercing. And Joy knew immediately that something serious had happened. Then Mathilda and Aidan raced up and down the landings of Elm House and began shuffling prisoners back into their cells, while yelling for lockdown.

'What is it, what's happened?' Joy asked Aidan as he raced towards her.

He looked around himself, his face paler than normal.

'We, eh... we just found Stella Cantwell in her cell. She was hanging.'

Joy held a hand to her mouth, then stepped back into her cell to perch herself on her mattress while Aidan locked the door from the outside.

It didn't take long for the doors to click back open, because it wasn't the prison staff's first rodeo in terms of cleaning up a suicide mess. Though it was the first time a hanging had happened in Elm House for many a year.

Aidan was still pale when Joy bumped into him on her way to visit Christy's cell.

'You okay?' Joy asked him. But he either didn't hear or didn't want to hear her. He just strolled on by as she rattled her knuckles against Christy's cell door.

'What the fuck?!' she shouted when she saw Christy's yellow stained teeth grimacing at her.

'I told you, I told you, Joy. She not long for this world and then within half a day, Our Lord Jesus Christ took her from us.'

'Christy,' Joy said, her eyes heavy. 'Did you murder Stella?'

Christy's bloodshot eyes almost popped out of her head.

'What you talkin' bout, girl? I ain't no killer.'

'But... but...' Joy held her palms out. She was dumbstruck.

When all of Christy's Crazies had gathered around the worn sofa in the games room, they couldn't hide their awe of their leader.

'I can't believe God communicates with you directly,' one of them said. 'And just so randomly like that. God comes to you in your dreams to tell you Stella is not long for this world and then next night she does it... she kills herself.'

Joy was the only one who didn't laud Christy's gift. It simply couldn't be that she could tell the future. Not like that. Though Joy didn't say anything. She needed to pretend she believed in Christy. After all, it was Christy's gift that had exonerated her in the eyes of most of the prisoners who resided in Elm House. Going against the grain now would only mean she was arguing against her own innocence.

She did question Christy when they were alone, asking her where she had been the evening previous; though she did it in a very subtle manner. Then she realised, as did the other Crazies who might, like Joy, be sceptical, that Christy couldn't have had anything to do with Stella's hanging. She had a solid alibi; was doing a medical in the health room during the time in question and was escorted to and from that medical by Mathilda before she was locked back up in her cell for the night.

'Oh my God,' one of the Crazies said to Joy, 'Stella really did kill herself. She killed herself right after Christy had seen it in her vision. This girl is the real deal. The real deal.'

Joy found herself shaking, even though Stella had handed down the only beating she had ever received her whole life. Her hands were covering her face and slightly quivering when Aidan walked into her cell later that afternoon.

'What a day!' he said, his face still pale. 'You okay?'

'Just a bit of shock is all,' she said before getting to her feet.

'I'm a little bit shocked meself,' Aidan said. 'I mean, I didn't get on with Stella or anything, she just kept herself to herself... but I never thought in a million years she'd go and top herself. She just didn't seem the kind. She... I dunno... I guess I feel guilty. I should have known she was depressed. She's on my wing. My landing.'

Joy inched closer to him and could smell the never-changing scent of Lynx on his neck.

'You don't need to beat yourself up, Aidan. Don't be silly. We never see the most obvious things that are right in front of us. Human nature isn't it?' Joy said.

'You sure you're gonna be alright? You seem a little shaken yourself. Can I get you anything? Want me to see if I can get you a warm mug of coffee?'

Without hesitating, and with her emotions bubbling, Joy inched even closer, then looped both arms around the back of Aidan's neck before she leaned upwards to press her lips against his.

'Hey,' he said, baulking backwards and wiping at his mouth. 'What the hell are you playing at?'

∴

Delia pulls out the long drawer from the bottom of the stack of tall library shelves in her dimly lit office and removes a fresh robe.

She had ordered Aisling, as she was approaching her office all hot and bothered, to arrange a clean-up of the corridor that leads to the side entrance of the main courtroom.

'There's something funny along the tiles, there,' she shouted into Aisling's pokey office. 'As if somebody got sick or something. See to it that it's mopped up as soon as possible, won't you, my dear?'

She struggles to get her robe over her head, not helped by the fact that her glasses have been combed back into her hair. But when she eventually tugs it down and flattens it at the knees, she takes a seat at her desk. She doesn't necessarily need to don a new robe as court is over for the day, but she intends on working on the trial at her computer and always likes to be dressed for the occasion. Though she knows working on the trial won't be the first thing she does when she reawakens her computer.

She hovers her hand over her mouse, then wiggles at it frantically, bringing the screen to life. She doesn't want to watch it again. But feels she needs to see the whole video through, just in case there is a personal message or instruction at the end of it. All she'd seen of it so far was about six seconds before she'd slapped a hand at her computer monitor. And the video goes on for a full two and a half minutes.

She lowers the volume on her monitor, then covers a hand over her eyes before tapping at her mouse. A sound of repeated rustling, then a groan, cackles from her speakers.

Delia slightly widens the gaps between her fingers and turns her eyes inwards so that the image on the screen blurs somewhat and she doesn't have to take the full impact of it. The rustling continues, as another groan, this one more high-pitched, is followed by an elongated panting. Then the video abruptly stops.

'That's it?' she says, wiggling her mouse. She clicks back into the email, and rechecks to confirm that there is no message accompanying it. Just an email address in the sent bar and the video in the attachments.

She pauses her fingers, plastered thumb and all, over her keyboard, then lets out an audible sigh as she begins to type.

Who is this? What do you want from me?

She shakes her head and then pokes one finger at the mouse, sending off her two questions before she has time to stop herself.

She couldn't think of how else she could have conceivably replied to that email, even though her next move was constantly floating through her mind in between the silences of Mathieu Dupont's testimony.

Her stomach has stopped producing bile – her burping and vomiting all done – and her hands aren't shaking anywhere near as prominently as they were inside the court room. The time she spent in the women's' toilets, splashing her face with water, helped recede her panicking somewhat. But she keeps wringing her sweating hands as she stares at her email list, waiting on a reply to drop into her inbox. But her screen just shines back at her, unblinking.

'Feck it,' she mutters to herself. Then she clicks her email account off the screen and opens the Word document she had been working from.

She types 'Mathieu Dupont' underneath the minimal amount of notes she has taken so far, then taps her fingernail repeatedly against the mouse in contemplation before typing the word 'interesting' next to the name.

'Mathieu Dupont,' she mutters to herself. She imagines his face, the vertical dimple covered in stubble, the dark eyebrows framing his deep-set eyes. 'Well... he was definitely manufactured by Bracken, but certainly legitimate nonetheless,' she says. And then she types the word 'legitimate' next to the word 'interesting.'

'One hundred and fifty... what was it again?' she says, tip-tapping her fingernails against the mouse before she swiftly swipes at the receiver of her desk phone.

'Aisling,' she says, 'can you get me a copy of Mathieu Dupont's testimony, please? I, eh... didn't take many notes during the trial today, for some reason, and I need to know the exact height his 3D software measured the figure in the CCTV footage.'

'One hundred and fifty-four point seven, one five centimetres,' Aisling says without hesitating. 'I am literally reading through the transcripts myself now. I'll print you off a copy and bring them into you as soon as I can.'

'Thank you,' Delia says. Then she places the receiver back down and proceeds to type.

$$154.715 \; cm = five', \sqrt[3]{4}"$$

'Joy has never been measured at that height. Lots of different heights, yes. Likely because of her great big mop of curls. But never five foot and three quarters of an inch.' Delia holds a fist under her chin as she swivels left and right in her chair. Then she hears footsteps and a familiar one-knuckle rap at her door. Her stomach immediately turns itself over before she can shout 'Come in, Callum.'

Her son's eyes squint at her as he enters.

'Were you okay in court today, Mum?' he asks. 'You looked a little... distracted.'

She shakes her head back at him and puffs out a short snort of laughter.

'I'm fine, dear,' she replies.

'Distracted by the hunk in the witness box, huh?' he says, plonking himself into the seat opposite and giggling.

'Bit of a cliché, don't you think? Tall, dark, handsome, thick French accent, all wrapped up in a skinny designer suit,' she suggests.

'Well, if that's what cliché is, let cliché rain down on me any day of the week. And twice on Sundays.'

Callum giggles again, then stops abruptly when he notices his mother stare down at her lap, her face still, her fist to her mouth – just as she had been through most of Dupont's testimony.

'Mum... seriously, what's up with you?'

Delia shakes her head.

'Was interesting testimony, don't ya think?' she says, swallowing back the bile.

'Certainly was. Though I think Jonathan Ryan crossed well... did his best to undermine Dupont's credibility.'

'Did he, though? Did he really undermine him?' she asks.

'Made his testimony pretty darn unconvincing, seeing as he hadn't even measured the suspect herself.'

'Still... all-in-all, his testim—'

Delia stops as her speakers ping, and a flashing box appears in the top corner of her screen. Without hesitating, she drags her icon towards it and clicks at her mouse.

Return a Guilty verdict and this footage will stay between us. Deliver not guilty... then this goes everywhere.

'Mother fuck—' she mutters before stopping herself.

'Mum!' Callum says, his brow dipping. 'What is wrong with you today?'

Light footsteps followed by a knock at the door distracts them.

'In you come, Aisling,' Delia calls out.

Aisling enters, offering a friendly smile to Callum.

'Transcripts,' she says, handing a small pile of papers across the desk to her boss. 'Fascinating reading. Considerable testimony today, huh?'

'What? You think so too?' Callum says. 'You sure you girls weren't just swayed by that neat stubble... or was it the dimple?'

'Weren't you?' Aisling says. 'Pretty much a turning point in the case in my humble opinion.'

'Nah,' Callum says. 'The turning point, if it's ever going to come, will come tomorrow. Shay Stapleton takes the stand first thing in the morning, right? If anybody has come up with answers to this mystery over the years it must be him. Poor man must have obsessed about this case non-stop for the twelve years since his boys first went missing.'

'We'll see,' Aisling says, before she sweeps out the door, dragging it shut behind her.

'I mean, I get that Dupont came with new technology, but really? I thought Jonathan Ryan handled him well,' Callum says as he watches his mother rifle through the paperwork.

'You seem to be transfixed on how Ryan handled him,' Delia says, without looking up. 'But the gem of his testimony lies in the answers he gave to Bracken's questions. This is... this is...' Delia holds her fist to her mouth again and burps loudly into it. Then she bends down and drags the metal bin from under her desk closer to her feet.

'Mum, Mum,' Callum cries, standing up and chicaning himself around the desk. He hunkers down beside his bent-over mother and rubs at her back. And as he does so, glass crunches beneath his feet.

'What the hell?' He bends down to pick up the smashed photo frame and stares at it. 'Oh, it's the one of you, Dad and me,' he says. 'When did you break this... *how* did you break this?' He leans in closer to his mum, gripping her in a one-armed embrace. 'What's wrong, Mum? Tell me. You can tell me.'

He places the photo frame back on the desk, a large V-shape of glass missing from the centre of it, and then purrs a sorrowful look towards his mother. Delia sucks up the dribbles that are threatening to run on to her top lip before she pats her son's shoulder repeatedly.

'I know I can tell you anything, son,' she says, rubbing the ball of one of her palms into her eye. 'But you are the one person I can't show this to.'

'Show?' Callum asks, his voice all high-pitched.

'Forget it,' Delia says, waving him away.

'Show me what?... Mum?... Mum?'

Delia leans forward, her two elbows on her desk, her hands slapped to her cheeks.

'Callum... I... we...' She drops both forearms down onto the desk, then sits back in her chair and begins to wiggle her mouse. 'We're being blackmailed.' She opens up her emails, then reaches out to her computer monitor and tilts it ever so slightly, so that it's more face on with her son. 'I don't know what to do... who to...' she says, almost sobbing. Then she reaches for her mouse again, clicks on the video link and baulks backwards, wrapping her arms around her head.

Callum inches his nose closer to the screen, and realises the torso on it belongs to him; his penis throbbing, his knuckles wrapped tight around it. He watches himself tugging and grunting. Tugging and grunting.

'Holy fucking shit!' he says, turning to his mother. 'Holy fucking shit. That's my computer, recording me. My computer! Somebody hacked into my computer. They must have accessed my camera and...' He covers his mouth with his hand, then stands backwards against the wall of Delia's office. 'Who the fuck sent you that?' he asks.

Delia removes her arms from her head, then clicks at her mouse, bringing up the last email she was sent.

Return a Guilty verdict and this footage will stay between us. Deliver not guilty... then this goes everywhere.

'Eddie fucking Taunton,' Callum says. 'Didn't you say he wanted a guilty verdict? Mother fucker had somebody hack into my computer, triggered my camera while I was watching porn and... and... well... The dirty, fat, perverted bastard.'

'Callum, please!'

Delia holds her fingertips to her temple, her stare glaring down at the small pebbles of glass glistening beneath her feet.

'Well... y'know what... it's not that bad. It's not that bad,' Callum says, kneeling down beside his mother's chair and staring up at her. He grabs both of her hands. 'Yes, you are being blackmailed. Yes, somebody hacked into my computer and... yes, it seems we're in trouble. But we're not. Not at all. All you have to do is return a guilty verdict. Then this is all over and that video can... go away. Just get on with the trial as if everything is normal... then at the end of it just deliver your guilty verdict.'

'Even if Joy is innocent?' Delia asks.

'Mum... you don't... no. You don't think she's innocent, do you? You've never thought she was innocent...' Callum places a hand either side of his mother's face and stares up into her eyes. 'Mum, seriously, talk to me... you don't think she's innocent now... do you?'

'I *am* innocent,' Joy said, her hands on her hips, one eyebrow arched to mirror Debbie's glare. 'The only reason I'm in this kip is because of that pink hoodie, and that is not my pink hoodie in that CCTV footage.'

'It could only have been fuckin' you,' Debbie snarled.

'You don't know what you're talking about!'

Debbie stepped closer to Joy, and Joy's heart thudded. Debbie Hart was a new inmate at Elm House, but she had already made her presence felt. She was loud and brash and certainly stocky – as wide as she was tall. Her greying hair was all shaven on one side and she had a swirling tattoo on the side of her neck that looked as if it had been designed by a four-year-old. But thankfully, for Joy as well as the other smaller girls in Elm House, Debbie wouldn't be hanging around for too long. Two months. Max. Inside on a GBH charge. Which is why Joy's heart was thudding right this minute. Because she knew all too well that Debbie could handle herself. Yet, despite her fear, Joy still couldn't stand there and listen to a prisoner insist she was guilty of killing her sons. Not to her face. So, she plucked up enough courage to take a step closer to Debbie and held her breath.

'You're a fuckin' child killer,' Debbie snarled.

'I am no child kill—'

Before Joy had finished her retort, Debbie shoved her, and the other prisoners gathered around them to watch the fight in as close proximity as they possibly could.

'That's enough!' a voice boomed.

And as it did, the crowd parted to allow Christy to walk through.

Joy was leaning on her forearms on the concrete floor, Debbie hunched over her, her fist balled.

Christy stepped towards them and offered Joy a hand while curling her top lip at Debbie.

'You wanna pick on someone, pick on someone yo own size. Wanna piece of me, bitch?'

Debbie stared into Christy's bloodshot eyes, contemplating. Then she broke her stare to glance at Joy before grunting and storming back down the grated landing and towards her cell at the far end of Elm House.

'What was all that about?' Christy asked. And as almost everybody in the crowd tried to explain that Debbie had approached Joy for a fight, Joy sulked away, chicaning through the crowd until she found herself back in her own cell. Alone. And crying – sobbing as heavily as she had done the first night she had arrived.

It wasn't long until Christy had come to her rescue, perched, as she had done countless times over the past two and a half years, on the edge of Joy's bed, consoling her with words of wisdom that were filled with profanities and verses from the bible that weren't.

'You very emotional, sista... you wanna tell me why yo face look like Niagara Falls... and don't say it's cos that Debbie Hart bitch be intimidatin' you. I know you stronger than that.'

Joy sniffed up her tears.

'Fuck Debbie Hart,' Joy said. 'She doesn't mean anything to me. Besides, she's gonna be outta here in a matter of weeks. I would've fought her, though. I was willing to stand up for myself, even if she did hand me a beating. I'm not gonna just stand there and have somebody call me a child killer to my face.'

Christy dabbed at Joy's eyes with the sleeve of her sweat top.

'Then tell me, what else got you all emotional?'

'I dunno,' Joy said, lying back onto her bed, her legs hanging over the side. 'It's loadsa different things but most of all... I guess... I mean... I don't know what to tell you, cos I'm embarrassed about it... but a few months back I tried to... I tried to kiss Aidan.'

'Kiss him?' Christy's red eyes widened, and she held a hand to her mouth.

'I mean... I was a bit... I don't know. He was just standing there one day, and I was vulnerable and alone and sad. And I just threw my arms around him and... and...'

'Ah!' Christy said, 'That's why that boy ain't been around us much these days, huh? He keepin' his distance from you, ain't he? That's why you haven't been yourself.'

Joy answered by sobbing. So, Christy lay beside her, to hold her in a tight embrace and whisper into her ear, life lessons filled with profanity and bible verses that weren't.

'Ah, good. I got the two of you together,' Mathilda said, interrupting their moment. 'Stapleton, you're coming with me. Jabefemi, you've an appointment in the Governor's office.'

'The Governor's office... wot I do?' Christy asked.

Mathilda shrugged her shoulders.

'How t'hell would I know? Just get your lanky ass up there. Meanwhile, Stapleton, step outside with me.'

'She didn't start anything,' Christy said. 'Debbie came over to her, pushed her to the ground and then I stepped in and put a stop to it.'

'I don't know what you're talking about, Jabefemi,' Mathilda said. 'And I don't care either. Stapleton, c'mon, let's go.'

Mathilda led Joy down the steel staircase, across the landing of Elm House and deeper into the bowels of the prison. It had been pretty much close to a year since she was last in this vicinity; when she was being led to a surprise meeting with her husband.

'Here y'go,' Mathilda said, stopping outside the exact same yellow door Joy was certain they had stopped outside that time last year.

'It's not... it's not Shay again, is it?' she asked. And then without saying anything, Mathilda gingerly pushed open the yellow door to show Joy the greying face of her husband.

'I gotta put these on first,' Mathilda said, whipping a pair of cuffs from her waistband.

'Well, well, to what do I owe this pleasure?' Joy said as she sat across from her husband, chained once again to a loop under the desk. She stared at him, noticing that some of the blue had returned to his eyes. 'You look good, Shay. How's the outside world treating you?'

'Eh...' he said, leaning forward on the table, 'I, eh... well, I'm doing good. Better. How about you?'

'Same as you. Better. I'm getting used to it, aren't I? But I guess I may as well. Ain't nobody coming to rescue me, are they? I had to get rid of my last lawyer. Think the creepy prick fancied me or something. He'd turn up all smiles and compliments, but he never did anything. For eighteen months he tried to work around things so he could get me a retrial, but... I'm not sure he was doing anything at all to be honest.'

She shrugged her shoulders, causing her cuffs to clank.

'So, who's representing you now?'

'I haven't got anybody. Don't see the point. I'm gonna be here the rest of my life and I guess I've just had to come to terms with it.'

Shay thinned his lips at his wife, then he reached a hand across the table and placed it on top of hers. It was the first time they'd touched since the week before Joy's original trial – just over two and a half years ago.

'I, eh... I didn't actually come here to talk about this place.' He looked around himself. 'I came here to ask for a divorce.' Joy was surprised that she was surprised. She had expected this request as soon as she was found guilty, yet Shay had never so much as raised the topic. 'I, eh... I met somebody else. Jennifer. Jennifer Stevenson. She's a vet.'

Joy held her eyes closed.

'How old?'

'How... sorry? Your first question is how old is my fiancée?'

'Fiancée?' Joy threw her arms to the air, but the chains clanked and dragged them back to the desk, causing an echoing racket. Though the shooting pain in her wrists wasn't as severe as the throbbing pangs in her heart.

'I had to move on. Course I had to move on. I, eh... I met her last Christmas, at a charity function and we... we hit it off. I asked her a couple of weeks ago to marry me and she said 'Yes'. So, I, eh...'

'So, you've come to see me to ask me to sign a piece of paper that'll free you up to marry her?'

'Well...' Shay shifted himself uneasily in his chair, 'I don't have any papers with me. I am just here to tell you – face to face – that I'm filing for divorce. I'm sorry. I'm so sorr—'

'You don't need to apologise,' Joy said, cutting her husband short. 'When you have the papers, send them in and I'll sign 'em. Shay... congratulations. I'm glad you're happier. Your eyes have turned blue again. Mathilda!' she shouted, 'I'm good now. You can take me back to the cell.'

Mathilda pushed the yellow door slightly open and peered through the crack.

'You have fifty-five more minutes, you two. Might as well make the most of it.'

Joy sighed, then stared across the cramped desk to look into the eyes she once thought she'd be spending a lifetime getting lost in.

They didn't talk about much, aside from a quick catch-up, before Shay eventually left. Joy relented and then exaggerated; telling him she was having a hard time of it with the bullies in the prison; that in fact just before he had come to visit her, she had been beaten up. He could well believe her, what with her face swollen from all of the crying she had done earlier.

'So, there we have it, after all these years, Shay Stapleton finally gonna divorce your ass,' Mathilda said as she led Joy back around the maze of landings.

'Mathilda,' Joy said, stopping. 'Shut the fuck up and stop listening into my visitations.' Then she stomped herself all the way back to her cell, like a fourteen-year-old who'd been sent to bed early for misbehaving. But she only stayed in her cell for a matter of minutes; too emotionally drained to be in her own company. She knew what she needed; the calming Texan/Nigerian drawl of her best friend. Her only true friend. The only person who could right her wrongs; who could stop her mind from travelling to the darkest of places. The only person who truly believed she was innocent.

She paced across the landing and pushed at Christy's cell door, but it wouldn't budge.

'Christy. Christy, you in there?' she said as she slapped her open palms against the door. 'I need you. I need you. You're not gonna believe this. Shay wants a divorce. Mother fucker's getting married again... Christy? Christy?'

She hunkered down, to stare through the boxed gap in the centre of Christy's cell door. But the cell looked vacant.

'She's gone,' Aidan's voice echoed. Joy, stunned, spun around and looked up to see him standing on the landing above her, leaning over the rail. 'Governor came to her about an hour ago, told her her time was up. She's a free woman now, Joy. Christy's already back on the streets.'

1,977 days ago...

Linda rubbed at Joy's legs, but it didn't seem to be having the calming effect she was aiming for. Joy was still stretched out on her mattress sobbing, just as she had been for almost the entirety of the past twenty-four hours.

'We'll get through this. We can take everything Christy taught us and just continue to learn from it through the rest of our time here,' Linda said.

Joy gulped, then wiped at her nose with her sleeve, causing a streak of snot to stretch across her cheek. She didn't notice. And Linda felt it best left unsaid, given the sombre circumstances.

'S'all right for you to say, Linda. You've only got a couple of years left. I'm gonna be here the rest of me life. I can't do it... I can't do it without Christy. Besides...'

Linda continued to rub along Joy's short legs.

'Besides what?'

'Christy getting out isn't the only reason I'm in this state.'

'Huh?'

'Shay.'

'Shay... your husband? What about him?'

'He came to see me yesterday. He's met someone else – asked her to marry him.'

Linda rubbed even more fervently, while producing a sympathetic purr.

'I know you've loved that man so much, Joy. But aren't you better off detaching from him once and for all? You talk so much about what he thinks; what he does and doesn't believe. Maybe, just maybe this could be a fresh start for you.'

Joy sobbed again. Then she sat up in her bed and rested the cheek with the streak of snot stretched across it onto Linda's shoulder.

'I wish I could be more positive like you are, Linda Wood. It's just...

uuuuugh... two body blows in the space of one hour yesterday. First, Shay asking me for a divorce. And then I come back to tell Christy and she's just... she's gone. Pfftt. Out of my life like that... forever. But ye know what seems to be hurting the most?'

'What's that, baby?' Linda said, now rubbing in circles at the small of Joy's lower back.

'I spent the guts of an hour with Shay yesterday. Mother fucker never once mentioned our boys. He never mentioned the case at all. All this time has passed... and all this drama has passed... and ye know what? The most painful and frustrating part for me in all of this is that I've simply never, *ever*, truly known what's been going on inside my husband's head.'

SHAY STAPLETON

Nine autographs I signed between getting out of the car and reaching the front doors of the Criminal Courts. I counted as I was signing. Only because I was miffed. Though I often am when I sign an autograph these days – not quite sure if I'm more famous for being a footballer or for being Joy Stapleton's husband.

There used to be a time I'd love to be asked for my autograph. In fact, I'd often walk up and down Grafton Street in my spare time just so Dubliners would recognise me and ask me to sign a slip of paper for them while they told me where they were when I side-footed home the winning goal in the 2005 Leinster final. But now I do the total opposite of that. I stay indoors. So that I can stay out of sight of the general public as much as I possibly can.

I'm only out today for her. For Joy. Her torture has been going on way too long. Though so, too, has mine. I guess I'm just hopeful this trial will go some way to diluting my torture. I came here to let the judge know that I feel, after all this time, that Joy is innocent; that she isn't responsible for the fact that our two boys' skeletons were found in wasteland up in the Dublin mountains. But the truth is, as it's always been, I really don't know what to fucking believe. All I can hope for at this stage is that if Joy is to be set free, then so too might I. I know that's selfish. But I need it. I need the freedom. I need to be able to breathe fresh air again.

Nobody in this world feels more guilty about Oscar and Reese's murders than I do. I wasn't there for them when they needed me most. Guilt riddles me. It eats at me. And it has done ever since I received that phone call from Joy – screaming at me that our boys had been taken.

My best friend Steve pats me on the back as Gerd Bracken calls out my name, and as I stand, my ears are immediately enveloped by humming. I feel a slight sense of dizziness, almost vertigo-like, as if the red carpet wants me to lean towards it. But I make my way up the three steps to the witness box, without falling; avoiding eye contact with Joy as I sidle by. Though as I sit into the leather cushioned witness box, after I've been swiftly sworn in, I allow myself a glance at her. So many years have passed since I last saw that face. She looks as if she's aged. But haven't we all? Her eyes glance upwards to meet mine, but I immediately blink away. Last time Joy laid her eyes on me, I was, dare I say it, still handsome. Now I just see an old man staring back at me every time I look in a mirror. Like proper old. I'm only thirty-eight, but I see a fifty-eight-year-old in my reflection. I actually remember, distinctly, just waking up one morning and noticing I had two extra chins. As if they just appeared overnight. And the blue in my eyes, which I used to be complimented on constantly, has turned grey... a bit like my hair. A bit like my skin. I'm just grey all over these days. Grey and chubby. A bit like the cloud that constantly floats above me.

'Mr Stapleton,' Bracken says, appearing in front of me with his hands clasped against his belly. 'I and the court sincerely thank you for being here today. Can you start by stating your profession for the court, please?'

'Eh... well, I work in public relations for Jameson Hotels.'

'But it's fair to say the population of this country would know you in another capacity...'

'Yes, as the man whose two sons were murdered.' Before Bracken can react, I hold my hands up. 'Sorry. Yes. Of course. I, ehm... was also a member of the Dublin football squad from 2002 up until... well, 2009. I stopped playing when Oscar and Reese went missing, then came back eighteen months later and played a couple more games, but my heart just wasn't...'

'It's understandable, Mr Stapleton. You were, it is fair to say, a well-known sports star in the mid part of the noughties, correct?'

'Correct.'

'You crossed paths with Joy Lansbury as she was then in December of 2002. You guys had Reese just shy of one year later. In May of 2006 you got married. Then in March 2007, Oscar was born. Four Stapletons living in a beautiful four-bedroom semi-detached home in Rathfarnham... correct?'

'Correct.'

'How would you describe your family life in those days... the days before your boys were first reported missing back in November of 2008?'

I shift uneasily in the witness box, my fingers drumming on my lap.

'Well... I would describe it as normal.'

'Happy?'

'Objection, Your Honour, Mr Bracken is putting words into the witness's mouth,' the lawyer on the other side of the room calls out.

'He's only asking a question, Mr Ryan,' the judge says.

I look at her and then she looks at me. And nods.

'I would say happy, yes.' I sniffle up some tears that are threatening to fall. I promised myself I wouldn't cry. Though I knew I couldn't guarantee that promise. I reach inside my suit breast pocket and take out the photograph of Oscar and Reese, just to squeeze it in the hope that it will gift me some strength. I stare at this photograph every day. Truth is, I often spend hours just staring at it. Their two little faces smiling back at me. It's so odd. It seems it's all I've got left of them. One flash of a camera. A moment in time captured forever; a moment I will never get tired of staring at.

'Although you were a footballer at the height of the sport – and I'm sure most will know you scored in a Leinster final in 2005 – you still worked for Jameson Hotels, correct?'

'Yes.'

'GAA stars are, of course, not paid for their efforts. They need full-time work for their livelihoods. And you travelled for work, yes?'

'Yes. I had to stay in a lot of our sister hotels in different counties regularly... that was part of my job.'

'Yet despite the amount of travelling you did, you were utterly faithful to your wife and children and couldn't wait to get home to them each time you travelled, correct?'

I clear my throat, and lean closer to the microphone.

'Mr Bracken, I will say under oath, that I was always faithful to my wife and boys. I never once committed adultery. I always wanted to come home to them. Yes.'

That's not entirely true. I didn't always want to come home to them. I have to admit, I liked the solitude working in the hotel industry offered me. That's why the guilt riddles me. I was in a bloody hotel doing absolutely nothin', when my boys were taken. I should've been home. I should've been a better father. A better husband. And I guess that when Joy and I first started dating I was seeing other girls at the same time. It was part and parcel of being a sports star. Girls would offer themselves up to me. But once Joy fell pregnant for the first time, I didn't dare look at another woman. In fact, I stopped socialising altogether so that the temptation of other women would die. And it did. I never cheated on my family. Other than to pretend to them that I really missed them while I was being pampered in a five-star hotel.

'And you knew Joy Stapleton better than anyone? You lived with her for five whole years and you shared some amazing memories, correct?'

'Those five years were the best five years of my life. We had two children.

We got married. We honeymooned in South Africa. We travelled to different countries on many different holidays. We were... we were two young people in their early twenties very much in love and very much looking forward.'

A tear threatens to race out of my eye, so I pinch the photo of Reese and Oscar tighter.

'In 2008, may I ask you, Mr Stapleton, did you notice any change in your wife's behaviour?'

I shake my head.

'You must verbally answer the question, Mr Stapleton,' the judge says, looking down at me. The judge seems firm, but fair. Though I've noticed her out of the corner of my eye every now and then get distracted by somebody sitting at the back of the gallery. Her eyes seem to flicker there every now and then.

'Oh... sorry. I, eh... no! I've been asked this question I don't know how many times over the years. I've even asked myself it. Did Joy murder the boys because she was suffering with postnatal depression, or some mental health condition? Truth be known, Joy was the same Joy she had always been to me. I am just here to tell the truth, Mr Bracken... as you well know. I have to say, hand on heart,' I push the photo of the boys to my chest, 'I didn't notice any behavioural differences in Joy before... before...'

A squeaky sob pulses from the back of my throat and forces its way out through my mouth. I sound like a puppy dog who's just has his tail trod on. And then my dam breaks, and tears begin to race down both of my cheeks.

'It's okay, I can give you time to—'

'No,' I sob, pressing the ball of my hand into my eyes. 'Let's keep going.'

'Well, eh... what I was going to ask next, Shay, is... because of the fact that you never witnessed any behavioural differences in Joy, you have never been convinced by the verdict of the original trial, have you?'

I sigh out what probably sounds like a laugh, though it's a laugh hiccoughed through snot and tears. This is one of two big questions Bracken rehearsed with me. I just need to remember what my answer is supposed to be, which is not easy when dozens of people are sat in a gallery gawking at my swollen face.

'No. The original trial, for me, had too many holes in it. I've never been convinced by anything in this case. It's just been... it's just been...'

I wipe my entire hand across my face as another sob throws itself up from the back of my throat, then I look back up at Bracken.

'Take your time, Mr Stapleton,' he says. He has been so nice to me, has Bracken. But I'm not sure I've ever made my mind up about him. He begged me to testify when the retrial was granted; begged me to get on the stand and state for the record – once and for all – that I didn't believe Joy killed Oscar

and Reese. I agreed. Not because I'm certain. But because I just want this whole thing over and done with. It's consumed my life. It has ruined my life. I can't move on... I just can't. I hope Joy being set free will help free me too. I know that is so damn selfish. But I'm half-way through my life right now. I'm going to be dead in about forty years. I just need... I just need... to move on. I need to turn the grey cloud that hovers above my head into a white one. And that can only happen when people finally stop asking me about Joy. If she gets out... maybe, just maybe I can move on. My whole existence has just been so static for over a decade now. So insignificant. And numbing. As if I can't get my life into another gear. I got engaged once. About four years ago to a beautiful Galway girl called Jennifer. She's adorable. In every way. We met, fell in love, got engaged and then... and then I left her. Because... because I just couldn't move on. Some other lucky bastard is engaged to her now.

'So, let me ask you this more specifically,' Bracken says. 'Have you ever been convinced of Joy's involvement in the murder of your two sons?'

I swipe my sleeve across my face, mopping up the last of the tears, then steady myself by gripping the shelfed edges of the witness box, the photograph now resting on my lap; my boys smiling up at me.

'Sorry,' I say, composing myself. 'No. I've never been convinced of Joy's involvement in Oscar and Reese's murders.'

There... I finally got out the sentence Bracken and I rehearsed. A sentence that I'm sure will be splashed all over tomorrow's newspapers. I only said that sentence because it's true. I am not, nor ever have been, convinced of her guilt. There were times, especially during the first trial, that I was growing in certainty that she did it. Then holes would appear in theories and it just became impossible to have any definitive opinion, let alone proof. I've literally never known what to believe since the day my boys went missing. But even if she is guilty; even if she did flip one day and did the unthinkable – under the stress of raising two young boys all on her own while her husband was away being pampered – then I'm as much to blame as she is.

I allow myself another glance at her and, this time, she meets my eye immediately, as if she was waiting to catch my eyes darting towards hers.

'Mr Stapleton,' Bracken says, approaching the witness box and forcing me to blink away from Joy. 'May I say that, under the circumstances, it is very brave of you to not only be here, but to testify under the strains of such unimaginable emotion. I cannot fathom your experiences. It is heroic for you to be here today to tell your truth; for the one person who knew Joy more than anyone else to say under oath that you have never been convinced of her involvement in your sons' murders. I used to watch you in Croke Park, Sir. Was a big fan. Am a big fan. You were always a hero to so many people. But *you have never been so heroic as you have been here today. I thank you. The courts thank you.'*

Bracken stretches his hand towards me and I take it and shake it. I've never seen that done in a courtroom before. I'm still feeling a little shocked that his questioning has come to a sudden halt, when the lawyer on the opposite side of the room is striding towards me, unbuttoning his blazer.

'Mr Stapleton,' he says, 'you have just testified here that you have never been convinced your wife is guilty of your sons' murders, yes?'

I cough. Then nod my head.

'Mr Stapleton, you must verbally answer for the record of the court,' the judge reminds me.

'Yes. That is what I have just testified,' I say, taking the picture of the boys from my lap and pressing it to my chest again.

'So, let me get this straight. You are a loving husband, who has just lost his two sons. Then their bodies are found two years later, and soon after that your wife is arrested and sent to prison for two life sentences for those murders. Yet you have never been convinced of her guilt?'

I nod my head a little, while whispering, 'Yes.'

'That is some tragedy. Not only have you lost your sons. But your wife... As Mr Bracken said, that must be unimaginable. Now, can you tell me, Mr Stapleton – and I would like to state for the record that you very much have always had my sympathies and my sympathies remain with you as I ask these questions, but – can you tell me why in all of the eight years your wife has spent in Mountjoy Prison, and given that you have never been convinced of her guilt, you have only ever visited her on two occasions?'

I squeeze the photograph as firmly to my heart as I possibly can.

'Well... in the same way that I've never been convinced of Joy's guilt, I've also never been convinced either way. You have to understand... I know as much as anybody knows about this case. And nobody seems to know the truth.'

'Ah... so, Mr Stapleton,' the lawyer says as he takes a step closer to me. 'Not only are you testifying that you aren't convinced of Joy's guilt, but you are also not convinced of her claims of innocence, yes?'

I open my mouth, but nothing comes out. Not before the tears do. I snort and wash my hands over my face again. What a question to be asked. Though it's not as if I didn't know it was coming. We knew it would. Bracken had told me I would be asked if I was convinced of Joy's innocence after testifying to him that I wasn't convinced of her guilt.

'I am more convinced of her innocence,' I say, just as we had rehearsed, 'because I knew Joy better than anybody. And I am quite certain she is not a killer.'

It stuns the lawyer a little bit. His chin tilts upwards and his eyes squint. He didn't think I'd answer that so emphatically. But I did. Because it was what Bracken had manufactured. And I was fine with it. Because I just want this nightmare to end.

'Well,' *the lawyer says, still a little taken aback,* 'you say you knew Joy well enough and of course you wouldn't have married a woman or started a family with a woman you believed was capable of murder... but given that you were away travelling so much for work, is it possible that you didn't notice your wife transforming into a killer?'

'Objection!' *Bracken stands up.*

'Fair question,' *the lawyer says, turning to judge Delia.*

I stare at the judge... and wait...

'You may answer,' *she says to me.*

I look back at the lawyer, through new tears that have just snuck up on me.

'If you are suggesting she may have suffered some mental health problems to an extent that she would kill our two sons, then I am already on record as saying I don't believe that to be the case. I testified ten minutes ago to Mr Bracken that I did not witness Joy suffering any depression after our boys were born. She was happy. We were happy.'

The lawyer looks about himself, and as he does I turn the photo of my boys' smiling faces towards me and stifle a smile back at them. Though all I manage to do is blink more tears down my cheeks.

'Mr Stapleton, I cannot possibly comprehend the amount of emotion you must be feeling. But I must do my job properly... so forgive me. But you are here today testifying that you do not believe, after all these years, that your wife is guilty of this crime, yet you have only visited her two times in eight years. And we also know that the second time you visited her was to seek a divorce... wasn't it? Because you had just got engaged to another woman, correct?'

My chins quiver.

'Please,' *I sob.* 'Please... can you not just let me move on? I came here to say what I had to say so I could move on... please.'

∴

Delia remains upright in her highchair, her two arms folded and resting onto the desk, her lips ever so slightly pouted. She had learned, many years ago, how to refrain from showing emotion inside the courtroom. A turning out of her lips is about as much as she has ever skirted the lines of what is deemed appropriate for a trial judge. Though she is holding up well, especially in comparison to those in the gallery; some of whom are dabbing at their eyes, most of whom haven't bothered and have decided, instead, to just allow the tears to flood down their cheeks.

'Mr Stapleton,' she says, intervening, 'the question is pertinent. Given that you have come here to testify, I would like you to answer it. If you need more time, I am happy to adjourn the court and allow you to—'

'I'll answer the question,' he says, sitting more upright and sniffling up his nose. Delia's lips pout even further and her brow dips, heavy with empathy. 'Yes, I was engaged to Jennifer a few years ago. I met her at a charity do one Christmas, we hit it off... we were going to restaurants on dates. I was finally getting back out there. Living myself a life. Then after I asked her to marry me and the media got wind of the story, they started to follow us about. They wanted a picture of Jennifer's ring, and me and her all cosy or something... I don't know. But it frightened me. It made me want to stay home and I started to suffer with more grief and... and... eventually, I just told Jennifer that she needed to move on. That is the truth of it all. I don't understand what this has to do with the trial. Yes, I once asked Joy for a divorce, but I never went through with it. There was no divorce.'

Jonathan Ryan coughs, unsure whether his line of questioning is working. He wanted to display Shay as somebody who couldn't possibly have thought Joy was innocent all these years, not when he had only visited her twice and had since got engaged to another women. But the witness's raw and emotive responses seem to only have endeared him more to the gallery.

'Okay, Mr Stapleton,' Ryan relents, 'I just want to ask you three more questions, to re-establish some points, then you are free to leave. Firstly, you say you are not convinced of your wife's guilt in this case, but you have only visited her twice in prison in the past eight years, correct?'

'Yes, I've already confirmed that.'

'Okay, Mr Stapleton, we are just re-establishing some points. Secondly, you got engaged to another woman in 2016, correct?'

'Yes,' Shay says, before allowing a frustrated sigh to blow through his lips.

'And whilst you are not convinced of your wife's guilt, you are also not convinced by her innocence, yes?'

Shay shrugs his shoulders.

'I guess so,' he says.

And then Ryan turns to Delia and nods at her before returning to his desk.

'Mr Stapleton,' Delia says sombrely, just as the witness is getting to his feet, 'I don't often break protocol in the court, but feel it's warranted to add an extra thank you to the one already offered up by Mr Bracken. Your time is really appreciated.'

Delia was genuinely moved by Shay Stapleton's testimony, not because he got so emotional discussing the unfathomable murder of his two young sons, but because he was willing to support his wife after all these years. Delia knew next to nothing about sports, but even she could tell why Shay had been such an outstanding athlete for his county. He was strong. He was brave. And he was undoubtedly loyal. But as he was stepping down from the witness box, Delia was trying to filter through her mind whether or not Shay being all those things truly counted towards her judgement.

As the witness walks his sizeable frame down the aisle of the court, Delia's eyes burn again towards the bushy v-shaped eyebrows in the back row.

She waits until Shay, in total silence, sweeps open the double doors and disappears out of them before she twists her wrist towards her face.

'It's just gone one p.m.,' she calls out. 'We will take nigh on ninety minutes for lunch. Court will reconvene at 2:30 p.m. precisely.'

She hammers down her gavel once and then stands abruptly, her eyes fixed once again on those eyebrows.

Eddie squints back at her, then rises to his feet as a sea of heads pass him to rush towards the same double doors Shay Stapleton had exited just moments ago.

'Edward Taunton!' Delia calls out as his eyebrows get lost in the crowd.

There is no answer to her call as those attempting to exit swivel their heads back and forth from the judge to the double doors.

'Eddie!' Callum, standing on the other side of the courtroom, shouts. The crowd stop in unison, and stare. But Callum just waves them on, and as they finally disperse through the double doors, Eddie's obese frame comes into view, his hands in his pockets, his tiny eyes squinting under the arch of his bushy eyebrows.

'I need to have a discussion with you in my office. Now!'

'I, eh... I need to—'

'Now!' Delia shouts.

Then she takes the three steps down from her highchair and storms out the side entrance of the courtroom. She whips off her robe as she paces down the corridor; the emotional gut-wrench she had felt during Shay's touching testimony well and truly replaced by a fierce doggedness.

When she snatches open her office door, she tosses her bunched up robe to one side and wiggles at the mouse of her computer as she sits into her leather chair.

'How the hell am I going to deal with this?' she says to herself as she waits on her monitor to blink back to life.

She stifles a yawn, only because she is so mastered in the art of doing so that it has become her usual yawning practice. She's spent twenty-five years as a criminal judge, overseeing many, many a dour hour of needless interactions in the midst of trials, and has therefore grown accustomed to mastering the stifling of a yawn. She *is* tired, but not just mentally today. She hadn't slept last night. Not much, anyway. She kept tossing and turning in her bed, the images of her son masturbating flashing in front of her eyes every time she tried to concentrate on the specifics of the retrial. Then Eddie's eyebrows would make their way into her thoughts and her fists would form into a tense ball under her duvet. She gazes around her desk, while waiting on the screen to blink to life, and looks at her son's proud smirk in the cracked photo frame, then the monitor hums and the screen blinks on at the same moment footsteps make their way to her door. She anticipates a knock, but none comes. The door just sweeps open.

'Where is he?' Callum says.

'You beat him to it.'

'Mother fucker better get here.'

'Callum McCormick, mind your language.' Delia snaps at her son as if he's a teenager again.

'How you going to approach this, Mum?'

'Oh, good afternoon, Mr Taunton,' Aisling calls out from the hallway, before heavy footsteps thud closer and knuckles rattle ominously against the door.

'Come in, Eddie,' Delia shouts.

He walks in, stares at Delia, then at Callum, before he ever so slowly glances around the dimly lit office.

'You need to talk?' he says.

'Sit down, Eddie,' Delia orders.

Eddie puffs out a snigger, then shuffles around Callum and takes a seat opposite the judge.

'I thought Shay's testimony was very touching—'

'Shut up, Eddie. And listen to me.'

'Excuse *me*, Delia,' he protests, sitting upright and pointing his finger. But Delia slaps her hand to her desk, causing another thin shard of glass to fall from the cracked photo frame.

'*You* are listening to *me* now,' Delia says. She leans more forward in her chair, mirroring Eddie, her eyes wide over the rim of her glasses. 'Tell me about the video.'

'The vid.... What? The CCTV footage of Joy?'

'Wise up,' Callum says from behind Eddie. 'And grow up. You know what my mother is talking about.'

Eddie stares over his shoulder at Callum, then fills his cheeks with air before slowly exhaling through tightly pursed lips, producing a rasping sound.

'Shay Stapleton's testimony, whilst tragic and touching, was largely a nonsense, right... you know that...'

'We're not talking about Shay Stapleton, Eddie. We're talking about the video,' Callum says.

'Calm down, little boy,' Eddie replies, turning in the chair again to eyeball Callum. Delia keeps her eyes wide. Then Eddie turns to her and continues. 'He's just a grieving father who's never been allowed to grieve. And now he's just happy for his wife or ex-wife or whatever she is to him to be free... regardless of whether or not he thinks she had anything to do with it. He's been asked about his sons and his wife every day for twelve years. The man is sick of it. He's testifying so Joy can get out of prison, because he thinks it may end his pain, too. Yes, his testimony was touching. Yes, his testimony was emotional. Heck, I almost cried. He used to be a hero of mine, y'know? I used to cheer him on from the Hogan Stand. But you don't need to view his testimony in any way other than testimony from a grief-stricken father who is not a professional in any line of investigative work.

Nor judicial work. You – Delia – are one of the best trial lawyers this country has produced. You know that. You know you can't let the emotions of a grieving father change your mind. Joy Stapleton did this.'

'The reason we called you here was not to discuss Joy Stapleton—'

'Calm down, Callum,' Delia says, dropping the curtness in her tone. 'Keep talking, Eddie.'

'Well, what more do you want me to say? This retrial has offered up tidbits of interesting anecdotes, but nothing should change your mind on this, Delia. You need to protect the original verdict. It's as simple as that.'

'And that's why you sent me a video of my son in a private moment? To blackmail me into protecting the original verdict?'

'Have you any idea what a not guilty verdict would do for the whole judicial arm of our nation? The whole house would come crumbling down. They'd totally drain the swamp. A not guilty verdict here would be detrimental not only for the judicial system, but our nation as a whole.' Delia gets to her feet and begins to pace the small square of floor to the side of her desk. 'C'mon Delia... You know Bunny the dog had fuck all to do with the guilty verdict in the original trial anyway. So, it shouldn't have anything to do with this retrial. We have Joy, for crying out loud, on camera walking away from the scene of where her boys' bodies were dumped.'

'That's not what Mathieu Dupont's testimony suggested. The height of the person in that footage doesn't compute to Joy.'

'That's bullshit testimony, Delia. Dupont is a fit-to-type witness. You know it. I know it. Anybody who knows law knows it. Gerd Bracken wanted to find somebody who could throw doubt on the figure in that footage and he found it in Dupont. He had to get to France before he could find somebody who *might* pour cold water on the fact that that is – without doubt – Joy Stapleton in that CCTV footage. This trial doesn't come down to coincidence, Delia. You told me that yourself years ago. Joy Stapleton is guilty. I don't care what fit-to-type testimony the court has heard over the past week. Besides... you've only heard the defence arguments so far. You can't let your head get swayed. What you have to do here is simple. Protect the original verdict. And let's all move on from this.'

'Drain the swamp? You think this whole place is a swamp just because you yourself happen to be a sloth? Don't lump me and all the other great judges in these courts in with the likes of you, Eddie. You think I'm dirty? You think I play dirty? Don't you dare...' She continues to pace the small square of floorboards. 'Y'know, I was lying in bed last night wondering why you picked on Callum. And you know what I realised? It's because you could get nothing on me, isn't it? You would have worked trying to find dirt on me so you could blackmail me into delivering a guilty verdict, but you found nothing... right? You looked at my exemplary work record... nothing dirty in that. You would have hacked into my computer as you did Callum's. No dirt in that. So, you had to turn to my son. And even then, you got nothing. What? An innocent man masturbating? Think about it. That's the worst you could find on *me*... The fact that my son masturbates? You think that's a sin? I masturbate too... we all masturbate, Eddie.'

'Mum!'

'Sorry, Callum,' Delia says without looking at her son.

Callum audibly shivers.

Eddie remains seated, the two McCormicks gazing down at him, as his grin turns into a chuckle.

'Delia, if you don't mind sitting. Please,' he says trying to compose himself. A silence settles between them before Delia finally relents and takes the seat opposite him. 'We're a country of what... ninety-nine years of age? Our judiciary system is much younger than that. It was only born in 1961, for crying out loud. It's a baby. It's younger than you and I... And it's vulnerable. You know it's vulnerable.'

'It's only vulnerable because you've been running it for over twenty years.'

'Delia, please,' Eddie says as Callum begins to pace back and forward behind him.

'It's true, Eddie. The system's a mess because you allowed it to become a mess on your watch.'

'That is ridiculous to suggest,' Eddie snaps back. 'This nation is growing at such a rapid rate that it is nigh on impossible for any sector to grow with it. We do the best we can here in the—'

'Is bribing the judge of the biggest retrial in the system's history "doing the best you can", Eddie?'

Eddie snorts.

'If Joy Stapleton is to be acquitted, everything falls down. Have you any idea what the newspapers are speculating her pay-out will be if she gets out?'

'I don't read the newspapers, Eddie.'

'Fifty million.'

'That's why I don't read the newspapers, Eddie. They're full of shit.'

'It will collapse us. The nation would lose total faith in the judicial system. Heads will roll. A whole review will be done. It will regress the whole progress the judicial system has made over the years. We'd be set back a hundred paces.'

'You keep saying that, Eddie. What you seem to be missing is the fact that you are willing to keep an innocent mother behind bars for the rest of her life just because you want to protect a system you have failed.'

'She's not fucking innocent, Delia! Listen to me. You know she's not. You told me that before.'

'I am looking at this trial—'

'Yeah, yeah... with a fresh pair of eyes. I get it. But that's what's worrying me. The evidence this retrial was granted on is bullshit. We can't afford to lose this one. That's her... that is Joy Stapleton in that CCTV footage. It's no coincidence. Just do the right thing, Delia. Let this whole mess go away. For everybody involved. All you have to do is protect the original verdict.'

Callum stops pacing, and places the tips of his fingers onto Delia's desk.

'Eddie's right, Mum,' he says.

Joy was pretending – not just to everyone around her, but to herself too – that she was finding solace in the responsibilities she and Linda had undertaken in the wake of Christy's release. They had tried, hard, over the past two and a half months, to ensure Christy's Crazies were maintained as a functional and, more importantly, peaceful group within Elm House. They followed pretty much the same routine they always had done when Christy was around; they assembled at the same bench for breakfast as soon as the cell doors clicked open – to begin their day with prayer, even though Joy wasn't sure any members left in the group actually believed in God anymore. Then they'd laze around the worn sofa at the back of the games room after work or school, catching up on prison gossip, by often exaggerating stories they'd heard about prisoners in the other Houses. Or sometimes the Crazies would all sit together in the TV room, watching reruns of old British quiz shows and giggling along because their attempts at answers were often so terribly wide of the mark. Their days pretty much ticked by in much the same way as they had when Christy was there, only this time the group lacked leadership, no matter how hard Joy and Linda had tried to take a reign on affairs. Neither of them had the gravitas Christy had; they certainly didn't have her presence, nor her voice. Two softly spoken south Dublin accents couldn't compare to a brash and husky Texan/Nigerian drawl. And so, despite Joy and Linda's efforts, all the twenty or so members of the Crazies did on a daily basis was follow each other around in packs like lost penguins during the seven hours they weren't locked inside their cells.

Though despite the Crazies' lack of direction, they still managed to remain peaceful and unharmed, even though Joy kept repeating that a grey cloud was hanging over them. Nancy Trott had been sent to isolation not long after Christy was released ten weeks ago having been caught with three mobile phones in her cell, and would be due back on the wing any coming day.

Joy had pretty much curled up on her mattress for the first fortnight in the wake of the double blow that was Christy's release and Shay's request for a divorce. Though slowly but surely, she crawled herself back to her feet. And because Linda had such willingness to have a companion whilst in prison, she pushed Joy to get off her bed and try to take a rein on the Crazies.

Aside from the grey Nancy-shaped cloud that was hanging over her, Joy was starting to gain some semblance of prison normality. Though images of her husband bedding a younger, hotter model sometimes tainted her thoughts.

She was literally thinking of Shay while flicking her way through the previous day's copy of the *Irish Daily Star* when he stared right back at her. Her mouth popped open. And she had to stand to soak him all in. A head-shot of him was placed below a headline that read:

Stapleton ends engagement

She whizzed through the story, sucked in by the quotes from a 'close family friend' who suggested Shay had gotten cold feet not long after asking young veterinarian Jennifer Stevenson to marry him because he was so overcome with a heavy and nauseating sense of disloyalty to his sons.

'That's why he hasn't sent in the divorce papers,' Joy whispered to herself, 'he doesn't need a divorce anymore.'

'Huh?' Linda asked, overhearing her friend's mumbling.

Joy looked at her, then sucked in her cheeks and turned the newspaper around so Linda could see it.

'I feel so sorry for him,' Joy said, almost sobbing as she sat back down on the worn sofa next to Linda. 'Almost as sorry as I feel for myself. Neither of us deserved this mess of a life we got. We were so happy... honestly Linda – the two of us really were so happy.'

Linda threw an arm around Joy and they both sat in silence, Shay's aged face staring back at them from the newspaper, until the mumbling of voices behind them began to rise in volume. Then a screeching and a howling sounded.

Joy and Linda both turned to look over their shoulder at the gathering crowd, and when the crowd parted, there she stood. Nancy Trott. High-fiving members of her cohorts with a grin stretched wide across her face.

'Bollocks!' Joy whispered out of the side of her mouth.

1,805 days ago...

'Not hungry?' Linda asked.

Joy shrugged her shoulders, then played around with her spoon, patting it down repeatedly to crush her Corn Flakes.

'Nope.'

'What's wrong?'

'Been dreading her coming back,' Joy said nodding over to the bench in the middle of the dining room to where Nancy had her cohorts in fits of giggles.

'We've just got to keep our heads down like we always have. We don't need to talk to them or do anything with them. Same as always. Besides, that bitch isn't going to cause any drama is she? She's only just back from isolation... she won't wanna be going back there again.'

Joy sighed, then pushed her bowl away.

She liked Linda. A lot. Linda was one of the Crazies most awed by Christy's visions. And because Christy had a vision that Oscar and Reese weren't killed by their mother, it meant Linda truly believed in Joy's innocence. But she didn't admire Linda. Not the way she wanted to admire a best friend. Not the way she admired Christy, even though she thought her bat-shit crazy. And certainly not how she once admired Lavinia. Lavinia could be bitchy and judgemental, but she never allowed anybody to control her. Linda was weak in comparison to the types of women Joy liked to be around. And she knew all too well that if Nancy started something, there would be fuck all her new best buddy could do about it.

'Okay, listen up,' boomed a voice.

Joy looked up to see Nancy stepping onto the table she had been sat at, before she began to clatter a wooden spoon against one of the kitchen's soup pots.

'Get down from there,' Aidan cut in, ordering Nancy with a wave of his hand.

She grinned at the prison officer, then took one step down so she was standing on the bench she had just been sitting on, and not the table top.

'Ah... I see you've grown some balls over the weeks I've been away, Aidan. Heard you got yourself a promotion, too.' Then she clanged the soup pot again with the wooden spoon before she began to shout. 'Girls. I am calling a truce in Elm House. There is no need for there to be separate groups among us. We are all one. All in this shithole together. So, let's get through it together, yes?'

A chorus of 'yeses' erupted from around Nancy, but the Crazies table at the far end of the dining room remained mostly subdued, save for some mumbling.

'For the past three years, we've had two separate factions on this wing. That ends today!' Hurrahs and applauses rippled around Nancy. 'Some of you only have a couple of months to serve, some of you a couple of years... some of you gonna be here the rest of your lives.' Joy looked up through her curls at Nancy, assuming she was talking not only about her, but to her. But

Nancy barely looked her way. 'Wherever you are in your sentence, whatever time you have left to serve, you are going to serve it in a peaceful wing. No more Nancy's Cohorts. No more Christie's Crazies... not now that Queen Crazy herself is no longer with us. We are Elm House. That's the only group name we need. Though having said that, every group needs a leader. And while I believe in democracy, I also believe in power. So, ladies – and gentleman,' she said, eyeballing Aidan with a grin as he stood looking helplessly up at her, his hands on his hips, 'I will be the leader of prisoners in Elm House and I promise to represent each and every prisoner in here equally. I will represent the guilty, the innocent, the thieves, the murderers.' Joy glanced at Nancy again. But Nancy still hadn't looked her way. 'Don't matter who you are or how you got here. We are all in this together, and we will all get through this together. But...' she said, before pausing and sucking on her lips, 'I can't do it alone. I can't keep track of ninety women all by myself... so I need me a deputy.' The hurrahs roared from the benches around Nancy, lasting so long she had to calm them down with a wave of her hands. 'Now, I've had a long time cooked up in an isolation cell to think about this. And I know who my deputy should be.' The raucous chanting around Nancy died, and there seemed to be a synchronized sucking in of breaths. 'So, without further ado, I give to you, Elm House, your new deputy leader. The one. The only. Missus Joy Stapleton.'

This time, when Joy looked up through her curls, Nancy wasn't only staring at her, but pointing her wooden spoon at her. Then Nancy started to clank the spoon against the soup pot again, generating louder cheering from those all flanked around her that created such a raucous noise that Aidan had no choice but to squeeze at the button of the walkie talkie on his shoulder and frantically ask for assistance.

⋰

'Judge Delia, you're due back in court now – it's two-thirty.'

Delia rises to her feet and stabs a finger at the standby button of her computer monitor, all in a bit of a fluster, knocking over the already-smashed photo of her family again.

'Coming, Aisling,' she calls out.

She picks up the photo, rests it on the table, then sweeps away teeny glass shards from her desk with her hand before eyeballing the two men standing opposite her.

'Protect the verdict, Delia,' Eddie grunts.

She doesn't respond. Instead, she spins around, pulls at the bottom drawer under her library shelves and takes out a fresh robe.

'Mum, we need to sit down and talk this through,' Callum says as she yanks the robe over her head where it gets caught on her glasses that she had, once again, forgotten she'd combed back into her hair.

'In case you haven't bloody noticed, Callum,' Delia whisper-shouts through the robe, 'I'm in the middle of one of the biggest trials in the history of these courts.' She frees herself, by yanking the robe fully down, revealing her face again. 'I have to sit down and listen to everybody. The witnesses. The lawyers. And now you want me to sit down and listen to you, Callum. And you Eddie. Over what... stupid bloody blackmail games? How dare you. How fucking dare you, Eddie Taunton.'

She swipes her door open, startling Aisling, and begins to pace down the corridor.

'Mum, Mum,' Callum calls, racing until he catches up with her just as she's turning on to the long corridor.

'He's right. We're all in a mess,' he says. 'And you're the only one who can clean the mess up. You can't let that video get out. It'll ruin my career. I'll never be seen as a serious contender in the courts.'

Delia keeps pacing, saying nothing, her breathing heavy. She notices the young woman dressed in black up ahead open the courtroom side door and nod into it. Then the call goes up.

'All rise.'

'Mum, please.'

Delia stops, grabs her son by the collar of his shirt and pins him against the wall.

'Shut up, Callum,' she says. 'I have a trial to judge.'

She stares into his eyes before releasing her grip. Then she turns around and smiles at the young woman dressed in black before she paces into the courtroom and up the three steps that lead to her highchair.

Courtrooms are normally silent, save for the hum of the air conditioning machines. But there certainly seems to be a stretched sense of eeriness in this courtroom today. Maybe it's because the trial is at the half-way mark and minds are working overtime – soaking in the entirety of the defence's arguments. Though the eeriness is most likely down to the impact of Shay Stapleton's testimony this morning. It had cast a huge wave of emotion right through the room. And it doesn't seem as if that wave has fully receded. Not yet anyway.

Delia gulps when she finds the correct hymn sheet she is supposed to be singing from and when she pulls the page out from the middle of her pile and stares at the name on it, she lightly gasps. She hadn't realised such contrasting testimony would follow Shay Stapleton's. Had she been paying more attention to the trial, instead of getting caught up in Eddie Taunton's games, she likely wouldn't have allowed the next witness. Not today. Because whatever emotional wave Shay had tsunamied over this courtroom this morning was about to come right back the other way.

'Mr Ryan,' Delia calls out. 'The trial turns to the evidence the prosecution will argue. Can you please call your first witness?'

'Of course, thank you,' Ryan says, standing and straightening the knot of his tie. 'Your Honour, we call Lavinia Kirwan to the stand.'

The back doors of the courtroom sweep open and in the large doorframe, silhouetted, stands a tiny figure. Lavinia can't be much taller than Joy, if at all. But she's not 'all hair' like Joy is. Her hair, fine and mousy brown in colour, is swept back into a tight bun.

Delia notices as the witness walks up the aisle that she doesn't once acknowledge the defendant. Lavinia stares straight ahead as she is sworn in. Then she sits her boney frame into the oversized square witness box and tilts the microphone lower.

'Ms Kirwan, thank you for taking the time to be with us here today,' Jonathan Ryan says. 'You met Joy Stapleton when you were... how old?'

'We were four, I guess. First year of primary school.'

'And you are now aged... if you don't mind me asking?'

'Thirty-six... I just turned thirty-six earlier this week as it happens.'

'Well... many happy returns, Ms Kirwan. So... even with my bad maths, that tells me you have known Mrs Stapleton for thirty-two years, correct?'

'Even with my bad maths, I believe you are correct, Mr Ryan, yes.'

'Okay. So, you have known her much longer than Shay Stapleton has known her, right?'

'Your Honour,' Mr Bracken shouts, scooting himself to his feet. 'This is not a competition between witnesses.'

'I agree. No need,' Delia says turning to Jonathan Ryan. She knew what he was getting at; knew he just wanted to point out that this testimony was just as worthy, if not more so, as the emotional heart-tugging testimony offered up by the defendant's husband this morning.

'Okay... well thirty-two years, nonetheless. And you were best friends all that time?'

'Yeah. I mean everybody in primary school was best friends so I'm not sure I had one best friend at that stage. But by the time we got to secondary school, me and Joy used to walk with each other to and from school every day and we became really close. We shared most of our teen years in each other's bedrooms listening to boybands.'

'So, you know her as much as anybody, it's fair to say.'

'I would say so, yes,' Lavinia replies.

'Well then, let me ask this question: do you believe the jurors in the original trial in which Joy Stapleton was convicted for the murder of her two sons, Reese and Oscar Stapleton, got their verdict correct?'

'Objection,' Bracken calls.

'Ma'am,' Ryan says, 'I am not asking an independent witness. I am asking the opinion of a witness who we have just proven has known the defendant for over three decades.'

'Not allowed, Mr Ryan. Be careful with your line of questioning,' Delia says.

Ryan stares back at the judge, his eyebrow creased. She knows she's already been harsher with him than she has been with Bracken through this trial. But that's because it's justified. Bracken is better at skirting around the legalities of what is and what isn't appropriate when it comes to lines of questioning. Ryan's turn of phrases in trying to get his witness's points across aren't quite as subtle or mastered. She understands what he is trying to do; open up by having Lavinia explain how close she and Joy were, then hitting the judge with the whopping gut-punch that Lavinia has believed all along that her best friend is guilty of these murders. But he'll have to go about it another way.

'Okay, well, let me put it to you this way, Ms Kirwan... Since Reese and Oscar Stapleton were reported missing, you have gone on record to say you felt Joy was acting differently to how she normally acts, is that correct?'

'Yes, it is.'

'Can you elaborate?'

'There wasn't any standout moments where I thought, "Wow, Joy is losing it." I don't have absolute proof. It's just small things. Things that maybe only a best friend would notice. She was off schedule in different ways. She used to obsess about time... she'd never be late, would Joy. But in the months leading up to Oscar and Reese going missing, she just always seemed to be late. She'd never turn up to anything on time. And she got more forgetful.'

Joy lets an audible sigh erupt from the back of her throat. The only time she's made a peep throughout the entirety of this retrial. And it stuns the court into a silence.

LAVINIA KIRWAN

He nods at the judge, then readjusts his standing position to face me again.

'Okay, well, let me put it to you this way, Ms Kirwan... Since Reese and Oscar Stapleton were reported missing, you have gone on record to say you felt Joy was acting differently to how she normally acts, is that correct?'

'Yes, it is,' I reply, without hesitating. Just as we'd rehearsed.

'Can you elaborate?'

I sit more upright.

'There wasn't any standout moments where I thought, Wow, Joy is losing it,' I say. 'I don't have absolute proof. It's just small things. Things that maybe only a best friend would notice. She was off schedule. In different ways. She used to obsess about time... she'd never be late, would Joy. But in the months leading up to Oscar and Reese going missing, she just always seemed to be late. She'd never turn up to anything on time. And she got more forgetful.'

There's a beat of silence before she gasps. Loudly. Like, loudly enough for everybody in the courtroom to hear. It makes me instantly snap a stare at her – the first time I've seen those eyes in over a decade. She's aged. Definitely. Her skin is a lot paler – almost like milk. And her hands look really wrinkled. Much more wrinkled than mine. I might even be prettier than she is now. If we went out to some pub or club tonight, maybe I'd be the one who got all the attention.

The court has stayed silent since her gasp. I don't really react but to stare at her. I'm not going to let that murderous bitch intimidate me while I'm up here. Typical Joy though. Trying to steal the limelight from me.

'Okay,' the judge calls out. 'Mrs Stapleton, if you could refrain from making any noises.'

Then the judge nods back at Jonathan Ryan and he readjusts his feet to face me again.

'Can you give the court any specifics on Joy Stapleton getting more forgetful and not being herself in the lead up to Oscar and Reese being reported missing?'

'There was one time that I was supposed to meet her and the two boys in Dundrum shopping centre. We were supposed to meet at one p.m., so we could have lunch together. She didn't get there till gone two... about ten past two. I ate alone. Other times she would phone me and then we'd be on the call for a few minutes and when I asked why she'd rung, she'd say she'd forgotten. I could tell her mind was going a bit... a bit different. She was tired all the time.'

'Tired?'

'Yes. She wasn't getting much sleep. She'd do all the night feeds. Shay was rarely there and on the rare occasion he was, it was still all left up to her. I think Shay's idea of having kids was old-school and traditional. He thought his role as a father was to genuinely just assume that the mother did everything.'

'Objection,' Bracken shouts.

'It's pertinent,' the judge says, staring down at me again. I can understand why Bracken objected to that; I'm not here to testify about Shay's parental abilities, and he's not the one on trial. I don't hold anything against him. Never have. So, he wasn't a great husband or a father... big deal. Neither was my father. But that never turned my mother into a killer. Truth is, I never really got close with Shay. I would have liked to, and in fact I actually fancied him long before Joy happened to bump into him in town one night, but he was the type of guy who didn't really hang out with his girlfriend's best friends; the type who wouldn't even make the effort to. He was a lad's lad. As most sports stars are. He'd spend his time either hanging out with his teammates or being away in some plush hotel for work. Sure, if he rarely had the time for his wife and kids, how could he ever have had the time for his wife's best friend?

'So,' Jonathan Ryan says. 'She was tired?'

'Yes. And apart from her not getting a great amount of sleep due to the night feeds or whatever, Oscar in particular was high-maintenance for Joy, even in the daytime. He needed constant attention. It drained her.'

Hell, Oscar used to drain me. And I only had to see him a couple of hours a week. He was just one of those annoying little boys with one of those high-pitched voices that would never stop asking question after question after

606

question. He'd even ask questions he already knew the answers to, just to get attention. But I can't say that out loud. Course I can't. Ye can't speak ill of the dead. Especially not the young dead.

'Thank you for being so honest,' Ryan says. 'Now, to move on slightly... when Oscar and Reese were reported missing, you helped out with combing the streets in search of the boys, correct?'

'That is correct.'

'By this stage, you didn't suspect Mrs Stapleton, right?'

'No. I didn't. I genuinely believed her. I thought someone had taken them – that they'd been snatched. I prayed every day and every night for them to come home safely. It didn't cross my mind at all that they were dead, lying in a ditch in the Dublin mountains.'

'So, when did you become suspicious that your best friend was involved?'

'It was dawning on me as time went on... but when the bodies were found, I immediately said to my brother, "I bet she did it. I'm sure she did it." Then a while later the CCTV footage was made public and as soon as I saw it... and I mean this from the bottom of my heart... as soon as I saw that footage, I pointed at the screen and said, 'That's her! That's Joy!'

The courtroom falls eerily silent. Just as Jonathan Ryan had told me it would after I'd said that line. I'm not saying it for effect or anything like that. I'm saying it because it's true. I know Joy. I know that's her in that CCTV footage.

'Well, that is very powerful testimony, Ms Kirwan, indeed. Before I let you go though, there is something else I must ask. About five years ago, your name came up as a possible suspect in this case, correct?'

I offer a light snigger into the microphone.

'Yes.'

'By whom?'

'Joy. From prison. I'm not quite sure where her head was at then, I hadn't seen her in years. I just remember seeing it online somewhere, that Joy was trying to scream from prison that I was the woman under the pink hood all along.'

'Now, the defendant has chosen not to testify at her own retrial here, so she can't answer this herself, but do you know where she got that theory from?'

'I had my lawyer look into it, to try to get some answers. Apparently, Joy was making this noise through the Joy is Innocent campaign from within the prison. But when my lawyers spoke to some people, they couldn't get much info on where her theory originated from. Apparently one of prisoners just dreamt it up or something and tried to convince Joy of it. It all came out of nowhere.'

'And of course, this theory proves Mrs Stapleton was not making any sense, right?'

'Yeah. This is more proof that she's not of sound mind. The police did look at me in the days after Oscar and Reese went missing; they looked into all of us. Of course they did. But I was at the cinema the night they went missing. I was on a date with a bloke called Andy Harkness, and we had drinks afterwards... So...'

'So, the police ruled you out?'

'They did indeed. They checked everything, and in fact I rechecked everything after Joy started making stuff up about me from prison. On the night Joy killed and buried Oscar and Reese in the mountains, and when she was caught on those three seconds of CCTV footage, I, myself, was caught on a CCTV camera going into the cinema, and coming out of the cinema two hours later. Then there is more footage of me walking up Parnell Street and then going into Murray's pub on O'Connell Street at 10:45 p.m. and leaving at just gone one-thirty a.m.–my whole night is accounted for.'

'Thank you so much for your time, Ms Kirwan,' Jonathan Ryan says. Then he makes his way back to his desk and offers me an approval of my performance by winking at me subtly.

'Mr Bracken,' the judge calls out. And suddenly Bracken is on his feet before I can even take a sip of water to compose myself.

'Ms Kirwan, can you state for the record what your occupation is?'

'Mine?'

Bracken nods his head, showing me his bright-white veneers. The cheesy prick.

'Eh... well right now I work in a shop, as a shop assistant, I guess. Before that I worked in a bookies. I worked as a cleaner. I was also a receptionist in Fullams Accountancy once.'

'Ah... so lots of different career paths, yes?'

'You could say that, yes.'

'Yet despite your many careers, you were never a detective, right?'

I tut.

'No.'

'So, you don't know Joy is guilty with any degree of certainty, do you?'

'I know it was her.'

'Well, let me stop you there, Ms Kirwan. Are you saying you knew Joy was capable of murdering her two sons?'

'No. I'm not saying I knew beforehand. Of course not.'

'Exactly. So, you didn't know she was going to do it in the same way that you don't know in the aftermath. What definitive proof do you have to suggest Joy Stapleton is guilty? Any forensic evidence this court doesn't know about? Any eye witnesses the court have yet to hear from who saw the crime?'

'No.'

'No. So, you can't know with a degree of certainty that Joy was involved in these murders at all, can you?'

I take a sip of my water. And as I do, I take in the state of his leathery orange skin as he stands staring up at me from just below the witness box. Jonathan Ryan told me Bracken would lay it on thick with me. I just didn't know he'd look so smug while doin' it.

'I know in the way only a best friend would know.'

'Hardly definitive proof of murder is it?' he replies, the grin still on his face. 'Okay, so let's move on slightly. I need to ask you this question, Ms Kirwan – and I guess the answer is in the title I just called you – you are not married, have never married, is that correct?'

I silently tut again.

'I don't see what this has to do with anything.'

'Answer the question, Ms Kirwan,' the judge says, kinda bluntly at me.

'Eh... no. I have never married.'

'Never had any children? Never been a mother?'

Ah. I see where he's going. I cough into my fist, then take another sip of water.

'No. I haven't been married and have never had any children... So?'

'So, you have no first-hand experience of the ailments you accuse Mrs Stapleton of having after she had given birth to two boys, have you?'

'Ailments?'

'You suggested here today that Mrs Stapleton was suffering with some mental health fragilities in the weeks leading up to Oscar and Reese Stapleton being reported missing, yes?'

'Yes. And?'

'And, I am asking if you have any first-hand experiences of these post-partem mental health fragilities you accuse her of having?'

'Well, obviously not if I've never had kids.' I tut. And because I do it loudly, I look up at the judge to see if she is going to snap at me. She frowns over her glasses, then diverts her eyes back to Bracken.

'Do you have any academic qualifications in post-partem depressions, Ms Kirwan?'

I huff silently though my nose. I knew the cross-examination would end up as an examination of me. But I'm not the one on trial here. She is. She's the murderer. All I'm guilty of is not reporting to Shay that she was acting all strange before she killed her boys... before it was too late.

'No, of course I've no qualifications in post-partem depression.'

'Right. So, you have no first-hand experience, and no qualifications in post-partem depression. And you have no qualifications in detective work. Yet, despite all that, you think you are capable of solving the country's biggest ever crime, yes?'

'I know Joy better than anyone!'

'Really? Did you ever live with Joy?'

'No.'

'Ever marry her?'

'Course not.'

'Ever carry her children?'

'Objection!'

'No need, Your Honour, I'm done,' Bracken says. The tangerine-coloured cunt. I could strangle him. I see what he's doing. Trying to suggest Shay knew Joy better than I did and that means his testimony should hold stronger than mine. Gerd Bracken should be ashamed of himself. Defending her. Making it out as if she's innocent. She's a fucking murderer. There's no doubt about it in my mind whatsoever... and there shouldn't be a doubt in anyone's mind. That is Joy in that CCTV footage. There is no such thing as a fucking coincidence in this case.

1,625 days ago…

Aidan told Joy, in confidence, that the Governor had mentioned in passing that he wouldn't have sanctioned Christy Jabefemi's release the year previous had he known it would cause such a dramatic turn in Elm House. Her presence had ensured a somewhat peaceful ambience on the wing; extraordinary given that some of the most notorious inmates in the country were incarcerated there. Although Christy was a bat-shit crazy meth head in the eyes of almost all of the staff, they were aware that her athletic physique and bulbous bloodshot eyes made her an intimidating prospect for the other inmates. Even Nancy Trott.

'I told him it was getting out of hand on the wing now, but there's not much he can do – resources are stretched,' Aidan said.

'It's not that bad here, is it?' Joy shrugged, unable to look him in the eye.

She was glad that Aidan was back confiding in her. He had steered away from his friendly banter with Joy ever since she took it too far and tried to kiss him. But whilst she appreciated his rekindled support, she didn't want him coming this close to her. Not because she may feel an urge to kiss him again, but because Nancy had warned her to stay well away.

'I know you fancy the pants off him, but he's one of them, d'ya hear me?' Nancy had said to her numerous times over the past months. 'I know how these guys operate... been around the block too many times. They pretend to be all pally-pally with you so they can get you to open up, then they're sneaking back to the Gov and spewing everything you said. Aidan doesn't like you, Joy. Not the way you like him. Besides, he likes dick. Not pussy. S'what I heard anyway. If he comes up to you to talk, just keep your mouth shut and walk away.'

Aidan wasn't the only person Nancy had tried to turn Joy against.

'She was a junkie clown,' she had said of Christy. 'You thought she was protecting you all in here, she wasn't. She was deluded. Is back out on the streets now high as a kite, I hear. Bitch could never be trusted. Somehow you fell for her shit. Hell, I even saw you doing prayers with her. And the talk is she was only getting close with you so she could sell a story on you when she got out.'

Joy didn't have the inclination, nor the energy to ask Nancy why, if that was the case, Christy hadn't yet sold her story, despite being out for over a year. So, she just silently sighed instead. Which was becoming a regular tic for Joy. Her energy levels were low; lower than ever. She was fatigued by her role as Nancy's second-in-command. And as a result, she became insular, and mute; doing more listening than she did talking because Nancy's orders were so plentiful and exhausting. So, rather than arguing or even talking back, Joy just nodded along and did as she was told.

Nancy would hold court first thing in the morning, inside the dining-room, ensuring all prisoners sat together and not in cliques. Then she'd bang on the soup pot with her wooden spoon, call everybody's attention and introduce new prisoners or rattle off a eulogy or two about those who had just been released. The contents of what Nancy would talk about, openly in the dining room to every prisoner as well as the prison officers on duty, seemed genuinely caring and inclusive. But Joy knew better than anybody by now that that was all just a front. All Nancy was doing by coming across as the caring leader of the wing was getting everybody onside, so that they wouldn't rat her out.

Nancy had been smuggling in valuable prison assets; from sweets to mobile phones. She'd come up with the plan when bored out of her head in isolation at the start of the year. An associate of hers in the outside world had come into contact with one of the screws on another wing whom she had a hold over. He was bringing the phones and treats into the prison and then placing them into a marked laundry basket which one of the prisoners would eventually wheel to Joy's cell. Joy would then be tasked with distributing the goods to prisoners who had already paid Nancy in advance. It was a terribly dangerous game for Joy to get involved in, especially as she could have been housing anything up to a thousand euros worth of phones at any one time, but she had no choice in the matter. It was to her advantage that the screws in Elm House would never have thought of Joy getting involved in such affairs and that she would never be considered suspicious. Though that had actually been a part of Nancy's plan all along – getting goody-goody Joy Stapleton involved as her distributor. That way they'd never get caught.

'What the fuck were you doing talking to him?' Nancy asked, appearing in Joy's cell doorway.

'I, eh... he, eh... he just came to talk to me... that's all. I can hardly kick him out of my cell.'

'What did he want to talk to you about?'

Joy shook her curls.

'Nothing really. He just said I look tired and that...'

'And what?'

'And that if I was having any trouble that I should come talk to him.'

Nancy stepped towards Joy, pressing her fat tits against her.

'I've told you before. Don't—'

'Talk to Aidan. I know. I get it, Nancy. It's just... what can I do when he comes to my cell?'

Joy shrugged her shoulders and then Nancy snarled up the corner of her lips before spinning on her heels.

'Okay, come in, Tina,' she whispered.

Tina appeared, the cold sores on her lips looking nastier than ever, pushing a laundry basket into Joy's cell.

'Not more phones,' Joy said, almost sighing. 'I just got rid of six for you on Monday.'

'Relax,' Nancy said, placing a hand to the back of Joy's neck.

'We've been providing the whole fucking prison with phones for six months now, everybody's practically got one. Orders are drying up. Besides,' she said, squeezing at Joy's neck, 'the phones were only a trial run.'

'Trial run. Trial run for what?'

Then Nancy nodded at Tina and Tina removed the dirty laundry sheets from the top of the basket.

'Oh, for fuck sake,' Joy said. 'What is that?'

'Meth,' Nancy whispered. 'The purest meth available on Dublin's streets right now. Well... *was* available on Dublin's streets. Cos we've just done the cops a great turn by taking it off the streets. And now it's gonna be your job, Joy, to hold it here in your cell, before you distribute it to the prisoners on my orders. This,' she said, slapping her hands to both of Joy's cheeks, 'is gonna make us a lot of money.'

'*You* a lot of money,' Joy said, 'I don't see a cent.'

Nancy grinned.

'No... *us* a lot of money. Only your share pays for your protection, doesn't it?' Then she slapped Joy on both cheeks again, only harder this time, before she turned on her heels.

'Now, find a good hiding place for that stuff somewhere in here. And don't get fuckin' caught with it.'

1,624 days ago...

Joy had delivered two small bags to a prisoner from Maple House while she was out in the yard after lunch. But the majority of the meth was still taped to the underside of the toilet bowl in the corner of her cell.

She wasn't overly stressed about it – it may as well be meth as phones. If she was caught, there was very little that could be done about it, aside from the goods being confiscated. Joy was serving two life sentences after all...

what were they gonna do? Add an extra couple of months for drug possession?

'How long ya inside now, Joy?' Tina asked, showing her gummy teeth.

'Four years in September.'

'Jeez, is it that long, love? Fuck, I remember your trial. Was in the papers and all over the news for weeks... months.'

'Years!' Joy said, unmoving, still staring at the concrete floor of the TV room, which was all she seemed to really do when mixing with the other inmates these days.

'No offence. And I know we aren't really supposed to question prisoners on whether or not they're guilty, cos it's what's-the-word...?'

'Prison code,' one of the prisoners offered up.

'Yeah... it's code. But I have to say, I didn't know what to believe in your case, Joy. It was a real did-she, didn't-she, ye know what I mean?' Those sitting around nodded their heads, but they didn't offer their opinion. 'I thought you did it, I have to say... but now that I've met you in here. I'm not so sure. You seem too quiet to be a killer.'

'Thought killers normally were quiet,' one of the elderly women said.

'Suppose,' Tina replied, shrugging her shoulders. 'Anyway, what's going on with your appeal... haven't seen you shouting about your innocence in a long time. Weren't you saying it was yer old best mate or somethin' that killed your boys? That's gone all quiet...'

'She's stopped with the Joy is Innocent campaign, haven't you?' Nancy said, joining the group. Joy slowly nodded her head while still staring at the concrete floor. 'Okay... I need you, Joy. C'mon with me.'

Like the sheep she had morphed into, Joy followed Nancy out of the TV room and down the narrow landing that led to the laundry room at the back of Elm House.

She wondered, as she walked, how she had allowed Nancy to distract her from the Joy is Innocent campaign. While that candle was still burning on social media channels and in pockets of the outside world, Joy had pretty much given up the ghost. Nancy had tried to convince her that the lawyers were only looking out for themselves; that there was no chance of Joy's sentence ever being overturned, simply because the justice system wouldn't allow it. They couldn't allow it. It would make them look inept.

'You're fucked no matter what you do,' Nancy had told her repeatedly. 'They ain't never gonna acquit you, it'd bring the whole system down. There'd be outrage around the whole country if they thought an innocent young mother had been put behind bars for killing her own kids. You just keep focused on spending your time in here and forget about those scum lawyers, ya hear me?'

So intimidated by Nancy, Joy had even begun to turn down meetings with her lawyers and resigned herself to being inside for the rest of her life.

'What's this?' Joy whispered after Nancy had led her behind the tumble dryers. Barbara and Rosemary were sat on the ground, their backs against the wall, their knees up by their ears.

'This is... this is introduction class,' Nancy replied.

'Introduction... an introduction to who?'

'Mr Crystal.'

'Huh?' Joy replied. What are you talking...'

She tailed off her sentence because she noticed Barbara was crunching tiny crystals into rizla papers that were resting on her crotch.

Joy shook her curls.

'No. I can't. I'm not—'

'Oh yes you are, girl,' Nancy said, gripping Joy by the back of the neck and squeezing hard.

When the meth joint had been rolled, Nancy took it from Rosemary and held it in front of Joy's face.

'I, eh... I don't even know what to—'

'It's just like smoking a cigarette, Joy. You'll be fine. If you're gonna be shifting this for me, you need to know what it's all about.'

Then Nancy took a lighter from her trouser pocket and sparked it.

∴

Callum sits in the corner of Delia's office, his back against the wall, his arms hugging his bent knees.

'You can't deny that was convincing,' he says.

'Callum, for goodness sake – can you just, please, go home?'

'I'm just saying... that was convincing testimony, that's all.'

'I don't need telling what is and what isn't convincing testimony, Callum.' Delia is pacing from side to side on the small square of carpet to the right of her desk.

'Shay's testimony was all emotion, Lavinia delivered much more analytical proof—'

'Shut up, Callum!' Delia shouts, holding a flat palm to her forehead. 'I don't need you to analyse the witnesses in a trial only *I* am presiding over. And I don't need your input on a trial only *I* am experienced enough to judge.'

Callum scrambles himself to his feet and dusts down his numb bum.

'I'm only trying to help. This is more than just a trial. Lavinia said that was definitely Joy in that CCTV footage. And nobody knows Joy better.'

'Not even her husband?'

'Mum... women know women best. You think a sports guy like Shay Stapleton could read the signs of some sort of post partem depression? Or do you think a woman could do that better?'

Delia shakes her head while holding her hands to her hips.

'Callum, let me just point out that, right now this moment, you are in the midst of explaining to me how women work. Let that sink into your mind. What's the phrase... mansplaining... yes. You are mansplaining women to a woman.' Callum holds his eyes closed, then releases a long, slow sigh. 'This is my trial, Callum. You need to take yourself out of it.'

'I'm right in it. My bloody whole career is on the line.'

Delia swipes her coat from the standing rack to the side of her office door.

'You sound like a petulant little boy,' she says as she throws her arms into the sleeves.

Callum just stands there, staring at his mother, his eyes heavy, his hair all tossed from the countless times he has run his fingers through it.

'Do you not understand how much this would damage me?' he says. 'I can't believe you are even contemplating listening to the evidence of this trial... just protect the original verdict, Mum. She's guilty. Stop playing games.'

'Callum, when you calm down, come home and have some tea. Perhaps go for a long walk, get some fresh air before you decide to come home though, huh?'

Delia pulls her office door open, but she doesn't get much further, not without her son's fingers gripping her shoulder.

'Mum. I want to be just like you. I want to be a judge. I want to preside over the biggest trials these courts have to offer. If I don't get to be you when I'm older, my career will mean nothing to me. My life will mean nothing to me. I've been working up to being a trial judge... hell, *you've* been working me up to being a trial judge ever since I was a teenager. It's been all laid out for me. A Law degree from Trinity College. A job guaranteed at Wincott & Abbott before I'd even graduated. I am still the youngest ever board member of the Law Society. I've been walking the corridors of these courts for almost twenty years. I've always been taking the roads that lead to one of these offices. But I'm not going to get here if there is a video on the fucking internet of me pulling the fuckin' mickey off myself!'

Delia stares over the rim of her glasses at her son. Then she removes his hand from her shoulder and lets it drop.

'Like I said, Callum... when you calm down, come home and have some tea.'

Delia opens and closes another cupboard and moves on to the next one before slamming that one shut too. Then she sweeps her slippers back to the fridge. Back to where she started.

She shrugs her shoulders, grabs at the bruised apple from the top shelf and takes a large bite from it. Then she chicanes herself around her island, lifts a bottle of Massolino Parussi Barola from her cubed kitchen shelving unit, as well as a long-stem glass, and potters herself down her narrow hallway and into her living room.

It's an unusual living room. No TV. Instead, in each corner, stands floor-to-ceiling library shelves, filled with books of all sorts; from law manuals and non-fiction psychology, to classical works of fiction going as far back as Aristotle. The shelves reach all the way up to the eleven-foot high ceilings of her Georgian home and come with a sliding ladder. The room is always fully lit and is decorated, in its entirety, in the subtlest of pastel colours – the total opposite of her office in the courts, where it may seem to some visitors as if she is rationing electricity.

She rests the bottle and glass – with the apple gripped between her teeth – on to the drinks tray to the side of her large fireplace, then wrestles with the corkscrew until the cork releases with a pop. And just as she's about to pour herself a well-earned glass, the key crunches in the front door. She pauses, her eyes squinting, her mouth pursed... until the scent of Black Bean sauce wafts towards her.

'Thought you might be banging around in the kitchen looking for something to eat,' Callum says, holding a bulging white plastic bag aloft as he stands in the door frame of the living room.

He winks, then disappears into the kitchen where he makes a racket of himself, before arriving back into the living room with two trays.

Delia stifles a smirk, then she sits on to her floral-patterned couch, and allows Callum to remove the small cartons of food from his plastic bag before placing them on to her tray for her.

'So, you took my advice... you came home for some tea after you'd calmed down?' she says.

Callum snorts out a laugh before racing back into the kitchen. When he returns, he hands his mother a knife and fork before sitting down himself and taking a tray to his lap.

'How calm am I supposed to be when you are being blackmailed by a video of me masturbating?' he says. Delia cocks her head as she shovels a forkful of rice into her mouth. 'But yeah... I'm a little calmer. I, eh... had heard about this sort of thing before. Guys being hacked and caught masturbating when their own laptop camera records them. An old client of mine had told me about it a while back. He's put me in touch with a private investigator who might have a few answers for us.' Callum raises his eyebrows, then in the silence that follows, picks up a forkful of rice himself and shovels it into his mouth.

'Yes. Well... although I have a trial to judge, I want you to know that I am sympathetic to the plight you – *we* – find ourselves in. But no matter what, I will be judging this trial fairly. How we deal with Eddie Taunton is a separate matter entirely. But I have to judge this trial as I see it in that court room, Callum.'

Callum washes a hand over his face.

'She's guilty, Mum. You know she is. You told me before that you've always felt she was guilty.'

'Callum, in case you haven't noticed, there is a fresh trial on-going with fresh evidence.'

'The fresh evidence is bullshit, Mum. You know it. I know it. Shay Stapleton's testimony was nothing more than that of a broken man who just wants this entire nightmare over and done with. Mathieu Dupont is a fit-to-type witness who didn't even get his measurements right. And Bunny the Dog... I mean, c'mon... This trial was granted on the basis of new evidence... well, we've all heard the new evidence and it's nonsense, Mum. All you have to do is protect the original verdict. Deliver guilty. And we can all move on.'

Delia sighs her nostrils into her glass of wine as she takes a sip, fogging it up.

'Your father would be ashamed listening to you now, Callum McCormick.'

'My father would beat the shit out of Eddie Taunton, that's what he'd do.'

Delia scoffs.

'Your father never hit a man his whole life.'

'Well... he would have sorted this mess out in some way.'

Delia heaves a heavy breath, then takes the tray from her lap and places it on the couch next to her; her appetite waning.

'I'm not sure you know your father as much as you think you do, Callum. He was a superhero alright. But only in the sense that he was a fine trial lawyer. One of the best ever.'

'He'd certainly have found Lavinia Kirwan's testimony interesting today, that's for sure,' Callum says.

Delia picks up her glass of wine and takes another sip.

'It was powerful testimony... nobody could deny that. But I'm not going to be deliberating this trial with you, Callum. Not after everything that's happened. We have to remove ourselves from this. Our fate must be separate from the fate of Joy Stapleton.'

'But, Mum—' Callum gets distracted by his phone vibrating in his pocket. He reaches for it, stares at the screen, then stabs at the green button.

'Hello,' he says. 'Callum McCormick speaking.'

His eyes squint as he listens to the voice on the other end of the line, then he places a hand over the receiver.

'It's the private eye I was telling you about,' he whispers.

Joy no longer moved when her cell door clicked open first thing in the mornings. She didn't have the energy. It'd take her an age to roll over on her mattress before she'd eventually mope herself to her feet. And by the time she'd drag herself into the dining room, all of the best cereals would have been eaten up and only the deformed slices of toast were left. But she'd munch on a crust or two while swigging a glass of water, then head back to her cell to curl into a ball atop her mattress again. Mornings had turned grey for her. It was only in the evenings when she would come alive – because that's when she'd share a joint with Nancy.

She'd been taking an almost daily hit of meth for nigh on six months; only failing to get her high when Nancy's source couldn't follow through with delivering into the prison. Though it was rare when that happened. The majority of the ninety prisoners in Elm House were getting involved and were, like Joy, often walking around like zombies; jaded and fatigued. The screws had picked up on the eerie change in ambience on the wing, but it was pretty much impossible for them to put their finger on why, simply because each and every person under the influence of meth experiences different symptoms; different highs and different lows. Whereas Nancy was chatty and talkative, Tina sat there quiet, with a huge grin stretched across her face. And whereas Claire would go on a spring clean, helping with all sorts of maintenance around the wing, Linda liked to lie on her bed and get lost in a book. Joy, well, she would float around the landings of the wing, sometimes checking in with Nancy to laugh at her jokes; sometimes annoying Linda by asking what her book was about. She liked the evenings, did Joy; liked the airy sensation her mind would float into as soon as she sucked an inhale of meth to the back of her throat. But the mornings – the hangovers – they were tough for her to handle. Her head would be heavy, and her posture would slouch. And she couldn't care to summon up enough energy to engage with any of her fellow inmates. Nor any of the prison officers. She and Aidan had long since been buddies. He would drop by to talk to her, but not as frequently as he used to do. Joy certainly felt safer when he was with her, but there was always the nagging feeling that Nancy would catch them talking and then have to deal with Joy later by slapping her or kicking at her shins.

'Where you off to?' Mathilda asked as Joy was slouching her way back to her cell, munching on the last of her crusts.

'Just gonna lie back down,' Joy said. 'Is that a crime?'

'It's not a crime,' Mathilda said, 'but that's not where you're going.'

'Huh?' Joy creased her brow into a vertical wrinkle; though she was starting to do that so often that the crease was becoming a permanent fixture.

'You've got a visitor. He's been here bright and early, demanding he talk to you. He's up in the Governor's office right now. Been told to bring you to him.'

'Who is he?' Mathilda shrugged. 'S'not my husband, is it?'

Mathilda shrugged again.

'I've told you all I know. Now, come on, follow me.'

'I'm, eh... really not feeling up for a visitor. I've got a splitting headache and I—'

Mathilda scoffed and scowled.

'I'm not asking you. I'm ordering you. Now come on, we're heading to the Governor's office. And may I just say, Joy, if you don't mind, but,' she sniffed up her nose, 'you look and smell like shit.'

Joy looked down at herself, taking in the stained tracksuit bottoms she hadn't bothered to wash for months, even though she was literally working in the laundry room five days a week. Then she heaved out a depressing sigh, before pacing after Mathilda. She knew she looked like shit; knew she was wasting her life by feeling so shitty for the first half of every day, then high as a kite for the second half. But she couldn't help herself. The gravitas of meth was, as it is for most, too alluring. Once she'd felt the high of the drug for the very first time, she couldn't help but keep coming back for more. They all did. Nancy let slip to Joy once that she was taking in over five grand a month; all distributed through outside channels. If the prisoner couldn't have somebody on the outside transfer money into Nancy's account for them, then they simply didn't get their fix. Though some desperate inmates would do Nancy the odd finger favour every now and then, just to get their high. But only the ones she fancied. Joy was told her fix of the drug in the evenings was payment enough for her distribution of the drug. Though she really didn't care. Money was insignificant to her. She was never going to experience the outside world again. Whereas Nancy, despite being inside for attempted murder, would have a chance of parole at some stage... whenever that time would come.

Joy would spend some mornings, with her head and heart heavy, wishing Nancy would disappear one day, just like Christy had. But that day never seemed to come around. And it didn't look as if it was going to come around any day soon. Not with the multiple misdemeanours Nancy kept getting picked up for in prison.

624

It wasn't all bad. Some of the times she spent with Nancy could be fun. They had a smart phone hidden at the back of the laundry room and would spend their time, while taking their hit of meth, doubled up in laughter while watching random YouTube videos.

When they first realised they could access the prison's Wi-Fi, they spent their time watching epic fail clips; giggling away at models tripping over on catwalks, or toddlers getting hit on the head with footballs. As inevitably happens when granted access to the internet, their searches eventually took them down the rabbit hole everybody ends up going down. It was Nancy who had suggested it. She was horny – one of her side effects of meth. And Joy agreed. Because she was suffering the same side effect. They'd giggle along as they watched middle-aged men with oversized cocks fuck young women with bald pussies until they returned to their cells to bring themselves to their own climaxes. But one night Nancy didn't want to wait until she got back to her cell.

She shuffled herself out of her tracksuit bottoms and pulled down her stained knickers, revealing a fiery-red bush. Then she began to play with herself while Joy giggled along, high as a kite. The night after that, Nancy didn't bother to do the work herself; instead, she grabbed Joy's hand and pushed it against her pubic bone, then began to roll it around in a circular motion. Joy held her eyes closed, while still grinning from her high, and only really reacted when Nancy curled one of her fingers against Joy's and slowly began to enter it into herself.

'No. No. No. It's beyond a joke now,' Joy said, whipping her hand away. Nancy raised an eyebrow.

'Bitch. You wanna keep getting your fix of this,' she said, the joint pinched between her lips, 'then you need to play this little game with me. C'mon... when's the last time you had an orgasm at the hands of somebody else, huh?'

Nancy took the joint from her mouth and leaned forward to press her lips against Joy's.

'No,' Joy said, shaking her head, 'no kissing. I'm not gay. I don't wanna kiss.'

'Okay, okay,' Nancy said. 'No kissing.'

Then she gently took Joy's hand again, pressed it down to her groin and gingerly – *very* gingerly – curled her finger against Joy's until the tip of Joy's finger flexed inside her.

'Ye know where the office is from here, don'tcha?' Mathilda asked. Joy didn't bother to answer. Instead, she continued to the end of the landing, slodging like a grumpy teenager, until she eventually turned into the Governor's office.

But sitting there, at the Governor's large desk, wasn't the Governor himself. This man was, like the Governor, middle-aged, but he dressed entirely differently. He was wearing a pinstriped navy suit and a super shiny pair of brown leather shoes. He uncrossed his legs, grinned a smug smile at Joy and then got to his feet.

'Am I pleased to see you,' he said. He held his hand out for her to shake, but she was too taken by his leathery orange face that she failed to notice. So, she just frowned while he awkwardly put his hand back into his suit trouser pocket.

'Who are you?' she asked.

'My name is Gerd Bracken,' he said.

❖

Delia brushes down the creases on the front of her robe before pulling at her office door.

'Morning,' she calls to Aisling.

'Morning, Judge Delia,' Aisling replies. 'Another big day today, huh?'

'Oh, aren't they all? I've just been going through my notes and there's going to be written statements offered to the court today, as well as a key piece of evidence. Can you collect them all for me and have them back in my office by the time I return? I'll need to analyse that paperwork as soon as I'm done in the courtroom.'

Aisling smiles, then nods her head.

'Course I will.'

Delia mouths a 'thank you' to her assistant while squeezing the side of her shoulder, then she paces down the corridor. When she turns the corner, the young woman dressed in all black greets her from afar with a shy wave. Then she opens up the court's side door and nods into it before a bellow of 'all rise' is shouted.

Delia doesn't have to stare over the rim of her glasses to know the gallery is already packed as she climbs the three steps to her highchair, because she can already tell by the rumbling and mumbling. There seems to be a buzz circulating the room. She can never really predict what ambience is going to be present in a courtroom on any given day. Though she was well aware that yesterday's contrasting testimonies from Shay Stapleton and Lavinia Kirwan must have played havoc with everybody's opinions. They had certainly played havoc with hers. That and the fact that everybody knows this entire case all comes down to the coincidence of somebody walking near the scene of the crime wearing the exact same hoodie Joy had owned, and that coincidence was finally going to be examined today.

Delia eyeballs Joy over the rim of her glasses then looks to Jonathan Ryan and nods.

'Mr Ryan, can you call your next witness?'

'I can indeed, Your Honour. The prosecution calls Tobias Masterson to the stand.'

Masterson's suit looks at least two sizes too large for him as he sweeps his way down the aisle to a sea of synchronised swivelling heads on both sides of the gallery. He has a lacklustre presence, like that of a clichéd geek, what with his round John Lennon-style specs sitting loose on his pointed nose and his tie hanging below his nether regions – ironic given that he is the managing director of Pennsylvania's largest fashion distributor.

'Do you swear to tell the truth, the whole truth and nothing but the truth?' the court clerk asks as Masterson stands, awkwardly fidgeting, in the witness box.

'I do.'

'Mr Masterson, can you state your occupation for the court, please?' Ryan asks when the witness has sat.

'Sure. I run the company PeppaTrue – we are a stockists and distribution company based outta Pennsylvania.' Masterson spoke with a high-pitch nasal squeal, as if somebody was constantly pinching his nose.

'You stock fashionwear for some well-known high street stores, correct?'

'We stock up to eighteen different retail brands throughout the United States.'

'And you are managing director for the Pennsylvania branch of that company, yes?'

'I am.'

'And that company stock and supply Urban Outfitters with some of their fashion wear?'

'We do.'

'Did your company distribute the Pink Sasoon Ladies Hooded Top in the early spring of 2005 to Urban Outfitters?'

'We did.'

'Interesting. And just for the record...' Jonathan Ryan walks over to the television screen and presses at a button, 'this hooded top, seen here in this footage...' the screen blinks to the infamous three seconds of a figure walking into shot just outside a small residential garden, a mere one-thousand yards from where Oscar and Reese's bodies were found some two years later, 'is the Pink Sasoon Ladies Hooded Top, right?'

'We are without doubt certain it is. The Pink Sasoon Ladies Hooded Top has distinct trimmings. They are all red. A red zip as is visible in the footage at some points; the red band at the waistline and the red band on each cuff are also visible on the footage at some points. On certain freeze-frames the stitching on the side pockets and around the shoulders is also visible. It's the Pink Sasoon Ladies Hooded Top. One hundred per cent. The top is that distinctive. And even though this footage was shot in the early hours, we know the colours, we know the details.'

'Okay, thank you for your expertise in that regard, Mr Masterson. And for the record, Your Honour, that has never been disputed by anybody. All concerned are willing to accept that the hooded top in this footage is the distinct Pink Sasoon hooded top.' He narrows his lips, then turns to the witness again. 'Now, Mr Masterson, I want to move to another side of your expertise. I am right in saying that Urban Outfitters were the *only* store to stock the Pink Sasoon Ladies Hooded Top, yes?'

'Yes.'

'But more specifically, it was the Pennsylvania-based Urban Outfitter stores, only, right? This product didn't go nation-wide?'

'That is absolutely correct. It was a trial run of a fashion item by a local designer who Urban Outfitters' buyers are often willing to give a break to. That kinda thing happens often. Items come and go all the time.'

'Interesting. Thank you, Mr Masterson. And as managing director, you keep records of all stock coming to and from your warehouses, right?'

'Of course.'

'So, can you tell me and indeed the court how many Pink Sasoon Ladies Hooded Tops you supplied your Pennsylvania-based Urban Outfitter stores with?'

'Yes. They went on a trial run in three of their stores. And in total, we distributed ninety items.'

'Just ninety, for the whole State?'

'According to our records, each store received thirty Pink Hoodies; ten in size small, ten in size medium and ten in size large. It was a typical trial run.'

'And were any of the hoodies returned to your warehouses unsold?'

'Yes, almost half of them. Forty-three of the ninety.'

'Meaning only forty-seven were ever purchased from an Urban Outfitters?'

'Yes.'

Delia moves to pick up her pen, but she doesn't scribble any notes. Not yet, anyway. Because the witness hasn't revealed anything knew – nothing that hadn't been revealed in the original trial. But she knew something was coming...

'Now... a Mr Mathieu Dupont testified on that very stand two days ago, Mr Masterson, and was questioned about the figure in the CCTV footage being five foot, and three quarters of an inch, or five foot, two inches – but in regard to the hooded top itself, that wouldn't make a difference, right?'

'I, eh... I'm sorry. I don't know what you mean, Mr Ryan.'

'I mean, you don't make individual hooded tops for specific individual heights, right? There isn't one for somebody who is five foot, one and a different one for somebody who is five foot, two.'

Masterson puffs out a laugh.

'Of course not. These particular hooded tops only come in three sizes. Small. Medium. Large.'

'It's that straightforward?'

'That straightforward.'

'So, in that case, somebody whether five foot or five foot, two would be wearing a small hooded top, correct?'

'That is most likely, yes,' Masterson says, biting on his bottom lip and then looking to the judge as if fearful he had said anything out of turn. She glances at him, then looks towards Ryan, her eyes squinting. But she doesn't say anything.

'So, do you know how many Pink Sasoon Ladies Hooded Tops were distributed to Urban Outfitters in size small only?'

'Yes. As mentioned, each of the three Urban Outfitters received ten small hoodies, so that means thirty.'

'Thirty. Interesting. And how many out of that thirty were sent back to your warehouse unsold?'

'Fifteen. The hoodie wasn't a big hit.'

'So, if only thirty of these small pink hooded tops were ever distributed, and fifteen were sent back, that means this hoodie here in this footage,' Ryan points to the screen again, 'could only possibly be one in fifteen, too, right?'

'One in fifteen, correct. That is the famous fraction.'

'You see, Your Honour, our defendant here today was one of those one in fifteen. Because she purchased this small Pink Sasoon Ladies Hooded Top when visiting Pennsylvania with her husband, Shay Stapleton. He was away on a tour with the Dublin GAA squad when Joy flew out to meet him for the last five days of that tour in April 2005. She purchased this hoodie for seventy-nine dollars on April tenth, during that trip.'

Ryan walks to his desk, bends down and picks up the infamous hoodie, all wrapped in a clear plastic cover, as if it had just come back from the dry-cleaners and hadn't, in actual fact, been hanging in a dusty warehouse filled with shelves of trial evidence for the past eight years. The problem investigators had when it came to the hoodie was that it gave no indication of Joy's involvement in the death of her two young sons. The top wasn't of interest to investigators until the CCTV footage had been found some two years after the children had been reported missing. And in that time, the top had been worn and washed by the defendant an incalculable number of times. Meaning that, like the scene of the burial itself – given the two years it took to come across it – the hooded top had been rid of any possible DNA evidence dating back to the time of the crime.

'Also, for the record, Your Honour, in the original trial this was stated, but I would like to highlight again, investigators put a call out through national channels looking for anyone in Ireland who might have, coincidentally, like Mrs Stapleton, purchased one of these tops back in Pennsylvania in 2005. Nobody came forward. Not then. Not since. Which means, we firmly believe that Joy Stapleton was the *only* person in this entire country who owned a Pink Sasoon Ladies Hooded Top at the time Oscar and Reese Stapleton were murdered. However... since then, and for extra investigative measures for this retrial, we also put a call out to people in Pennsylvania to speak with women who may have owned the small version of this hooded top back when it was on sale in 2005...' Ryan walks towards the judge. 'Your Honour, I give you twelve statements from witnesses from Pennsylvania, all of whom say they did indeed buy that top back then, and, crucially, confirming they were not in Ireland during the period in which Oscar and Reese were murdered. We have narrowed the field even further. If it was hard to believe the coincidence excuse back when Mrs Stapleton first blurted it out, then it's almost impossible to believe it now.'

'Mr Ryan,' Delia calls out, hammering her gavel repeatedly. 'You will not assume the belief of this court. I am the judge here.'

She eyeballs him over her glasses. Though she knew what he had just delivered was pretty golden. He had literally chipped away at any notion of coincidence.

'Sorry, Your Honour, what I'm trying to say is... it was always argued by the defence that it was mere coincidence that a figure wearing that exact hooded top was seen so close to the scene of where Oscar and Reese were buried. And now we know it to be an even bigger coincidence than was claimed in the first place. In the original trial it was stated that it could only have been one of fifteen people in the entire world in that footage, well today we know that it could only have been one in three.' Ryan turns and faces the witness. 'Thank you, Mr Masterson. Your time is very much appreciated.'

Delia scribbles onto the paperwork in front of her as Jonathan Ryan takes a seat. Then she glances at Joy before raising an eyebrow at her defence lawyer.

'Mr Bracken, I assume you have questions for this witness...'

'I do indeed, Your Honour.'

Bracken gets to his feet, walks himself directly to the witness box and grips the edge of it, squinting up at Masterson.

'Mr Masterson,' he says, 'you are Pennsylvanian, are you not?'

Masterson's brow dips, causing his glasses to slip down his narrow nose.

'I am indeed, yes,' he says, pushing them back with a stab of his boney middle finger. 'I was raised in Roxborough, but have lived in Philadelphia practically my whole adult life. Since I was twenty-two in fact. So that's thirty-four years.'

'I'm an Irishman,' Bracken says. 'And like you, I have moved towns. I was born in Cork. I moved to London. Then to Dublin. So, what I'm getting at here is, we move around, don't we?'

'Move?'

'As in, we don't just stay in the same place, do we?'

'I, eh... guess not,' Masterson says, turning to the judge as if to ask if she is as flummoxed by Mr Bracken's questioning as he is.

'It's human nature to move around,' Bracken says, holding his hands out and shrugging his shoulders. 'It's not just Irish folk who move around, is it? American people move around too, don't they?'

'Yes.'

Masterson hunches his shoulders up and down, the wrinkles on his forehead now forming a deep V.

'In fact, Americans like to move around Ireland specifically... Let me tell you that in the year 2008, nine-hundred and eighty-seven thousand people travelled from America to Ireland. On November 2nd of 2008, when this footage was filmed,' Bracken says, pointing at the screen still on loop, 'and according to Fáilte Ireland statistics, eighty-eight thousand Americans were travelling in Ireland.' He inches closer to Masterson. 'I assume you haven't spoken to all of those eighty-eight thousand people, right?'

'Mr Bracken,' Delia calls out.

'Sorry, Your Honour. It's just that this witness seems willing to sit in this witness box during this very important trial to rule out the possibility of coincidence when indeed the coincidence cannot *totally* be ruled out. This witness hasn't spoken to everybody who owned a Pink Sasoon Ladies Hooded Top. We don't even know that the top in this footage is definitely a small, do we, Mr Masterson?'

Mr Masterson looks at the judge, as if she is going to protect him again. But she just looks over her glasses at him, awaiting his answer.

'It looks like a small,' he says.

'Sir, you do not know for certain whether that top is size small, do you?'

'No.'

'And, Sir, you do not know everybody who travelled from the States to Ireland in November, 2008, do you? So, therefore you cannot totally rule out the fact that one of those many travellers might, just might, have been from Pennsylvania and just might have been wearing one of those tops.'

'Well, as Mr Ryan has proven to the court with that new paperwork... he has ruled out many more people since the original trial. That dilutes the possibility of coincidence to one in three—'

'Mr Masterson,' Bracken shouts, his irritation stretched. 'Is it or isn't it a fact that you simply do not know for certain that somebody may have travelled from America to Ireland in November who owned one of those Pink Sasoon Ladies Hooded Tops?'

'Yeah... It's a fact.'

'You can't possibly know for certain, can you?'

'No.'

Masterson shakes his head and looks down at his own lap, as if he's just been scolded by his mother.

'Exactly,' Bracken says. 'You can't possibly know for certain. That's our questioning complete, Your Honour.'

Joy's cell door swept open, but she didn't turn in her bed; assuming it was just one of the prisoners dropping by out of sheer boredom. But then she heard the squealing whistle of hard-soled shoes against her concrete floor, before a familiar, agitated sigh exhaled.

'What are you still doing lying in bed? It's gone half eleven.'

She held her eyes closed with annoyance before mustering up enough energy to turn over on her mattress.

'Chill out, Aidan. Ye sound like me da. Ye think you can order me about?'

Aidan swung his jaw from side-to-side.

'Well, actually, I *can* order you about. I am a *prison officer* in Mountjoy Prison, and you are a *prisoner* in Mountjoy Prison,' he hissed through his clenched jaw. 'Now listen up... you have a visitor. And you need to go see him now.'

'Is it my lawyer?' she asked, sitting upright and rubbing at both eyes. 'Is it?'

'I think it is, yeah,' Aidan said, sounding exhausted. He stepped outside and waited for her to throw on a sweat top and slip herself into her trainers before she joined him.

They didn't say another word to each other as he escorted her around the maze of landings and into the bowels of the prison, eventually leading her into an office she had never been in before. Aidan had grown frustrated with Joy's moping about and had long since started to treat her as just another prisoner. He had no idea she was constantly moping about because she was hungover from the effects of the meth she was smoking most nights.

'Howaya, Mr Bracken?' she said, entering the office with as much of a smile as she could muster.

Like all of the offices in Mountjoy Prison, this one was freezing cold. The walls were bare concrete, as was the floor, and a cramped, cheap wooden white desk took up pretty much the entirety of the floor space.

Bracken stretched a hand across the desk and gripped hers in it.

'I've got some great news for you,' he said.

It had been a year since Gerd Bracken had first surprised Joy out of nowhere. They had sat then, for that first meeting, just as they were now – across a cramped white desk in a freezing cold office – where he explained to her that Bunny the dog, who had been a key cog in her original trial, had been exposed as a fake. Bracken promised Joy there and then that he was going to do all he could to get her conviction quashed. And she became fully convinced he would get her out, because he proved to her that he had a history of overturning convictions. None of them were murder convictions, of course, and none held the magnitude her case did. But she couldn't help but get excited; especially as prison life had turned so unbearable for her – much, much worse than it had ever been. If it wasn't for the crack of light that Bracken brought to her, Joy was sure she'd be contemplating suicide by now.

'Remember I said to you that we'd need something more than the dog?' Bracken said as Joy stared across the desk, heavy-eyed.

'Yeah,' she replied.

'Well, what we've figured out is that we need to convince the judges in the Criminal Courts of Appeal that it's feasible that when you claimed that a woman captured in the CCTV footage with the same unique pink hoodie that you owned was merely a coincidence, that you may very well have been telling the truth. You know this, right? Either the woman in that pink top is you and you murdered Oscar and Reese, or the woman in that pink top isn't you, and the police have got this wrong from the start.'

'Yeah,' Joy said, nodding her head.

'Well, we found an expert – he's from France – who is willing to testify that the girl in the CCTV footage couldn't have been you.'

'Couldn't have been me...' Joy said, changing the direction of her head from nodding to shaking, 'how?'

'He invented some technology that can read a person's exact height from camera footage. And he is insistent that the girl in that footage is too small to be you.'

Joy's mouth popped open and she held two fists up and shook them, as if the football team she supported had just bulged the back of the opposition's net.

'And this will seriously be enough to get me outta here?'

'Well...' Bracken cocked his head to the side, 'I'm confident it's enough to win us a retrial... and if we get a retrial, we'd certainly have a good shot of getting you out of here.'

Joy leaned over the table and bear hugged Bracken's tanned face, smothering it into her boney chest.

'You look a little better,' he said when he was finally released from the hug and was flattening down his hair with his hand. 'Have you stopped using?'

Joy nodded her head, then swallowed the lie. She hadn't quite stayed off the meth as she'd promised Bracken she would, but she wasn't taking it on such a regular occurrence as she had been months prior. Though only because Nancy couldn't get the stuff into the prison as readily as she once could. The dodgy screw from Maple House who had been smuggling the meth in for her had left his post, and so they couldn't get as many crystals into the prison as Nancy would have liked.

Although Joy found it tough to wean herself off the drug, she also took solace in the silver lining not being able to get the meth inside afforded her. Not only did she no longer have to stress about prison officers finding the drugs sellotaped to the understem of her toilet bowl, but she had promised Bracken – the only person in the world who seemed as if he wanted to help her – that she would stay clean. Though it was still a prison she was residing in, of course, and so every now and then a prisoner would manage to smuggle some measurement of meth inside. And when that happened, Nancy would jump all over it. And Joy would be expected to join in.

On the rare occasions that Nancy would get her fix, she was fine with Joy – as if they were in a happy coupling who would laugh and joke and smoke and orgasm together. But during her come downs, Nancy could be a nasty bitch. She would physically attack Joy; not in any extreme way, but she would often take her frustrations out on her by shoving her or slapping her or kicking her.

Just two months prior, during a comedown and whilst she was judging Joy to be turning the pages of the newspaper too loudly, Nancy took two handfuls of Joy's curls and pinned her against the cell wall. Then she grabbed at Joy's throat and held a firm grip until Joy's face turned puce and she eventually collapsed. Nancy ran, leaving Joy to be later found by Aidan who, in a panicked state, had to scream for medical attention before Joy eventually came back around. She claimed she fainted from low blood pressure, but Aidan was far from convinced.

Although Joy was wary and constantly conscious of Nancy's bi-polar episodes, she never really felt in fear of her life. She knew she'd be subjected to the odd shove or slap, and that a small cut on her lip or a bruised hip from crashing off the concrete walls would often appear on her skin. But trying to stay on Nancy's good side was the best way for her to survive Elm House.

'Are you sure?' Bracken said. 'You don't seem very convinced, even if you do look a little more pink in the face.'

Joy held her eyes closed for a second, and within those seconds she decided she couldn't risk lying. Not to him.

'Well, once or twice somebody has snuck some meth in and I've had a drag off a joint, but that's it... it's seriously only been once or twice since I last met with you and made a promise that I wouldn't touch it again. Twice... maximum.'

Bracken leaned his forearms onto the desk and pouted a sorrowful glare at his client.

'You promised me you'd stay off the drugs if I was going to help you, Joy.'

'I will,' she said, grabbing his arm, 'I won't take another drag. I promise. I won't. I'll do whatever it is you need me to do in order to get me out of here.'

'Well,' Bracken said, leaning back in his chair, 'it may take a while, but I am certain we have enough new evidence to convince the Court of Criminal Appeals that you should be awarded a retrial.'

'How does that work?' Joy said, her eyes squinting, her curls shaking from side to side.

'Well, three judges sit on the Court of Criminal Appeal and, in basic terms, the only way to convince them to order a retrial is to bring new evidence to the table. They really need two pieces of new evidence – two things that would pour doubt over the original trial that convicted you.'

'And we have the fact that Bunny the dog is a fraud... and now this guy... the French guy... suggesting that whoever that was in the pink hoodie in that CCTV footage can't be me...'

'Exactly,' Bracken said, grinning his veneers, 'well, really what's new is the technology this guy has come up with. That's what the judges in the Court of Criminal Appeal will be swung by; something that's been invented in the intervening years since your original trial that can further pour doubt on the original case built against you.'

'I'm gonna get out!' she told Aidan as he escorted her back to her cell.

He stopped at the top of a set of stairs and turned to face her.

'I'm happy for you, Joy. I am.'

'Well... tell your face,' she said, grinning.

He fake-smiled, then dropped it abruptly as he turned to continue down the steps.

'Hey... what's up with you?' She grabbed his shoulder, 'Didn't you just hear me. I'm gonna get out. Why aren't you happy for me?'

'I am happy for you. I just wish... listen,' he said, looking at her square in the eye as she now matched him for height what with her standing one step taller than him, 'getting through the Courts of Criminal Appeal is as far from easy as you think it is. Very, *very* few get offered a retrial. And I mean *very* few. They don't like to order retrials because it really is the justice system admitting that the justice system might have got something wrong. Then if... even *if* you get a retrial, there are still no guarantees.'

'Jeez,' Joy said, blowing out her cheeks, 'way to piss on my Corn Flakes.'

'I'm not pissing on your Corn Flakes.' Aidan leaned into her to whisper, in fear of anyone overhearing them; his face inches from hers. 'I'm happy you are getting this opportunity to get your case heard again. I am. It's just... I know these things can go on for ages... years. And in the meantime, you're still in here, and you're still under her thumb. And you're still vulnerable.'

'Nancy?'

'Shhh,' Aidan said, before he turned around to continue descending the stairs. 'Joy, when you first came in here, I was worried for you, but you seemed to fit in well. You were much nicer than you... than you've been the past couple of years. When Christy left, you seemed to wither right into the arms of Nancy Trott. I've seen the cuts and the bruises, and I hear stories about how she treats you. I found you flat out in your cell a few weeks ago, don't forget.'

'Wow... are you, eh... are you in love with me or something?' Joy said, grinning again.

'Shhh,' Aidan hissed, then he paced down the landing as quickly as he could, her jogging behind to keep up, until they reached her cell without a further word said.

Though Joy didn't have to stay locked up in her cell for long. She, along with half of the prisoners from Elm House and half from Maple House, were due their hour in the yard.

The yard didn't offer much. It was a long rectangular tarred stretch, fenced off by sixteen-foot fences that were topped off with swirls of barbed wire. There were some cigarette packets and paper bags, likely filled with weed or other contraband, caught in the barbed wire that were too tricky for anybody, even the officers, to get to. There were also two basketball courts lined out on the ground, and two hoops at either end, minus the nets. Though nobody ever played basketball. In fact, Joy hadn't remembered ever seeing a basketball in the five years she'd been inside. The prisoners would just stand around the yard, shooting the breeze as if they hadn't spent much of the last few years doing exactly the same thing. Joy often found it odd that they could come up with new things to talk about. Though she rarely came up with anything, because she rarely talked anymore. She'd just stand around Nancy and her cohorts, nodding when she needed to nod, shaking her head when she needed to shake her head and laughing when she needed to laugh. But today she was bursting with an energy she hadn't felt in years... not since way before she was an inmate.

'I think I'm gonna get out!' Joy excitedly spat out, holding up her fists and shaking them. 'My lawyer says they have the cadaver dog and now another expert who is going to prove in court that it wasn't me in the CCTV footage with the pink hoodie.'

'Wow,' Nancy said, exhaling her cigarette, 'you've finally got somebody who's gonna say it was a coincidence after all, huh?'

'Huh-huh,' Joy said as those around her laughed.

'Yeah, right,' Nancy said.

'Whatcha mean 'yeah right'?'

'I mean, you seriously think anybody's gonna believe that's not you in that pink—'

'Holy shit!' Linda said, interrupting Nancy by tapping her on the shoulder. Then she stretched her arm over that shoulder and flexed her index finger into a point. 'Look who's coming this way.'

Joy turned, but as she did, Nancy leaned into her.

'Don't you fuckin' dare say anything to her, you hear me?' she whispered with a snarl. 'You're mine now. If she tries to get pally-pally with you again, I will make your life miserable. Just tell her to fuck off, okay?'

'Well, if it isn't Missus Joy Stapleton,' a voice called out.

And before Joy turned around, she knew that she was going to be greeted by beautiful brown skin, stained yellow teeth and heavy, red eyes.

'She has nothing to say to you, Christy,' Nancy said.

'Huh... Me and Joy are best friends, ain't we, Joy?' Joy stared wide-eyed at Christy, the life she once lived inside the confines of this prison flashing before her eyes. 'Joy?'

Joy said nothing.

'She ain't talking to you, you crazy ass junkie hoe.'

Christy tutted.

'Nancy Trott, I will fuck you up. I will tear you to shreds in this very yard, you hear me, girl?'

'We're not surprised to see you back in here, Christy, whatcha rob this time?'

'Bite me, Linda,' Christy said. Then she put her arm around Joy and pulled her closer. 'Was hoping we'd be on the same yard times... I'm in Maple House this time. Now let's catch up, sista, huh? How you been getting on without me?'

Joy's heart stopped momentarily, then she shrugged Christy's arm from her shoulder.

'You heard Nancy,' Joy said, her voice shaking 'I don't wanna have anything to do with you. So do one, Christy. Fuck off. And don't ever come near me again.'

640

Joy's routine hadn't changed in the five years she'd been inside, because the prison system's routine hadn't changed in those five years either. Her door would click open, as would the majority of them on the wing, for breakfast at eight-thirty a.m., then she'd be locked back in her cell from nine-thirty for an hour before she'd have to go for her first shift at work in the laundry room. Lunch would then be between one and one-thirty, before another hour-long lockdown after which there'd be an hour's access to the games room or the TV room before another two-hour shift back at laundry. Dinner at her usual bench, and sat right next to Nancy, would follow for an hour before all of the prisoners were locked back up in their cells from seven p.m. until the doors clicked back open again the next morning, just for that whole routine to start up again.

For the hours that she was locked in her cell, Joy really only ever did one of two things; she either read a fiction book which she would swap with the librarian who called by, cell to cell, each and every Thursday afternoon, or, when she didn't feel like reading, she'd lie on her thin mattress in foetal position and stare at her photograph of Oscar and Reese. It was still hung in the exact same spot she had hung it on the very first evening she arrived here, after Aidan had gone to the trouble of finding her some sellotape.

She felt bad about telling Christy to fuck off the day before. But that guilt was battling against the waves of optimism that were also swaying in the pit of her stomach. Gerd Bracken seemed rather confident he was going to put an end to this nightmare for her. And when she got out, she wouldn't have to worry or stress about junkie criminals like Christy Jabefmei or Nancy Trott no more.

'Psst,' Nancy said, standing in the doorframe of Joy's cell as Joy was laying there, staring at the smiling faces of her two sons. 'C'mon, time for our shift... and time for us to celebrate.'

'Celebrate? Celebrate what?'

'To celebrate whatever it is your lawyer said to you yesterday. Look...' Nancy held a small plastic bag in the air and it twisted from her pinched fingers, making the crystals glisten. 'Cost me a few quid, but I wanted to celebrate... with you.'

Joy didn't say anything, not until they were both hid at the back of the laundry room where Nancy was licking two rizla papers together.

'I, eh... I'm not gonna have any,' Joy said. 'Not this time.' Nancy glared up at her as she lit the joint. 'It's just my lawyer made me promise I wouldn't do it anymore... I don't wanna ruin my chances of a retrial. You understand, don't you, Nance?'

Nancy took one step closer and lit the joint just inches from Joy's face.

'Don't be fuckin' ungrateful. Get some of this into ya. We're celebrating. We're celebrating you. I had to transfer a hundred quid for this. And I did it to spend some time with you. C'mon... it's been ages since we had a little fumble. Linda's keeping eyes out for the prison officers for us... Let's enjoy ourselves.'

Nancy exhaled a large cloud into Joy's face.

Joy gulped, then waved away the smoke before stiffly shaking her curls from side to side.

'No, I'm not taking it... I don't want any.'

'Get it fuckin' into you. I want a good high and a hell of a finger fuck from you this evening. It's been way too long. C'mon, baby,' Nancy said, softening her voice and rubbing a fingernail down Joy's cheek, 'I miss you. I miss us doing this together.'

She pressed the joint to Joy's lips, but Joy shook her curls even more fervently.

'No.'

The slap was loud, though not loud enough to be heard by the prisoners who were down the other end of the laundry room, overseeing the unloading of bed sheets with washing machines tumbling around them. Joy inhaled sharply through the gaps in her teeth, trying to rid the stinging sensation, but then Nancy's fist struck her nose. Hard. And when Joy fell to the ground the kicks were plentiful. And painful. *Very* painful. Especially the kicks to the ribs.

1,118 days ago...

'C'mon. I love you. You're my best friend. You're more than a friend,' Nancy said.

She was sat, on the grated floor of the landing, her back against Joy's cell door which Joy had requested be locked after her attack the previous evening. The prison officers agreed to her request, though Aidan was furious that she wouldn't go on record as admitting it was Nancy who had beaten her up. She was well aware by now, used to prison life, that ratting would only cause her more harm. She had learned that was why the nastiest prisoners, like Nancy Trott, thrived inside; because snitching is seen as being a totally unforgiveable act in the eyes of every prisoner. It was the one trait that was frowned upon more than any other. Ratting was deemed worse than the most heinous of crimes; even murder – even the murder of your own sons.

Joy slowly sucked in a painful breath while moving over in her bed; her ribs burning. Her two eyes were bruised yellow; much like they had been for her first full month inside prison.

'I didn't mean to hit you. Or kick you. I just wanted to celebrate. And I took offence to you turning me down, that's all. Come on. You're my best friend. I love you.'

But for the entirety of the one-hour Nancy was sat on the landing with her back to Joy's cell door, only distracted by Mathilda strolling by on three separate occasions as she walked her rounds, Joy didn't answer her pleas for a truce. She kept quiet as a mouse.

When the call came up for all prisoners to return to their cells, Nancy slid a note under Joy's door and then slumped back to her own bed for lock up.

Joy turned on her mattress upon hearing the note being slid inside, sucking in further breaths through gritted teeth. Then she mustered up enough energy to bend forward, through the pain, and pick it up.

I love you. I can't go on without you. x

She squinted at it; feeling it odd that Nancy was going on and on about how much she loved her when she had never so much as uttered that word before. Perhaps Nancy's emotions were being smothered by guilt. Or perhaps she was just being the manipulative and conniving cunt Joy knew she could be.

'Fuck you, Nancy,' she whispered to herself.

Then she heard a key turning in her lock and, in a panic, she grabbed at her bible and slid the note inside the back cover, just before Aidan appeared.

'I heard she was sitting outside your door the whole of the past hour. You need to make a formal complaint about the beating. We can't do anything until you do. Come on, do this. We can get you off this wing, onto another one.'

'You've been saying that to me for years, Aidan,' Joy said, while grimacing in pain as she sat back down on her mattress.

'She's never gonna leave you alone, y'know?'

'I'm fine, Aidan. Anyway, I'll be getting out soon.'

Aidan pursed his lips, while staring at the bruises under Joy's eyes.

'Joy. There's still every chance you are going to spend the rest of your life in prison. Nancy's in here for a long time, too. You don't want this to be a regular occurrence.'

'I told you before, Aidan,' Joy said, grimacing again while pressing a hand to her ribs, 'you're not me da. You can't tell me what to do. So, with the utmost politeness and respect, can you please just fuck off and leave me alone?'

Aidan raised his eyebrows, then let them drop back down before he paced out of her cell, slamming the door shut behind him.

Joy slapped the pillow in frustration. Then she turned to face her two boys, as the tears began to stream down her face.

⁖

Delia licks the tip of her thumb, then flips over the top sheet of paper and continues to read.

She has been going through the testimonies of the twelve females from Pennsylvania who had provided witness statements and proof that they once purchased a Pink Sasoon Ladies Hooded Top, in size small, for the past half-hour. She's just beginning to read through the last of these statements when Aisling walks into her office; a bottle of water, a packaged sandwich and a fruit bar in her hands.

'Here you are, Delia,' she says. 'They didn't have the ham and cheese one, so I just got you plain ham again.'

'You're a darling, Aisling. Thank you.'

Aisling places the lunch on her boss's desk, beside the shards of glass that have fallen from the photo frame and then turns to leave.

'So, eh... what did you make of Tobias Masterson's testimony this morning, Aisling?' the judge asks, looking over the rim of her glasses at her assistant.

Aisling smiles to herself before spinning back to face Delia. She loves being asked about the trials; feels really valued when probed for her opinion.

'Well, if the chance is now just one in three of that being Joy Stapleton in the footage and not one in fifteen as we've always thought, then that sure is a big difference... Those statements you are reading, they sure do make a huge difference to this trial, right?'

'But what about Bracken's cross examination... suggesting that

Masterson couldn't have known everything; that it may not even be a small-sized hooded top in that footage?'

'I mean, it was good cross... under the circumstances. You've taught me the difference between good and bad cross. And there aren't many better than Gerd Bracken at delivering one.' Delia smirks a proud grin. She loves how enthusiastic and studious Aisling is about her chosen career. She reminds her of herself. 'But is his cross that pertinent when you think of how coincidental it would all have to be to actually align? I mean, this footage was shot one-thousand yards from where Reese and Oscar were buried. On the night detectives are certain they were buried – the night before Joy rang in her missing person's report. It'd be some coincidence to think that isn't Joy in that footage, right?'

Delia winks at her assistant.

'Thank you, Aisling,' she says. 'I, eh... appreciate your input. Now, I got to get through this.' She nods down at the paperwork on her desk.

'Okay, well, I'll leave you to read while you are eating lunch. I'll knock on your door ahead of the resumption.'

Delia rips open the sandwich packaging as Aisling exits her office and takes a large bite before continuing to read. But she doesn't get very far before she is disturbed again. This time by her phone vibrating against her desk.

A text message.

From Eddie Taunton.

Convincing testimony today, huh?

'Conniving mother fuc—'

Delia only gets out half of her mumble, just about stopping herself from producing another swear word. She hadn't sworn since she was a teenager up until this week. Now she can barely stop herself; certainly not when Eddie Taunton pops into her mind.

She picks up her phone and finger taps a response.

Depends on your definition of the word 'convincing'.

Then she places her phone back down and continues reading. The witness statements have all been flawlessly prepared, clearly overseen by Jonathan Ryan for a final edit before they were signed by the witnesses and handed over to the judge. The statements don't throw up any surprises. Most detail how and when each witness purchased a Pink Sasoon Ladies Hooded Top from Urban Outfitters. Some even go so far as providing photographic evidence of them wearing the top. One statement even had the actual receipt from the hoodie's purchase, dated October 10th – the exact same day Joy had purchased hers.

Some investigative work had been done ahead of the original trial to track down Pennsylvanian owners of the hooded top, but the prosecution didn't deem it overly necessary. They were certain Joy was the only person in Ireland with one of those hooded tops, and they were convinced they would get a conviction from a jury based on that. Besides, it wasn't that easy in those days. But the evolution in social media in the years since Joy was first convicted has been so dramatic that it became much easier to track down folk anywhere in the world. And so, when Ryan put out social media posts to Pennsylvanian folk with an image of the pink hooded top, it was no surprise that a few women, who had purchased one back in the day, finally came across the posts. He knew if he got statements from as many of those women as possible, then that would be viewed as pretty convincing evidence to a judge. He outdid his expectation. He got twelve. Leaving the chance of the woman in the CCTV footage being Joy as only one in three in the whole world.

Delia flipped over the penultimate page of the written testimonies but got distracted by her phone vibrating again just as she was finishing up.

She's guilty. Can only be her in that footage.

Delia stares at the message, then puffs out a snort of laughter. Not because she finds the text particularly funny. But because she still can't get over the brazen manner in which Taunton is transparently blackmailing her. So, she thumbs at her phone again.

I will be the judge of that.

Then she places the phone back down on her desk and gets back to her reading.

'Judge McCormick,' her desk phone spits out Aisling's voice, causing Delia to tut, 'Mr Bracken and Mr Ryan are both here to see you.'

Delia holds her two hands over her face and silently grunts into them.

'Send them in, Aisling,' she says.

A light knock is heard at the door, before it swings open and Bracken appears, grinning his veneers into the dimly lit office. Jonathan Ryan, taller but much slimmer, is stood behind him, peering over his shoulder.

'Come in, gentlemen. I've only the one visitor's chair here, so rather than look favourably on one of you, how about you both just take one step inside, close that door behind you and stand where you are... what's the issue? Why are you here before I've even finished my lunch?'

'Ma'am,' Ryan says, 'I have reservations about the cross examination Mr Bracken has led me to believe he has planned for the next witness.'

Delia sighs loudly, before rifling through the larger document on her desk until she locates the sheet of paper she is looking for.

'Mr Bracken, is this true?'

'Your Honour, the next witness cannot be relied upon to offer honest testimony.'

'Excuse me, Mr Bracken. *I'll* be the judge of that. In fact, I already *have* been the judge of that. I've allowed the witness. You've known this witness would be testifying for weeks and although you raised an argument against it before, you are already aware of my judgement on this. Testimony from this witness is valid. Very valid.'

Bracken sucks on his cheeks, then slides himself into the chair opposite the judge, crossing his legs as he sits.

'With all due respect, Your Honour. This witness has history of very heavy Class A drug use.'

'She's clean now!' Ryan spits.

Delia waves an open palm upwards.

'Mr Bracken... firstly, stand!' she says. He heaves himself to his feet and throws his hands into his trouser pockets. 'Secondly, you're bringing this argument to me at the eleventh hour. I'm not quite sure what your ploy is with regards delaying this trial. You seem to be throwing clinks into the mix constantly. We spent much of the first day of this trial arguing witnesses and written statements when you had been made privy to the witness structure three full weeks before the trial began. I thought you were a much better prepared defence lawyer than this, Mr Bracken.'

'Your Honour, with all due respect, I am one of the most prepared lawyers in this country. I am not delaying this trial at all... in fact, I am aiming to have a quick resolution to what has clearly been a grand miscarriage of justice. I am eager to get my client out of prison as soon as possible.'

'Well then what is your problem, Mr Bracken?'

'The fact that the next witness is a heavy drug user and cannot be relied upon to tell the truth.'

'You have known about her appearing as a witness for quite some time... this is what I mean by you coming to me with issues at the eleventh hour.'

'Your Honour, this witness—'

'No. No, Mr Bracken. We will not be having this discussion now. The time for that argument was weeks ago. You raised some concerns then, but I informed you of my decision. And my decision still stands.'

'But, Ma'am.'

'Enough!' Delia shouts. She picks up her sandwich and takes another large bite from it, leaving Bracken and Ryan standing and staring at her as she chews.

A light knock is heard at the door, before Aisling enters.

'Delia, shall I delay the restart of the trial, seeing as you three are...'

'No need,' Delia says, swiping the sleeve of her robe across her lips and then snatching at her bottle of water, 'these two gentleman will return to the courtroom ahead of resumption. I shall be there in a couple of minutes.'

'But, Your Honour—'

'Off you go, you two,' Delia says, brushing her hand at them, unwilling to listen to any more of Bracken's groaning.

The two lawyers turn around like two sorrowful teenage boys to be greeted by the infamous hooded top, hanging from the back of Delia's door. Then they pull that door open and leave.

'I'm sorry,' Aisling says. 'I didn't want to disturb what was going on... but just felt I'd need to inform the court clerks if there was going to be a delay. Is everything okay?'

'No problem at all, Aisling,' Delia says as she twists the lid back on to her water bottle. 'Just Mr Bracken chancing his arm, trying to get the next witness null and voided.'

Aisling thins a smile as she picks up the empty sandwich packaging from Delia's desk.

'I've ordered a new frame for this photo,' she says. 'From Amazon. It should arrive by the end of the week.'

'You are a darling,' Delia says as she stands up, sweeping the crumbs down her robe with her fingers while taking in her husband's smile through the cracked frame. She misses him so much. No more so than when she has a major decision to make. Bouncing arguments off Callum is just not the same as bouncing them off Ben. Callum didn't quite inherit the genius level of constructive nous his father had, even if he is proving to be a fine trial lawyer himself.

'Right, I need to get back to the grind. This witness should be interesting.'

'She sure will,' Aisling says. 'If anybody knows the defendant's state of mind straight after she was found guilty, it's this witness, right?'

Delia arches one of her eyebrows and nods slowly at Aisling, then she makes her way back down the corridor, turning left to face the young woman dressed in black up ahead of her who carries out her usual routine of opening the side door and nodding into it to note the imminent arrival of the judge.

Delia glances across at Bracken as she climbs the three steps up to her chair, then she knocks at her desk once with her gavel, silencing the murmurs of chatter.

'Mr Ryan,' she says, 'can you please call your next witness?'

'I can indeed,' Ryan says getting to his feet. 'Your Honour, we call Miss Christine Jabefemi to the stand.'

CHRISTINE JABEFEMI

Ain't normal I see the inside of a courtroom. The four times I been sent down, I cut deals every time. I always admit I'm guilty if I get caught. That way I get less time. Don't think I'd ever have the patience to sit through a trial anyway... barely able to sit through this. But I promised Jonathan Ryan that I'd be here, dressed all nice and being all sober. So, here I am. Dressed all nice. And being all sober. Don't know how people manage to do this all day, e'ry day.

'Ms Jabefemi, thank you for taking the time to be with us today.'

'Call me Christy,' I say, 'Christ with an extra Y.'

He smiles. Like a little pretty boy. The exact same smile he offered me when I first asked him to call me Christy all those months ago now, after he dropped by to talk to me bout this retrial. He wanted to know all about my relationship with Joy after she had been first sent to Mountjoy.

'Christy it is then,' he says. 'So, Christy, can you tell the court about a prison sentence you served in 2012?'

I snort, then move the microphone closer to me.

'I was in for burglary and theft in 2012. For a seven-year stretch. Ended up doing almost three years. Should have been less. But the fuckin' parole board—'

'Excuse me, the witness cannot use such language in the courtroom,' the judge says, smackin' her hammer off her desk like a crazy lady. If she thinks that scowl is supposed to frighten me she can think again. I ain't the bitch on trial here today.

'We apologise, Your Honour,' Jonathan says as he walks towards me. He leans in, covering the microphone with his hand.

'Christy... as I said, no foul language. Let's just get through the questions and answers like we said, okay?'

I wink at him. He's such a cute little man-boy; I likes me them cute little man-boys sometimes; especially if they have dimples like he does. He walks backwards a few steps, then looks up at me again.

'Christy, if you could just answer the question directly... You were sentenced for seven years in 2012 for burglary and theft, and served almost three years of that in prison?'

'Yeah.'

'Okay... and you happened to be sent to Mountjoy on September sixth of that year, yes?'

'Yeah,' I say nodding my head. Though I only know that cos he told me. Otherwise I don't remember dates.

'That happens to be the day Joy Stapleton was also sentenced. Is it true that you both travelled together to Mountjoy Prison in the back of a police van?'

'Yep.'

'Good. Now, you spoke on that journey and when you entered the prison, you were both sent to the same wing within the prison, yes?'

'Uh-huh. Elm House.'

'Did you strike up a friendship with Mrs Stapleton?'

'Yeah. We sure did. I guess. I mean we spent time with each other. I tried to protect her. I'd been in prison befo', so I just tried to help with the small details. Ye know it's the small details in prison. How to get your hands on a new toothbrush. What books you can take from the library... how to keep yoself warm at night... those kinda details.'

'You, in a sense, took her under your wing, correct?'

'Like a Mamma birdie,' I say. And I laugh. But nobody else does. Cos this courtroom full of snooty-ass bitches.

'And, as you said, you spent almost three years in prison then. Did you spend all of that time on the Elm House wing?'

'Yep.'

'And did Mrs Stapleton serve all those years with you on that wing, too?'

'Think she's spent all her time on that wing... I don't know. It's been a lot of years since I've been back inside.'

'But, you were in effect neighbours in Mountjoy for all the years you were there that time?

'Yep.'

'Friends?'

'Yep?'

'Close?'

'I took her under ma wing, as I told you. I was her mamma birdie. There are a whole lotta screwed up women in prison, and I guess she looked so small and lonely and frightened. Hell, she was shakin' in the van the first day I met her.'

'Thank you, Christy. So, you were close friends for almost three years. Then you were let out of prison, but arrived back there some two years later, correct?'

'Yep. But that was bullshit. I shouldn't—'

'Enough, Mrs Jabefemi,' the judge says, slamming her hammer again.

'Sorry,' I say.

'If the witness could refrain from profanities.'

'I will, Ma'am,' I say, noddin' ma head at her.

'It's insignificant whether you feel you were rightly or wrongly sent back into prison, Christy, in terms of this trial. What is significant is what Joy Stapleton said to you during the small stretch of time you spent in prison during that sentence, isn't it?'

'That it is. That's when she told me she did it. That she killed her two boys. She confessed. Came crying to me one day, saying things hadn't been the same in prison since I left, and everything came out. It all poured outta her.'

I look to Joy. Her lawyer has his hand lightly gripped around her wrist, just in case. But she doesn't react. She just stares straight ahead.

'She confessed to you that she killed Oscar and Reese?'

'Yep. And that she buried them in the woods in the mountains. And that it was definitely her in that CCTV thingy... everything. She poured her heart out to me.'

'Wow, Your Honour,' Jonathan says, turning to look up at Judge Delia. I don't know whether she believes me. I hope she does. But she looks like the snootiest bitch of all the bitches in this courtroom. So I dunno. 'Now carefully and to the best of your memory, can you detail what Joy said to you exactly?' Jonathan asks.

'It was a long time ago, but I remember. I remember like it was yesterday because it was, well... it was Joy Stapleton finally confessin'. She said, "I did it, Christy. I couldn't put up with them crying no longer. I strangled them and killed them. Then I went up the mountains and buried them." She told me it took her three hours to dig out a grave and then she dumped the bodies in there and then she went home and got drunk.'

'Quite a lot of detail...'

'Yep. She just opened her heart to me.'

I look at her again, through the curls covering her face so I can see her eyes. But she won't look at me. Little bitch.

'So, you are here to testify today, Christy, that Joy openly confessed to you inside the confines of Mountjoy Prison during your six-month sentence in 2017, yes?'

'Yep. Sure am. The Lord God sent me. He said, he said, "Christy, you need to make sure o' justice for those two little innocent boys." So here I am. Making sure justice is served. She can't get out of prison. She's a killer. Worse than a normal killer. She kills her own.'

I stare at her again. I really want her to look at me, to see me. Bitch embarrassed me. She made a show o' me, telling me to fuck off in the yard that time. She payin' for that now. You don't fuck with Christy, sista.

She just keeps looking down at the desk in front of her, her lawyer still holding a loose grip round her wrist. Then I see him let go, and he stands up and stares at me. I didn't even see Jonathan sit down. Now it's this guy's turn? Jonathan told me not to be intimidated; that this fella will bring up my past and won't paint a pretty picture. But all I have to do is sit here and take it and not overreact. Then I can walk out those double doors, back to my freedom, back to ma little bedsit. While Joy here will be going back to Mountjoy. Back to those shitty little cells the rest o' her life.

'May I call you Christy, too?' he says.

'You may indeed, Sir.'

'Christy, you just said Joy Stapleton confessed to you that she killed her two sons. Can you detail for the court where this conversation took place?'

'Eh...' *I scratch at the side o' my hair.* 'In her cell in Elm House.'

'Really?'

'Yep.'

'It's just that during this period, in 2017 when you were in for a six-month sentence for theft, you were not based in Elm House, were you?'

'Eh... nope.'

'So how could you possibly have been present there for a conversation with Joy Stapleton at this time.'

'I must have... must have been allowed in. Somehow. Sometimes we wander.'

'You must have been allowed in... to Elm House? But this simply doesn't happen, does it? Prisoners don't wander block to block in Mountjoy Prison, do they?'

'Well, eh... maybe it happened somewhere else and my memory is a little... I don't know... fuzzy?' *I laugh. But none of the other snooty fuckers do. I know Jonathan certainly won't be laughing. He be screamin' inside. He told me this lawyer fella would ask all about where this conversation with Joy is supposed to have taken place. Because when I first told him, he recorded me and I said it had happened in Joy's cell in Elm House. So, he told me I should just stick to that, even if this lawyer fella kept suggesting it couldn't have happened there. But I didn't stick to it like he told me. It don't matter.*

'So now your memory is a little fuzzy on where this actual conversation took place? Is your mind fuzzy on the content of the conversation, too, perhaps?'

'Nope. She told me e'rything.'

'Really?'

'Yep.'

'She just spat it out one day to you... just like you testified here today?'

'Yep. She wanted to get it off her chest. She had been depressed since I left the prison and just wanted me back as a best friend, y'know, so she just told me e'rything.'

'Well, Mrs Stapleton says no such conversation came up during your six-month sentence in Mountjoy Prison in 2017. In fact, she says she had no conversation with you at all during this period. That she saw you one day in the break yard, but that she ignored you.'

'She lyin' cos we did talk.'

'Did you talk many times during that six-month stay?'

'Nope. That was it.'

'Hold on. You are telling me you only had that one conversation in 2017 and she openly admitted everything to you?'

'Yep.'

'Now I find that hard to believe. Especially as you've already admitted to your mind being fuzzy – which is the exact word you used.'

'Well you should believe it, cos it's true, Sir.'

'And you are to be trusted, Christy, yes?'

'I am a woman of God, Sir. I am honest and true.'

'You were fired from your job as warehouse worker in Cribbins Closets in 2019, Christy. Yes?'

'Yep.'

'For what reason?'

'Because they ass holes.'

'Mrs Jabefemi,' the judge calls out, slammin' that hammer again. It's a good job I don't have a hang-over... good job I kept clean these past three weeks.

'Sorry, Yo' Honour,' I say, 'won't happen again.'

'You may answer the question properly this time, Christy,' Bracken says. 'You were sacked from Cribbins Closets for what reason?'

'Cos they say I stole from the till.'

'You stole from the till?'

'That's what they say. Sacked my sorry ass in front of all the folk working there.'

'So, you were sacked for stealing on the job?'

'I didn't steal nothin'.'

'But that is the reason they sacked you, yes?'

'I guess so.'

'And you were thrown out of a hostel called The Inn Take in early 2011. why was this?'

I breathe out loud. Right into the microphone.

'I stole somebody's watch.'

'You stole somebody's watch?'

'I didn't do it.'

'You just said you did.'

'Well, I just sayin' why I was thrown out, s'all. They threw me out cos they say I stole the watch. But I didn't steal jack sh—' I stop myself befo' the judge slams that hammer again.

'Okay, Christy. Now let me go back a bit. You were first sentenced to prison in 2008. Yes?'

'Think that was ma first time, yep.'

'For what?'

'Theft.'

'Theft. Correct. And you spent nine months inside. You then went back to prison in 2010 correct?'

'Yep.'

'For what reason?'

'Theft, I guess. And I got eight month that time.'

'Yep. That's correct. Then the third time you got caught, you were sentenced to seven years for theft with use of an illegal weapon in September of 2012. Which is when you spent almost three years on the same wing as the defendant. You got out in 2015. Then in late 2017 you were back in Mountjoy for six months for...'

'Theft.'

'Yep. Theft.'

'See where I'm going with this, Christy? You were sacked from the only job you've ever held, according to my records, for theft. You were thrown out of a hostel for theft. You have been arrested, charged and imprisoned on four different occasions for theft. And yet here you sit before us, asking us to trust you as you testify about a conversation that simply didn't happen because it couldn't have happened.'

'It did happen!' I say.

'You ever been reliant on illegal substances, Christy?' he says, taking a step closer to me. I was told this would come up.

'You know I have.'

'When did you start taking drugs?'

'When I left home, back in... I don't know... late nineties or whatever.'

'And when was the last time you took drugs, Christy?'

'A long time ago. I'm clean now. I don't do nothing like that no more. I am a woman of God, Sir.'

'Last time... roughly?'

'I don't know, Sir.'

'You don't know... has it been weeks? Months? Years?'

'Years.'

'Years? Well, now that can't be the case, can it, Christy? I mean, I have here...' he walks back to his desk and picks up a sheet of paper. 'Records of you being accepted onto the Desoxyn trials at the Lilac Clinic in Blackrock back in February of this year, for a course of Desoxyn. Desoxyn, for the record of the court, is a legal substitute for methamphetamine. Did you need a substitute for meth in February, Christy?'

'Well, maybe it hasn't been years. But I bin clean fo' months. Ever since I did that clinic trial at Blackrock,' I lie.

'Really? It says here that you left the trial after only four days?'

'Whatever.'

'Whatever? Christy. Your history suggests you are a woman who has relied on Class A drugs for the best part of twenty-five years. It also suggests you are untrustworthy, given your records of consistent theft, isn't that correct?'

I start swishin' ma hands around on ma knees. This ass hole really rilin' me up. Jonathan told me he would. But I thought I be strong enough to get through it. Any time I play with my hands like this, I know I need me some meth. It's been three weeks now since Jonathan put me up in a hotel and told me to sober maself up befo' I took the stand. But tonight... tonight when I get back home, I'm gonna get straight on the phone. I need ma fix. I gotta get me some shit, just to get over this shit.

'Yeah. I guess ma history does suggest I'm a drug taker and that I'm untrustworthy,' I say. Then I shrug one shoulder at him. 'But I tell ya somethin', mister lawyer man, I ain't lyin' bout this. She told me she done it. That gal confessed to me.'

Joy was practically skipping behind Mathilda, her arms swinging by her side, a smile stretching across her face.

'And he said – and these are his words because I chose there and then to remember them – "there's a great chance" – a *great* chance, Mathilda!'

'Cool,' Mathilda said as she waddled her way around the maze of land-ings to lead the excitable prisoner back to Elm House.

'Are you not happy for me?' Mathilda shrugged her shoulders, not even bothering to turn around. 'Where's Aidan? I need to tell Aidan. Why didn't he bring me to my meeting with Gerd Bracken, I know he's rostered to be working today?'

Mathilda cleared her throat.

'He eh... was called up for a meeting with the Governor.'

'Well, I guess I'll tell him when I see him.'

Joy continued to skip and grin while following Mathilda all the way back to Elm House. Bracken had just informed her that her retrial had been officially granted – all three judges in the Criminal Court of Appeal agreed that the fresh evidence brought to them was enough to warrant Joy another day in court. The consensus seemed to be, in the judges' summoning up, that while they felt Mathieu Dupont's technological breakthrough to be less than one-hundred percent scientific, the fact that Bunny the Dog had been found to be a fraud in a court of law overseas was ample reason to order the retrial. Which was odd, Bracken had told Joy when delivering the news, because he thought it'd be the other way around.

'So now we have to start planning for the retrial... what we need to concentrate on is convincing a jury or a judge or whatever road they go down with this that you are not the woman in that CCTV footage. If we can pour doubt on that, then I think we have a great chance of finally getting you out of here.'

'When will the retrial be d'you think?' Joy asked, her face beaming, 'think I'll get out before Christmas?'

Bracken puffed a laugh out of the side of his mouth, then he leaned forward.

'Joy... this will take some time. Again. It may even be up to another two years before we get back into a courtroom. We gotta join the queue... and I can't tell you how long that queue is. Besides, with your retrial, who knows what way the justice system will even try it. They might not see a jury as being suitable... I mean, who doesn't know about the Joy Stapleton case? So, this could rumble on and on...'

'Two more years?' she said, grimacing.

But it didn't dampen her spirits. She was high as a kite. Especially after Bracken said he had to leave her to it because he had scheduled a press conference and was about to let the whole nation know that Joy Stapleton had been ordered a retrial – and that Ireland's most infamous prisoner may have been innocent all along. The Joy is Innocent campaign will be abuzz. Half of the nation will say, 'I told you so.'

'Listen, listen,' Joy squealed, clenching up her fists and excitely shaking them at her fellow inmates as soon as she arrived back in the TV room, 'I've got it! I've bloody got it! A retrial.'

'Well, holy shit,' Linda said, standing up and hugging a bouncing Joy.

Nancy remained seated on the worn sofa, her arms folded as she stared over Joy's shoulder at the TV.

'Right Said Fred.'

'Huh?' Joy said, her face scrunching up at Nancy.

'Right Said Fred. Which 80s pop band had a hit with a song titled *Don't Talk, Just Kiss*? Right Said Fred. It wasn't one of their big hits, but I was a fan back in the day....'

Joy looked over her shoulder at the repeat of *Tipping Point* playing on the screen.

'Didn't you hear what I just said, Nancy? They're giving me a retrial. They confirmed it at the Courts of Criminal Appeal this morning. My lawyers out there talking to the press right now as we speak. It's official.'

Nancy heaved herself up from the sofa, by griping a clawed hand to Linda's knee.

'I'm happy for ya. I am.'

She slapped Joy on the back, then refocused her stare to the TV screen.

Joy's relationship with Nancy had been awkward and undefinable ever since she beat her up almost a year ago. But Nancy kept claiming her undying love for Joy until Joy eventually gave in and forgave her, but only because it made her life easier to not be ignored by the entire wing, all of whom had begun to blank her because she wouldn't speak to Nancy. The two of them had been back talking for months now, but their relationship was undeniably strained. And awkward. They rarely spoke, not until Nancy felt horny and would sidle up to Joy and insist on being fingered. Joy wasn't receiving any fingers in return, not anymore. But that was fine by her. She'd just close her eyes, give Nancy all four fingers until she couldn't take them no more, then they'd both get back to folding bedsheets before being locked up for the night.

'Has anyone seen Aidan?' Joy asked, her fists still clenched with excitement.

The heads around her shook, then some of the inmates leaned into her for a celebratory embrace; though they seemed unsure. But only because while they knew they should be happy for Joy, Nancy had set an unenthusiastic tone to receiving Joy's news, and the ambience had fallen flat. Joy's fists released and the bubble of excitement began to dilute in her stomach.

But just as it did, in the midst of the awkward silence that followed a couple of the loose hugs she received from her so-called friends, she heard the voice she'd been waiting to hear. He was outside, asking if Joy was back from her meeting yet.

'Aidan, Aidan,' she shouted, running towards the door of the TV room, 'I got it! I got it! They're giving me a retrial.'

She stopped short of hugging him, only because she knew it to be frowned upon. But she so desperately wanted to. Instead, she stood in front of him, ringing her hands and smiling from ear to ear.

Aidan bit the bottom of his lip, then, in seeing Joy's excitement, beamed a grin at her, before reaching a hand to her shoulder.

'I'm so happy for you,' he said. Then the grin dropped from his face.

'What is it? What's wrong?' she asked, her smile dropping too.

'It's your father,' Aidan said, his fingers squeezing at her shoulder, 'I'm sorry, Joy, but he didn't wake up this morning.'

---

774 days ago...

She closed her eyes softly, allowing the gentle breeze to tickle her curls. Then she inhaled a fresh breath of air. It had been a year since she'd felt a breeze. The large sixteen-foot fences and walls around the prison made it nigh on impossible for winds to penetrate.

When she opened her eyes again, it was the green that stole her gaze; the grass, the stems of the flowers, the leaves of the trees that stood tall only fifty-feet away. She'd never found a tree more interesting to look at; had never even thought to stare at one for so long. But here she was, enraptured in its bulging trunk and the thick branches that bent and arched away from it. The leaves seemed luminous, and the flowers, in rows all around her, were so multi-coloured that it seemed as if the brightness of the outside world had been heightened since she'd last been out here.

Aidan stared at the profile of her face as she soaked in the tree, then he jangled the cuffs a little, and ever-so-slightly rubbed his knuckles against hers.

She blinked herself back to the present, glancing at Aidan quickly, before glaring down at the hole in front of them.

'We lay to rest Noel Benjamin Lansbury. Noel, may you rest in peace in the arms of our Lord.'

Six strange men, all dressed in black suits and shaking with cold, balanced the coffin on to two leather straps, before slowly lowering it to the bottom of the grave.

Joy looked around herself at the pitiful attendance. Two of her father's old workmates – one of whose name she had forgotten – and good old Pat Traynor; the one friendly neighbour everybody adored from the tiny cul-de-sac Joy had grown up in. There were a gaggle of women, none of whom Joy recognised, and two nurses from the home Noel had spent the past six years residing in; noticeable because they wore a ribbon around their necks that was emblazoned with the care home's logo – just to ensure their attendance was noted, Joy assumed. And then there was Ray De Brun. For some reason. The detective who spent all that time with her, telling her he was going to bring her boys back before he finally showed his true colours and arrested her for their murder. She knew he had spoken to her father multiple times during the investigation, and that he had once paid a visit to his care home to pass on his regards, but she was surprised he was here for the funeral. He had thinned his lips when he saw Joy enter the small church cuffed to Aidan. In fact, he made the same face everybody in attendance made at her when she met their stare. They all seemed to lose their lips and offer a very subtle nodding of their heads.

She got distracted by the breeze picking up, rustling through her tight curls, so she closed her eyes again as the priest mumbled a prayer, and inhaled fresh air through her nostrils. Then she noticed everybody blessing themselves and before she caught up with the act, not easy when you're handcuffed, most of the crowd had begun to disperse.

'You, eh... you wanna go, or hang on a bit?' Aidan said.

Joy looked back over her shoulder, towards the marked police car in the car park that had two police officers inside, waiting to escort her back to Mountjoy.

'How long will they give me?'

Aidan shrugged a shoulder.

'Let's stay until they call you, huh?'

She smiled at him, then subtly allowed her knuckles to brush off his again. He looked so handsome in his long navy double-breasted overcoat.

'Wanna join me on my hunkers?' Joy said, raising her cuffed arm. And then Aidan slowly lowered to his hunkers, before Joy joined him, staring down on to the top of the coffin.

'That was weird seeing all those old faces,' Joy said.

'Nobody really said anything to you, did they?' Aidan replied, squinting through the breeze towards the gate at the far end of the cemetery where the small gathering were filing through the oversized gates.

'Nope,' Joy said, 'But I know what they all would have said to try to console me: that he died in his sleep, so he went out in a good way. But he didn't. Did he? You actually couldn't go out any worse than my dad did. First, he lost his wife just half-way through her life, then his two grandkids go missing. Then his daughter is all caught up in the storm and wrongfully sent down for two life sentences. I mean... no wonder he was in a mental home by the time he was in his mid-fifties...' She sobbed a little, but then steadied herself. Her dad was only sixty-one when he passed; he got a decade more than her mother. But those ten years were as miserable as life can possibly get. The Lansbury's were once one of those enviable families – always by each other's side. Noel and Monica had been a proper partnership. Never shaken. They had tried for almost seven years after getting married in 1979 to have children, but it turned into a struggle. It wasn't until they had been for multiple tests that doctors got to the bottom of the problem. It was Monica; her eggs were limited. *Very* limited. She had one chance at IVF, and even at that there were no guarantees. But it worked out. Nine months later Joy arrived, kicking and screaming. The trio were inseparable until Joy was swept off her feet by a Dublin hero when she was just eighteen. And then, sometime not long after that, their whole lives turned into a nightmare from the first day Monica was diagnosed with breast cancer. She passed away not knowing Joy was pregnant with a grandson she would have just doted on. Joy didn't know she was pregnant either. Not until the following week, when she was still in the throes of her grief.

'It's such a shame you never got to tell him you had been offered a retrial.'

'Pffft... that's typical me though, isn't it? I had literally come looking to tell you in the prison, then I wanted to go call him to let him know. He would've been so happy for me.'

Aidan glanced at Joy's profile.

'At least you've got all that to look forward to though, huh?'

'What have I to look forward to, though? Even if I do get out... where would I go? Who am I getting out to? I've nobody. Not a husband no more. Not a son no more. Not a parent... Not even a friend.'

She sniffed up her nose, determined not to cry, then she gently took another of those fresh inhales through her nostrils, just to steady herself.

'Listen,' Aidan said, pinching Joy's fingers between two of his. 'I just want to say, cos I didn't really get a chance to yesterday, but... I'm super happy for you. Thrilled. You gotta keep this to yourself because us officers, we're not supposed to say anything like this, but...' he looked back over his shoulder, towards the car park, 'I've always thought you to be innocent. Always. From before I even met you.'

Joy stared into Aidan's blue eyes.

'I know you did.'

'I was glued to the coverage of your trial just as I was finishing my training as a prisoner officer. It's funny. I often wondered that if you were convicted whether or not I'd ever get to meet you in Mountjoy. And there you were on my very first day, the very first prisoner I ever got to escort to a cell. Funny how life works out sometimes, innit? But I was hoping I'd never meet you, because I never believed you should have been sent to prison. I thought your trial was bullshit. I knew the dog was bullshit, knew the CCTV couldn't be proven. I truly hope they overturn your conviction at this retrial. I mean, I'll miss ya 'n' all... but...'

He shrugged a shoulder at her and smiled.

'Why d'ya have to be fuckin gay?' she asked, beaming a smile back at him.

'Why? Do you still fancy me?' He laughed out loud. 'Don't think I've ever forgotten you tried to kiss me.'

Joy held her free hand to her face, to smother her embarrassment with it.

'Has anyone else been trying to kiss you lately?'

'Ahh, that'd be telling, wouldn't it?'

'Go on... tell me.'

'No. It's nothing. Nothing. It's the gay scene, isn't it? Loadsa chances of one-night stands, very little chance of actually finding somebody you want to see again after those one-night stands... typical.'

'Ye filthy sodomists,' she said, giggling. And then Aidan shouldered her. He didn't mean to push her that hard, but she stumbled and fell, and then he fell on top of her as the cuffs dragged him down. He immediately got up. Offered his free hand to help Joy to her feet, before he brushed down his knees in a fit of giggles.

Then he stared over at the two officers sat in the front of the police car and was relieved to see them sat still, unmoving.

'I'm serious, Joy,' Aidan said, gripping her hand again. 'I looked into your case as much as I could. And I know you. I've gotten to know you well over the past six years, despite our ups and downs. You're no murderer, Joy Stapleton. I know you're not.'

⁘

Delia's stare hasn't left Christy in quite some time – not even to glance at Jonathan Ryan as he is posing his questions. She has been fascinated by this witness, intrigued by the testimony she has just provided. Though the witness certainly has come across as troubled, what with her swearing on the stand and Bracken delving deep into her long history of theft. Yet Delia has been left feeling there was a sense of sincerity in how the witness spoke about Joy. Delia was wondering, as she studied Christy's heavy, bloodshot eyes, whether the witness possibly believed wholeheartedly that Joy confessed to her, even though Joy never did. Perhaps the drugs had played their part in convincing Christy she heard what she wanted to hear. The alternative theories were probably just as likely. Maybe Christy is aware she is lying, and at some stage decided to just turn on Joy. Or maybe, just maybe, Christy was actually telling the truth. Maybe Joy did confess to her.

Delia scribbled a question mark in her notes, then turned to Jonathan Ryan as he approached the witness box again.

'You have been clean of drugs for some considerable time, Christy. And you have begun to turn your life around... correct? I mean you haven't been in prison since 2017. And here is Mr Bracken trying to tear down all of your progress by bringing up your past. Christy, if I can ask you to say again what it is you came here to say... is it true that inside Mountjoy Prison in 2017, Joy Stapleton confessed to you that she had murdered her two sons?'

'Yep, it sure is. She confessed to me. She did.'

'Thank you, Christy Jabefemi, for your time. You are now free to leave.'

Delia stares over the rim of her glasses at the witness as she climbs down from the box before hobbling her way down the aisle. Then the judge pulls back the sleeves of her robe to check her watch just as Christy is pulling back the double doors, and notes that it's just gone two p.m. So, she sucks through her teeth, and stares down at Jonathan Ryan.

'Are we calling it a day, Your Honour, or would you like me to introduce my next witness?' he asks.

'Let's, eh...' Delia hesitates, 'let's take a quick recess. Fifteen minutes. Court will resume at two twenty precisely.'

She bangs down her gavel once, then gets to her feet and rushes out the side door. She offers a thin smile to the young woman dressed in black and – all of a sudden – she just collapses, her back sliding down the wall until her ass reaches the cold tiles.

'I just need to sit... sit anywhere but in there,' she says to the woman dressed in black, before producing a long sigh. 'You couldn't just give me ten minutes, could you? I, eh... I know my office is only twenty paces away, but I just feel as if I need to breathe before I walk again.'

'Sure thing, Judge McCormick,' the woman dressed in black says. Then she turns on her heels, leaving Delia to sit alone in the overly-lit hallway, her head in her hands.

She tries to steady her breathing as she soaks Christy Jabefemi's testimony into her mind; trying to gauge it within the context of everything else she has heard over the course of this retrial. She couldn't make it all the way to her office because she was jaded; and she is jaded because her filtering system has been working overtime – her mind splintering in so many different directions.

Then the side door sweeps open beside her, and her son appears.

'Oh hey,' he says, blinking at the sight of his mum's legs stretched across the tiles. 'Was just coming to see you.'

'Course you were,' she says, puffing a laugh into her hands.

'That was some testimony, huh? This is over – she's guilty. This retrial paints her even more guilty than the original.'

Delia removes her hands from her face.

'Really?'

'Mum... don't tell me you don't agree? I mean, you're not still thinking about that bloody cadaver dog, or Mathieu Dupont's testimony, are you? Mum...' Callum takes a step closer and stands over his mother. 'This is open and shut. Just deliver the guilty verdict and get me out of this mess.'

'Making it all about yourself again.'

'Mum, this will destroy me.'

'Calm down, Callum,' she says, whispering and then pointing at the

668

courtroom door he had just exited. 'You think that witness was reliable... really? Ponder this for a second, yes? Joy Stapleton murders her two children, then keeps it secret from the entire world for the past twelve years. She doesn't tell a soul. Not one of her loved ones, not her best friend, not her husband. Not a police officer. Nor a doctor. Nor a psychiatrist. Yet despite keeping it a secret for so many years from so many loved ones and so many professionals, she just happened to let it slip to a prison junkie? Of all people. Really? You think that's plausible?'

Callum circles his foot on the checkered tiles.

'You allowed the witness.'

'I allowed her because I thought it'd be beneficial to hear the testimony of the person Joy spent most of her time with just after she was incarcerated. I was intrigued to understand how different Christine Jabefemi's opinion of Joy Stapleton would be compared to anybody else. Even as much as Shay Stapleton's. Or Lavinia Kirwan's. I wanted an insight into the convicted Joy. The Joy who was behind bars... to see if she was any different post-conviction to how she was pre-conviction.'

'Exactly,' Callum says, 'and that's what you got. Joy admitted to a prisoner that she did it. You got what you wanted...'

'Just because I allowed the witness, doesn't mean I have to buy everything she testified. Christine Jabefemi is hardly a model witness.'

'She is a witness who knew the defendant—'

'Shhhh,' Delia whispers. 'Keep your voice low. Besides... I'm the bloody judge here, okay? Only I know why I allowed Christine Jabefemi to testify. Only I can glean from her testimony whether or not she is being sincere.'

'Mum, I don't give a shit,' Callum says, keeping his voice low, but his tone curt, 'about Christine bloody Jabefemi's sincerity. I just want to know you are going to do the right thing; that you are going to get me out of this mess.'

'I thought you were getting yourself out of the mess,' Delia says, folding her arms.

'The private eye hasn't got back to me. I've left about half a dozen missed calls on his phone between last night and this morning. He said he was looking into things... But I'm not sure he's going to be quick enough. He might not get much information for me before this trial ends. You've only one bloody witness left now anyway, haven't you? Final arguments will be tomorrow. You might even have a verdict back by tomorrow afternoon.'

Delia rolls her eyes to stare up at her son, and then snorts out a laugh.

'That won't be happening. I'll be taking my time. Let's see what Detective Ray De Brun has to say anyway.'

'Well, hopefully De Brun will be able to convince you of Joy's guilt again. Because I think you have somehow been slanted on this... you seem like you're determined to acquit her...'

'Slanted? Me?' Delia holds a hand to her chest. 'Determined to acquit? Where did you get that from?'

'Well you keep constantly arguing with me about it. I keep telling you she's guilty, you keep pushing back.'

'I'm not pushing back on guilty. I'm just not jumping the gun like you are. Besides, I've taken all of my emotion out of this. You clearly haven't. I haven't told you I am leaning either way yet. Because I'm not leaning either way. It's too early for a judge to pass judgement. And you need to learn that, son. You should have learned that already. I'm assessing every witness testimony and every slice of evidence being offered up just as I'm supposed to. So, stop assuming you can read my mind. If you could, you'd be able to tell that I haven't made my mind up at all, yet. Far from it, in fact.'

They both pivot their heads and stare up the hallway as a sweeping of feet brushes its way towards them.

'Sorry, Judge McCormick,' the young woman dressed in black says as she walks into view. 'I was asked to get back to my post because it's 2:18. Court is set to resume in two minutes.'

'Oh crikey, that fifteen minutes flew,' Delia says, readjusting so she's on all fours before she steadies herself to her feet. She then puffs out her cheeks and slaps her son between his shoulder blades. 'Time to get back to it, Callum,' she says. 'Take your seat. I'll be in in one minute.'

Callum pulls at the side door and disappears, but not without huffing and puffing.

'You can let them know I'm coming,' Delia whispers to the young woman dressed in black, then she, too, pulls open the side door Callum has just disappeared through, and nods inside.

'All rise!'

Delia winks at the woman as she passes her, then she climbs her way to her highchair.

There is a lot of chatter in the courtroom, but that's only because most of the gallery didn't bother leaving their pews for the short fifteen-minute break, preferring instead to debate Christine Jabefemi's testimony with the folk sat next to them.

'Mr Ryan,' Delia shouts, arching her eyebrows over her glasses and putting an end to the chatter.

Ryan stands and straightens his tie.

'Your Honour, I call Ray De Brun to the stand.'

A rotund, bald man with an overgrown grey moustache, rises from the middle of the gallery, apologising with whispers as he brushes past attendees in his row, before pounding his heavy frame down the aisle and up into the witness box.

Instead of paying attention to the witness being sworn in, Delia reshuffles the paperwork in front of her, then gives up looking for the sheet she needed when Ryan takes to the middle of the courtroom floor.

'Thank you for your time, Detective De Brun.'

'Ex detective.'

'Yes; ex detective. You retired in...'

'2016.'

'After how many years on the force?'

'Forty, exactly.'

'Impressive. And how many years as a detective?'

'Thirty-two.'

'You were one of longest serving detectives in the history of the state when you retired, correct?'

'So they tell me.'

'Well, thank you for your service, Detective De Brun. Let me ask you this... in those thirty-two years you led the investigation on some of Ireland's most notorious cases... But, of course, the reason you are here today is because you were lead detective on the Stapleton case, correct?'

'Yes. I certainly was.'

'From day one, right? When Reese and Oscar Stapleton were reported missing, who was the first detective assigned to the case?'

'I was.'

He fingers the blunt-edges of his moustache, then scratches at the aging freckles that are forming a map on his scalp.

'You worked on the case for over two years; two as a missing person's case and then a further two months after that when it turned officially into a murder investigation, right?'

'Yes. And I stayed with this case all the way through to conviction.'

'So, it would be fair to suggest you know this case better than anybody?'

'I've certainly poured more hours into it than anybody. And I can also say that I've poured more hours into the Stapleton case than I did any other case in my entire career.'

'Impressive. And you say you saw the case all the way through to conviction. It was you who literally arrested Joy Stapleton for the murder of her two sons in January of 2011, correct?'

'Yes, I did.'

'And can you tell us why you arrested her?'

'Why I arrested her?'

'Yes, Sir.'

'Well... because she murdered her two sons.'

RAY DE BRUN

'So, it would be fair to suggest you know this case better than anybody?'

'I've certainly poured more hours into it than anybody,' I say. 'And I can also say that I've poured more hours into the Stapleton case than I did any other case in my entire career.'

It's true. This case was a nightmare for me right from day one. And it's a nightmare that never seems to want to end. Not with half the country believing she's innocent – judging the entire case on tabloid headlines. They don't know the case like I do. Nobody does.

'Impressive. And you say you saw the case all the way through to conviction. It was you who literally arrested Joy Stapleton for the murder of her two sons in January of 2011, correct?'

'Yes, I did.'

'And can you tell us why you arrested her?'

'Why I arrested her?'

'Yes, Sir.'

'Well... because she murdered her two sons.'

Ryan pauses for a gasp from the gallery after I say that. And it arrives right on cue. Only because he set it up. He told me, when we rehearsed what I was gonna say up here, that there'd be a gasp when I bluntly delivered the line "She murdered her two sons." I think it's a guy who works in his law firm who produced it. But it seems to work. The courtroom has fallen silent, and the judge is scribbling away on her notes.

'So, you investigated this case from day one, Detective De Brun, and worked on it for over two years – put more work into this than any other case, you say?'

'It was more than two years. It was two years between the case opening as a missing person's case and the eventual arrest for double homicide. But I worked on it a lot more after that. The original trial took almost a further two years to come around... and I worked hard on the case all the way up to that. Heck, I'm still working on it today.... sitting here.'

'Yes... much more than two years, that is correct. And the state thanks you for your dedication to true justice. But just to go back a bit... past the second year you worked on this case, you arrested Joy Stapleton because, as you have just said, she murdered her two sons. Why were you and the police force so convinced of Joy Stapleton's guilt?'

I blow through the bristles of my 'tache.

'In missing children's cases, in particular, it is always key to look closest to home. In eighty-four percent of child abduction cases the culprit is found to be a family member or somebody closely associated with a family member.' Jonathan Ryan told me the statistic last week, told me it would fit in nicely with my testimony; certainly after Sandra Gleeson tried to throw me under the bus when she was sitting up here last week. 'I know an ex-colleague of mine testified here to say that we were focused on Joy Stapleton from the get-go, and that's because the statistics inform us that is the right approach to take. We rule out who we can with a matter of urgency. And we managed to rule everybody associated with Oscar and Reese out – all except for Joy. In fact, we only got more and more suspicious of her involvement as time went on.'

That's all totally true. We ruled out Shay straight away because he had been in Roscommon, lounging about in the Grand Hotel on a work trip. Shay's parents had alibis, as did Joy's father. Their closest friends and associates all accounted for. Lavinia Kirwan was on a date; Shay's best mate Steve Wood was at home with his then-girlfriend. One by one we found we could strike all family and friends from the list. Yet Joy's name remained there. In capital letters. Highlighted.

'Can you tell me when you, personally, first became suspicious of Joy Stapleton?'

'Personally? At the end of day one of the investigation... when I heard the phone call for the first time.'

'You mean the phone call Mrs Stapleton made to 999, to report that her boys had been abducted?'

'Yes. I listened to it at about eight p.m. on the first evening, and I was shaking my head listening to it. Especially as I'd just spent much of the day with Joy, consoling her.'

'Well, I think now is a good time, Your Honour, for the court to listen to the tape.'

The judge nods her head and then Jonathan Ryan holds a finger to the ceiling as if he's the conductor of some invisible orchestra up there. There's a small clicking sound, then a pause, before a crackling ringing blasts through the speakers.

'Hello'

'Somebody took my boys. They are gone. They are gone.'

'Your children are missing, ma'am, is that what you said?'

'Yes. They were on the green in front of my house. And somebody took them. My boys have been taken. They're gone.'

'Give me your address, ma'am.'

'Yes... yes... It's ninety-three St Mary's Avenue, Rathfarnham... please get here as quick as you can. My boys! My boys!'

Seventeen seconds long that call is, before Joy hangs up. It must be the thousandth time I've heard those seventeen seconds. And I am under no doubt that I have heard a guilty mother every single time.

'Can you tell us why you felt suspicious of Mrs Stapleton as soon as you heard that call, Detective De Brun?'

'The whole country has heard that call by now... it was all over the news for many a year. There's still people arguing about it online today. And I see people arguing that Joy sounded too over the top when she was screaming down the line; that she was being too dramatic an actress... but her screaming is not what was suspicious about the call for me.'

'Well, what was suspicious?'

'Her words, "Somebody took my boys".'

'And that was suspicious because?'

'It sounded to me as if she had already decided what her narrative was going to be – that her sons were abducted. She said it right from the off. She didn't say they were missing. She said they were taken. That somebody took them.'

'Interesting. But that only raised your initial suspicion, correct? It wasn't a smoking gun for you. You couldn't have been certain she was guilty because of the phone call alone?'

I shake my head and mouth a 'nope' – popping the 'p' sound into the microphone.

My thoughts on the phone call were, in truth, just instinctual suspicion, but detectives live and die by the art of using their instinct, and it always pisses me right off that so many people are keen to play that skill down. My instinct... my gut... it never let me down in forty years on the force. Certainly didn't in this case. I believed Joy Stapleton murdered her two boys from day one of this investigation. And I was dead right. We didn't take our eyes off her during the process of the missing person's case, but we had nothing to go on for such a long time. The dog evidence was never a clincher for us. In fact, there was no clincher for two years – not until the bodies were found. Then we turned the heat up on her. Nobody else seemed to suspect a thing. I remember Shay, God love him, storming up his garden path one day when he saw me coming to his house and asking me out straight if I was genuinely considering Joy as a suspect. He had tears running down his face. I'm not sure Shay has ever been fully convinced of Joy's guilt, and he certainly let that be known at his testimony yesterday – but his mind has been clouded by too much emotional attachment. It's been really sad watching him go down-hill over the years. The poor man is living in a warped universe. I'm surprised he hasn't gone mad. Though I did notice when I saw him at the courts yesterday that he has aged terribly. Such a shame. He didn't deserve this life.

'Even though you brought in the cadaver dog who indicated a body or bodies may have decomposed in the Stapleton household, you still didn't arrest Joy Stapleton, did you?'

'We had so little to go on. No bodies, no evidence whatsoever. It seemed to the naked eye as if the boys had just vanished into thin air. Only we had spoken to Joy's best friend Lavinia Kirwan who I know also testified at this trial and she had told us Joy had been acting strange for a couple of months leading to the boys' disappearance. We also observed changes in Joy as the case was on-going ourselves. The psychologists who spoke to her during the course of the investigation very often reported that Joy would speak like a fantasist; saying she always felt Oscar and Reese would grow up to be superstars or superheroes or something like that. And she was also observed as having a natural ability to emotionally manipulate... we saw her manipulate those out searching for Oscar and Reese, she tried to manipulate some of our police officers, too. She even manipulated her own husband, Shay. It was just a subtle personality trait she had. But we zoned in on it. She was a strong voyeur, too. She would stand back and watch everybody; watch the investigation unfold... She knew every-body's business. She also had a history of abuse, albeit small. Her father used to smack her when she was younger. And I have to tell you, Mr Ryan, that all these traits I have just mentioned; a fantasist, emotionally manipulative, a voyeur, a history of abuse... they are all the traits associate with killers. It's just that Joy Stapleton doesn't look like your everyday killer. Even though she is one of the most cold and calculated killers I have ever come across.'

Everything I'm saying is true, apart from the history of abuse thing. That was minimal. One time at the start of the investigation, during what he thought was routine questioning, her father, Noel, admitted he used to smack her as a toddler – only if she was naughty, mind. It was no big deal. But it helped with our argument of listing traits Joy has in common with other murderers. The other traits I've listed – a fantasist, emotionally manipulative, a voyeur – they are all traits Joy genuinely possesses. In abundance. She killed those boys and tried to hide it from us as we investigated. But she wasn't doing quite as good a job of it as she thought she was. We were on to her all the time. We just couldn't find the bloody evidence to nick her. Which is a great shame. I'm aware more than anyone that the evidence is light-weight in this case. But I always felt when we got that CCTV footage of the pink hoodie, even though her face wasn't shown in it, that we had enough to put her away – certainly enough for a jury made up of everyday people to put her away. But a judge, somebody who knows law inside out, well... now that is a different type of persuasion. And I'm worried... I'm worried Joy might get out. She doesn't deserve her freedom. That's why I'm testifying again here today. And why I rehearsed with Jonathan Ryan what I needed to say. We have to get this right. We need to convince the judge she has to uphold the original verdict.

'And then two years later, a member of the public happened upon the bodies and the investigation dramatically changed from there, isn't that correct?'

'Yes. A dog walker.'

'But the scene or the bodies didn't give you as much evidence to go on as you would have liked...'

'Nope,' I say, shaking my head. 'All that was left of Oscar and Reese was bone. And the scene itself had long since weathered away any indication that might have led us to a suspect. I mean studies on the bones suggest there was no sign of a struggle and therefore it is likely Oscar and Reese knew and trusted their killer, but there was no direct forensic evidence at the scene by the time we got to it, no.'

'But then, a few days later you came across the CCTV footage.'

'Then we found the CCTV footage, yes. And everything changed.'

'Everything changed?'

'We knew we had her. That is Joy in that CCTV footage, just yards from where the bodies were found. She is walking back down the mountain on the night we believe her sons were murdered and dumped in that wasteland. It was the night before she reported them missing with the phone call you just played to the court.'

'You have no doubt she is responsible for killing her two sons, do you, Detective De Brun?'

'None whatsoever,' I say, leaning closer to the microphone. 'Listen, Joy Stapleton had no alibi for the night we believe the boys were killed. She says she was at home alone with them, but she has no witness to back that up. There are also no witnesses whatsoever to the crime Joy claimed; that they were snatched from the green area in front of their garden. Then she makes a mistake by telling 999 when she made the emergency call exactly what she wanted her narrative to be. Then she acted with all these strange behaviours over the course of our investigation, right in front of us. And then, low and behold, she was spotted on CCTV footage not far from where the bodies were buried. She is as guilty as they come. It just took us a couple of years to be able to provide proof of her guilt. Which we did, of course. This case went to court, let's not forget that. And that court found her guilty. And the court found her guilty because she is guilty.'

'Detective Ray De Brun, thank you for your time.'

I release a sigh of relief as Jonathan sits back down beside his legal team, but I know I'm only half-way through this – with the worst half yet to come. I can't stand Gerd Bracken. I mean, his cause should be so worthy – trying to get innocent folk out of prison. But this guy isn't interested in the justice of it at all. He's only interested in making a name for himself. He's a narcissist – there's no doubt about that. As soon as that cadaver dog, Bunny, was outed as having made a mistake in a case in England a few years ago, he jumped all over Joy Stapleton because he thought if he could overturn the most infamous case in Ireland's judicial history then he'd make an even bigger name for himself. He's a disgrace. There's no way even he can believe Joy Stapleton is innocent. The smarmy prick literally lies to himself for a living.

'Ex Detective,' he says appearing in front of me, his legs standing slightly wide apart, his hands clasped against his stomach, 'correct me if I'm wrong, but you have just testified here today that you felt Joy was guilty for two whole years but you couldn't arrest her because you couldn't prove it in a court of law, correct?'

'Correct.'

'Correct? So, the cadaver dog. The voyeurism you accuse my client of having, the personality traits you have testified here today suggesting she proved to you, without providing us any proof whatsoever, the phone call that in your opinion she is acting in... all these pieces of evidence you were building up against my client... they weren't enough for an arrest?'

'No. They weren't.'

'Good,' he says, 'then I can throw most of my questions away. Because, ex

Detective, I was going to ask you about all these nuances and redundant pieces of evidences, or opinions as I would label most of them. But you have just admitted to us all under oath that these are pretty much redundant because they weren't enough to warrant arrest.'

'They weren't enough to warrant arrest, but I wouldn't call them redund—'

'Now, ex Detective,' he says, talking over me and looking all smug, 'that only leads us to the CCTV footage then, doesn't it? The only reason you arrested Joy Stapleton is down to that CCTV footage, correct?'

'It's not only down to the CCTV. We built a case around her....'

'Yes, but a case that wouldn't, in your words, have led to a conviction without the CCTV, right?'

I cough and fidget in the chair.

'I guess so.'

'Well, not "I guess so". I know so. Sure, you just said that yourself on the stand.'

'Okay. Then, yes. We would not have got a conviction without the CCTV.'

'And yet we've all seen the CCTV footage. And nobody can see a face in that CCTV footage. All we see is a figure walking past a garden wall in a pink hooded top, isn't that correct?'

'We know it's Joy.'

'You don't know it's Joy. You can't possibly know it was Joy. Besides, there was never any footage found of this figure going up the mountain. Only down. How do you explain that?'

This argument irks me. Has always irked me.

'She likely walked up on the other side of this street where the CCTV didn't reach. Or maybe she even went up the mountain via a different way. Truth is, we've never quite known exactly how she got up there. How she got the boys up there. But we know she did it. Because we found film of her coming back down that mountain. On top of that, Mr Bracken, this argument was addressed in the original trial. We only found footage of Joy walking back down the mountain. But it is Joy. We know it's Joy.'

Bracken puffs out a small laugh.

'You keep saying that, ex-Detective. But you can't possibly know for sure that is Joy in that footage, can you? You can't see more than the rest of us can see with all due respect. You're not a superhero. You don't have x-ray vision, do you, ex-Detective?'

'Mr Bracken,' I say, leaning towards the microphone, 'don't let the conspiracy theories fool you. A woman walking away from the scene of the crime wearing the only hooded top in the whole country which we know Joy owned, a woman of Joy's height and description, on the exact night the crime took place... Let me tell you, Sir. There is no conspiracy to be had here. There is no coincidence. There has never been any such thing as a coincidence in this entire case.'

349 days ago…

'We don't even have to prove it was a coincidence,' Bracken says. 'We just have to pour doubt on the case the state proved against you in the original trial. When Ray De Brun testified in that original trial, his expertise was given too much credence. The jury bowed down to him. They took him at his every word. But I'm gonna tell him out straight when we get him on the stand in the retrial that he's not superhuman, that he doesn't have x-ray vision and he can't possibly know that was you in that CCTV footage more than anybody else on this planet can. I'll prick his ego a little bit.'

Joy smiled, while both of her knees bounced up and down under the desk. She had been animated anyway; because the opportunity of freedom was now very much in sight. But after Bracken just informed her she could be set for millions in compensation if she got out, her elation has immeasurably elevated.

She was still grinning, still bouncing her knees when Aidan knocked lightly on the door before pushing it open.

'Time,' he said.

He winked at Joy when she joined him on the landing, and after she had said her goodbyes to Bracken, and she and Aidan were alone, she gripped onto his arm.

'I've got a date. Eighth of December.'

'Really? Less than a year away. You could be out for Christmas, huh?'

She gripped his arm even firmer, but then he had to shrug her off when they heard the footsteps of another prison officer coming up the stairs behind them. So, they walked, as they were supposed to, the inmate in front of the prison officer and in total silence, until they arrived back at Elm House.

She updated the prisoners she normally sits next to for meals, and while some were already excited by her court date, interest really began to inflame when she mentioned compensation.

'He said it could be millions. I mean… if I get out in December that'll mean I'll have spent eight years in prison. Wrongfully. Think they'd give me a million for each year? I'd be super rich!'

'You'd take that eight million over having your two sons, would ya?' Nancy said, cutting right through the excitement that had just fizzled across both sides of the bench.

Joy chose to ignore Nancy's negativity, and turned away to stare down the line of women on her side of the bench.

'He said the reason it took so long for them to agree to a court date was because they couldn't figure out how to run a retrial for me. Some members of the judicial board wanted a jury, but they were overruled by the Chief Justice, because they don't think they'd be able to find an unbiased jury. Too many people know about me, apparently. The Joy is Innocent campaign has lovers and haters in equal measure, my lawyer said.'

'Well, if I was a juror on your retrial, I'd let you out,' Linda said, pouting her lips and blowing a kiss across the bench. 'So... what way are they gonna do it?'

'One judge, and that's it.'

'So, all your lawyers have to do is convince one person, huh?'

'That's all,' Joy said, 'and my lawyer said I have a much better chance with somebody who knows law inside out rather than a jury of nobodies. He's really confident I will be let out. *Really* confident.' She made a screeching sound that cackled from the back of her throat and those sat around her, gripped by her excitement, squealed too. Nancy Trott didn't, though. She just stood up, snatched at her tray, whispered something into Linda's ear and then left them all to it to giddily celebrate Joy's court date. Joy had noticed everybody around her was smiling just as wide as she was. Except for Linda. Linda's smile had well and truly been wiped off her face by whatever it was Nancy had just leaned in to whisper to her.

---

348 days ago...

'Oh, hey,' Joy said, pushing the door to her cell wide open.

'Hey,' Linda said.

'Whatcha doin' in my cell?'

'Just lookin' for you.'

'Sure, you know I'd be in the laundry room now – it's my shift time.'

'Oh yeah,' Linda said, her brow frowning. 'So whatcha doing back so early then?'

'I, eh... have a headache. Think it's all the excitement of yesterday. Mathilda said I could come back to my cell and have a lie down.'

'Oh...' Linda said. 'Well, eh.... Hope you feel better soon.'

Then Linda pulled open Joy's cell door and walked out.

'Eh... well what did you want me for?' Joy shouted after her.

682

'Oh, don't worry about it. I'll come back to you when you're feeling better.'

Joy scrunched up her face in confusion, then picked up the book she had loaned from the call-by librarian the previous Thursday and sat up on her mattress, her back resting against the cold concrete wall beside Reese and Oscar's photograph.

She was only three chapters in when she had another visitor. It was the fat red-headed prison officer who she remembered from her very first day who escorted her and Christy to the prison in the back of the van. She was never given his name, and had only ever seen him in passing when she was brought through Maple House on her way to her own private visitations.

'Joy Stapleton, stand up!' he ordered.

She looked confused, but slammed her book closed before slowly getting to her feet.

He pulled back the sheets on her bed before pivoting his head from side to side, his hands on his hips, whistling. Then he strolled towards the toilet seat in the back corner of her cell and immediately reached downwards.

Her mouth popped open when he stood back upright and held out his hand, from which was hanging a rather large bag filled with glistening crystals.

---

347 days ago...

Joy was worried; stressed. But her overall feeling was one of sheer anger. She knew she'd been set up; knew who had set her up. So, as she sat on one of the uncomfortable office chairs – which reminded her of the chairs she used to sit on at school – in another cold office, she dug her fingernails into her palms to try to dilute the frustration erupting from within her.

'If you don't mind, Gov, I'd like to sit in on this meeting. I, eh... I was asked by the prisoner to be here, and with your agreement, I'd eh...'

'Stop stuttering, Aidan,' the Governor snapped. 'Why on earth would a prison officer ask to sit in on a disciplinary hearing at the behest of a prisoner? I've been working here thirty-two years and I've never heard of such a thing.'

'It's just, eh...' Aidan looked at Joy and swallowed, before turning back to the Governor. 'Literally my first job as an officer here was to escort Joy to her cell. We've been in this prison the exact amount of time, only difference being that I get to go home every so often, though not that often, right?' he said, puffing out a laugh. He paused to allow the Governor to catch up with the joke, but too much time passed and the Governor's face remained stern and unflinching. He just glared at Aidan, waiting on him to explain himself. 'And, eh... I guess what I'm saying is that I know the prisoner well. I have worked in Elm House since my first day, and I see first-hand what goes on down there. It's not the worst House in this prison by any stretch, but I know who's in control and who's up to what. I firmly believe Joy was set up, Gov.'

'No!' the Governor said, and Aidan's face dropped. 'You can't sit in on this hearing. Get your ass out of here and you,' the Governor said pointing at Joy, 'better explain yourself! Over three hundred euros worth of methamphetamine... what in the world are you playing at?'

Joy dug her nails deeper into her palms as Aidan squirmed his way out of the office. She had never been intimidated by the man sitting in front of her. In fact, she always thought him to be fair and reasonable – as the majority of the prison staff had been. But this was different. The Governor wasn't being his usual jovial self with her. He was pissed. Really pissed.

'Please, please don't tell my lawyer. Please don't let this story get out to the newspapers. Please. I beg you. I'm only eleven months away from my retrial, Sir, and I... I promise.' She held her hands up. 'I was set up. Linda Wood and Nancy Trott set me up. I know they did. I saw Nancy whisper something into Linda's ear yesterday. Then I found Linda lurking in my cell for no reason. Next thing I know that red-headed officer was calling by and searching my entire cell.'

The Governor leaned back in his chair, removed his glasses and washed a hand across his jowls.

'Oh, Joy, you haven't given me an ounce of trouble in all the time you've been here...'

'I know, Sir. Because I'm not one for trouble. I shouldn't even be here in the first place. I've never done anything wrong in my life. Stole a pencil off a friend of mine in primary school once... s'about all I can ever remember doing wrong. I didn't kill my boys. I didn't. And my lawyer will prove it in my retri—'

'Enough!' the Governor said, raising his voice and holding up his hand to signal that Joy should put a stop to her rambling defence.

He sat more upright, hooked his glasses back over his ears and sighed.

'I will keep this internal. Nobody else will know. I will ensure this story doesn't leak. But I'm gonna remove you from Elm House and place you in isolation for two reasons: one, as punishment for holding contraband in your cell, and two, for your own protection.'

'Eh... thank you,' Joy said, unsure of herself. 'How eh... how long will I need to spend in isolation, Sir?'

'Eleven months.'

'Eleven months! But, Sir, that'll bring me up to my retrial.'

'Exactly!' he said.

❖

Delia felt refreshed; as refreshed as a Criminal Court Judge could possibly feel at the tail end of a major trial. The uptake in her mood was somewhat influenced by the fact that the trial was coming to an end. But she was mostly feeling upbeat because she turned off her phone last night, poured herself a full bubble bath – as well as a full glass of Massolino Parussi Barola – and ordered Callum out of the house. She wanted, no, *needed*, an evening without distraction; does her best thinking when bubbles are hugging the cheeks of her face, and a glass of red is swirling in her one dry hand. The bubbles and the wine have proven, over time, to be the best lubricant to start the cogs of her mind-filtering process.

She lay there last night filtering out the fascinating new evidence brought by Mathieu Dupont, suggesting it simply can't be Joy Stapleton in that infamous CCTV footage; filter-processing what was and what wasn't significant about the fact that the cadaver dog, Bunny, from the original trial had since been exposed as a fraud; filter-processing the emotional pull of Shay Stapleton's testimony – and that, in stark contrast, to Lavinia Kirwan's; filter-processing the alleged confession made to former inmate Christy Jabefemi, and then filter-processing the rather convincing and direct testimony of lauded ex-Detective Ray De Brun.

She circled through the entire trial and then back through it all again while she soaked. She even had to refill the bath with hot water when the temperature dipped too cool an hour and a half in. Yet she was still far from making up her mind. Which was fine. Because she wasn't supposed to make up her mind. Not yet anyway. Not until final arguments were heard.

There were times, during her filtering process, when images of her son's erect penis would flash before her. Then arched bushy eyebrows would stain her thoughts further. But the warming serenity of the bath and wine saw to it that those flashes were kept to a minimum. She knew Eddie Taunton would have tried to reach her multiple times last night – which is the main reason she'd turned her phone off. So, it was no surprise when she arrived at her office just gone eight a.m. to find he'd left four voicemails on her desk phone. She didn't listen to any of them though; didn't need, nor want to. Whatever Eddie had to say for himself, Delia was going to judge this trial independent of his meddling. She'd get to his blackmailing in time.

'Morning,' Aisling calls out as she opens the door to Delia's office, she too looking more relaxed than she has over the course of the retrial – most likely because she has a tendency to mirror her boss's moods. Though Aisling was also aware that her workload and stress levels were about to dramatically reduce after today. And she needed a break... even more so than Delia did. She had two children at home; both under six years of age.

'Final arguments, then we're done, huh?'

'Yes. Sorry about all the late hours you've been doing over the course of this trial. You can get back to seeing your children soon.'

Aisling giggles.

'Seeing them for bath time and putting them to bed is enough,' she says.

Then Aisling's desk phone begins to ring outside and her assistant turns to rush towards it.

'No need... I can pick it up here,' her boss says.

Delia stabs at a button, answering the call and placing it on speaker.

'Hello.'

'Oh, Judge McCormick herself,' the familiar voice of Gerd Bracken says. 'I, eh... we need to talk, Your Honour. As a matter of urgency.'

'Well, we are talking, Mr Bracken. Used to be the only useful thing you could do on a phone in my day.'

A silence breezes through the speaker, and in the time that it does, Delia creases her brow at her assistant, aware something intriguing was about to be said.

'My client has had a rethink. She eh... she wants to go on the stand.'

'What!?' Delia replies, her voice high.

'Joy Stapleton wants to testify, Your Honour.'

'Is this your idea of a game, Mr Bracken?'

'No... no, Your Honour. We're being totally honest. Joy has shown more eagerness to put her own version of events across as this retrial has gone on, and especially so since Lavinia Kirwan's testimony earlier this week.'

Delia stretches both arms across her desk, spreading her fingers wide.

'I wouldn't put it past you to have planned this out, Mr Bracken. The defence have had their time... Mrs Stapleton opted not to take the stand before her retrial.'

'Your Honour, with all due respect... Joy Stapleton on the stand suits both the prosecution and the defence. I'm sure Jonathan Ryan has many a question he would like to ask her. And, personally, I'm glad I will have the opportunity to get her innocence across when she's up there. Either way, two trials have now taken place over whether or not Joy killed her two sons back in November, 2008 and not once have we ever heard from the defendant herself. She was advised not to testify in her original trial by her defence team and – to be totally transparent with you, Your Honour – we also advised her not to testify during this retrial. But now she is insistent... she wants to go on record. Under oath. She told me last night that she feels she has to do this... that she has to stand up for herself. She can't go back to prison, Your Honour. She wants to fight for the freedom and justice she is owed. She is entitled to fight for herself...'

Delia stares up at her assistant to see Aisling squelching her lips before quietly leaving the office, pulling the door quietly behind herself.

'Your Honour...'

'I'm still thinking,' Delia hisses. Then she swipes up the hand receiver of her phone and exhales heavily into it.

'Okay,' she says. 'I'll allow the witness.'

Isolation had been long. And boring. *Really* boring. It was as if the days had lasted weeks and the weeks had lasted months.

Joy had to keep reminding herself that the Governor had done her a good turn by not allowing the story to leak outside of the prison walls. But while her excitement for her retrial was growing, she still felt largely frustrated by the fact that she was punished so harshly when it was so clear and obvious that she had been set up.

Initially she didn't mind being sent to isolation, but that's because she was comparing it to her time spent there in the early days of her incarceration. Back then, she was sent to isolation under caution, because her life was under threat. So, she was given all the luxuries and protection prisoners get, such as multiple hours of yard time, and a TV in her cell. But this time, because she was there under the grounds of punishment, there was no TV – and she could only visit the yard once, on her own, for one hour a day. The first time she had been in isolation was also bearable because she often had Aidan for company. But this time it was Mathilda and a new female prison officer called Anya – who was tall, thin and beautiful, like an Eastern European model – who took shifts looking after her. And neither fancied much conversation with Joy, except to order her around.

Joy had hoped Mathilda at least, who she had known for eight years now, would have melted her hard exterior somewhat, seeing as Joy's retrial had been granted and many of the national newspapers were now beginning to lead with stories suggesting her innocence. But Mathilda still treated Joy the same way she treated every other prisoner inside Mountjoy – with an evident air of superiority that she almost thought it beneath her to converse with her.

Joy's spirits had been further dampened when Aidan paid her the only visit she had had from him in all the months she was in isolation. He had been allowed to come see her, to let her know face-to-face that he was leaving the prison. The catering business he had started with his brother had finally taken off – enough for both of them to move into it full-time anyway. Besides, his relationship with Joy had been, for years, too much of a concern among the staff of the prison, and his insistence on backing her after drugs had been found in her cell was the final straw for the Governor. Although he informed Joy that he was standing down to concentrate on his catering business, she knew it was more likely a mutual agreement with the prison's board. While she painted on an excitable face for Aidan as he revealed his new business plans to her, her stomach was tossing and churning like a washing machine. She knew in that moment, more than any other over the years, that she *had* to win this retrial. There was no going back to Elm House for the rest of her life. Not without Aidan there.

Though it was Elm House she had been led back to last night. But for the first time since she'd arrived in Mountjoy she wasn't holed up in E-114, but E-108 – the cell right next to Nancy. She taped the photograph of her two boys to the wall, hoping that she'd be taking it down in a few weeks' time once her retrial had granted her her freedom, then she left her cell to go to the dining-room, flanked by Mathilda.

The atmosphere fell silent as she walked to the counter and took a plateful of lasagne from the prisoner serving it. Then she turned around and looked about herself, wondering where she should sit, feeling like the new girl all over again. Those eleven months had seemed a hell of a lot longer than eleven months, even though nothing on the wing seemed to have changed.

'Over here,' Nancy shouted from the middle of the largest pack of prisoners. Then she stood up, showing her shock of red hair, before waving her hand, beckoning Joy towards her.

Joy wandered over, slowly and uncertain, as Nancy ushered some prisoners to move along the bench so that there was room for Joy next to her.

'Great to see you,' Nancy said, wrapping both of her arms around Joy while trying to avoid the plate of lasagne she was gripping with both hands. 'Sit down. Sit down.' Nancy patted the bench next to herself. Then she immediately began asking Joy about isolation until they were finally conversing as if no time had passed at all. As Nancy repeated how much she missed Joy, all Joy could think was, '*You set me up, you devious cunt*'. But she didn't tell her face what she was thinking. Because her face smiled and frowned along with whatever it was Nancy was saying.

Although Joy's pleas to the Governor, that her drugs bust wouldn't leak outside the prison walls, were adhered to, she couldn't keep the punishment from her lawyer. Gerd Bracken was initially fuming, but Joy was keen to put his mind at rest.

'I swear I was set up. I was set up. Believe me. Please.'

Bracken made her undergo a urine test, just to prove that she hadn't been using, which did return, thankfully to him, a negative result. He needed those results in case the story ever leaked out and was brought up in the retrial. That way he'd have some proof of her innocence with regards use, at least. Though he doubted it would be brought up in the retrial. He only knew the Governor of Mountjoy to be a man of his word.

She took a seat opposite Bracken and let him know that her reintroduction to Elm House the night previous had gone as smoothly as she could have imagined.

'It's as if I hadn't been away at all,' she said, shrugging her shoulder.

And then they got down to the business Bracken had called in to the prison to discuss.

'Okay, it's less than a month until the retrial starts,' he said, 'and my assistant and I have finalised the layout of the case we're bringing to the court.'

Joy's knees began to bounce under the table.

'We're going to start with the cadaver dog, bring its owner to the stand and have him admit to the judge that the dog never had the pedigree to determine the presence of decomposing bodies. But even if he's arrogant enough to not openly admit that on the stand, we'll easily be able to get him to say that the dog had been found as a fraud in another case – and that will make an instant impact on Judge Delia. She's a stern judge, but one of the finest in the country. So, what we've been working on for the past months is a strategy of trying to convince her that a lot of doubt exists in this case, which is totally different than trying to convince a jury of twelve.'

Joy nodded her head, then muttered, 'go on.'

'Then we'll bring Mathieu Dupont to the stand. I've mentioned the name to you before... he's the French guy whose technology may or may not have a huge impact on the judge. We're taking a small risk in that we'll be comparing the height he deems the woman in the CCTV footage to be against the height you are on all of your prison records... which is out of sync when we look at them. But I'm confident his testimony will go over well. If it does, you'll be a free woman in a matter of weeks. If it doesn't, the whole retrial could go either way.'

'Well, just make it go well,' Joy said, her two knees bouncing now.

'We're going the best way we can, Joy,' Bracken said. 'And then... and then... listen, because this might make you happy, or upset in some way or... I don't know what...'

Joy's knees stopped bouncing and her nose stiffened.

'What?' she said.

'It's great news, I want you to know it's great news.'

'What is it?'

'Shay is going to testify. For you. He's going to say on the stand that he doesn't believe you murdered his boys... *your* boys.'

'Really?' Joy said, her eyes widening.

'We think it'll win the judge over. This could be the game-changer, Joy. Depends on how well Shay does up there.'

'Oh my God,' Joy said. And then she puffed out a laugh that produced both snot and tears. Bracken had to rise from his to lean over and rub her back in consolation.

'I should also say, in opposition, that the prosecutors have a big bullet in their gun, too,' he said, sitting back down. 'Lavinia Kirwan. She's still convinced you did this, Joy. And she's been added to the witness list for the prosecution. We just need to hope Shay's testimony outweighs hers in the eyes of the judge.'

Joy wiped the tears away from her cheeks, using the sleeves of her sweat top, then shook her curls at Bracken.

'It's crazy... my life in the hands of all these people... husbands, friends... detectives... bloody dog handlers. I mean... ahhh, I actually don't know what I mean.'

'I understand what you're trying to say,' Bracken said, placing his hand on top of hers. 'It can't be easy.'

'I mean why can't I get up there? Why don't I get to defend myself? If Lavinia is gonna get up there and call me a child killer, then surely I have a right to let the court know that she's just a jealous bitch who has always envied me.'

'No, no, no,' Bracken said, shaking his head and taking his hand off Joy's.

'Why? Why can't I defend myself?'

'I've told you, Joy. It just gives the prosecution too many opportunities to trip you up. Even though you're innocent, their job will still be to get you to act on impulse. And if they wind you up on the stand, it could go horribly wrong for you. It's never a good idea for the accused in any murder trial to take the stand... trust me.'

'It's just so unfair. The whole nation has had a say on whether they think I'm guilty or innocent. I seem to be the only one who never gets a say. That's just... it's just...'

'Listen.' Bracken placed his hand on top of hers again. 'We would consider putting you on the stand at the very end of the trial,' he said, 'but if we do, it's only because we'll be feeling things haven't gone as well as we would have liked. If you do end up on the stand, Joy, it would literally be a last roll of the dice kinda thing.'

JOY STAPLETON

I comb my fingers through my hair, then retighten the scrunchie around my heavy pony-tail. Gerd Bracken said it'd be a good idea if I removed all the hair from my face, so that it doesn't look as if I am trying to hide.

Playing with my hair seems to have stopped my hands from shaking. And my heart doesn't seem to be thumping as much as I thought it would as soon as I sat up here. Maybe I can do this. Maybe I just might be able to turn this whole trial around.

'Mrs Stapleton,' Bracken says.

'Call me Joy, Mr Bracken, please,' I say, snapping the scrunchie tight and then bringing my hands to rest on my knees.

'Of course... Joy.' He smiles his big teeth at me. 'Your world turned upside down on November 3rd, 2008, correct?'

'It did, Mr Bracken. That's the day my boys were taken.'

'Can you tell the court when you first realised they were taken?'

'Where I live – lived – there's a green patch of grass straight across from the house. I often brought the boys over there. Reese would kick a football around and Oscar would bundle about after him. It's all very safe. It has a rail around the edges of it. Well, most mid-mornings the three of us would potter over and have a bit of play time there. It's literally thirty yards straight across from the house... Well, on this particular day, we were there playing and then I realised I hadn't put the dinner on. I was going to do a chicken, and wanted to oven-roast it for a couple of hours. So, I went back to the house... which is the biggest regret I'll ever have in my life... to baste the

chicken and throw it in the oven. I was four or five minutes. Four minutes. That was all. And I left the hall door open.'

'And when you came back outside?'

'They were just gone. They weren't there no more. I knew instantly somebody had taken them.'

'And what happened next?'

'I called out their names. But there was nobody around. Nothing. I knocked into my neighbour – it's the only other house that overlooks the green – but he wasn't in. Then I panicked and...' I sob. My first sob on the stand. Only one minute in. Shit. I need to get my act together. 'And then I rang the police.'

'That's correct, Joy. Almost immediately upon noticing your children were gone, you made this phone call.'

Bracken points his finger to the ceiling and there's a click sound, before the ring tone starts.

'Hello'

'Somebody took my boys. They are gone. They are gone.'

'Your children are missing, ma'am, is that what you said?'

'Yes. They were on the green in front of my house. And somebody took them. My boys have been taken. They're gone.'

'Give me your address, ma'am.'

'Yes... yes... It's ninety-three St Mary's Avenue, Rathfarnham... please get here as quick as you can. My boys! My boys!'

Every time I hear that recording even I find myself listening out for my acting skills. As if I can't even convince myself that I didn't kill them.

'Joy, it is the prosecution's claim that you are acting during that phone call. Given that I've now heard that recording about two hundred times, I'm a little baffled that they would suggest you were acting, because it sounds so legitimate to me. So raw. So emotional. For the record of the court, you weren't acting, were you?'

'Of course not.'

'You've never studied acting, never did an acting course?'

I sniffle up my nose, then remove a tissue from the pack Bracken had promised he'd place in the witness box for me.

'No.'

'No amateur dramatics... nothing like that? You weren't part of the local theatre group?'

'No.'

'The prosecution have argued, during this retrial and indeed at your orig-

696

inal trial, that you were too keen to suggest your boys had been taken, but that's easily explainable, right?'

'Well, I was right. Wasn't I? They were taken. Two years later their bodies turn up, so I was right all along. They were taken. Somebody took them. It's not as if a four-year-old and an eighteen-month-old went on walkabouts and ended up in a shallow grave, is it? I never quite understood why they fixate on me saying they were taken. It's obvious they were taken. It was obvious at the time. There was nowhere else for them to go.'

'Thank you,' Bracken says, pursing his lips at me. He told me he'd do that every time he felt I needed to take a sip of water. So, I do. He's planned this all out. Well, apart from the fact that I'm up here in the first place. He said to me two days ago that he needed me to take the stand, that he felt the judge would really benefit from hearing from me. I'm not sure I believe him, though. Because he told me only a few weeks ago that I shouldn't testify; that if I had to it'd only be because the trial wasn't going so well. But I'm gonna turn this around today. I have to turn it around. I have to convince Judge McCormick that I didn't do this; that the only reason I'm in this mess in the first place comes down to a stupid fucking coincidence.

'Almost two years passed before you realised you were a person of interest for investigators. Can you tell me when you first realised you were being investigated yourself for the disappearance of your sons?'

'At first, I knew I was a suspect, so was Shay, so was my father, our best friends. We weren't stupid. We knew they always look closest to home in investigations like this. I just wanted them to question me, then get out there to go find out who had actually taken Oscar and Reese. So, I thought they had moved on, after ruling all of our nearest and dearest out. I thought they were looking for their kidnapper. Then they started playing silly games by bringing the dog into our home and pretending he could sniff evidence of dead bodies... I mean...' I shake my curls and then gulp.

'Yes. And as a reminder for the court, that dog has since been found to be a fraud when it comes to investigations like this.'

'I knew he was a fraud at the time,' I say. 'Well, either that or somebody who used to live in our house before us maybe died in that bedroom or something. I really didn't know. I still don't know. All's I know is that I had nothing to do with this. But they fixated on me because everybody else had alibis... whereas I was just home with the boys until...' I sob. 'Until they were taken.'

I snatch at another tissue and press it into my eyes.

'A lot of time passed without any progress in the investigation, then a dog walker came across the bodies in a remote part of the Dublin mountains... what happened then?'

'After their bodies were found, they started bringing me into the police station again, asking if I knew anything about the place where Reese and Oscar had been buried.'

'And did you?'

'Of course not,' I say. 'I knew nothing. I still know nothing. I still don't know who buried my boys in that shallow grave. And neither do the police, because they haven't looked past me.'

'And soon after the bodies were found, you were arrested, correct?'

'Yeah – five weeks later. But only because of a coincidence. I swear, Your Honour,' I say, turning to the judge while balling up the tissue in my hands, 'it's just a coincidence. That's not me in that footage. That is not me. That is not my hoodie. I swear.'

Her face softens a bit, probably to match mine. But I genuinely have no idea what she thinks of me.

'So, you have been through the unimaginable, Joy,' Bracken says. 'Your boys are snatched from just outside the house and after two years have passed a detective comes to you to say a dog-walker has found their bodies. Then within a few weeks of their bodies being found, you are arrested for their murder?'

I nod.

'If you can answer audibly,' the judge says.

'Yeah... yeah. I mean, it's such a big tragedy in so many ways. How can they do this to me? How can the justice system get this so wrong?'

Bracken purses his lips at me again and I reach for the glass of water, noticing that my hand is now quivering.

'It's terrible... terrible.... terrible,' Bracken says holding his chin and shaking his head. I know that he is biding time for me to compose myself. 'This is the biggest injustice this country has seen, in my opinion. And it all came down to three seconds of CCTV footage that shows a video of what looks like a woman walking past a house wearing the same hooded top as one you happened to own, yes?'

I place my glass of water, using both hands to hold it steady, back down onto the shelf.

'When they showed me that footage, I knew it couldn't have been me. But then when they started to suggest it couldn't be anyone else, I just told them that it was a coincidence that somebody was wearing the same hoodie as me. One of the police started laughing at me when I kept saying that word. Then it was all over the newspapers, that I was defending myself by claiming a coincidence... but it's true. It is a coincidence. I don't know what else to call it. That is not me in that footage.'

'I know it's not, Joy. I do,' Bracken says. He told me he was going to say that. "An extra blanket of security while I was on the stand" he called it.

I take another swig of water, and in the time I do, I notice he has moved closer, glaring up at the witness box from just below.

'Joy, you didn't suffer with post-partem depression after the boys were born, did you?'

'No,' I say. And I say it as clearly and frankly as I possibly can. 'We were happy. I was happy. We were one big happy family. I don't know what else to say about being accused of having post-partem depression, because it's just not true. I know Lavinia Kirwan sat up here earlier in the week and said that I was suffering with depression before my boys went missing, but that is a very obvious lie. Shay admits he didn't think I was depressed around that time. My dad admits he didn't think I was depressed. Because I wasn't depressed. I wasn't suffering with depression at all. I was happy. We were happy. Then it all.... Then it all....' A loud sob leaps itself up from the back of my throat. And suddenly the tears pour from eyes. And my nose. I pinch at the tissues and cover my face with them, my shoulders shaking. That fuckin' bitch Lavinia. She's such a jealous fucker. Always has been. She hated that I was prettier than her. Hated that I snagged myself a Dublin footballer while she was left on the shelf.

After steadying my breathing behind the mask of tissues, I remove them from my face, then mouth a sobbing 'sorry' at Bracken.

'You have nothing to apologise for, Joy,' he says. 'It's the entire state who owe you an apology. Now,' he says, moving even closer, so close his fingers are clinging on to the edge of the witness box, 'do you know how many days you have spent in prison for this crime that you did not commit?'

I spray from my mouth as I let out a puff.

'Days... no?'

'Two thousand, nine hundred and ninety-nine,' he says. I make on 'O' shape with my mouth. 'That's right. Tomorrow will be your three-thousandth day inside Mountjoy Prison. Three thousand days, Your Honour. Three thousand days for a crime she did not commit. Three thousand days incarcerated for a crime that unearthed zero eye-witnesses. Three thousand days incarcerated for a case that offers up zero forensic evidence. Your Honour, this is the biggest miscarriage of justice in the history of our nation, and you are the only one who can put it right. I am done with my questioning, Your Honour.'

He reaches out his hand to me and squeezes my fingers, and as he does, I wipe another tissue across my face with my other hand. Then Jonathan appears, standing in front of me – all set and ready to convince this judge that I am a fucking child killer. I hate him. I hate Jonathan Ryan. He's an arrogant cunt.

'You are the only person in the country who owns one of those hoodies, Joy – right? You know it is not a coincidence that that hoodie was filmed a thousand yards away from where your boys' bodies were found on the night we believed they were first buried there.'

Wow. Straight into the coincidence. Fucker wants to squash my argument from the get-go. But I'm not for moving.

'It wasn't me. So, it has to be a coincidence.'

'I find that hard to believe, Joy.'

'What I find hard to believe, Mr Ryan, is that my boys are gone. Forever. And I've been holed up in Mountjoy Prison ever since, accused of murdering them. That's what I find hard to believe.'

He hangs his bottom lip out, then inches closer to me. And in the time he does so, I look over at Bracken, to see if he was impressed with how I answered that question. But his face is void of expression.

'Joy, your mother passed away... when?'

'Second of February, 2003.'

'2003... so just before you gave birth to Reese, right? Your first son came along eight months later?'

'Yes.'

'And then Oscar was some two and half years after Reese?'

'Yes.'

'Okay... I just wanted to get my timeframes right. So, your mother passed just before you became a mother yourself?'

I sigh out loud.

'Yes.'

'Get to your point, Mr Ryan,' the judge calls out. And I stare at her, surprised she's sticking up for me. Maybe I'm not as far behind in this race as I thought I was. Maybe the judge likes me. Maybe she believes me.

'Sorry, Your Honour,' Ryan says. 'Joy, you have testified on the stand here today that you did not suffer with any depression when your boys were born, but in truth you must have been feeling grief stricken, right?'

'I grieved the death of my mam, yes. But I'm not one to... to...'

'Not one to, what?'

'To mope. Life is what it is. I was sad my mother only got half a life. But I was also looking forward. I knew I had lives yet to live. One was literally inside me when I was at my mother's funeral.'

'So, you did grieve your mother's passing, or you didn't?'

'No, I did. Of course I did.'

'Of course you did,' he says, unbuttoning his blazer and looking smug. Then he strolls back to his desk and picks up a sheet of paper. I've no idea what he has in store for me.

700

'Do you know what the second most prominent trigger for post-partem depression is, Joy?'

I sigh out of my nostrils, then shake my head.

'Out loud, Joy, please,' the judge orders.

I lean closer to the microphone and whisper, 'no'.

'Grief.' He stares at me, while scratching under his chin. I don't know whether he's expecting me to answer that. But he didn't ask a question. So, I just eyeball him back while pinching at the balled tissue in my hands.

'You gave birth to two sons within the immediate years following the tragic loss of your mother and you don't feel you suffered from any post-partem depression?'

'I didn't. I loved being a mum.'

'You were spotted one thousand yards from where you buried your sons after killing them, Joy.'

'I did not!' I stand and scream. But my screaming is drowned out by Judge Delia hammering onto her desk.

'Mr Ryan, you know well it is your job to ask questions and not make judgements in my court room.'

He stands there still trying to look smug, but she just made him look like her bitch.

I toss the hard ball of tissue onto the shelf, then sit more upright and try to steady my breathing. Bracken told me that Ryan would do this, that he would constantly try to wind me up. I swore I wouldn't react. But I couldn't help it that time. Besides, the judge seems more pissed off with Ryan than me.

'Let me rephrase that, then,' Ryan says, 'I put it to you, Joy, that in a bout of depression, after you lost your mother and then gave birth to two boys, you lost control of yourself, killed your sons and buried them in the Dublin mountains.'

I grind my teeth. And as I do the judge looks at me, as if it's my turn to talk, even though he didn't ask any question... did he?

'Mrs Stapleton, the lawyer has put a claim to you... how do you respond?' the judge says.

I unclench my teeth.

'You can put that claim to me all you want, Mr Ryan. I didn't kill my boys.'

'So, after all these years you are still saying it is a coincidence that your unique pink hooded top – the only one in the country – was filmed near the scene of the crime?'

'It is a coincidence.'

'Well, it's a coincidence that didn't convince your best friend, isn't it? A coincidence that didn't convince the detectives in charge of your boys' *murder investigation. And a coincidence that didn't convince this very court of law over eight years ago.' My teeth immediately snap tight again. I'm literally keeping my mouth shut until he asks a question. Bracken made me swear I wouldn't offer up any information that Ryan doesn't specifically ask for. 'Mrs Stapleton, isn't it quite apparent to you that this defence you have – of coincidence – is difficult to be believed by anyone... not even your best friend?'*

'Former best friend. I haven't spoken to her in a decade.'

'Yes. Because she believes you killed both of your boys in cold blood.'

The whole room goes silent... waiting on my response. But I just sit there, staring back at him, not saying a word, my teeth snapped shut.

'Now, Joy,' he says, taking a stroll back to his desk to pick up a sheet of paper. What the fuck has he got for me now? 'I'm going to read out a text exchange between you and your husband Shay from February 14th, 2008. This is just over half a year before you reported Oscar and Reese as missing persons.

What. The. Actual. Fuck?

"'Hey," it starts, "you didn't think to check your schedule?" And then Shay replies, "Jesus it's only one night a year, we can rearrange." And then you reply, "I'm thinking of rearranging my whole life, never mind one fucking dinner." Rearrange your whole life... what does that mean, Joy?'

'Oh, please,' I say, gripping on to the shelf. 'We were having an argument about Valentine's night. I thought Shay was going to arrange something romantic for us. But I had just found out, because he had rung me just before I sent that text message, that he wouldn't be home that night; that he was in some other county... staying at some hotel.'

'You were having an argument?'

I sigh, and then throw both of my hands in the air before they slap down on to my lap.

'Seriously, Your Honour,' I say, looking to the judge. 'Is he seriously trying to convince you I murdered my two boys because I was expecting dinner with my husband on Valentine's night?'

The judge doesn't answer, she just turns back to Ryan.

'Well, that's not all, Joy,' Ryan says, 'I have another text message here dated earlier than that, December, third, 2006. This is Shay texting you, "Where are you?" You took almost three hours to reply to him. And when you did, you wrote, "I am taking a little time for myself. Jesus." He replied straight away saying, "Well, of course that's no problem. But perhaps we can talk about it rather than you just racing off without telling me. The boys were just left here. I don't know what to even make them for lunch." Joy, you never replied to that text.'

702

'So,' I say, shrugging my shoulders.

'Well, it just makes me wonder... fond of abandoning your sons, were you, Joy?'

'You little,' I grip the shelf, digging my nails into it, the blood shooting up my neck and into my face, 'you little—'

'Calm down, Joy,' Bracken shouts towards me.

I try to steady my breathing, then I turn to the glass of water Bracken said I should turn to every time Ryan tries to rile me.

'Your Honour, if she could answer the question.'

I look to the judge. She just nods at me and I audibly sigh. What am I playing at? I need to calm the fuck down.

'I went into town to treat myself for the day,' I say as calmly as I possibly can. 'It was one day out of I don't know how many that I had to myself. What do you want me to say? You found, out of hundreds of text messages, two that might suggest me and Shay were arguing. Well whoop-de-doo, Mr Ryan — ain't you a genius. Yes, on one or two occasions me and Shay had an argument. Do you know a married couple who don't argue?'

'Joy, I asked you a simple question, and the court would appreciate an answer to it. Were you fond of abandoning your sons?'

'Of course I wasn't,' I shout. At the top of my voice. Then in the silence that follows, I manage to become conscious of reducing my tone. 'As I said, that was one time I went and had an afternoon to myself. I never abandoned Oscar and Reese. Ever.'

'Well, that's not true, is it, Joy. It says right here in this text from Shay that you left the boys without any lunch.'

'They were with their father, for crying out loud. I left them at home with their father! Do you have children, Mr Ryan?'

He glances at the judge briefly, then nods back at me.

'I have a son, yes.'

'Your wife ever leave your son with you?'

'With all due respect, Joy, I am not the one on trial here today for killing his son, now am I?' I grip the shelf again to try to contain my shaking hands. The arrogant smug bastard. 'So, let me move on, Joy. Tell me this, why did you confess to the killings of Oscar and Reese to Christine Jabefemi.'

'I did no such thing.'

'Well, now, Christine, despite her personal struggles, is a woman of strong faith. She stands to gain nothing from this trial. So, why would she admit that you confessed to her?'

'Because she's crazy. That woman does more meth than I knew even existed in Ireland. She is a thief. She steals and robs and lies her way into getting her fix.'

'But you did confess to the murders to her, right?'

'No, I did not!'

'Joy, I have met with Christine Jabefemi multiple times over the past months. We have tested her for drug use. She has not used in all the time I've known her. In fact, I've just known her to be a fighter who is determined to stay clean. She has proven to be a courageous and honest and hardworking woman to me. Now, you on the other hand claim you had a happy marriage, and now here we have proof that things were not so rosy in the Stapleton household at all, sure they weren't?'

'You're a liar,' I snap, 'you are lying right now saying that Christy is hardworking and honest. She's a thief, for crying out loud. She's been a thief her whole life.'

'Calm down, calm down,' the judge says, hammering again. 'The court will ask this witness to refrain from raising her voice and reacting in the manner she just has.'

'But... but,' I stutter to the judge, 'but he's... he's...'

'Just answer the questions put to you, Mrs Stapleton. This is the reason you have been allowed on the stand... so you can answer the questions put to you.'

I swallow, then find that I'm rubbing circular patterns into my thighs with my hands. As if that's the only way I can remain composed.

'Our life together was happy. Just like Shay said when he was sitting up here earlier in the week. There were two of us in that marriage, and both of us are saying we are happy. Yet you somehow think you know better, Mr Ryan, do you? You know more about my marriage than me or my husband do?'

'Well, I wasn't asking about your marriage,' he says, offering me a smug grin, 'I was asking about your family. And while it was good to hear from your husband during this trial, and whilst it's good to hear from you, we can't hear from Oscar or Reese, can we? Because they're dead. And they're dead because you killed them.'

'I... I.... Your Honour, Your Honour,' I say, spreading my arms out with panic etched all over my face.

'Mr Ryan,' the judge says, 'please ask a question, or be done with your witness.'

Please be done with me. Please be done with me!

'I have a few more questions, Your Honour,' he says.

Shit.

He walks back to his desk, picks up a small remote control and then pinches his fingers at it. And when he does, an image flashes up on the screen in the middle of the courtroom. A picture of my boys. The same picture I have sellotaped to the wall of my cell.

'They were very handsome boys, very handsome boys, don't you think?'
he asks me.

I just hold my eyes shut, then I rework the scrunchie in my hair, because
my palms are actually beginning to burn with how hard I'm rubbing them
against my thighs.

'Yes. Very handsome. They looked like their daddy.'

'What would you imagine they'd be doing today, if they were still alive?'

'Huh?' I say, before eyeballing the judge. But when she doesn't look at
me, I glance across to Bracken. He just nods his head. So, I lean closer to the
microphone.

'Well,' I sob, 'Reese would be sixteen now. And Oscar would be almost
twelve. They'd be... I don't know... typical boys.'

'Think they'd have been training to get into the Dublin football team like
their daddy?'

I take another tissue, then fold it over in anticipation of another loud sob.

'Probably. I mean... Yes. Who knows?'

'They would have been happy children though, right? With the world at
their feet. A whole life ahead of them?'

A sob does come. But it's a quiet one. And I just find myself ripping at
the tissue while nodding my head.

'Yes.'

'Well then why did you take their lives away, Joy?'

The smarmy cunt.

I'm on my feet. My arm fully outstretched, my finger pointing. The tissue
raining to the ground in pieces.

'How fuckin' dare you!' I snarl through gritted teeth.

And then Bracken is suddenly on his feet too, rushing towards me while
the judge is hammering down a racket.

And the flashes I get when my head is spinning start illuminating in
front of me. Those fucking flashes. They haunt me; have haunted me all these
years. But it's not the flash of their lifeless bodies that haunts me. And it's not
the flashes of holding a chloroform-filled rag over their mouths to shut them
the fuck up that haunts me either. Nor is it the flashes of dragging their
bodies into a shallow grave. It's the flash of a camera that truly haunts me. A
stupid fucking camera. I still see the flash of it every time I close my eyes.

∴

When the gallery finally settles, Delia consciously begins to inhale and exhale deeper... just to dampen her own emotions.

She stares at a Joy, whose sobbing shoulders are being dragged into a one-armed squeeze by Bracken, before announcing that the court will take a recess for ten minutes, ahead of each side's closing arguments.

Her heart feels heavy as she solemnly takes the three steps down from her highchair and pulls at the knob of the side door.

'Oh my,' she says, bending over to rest her hands on her knees as soon as the door has closed tight behind her.

'You okay, Your Honour?' the young woman dressed in all black asks.

Delia pants for breath, then shakes her head, still folded over.

'Tough going,' she says. 'I, eh... I'm just gonna sit here for a few minutes. Can you please make sure nobody disturbs me; that nobody comes out that door?'

'Sure thing,' the young woman says. Then she moves to stand in front of the door like a guard and clasps her fingers together.

Delia sits on the floor, her back upright against the wall, her legs stretched across the chequered tiles. She squints her eyes, the cogs of her filtering process beginning to churn. That may well be the heaviest testimony she has ever heard in all the years she's sat atop one of those highchairs. She looked so pained, did Joy, while she was up there. But why wouldn't she? Whether she's guilty or not, she's still bound to be pained. Of course she'd be hugely emotional. Of course she'd be prone to outbursts.

'Ryan certainly was trying to wind her up,' Delia mutters.

'Sorry, Your Honour?' the young woman asks.

'Don't mind me,' Delia says without looking up, her eyes still squinting down the length of her legs. 'Just thinking aloud.'

There's a scuffle at the door, as somebody from inside tries to open it while the young woman spins to grip at the knob with both hands, dragging it back shut.

'Excuse me!' Callum's voice sounds agitated, curt, rude.

'Judge McCormick has asked me to keep this door closed during recess,' the young woman says.

'It's her son. Callum. Let me out.' He yanks the door so forcefully that he almost sucks the young woman into the courtroom, then he paces outside without an apology where he almost trips over his mother's outstretched legs.

'Get back in that courtroom,' Delia snaps.

'Mum, you need to—'

'You heard me. Get back in that courtroom, Callum. The court official here has just told you *nobody* can come outside that door. You are now in breach of the court. Do I need to call security?'

'Mum, listen. The Private Eye—'

'Callum!' she screams, forming both of her fists into balls atop her lap. 'I need these minutes to consider everything I've just heard.'

'Course you do, but—'

'Callum!' she screams again.

He holds both of his hands aloft, then looks back over his shoulder at the young woman dressed in black.

'Okay... okay, Jeez,' he says, swivelling, then strolling back into the courtroom in a sulk.

When the young woman dressed in black pulls the door back shut, Delia offers her a smile.

'What's your name, sweetheart?' she asks.

'Ivy. Ivy Malone.'

'Well, thank you for your continued service of the courts, Miss Ivy Malone,' Delia says. Then she drops the smile from her face, re-squints her eyes and stares back along her outstretched legs.

She doesn't know where to begin dissecting Joy's testimony from. She is aware the media will make it all about Joy's outbursts. But Delia knows she doesn't have to complicate her filtering process by concentrating on the two occasions Joy stood in the witness to shout back at Jonathan Ryan. Delia needs to dig deeper than that. She needs to reach the fine lines in between the lines, and then begin the process of filtering them into the appropriate pockets inside her mind.

'Your Honour, that's the ten minutes you called for,' Ivy says, startling the judge. It didn't seem as if she had been squinting that long. The judge tuts, then scrambles herself to her feet, squeezes the shoulder of Ivy's black blazer and pulls the door open herself.

'All rise.'

The shout goes up late from the clerk as Delia settles herself back into the highchair, gripping her gavel tight.

She sighs heavily, then knocks lightly once.

'We have heard from the last of the witnesses in this retrial. It is now time for both the defence and the prosecution to deliver their final arguments. Mr Bracken...'

Bracken scoots back his chair to get to his feet, then strolls purposely to the centre of the courtroom floor, leaving behind his client whose face is still swollen from all of her crying.

'Your Honour,' he says, adopting his familiar stance of forming a steeple with his fingers. 'If there is doubt, then you must let her out. And there is plenty of doubt in this case. In 2010, my client was arrested and eventually sentenced to two life sentences for a crime she simply did not commit. Nobody has ever been able to say with any degree of certainty that she is guilty of the horrendous and heinous crimes she is accused of. Two life sentences for a crime one police officer working on the case testified in front of you to say was a deeply... flawed... investigation. Let me remind you what Sandra Gleeson said when she was on that stand, Your Honour. She testified that investigators, "were only focused on one suspect from the outset." She said that only three seconds of CCTV footage out of five thousand hours that were viewed were ever deemed necessary to the investigation. Three seconds out of five thousand hours. That is a decimal of a percentage that begins with three zeros, Your Honour.' Delia scribbles notes on the paper in front of her as she maintains eye contact with Bracken. 'If investigators were only looking for Joy Stapleton in all of the footage they viewed, Your Honour, then what did they miss? Sandra Gleeson was an assistant detective on this case, and she believes the investigation was lacking from the outset... and flawed from the outset. That, in itself, Your Honour, is enough to excuse Joy Stapleton with an apology for her wrongful conviction. Sandra Gleeson's testimony pours all sorts of doubt onto the original verdict. And if there's doubt, Your Honour, you must let her out.' Bracken readjusts his standing position, shifting his weight from one foot to the other. 'But that is not the only doubt that has been poured onto the original verdict over the course of this retrial. Bunny the dog, Your Honour, who had been instrumental in Joy's original trial has, since that trial, been confirmed as a fraud. The dog did not have the skillsets required to even attempt to confirm the presence of decomposing bodies in the Stapleton home in early 2009. Bunny's handler, Mr Grimshaw – who sat in that witness chair last week – also lacks the skillsets and indeed qualifications for such a claim. Again, Your Honour, we managed to pour more doubt onto the original verdict in this case. And if there's doubt... you must let her out. Then we brought, to this court, brand new technology which was able to pour more doubt over the woman in the infamous CCTV footage... letting us know that this couldn't be Joy Stapleton. Because the height of the woman in that footage simply doesn't measure up to Joy. Y'see that's a metaphor for this whole case, Your Honour. Nothing measures up. Nothing measures up at all... Judge McCormick,' he says, taking two steps closer to the judge and staring up at her with his heaviest puppy-dog eyes, 'when there is doubt poured onto a case brought by the state – any case at all – it is proper legal procedure to dismiss the charges. After all, a case must be proven beyond *all* reasonable doubt. We, here, haven't just poured doubt on to this case, Your Honour, we have flooded doubt onto this case. My client has spent eight years, two months, two weeks and two days inside Mountjoy Prison for a crime she did not, and could not, have committed. If you are to release her tomorrow, which we strongly believe you should do given the amount of doubt flooded onto this case, my client – Mrs Joy Stapleton – will have spent three thousand days exactly behind bars. Three. Thousand. Days. For a crime she simply did not commit.' Bracken softens his face and releases his fingers from their steeple. 'I and my client thank you for your time, your diligence and your expertise, Judge McCormick, and believe that you will faithfully do what is right by these courts. That is our final state-ment – thank you, Your Honour.'

He produces his tilted head bow again, then paces back to his desk, and as he does Delia pulls back the sleeve on her left wrist before tilting it to her face.

'Mr Ryan, it is lunch time. But I'll leave it up to you. Would you like to deliver your final argument now, or...'

'Let's take the recess, Your Honour,' Ryan says.

'That okay with you, Mr Bracken?' Delia asks, flicking her eyes to the opposite bench.

Bracken curls up his mouth, shrugs his shoulders and nods his head. Then Delia bangs down her gavel once again.

'Okay, let's take half an hour. Court will resume at 1:40 p.m. precisely.'

Delia sucks on her cheeks as she heads out the side door, nodding to Ivy as she passes her.

But she's barely turned the corner of the first corridor by the time she hears a familiar calling – a calling she's heard almost every day of the past thirty-five years.

'Mum.'

She stops, and sighs as she spins.

'What is it, Callum?'

'I've got something to show you, though it'll make you wanna vomit.'

'Vomit?' she says, placing her hands on her hips, then squinting at the wry smile flickering on the corner of her son's mouth as he approaches her, his phone cupped inside his hand.

He swivels when he reaches his mother, to show her the screen, then he presses at the play button. As soon as he does, a scratching sound hisses from the speakers, before Delia baulks her face away.

'What the hell is that?'

'Keep watching, Mum.'

'Callum,' she says holding a hand to her face. 'Have I not seen enough penis for one woman this week?'

'Keep watching.'

The camera was between his legs, his balls hairy and tight at the bottom of the screen, his hands tight around his tubby mushroomed-shape shaft. Over his fistful of penis lay a hanging belly, all hairy and matted with sweat. She couldn't see a face. Not until a neat side-parting of grey hair made itself visible. Followed by those unmistakable bushy V-shaped eyebrows. It looked as if Eddie was staring up over his belly at whatever footage he was masturbating to, totally unaware his laptop was filming him.

'Men. You really are all stupid, huh?' Delia says. Then she glances up at her son, producing a wry smile to mirror his.

'Where is he?'

'Canteen, I bet,' Delia says.

She pats her son on the back and then they both pace back up the corridor they had just walked down, before entering through the side door of the courtroom so that they can take the short cut to the canteen. But they don't need to travel so far. Because heading towards them are the same bushy V-shaped eyebrows that had just appeared in the video.

'Eddie...' Callum calls out, his voice echoing around the empty court-room. 'You might wanna take a look at this.'

1 day ago...

Joy sighed with every exhale of breath she took as she slodged behind Anya. The cringing hadn't diluted. Nor the anger. She was furious with herself... so much so she formed both fists into balls and let them hang heavy by her side as she was being led back to her cell. That was her one chance – the only chance she'd ever have – of defending herself. And she fuckin' blew it. Or at least she felt she had.

In between bouts of heavy sighing, she held her eyes closed and replayed all the times she had stumbled or stuttered on the stand. Then she'd cringe when she'd picture herself standing and shouting back at Jonathan Ryan.

'I'm a fuckin' idiot. I should've listened to my lawyer. I shouldn't have gone up there. I think I might've fucked it all up for myself,' she said to Anya, who looked even more like a model today because she had her hair all tussled into a loose bun and was dressed in a designer fitted suit to accompany Joy to and from the courts. But, as always, Anya didn't return conversation to the prisoner. She just kept her sculptured face stern until they reached cell E-108, before she pushed open the cell door, pointed Joy inside and then slammed it shut – even though Joy would have been allowed to roam around, given that cells were open and most of the other prisoners were in the TV room gossiping – about her, no doubt. Though Nancy wasn't. Joy had peered through the crack of her cell door when walking past just moments ago, noticing she was having her usual post-dinner nap.

But Joy chose to do just as she had done every evening of the past two weeks when she returned from court – she lay on her mattress in foetal position, and stared at the smiling faces of her two boys.

She didn't feel up to mixing with any of the inmates since she'd returned from isolation – and knew the only likely place she'd find peace and quiet during her retrial was on top of the plastic, blue mattress of her own cell, with the door shut tight. She had heard the prisoners were getting updates on her retrial through the RTÉ evening news, which, she realized as she lay staring at her boys' smiles, is what most of them were likely doing right now.

She thought about crawling out of her bed and heading down to the TV room just to listen to what the RTÉ reporter had to say about her time on the stand. But she couldn't summon the energy. Nor the courage. She felt that if she heard him report that she had made a fool of herself up there today then she might as well head back to her cell and end it all.

So, instead, she rested her ear onto her thin pillow and attempted to relive her testimony. She cringed when she replayed the first time she'd stood up to shout at Jonathan Ryan. "How fuckin' dare you!" she'd snapped. And then she filled with rage when she heard him accuse her, straight to her face, of murdering her sons. Especially as he was so close to her, almost all up in her face, just below the witness box.

'Uuuugh,' she squirmed, tossing and turning on her mattress. 'I'm gonna be here the rest of my fuckin' life.' She stared at the photograph of the boys, then turned over on her pillow, away from their faces and began to sob, her shoulders shaking, her throat gurgling. She was so overwhelmed. So exhausted. So devastated.

'Fuck. Fuck. Fuck,' she said, slapping her palm to the pillow right next to her face. She had done the exact same thing during her first night inside. Eight years, two months and two nights ago now. Three thousand days tomorrow. Sometimes those three thousand days feel like a lifetime ago to Joy... and yet on other occasions, her first night inside a cell seems as if it were only last night.

She managed to stop sobbing, then mustered enough energy to sit up; her teeth grinding, her jaw swinging. She knew the rest of the prisoners would be heading back to their cells for lock up soon. So, she stood up, yanked the sheet from the four corners of her bed and then pinched one end of it between her chin and chest so she could fold it neatly in half. Then she knelt down and began to roll the sheet up so tight that it turned into a long scarf. Seconds later, she was looping the scarf around one end, before gripping and yanking the noose as tight as she could get it.

'Fuck this shit,' she whispered to herself.

Then she reached for her bible.

⁛

'Get your filthy hand off me,' Delia says, shrugging her shoulder until Eddie's arm drops. 'I know what you do with that hand.'

His eyes widen, his neck roaring red under the collar of his creased shirt.

'Delia, you can't... you can't...'

Delia pushes a laugh through her nostrils, then tucks her chin into her neck so that she can look up at her boss over the rim of her retro-styled glasses.

'I mean, how stupid can you be, Eddie, huh? You know... *you know* people hack into laptop cameras... Sure you did it to him.' She flicks her head back towards her son who is beaming with smugness over her shoulder. 'You got beat playing your own game. But nothing seems to get in between a boy and his tiny best friend, does it?' She puffs out another laugh, then spins on her heels, storming back out through the side door of the courtroom, ignoring Eddie's calls.

'You gotta protect the verdict regardless, Delia,' he whisper-shouts after her. Callum has to hold a hand to Eddie's chest, to stop him from following the judge as she paces her way back down the corridors, where she eventually kicks her way into her office and plonks herself into the leather chair at her big oak desk.

She nibbles at half of the sandwich Aisling had left for her as she attempts to soak in the absurdity of it all. Then she holds her eyes closed to clear her mind of Eddie's hairy ball sack, so she can turn her focus back to the trial. Though her thoughts are delving much, much deeper than just the trial itself. Well beyond this one court case. She finds herself questioning everything she has ever believed in; the system in which her family had given over almost the entirety of their adult lives. Then, in the midst of her inner deliberation, Aisling's voice cackles through the speaker of Delia's phone, stunning the judge back to the present, informing her that she's due back in court again. Time is flashing by for her. It seems as if every time Delia begins to squint her eyes in deep thought, she is instantly snapped back out of it.

When she is sat back into her highchair in the courtroom, she eyeballs Eddie in the back pew, watching as he fidgets, firstly by folding his arms, then dropping them down by his side before he begins to comb his fingers repeatedly through his hair with both hands. He doesn't know what to be doing with himself. His face is now hot pink, his neck flaming red.

'Your Honour,' Jonathan Ryan says, approaching Delia's highchair. 'Mr Bracken's final argument kept trying to suggest that there was no evidence in this case.'

Ryan holds aloft a tiny remote control, then pinches his finger at a button that blinks the large screen at the side of the courtroom floor back to life. An intriguing opening to his final argument.

'There's your evidence,' he says, pointing at the footage playing on loop of a figure in a pink hood walking by a garden wall. 'I'm not sure evidence gets more red-handed than that. This is Joy Stapleton walking away from where her boys were buried, about one-thousand metres from where her boys were buried, on the night we believe they were buried. The defendant was practically caught red-handed.'

He pauses, with his finger still pointing at the screen, allowing the footage to play on loop three more times.

'Talk about evidence,' he says, shaking his head. 'That is literally evidence in front of our own eyes. Mr Bracken says there is no evidence. Well, he should know that most murder cases don't get the luxury of evidence as hot as this. In most murder trials we don't get to see footage of the defendant walking away from the scene of the crime. The defence's argument, that this is mere coincidence, is frankly laughable, Your Honour. We know that Mrs Stapleton was the only person in Ireland to own this particular pink hooded top even before this retrial. But during this retrial, we had Mr Tobias Masterson testify on the stand to reaffirm that, and we also produced written statements from other purchasers of this pink hooded top from Pennsylvania which only further rules out the plausibility of coincidence. If a coincidence was difficult to believe for the original jury in this case eight years ago, Your Honour, then a coincidence must be impossible to believe now. This,' he says, pointing his finger at the screen again, 'can *only* be Joy Stapleton. This is the evidence that proves she murdered her two boys. Don't let it be said we don't have evidence. We have evidence.'

He strolls back to his desk, picks up his glass of water and takes a short, sharp sip from it.

'Your Honour, the accused's best friend since Primary School testified on the stand that Mrs Stapleton was suffering with some form of undiagnosed depression around the time Oscar and Reese Stapleton were murdered. After her mother had died, and with very little support from her overworked husband, Joy Stapleton slipped into an undiagnosed depression that drove her to do the unthinkable. The testimony from Lavinia Kirwan proves motive, Your Honour. Which means that, to this court, during this retrial, we have proven motive. And we have proven evidence.'

He points his hand at the screen again where the footage is still playing on loop.

'We also had distinguished Detective Ray De Brun testify during this retrial. Ray De Brun has been the lead detective on many of Dublin's most infamous cases. He testified here, in this courtroom, this week, that he is under no doubt whatsoever that Joy Stapleton murdered her two boys. He was asked quite bluntly if he had any doubt that Mrs Stapleton is guilty of this crime. And his exact response under oath was, "none what-so-ever." This is one of Ireland's most decorated investigators in the entire history of our state, Your Honour. So, now we have expertise. We have motive. We have evidence.'

He doesn't point his finger at the screen this time, but he does notice that Judge Delia glances to the footage as he melodically repeats his tagline.

'Your Honour, the detectives in this case got it right by arresting Joy Stapleton. The jury in the original trial got it right by finding her guilty. And the judge in the original trial – Albert Riordan – got this case right by handing down a double life sentence. That double life sentence needs to be protected. It needs to be upheld. It has been made plain and clear during this retrial that the defendant is prone to outbursts. She made numerous outbursts directed at me today whilst on that stand; outbursts certainly not befitting a woman of innocence, outbursts that can only reaffirm to us that she ended the lives of her two young sons in the most inhumane act this country has ever—'

'You lying mother—'

Joy is dragged back down to her seat by Bracken, who has to add weight to both of her shoulders to steady her.

'See, Your Honour,' Ryan says. 'A hot temper. Another outburst. And that is numerous times today. It is far from inconceivable that on November

2nd, 2008, Mrs Stapleton had the mother of all outbursts. And that outburst led to her murdering her two boys, before burying them in shallow graves in the wasteland of the Dublin mountains. And we know she did this because we have expertise. We have motive. And we have evidence,' he says, pointing at the screen, this time with both hands. 'Your Honour, the prosecution rests its case.'

There's a humming of chatter in the gallery as Delia steps down and exits the courtroom.

Aisling chooses to stay quiet as the judge brushes past to enter her office; conscious the judge will be deep in thought.

Delia huffs as she sits into her chair, before wiggling at her mouse again. And as her screen takes its time to blink back to life, she stares at the sharp shadows the cupfuls of pens and the cracked photo frame of her family are casting due to the dim orange light above her head. She is thinking about the taglines used in both closing arguments, feeling both to be rather outdated. Though she does realise Ryan and Bracken were playing to the media as much as they were playing to her. They knew the newspapers would lap up the taglines for lazy headlines tomorrow, though she isn't quite sure whether 'If there's any doubt, you must let her out,' would be preferred by editors over, 'We have motive. We have expertise. We have evidence.' All she knows right this second is that she, personally, wasn't won over by either of the closing arguments. Though she won't be making any decision right now. That'll happen later. When she's sunken into a hot bath, with bubbles hugging her face and a glass of wine swirling in her hand.

A familiar knock rattles, causing her to tut.

'Come in, Callum.'

He shows his grinning face, then shuts the door quietly behind him.

'Did you see how puce he was sitting in the back of the courtroom? He's in some shock. He kept stuttering to me after you stormed off. The fat gobshite. I mean, I'll never get the image of his hairy balls out of my mind, but... drama finally over.' He sits into the chair opposite his mother and holds up both hands. 'You can, eh.... do as you were always hoping to do; see this retrial through a fresh set of eyes.' Delia thins her lips while continuing to squint at her screen, saying nothing. 'Mum... Mum. Whatcha thinking about?'

'Things.'

'What things? The closing arguments? I thought, personally, Bracken's was stronger, but Ryan's was more specific. I mean—'

'No, Callum. I'm not thinking about the closing arguments. I'm not even thinking about the trial. I'm thinking well beyond the trial. I'm trying to figure out a bigger picture.'

718

'A bigger picture? A bigger picture of what?'

'Things.'

'Things?' Callum sits upright. 'Mum... what the hell are you talking about? Things?'

'Just a bigger picture is all... anyway, my head's been stuck in this trial for way too long... I'm going to wait till I run a hot bath tonight, then I'm going to get my head into it. Tell me something. Anything to distract me. How's that fella you dated last weekend? You guys arrange a second date?'

Callum sniggers, then snatches at a pen from the cupful on his mother's desk and repeatedly clicks at the top of it.

'I'm actually seeing him tonight.'

'And have you told me what this guy does for a living, yet?'

'He's a cook of some sort. Runs a catering business with his brother.'

'Ah, nice. Someone who can cook, huh? So, he's gonna be the one then, is he?'

Callum sniggers again, then tosses the pen onto the desk.

'Why you wanna talk about me? I wanna know what you mean by 'bigger picture', you're not thinking of doing anything stupid, are you, Mum? What does *bigger picture* even mean?'

Delia swipes the glasses from her nose and rests them down beside her mouse before leaning back and twisting the butt of both palms into her eyes.

'Don't know...' she says, through a stifled yawn. 'I'm thinking beyond this trial – way beyond it. About the justice system as a whole.'

Callum creases his brow.

'So, you *are* thinking of doing something stupid. Are you gonna let her out, just to let the system come crashing down? You're not... you're not thinking of letting her out... are you? Mum, she's guilty. C'mon... you know that.'

'Well firstly, I don't know that, do I? Nobody does. Ryan says he proved red-handed evidence. He didn't. It's a figure in a pink hoodie. We see no face. So, we don't know for certain. Nobody does. But... secondly, does it even matter if we did know for certain?'

'Huh?' Callum says, sitting more upright.

'Eddie Taunton... I mean the absolute cheek of that man.'

'You're not... Mum... are you fucking serious?' He mouths the word 'fucking', the sound of the 'f' flicking off his bottom lip. 'You're gonna acquit Joy Stapleton just to throw a grenade on the system?'

'I don't know. I told you, I need a warm bath. I'll do my filtering process in there tonight and I'll... I'll—'

'Mum. Tell me you're not being serious?'

'I told you. I'm gonna think it all through tonight.'

'Mum, she murdered her two young sons. They were babies. She was videoed walking away from the scene for crying out loud.'

'We don't know for—'

'It's not a bloody coincidence, Mum. There is no coincidence in this case. You said that yourself. You said it years ago in your interview with Eddie Taunton. There is no coincidence in this case whatsoever. Never has been. This has been known as 'The Coincidence Case' for over ten years now, ever since Joy was first arrested. Coincidence this, coincidence that. As Jonathan Ryan said in his opening argument, there's no such thing as coincidences, not really. Hell...' Callum puffs out a snort, 'the only time I heard any coincidence in this entire trial was when they mentioned the date of the murders. Second of November, 2008. Same date as my graduation, wasn't it? Same night this was taken.'

He picks up the cracked photo frame from beside his mother's monitor and turns it to himself. He's still grinning back at his father when it releases from his grip, his thumb slicing on a shard, the frame swirling in slow motion until it crashes to the floor. Again.

'What the fuck?' he says, standing up and holding a hand to his chest. He bows forward to stare down at the photo; but not to see his father's proud face, nor his, nor his mother's. But to squint at the tiny figure in the background. A figure that had never caught his eye before. Joy Stapleton. Just over his father's shoulder. Her curls packed tightly into a pink hood.

Delia's brow is heavily creased as she chicanes herself around her desk. She stares up at Callum's paling face... then down at the photo. She lowers to her hunkers and inches her nose closer. It takes a long moment for her to finally see it; to notice the tiny figure in the background – a figure she hadn't noticed, not once, in any one of the ten thousand times she had glanced at this photograph over the years.

'What the fuck?' she says, opting for the exact same words her son had chosen.

Delia lifts her knitted jumper from the waist, taking her undervest with it and struggling, once again, to lift them over her head because she'd forgotten she had combed her glasses back into her hair. But she manages to untangle herself before tossing the garments to her bed. Then she unclasps her bra and pulls down her trousers – taking her cotton bloomers with them – before kicking her way to her birthday suit.

She normally basks in the quiet of the house; loves it when Callum goes out for the evening. But this quiet sounds too quiet. Eerily quiet. It's not calming her spinning head at all.

Callum didn't want to go out on his date and had actually texted him to call it off. But Delia forced him into a U-turn, demanding that she had the house to herself this evening; that she wasn't to be disturbed.

They had both sat for an hour in her office just staring at the photo, their jaws ajar, their eyes wide. Then, when Delia snapped out of her shock by shaking her head, she snatched at the photo frame and shoved it into her briefcase, loose glass and all.

'Mum... what you doing?'

'I'm going home to have a bath.'

'But... Mum... Mum,' Callum roared as she was pacing out of her office.

'Enjoy your date, Callum,' she shouted without looking back.

She stares at her body in the mirror, shrugging a shoulder at herself before tip-toeing the length of the carpeted landing that leads her straight into the bathroom. She dips her toe into the bath before sucking in through the gaps in her teeth. Too hot. So she runs the cold tap and begins to swirl her hand through the foaming water. The bathroom is consumed by steam, the glass of Massolino Parussi Barola standing tall on the edge of the bath fogged and dripping with condensation. She turns off the tap, then dips her toe in again for another temperature check. Perfect. She'd been looking forward to this all day. Even before she was stunned into the surrealist of silences by the most extraordinary of coincidences.

As soon as she rests her head on the back rim of the bath she squints through the swirling steam at the cracked photograph. She had sat it upright on the edge of her chest of drawers facing the bath so that she could soak it all in while the cogs of her mind-filtering process churned. She still can't believe it. Undoubted proof that Joy was walking back down the Dublin mountains on the night she dumped her son's bodies up there; caught in the background of a family portrait of the McCormicks as they stood, proudly, outside the Windmill pub celebrating Callum's graduation. One quick flash of a camera. And there it was. Proof; a single split moment caught in time forever.

'Justice?' Delia whispers to herself as she sinks further under the water. 'Or the justice system?' She picks up her tall glass of wine and swirls it before taking a tiny sip and resting it back down. 'Which is more important?'

She takes a deep inhale of breath before pushing her bum further forward, allowing her shoulders, then her neck, and finally her face to sink under the water. She opens her eyes when she's fully immersed and stares up through a gap in the bubbles at the steam as it swirls in a haze towards the high ceiling. Then one bubble releases from her mouth and buoys for a long moment on the surface... before it eventually pops.

0 days ago...

Joy glanced over at Mathilda and Anya who were both standing against the side wall of the courtroom all courteous and disciplined with their hands clasped behind their backs, their shoulders high and their chests puffed out. And as she stared at them, she was certain that Mathilda was smiling at her – her lips twitching, the sides of her eyes ever so slightly creasing. Joy squinted back for a moment, then lightly shook her curls from side-to-side, assuming she was just imagining things.

She pivoted on her chair to face forward when Judge Delia lightly coughed into the microphone, signalling she was about to begin. And as Joy sat more upright in her chair, Gerd Bracken reached a hand across to pinch two of her fingers between his.

'I have concluded my judgement of this retrial,' Delia said, leaning her forearms on to the desk in front of her. 'In all my years I have never so strenuously had to consider so many matters in one court case. Not only is this a retrial that meant I also had to consider testimonies from the original murder trial, but this is a unique murder retrial in that it is without a jury.' She lightly cleared her throat again and then swallowed, looking sincerely sorrowful. 'I meticulously examined all evidence and witness testimony brought to this court. And after considered due process, structured within the legal parameters in which I am honoured and proud to work in, time has now come for me to ask the defendant to please rise.'

Bracken squeezed Joy's hand. Then the entire defence team got to their feet in unison.

'Mrs Joy Stapleton,' the judge said, 'this court finds you not guilty of the crimes of which you have been charged and subsequently incarcerated for.'

There are audible gasps in the gallery. Joy releases from Bracken's grip so she can throw both of her arms around his neck, then she leans in and kisses him just beneath the ear. 'You are a free woman. You are free to leave this court a free woman. On behalf of the Justice System,' Delia continued, even though it was evident Joy was no longer listening to her – lost in a haze of elation, 'I would like to extend the first apology for your wrongful conviction.' She slams down her gavel. 'Court dismissed.'

A booming chorus of chaos sounded out as the judge stepped down from her highchair. Joy was sandwiched in a double hug; Gerd Bracken on one side of her, his assistant Imogen on the other. Then, over Imogen's

723

shoulder, Joy noticed Anya and Mathilda making their way towards her, Mathilda definitely smiling now, Anya's stunning face still sombre and pouted.

'Joy, we need to conduct due process before we free you, as per the court's orders,' Mathilda said, holding her fingers to Joy's elbow. 'If you could step into the hallway with us.'

Joy nodded her curls while beaming a huge smile through her tears and then, flanked by Bracken, she followed Anya and Mathilda through a side door that led to a monochrome tiled corridor.

As soon as the heavy door was closed behind them, the chaotic mumbling of debate and discussion humming from within the courtroom instantly drowned to a near silence.

'I told ya all them years I was innocent, Mathilda,' Joy said, bouncing up and down on the spot, much like she used to when she'd get high on meth.

Mathilda nodded and pursed a thin smile at her.

'Listen,' she said, leaning in to Joy, 'I know you have just had the best news ever, but eh... we just got word after we arrived here this morning, and I'm sorry to have to tell you this... but it's, eh... it's Nancy.'

Joy stopped bouncing.

'Nancy?'

'She, eh... she took her own life last night.'

'What?'

Anya nodded once, like a robot.

'I know you've got a lot going on, but I know you guys were close and I thought I should tell you,' Mathilda said. 'Because well... she did it because of you, y'see?'

'Because of me?'

'She left a note. A suicide note. It said, "I love you. I can't go on without you." She didn't want to do her time inside with you not being there, Joy. She musta feared you were gonna be acquitted today.'

Joy pouted her lips and shrugged one shoulder.

'That's sad,' she said, before she began bouncing on the spot again. 'Now, what's this due process we need to go through, cos I just wanna get the hell outta here?'

Mathilda stared up at Anya, but Anya, as usual, produced nothing – not even the flicker an eyelash.

'There is no procedure,' Mathilda said, turning back to Joy. 'I just wanted to let you know about Nancy... that's all.' Then she pointed her whole hand to the back end of the corridor. 'Let your lawyers take you out that entrance down there... there'll be less media that way.'

Joy spent her first hour of freedom bouncing her knees up and down under a desk inside Bracken's office, celebrating with men and woman dressed in suits – most of whom she'd never even met before. She was buoyed, but already bored by her new-found freedom. Only because she felt she had to keep a fake smile plastered wide across her face for the sake of those in suits she knew she had to consider her heroes.

'I, eh... gotta go, I gotta go do... *something*,' she finally said. Bracken was reluctant to allow her to leave. He knew all too well that she had nobody on the outside world she could consider a friend. And when he informed her he had already booked a hotel room, she resisted – insisting she couldn't spend another moment of her life being holed up.

'I just wanna walk. I wanna feel... *free*,' she told him. Then she held him close, whispered a 'Thank you' into his ear, and left his office to wander the streets of Dublin city with the four fifty-euro notes Bracken had insisted she take from him stuffed into her back trousers pocket.

She strolled up and down the boardwalk of Bachelor's Walk, sniffing in the scent of the River Liffey as if, despite its stench, its air was as fresh as any air she had ever inhaled. She turned heads as she walked. There was no mistaking Joy Stapleton. But nobody approached her, except to shout an odd, 'I always believed you, Joy' or a 'Oh, look, it's yer wan' in her direction. Though most of the folk she passed were too silenced by their own shock to say anything. They just stood there, open mouthed with shopping bags hanging heavy from both hands.

It was only when she sat in the back of a taxi that she felt her thighs and calves begin to burn from the mileage she had covered. She only realised when she stared at the clock on the taxi's dashboard that she had been walking non-stop for over three hours.

Her thighs and calves still feel stiff now as she holds a finger to the door-bell while inching her ear to the glassed porch door so she can hear it chime through the house. Then she stands back and stares up and down the street, nibbling on her bottom lip. It doesn't look as if eight years have passed. Aside from the car in the drive next door being larger and wider than it used to be, she genuinely can't notice anything else that's changed around here.

He appears, standing in the frame of the front door glaring out at her from behind the glassed porch. His face is still as grey as his hair; his eyes a diluted blue.

She thought about what she would say to him repeatedly as she wandered the city centre streets, but as he is sliding the porch door across, she begins to lose all sense of herself and has to grip the wall that separates their garden from their neighbours with her fingers – just for some semblance of support. In case Shay is unreceptive. In case he steps out and snaps 'What the fuck are you doing here?'

'Joy,' he says. As soon as he steps into the garden path he glances up and down the street, much like she had done seconds ago. 'Come in. Come in.'

She stares straight into the living room as soon as she steps back inside the squared hallway. Shay hasn't changed much, aside from the overly-wide flat screen TV hanging over the fireplace. Her own face stares back at her; the mug shot of when she was first arrested. Then the screen blinks to a reporter standing outside the entrance to the courts, speaking into an overly large squared microphone.

'*Judge Delia McCormick delivered her verdict at 10:40 this morning; shocking some members of the gallery—*'

Shay stabs his finger at the remote control making the screen blink to black. Then he walks across his wife, taking her in as she glances around the room.

'I, eh... I don't know... eh... don't know what to, eh...' He scratches at the back of his neck.

'You don't have to say anything,' Joy whispers. 'You said it all on the stand, Shay. I'm just here to say... to say thank you.'

'I'm so sorry for all you've been through. I can't even begin to... I mean, my mind has just been jumping from one theory to another to another to another over the years and I...'

Joy steps closer to him and holds a hand against his elbow.

'You don't have to be sorry for anything.'

'I left you alone. With the kids. I mean... what was I thinking? All's I ever thought I wanted to be was a father. And when I became one, I bloody left you all to it... didn't I? I just went to do nothing in hotels. For no reason whatsoever.'

'Not for no reason,' Joy says, gripping his elbow tighter. 'You were earning crust for your family. You don't have to be sorry for anything, Shay. You've never needed to mutter the words 'I'm sorry'. I'm the one who left them on that green over there. I'm the one who's had to deal with that—'

'Joy,' Shay says, looking down at his wife, his eyes filling with tears, 'you need to stop blaming yourself. The entire state has blamed you for eight years and today that entire state has stopped blaming you. So, you need to stop blaming yourself.'

She takes one step closer and holds both her hands to his hips.

'I'll stop blaming myself, if you stop blaming yourself,' she says.

Shay stiffens his nose in an attempt to stop the tears from falling, then he leans down and kisses the top of his wife's curls. But as he does, his dam breaks, and he sobs snot and tears into her hair; his shoulders shivering. Joy reaches both hands up his back, and drags him as tight as she can to her, resting an ear against his chest.

'It's okay, Shay,' she whispers. 'I'm home now.'

SEE THE PHOTOGRAPH!

And see the real photograph from the true coincidence that inspired this novel.

Both photographs are shown at the start of this short video interview with author David B. Lyons in which he discusses all of the clues that lead up to the twist ending; clues you may have missed.

Click the below link to access the video right now.

www.subscribepage.com/coincidence

The End.

ALL OF DAVID B. LYONS'S NOVELS

The Tick-Tock Trilogy

Midday

Whatever Happened to Betsy Blake?

The Suicide Pact

The Trial Trilogy

She Said, Three Said

The Curious Case of Faith & Grace

The Coincidence

ACKNOWLEDGMENTS

Each of these books are dedicated to a special woman in my life.
Kerry, Debra, Lin — thank you for being awesome.
And thank you to *you* — the reader. You're a treasure.

Printed in Great Britain
by Amazon

59051237R00442